BYRON

A Novel

BYRON

A Novel

SIGRID COMBÜCHEN

Translated from the Swedish by Joan Tate

HEINEMANN : LONDON

William Heinemann Limited
Michelin House, 81 Fulham Road, London SW3 6RB
LONDON   MELBOURNE   AUCKLAND

First published in Sweden as *Byron: en roman*
by Norstedts, Stockholm, 1988
Copyright © Sigrid Combüchen, 1988
This translation first published in Great Britain
by William Heinemann Limited, 1991
Copyright © in the translation, Joan Tate, 1991

This publication was produced with the
assistance of the European Commission.
The publishers gratefully acknowledge
their help.

A CIP catalogue record for this book
is available from the British Library
ISBN 0 434 14106 2

Typeset by Deltatype Ltd, Ellesmere Port
Printed and bound in Great Britain by
Mackays of Chatham PLC, Chatham, Kent

BYRON

A Novel

Preface

Everything surrounding Byron has been abundantly documented, and that documentation forms the foundations of this book. Truth, or veracity, is the essential core when one is conveying a myth. Equally important is the sense of 'Truth' which can only arise when the old story finds a new human being, is prepared to understand that person – and do violence to that person – with his or her own favourite ideas as a guideline.

'The Byronists' in the novel lurch between truth and 'Truth' – as my representatives. They make references and quote, interpret and speculate, pick the raisins out of the cake and surround them with a new dough. Methods of adjustment are occasionally discussed in the book, first and foremost in connection with the sections of 'Hobhouse's diaries', which are said to be half authentic and half developed further by Link the dentist. In actual fact, they consist of very few direct quotations from Hobhouse's *Recollections from a Long Life*, published by Murray under his title Lord Broughton in the early 1900s. These are used to allow the spirit, environment and linguistic manners of the day to appear here and there, undisturbed by the technicalities of fiction writing, and to reproduce an interview with Napoleon, a conversation with Stendhal and a review of the troops in Paris – details which would have suffered from 're-creation'.

Elsewhere reference is made to sections of letters. On one occasion, for instance, some of Byron's letters to Lady Melbourne are read aloud. They are not direct quotes, but essentially in order – as the reader states – to allow us to hear Byron's own voice. The original texts can be found in most collections of Byron's letters, the latest being the complete edition edited by Leslie A. Marchand and published by Murray.

If direct quotations lie at one end of the narrative scale, there are deliberate inaccuracies at the other. They extend from important details – Clara Shelley died in less carnival-like circumstances than are described – to trivialities – Frank Sinatra had not yet made his début as a singer when his voice floated over Nottinghamshire from Brenda's wind-up gramophone.

Between these extremes lie years of reading and forgetting and wandering round Byron's old haunts in Europe, which in several cases still remain as he saw them. I started by reading about Byron; first the new, truth-seeking monographs, then, bearing the stamp of 'Truth', the memorial pieces from friends and adversaries such as Trelawny, Leigh Hunt and Thomas Moore. Finally, I went on entirely to reading Byron, the most enigmatic and least finite alternative, when it comes down to it.

Sigrid Combüchen
Lund, January 1st, 1990

Prologue

Fifty years ago, a handful of people took hammer and chisel and opened the vault in the country church of Hucknall Torkard, Nottinghamshire, England. One of them waved his hand about to disperse the dust loosened from the inner walls as the hammer struck from the outside. He switched on his torch.

At first the filament glowed alone in its capsule, the spark running back and forth without producing any light. Then the dust and mould settled, a cone appeared, and as the laws of gravity grew even more effective, the light penetrated deeply and started to bring the room up out of its hundred years of darkness.

Large spiders swirled over the walls and dusty cobwebs fluttered as the air rushed in. Once eyes became used to movements in the stillness, they noticed the stacked coffins: generation after generation of the Byron family, the oldest decayed, not too badly, but sufficiently for the top one to tilt. That was also the way life went. A glimmer of gilt, a crown with eight pearl points still lying at the head of the grandest sarcophagus, like a grieving dog turned into matter. Ten whites of eyes glimmered in that direction. One of the gentlemen, who could read upside-down almost as quickly as the right way round, told the others that the coffin was Ada's. But on that particular evening no one wanted guidance. They all wanted to experience it themselves, unprepared. So they followed in his tracks, though with some labour: 'Lady Augusta Ada, wife of William, Earl of Lovelace, only daughter of George Gordon Noel, Lord Byron. Born 10th December, 1815. Died . . .' The date was concealed by a patch of mould or mortar, but they all knew it should be 1851, for Ada was thirty-six years old, as her half-sister Medora had been, and her grandfather. As had been her father – in the next coffin.

Eyes and minds mist over when they take in the first firm evidence of an existence they occasionally thought they had dreamt, had been persuaded into. The mist does not come from emotion, but from the precipitation of the dream, as it defends itself against what is indigent, though powerful and incontrovertible, in a piece of dry wood.

There is a glimmer of Atlantis in the eyes of an archaeologist standing on a hill and seeing an unusual contour in the landscape just where he had expected it, but that mist disperses. This mist also disperses and the man with the torch uses a short ladder to climb down, his back to the vault. It was shallower than they had imagined; as he stood down there, his head and shoulders protruded out of the opening.

To begin with, he took the flat baronial crown off Lord Byron's coffin and four pairs of hands groped down into the pool of light. It was wiped and examined for hallmarks and engravings: it was nothing but a broad band, a kind of ancient ring, three of its milk-tooth points missing. Toothless. Gilt. Next out of the tomb came an ornamental box in which the four doctors had deposited most of Byron's internal organs when they had embalmed him.

Then there was room for another person to climb down.

That person was Link, a Nottingham dentist – a trifle shakily, in fact, but he was the thinnest of those present. He shuddered as something ran across the earthen floor. Out of the corner of his eye, he could see signs of life in the tomb. Everything grows over. He knew that what has recently died is already covered by a membrane of new life, and what has been long dead is inhabited by new worlds. That was a horrible thought.

There was a smell of earth, worms and mice. They worked with parsimonious movements, fearing to bump into things and tip them over. Link had read somewhere that the coffin beneath Ada contained Lord Byron's mother, and that the plinth had been judged to be too weak as long ago as the summer of 1824, when they had considered placing her son above. Since then, the decay had continued for another hundred years, and he imagined an incautious gesture and a groundswell of horrors every time he had to stick out his elbow.

2

With rope and their bare hands, they finally hoisted up the coffin, and with the minute steps of a centipede, shuffled across the paths of moonlight with their burden. In a smallish room, an oak table was prepared with rags and old blankets, but Mr Hazell flung across a clean sheet as well to protect the surface. They unscrewed the lid of the outer coffin. There was a very faint smell of spirits, like a barrel in a back yard. They all helped unscrew. As they lifted off the last lid, Mr Cohn averted his eyes.

It is actually true that at the end of the 1930s, some people took the poet Byron out of his tomb to have a look at him. They noted down what they saw and their neat disposition of his anatomical details is today on view in glass cases at his ancestral estate, Newstead Abbey, some twelve or so miles from Nottingham. An intimate study of his remains is described there. Measurements, cogitations. Admiration. Curiosity, an inability to let things alone. They lifted up the amputated right foot and found it flawless. A little hair fell victim to the scissors. They really were far too intimate, and with that perpetrating a literary and quasi-literary tradition of never allowing the character of Byron to rest in peace, always demanding of him new sensations.

Though curiosity does not come from earlier sensations. It comes from a faint repeated cry in the sky approaching the earth and welding its wisp into the smoker's pipe.

A circle of smokers are sitting there.

The grave-openers were the most extreme Byronists in a multitude of curious people intoxicated by faint cries. I know nothing about them, except that they gave in to a whim, and this provides them with a place of their own in the lengthy mythology of Byron. Their names, professions and personalities – even their number – are the only things that are entirely fictional in this story. Everything else is my hypothesis on the story of Lord Byron.

3

Part One

Pale sherry

The first time she came into the shop, she was wearing a brown coat that had been turned and rubber boots with patches of a different colour, the kind you use for mending bicycle punctures. She asked for a bottle of 'pale sherry'.

'Consumptive or vapid?' he said.

'What . . . ?'

She said the little word in a strange accent he hadn't noticed in the sentence. Perhaps it would have passed if the 'what' hadn't at the same time revealed that she didn't understand English jokes. He looked at her. She must be thinking the joke was aimed at her personally.

'What sort?' he said, clarifying, and speaking clearly.

She looked down into her wallet, pretending to read from a list, but he saw she was counting her money. Mr Cohn went away and took the cheapest but one bottle of dry sherry off the shelf. In situations of this kind, you should take one or two steps away from extremes. That is what he usually did, for himself, his wife, and waiters, when he found himself in too expensive a restaurant.

He had taken particular notice of her when she had come in. It was a wet Friday in early autumn when November looms and you feel like a drink. He had just decided to shut up shop, and as usual the thought alone was tempting in the throng of customers, some of them passing motorists on their way to or from Nottingham, but most of them friends, acquaintances and people he at least knew by name or sight. They wanted the usual, which meant cheap brandy of the kind you splash soda-water into, two bottles of gin, 'pale sherry' and perhaps the occasional bottle of wine. Most people preferred to wash down their

7

Sunday joint with beer, preferably home-brewed. So did he, for that matter.

His wife used to maintain that he saw things with 'feminine observation, like a tailor or a lady's hairdresser'. So he noticed at once if a coat had been turned, for then the owner had it buttoned up the wrong way and tried to correct this sense of a reflection by fumbling buttons and buttonholes together with the left hand. In addition, the reverse side of the material quickly wore at the seams. Such elegance – complemented with patched boots – did not indicate someone passing through. He decided the woman was from the locality, as a guest perhaps or just moved in, so he prepared an appropriate form of address as he dealt with the nearest customer; a pale sherry; listlessly praising a 'yellow' Bordeaux to go with shortbread and éclairs. He himself detested the sickly stuff. An inhospitable (or simply all too typical) French waiter during the young Cohn's first trip to the continent had allowed him to go astray in the menu and compose a meal of pork sausages and Sauternes. The waiter hadn't reacted until he had pushed open the swing door into the kitchen regions and with a guffaw indicated he was about to share the joke with his colleagues. Mr Cohn had not then had the courage to withhold a tip and even that was accepted with superiority.

Why do people talk about their youth with regret? It's a dispiriting, limited time, lacking real originality. Mr Cohn thought you were really missing someone else's youth, a youth that you only see in its occasional boldness so that you confuse it with your own, confuse it with Youth itself. And the French have remained blinded by their self-righteousness.

The woman was now looking round the shop interior with a curiosity that revived the owner's own. The oak leaves carved on the window frames and which after two hundred and fifty years had sweated out their own varnish; the mahogany counter's inlays of ash, hazel and ivory in the forms of medicinal plants; the snake's symbolic curves round the staff . . . She was thinking something. He could see what she was thinking.

He thought: So. If an old customer said 'pale sherry', they both knew what was meant. After ten years, he was intimate with people's habits and requirements, the catchword a symbol leading along the corridor into his brain's card index of his customers. But if she were

8

already trying out such a catchword, just because she had heard it crossing the counter, just to take a quick short cut in the style prevailing here, then she was being obtrusive! And Mr Cohn declined to complete the form of address he had prepared. He was the first to admit that he could be grumpy about that kind of thing, but he also considered he had been born with an ear for what was natural and what artificial – a very sensitive ear. Everyone must take pains over details in a culture, its entirety, before claiming to be participating. It was naive to imitate a style with nothing but goodwill as an argument.

Her body was also naive, strong and broad across the shoulders and hips, with a pair of sturdy shanks to fill out the boot legs.

'No,' she said. 'Not that sort.' She smiled slightly and asked for his most expensive but one kind instead.

Really . . . thinks Mr Cohn, smiling himself and wiggling his eyebrows as he stands with his back to her to make the exchange. For the second time he thinks about that repulsive dish, the pork sausage, and the handsome tip he gave as the waiter went on grinning behind his hand.

He helped the woman put the bottle into a string bag which already contained root vegetables and a newspaper parcel concealing every-thing of the chicken except its scaly feet.

'You can tell a chicken by its feet,' he said.

'What . . . ?'

'You can tell the quality of a chicken from its feet. A good poultryman always leaves the feet on a plucked and dressed chicken.'

'I did *not* know that,' she said, a polite emphasis on the not. On the threshold, they exchanged a few words about the weather, which she said she loved. 'You breathe so easily in the rain.' A dog joined her. She called it Cass, and together they walked down the street, neither hurrying nor trying to get out of the rain. The dog's feathery tail waved gently in time with the hem of her coat. They walked in step like two friends talking, until she flicked the dog playfully over the head with her rain hood and then pulled the hood over its head. It looked comical as it backed between her legs, its hindquarters lifting her coat and its tail wagging like her tail. He smiled and heard her laugh and saw their flirtation disappearing into a cloud of water from the dog's coat: before seeing each other again in the same amused calm under the light of a street lamp.

9

Mr Cohn went upstairs to take a bath in his wife's bath water, first walking through the shop and the store and locking the grid at the back. The car was there, full of uprooted plants, his wife's oilskin and muddy boots on the radiator. The rain was warm and, actually, easy to breathe. The darkness made a neatly packed leafy jungle of the car. When he got upstairs, he heard a splashing in the bath and exchanged a few rhetorical phrases through the closed door. He asked about the main dish for tea and whether he should prepare something before they changed places. She told him, and on her rosy linen-white arrival, the table was laid with porcelain and domes and tea-cosies, hot water steaming out of the kettle and the oven on.

'Oh, thanks a million. How good!' Mrs Cohn's cheeks were broken-veined, for a few years ago she had inherited a market garden, and instead of selling it (as he had thought), after nearly twenty years of being a housewife, she had started running a business – in a trade she had no training in. One way of throwing away a university education, Mr Cohn considered, not having had one himself. But he had never expressed such thoughts when she was looking after their home and children (said Mrs Cohn). She learnt to deal with her employees, who also had no other training except experience in life, and the business was profitable. Even when people think they can't afford anything else, they still put their money into expensive failures on vegetable plots. Mrs Cohn became more and more weatherbeaten, her eyes like small laughing lakes of ice in Spanish clay.

She was not pleased with her husband's re-use of her bath water.

'It's unsavoury, if not repulsive,' she said. (The Cohns conversed in a strange jerky jargon of résumés, abbreviated expressions and dropped words.) 'What makes you think I'm clean when I launch into it. One day in the soil is rewarded with more than double the sweat and muck you come across in a month in your cuffs.'

'If not clean then comely,' he used to reply, letting out half her tepid water and filling up with hot. 'Intimate, my dear.'

'I'll never do the same for you. As long as you know,' she called out above the noise of the taps. (But she did so later, when the war came.) 'Read the other day in an agony column, gentle maiden fears pregnancy alternatively shameful disease if visiting one-bathroom houses for Christmas in the company even of gentlemen.'

'Ho, ho,' chuckled Mr Cohn, snail-white gliding on light reflections playing with rust spots. 'You can't on the one hand blame me for fleeing into the male climacteric and on the other suspect me of playing at being doctor.'

And so on in an old marriage. The Cohns had become parents at a very young age and couldn't remember moving or talking freely in their own home until recently, after their third child had moved out along with his censorship. They were surprised that the censorship had really ceased, for they had thought they were its sole basis and nourishment. Neither had they expected to have saved up enough vitality to fill the space left behind the children. Then they had felt relief at being able to free themselves to the same degree as their issue had. On Sunday they said to each other that a mutual gift of freedom is the foundation of continued love. It sounded beautiful and mendacious, like a liberal sermon, and they were far from sure it was true. But life is a series of postponements of inevitable griefs and every postponement demands its liturgical phrase. The situation was still unfamiliar, almost abstract, apart from Mr Cohn being able to use Mrs Cohn's bath water without pleading economy, being able to swear and – most of all – having an ample, a hands-and-eyes filling sense of something flower-like, which was really his aloneness, his self-perception rather than of her.

Her. Naturally she knew the new customer. The woman and her husband (and their dog) had already been to Mrs Cohn's market garden several times to talk about clearing and replanting the orchard, thinning out perennials and rearranging the vegetable garden. They had bought a house just outside town, a red-brick cottage with a thatched roof, the foreigner's dream of England, although it had been in a state of decay for a couple of decades, inhabited by an unsociable old lady, who had dropped dead between the well and the kitchen steps the previous winter. Dead, she was accessible.

'They're doing the top floor and they've laid on water and gas, so it'll be quite modern,' Mrs Cohn told him, trying to sneak a look at the newspaper as she ate and talked. Mr Cohn remembered white rims round the cuticles on the right hand accepting the bottle of sherry. Paint.

'Thought I caught an accent,' he said.

'Mm, her husband', replied Mrs Cohn easily, reading, 'comes from northern Australia and what they're doing here I really don't know, because she seems to be missing it already. All that space, the warmth! Anyhow, that's how it is, and . . .' (raising her eyes and looking gravely into his) 'she, of course, is German.'

That it should be so difficult. They keep their eyes on each other, she testingly, just as when you let go a toddler to check that it can walk.

As recently as six months ago, Mr Cohn has not been capable of hearing that last word without something frightening happening to him. Something deathly pale. Something blood-red. He has been unable to explain it.

No one can explain. Everyone has understood why he reacted, but not why he reacted in this way: by being painfully affected, ashamed. 'What's up?' you say to a man who starts stammering or is struck dumb. That feeling as if a black hole had opened inside him ('a cave-like hollowness') and then a flush that almost suffocated him.

It doesn't happen now. It doesn't happen often, not any longer. Mr Cohn has worked on himself and forced the reaction back into the depths of his mind.

Mrs Cohn returns to her newspaper, but is still aware of him with a small part of herself.

No, it doesn't happen any longer. He has worked hard on himself to tame that reaction. It's not reasonable. It was wretched, like the helpless shame of someone mocked for his ugliness.

Earlier on in his life, he had counteracted ordinary cases of anti-semitism with his self-esteem. But this German was not a case and everything personal was out of the running: faced with what was massive in the message, the individual was no argument. What had really happened?

Mr Cohn knew nothing about what was about to happen. The time was not ripe for such knowledge. He thought that despite everything he lived in 'modern' times, permanently beyond the pogroms of the 'old' days. He knew that everything in the world grows and thrives towards annihilation. But he thought modern times were always being established. It was himself he saw as the problem. He felt his private defence cracking.

You never become experienced. You don't make experiences, thought Mr Cohn. For he knew he had overcome occasions of undeserved shame in the past, worst of all when their middle boy had been small.

The eldest of the couple's children was a girl, a pretty red-haired girl of the kind who seem perfect from birth. The youngest boy was lazy and under no obligation to anything, but life was easy for him and he made tracks of his charm through life like the glittering trail of a snail. But Joe was born too early and had suffered from lack of oxygen during his birth. The doctors and Mrs Cohn called it 'insignificant injuries' and presumed he would grow out of them in puberty (which he did). Mr Cohn, however, had no aptitude for that kind of consolation. He suffered his son's sufferings and made them worse by turning him from a growing child into a growing problem, trained, tormented, exercised. The child's nevertheless intelligent eyes looked on, understanding.

Mr Cohn forced the boy to play with his contemporaries, whose games he didn't understand. And when after a while, he saw him sitting abandoned – often crying or bleeding and his marbles stolen – he himself might offend his son by letting him see his intense dislike. These memories were to adhere like skin in his mind, but unfortunately it was not himself he was ashamed of on such occasions.

When the boys played football in his second year – his dark vague cloud and the ordinary grey stone of the others – and the teacher came up to him afterwards in the presence of parents and children and said, smiling: Little Joe was half-back today, and rejoiced with the opposite side when he kicked an own-goal. Fun for him to get a goal, all the same. Ha ha ha ha.

That was when for the first time he felt the full significance of this 'cave-like hollowness' and an almost bleeding feeling welling up in his throat and spreading over his face. It was not righteous anger. (Everyone's eyes were turned in their direction, or were obviously turned away.) No, it was that he was ashamed of the child who had put him in this situation and was now just standing there glowering, indifferent. He was so *ashamed* he could have thrashed him in full view of everyone.

Somehow or other, civilisation had been victorious. He had managed to keep a cool head and find an answering salvo:

'And to think one was under the illusion that the task of England's games masters was to inspire honesty and fair play, and what does one see? A creature vilifying his pupils in front of each other, in front of their parents and – ' just think that he managed to put on an expression of comical surprise, with no heartrending nuances – 'in front of them*selves* . . . Strange,' he ended with a grimace which, to be sure, did bring the laughs over on his side.

Yes, he had the laughs on his side. Won them by controlling and channelling and civilising his rage. And in England nearly everything is won if you can conquer laughter in that way. But anger and shame continued to hurt inside him.

On the way home, they had walked along side by side. Small men. A large step, two small steps, a large step, two small adjusting change of steps. Then a sudden loss of pressure occurred in this inner discomfort. His heart started ticking, tittering at the memory of the teacher's defeated face, slipped and draped over a crooked smile. He squeezed Joe's hand in the discovery that you have to be unpleasant. You mustn't be upset. You must be unpleasant and think of yourself and your kin and hit back. Be ironic, ridicule and be relentless in the face of insults. Mr Cohn's understanding of human co-existence had hitherto always been built on explanations as means and harmony as the aim. Suddenly he had found himself an interested party, and he reacted just as when you happen to become aware of your new and beautiful profile in a side mirror.

But feeling has no axiom. Experience is never established. One never becomes experienced. The same feeling seeks out its human being again and again, biting in the same place. Mr Cohn knew that Freud considered one should seek them out oneself and allow oneself to be bitten, and that at best man should grow up and become experienced round his cave-like hollowness. Though inevitably in life one is attacked by facts. Strangers.

And then he had had a weakness for Germans before. After all, a German and an Englishman were very alike as they went around in their shirtsleeves worshipping their patch of earth. With pink cheeks, china-blue eyes and chalk-white hair. It hadn't helped to hate that scum who had called him and his children scum. They didn't even see him in a way that enabled them to discern his contempt. He became embittered by despising, unseen by his object, at the same time receiving its cruel summary message about him.

A year or two passed.

In the end, something had helped. Mrs Cohn blinked and, reassured, folded up the paper.

The start of the change could be dated to the twenty-second of

January. If that were so, in four months (thought Mr Cohn), it would be a year since the change – or the help, if you like. The memory almost at once became a reminder of a duty he had to fulfil. He rose from the table and felt under the tap in case the water-heater was ready to provide the washing-up water. As the weak trickle slowly filled the bowl, he cleared the table, and at every turn bent over and blew across a patch cut far too short on the top of Mrs Cohn's head, where pink skin shone through the reddish-fair hair. She mechanically waved him away, but went on reading.

Mr Cohn's duty was self-imposed. This is what it was. In four months' time, it would be the twenty-second of January, nineteen hundred and thirty-eight. That day would be the hundred and fiftieth anniversary of the birth of the poet Byron. As the Byron seat, Newstead Abbey, was scarcely half an hour away, and the poet himself was laid to rest in the church on the corner, this had aroused expectations that the community should celebrate the occasion.

All these 'shoulds' were confirmed into 'shalls' on New Year's Day, 1937, when a large circle of acquaintances had as usual gathered at the Hazell family home. Their host was what is called a devoted Byronist, a collector of first editions and autographs, a traveller – to Brighton, Cheltenham and Aberdeen, but also Drachenfels, Waterloo, Lac Leman, Venice, Pisa and Missolonghi (or Mezologgi, as he preferred to pronounce it). During his improvised chairmanship, and round a bowl of strong mulled wine, a Jubilee Committee was formed. People were more than willing to take on both practical and intellectual tasks. Offers poured in: they should arrange a week-long festival; they should invite guests from every corner of Europe and trim an avenue of evergreen thujas into topiary statues with connections with Byron (a dispute arose over the extent to which the poet's work really contained sculpturally characteristic characters).

The afternoon turned to evening and cheeks were as red as holly berries. Ideas began to run out. In the heat and the twilight, each one of them found something to remember dimly, or sing: quotes, even declamations rattled in one after another like chipped pearl beads on a thread. At about ten, after reinforcing the bowl for the third time, Byron was alive to people who had otherwise never given him a thought.

But when the committee's first meeting actually took place three weeks after the New Year, of the original fifteen members, only five remained. Mr Hazell had spent the intervening time autocratically drawing up rules which were sent out together with the invitations. They contained among other things a clause on 'accomplishments'. Every member of the committee was expected to give a brief address on 'some aspects of the life and work of the poet'. This obligation was deemed to be just within the capabilities of everyone except the established Byronists. They, on the other hand, considered themselves capable of pouring out their surplus knowledge with no effort at all. What an illusion!

Apart from Mr Cohn himself, his good friend Eric Watson was there, plus a dentist called Link who wasn't actually from that part of the world but lived in St James's Street in Nottingham, and Mr Hazell's twenty-two-year-old son, Rupert, named after Rupert Brooke, after his father had been persuaded to abandon the four Christian names George, Gordon, Noel and Byron.

At first they talked for quite a long time about which subjects they should choose for their addresses. The dentist said that even if this meeting hadn't happened, he would sooner or later have put together a brief paper entitled 'Byron, Napoleon and Edmund Kean' to allow those three romantic characters who were so markedly non-romantics to illuminate each other. 'The military man who became a statesman, the poet who became a military man and the jester who became the royal purveyor of the art of drama.'

Rupert had at once signed up for Byron's last six months, his claim being fresh impressions. During the past year, father and son had been on a pilgrimage to Italy and Greece, including, of course, western Greece. And to *Missolonghi*, where the house 'that stands where Byron stood is in a state of filth and decay, and we sought out the caretaker with a request to remove the urinoir on the long wall, which in fact is not a facility but a fence. Harold Nicolson had already asked them to do this ten or more years earlier, but on the whole absolutely nothing ever gets done in Greece. And should they start on something, then they never finish it. Repairs on the house are never more than half-finished. You can never find out whether they are building or demolishing, or whichever it was that was started thirty days or thirty years ago.'

After a couple more hours' discussion on the actual programme –

16

laying wreaths, salutes, a memorial service, a chamber music evening combined with dramatic performance, and Rupert's suggestion to arrange a swimming competition in one of the pools at Newstead Abbey (in January? Well, you go and test the temperature tomorrow) – the evening levelled out into the informal conversation considered appropriate to round off the world's agendas, but which is really the only useful result of them.

It was hot in this room where five people had warmed up an ordinary evening, and the coal fire had been burning all the time. Mr Cohn had brought with him a friendly, yes, pale sherry, which they had started sipping and then had finished off although it was late. They talked about their subject with the same absolutely fresh, dew-fresh bias that all Byronists do, and the character escaped them – as it also always does – by contradicting their interpretations, splitting all their cells into a smiling blur, and slithering out of their contours. It was a wonderful evening, with small gaps in which Mr Cohn heard the echo of German lederhosen music ('Crimson blooms the briar rose, lusty loves the sailor boy') and Eric Watson listened for his wife's admonishing tears.

Link the dentist said: 'For instance, I have never succeeded in ascertaining whether Byron really did occasionally feel like a *monster*. He might say so. He might sound like that. But was it seriously meant? We know that for his – and our – day he had modern opinions, and I have always thought he was above all a sensible and moderate person. But there are multitudes of sensible moderate people who don't arouse even the remotest interest in me because they lack *the other side*. Byron was not only wise but also honestly superstitious. He really believed in sin and he himself was tremendously involved in *original sin* – '

'Yes, but I give him credit for that,' interrupted Mr Hazell. 'In my opinion it's very civilised and discerning to believe in original sin. Nowadays people think they're innocent individuals in an evil world. They think original sin is a difficult Christian concept and so they act all innocence and pretend not to know everyone, every new-born one of us, shares in the evil and the good that occurs. No, it was very sensible of him to believe in original sin.'

'Now I've lost the thread,' said Link crossly. 'Don't you know that you must never interrupt a middle-aged person who finds it hard enough to keep his thoughts in his head . . .

'Where was I,' he muttered. 'Where was I?' With the considerate whispers of the others in the background, he searched for the thread he had lost and found another.

'Is there a ghost that has penetrated closer to reality than Byron? Sometimes he seems to be again among the living. Perhaps he is? I feel his dissatisfied presence as I rootle round in his life for the five hundred thousandth time. No, dissatisfied is the wrong kind of word: a *swelling* presence, like an abscess in the room. Sometimes it's made me stop – stop bothering with Byron, I mean. They say that on certain days the caretaker at Bennet Street in London hears his ghost shuffling about in the attic, with a special sound for his club foot.'

'For heaven's sake, what kind of idiocy is that!' said Rupert.

'But he believed in ghosts himself,' cried Link. 'He was terrified out of his wits one day when he saw an empty Venetian mask on a wall start glowing as if from within. It was some phenomenon, something to do with sunlight and foliage. This combination of objects and chance was no matter of chance to him, but *meaning*. He saw it as a possibility to reckon with; that the supernatural was seeking him out for his sins, and had found him and was *looking* at him through a mask he himself had hung up on the wall, his own face in it.'

'Would we be allowed to get him up and take a look at him?' said Rupert scientifically. 'Would they give us permission?'

'What he called his monstrosity' – Link dismissed the question with a single look – 'on a larger scale was something I think all civilised people share. I'm not only looking for the sugar and spice but also for the universality of Byron. What he had on a large scale was that cold inner twin men have, the one who always chooses the worst alternative whenever he has a choice. The one who, with your eyes wide open, makes you choose faithless friends, the wrong education, a wife it takes years to reconcile yourself to, the wrong queue, the train north instead of south – all without being able to explain it except as a bad day, a self-destructive compulsion. You all recognise that twin; with no motivation, it fills wonderful moments with a feeling of ashes and loathing. What I think is that Byron's inner stranger was more capricious than mine, and drove him to greater exaggerations and greater regrets. Exaggerations and regrets are a prerequisite to art. Artists exaggerate – and then regret it, for the sake of balance. It gives breadth to what they are doing.'

18

For the second time, the thought ran out of Link's words. For a while, he sat chatting to himself, but then he noticed that Mr Cohn was looking at him, waiting for him to go on, and when their eyes met, he suddenly found his original thread again.

'Byron was freed from the sense of housing a monster when people started *accusing* him of being a monster. The press fell over themselves in their efforts to invent sins in him after his wife had left him. After a year in his house, she fled at dawn, leaving behind gross hints about the reasons why. As they were only hints, the press had an opportunity to search their imaginations for truly grotesque sins. Satan would have blushed at their lack of sophistication. All this made Byron unite with his inner twin for their mutual defence. The public image of him became so absurd, it tickled his sense of humour. And you all know, once he was amused, he couldn't even take his own work really seriously.'

Mr Cohn, Mr Hazell, Eric Watson and Rupert do indeed all know. (But perhaps the reader doesn't. The reader is ninety per cent certain to be ignorant of the facts to which Link the dentist is alluding, and wonders whether the author is even considering letting the argument out of Mr Hazell's library and making it accessible to everyone. Calm. Our Byronists are only reinforcing themselves with a little philosophy before starting on their labours of transforming the actual flesh into words.)

'What was interesting to the *modern* man Byron,' Link went on, 'was not least the general public's perception that a monster is denoted by immorality. But his own sense of being a monster contained a profound quality of *guilt*. He had discovered that the general public doesn't care a fig about guilt and considers offences much more serious than sins. And then he discovered that he himself was one single indivisible creature with all his qualities interdependently mixed, interwoven with each other. This insight can be seen in the later parts of *Childe Harold*, which lack the mannered resonances of the first and second cantos. But maturity depressed him. Man is inevitably depressed by great insights into life. They reduce you. They break you down to strengthen you, and Byron was broken in 1816. Not because his wife had left him, together with the child – nor that he had lost his position in society, or his Grass-Goddess Augusta. No, he felt robbed of his youth, in which you can distinguish your innocence from your evil genius.'

That was what had helped Mr Cohn. He had begun a process that was to lead to Mrs Cohn's now being able to mention the German lady without risking hours of lulling dialogues. True, there were neither comparisons nor analogies with his own rôle as 'monster', but words had come like drips of vinegar. The surface tension had gone and he could see down into the murky sludge of words about 'Die Juden'.

When Mr Cohn was consoled, it was nearly always because of something he had found in the margins. When he read books, he turned side issues into main themes. He had most recently been reading *Anna Karenina*, and passion, the despair of doubts – Anna and Vronsky and their sins – had left him cold. The Levin theme of Country versus Town was his way through the novel, all about how work occupies man in human life and the countryside, while society life (and for that matter unemployment or a purely intellectual existence) was sweated out of him in isolation, as when wax is sweated out in taut greasy drops.

When Mr Cohn talked to his acquaintances, far too often he found his own train of thought among his friend's subordinate clauses and then followed it, while allowing his friend to talk himself dry. Rather ill-mannered, of course, but he could not make his ideas uniform with those of others. He had no desire for his problems to be uniform with others. Certainly not.

He clattered and splashed in the washing-up bowl. He liked washing up. It stimulated his thoughts, not to mention his fingers. He had low blood pressure and poor circulation. Sometimes his hands were icy cold and the only thing that helped was the washing up. He knew how he would die. Everyone has some inkling of his weak point – whether it's the heart or the brain.

After their meal, Mrs Cohn powdered the two small cheeks she would soon be washing and creaming for the night. She fluffed up her reddish curls and sat down with a book and her knitting in an armchair by the wireless, at the time broadcasting the third part of a dramatised version of *Jane Eyre*. Mr Cohn looked at the picture before him: she was reading and knitting at the same time.

Women who don't like wasting time are also hectic when relaxing. He listened to the first few lines, then lost interest: a cloud of light falsetto female voices twittering into a cloudbank of words, its silver lining apparently a gentleman called St John.

He looked out of the window. He looked at the window, also a picture, a work of art of deep dusk, of reflection, rivulets. Those layers were much more evocative than just the view.

Mr Cohn was sitting beside a small oval table that normally fulfilled no other function than standing there covered with family photographs. At the moment it was laid out with a pile of lined paper, some books and a fountain pen with a gold feather on it. The filler was broken, so there was also an inkpot. One of the books was open at two full-length portraits protected by rice-paper. On the left was the only *en face* picture of Byron. Curly hair, very large eyes, a slight squint, a delighted smile and a strong round neck. Over one shoulder – carelessly – lay a fur, the coarse, apparently sticky hairs indicating a nordic and heathen breed of animal. On the right was a picture of a woman with the same kind of enormous eyes. But they were not cheerful. There was no vitality in them. There was no expression in them at all, and yet they completely dominated her face. The other symbols in the portrait were equally cool and quiet and in accordance with early nineteenth-century fashion. Her coiffure was ornamental, piled up and hanging in corkscrew curls – her head was dripping with curls and jewellery and she held it with elegant indifference. The woman consisted of coiffure, eyes and pearls in row upon row. Mr Cohn was unable to extract any more than that out of this picture of the 'Grass-Goddess'. It was one of two existing that might *possibly* be of Byron's sister, Augusta Leigh.

He leafs through the book. He looks at his wife. He looks at the window. Like every author's pen, Mr Cohn's hovers over the first word. The moment it is written, the direction has been given. The whole intuitive arsenal of the story rushes in, spreads itself out in the service of that word. He wanted to believe that he was going to write something humorous, something entertaining to emphasise the modesty of his project – though modesty must not lead to poor story-telling. That can easily happen and often does. A lecturer who does not dare be sensitive and emotional about his subject can easily start reducing and scorning it. On the other hand, you mustn't allow yourself to be swallowed up by conditions you have no control over. And then again . . .

But let us not follow all the way into Mr Cohn's meandering thoughts on how best to deal with historical material. On Mrs Cohn's wireless, a modern play is flowing along quite smoothly, a radio dramatisation of *Jane Eyre*. Jane is just being proposed to by the loveless, chilly St John, and the actors' voices betray no embarrassment, despite the limitations of turning meticulously drawn characters from a novel into voices. Mr Cohn raised his pen: the first word, the first sentence, the first page must be something quite special! Jane Eyre said: 'I am extremely honoured, but . . .' The pen hovered. He put it down.

Half the summer had run away in sunshine and hesitation.

'I intend these written contributions together to produce at least the contours of an overall picture of Byron,' Mr Hazell had stipulated in the invitation to the first committee meeting.

On the way there, one cold January evening, Eric Watson caught up with Mr Cohn, who was moving with caution, for there were patches of ice on the street and under his arm he had a bottle of Tio Pepe in a brown paper bag with string round it. Even at a distance, Mr Cohn recognised the sound of those seven-league strides of the sturdy police boots Eric Watson had inherited from his father and wore when the roads were bad. Then came the smell of old dubbin. Then he came himself. They were old friends, although they lived very different lives, such good friends that Eric Watson told him about a dream he had had that morning. Then they slowed their steps and gradually stopped altogether, because they had started discussing what subjects they were to choose for their respective lectures.

Eric Watson said that the crossroads of narrative had four signposts. The one pointing to the north was The Right Way. The final goal is that cool place Harmony. It is a thousand miles away and the stages on the route have small unreliable resting places like Moderation, Fidelity, A Sober Outlook, Think Before You Speak, Restraint and Look After The Pennies.

On the south signpost is written The Way of the Senses, 0.0 metres, because it starts in the present and ends in the present and moves through the present, though no one knows its extent. It is a modern and discerning way. On the third signpost is Concentration. That's the way of ideas. Anyone going that way with his head in the clouds has never noticed whether the road is asphalted or paved with gold. And the fourth signpost – finally – points to Triviality. That way you take step by step, through the uninterpreted junk of reality, beauty and morass, without emphasising anything at someone else's expense.

Eric Watson said that his own lack of success was due to the fact that he was always trying to go in all four directions at once. And the rope you pull in four directions is inadequate everywhere and *jerks* you back to the starting point, where you could regularly find him, confused and not a little bewildered.

Mr Cohn smiled to himself. Yes, you could describe Byron like that.

Then they stopped again and continued the discussion, and a veterinary surgeon who had just got out of his car to visit a cowshed heard peals of laughter rolling across the field. They had decided that Eric Watson was to write along the Right Way, while Mr Cohn trod the Carnal Way. Anyone superficially acquainted with the two gentlemen and knowing their leanings and tendencies would certainly also have laughed. In practical terms, this meant Eric Watson had signed on for a discourse on the poet's brief marriage with the intelligent 'model of virtue', Annabella Milbanke, while Mr Cohn was to devote his labours to the incestuous passion between Byron and his sister, Augusta.

But time had gone by and nothing had been written. Eight months had passed without a line. Mr Cohn did make a discovery about time factors: you could keep time back in a project at the eternal 'beginning' while the present swept past. Like a thumb marring the flow of a veil, like the stone in flowing water. But that was no fertile discovery, for nothing got written. When the committee members met, it was more and more often with half-averted looks indicating that the eagerness to get started had faded and that everyday life had hollowed out any sense of necessity.

It says a great deal about Lord Byron's attraction that it is always half a head taller than the difficulties he piles up for you. The five Byronists struggled on with their plans. Spring came and grew into summer. At the height of its beauty, it turned to autumn. From Rupert and Link, there were indications their labours were beginning to show results. But Mr Cohn and Eric Watson had not produced a line.

To get going, they talked, but the more they talked, the further they got from the start. They asked each other how you encircle a subject – at which point do you start a circle? The answer came suddenly out of the blue. Eric Watson had an abscess on his middle finger from playing the guitar and went to the doctor to get it lanced. In the waiting-room, he leafed through a three-year-old magazine and came across an article on Brest-Litovsk – a list of the occasions when railway lines had served as 'neutral ground'. Most of the examples were military, but politicians had also used railway carriages in which to sign treaties, make agreements and draw up truces. This modern vehicle offered an impersonal coolness where you could give and take without being bound by guest and host status. There a man was a glint, a photograph in the other man's eye. It was the point of issue that mattered. The individual retreated untouched.

This insight had had a predecessor in Annabella Milbanke, Lady Byron. For right in the middle of all the pictures of spiked helmets, seals and gold braid was a scrap of information: 'In the winter of 1851, Lady Byron, wife of the poet Lord Byron (1788–1824), met his half-sister Augusta Leigh at a railway station after each had been taken half way. The journey had been demanded by Lady Byron and it was said that, before the death of Mrs Leigh (which occurred shortly afterwards), her aim was to receive her confession on the question of assertions about an incestuous relationship between her and her half-brother.'

Bandaged half way up to his elbow, Eric Watson left the surgery filled with the eureka that floats on every author's lips during those brief moments when he thinks he has found the ideal form for his content. He had a circle for the subject, a double circle, in fact. Fantastic! That train journey from opposite directions, with Truth as the objective. It was like a find. So Mr Cohn could account for Augusta's memories with London as the starting point, and he could follow Lady Byron on her way from Leicester, where she presumably had boarded the train. Then the lectures could meet half way, where in the fullness of time they would have occasion to summarise their views on the case.

But Mr Cohn made difficulties, embarrassed, as usual. It was too calculated. It might be like a film, or rather something like Mrs Cohn's radio play. It could be embarrassing to propound it. Eric Watson said: 'Joel, anyone who worries about starting wrongly never even gets started.' He said it so fiercely that after weighing it up briefly, Mr Cohn decided to submit and listen to the scenario that was to be his starting point.

*

In 1851, Lady Byron had been separated from her husband for thirty-five years and his widow for twenty-seven. She lived a decorous life in the country, devoting herself to intellectual and spiritual matters. She had a faithful and uncritical circle of friends, as well as her daughter, Ada, herself a mother of three children and in addition quite an eminent mathematician. But this winter, Ada was already showing symptoms of the cancer of the womb shortly to lead to her death. And beneath Lady Byron's intellect and spirit still ran a minute commentary on everything said or written about Byron. She went on snapping at the name Byron like a waiting pike, seeing in every bait a promise of evidence. For Lady Byron was still waiting for the incontrovertible evidence that would justify her leaving Byron without warning or explanation, then mobilising a campaign of slander that drove him into exile.

Augusta Leigh herself had a weak heart, poor eyesight and was slightly senile. Her family had been wrecked in the storms of life and had left her to the inevitable, hopefully chastening miseries of old age. The two ladies had not seen each other for years. As long as Byron had been alive, Lady Byron had been able to threaten him with 'revealing all' and exposing Augusta, this also being a means of intimidating Augusta and subjecting her to minor degradations. When he died, some of the need for revenge evaporated, and thus also any contact between the two ill-matched sisters-in-law. A bond snapped like a silk ribbon tied in spring between two saplings, forgotten by autumn, when it fades, turns brittle and breaks.

When Lady Byron heard how ill Augusta was, however, she was reminded of a fundamental obscurity. Everyone knew Byron had had an illegal relationship with his sister for two years, and that he was perhaps even the father of her fourth child. He had told several people and implied it to others ('that man could never keep his mouth shut!'). Augusta reacted with anguish and *obedience* when the matter was mentioned in roundabout ways. But she had never confessed to this horror in so many words. Lady Byron had never heard her answer yes or no to the question, nor heard her say the words everyone was waiting for. She hadn't even seen the admission that can be observed on a naked face caught red-handed. Augusta seemed to have managed to maintain a neutral mask in the obstinacy of conscious amnesia.

The waiting pike (Annabella), her Case – her reason for leaving

25

Byron – had always been substantial. But as long as she lacked Augusta's confession, her argument was based on circumstantial evidence, a bridge with sawn-through piles.

No wonder she was hoping for a dying woman's confession, Eric Watson said, rounding off his sketch.

So we are back in the Cohns' living-room, Mrs Cohn knitting stocking-stitch, her book on her lap. Jane Eyre had just received the letter telling her Rochester is seriously injured. The actress rustles something supposed to be a letter pressed to her bosom. Mr Cohn writes his first line:

In the winter of 1851, two trains cross England on passing tracks. Two women, each coming half way.

That was two lines, to be more accurate. And then? He looked at his wife, at that moment neither knitting nor listening nor reading, but sitting leaning slightly forward with a thoughtful pale golden smile on her face. What a strange expression. The same as when she once listened to foetal kicks. It disappeared. It disappeared tremendously quickly, disappeared almost like a memory before he got it down on paper:

From east to west, the older woman, alone now and clad entirely in black, a few months before her own funeral. But her body well under control. Her hands clasped, she leans her forehead against the window, desiring sun, like a flower in the shade of large leaves, not eagerly, not avariciously but gently, with a sleeping smile, to which the warmth is persuaded and stays, right next to her final desire.

And why not go on:

She is thinking no words. No thoughts apart from the three which are regularly needed to keep her head up and to ensure breathing in is followed by breathing out. But when the world – a wall or a yard or a bridge – comes so close to the carriage that the air is compressed into sound, she tries to observe what they call 'speed'. Though she is not attentive. Each time she is surprised for the first time. And is half-blind: a dazzle of sunlight flickers over her face when she opens her eyes and wrongly fixes her gaze. It comes from within herself, with a touch of her youth. It is an expression of coquettish helplessness which was never convincing when it was a lure call and she was a girl. But now her helplessness has become real and its warm troubling spot searches over her face as she herself seeks an eye to catch.

Mr Cohn noticed he had stopped modelling his wife, but instead had been thinking about a woman who smiled a shortsighted smile at him in the street, uncertain whether he was the person she thought he was. Then he thought about the dim, black-spotted mirrors at the chemist's and then about his mother's mirrors, which had been in a fire but hadn't cracked and had become laughing distorting mirrors. Finally he thought about his mother's ear-lobes, stretched by sixty years of gold. Three of his fingers were inky. He decided not to write any more until he had the pen mended. Then he read through what he had written. It was like a blot of ink! He stared at it with the utter confusion of a man thinking he has put out a net. He thought he must think, think out things before he wrote them down. But before he began his thoughts, he wrote a heading above the ink blot: *When I think of leaving you, Jerusalem.*

When I think of leaving you, Jerusalem

In the winter of 1851, two trains cross England on passing tracks. Two women, each coming half way.

From east to west, the older woman, alone now and entirely in black, a few months before her own funeral. Her hands clasped, she leans her forehead against the window, desiring sun, like a flower in the shade of large leaves: not eagerly, not avariciously but gently, with a sleeping smile, to which the warmth is persuaded and stays, to her final desire.

She is not thinking, no words, no thoughts apart from the three which are regularly needed to keep her head up and to ensure breathing in is followed by breathing out. But when the world – a wall or a yard or a bridge – comes so close to the carriage that the air is compressed into sound, she tries to observe what they call 'speed'. Though she is not attentive. Each time, she is surprised for the first time. And is half-blind: a dazzle of sunlight flickers across her face when she opens her eyes and wrongly fixes her gaze. It comes from within herself, with a touch of her youth. It is an expression of coquettish helplessness which was never convincing when it was a lure call and she was a girl. But now the helplessness has become reality and its warm troubling spot searches over her face as she herself seeks an eyeful to catch.

At a distance, the landscape slowly changes. What is closest to her rushes by, occasionally hidden by the smoke coming out of the engine and turning white in the cold and, depending on the direction of the line and the wind, falling on either side of the London to Birmingham line. Only by noticing details on the way can she imagine herself being carried along. For long spells, she forgets even to think about the journey, just shivers and rests in the rare pearl of freedom between departure and arrival.

And rare, inherited pearls in the shape of drops hang from her lobes, swinging and meeting and measuring the train's shifting weight. When Augusta was young, the mirrors were also young, not yet dimmed by silver oxide. From the depths of the mirror, Europe answered with its blind young face, the one she uses when young men talk dreamily about premature death. But Augusta saw only the surface of the mirror, where all those dead were men. And shook her head, but only to enjoy the effect of polished stones making the light explode furiously round her pious countenance. She had no idea that effect also enjoyed her. The glittering sparkling ear-rings danced and jerked in the opposite direction to her head, measuring out the price of vanity: everything contrary to her whim. And now the holes in her lobes have stretched into slits, into ear-patches as long as empty lips, limbs. And the weight goes on weighing heavily, weighing and swinging. To and fro. The laws of gravity are reinforced in Augusta, although they have long since possessed her. Those who spoke of it also died young. And dark showers of hail came out of the mirrors.

The train does not take the shortest route. The early tribal routes wind round, following the landscape as it opens and closes, softly, as England does where the mountains are hills and the rivers streams, the earth itself old, shaggy groundswell. Snow swirls in the plough furrow, the way wind swings in the horse pasture, a thread running beneath the rail-bed, and over the horizon glide banks of cloud soon to unfold into new downy calm. Long before the cloud hides the sun, it is predicted by red sky: a half sphere of threads, glistening like hair or cobwebs. The square church tower changes colour as new light seeks other patches in the sandstone. The dog turns on the road, and four girls run homewards holding on to their hats.

All this plus a bolting pony look on the person in the carriage of iron and wood. She leaves a veil of soot on the snow behind her. And doesn't notice. And forgets it. The girls point at 'the speed', which snatches the expression off each of their faces and drags it along with it. Once again something has happened, with human time. It has torn itself out of the rhythm of its days and confirms it with a triumphant scream from the pipe for the release of steam. At every curve, a desolate cry of warning. And again. Behind the train, the air closes in again like two halves of an apple. But what had been whole goes on swirling in halves. The silence also remains divided after the cry. A tube of iron and wood. Inside, the person sits like an infectious vulnerable preparation sealed in glass. She turns to the sun with her unborn smile: Augusta.

The dog turns on the road. The pony stumbles at the bottom of the embankment. She senses it. It bolts in the pocket of air between the train and the groundswell of air behind it. But when the fence and ditch block its way, and with great shudders it rears and loses its fear, it falls back into undisturbed peace and nibbles off a chestnut shoot sweetened by the frost.

If Augusta had ever thought about herself, that kind of simultaneous panic and calm would have aroused her affinity: to adapt, not in obtrusive closeness, nor in resistance, but with gracious dependency. Graciously dependent. Though she is not thinking about herself, but clasps her hands and starts counting on her fingers.

Yes, now, the children had one just like it before, with a yellow mane. It had a white square round the tail's . . . inside, and a patch over its eye. Hm, I remember when Leigh came home with it one night. He had lost a boot and it was raining so he wanted to ride, but that pony, it backed and bucked and tossed its head so that you could hear their exchange of opinions a long way away. I'm sure it didn't want him! A coarse man who breaks your back and sits as comfortably as he can and rides off! Then I heard him whistling on the steps. He had lost one boot, so half the creature pattered and the other half clumped, then he came in to show what he had won. Money, IOUs hauled out of his pockets and sleeves and showered down over me in bed. I told him to go on with that kind of gambling (whatever it was) instead of horses, for which he had only a passion, but no luck. Then he showed me the pony, which he had also won. But . . . that kind of horse was hardly what tested his gambling. It allowed itself to be harnessed to the children's trap on the very first Sunday, and managed to pull them all.

. . . and then she sees her children in lovely weather, between fields of silver-green wheat shimmering spike-like in the poppies. Coloured by memory, the picture floats in behind the optic nerve, shaped by memory. Sometimes the road dips, the waves of corn rising so high that the little ones in the trap are obscured. She uses her fingers to count them, but after every crest of a wave someone is missing, and it is laborious to fish him out again. And: they are all equally young. All eight of the siblings had arranged a meeting at the same age instead of the same time! That's why no one is old enough to look after the others! They keep losing someone. After a huge long wave of stems and foaming ears of corn, they suddenly change vehicles and are sitting in a – boat! The pony's tail has become a – wind flying high above only *two* children.

This makes Augusta very uneasy and she fidgets and grumbles as she sits forty years away. She knocks on the window and another passenger starts looking at her. But after a while she pulls herself together, and when she looks more closely at the two girls, she realises the other children aren't yet born, or are 'far too small to be in a boat'. Her sense of reality pours back to the present and fades. Her hands quieten. Augusta is worn out. Her memory has become sludge.

But the boat with faded sails, compass rose and white-clad girls refuses to sink back to the bottom. Instead it stays afloat and keeps on rising with the same picture from different angles: it fills her pupils like a miniature; it follows like a finger picture on a misty window. She holds firmly on to it, and reinforces it. The forest grows out towards the rails and its darkness dazzles the white. The train sways over the rail-bed, the boat plunges, swinging down on the curve of the wave – a steep incline, and Augusta sharpens all her senses to remember her daughters' names.

One is still really small, she sees, smelling the fragrance of her hair: neither cleanliness nor dirt, but the smell of hair as only children have. The girl tips back on the incline and her face is hidden under the brim of her hat as she leans forward, downwards, not to counteract her position but to admire her new shoes. The other girl is larger, 'a six-year-old', and is sitting framed by a man, between his legs, her hand on his hand on the tiller. The other hand holds a rope-end and between these hands floats the expression of pride at being entrusted with a task of her own. The man talks about compass roses as the 'most beautiful roses there are, because man has created them'. He instructs the girl, but only the mother understands: on earth there are two poles, two extreme places, but they are so cold no one wishes to go there. The other points of the compass are simply directions, not goals. But people long to go there, although east and west are always as far behind you as in front of you. Or perhaps because of that.

31

'. . . have *you* been, travelled, far away over there?' the girl shouts above the noise of the wind and rigging. 'I,' he replies, 'have travelled all round the world. Several times.' His reddish-brown beard moves above the girl's head as he speaks, a crackling beard full of late summer, but Augusta has qualms. She suddenly remembers her eldest daughter's future and now sees quite clearly the way it was furled in the child, like a rope, ready to be thrown forward, the whole of its vacillating uncertain length. Only her way of leaning inside him, the man: so unhesitatingly and trustingly . . . the warning throaty sounds she produces in the shelter of the noises of the train do not reach down into the past. The girl doesn't hear, she chokes with laughter with her nose against his waistcoat as a wave breaks and spray washes over them. And on the other side of time, her mother gives up. Again.

The engine now slows down before a bridge, a wooden bridge over the first, second and third water course. The engine stops flowing in sequence, dissolving its sounds in tones, its speed in cogs that stop-start with dull reverberations from the spans of the bridges. A thin layer of ice lies on the stream pools, dipping under and air-bubbling a mobile painting. The sky – now almost covered with snow clouds – drops three, drops four five warm flakes. 'Girls, flakes, white' . . . so impermanent, melting away. Augusta is old and her memory has become sludge, where patches of light float down to the surface and sink back before she has had time to establish fish or coins.

But on the other side of the bridge, the last rays of sunlight crowd out of a rent and sparkle through the bare treetops. This thousand-fingered light game does to the base of the eyes what the sea used to do, and out of that confusion the picture returns –

She herself is sitting in the prow of the boat looking out for shallows. She shades her eyes against the brilliant line of the horizon encircling the sea almost all the way round, a dish, green and glass-blown in curves and fragments, with anemones under the dusky shadow of the seaweed. Stillness outlines itself in the air. On the flat islands of ebb and sand far away, a white raven is hacking through oyster shell, year-ring by year-ring, and sucking out meagre fish-oil.

When what is distant is the closest of all, you grow there and are thinned out, swelling and cooling and *seeing* what clear days conceal: a mouth opening in space to swallow the sea water. The drops leap upwards, racing each other in a thick shiny column, and the mouth closes on the last. Growing there and being thinned out. The world is water, a landscape of curves and fragments, and a buoy is climbing half way to the horizon.

Augusta is resting on her side, listless, her arm stretched over the prow. In front of her flutter the lengths of ragged lace tied under her chin to keep her hat on her head. Ragged like so many of her things that she will never get mended, mend. It is easier to live forgotten in rags that hang together than to live purely and correctly. It is wiser.

Behind her – at the tiller – the man in white now has a face and so the threat to the girl in his lap fades. Ha ha, how can Augusta have suspected him of ever . . . but it is probably true that without his face, a man is approximately all men. Above the bright colours of the beard, this face is small, narrow and stern. It belongs to her cousin, George Anson Byron; he is steering, and on his lap Georgiana is also steering. Normally he is in command of royal ships and does not shout and swear, as inexpert men do in small boats. The little skiff moves compliantly under his eye and hand. There is nothing to be afraid of.

At sea, a buoy climbs sluggishly against the movement of the water. While she watches it, the boat goes from wave to swell and opens the world beneath her. You don't see it until you are already in it and the firm surface rolls away irregularly, chess-patterned. It makes you catch your breath. In the pit of your stomach moves a yellow patch that might be nausea. George obeys her protests and turns so that Augusta is pointing back towards Hastings.

As her fingers meet the wind, they give out small signals, hard, separated like hair. The wind runs on up her arms, into the sleeve of her dress, once a gift in yellow: it grows cool on the underside of her arm, cold in her armpit and envelops a breast, which shudders, goes goose-fleshed, a sparrow's egg. She draws in her arm and looks back at the buoy that has been washed over. Washed over, it comes up glistening black, not lying at anchor but with a direction like the point of a V, and soon the white arms it creeps with become visible. Soon a heel can be seen on the surface of the water and unbleached Nanking trousers swinging and dragging. Then the lace fringes of Augusta's shawl are flicked back against her eyes by a puff of wind, blinding her, while the old Augusta blinks something grey out of her eye. But she is used to it and goes on blinking, this time without losing the inner picture of 'my only holiday. . . ?'

*

33

It was August, 1814. 'Your evasions are simply a continuation of your old hero-worship,' said George Anson to Byron.

They were walking along the fortifications and embankments, on a shore of polished shingle in shifting pastel colours. He lent Augusta his telescope and she found you really do have to stand curved like a fishing rod to be able to see properly at eye-level. She had thought that the looking position belonged to a fraternity (captains like George) just as only tailors are supposed to sew sitting cross-legged; she thought people deliberately shaped their bodies according to a tradition in their profession. Though it might be that an occupation is independent and re-creates itself in postures everyone has to obey: as she grasped the narrow end with one hand and cupped the other under the lens, she at once began to lean back to find the field of vision, and out of the corner of her eye she saw her shadow imitating the position everyone takes when looking into a telescope.

There rose in her, indolently, from what was most patient in her character, a resistance, a nagging thought that everything can be done differently from the way it is done, and that the only thing that stops this is habit slicing through the multiplicity of things. The thought had no purpose, not even touching on her own daily life, which was smooth, rather offwhite, like the fly-leaf in the Bible on which she entered her children's names as they were born. But the idea was fixed, and the moving fabric of days, manipulations and thoughts ran over it like a blunt but upturned knife. 'He,' said George, continuing the summer's conversation – and the previous summer's – 'might have been a hero ten years ago, or fifteen, or perhaps even only seven. After that he had to become respectable (like us) and fat (like a satisfied *arriviste*). Now he has nothing (staccato) left and is a minimal man with the largest dead army in the world. He's never had a navy (the French don't understand the sea) and the economy is in ruins. But these Frenchmen – and you dreamers! – would have him back like a dead man preferring to have back his fatal disease.'

The sea lay still for an hour, at dusk dark green with a blood-red trace from the sun swelling at the end of the world. Only the surface water came from France, softly, its extreme edge going a little way up on the shore at floodtide, past the string of seaweed and mussel shells before beginning to turn back across the Channel.

Augusta saw the off-shore wind through the telescope. It blew twice

34

experimentally, three times, then steadied and at once, fumblingly and majestically, struck, filling and stretching the sails of the five or ten southbound warships, some of them completely, others half beyond the horizon. You could see figures clinging to a forest of masts, straddled, obeying orders that had gone from course to course, from dialect to dialect, but with the same content of terms.

More sails rose, the wind filling them or filling them with vacuum just where the figures were straddled. She imagined they were smoking their chalky clay pipes. The whole coast was chalky clay. 'No,' laughed George in answer to her question. 'The lens doesn't fill the telescope. You wouldn't be able to lift it. It's only at the end. Further inside is another lens that turns the picture the right way up. The lens alone shows everything upside-down.'

Augusta nodded and handed back the telescope. She never asked subsequent questions. What contradicted the testimony of the eye seemed believable: wind filling sails with a vacuum; the world having to be turned several times to reach the senses the right way up. George was about to replace the telescope in its case, but she reached out for it to try once more, now she knew.

'The revolution,' said George, 'was for him (as opposed to Lucien Bonaparte, whom one must respect, reluctantly or otherwise) nothing more than a chance occurrence that gave him the chance. A generation of dreamers imagine that he nevertheless spread it with his wars! Well, whoever brings down an old order and calls it despotic does not establish new times by installing himself as a dictator (and nepotist), even if he were to institute a score of new laws. What he has spread is a mass of unnecessary, fundamentally unmilitary deaths, which we have also had to experience in the family . . .'

'Oh, yes,' said Augusta.

'. . . and his own example. As victor, he himself became the yardstick of his time for government by the people. (Not that I in any way advocate government by the people, as they call it. What is it, really, government by the people? Should someone from the people govern, he would soon be ruler. If all the people govern, chaos reigns. If the people hand out a mandate, the ruler becomes an opportunist and self-contradictory!) But it's not logical for a tuppenny-ha'penny emperor with pretensions to rule the world to represent the people, is it?'

35

George paused. No one answered. Later, Byron told them that his 'Mamma' had been particularly proud of her birth and made him aware 'from the day I wore skirts' that he was a Gordon of the Gight clan, not a common Seton Gordon. And yet his mother had supported the revolution in France.

A moment later he said that the dreamers he knew were more *illogical* than fanatical creatures. They seldom followed their interests, which of course reduced their ability to govern. 'One must not underestimate the weight there is in personal interests.' And the sensible idea that only idealistic statesmen may displace bad ones had not yet got through to them. 'Mandate, of course one can doubt the mandate. Mandate . . . personally, I would never give anyone my mandate, but I think someone will take it all the same. As far as fat upstarts are concerned, then observe that the next most senior Hanoverian in this country is so grotesque with debauchery that he has to be hoisted out through the window to get into his carriage.'

'The royal family is German!' replied George.

Augusta shifted her view from the heavily armed warships on course for Lisbon, Cadiz, Gibraltar, Sardinia and Malta – and spun a half turn of swirling pictures to look at her brother:

Byron was leaning against the embankment on the shore, also studying the continent. He had a walking stick of bone and porcelain and hide in one hand, the point whipping and drawing in the sandy shingle. She saw signs, three, enlarged, three, drowning in the running shingle, three, then let her field of vision glide on upwards to frame his face. It had the same expression of annoyed arrogance it had had all week. He was unutterably bored by George's patriotic effusions against Napoleon Bonaparte and for the moral values of Englishness. On the left side, he had clenched his teeth and made a little leaping knot of muscles in front of his ear. On the right side, his lips were parted and commenting silently on the course of the ships: Lisbon, Cadiz, Seville, Gibraltar, Sardinia, Malta, Cephalonia, Zakynthos. But when he saw her looking, and looked at her – at first into the dead lens, then below it – satisfaction crept up through his arrogance and she lowered the instrument to answer a smile.

Only a year back in time since they had admitted, given way to the desire to smile in this way. It still felt warm, pungent, like waking up with a chewed rose hip in your mouth. And yet mild. It couldn't rest in

36

the curve of other smiles that would burst into *laughter*, when people were present.

As they were confirming each other – silently in the dusk and behind their cousin's back – Byron nevertheless went on talking about the lack of logic and practical disposition in dreamers. He was talking to George, but with Augusta. The words there, the tone here, the latter so private that George reacted to something he was too stupid to understand. Byron was saying in a tender voice that dreamers dream. And what is less filled with fanaticism and ideals than just dreams? Dreams of anguish and agony and seven-league strides and shameless longing with a hand in openings of clothing.

('I pray!!' said George.)

A dream is splintered by everything at the same time. Byron said nothing is as easy as splintering in the way an idealist does. An idealist can be convinced of anything.

He said anything would be good at that particular moment as long as it entailed an end to this bloody orgy that appeared to be so sadly linked with development. I don't want to know about it. By the way, have you seen my new little hand-pistol that came by the second post? They have a stronger striking force, as the lock is reinforced by an alloy ring of . . .

His tender voice. The words ran after him as he walked across living tinkling rows of shingle, beside George. With Augusta five steps behind.

A scream of rage was heard that night.

The thundery weather ran along the coast. It had grown out of the summer storm over the Bay of Biscay and combined its rolling hurtling darkness with that of the sea. All things not born or dying in cycles came up one after the other, pouring rain whipping milk out of the earth. Later on, a faint wind licked the fragrance out of thousands of dripping chalices.

If you looked out to sea, you could see the lightning flashing and casting the shadows that rose after sunset. You could see it pissing fire into the water. Anyone looking steadily saw more: corn-glow falling perpendicularly out of the night in an act of self-consumption already half completed, shooting stars like drips from a roof, quenching the darkness. The silence in the play of light was complete: delayed echoes of rough indifferent rumbles gliding out of the scene the further away they were from the thunderstorm. And as everything sank away and the clouds thinned out on land, half-grown young sea-birds rose on their long legs, trying to shake the water out of their feathers. But the old hands already knew everything and lay still, chattering quietly.

Clouds encircled the moon and the zodiac in a wreath of colour, and in warm corners the night flowering of creepers began. For a long time and briefly, gently and sharply, the scents licked around, in and out, in, out of pockets of buildings, running up walls and tall chimneys, down into them, to trickle through ventilators and right into the rhythm of human breathing.

In this silence, someone let out a scream of rage, jabbed again and opened the doors of sleep. An inkwell shot out of the second floor, showered black content over grass, gravel and boxwood and – at the moment of breaking – over a muse, who together with her seven sisters was a statue among the cypresses on the terrace.

The next morning, Byron was full of regrets over what his temper had done. He dispatched a few humble lines and money to the owner of the house. Yes, that morning was sunny and good company and happy laughter, as Byron used the rest of the page counting up what impetuosity, thoughtlessness and uninhibited temper had cost him over the last eight years. He came to the sum of one thousand, three hundred and thirty-eight pounds, four shillings and sixpence ('and I'm not counting unintentional paternities and rash purchases', the man said).

Together, they helped scrub with pumice stone.

'I'm a vandal,' he muttered, not without satisfaction.

Euterpe's position was laughable, a troubled movement of flight: with body twisted and arms entwined above her head, she was glancing over her shoulder down at the small of her back, where the inkblot grasped with eight ugly fingers. A man came walking across the lawn, his face bright with amusement as he caught sight of his Dear Friend! He shook hands with Byron, bowed to Augusta and together with the others admired the inkblot.

Cottages lean against each other among the headlands of Hastings, the herring slipping and dancing out of far too small nets at sea. The Society Outside All Laws moved about on the terrace of Hastings House, the dog lying indolently on its side, all four paws outstretched in the heat, the little girls playing dragonflies. Their nurse was plucking or darning something in her hand. White adults were circling round a plaster statue. The recently arrived friend asked Byron why he had thrown 'the inkwell in particular . . .' Byron replied with a suspicious 'What do you mean?' The friend mentioned 'the great ink-thrower'.

'Ha ha, I didn't aim. I never aim, except in fun, for sport. When it's serious, I've never done anything else but defend myself.'

The white adults sweep with their arms when he subsequently changes his mind and asks if his blots on the Muse could be called a satanic jest! His best friends used to say he was a lazybones selling his Muse piecemeal, in mouthfuls.

'They're right, of course. They're right when they say that anyone putting together a verse in ten days and scribbling another in four has undeserved success. But if the artistic act has to be carried out with a limed twig, then I'll fall by the wayside! The devil makes all this too sophisticated. And me too superstitious. Which I am. Let's drown our annoyance in tea.'

Augusta laughed again, seeing out of the corner of her eye his blasphemy taking shape as three owls came and perched in an elm. She laughed at table as Byron teased his servant Fletcher.

Augusta simply laughed. She listened to the way Byron and Friend gossiped about people she didn't know, places she would never go to and books she would never read. She breathed in her only holiday and heard their conversation, quietly in her outer ear.

*

Mr Cohn's concentration snapped there – or reveries, if you like. Mrs Cohn had dropped some stitches or done something wrong, for she attracted her husband's attention by sitting bolt upright. Her book had landed on the floor. He went across to pick it up for her. She told him roughly where she had got to and – with much the same spouse-like intuition with which she found the place on his back that was itching – he found the place in the book and put a piece of thread in as a bookmarker.

'Do you want anything more to eat before you go to bed?' she said in a certain singsong tone of voice. She knew that it irritated him. The actual question irritated him. The children used to get annoyed, angry when they came to see them and she kept going on about food. Her awareness of her family's displeasure enticed this anxious challenging song out of her. Always the same blind flirting with the same cooling growing No.

The BBC drama episode was over. After forty minutes, they had gone over to *At the Fireside*, a concert given by semi-amateurs before an audience once a month. Hitherto Mr Cohn had taken note of a piano extract for four hands out of *The Geisha* (in which he particularly liked the bit that began tadadimtimtimtim*tim*tada), a soprano who had sung of her sky-blue stockings, and then a bass (you could imagine his appearance, military and colonial, red-faced, starched collar squeezed round a square jaw as he prolonged the note) in 'The Road to Mandalay'. For the hundredth time the couple asked each other whether Kipling had written the words. Neither of them bothered to find the answer. The routine of a question keeps the question alive.

When the audience applauded, it sounded like someone shaking a gigantic handful of pastel-coloured shingle.

'Do you remember when we were in Hastings last summer?' The question was rhetorical. Why should she have forgotten it? But Mrs Cohn answered benignly.

'I certainly do! It was too cold to bathe, and I never saw the battlefield, because you simply had to go and look for something called Hastings House, which no one in the town had ever heard of. And we had scones that were frightfully expensive, although we'd chosen a place that looked cheap. So we had only one each and then when we were starving hungry on the train back to London, we shared a compartment with a family who were eating up what was left of their picnic. And it also drizzled all the time.'

'Something which in the fullness of time led to . . .

'A-magnificent-rainbow-over-the-sea', quoted Mrs Cohn and Mr Cohn in chorus. He had produced this defence (as if he had made the rainbow himself) the first time on the train home and several times since then.

Offended, he retreated from the conversation and went back to his notes.

*

Augusta was breathing freedom. Hot sweetened milk, over-ripe stone-fruit and red roses mingled their scents with sea salt and the harsh smell of sweat from the dog in the shade of a current of satisfied idleness. And she laughed loudly and wonderfully free of malice as she watched the Friend, who now had to go, and Byron said about him that his *love life* had been a *tangle*. He and a captain in the Guards were hopelessly in love with the same *whore*. Tears flowed and almost blood, for he gave the captain a slap on the cheek with his glove, which the captain took as a challenge to a duel. Letters were exchanged, weapons decided on. Time, place, seconds all prepared. But nothing ever comes of duels these days, thank goodness in this case. The whore called herself a *washerwoman* and therefore was appointed by my friend as *The Image of Cleanliness*. She received one hundred and fifty of his few pounds for her outfit. *He* got the clap and carried the image with him wherever he went, on a portrait he kept in his *armpit*.

Laughing, they went into the house, taking with them a train of light-heartedness and cheerfulness, which they unhooked on the threshold and left lying there. Augusta thinks she would be able to find the remains of it in the same place, that day as today . . .

But during the night, the household was woken by two furious yells, half-suppressed and hoarse with tormented energy.

People woke, lay half-awake in the depths of slits of eyes black, shiny and profound as dishes of rain. They rubbed their feet against the mattress to enjoin wakefulness to wakefulness, but fell asleep again from the actual effort. One of the girls twisted in her dream and complained, to punish an itch that neither woke her nor allowed her to sleep. Augusta sat up and listened. She took off her nightcap and listened again. The floor was flooded with a moonbeam and she waded through to the end of it to the largest of the children's beds. 'What's the matter?' she whispered, but the answer was meaningless and about a dream that had just been dreamt.

The little girl with the proud face was asleep and flushed, lips and cheeks and forehead pouting. One foot protruded, chubby with chubby toes. Augusta covered it up and it stuck out again. Augusta caressed the foot and peeped into the windowless room where the baby and nurse were sleeping. Something was happening round the basket: a weighty straddle, breasts, straddling, the broad hands stretching down, but the little one's reaching up and pulling the woman's dark centre-parted hair.

The dog moved under the stairs as Augusta pattered across the landing floorboards. It was used to the sound but too stupid to understand what it was. It got up on its hind legs (she was looking from above), its hackles rising in tufts, trying to interpret the thump of heels on the boards: the dog was still young, but knew the price of making a noise at night with no reason – two nights tied up in a flea-ridden kennel. Augusta enjoyed tormenting it like this, arousing its fussiness and mocking it. She didn't like the fussiness of dogs, preferring sheep and goats and cats.

In one of the many portraits framed and behind glass calculating the length of their host's genealogy was a reflection of an open balcony door, the full moon in its opening and in the swell of the moon a bird-cage swaying as the parrot changed feet.

She enticed it with soft fingers. A low sound from the bird-cage sounded like a bird shuddering; some more sounds, of claws on the roof, emphasising the silence.

The night was pure and clear after the thunder, not cold but chilly for the first time, a membrane of opal over the fruit. The silence outside expanded against her ear with a regularity full of nuances: the clockwork of the waves was not mechanical, some reaching further in, breaking more deeply and leaving behind in the sand a rougher lisping. From the horizon they came in on the tide with crests of brilliant fire. Everything moving in the darkness was pulsating with phosphorescence: the jelly-fish drove green bells out of their limbs; the fishermen shot out their boats and the swell and the oars together inexhaustibly formed new eels of light. Everything was climbing and striding on the slope towards the horizon, where darkness ran into quiet darkness and the light turned from water into Fire: the season – leaning, the constellations of autumn nodding to the east. Augusta had a premonition. The horrible dog above the grave. The premonition did not culminate, had neither beginning nor end, but was born and died in flight and left behind an intangible anxiety – over the children? the winter? money?

But the stone floor of the balcony was still warm and the warmth penetrated into her bones. She thought about old age. Or perhaps the old days, 'of Antiquity', where the oleander blooms in 'the wild! You should see it! You should see the barren rank Morea, you should see Smyrna or Cintra or Athens, which is nothing like the books, you know, but a town below the most extraordinary of moonlit cliffs, vandalised by the Greeks and the Turks and the Poles and Lord *Elgin*, curse him because he's still alive and is delighted with his ravages. And the blue trees in Seville called Woman Between Nights. And the white mirage of the town of Cadiz. Everywhere, the oleander blooms in the wild and dustily in three colours. Why in God's name didn't you come with me last summer as I wanted you to – and *you* wanted to? Think what we could've done! And we could have taken your whole mob of children with us. Why did you refuse? Everything was all right as far as Italy. You can live off nothing there. We would never have had to come back!'

'But my dearest Byron. That was no matter of will. The mail boat you decided on was full, don't you remember? There was only room for you. And while you couldn't decide whether to go or not, it sailed. Ha ha ha ha ha ha ha ha ha . . .'

In three earthenware jars, the oleander bloomed on the balcony, white, red and pink in a bed of narrow leathery leaves. She couldn't distinguish their scent, for the night flowering was now in full force, the scents all mingling along the walls, proposing to everything and in all directions, also in through the window of bubbled unrefined sugar glass, up into the roof beams and down over Byron, now after his outburst of anger dipping into the remaining inkwell, dipping and writing:

> A night-beam Sorrow watcheth to behold,
> Distinct but distant – clear – but, oh how cold.

and changed a word (moon, the sun of the sleepless). Augusta did not look at the moon. He wrote about it. The chandelier above and the light in front of him stole reflections of his body, clothing it in a kind of language of glitter as he moved. That was what caught her interest.

He did not see the buttons on his chest himself, the rings on his fingers or something darting out of the whites of his eyes. Didn't see the way they formed converging streaks of light as he breathed, as he dipped and wrote and crossed out and stared – brooding. He used to maintain that he wrote correctly first time, or didn't write at all; she saw

43

that he was industrious and pedantic and thorough, crooking his little finger in towards his palm and mastering the English language.

Augusta was silently spying on the language of light answering the movements of his body. She was aware of it without thinking, an innocence, a body language he did not know he was speaking, so did not master.

(In her memory, come and turn – his foetal movements under a black coat and a pink dress. It is late autumn, the year's first numbers reading seventeen. She is four years old. A Channel crossing from Ostend to Dover, in a sudden squall. Mrs Byron wishes to go to England to give birth to a half-sibling to Augusta and is leaving her in the hands of her grandmother. The boat lurches fiercely and Augusta's small hands grasp at the air. The great belly is at face height and she bumps into it, holds on, then lets her hand wander, inquisitively. A larger, fat but not large female hand slaps it away, not her mother, her stepmother, but not before she has felt something moving under the skin: a foot, a heel that stays in her hand and quite clearly decides how it will move over the outside of the belly. She is sad when she has to let go and the foetus misses – its sister.)

If she went in and asked what he was writing, he would laugh at her drowsy appearance or make a forbidding gesture.

Or take her on his lap and answer factually: 'By the waters of Babylon we sat down and wept.' He looked at her and everything about him was suddenly several shades deeper. 'My heart breaks when I think of leaving you, Jerusalem.' Augusta sat on his lap and nodded, satisfied with the biblical theme after all those Turkish tales such as *Lara* and *The Corsair* or whatever they were called, fascinating though they were, but distinctly heathen.

She rocked on his knee and listened comfortably to what he had to say. 'Everyone who was alive in the seventeenth century is dead now. Have you thought about that?'

That's what he said. Then he *imitated* her until she cried with laughter. He had otherwise entertained her with that talent for many an evening: he had enacted a whole choir of seamen, good men, merchants and whores from the gin palaces, where he maintained half the population of London was drinking itself to death, all in accordance with Malthus' recommendations and the government's blessing. He could imitate debates in the House of Lords. He joked

44

about the Tory lords and the Radicals, but whenever he had provided her with some understanding, he turned on his heel: 'we all have prejudices and always have had', defending their stupidity, 'when you think you're most free of prejudice you're black with opinions on other people. Only those standing outside all open-mindedness see that...' And in that way at once rehabilitated the slandered – disagreeing with him. He was musical.

His voice was music and he could imitate them all, his servant's complaints about a cabbage roll, a lover's lament over a lost gift. He aped Jackson, his boxing instructor, when he was the expert in a circle of admirers, and enticed her to laugh again, and again, and again by letting a circle of friends, at a twenty-course dinner, discuss named women. But while she laughed, he fell silent and turned stern, snuffing out all the voices, a flutter of helplessly reiterated jokes pouring back into gums of laughter, which then closed. He frowned and said what all male relatives said: watch out for men! Stay aloof. Don't stoop to their level. I know what they say to each other behind your back, you know, whatever they say to you. I would never... but a crowd of them together, oh ... when they talk about women, oh, dear me!

Then she stopped laughing, but he began again. He was just as he wished to be, and chose the mood. Attentive. If he allowed himself just to fall, and *whispered* ('apropos this biblical thing you like!') hey ho, Augusta, Gus, the land of Goshen, which is d-r-i-p-p-i-n-g. With milk. And. With honey ...

But now she was reading the play of light on his body, which he knew nothing of and was unable to control. He now also stopped writing and moved away with a grimace. Then he took his stick and struck the top off a bottle of soda-water. Splinters of glass flew, and he blew glass dust off the surface to let the soda-water dilute the hock. It didn't help. His grimace turned ugly as he pulled his knees up to his chest and, sighing, rested his forehead against them.

She was spying for one reason. A reason she called 'loneliness'. That was it. Everything between them and everything he said to her would be wasted if she were not occasionally allowed to recognise herself – in his mind – in what he did when he was not thinking about her. Once she had tried to describe her desire for him and had then laughed at it, but felt the shadow run back over his face, for he had had not one word to say in reply. Only words on his tongue which – in that

45

he rejected them – drove him down a long visible train of thought. And when he came back from it, he still had nothing to say, but just struck his forehead against hers, lightly – as if against an eggshell – three or four times.

One Sunday in
the park

Eric Watson was a lover. He did not talk about his conquests, not even to Mr Cohn, who had been his best friend for many years. But he said the man who maintains all women are alike and that one is as good as another provided she is pretty, is describing just how drearily uniform he himself is in his approach. A gentleman of that kind. Mr Cohn couldn't bring himself to reply that female perspective ought to guarantee success with women. That in extreme cases it is called philandering.

Eric Watson was mooching along the stream with his labrador, bending the water-lilies over with his walking stick and letting them whip up again to give a rainbow second. The Friday November weather was now but a memory in the reservoir of leaves, now heavy with rain. During Saturday night, the low pressure had passed, the small hours of Sunday morning had touched on below zero, still harmless to the flowers, but some people were out picking rowan-berries and sloes from the blackthorns. Eric Watson was mooching along in the sun and the renewed summer warmth, his jacket hanging from his forefinger over his shoulder, grey pullover, sleeves rolled up – tall, gangling and freckled, his thin sandy hair a prey to all winds. Mr Cohn, who occasionally considered he had himself regained his virginity after thirty years of faithful marriage, did not begrudge his friend all the compensations he could find.

They met where the stream swelled, widened and opened up into an artificial pond. On the other side of the pond was a waterfall of willows welling green up through the reflection of the water. On this side were handsome lilies and leaves of other water plants that had already

47

flowered in June. Then came a long slope with deck-chairs and – at the top where the ground levelled out, on the right of the yellow semi-derelict summer café – a cricket pitch. It was Sunday and no one was playing. Cricket and bull-fighting are performances that take place for a reason, not according to the calendar. But three youths were practising strokes, two feeding the third with intricate bowling at the wicket and without exception he blocked them all with his bat, although the ball often spun to a standstill at his feet. As Eric Watson had been – and still was on ceremonial occasions – in a cricket eleven, he stopped for a moment to watch.

No, not because of that. It took a long time before they were able to tear themselves away from this extraordinary desire to watch such degrees of monotony.

'Me, too,' said Eric Watson in answer to Mr Cohn's little pat on the brown file he had under his arm and which contained his notes on Augusta. Then he reinforced his answer with a fat little notebook he pulled out of his back pocket, where it had resided without spoiling his elegant contour. Mr Cohn would not have been able to keep it anywhere in his clothing without looking grotesque. 'Me, too,' he repeated. 'You know, Lady Byron had some cleric with her on the train. She was interested in a special sect within the Church of England at the time. I don't know which, but influenced by the Moravians, I think. But there's no reason why I should know that. If you delve deeper into all the subsidiary characters, you could soon become like Miss Mint, you know, that woman who keeps cats . . . well, good morning again!'

At a distance of fifty yards, the labrador had recognised a dog of similar shape and they were both at that moment studying each other's defecating regions, foolishly rotating on the principle that the nose approaching a tail distances its tail from the corresponding nose. 'Cass!' called the other dog-owner, more disgusted by such direct-ness, as ladies are. 'Phewit!' whistled Eric Watson, for his tolerance of ladies always weighed more heavily than that of dogs.

'. . . no reason why I should know that. If you delve deeper into all the subsidiary characters, you could soon become like Miss Mint, you know, that woman who keeps cats . . . well, good-morning again!'

The woman (Mr Cohn observed) had today covered her large body in a floral summer dress with a white lace collar and chalk-white canvas shoes. Her hair was loose as if she were a girl, almost down to the small of her back. She came over towards them.

The horrors themselves lasted a second, or fifteen. She seemed to step out of an old film and run up the slope. Something about the light – the sun whitened her face just as she herself had whitened her shoes. But there were deep almost black shadows under her eyes and nose. Eric Watson held out his hand and lazily pulled her closer as he shook hands. Then they stood in a row looking down at the dogs, now satisfied with each other's scents and playing instead, chasing, growling, fighting. They looked down on to the pond with its swans, grebes and ducks, reminding Mrs Somerset (for that was actually the German lady's name. She introduced herself with both first name and surname, and from that moment the English surname vanished from Mr Cohn's mind, leaving only 'Mrs Lisbeth'), reminding Mrs Lisbeth of her first piano exercises, the theme of which had been a children's song about what the ducks eat under the water.

Her face darkened as the sight of duck-tails evoked the memory of being shut in a room with closed shutters so that she should not be tempted by the warm spring day outside as she practised her scales. No, nor had she ever learnt to play, she replied. Her co-ordination was not good enough. She could have told them that from the very beginning.

'And how is your wife today?' she asked Eric Watson.

'My wife's always a little better than she imagines,' he replied with a jovial loyalty that nevertheless allowed him to say something.

Mr Cohn used to tell his wife (who didn't like Eric Watson) that you could summarise Watson's marital unhappiness on the back of a visiting card. At the same time, it was like the bowling practice up on the cricket pitch: as it went on (a listless seriality trying to the patience just to think about it) it kept on growing and changing. He had been married at twenty. Mary, for three weeks apparently the most wonderfully ethereal of women, became panic-stricken. And there was a tremendous hurry so that nothing should 'show' at their wedding, or should her mother count up to eight instead of nine months. Three days after their wedding, her menstruation returned and – he discovered during the first six months – it came and went at will in this thin girl, who was likely to vomit up her dinner even when she didn't think she was pregnant. On their honeymoon (five days in

49

Cumberland), she telephoned her mother eleven times and worried for the rest of the time. Eric Watson had been warmly welcomed by this mother, with whom they first moved in and who later moved in with them. Sometimes he felt rather like a common husband in all decency – gradually as far as Mary was concerned. (Sexual fidelity is an utterly idiotic concept, he said. How many walls have you got to hang the same picture on? It anyhow gradually ends up in the wardrobe. Mr Cohn did not reply. His own marriage was in itself a vulnerable confidence, and if that is so, you can't confide in anyone else about it.) The ladies made much of Eric Watson with material exaggerations and verbal subjection of the kind that package so many women's contempt for men for their – yes, for what? – for their very existence. After four years, he was told that his father-in-law, whom the mother and daughter mourned every year on July the nineteenth, had lived in enviable good health. He had escaped during a boat trip between Oslo and Newcastle, sensitively enough to give his wife a chance to keep up appearances. The 'funeral' had taken place in his home town outside London, from where mother and daughter had returned in almost Muslim-like deep mourning. He found out the whole story when his mother-in-law dispatched him to London, where the man lived with his new family. What had happened was that she had seen that *her* mother-in-law had died, and she now wanted the platinum and diamond brooch she had been promised during her engagement.

That was the first time Watson had tried to free himself with the help of the law. He would take the blame, with the help of a willing woman friend. In the ensuing emotional tumult, when Mary clung hard to him, she actually did become pregnant and all his plans came to nothing. The miscarriage occurred in the second month. Three more miscarriages occurred in the second month, then his mother-in-law moved into the bedroom to ensure yet another foetus would not be 'poked to death'. (Where do prudish people get it all from? Eric Watson asked. Poked to death! What raging passions must she be imagining!) He simply moved into two attic rooms and had stayed there.

'That was some visiting card,' muttered Mrs Cohn, turning away with a frown as Mr Cohn thus summarised the prehistory of the miseries of the Watsonian marriage. 'And you just accept his version, do you?'

The son born to the Watsons was lost in the fifth or sixth duel between his parents. His grandmother declared him sickly and made him unhealthy and fat with food and fussiness. Every time the boy threw a ball, the ladies caught it after the first few yards of flight and threw it again so that he should not strain himself. Now he was seventeen and knew they understood his grunts so well he had no need to make the effort to speak. A few years earlier, he had been caught cutting the throat of a swan in this very pond. Eric Watson had been so upset at the time, he had got drunk and in that state had told Mr Cohn his life history.

'Really,' said Mrs Cohn, irritably scattering peas all over the kitchen floor as she podded them. 'And why hasn't he done anything about it for twenty-five years? I don't know about fighting over that child. I do know only too well how men fight for their ideas of how to bring up children. This is what you should do, they say, then walk out of the door, expecting the wife to carry out the decision and the child to fall in with it. Bah! When they celebrated their silver wedding, he was the one to arrange a big party and then he danced with her all evening. The boy was pampered, but now that he has straightened up and lost weight, he is good-looking, and he waited at table all evening with a friendly word for everyone. Your fine friend has a very, very comfortable life with a great deal – ' she wagged a forefinger with a blue nail warningly – 'a *great* deal of freedom.'

It was Mrs Cohn's evaluation of Eric Watson – and not the lovely weather – that meant Cohn and Watson chose to meet away from home to show each other their first notes on Byron. For that matter, nor was it easy for Eric Watson to take friends home. Mr Cohn had been there occasionally. Whether it was true or only a preconceived notion – he thought he smelt the odour of unaired animosity. So they had decided to meet at the park café. And then this German lady had interfered in this disturbing way.

It was Mr Cohn who was disturbed. Eric Watson was so delighted, it was clear her presence had some prehistory. He was so delighted he didn't notice he had dropped his notebook. Mr Cohn picked it up for him, but when he caught up with him, he heard their conversation flowing out into professional terminology. There was a moment's silence. 'Parallax ? ? ?' Mrs Lisbeth filled the air with question marks. 'Tell me why I've got that word on my mind.' Eric Watson purred. As a surveyor, he used the same method as astronomers use to measure the distance to celestial bodies. He demonstrated the principle by angling three fingers and drawing imaginary curves between them. Mr Cohn saw the silhouette of those fingers. He could already observe the glow round the couple's common silhouette as she leant closer to see those curves in the air. The glow was the ruthlessness of mutual attraction. That made him aware that Eric Watson was concealing a prehistory – and that both of them were half a head taller than he was. It struck him all of a sudden, as if he were an innocent child.

When he reminded them of his existence, Eric Watson took him by the shoulders – a very rare touch. At the same time he grasped the German lady, who smiled an apologetic toothy smile. Together, the three of them walked towards the summer café with the two dogs behind them like the trimming on a train. Eric Watson chattered on: '. . . about our Byron project. Do you know Byron?' ('Do you mean *Lord* Byron?') 'He had a really grand mansion in the neighbourhood here. It's been owned by the city of Nottingham for several years now and you can go round it. You ought to go there. Mr Cohn would be delighted to show you round. So would I, if it comes to that . . .'

Eric Watson was struck dumb as he sat down and missed the knobbly feeling in his back pocket. It was a kind of pleasure to be holding what someone has lost and watching him looking for it. He ransacked all his pockets, the long body twisting and turning. All the time, Mr Cohn sat there with the notebook in front of him on the table and Eric Watson looked at it several times without seeing it.

Things had calmed down ten minutes later. Both dogs were lying down, one under the table, the other under a bush. Mrs Lisbeth pulled her hair over her shoulders like spaniel ears. First Mr Cohn read his notes about Augusta, and then it was Eric Watson's turn.

*

The second train is still in the middle section of the track running from north to south: it is black, in a landscape of reeds forming a frosty-white plain over a whole system of watercourses that have merged together. The roots are blocked, the strength returned to the soil. They are already turning up again, but in millions of new shoots no one can see. Millions of dead reeds remain standing, entangled with ice crystals.

This is what he is looking at and in what, from habit, he is seeking similarities as he sits there, tormented, his face parted from his body by a shiny dog-collar: the wind strokes across the chrysalis ears of the reeds, turns, swings and lets the ice break round the light in small almost imperceptible ghostly shiftings; and for every inch of its journey, the train releases a complex of movements and counter-movements in the nearest plants. It always ends by everything white loosening and swirling with them.

In the last carriage, the chandelier sways, the wall lights and the Sheffield plate vases fixed to the walls rattle as the train runs over repaired parts of the line. Objects clatter unguided across the floor as it sways, unrhythmically without allowing them time to collide. He tries not to alter position, or even adjust yet again the circular cushion he is sitting on. For Lady Byron is sitting still, upright and unmoved opposite him. He doesn't see what she is looking at, because she had already pulled down her veil as they had approached Hinckley. Sometimes there is a glimmer behind the fine grey lace, hesitant and sweeping like a white lighthouse in the mist. Like a *lighthouse*, her eyes have a way of slowly curtseying into focus and darting out before retreating back into the corner.

He is not in good spirits. He is this solitary woman's advisor, spiritual guide . . . friend, and risks losing an important part of his influence if nature plays too many tricks with the wrong parts of him and one day she notices that he lives in a body. Lady Byron is very considerate, devoting time and thought to the sick and disadvantaged, but when he is ill – or when he sets about enjoying life – it happens at his sister's house. She is benignly plump and curvaceous, the interior of her house brown and flowery, little steps between the rooms reminding you that ground settles over the centuries and low houses adapt to the change. His sister Sophie really does talk like a phrase-book, page after page of old sentences that just need warming up. She doesn't pronounce her name the French way, as Lady Byron does when she mentions her, but says shyly 'Soe-fee'. She really does speak like a phrase-book and he really does answer in the same way. But still, her duck eggs always whet the appetite, only increasing one's enjoyment of them. Like red and blackcurrants in the garden and hollyhocks against the wall, her words come according to circum-stances and seasons – 'repetitions provide life with its calm', he thinks with a warmed-up sentence, which at the actual moment of thinking opens up in two directions, one vague, with no words, something to do with Easter, the other in a carriage in northern Ireland many years ago, travelling through a village where the people eat earth, the children are muddy and barefoot in winter and – regularly – resort to eating earth. 'If you always think about everything you go mad,' he thinks, and then: 'If you keep making yourself think straight then you think about yourself.' But that doesn't help. Memory, or imagination, or conscience spreads its wings from his gentle sister-thoughts and flies him from her house to Lady Byron's. Kirkby Mallory is a mansion surrounded by a park imitating beechwoods, but it differs from surrounding woods by being cared for. No bushes grow between the trees, no undergrowth or brushwood, nothing but layers of soil, decaying leaves and last year's leaves, in March shaded white with anemones and in May with lilies-of-the-valley. The house itself floats white on a grassy slope, anchored to four mast-like chimneys. Otherwise nothing.

She is still working with ideas there, and at exercising influence, but perhaps most of all nowadays at preserving objects. He imagines he has seen her re-binding music scores with broken spines, touching up watercolours that have faded, mending rents in chair seats and polishing at the increasing numbers of black spots. He has seen her vainly rubbing, trying to clean the mirrors of internal spots of soot (oxide, he calls them).

Perhaps it is a matter of keeping your sense of life together by not letting anything in its pattern decay: several hours a day are spent on keeping up many lifelong friendships and correspondences, and gathering evidence of them in envelopes, herbariums and suitcases. 'If you live your life unseen, you cut a connection between history and the future,' she explains. 'People who don't keep up that connection in their lifetime never have it reconstructed. Anyone who despises life, who is driven to despise life – women – will never later obtain redress. Life that does not manifest itself while they are alive also later becomes dead paper. I could despise my life. My husband made me public to the whole world, and not favourably. If I don't preserve my own evidence, not even my descendants will remember who I was, the way people thought in my day and the way one could live simply. The obituary of the time would be his . . .'

54

Her companion knows this is an exaggeration. Times have frequently changed since Lord Byron's death, and these phases have been described. But he also realises there is a loneliness, when father and mother, husband and child have died, leaving one behind like a last island to be flooded by forgetfulness – then you construct reefs of memories in order to continue to connect with something. For Lady Byron's anxiety over her daughter's ever-increasing thinness, haemorrhages and fainting fits runs through this year like an undercurrent. In actual fact, Lady Lovelace has told him under oath of silence that the doctors think her womb is riddled with cancer. She thinks so, too, but up to now has allowed her mother and her husband to reproach her for working too hard at her research. Overwork is necessary, she would add. There are one or two things she wishes to find out before she dies.

So Lady Byron doesn't know, but has some idea. It is bad not to have the other parent with whom to share your anxiety. He is not only dead, but is so obliterated from her life that she can't even talk to herself and imagine his comments. Instead, she says her prayers. But these prayers are not to be trusted. The clergyman suddenly has to hide a smile behind his hand, not a suppressed laugh, but a gasp of human knowledge, for she is also a religious theorist, this lady. 'Prayers are simple mutual words filled with individual thoughts,' she says, but her own prayer disputes and argues at the highest level. She tries to convince God that she has found out something he has not yet had time to consider, and so tries to mislead him with intelligent formulations.

His smile fading, he runs his hand over his face and looks at her through his fingers. Lady Byron is living in the drawn breath now still above her corset, a garment she adopted as soon as it came back and of whose blessings to posture she has convinced all her women friends. He also knows that she is living in a wound in her arm which she herself ensures is kept open. She has denied it – it is rumoured. He believes it, has almost seen it. Self-confidence in a self-stigma ought to make him indignant. But a shiver runs through him, that's all, at the thought of a suppurating trial of strength there under one of her arms: foolish nature trying to heal and Lady Byron's culture, overriding nature, her arrogance-meekness which every day matter-of-factly takes the needle, sterile from fire, and whips new blood-foam from the crater. Once, or twice or at most three times, he speaks to her about

55

this artificial pain. She denies it, but says that *if*, then it might do to tame her spiritual pain, just as a stormy sea can provide an inner stillness.

Beneath this dispute runs his silent question: how can a person fret all her life because of injustices experienced in one single year? For he has no doubt that the wound also has its origin in that brief marriage and long separation. Just like this journey. And her despair over Lady Lovelace's request to be buried by her father, a despair that was not only because this desire implied mortality. How can she allow such a large part of her life to have been enacted within that one year and let so many of her actions allude to a trial of strength whose wounds to everyone else concerned (possibly still alive) had long ago healed.

Why, he thinks, and another lurch of the carriage renews his pain in sitting, why does sickly Mrs Leigh have to come and meet Lady B in a station building, in winter, ice and snow, when Lady B could just as well invite her to Kirkby? If it can be a good thing at all for the old lady to have to revive a past that has long ago been buried beneath a great many necessary memories.

In response to his silent question, Lady Byron once again turns the drama of her life between the two halves of her face, letting it work from brow to chin, for she is not seamed with a perpendicular line like other people, but horizontally across her face. A great deal more is seething on the surface and in the semi-depths of Lady Byron's life. She has much to live for. But every time they touch on the subject, he sees the great secret extend across her forehead, the desire and the memory of one single caress lowering her gaze transparently and turning, when reaching her nostrils, into open pores and unreasonableness, and furthest down, where her chin unfortunately recedes: revenge.

The reeds now open the landscape almost to the horizon; brittle, sterile and scaly with falling ice and reappearing out of the water vapour. All this downiness meets a dirty white sky and suddenly the veil in front of Lady Byron's mouth starts filling with words: 'In time,' she says, 'they will straighten out the line. All these bends are absurd for a modern means of transport and anyway make the speeds this sort of engine ought to be capable of impossible.' Such thoughts interest her and she goes on at length talking about strength tests, widths between rails and types of sleepers. 'Goods traffic will gradually lead to much greater wear and tear on the rails,' she informs him, then tells him what her cousin, Lord Melbourne (and the Queen herself), considered regarding the expansion of the railway network during his time at the helm of the nation. 'Really,' mumbles the priest, who, when he thinks about goods, is still thinking of wagons.

Once Lady Byron has started conversing, she likes to continue according to a kind of musical pattern, with sentences in various melodies that end in calm, andante. She cannot tolerate one day, or a fragment of a day, being broken off at its peak level; all must calm down, be still and level out in explanation. Nature follows reasoning on technology, words on good manners parrying tales of danger.

'One winter,' she says, after gazing at length over the reeds, 'I was in Ballantrae. The air was freezing, far below zero, and the ground was as hard as stone although there wasn't much ice or snow covering it. But do you know what? The sea was still warm and literally rose up out of the water! I've never known such a strong smell or taste of the sea. It was as if all the mussels and oysters and species of seaweed, which are said to be so good for you, had become steaming hot tea you took in just by breathing.'

He nods. He experienced something similar in Ireland at the beginning of the century. He asks her if she remembers the hideously cold February of 1816. She turns her head and he can feel both beacons fumbling inside the lace veil. He shifts position. Why has God created just haemorrhoids to try him? The affliction is not only painful – in some way or other it is *stupid*. How could he have asked her whether she remembered the cold February of that year? That was 'her' year, wasn't it? He starts nervously talking about Ireland and the Catholics and the question of religious freedom at that time and the Papists and a series of 'new liberals' in London that year, under the leadership of Lord Holland, who approved of Ireland in theory but never went there. 'The union between England and Ireland is like that between the shark and its prey,' quotes Lady Byron, who knows by heart most of what her husband had said and written. 'A unity of gastric juices.' The clergyman again thinks he might have abstained from mentioning that particular year at this moment, the year of their separation. He sees a shrill drum without music in her head. Drumming a series of thoughts thought so often that each and every one of them can be summarised by a short blow of a knob on skin.

She turns her head and watches a family of magpies swarming round an island in the reeds. What can they have found there? The black elm rises smooth-branched and rounded against the sky, the arms of the elm open to nest-building, jays, larvae, the whole wrinkled life that starts with the first sweating of the bark in the spring and dies away almost at once when everything is drowned by the first winter rains. 'Yes, it was a hard winter when my Ada was born. I have recently wondered whether her delicate health has been due to that,' she says as the drum falls silent, and much later – the train has already stopped at a station, exchanged passengers and filled up with coal – 'after all. A child. Particularly a daughter. To be childless would have been a dry and desolate life. Cowardly women wish for sons. Not me. You have to give something back to life.'

*

Mr Cohn was angry. He had finally put out his hand to retrieve the notebook hanging slackly in his friend's hand, while the latter took pains to explain the basic facts about Byron to Mrs Lisbeth. It started with Eric Watson interrupting himself – so that you'll understand this properly, my dear Mrs Lisbeth, I must first tell you . . . But soon it was she who lined up clumsy, obtrusive interruptions, laughing, giggling, pushing herself into the centre and then wanting to order some refreshment.

'Perhaps I'd better read it myself,' said Mr Cohn, holding out his hand, the offended lines Eric Watson knew so well appearing round his mouth.

Then the girl in the lace apron appeared.

'Now then. Let's take it once again,' he cried five minutes later. 'One with lemon and no sugar, one with milk and sugar and one with milk and no sugar. In addition two savarins with cream and one scones with cream, jam and butter.' This was the third version and he had now confused the girl with far too many contradictory orders. She flushed, sent a porcelain blue look in his direction and bit into her cherry-red bottom lip with her front teeth. A little lipstick fastened on the enamel. Mrs Lisbeth added to the confusion by laughing a horse-laugh and protesting about 'cream, jam and butter', and as she laughingly pressed her broad back against the chair, one of the slats broke.

Mr Cohn laughed. His eyes glittered as he laughed, a quiet, calm laugh that drowned the hysterical cheerfulness of the others. Truth penetrates through games. He rose from his own chair and suggested they change, at which she replied in her coarse way: of course, you're small and light. But when she placed her own body in floral muslin on to the body-warmth of his seat, her face acquired such a secretive expression of caution, he forgave her and kept some forgiveness in store for her in the future.

But now he tried to ignore them instead of being annoyed with them. He made a great effort to read Eric Watson's careful handwriting, which was not very well suited to a middle-aged eye. Mr Cohn squinted down his nose and held the book at an angle to favour his best eye; thus he had his best ear turned to the couple. For some reason, they had started talking about D. H. Lawrence, Nottinghamshire's other great pride. Why? Well, he seemed to be Mrs Lisbeth's favourite. Eric Watson objected slightly.

'Nonsense.' Mrs Lisbeth's voice trampled in between. 'Not man but "modern man", the civilised idiot.'

'Yes, yes. Civilised idiot. That opinion's easy to hold, but it has only contempt for people who can't bring themselves to be magnificent natural creatures.'

'Pork sausages and Sauternes,' said Mr Cohn.

'Eh?'

'He wrote pork sausages and Sauternes.'

Mrs Lisbeth looked at Eric Watson, who patted her hand and assured her that it was only a private joke.

'Yes,' she went on, the new chair also beginning to creak. 'What D. H. Lawrence defends with what you call "brutality" is the weak, a kind of living flame threatened by . . .' She searched for words and said hesitantly '. . . searchlights. In his novel, you know . . .' she chattered on. 'After he's gone away with his favourite pupil, a girl violinist who only knows his romantic name,' she went on and on. 'His little child sees him eating the bitter meal his wife had contemptuously put out. He sees that the child sees,' she sighed.

Mr Cohn found himself caught between constitutional short-sightedness and the long sight of middle age. He looked at the woman. His listless lenses slowly adapted to the distance from which she was sitting and talking. There was certainly something contrived in what she said. How far had things gone between these two? He screwed up his eyes and saw Eric Watson playing with a bottle top, snipping it away, exchanging a look with Mrs Lisbeth and mutely beginning to answer her mute questions. Mr Cohn stopped, but for no other reason than that he wanted his savarin. Instead of leaving, he turned his attention to Lady Byron.

*

Lady Byron has a vision. Deliberately. The train crossed a highway, not at right angles, but narrowly, running side by side for a long stretch. A carriage is coming towards her along the road, at first hidden by its two horses, two grey fillies with clearly marked faces, more and more familiar the closer they come. Both have dappled noses, two muzzles with frozen froth describing the same arabesque in the air as the final method of meeting the pulling movement. But one of them has extra white markings, a blond curiosity. The other is striving slightly crookedly in its harness, seeking its sister with its shoulder. Her left eyelid has a defect that means it can neither be fully opened nor closed. Lady Byron remembers the wasp sting that had caused it all, the bolting ride and their rescue. The train is now so close to the carriage, she can stretch out her hand and touch the gentleness of her horses and at the same time feel their reserve, what is left in them of the wild. They have stopped, the spokes of the wheel moving back and forth for stillness, the coachman immobile in his old-fashioned livery.

She has planned such 'mental meetings' on her way to the real one, with Augusta. Not because she herself has to activate her memories. She is strong and they are alive. But Augusta seems never to have had a memory. Like a rabbit. When she had refused to hear, or had circumvented all Lady Byron's questions over the years, she seemed to have said nothing in genuine innocence. She has always talked about 'poor B' as if he had been a brother at a distance, with unfavourable fortunes. She seems to have managed to forget even the intimate sibling-love Lady Byron herself had witnessed. Rabbits have no memory. One has to find a branding iron.

But now, when she has conjured up the first of these mental meetings, she herself cannot keep away, but notices the way she is drawn into a numbing melancholy: the young woman who was herself stares out of the carriage window, her eyes wide with fatigue, astonishment and dry tears.

60

She has taken off her glove and is squeezing it in her hand against a cheek which seems to blaze with pallor, like a snow-lantern. On her middle finger – even that too thin – is her mother-in-law's huge gold wedding ring. It is too big. She will have to wind wool round it to get it to stay on. She wound wool round it the next day and her superstitious husband cried out in horror when he saw she had used black wool. She cut it away and lost the ring on the third day.

In the carriage, her husband had drawn the curtains across his window four hours earlier and he is indistinct. Lady Byron insists that he should be distinct. He obeys, of course, but when he leans over the young woman to be seen, he turns to marble. The face glaring at her through two glass panes is white and blind. Familiar, not because she had known him, but because it is Thorwaldsen's bust of him. Pleased to have frightened her, he again sinks back into the interior of the carriage and goes on singing. Lady Byron makes the memory more transparent. She thinks up thirteen curses on the carriage, a sentence that has eaten its way into her life. Like a parasite, it enjoys her story and occasionally empties itself with a stream of venom. Five years ago yesterday I was on my way to our funeral wedding, he wrote to her, long after they had stopped seeing each other. And after having used those words to demolish everything, he added: As long as we don't meet, we can be gentle.

He wrote again: You have been a bitter liaison in all respects – it would have been better for me never to have been born rather than to have met you. That sounds hard – but isn't it true? Please observe that I don't mean you should have been my deliberate Evil Genius – but you were an instrument to destroy me – you yourself have also suffered from this designation, you poor creature. And the coachman smacks his lips and the horse's ears take their bearings as the carriage goes north through southbound trains.

The clergyman notices that his companion is preoccupied. Has she fallen asleep? Has she tired at last? The amethyst cross swings slowly as her straight shoulders begin to curve round a sunken chest. Her grip has also left him – he gets up and with poor seamanship walks round in circles to get some feeling back into his left leg.

A roar lifts from her senses as she glides out of the train, into the carriage. Her consciousness swells in all directions as the noise and speed turn into a quiet creaking, rocking, scraping. The hail of eight hooves and wheels cutting into gravel are indeed noise, but nevertheless noise interwoven with silence. While Lady Byron grows back into her young newly married self – just learning to call herself 'Lady Byron' but still thinking 'I, Annabella Milbanke' – the roar lifts.

The roar lifted. On the way out of Durham City, it followed behind them. Church bells swung over and over, swinging in clusters from the largest to the smallest, from top to bottom in the Cathedral, in St Mary le Bow, St Mary the Less.

Her Byron lifted the curtain to look out and said: 'The Blue Boar, Francis King, Apothecary, Willm Makepeace Armourer, Jeremiah Jolly Baker. Robinson's Hotel: Spa Water Effective Against Gallstones and Liver Complaints. John Slattery, cabinet maker and lace-maker. The Lonely Shepherd, what's that hellish *noise*!?' as all the city's bronze sang and thundered. A hundred men must surely be in the belltowers of Durham, each pulling on his rope to honour the newly wed. 'Is it war? Has by any chance peace been declared? On earth. What the hell is it all *about*!?'

Annabella said nothing. She didn't think her voice had enough strength to drown the sound of bells. She had no desire to shriek at him so soon.

But the roar lifted when they came out into the countryside. The great mother bell fell silent at the same time as the small ones faded into a monotonous jangling, like evensong over layers of hills, in increasingly silvery mist the further on they went. The landscape rose to the north again, more swiftly and violently as walking turned into trotting. The winter green pastures were hard with frost, sheep grazing on them. 'They were ringing – I think – for us.'

'Us . . .' He sounded as if he had never heard the word before. He let it fall and took it up again and started looking at her, regarding her, observing her, so impertinently that she felt herself inspected like cattle. His countenance was thoughtful, his eyes laughing and warm. He seemed caught out and – when their eyes met – compassionate.

Annabella suppressed her anger with an effort, anger now roused and beginning to unravel three weeks of wedding preparations. *He* had decided: no 'wedding', only a marriage ceremony – no guests, only a limited number of witnesses over and above the unavoidable kin. He had written from London that he would *hasten* to their nuptials. Later on, he wrote that he would hurry to the wedding. Then that he would be coming before Christmas, possibly for Christmas, if the opportunity arose, perhaps for the New Year. His journey from London to Seaham was extended like an ocean journey and wound its way via Cambridge and a number of small towns. From each place he wrote which books he had read, that he assuredly loved her, whether she didn't want to postpone the marriage after all? Or possibly cancel it entirely? And which book he had just read. That he loved her and wouldn't she like to postpone it all for a couple of years or three? For in truth, she was always in his heart.

Every morning, the torment was renewed. Her parents made such obvious efforts to hide their forebodings. Some relatives come to join them left again. The wedding cake went mouldy on its pedestal. Annabella joked about it, saying it was a performance of *Hamlet* with the main character absent because he was sick with doubts. One evening, they had heard the carriage. He had come in and paled at the sight of her.

It was like that every time they saw each other again; which is heart-rendingly prosaic in a creature you have remembered by imagining great things. Instead she now took great pains to keep her expression neutral. Everything too big or too small gradually adapts to the shape it is intended to fill. When you see each other every day, the personality is no longer the apparition, but nuances and details freeing themselves from the physical covering but at the same time suddenly brought out by it.

But he had come in and paled at the sight of her. He had his friend Hobhouse with him, a stiff, chilly, polite fellow holding 'our friend' by the arm when he appeared to sag. His politeness gathered itself into a gaze which could look on her without feeling. And his gaze tempted Byron's into him. They stood there, two men washed together into one pair of eyes, seeing that she was not particularly beautiful, and also carelessly dressed. Coming to that conclusion, they started to weigh better features against worse and continued their mute speculations round such things as character and state of health. When these quadruple eyes parted, only Byron's remained filled with tears. Hobhouse's had been dry and it had been time for marriage.

'Us . . .' The newly married man, however, seemed to find great pleasure in the word, which soon spilled its abundance over into 'we' and 'our'. Restful years. Out of air, children were born. His face crept into its angles as he played with 'us' and let it bounce back from the memory of loneliness – abundance of loneliness – no superfluousness. She saw him being amused, being gentle, distrustful, being tempted. At that moment, she was perhaps able to admit that her own gaze had not always been good. The first time she had met him, she had retreated from the worshippers surrounding his person. Too proud to intrude. He had recently published his desolate poem *Childe Harold* and had been a great success because that season, the spoilt young people who read poetry were hungering for darkness, rags and hopelessness. Despite this, Annabella had found it interesting and thought she might interest him with her critical views. But not here, in the drawing-room at Melbourne House.

A look of clarity and irony, appropriate for all those crowding round him, struck him and was returned with – *sympathy*. Confused over this misunderstanding, she stated her own irony. It was not personal. She was well able to understand that admirers wished to crowd round him and that pleased him. What she meant was that there he is, just standing there letting himself be exploited as the event of the season by these faithless people – in a year he will be forgotten and 'gossip in coteries burn only through real thoughts and emotions and destroy the proportions of life'.

She had learnt to mistrust that ability later on. Byron never allowed himself to be affected by the insights she gave him. He accepted them willingly – just as he had that time – but was not changed. In his character was unlimited space for critical self-insight, but neither the weight nor the quantity influenced him. He continued to be what he was and also continued to say 'I' with the same newborn delight as he now said 'us'. 'I,' he said tenderly and spitefully, 'me and mine,' he added sadly. At her aunt's house Melbourne House, for the first time, she lowered her eyes in face of his prominent ones. When she raised them again, he had retreated into himself and was conversing slowly, his lips tense for a moment round every word before it tinkled into the common bowl.

From adjoining rooms, the music came in a slanting melancholy waltz and Annabella, who was looking at the walls, thought the straight pale wallpaper pattern would soon be following the pattern of the waltz. Her attention was drawn like pointed embroidered edges along the many doors in the long wall, where people were coming and going. The buffet was set out in front of a row of windows, small Creole statues holding up blocks of ice, a rose cooling inside a swan of ice, the beautiful dishes remaining almost untouched, sometimes someone taking a glass of wine or preferably a cup of tea. The Whigs were sober refusers of food that season – in public. Byron himself was said to live off soda-water and ship's biscuits, but her cousin William said that he had regularly seen him eating fried potatoes and eggs at the Cocoa Tree coffee-house. A company of Whigs was moving across the floors here at Melbourne House, as on every evening during the season, discussing the same things in the same Whig salons. They were called 'new liberals' and considered themselves more farsighted than the old ones. However, there were certainly no impossible Radicals with whom people had no wish to mix. Two leading ladies were standing apart talking together as they looked and searched over each other's shoulders. The darker one was Lady Jersey, the lovelier one Lady Oxford, a less ordinary guest, for she was almost a Radical. She dipped her short upper lip into her cup to hide a smile. Annabella followed its direction and again saw Byron – suddenly anointed to lover – exchanging looks with a third person creeping alone through the room, leaning, tired of waltzing, nothing in her hands, no jewellery or other protection, leaning to one side to look under her sole and sitting down by Annabella as she licked her middle finger. Her presence was obstinate, the warmth of her body breathlessly vibrant all over after the waltz. 'Bell,' she said, pressing closer. A drop of red saliva glistened on her lip where her tooth had left an impression. 'Bell, I'm so restless, restlessly unhappy!'

'Oh, Caro,' exclaimed Annabella, irritated by a – presumably genuine – feeling that had been dragged through artificiality. 'Restless, restless . . .' not grasping that a little banality affirms emotion, nothing else.

Annabella Milbanke and Caroline Lamb, cousins by marriage, on a silken sofa. They look away from each other, the one full of reserve, the other interested in nothing except her own unhappiness. The one in a gown that is quite simply an appropriate dress in which to try to look pretty, a dress without the slightest origin in Annabella's character and longing. The other is in a peculiar mixture of transparency and uniform to expose Caro's brokenness. The memory of them gives rise to a profound time-swing in Lady Byron and causes her to search the air for an already vanished presence, caressing her skin like a draught of air from a bat. It rushes away from her, back through the years and past the bridal couple in the wedding carriage. 'What was that,' says Byron, 'flying by?'

Caroline's eyelids slanted down against her cheekbone and rested there, as if on a tragic mask. With the corners of her mouth drawn up, they formed a circle, a little black ring of face inside her face: the imprint of an iron coin. Her eye sockets were full of false gold. Hexagonal. Glistening where her eyes were moist with emotion, otherwise dead, as false gold is on land. Nature's whim, perhaps, to give her such an appearance. But in that case, it had brought with it her character. She really did *look* someone. Her appearance was that of a woman who gives up in advance in order then to offer underground resistance. It promised the inverted – the world below the mirror surface of the water.

As Annabella was thinking this, she saw a sunset on the horizon of the sea, islands floating like black clouds in the white sea, embodying the flight of white clouds over a coppery evening sky. The sense of diving and flying in such a sight must have its equivalent in Caroline's attraction to duped men. Instead of protection and reserve above the line where the soul goes, she hung a hairy pouch of secrets below it. Caro was exposed to anyone, but promised them she desired deeper falls and endless falls. 'No one has such depths,' said Annabella. 'Yes, he has them, despite everything, he has them!' whispered Caroline, returning her gaze to the middle of the room.

He was now standing there with her aunt, Lady Melbourne, leaning slightly forward, downwards to create sufficient distance between his ear and her mouth. In the heavy murmur, beneath the soft music and the mist of porcelain sounds, he was reading her lips, laughter ready on his own. Lord Byron laughed hugely. In eighty per cent of cases, he laughed for no reason as far as she could see. Annabella had to establish that his face was not at all good – intelligent features in themselves, but his semi-profile criss-crossed with careworn lines. She had heard so much talk of his beauty . . . 'Bell, you're so monstrously critical, you would only be able to enter into association with a marble bust,' complained Caro. 'Liveliness, the way to live! Beauty is a question of *movement*. Have you never seen a beautiful face become a blockhead when it starts rolling its eyes and addressing you?'

Byron was just about to answer a question from Lady Melbourne. His voice was no longer metallic as before, but round and small in honour of the elderly lady's delight. And gradually as this delight wormed confidence out of him, movement began to leap out of his face. He bestowed on her smile upon smile, giving his words orbits by slowly pushing them ahead of a series of facial expressions, so amazingly fresh, as if they had come into use for the very first time. 'You see . . .' said Caro, taking aim as he suddenly turned his head and looked at them from an 'underlook'.

At first he wasn't looking at Annabella at all but simply concealing a kind of insolence in his eyes by looking away from Lady Melbourne as he said 'a girl from the country'. His face was really very good from the front, his forehead a frame of two soft lines, like the gills on a violin, with life prodding behind sixty times a minute. The sculpting of the surface, born anew in every smile, made her think of sculptures someone gives life to, for an hour, to concentrate a whole past and a whole future.

The moment that thought had arisen, it reshaped the world. From the vault of the ceiling in Melbourne House, silence poured as gently as windless rain and the last sounds of feet against floors came to rest. Everyone stood still and looked round for the source of the silence. Only he, Lord Byron, went on throbbing out his tender, attentive smiles at her aunt and his voice was heard to say – with its slight Scottish intonation – 'girls from the country'.

Then the silence was complete and out of the middle of it came a voice with an Irish tone to it. The harp was tuned, trying out touches and dropped notes, and finally also finding response in the whispering Byron, whose merry, 'wonderful' eyes now turned to the short man at the centre of everyone's attention. A player was striding round with a hand harp against his cheek. But the singer was neat and squat, with a small head set directly on his shoulders – he bent it back to smile widely, revealing the instrument in his throat. He lubricated it with more wine, small sips, let his flax-blue eyes shine, his fine cheeks glow as he said thoughtfully: 'In Ireland, one usually . . .' Oh – the words touched each guest individually with a common memory – all eyes widened, ready. Then he sang a couple of songs from his book *Irish Melodies*.

> 'Tis the last rose of summer, left blooming alone,
> All her lovely companions are faded and gone;
> No flow'r of her kindred, no rosebud is nigh,
> To reflect back her blushes or give sigh for sigh.
>
> I'll not leave thee thou lone one to pine on the stem
> Since the lovely are sleeping, go sleep thou with them.
> Thus kindly I scatter thy leaves o'er the bed,
> When thy mates of the garden lie scentless and dead.
>
> So soon may I follow, when friendships decay,
> And from Love's shining circle the gems drop away!
> When true hearts lie wither'd and fond ones are flown;
> Oh! who would inhabit this bleak world alone?

Such a horrible song! What kind of *thoughts* were they it evoked anyway! Annabella pressed her clenched hands hard into her cheeks and tried to find an answer from her cousin Caroline, who, however, seemed unmoved. She looked at other people and some seemed slightly moved. But no one was thinking such difficult thoughts as she was: she was thinking about her mother and about her father and loneliness, the unevennesses of the seashore in the autumn. They had both been over forty when she was born and now she was already twenty. They had no wish to go into the future, which for their part contained little hope and even less desire, but they persevered, loyally, for her sake.

With an effort she held back the wave of tears trying to break through. She saw that a decorative tear or so really had fallen in the crowd, but they were tears of mere emotion. No one was tormented, as *she* was.

The poet, the singer, Thomas Moore said: 'Yes, it's sentimental. Sentimentality is a gatecrasher. Unannounced, it reaches emotions, but does not express them. And the right expression is the human deliverance. And yet . . .' He shrugged his shoulders, and what else could such a poet do?

During the last two verses, the singer directed his song at Caro but she – alone outside the thrall of the harp – shook herself free and denied the atmosphere, and infected Annabella, who nervously started sketching in the air.

When the music stopped and the applause died away, the listeners dispersed, but at the same time they had established something which now extended long hesitant lines, together resembling 'diagrams'. She read them off: lighthearted undertones, hyper-thin connections. Likenesses seeking each other – likenesses instead of spouses. 'Oh,' she said to Caro. She looked on the matter in this way: spouses were two who had powers of attraction to each other, but also sufficiently great estrangement to challenge each other and force out mutual – 'growth'.

She frowned at Caroline as, slithering and bowed, she made her way across the floor towards one of the far doors. 'That's the way you slither, that's the way you're bowed when you go in and out of relationships with *men* without thinking and without learning any-thing,' the young girl reflected, Anne Isabella (Annabella) Milbanke, only daughter, only child. 'Whenever I meet it . . . no diagrams in the air. Honour, trust . . . growth.' 'A girl from the country,' said Byron, now looking straight at her. The words resounded in the bowl, went through the bottom and ran out on to the floor. A girl from the country, he said looking at her carefully and something – which she caught red-hot – ran to meet her. No! With no time for consideration, she lifted her feet and slapped her knees together, but it was humiliatingly much swifter than her and made its way instinctively and matter-of-factly up her legs and in between them to spread out right up into her heart, her mind. She felt herself growing, softly pressing and sensing against material, feeling herself sealing and melting, sweet nuts scraping holes in her skin from the inside.

Now it was winter three years later and they were married and the carriage was heading north towards the Halnaby estate, where she had lived as a child and was to live for her first weeks (honeymoon) as married. They were sitting in this box made of wood, nails, glue and upholstery, scarcely protected from the climate that would freeze them if they were suddenly brought to a halt, sufficiently long, sufficiently alone with it. Only trust makes human beings secure. Trust between them makes people rely on human labour; the culture that protects against the climate.

Trust in the interior of the carriage would carry them straight to the Halnaby house, where logs were sure to be already burning on dog-irons, and brass warming pans full of hot embers lying between the sheets. But there was no trust. He was testing her, challenging her, threatening her.

'You've brought this on yourself,' he hissed.

He sang false little songs as twilight fell.

He was slumbering with his head on her shoulder. She became maternal. The head sank, sank down towards her breast and was warm there. She looked down on to his eyelids, which suddenly glistened, with two black holes, and simultaneously he made a wet patch on her bodice.

He sat up and snapped: 'You would have me. That *idée fixe* couldn't be got out of your head. Not even your mother could put you off. What did you want me for? You should have taken me three years ago when I wanted you. Now it's too *late*. Now it's too late . . .'

'Us?' he said mildly as the church bells stopped resounding. He repeated it once more, and it was the first day of the year and the shadow of horse and carriage wandered on across frozen fields.

Faun unveiling
a woman

Let us move ahead of events and introduce Mrs Lisbeth's penman-
ship. That autumn, the rains kept sweeping in swirling low-pressure
curves from the Atlantic over Ireland, over Wales and then northwards. They still tasted of salt as they arrived. The garden became
waterlogged. So did Mrs Lisbeth's eyes. She did not like rain at all.
Not after two days, not at *all* after a week. '*Do* something,' her husband
said irritably, slamming the car door. That was why she began
imitating the Byronists. Not to imitate them, but to have something to
do.

As the garden was waterlogged, she went looking for moorings. Eric
Watson and Mr Cohn were the only people she had met in this place
who seemed to have 'something to do', or considered themselves
useful as well, not just doing strictly economically useful things.
Everyone else worked and slept.

Her method as a writer was to take roughly as much as she gave.
Whereas the Byronists were inhibited by the respect knowledge
provides – or years of fidelity – Mrs Lisbeth ripped off pieces of the
poet's life and destiny much as one rips a plaster off a downy
moustache, and abruptly turned it into prose, flavouring some of it
with her own experiences and travel letters. Others she extracted just
as they were in Byron's letters, or in contemporary testimonies, fresh
from the detailed truth that can never be created from one century to
another. Before she showed the first ones to her friend Eric Watson,
she gave them a common heading. The year before, she had seen some
drawings (aquatints) by Picasso, six in all, all variations, nuances of the
same thing. A faun, kneeling or squatting, looking at a sleeping female

behind a veil. He was lifting the veil slightly, looking down, his neck straight, determined like an animal, hesitant like a human being. Mrs Lisbeth called each of her scattered efforts *Faun Unveiling a Woman*. The first one she produced took place during Byron's Grand Tour of Greece and Albania. The year was 1809. He was twenty-one and as Mrs Lisbeth had taken most of the facts from the diary kept by his travelling companion, John Cam Hobhouse, she let Hobhouse have the floor:

October 3rd, 1809 – Woke at unaccustomed hour with feelings of hunger. Went out and found all our packs drenched by rain. Fletcher helped drag essentials into the cabin. The guide had almost extinguished the embers in his efforts to revive the fire. Impractical man. Byron swore at him and broke off half of a cracked wall plank, then split it with his sword. When the fire looked promising, he took it into his head to crumble a little horse droppings on to it – a well-tried fuel in these regions, he had read – and was the first to make his way out . . .

The guide tried to dry out gunpowder by the fire. I explained that I would have let him go on had I not been present myself. Towards evening, he burst out laughing and aimed at his forehead as a sign that he had understood 'your amusing joke'. Impractical man! Outside the cabin, the Albanian soldiers stand on one leg drinking coffee, inscrutably chewing on the grounds. They keep dry under the eaves and carry out some kind of morning toilet consisting of scratching their backs against protruding parts of the building. Unfortunately the only kind of toilet I have seen them doing. But they rub themselves with great voluptuousness, like so many boars, though with no grunting.

These people reserve the best places on their bodies for their firearms, looking after them with a care resembling sorrow and tenderness. All of them have a pointed pipe constantly in their mouths, like a limb growing out of a hole between teeth and wet lips, in the crevice between their long moustaches. Byron's servant Fletcher thinks they smell 'monumentally' but otherwise everything is according to conditions peaceable. Eleven people in a forest cabin that is losing its foundations on the streaming ground. When Byron cut the throat of a goose he had come across and roasted it, we were fairly content.

October 5th, 1809 – Bad weather has continued for two and a half days. I have been given the guide to interpret between me and the sergeant. With considerable perseverance, Byron is trying to learn the technique of singing like the Albanians, muttering, creaking, boldly lamenting. We glimpse the mountains every time the rain lifts and a cloudbank induces itself to rise over the ridge into the next valley. Apart from these glimpses, we just hear – *listen* to the greyness of the massifs, their rugged heights, the alleys in a rock once blasted by water and the water now springing out of them, swollen by the rains from brook to waterfall. The dripping echo. Eagles and hawks circling inside, their swiftness and strength kept to a few feeble shrieks.

The sergeant said the people in the Albanian countryside on the whole ought to be content with their lot. Ali Pasha has been ruthless and successful in his war against the robber chieftains, to the extent that plundering of agriculture no longer occurs, except – naturally – his own. And this legal form – which seems to be a way of maintaining the army without middlemen . . . does not permit methodical terror. The destruction of crops and the taking of another man's wife are punished.

The sergeant says he earns his pay over about nine of the months in the year and in between allows himself the freedom he needs to supervise the work on the farm, increase his family, hitherto eleven (with two wives, although he calls himself Christian. So much for Greek Orthodoxy!) and adds to his income with a little – robbery! on the road between Ioannina and Tepaleni. He talked about it as if he were harvesting his vines or mulberry trees.

I asked whether he were not afraid of being discovered and sentenced to death. He blew out an endless stream of smoke and gazed at its annihilation. A man, he said, has his own rules to follow as well as the Vizier's. Ali Pasha, he said, persecuted equivalent robber bands, not loyal ones. I think people in the Levant are more pragmatic than at home. Outwardly, they show several simultaneous faces.

October 8th, 1809 – Outwardly, people in the Levant show several simultaneous faces. One should not try to look deep into those eyes. Velvet is obtuse. I remember a few years ago, when we were all still at Cambridge and Byron had a woman friend with an expression of a guttersnipe. Caroline someone. He always dressed her as a youth, though not a guttersnipe. He fetched her in London and took her with him when we all rode to Brighton one Whitsun, she astride her own horse, wearing Byron's breeches and neckcloth. She had an attack of hiccoughs – that's what happens when ladies use men's saddles – lost her hat in a brook and her whole pile of reddish-fair curls came loose and haunted us like a pale flame.

Byron confiscated another hat for her when we met three school-boys on a walking tour, and paid with a button.

Caroline went with us on our adventures. Impudent, mute. She stood on the shore and wrung her hands when Byron rode his 'Old Father Sea' and was naturally present on individual rides . . . She was no boy. Or perhaps just the right amount . . . His clothes effaced her femininity, which might seem more uncertain when she was wearing a dress and lace cap. The slim neck in the collar. Byron said disguise is instinct with what is ambiguous in people. 'It brings the snake up out of the well . . .'

So much for Brighton and early English summer. Yesterday it was Albanian autumn and we experienced the shadow side of disguise when we saw something called 'Virginesca'. The region's men of dignity were at the inn, assembled in a special group, as if it were the East. Chewing their coffee-grounds, smoking their pipes, and anyone who happened to drop a single word licked it carefully off the back of his hand. One of them was a woman. That could be seen not just because it was obvious but also it was self-evident, permitted. At the same time, she was dressed as a man and behaved like a man.

Fletcher pointed discreetly at his reproductive organs and explained to his master that the sight gave him 'substantial discomfort' there. Byron told him not to be a blockhead.

The guide said that 'the Virginesca' was a common phenomenon in these mountains where war harvested men. What happens is that if a family lacks a male head, a woman is appointed as head man to keep the family and the worldly property together. But as this is beyond a woman's capabilities, she became a man.

As far as I can understand, what happens is that when a girl becomes a virginesca, she gives up her femininity and becomes a kind of obscure worldly economical vestal. She wears men's clothing for ever after and can become a soldier. She has no relations with the opposite sex (whichever that is). She cannot become a father. As she has entered into the world of men, with its privileges and responsibilities, she cannot become a mother, for it is forbidden to turn back and take 'the secret home to the womenfolk'. But a virginesca naturally does not entertain such desires, the guide said finally. She is much respected and can achieve great age.

I couldn't help spying on the creature. Byron stared at her and turned pale several times, a kind of wave that seemed to take away his natural ruddiness. We said that her circumscription was perhaps so remarkable to us just because it was unlike all others. He said that by being made apart in this way she became *nothing else but apart*!

I have never before realised that gender is the centre of gravity of personality. I must repeat it. Gender is the centre of gravity of personality? The degree of gender gives it essence? Look at every mammal and every bird to confirm that matter in your recalcitrant mind. I would never have been able to admit such a thing if I hadn't seen that creature.

It liked it! There was a darkness over its body, as if the body were blind. A castrato is after all a condemned man. This creature was nothing. The transformation was nothing but will, and thus lost what it had renounced without reaching a goal. The will achieves nothing without the aid of chance. Byron said that it was 'theory realised'. He said it had no look for one's eyes to catch. But had knowingly dropped the snake into the well and was never going to bring it up again.

We talked about our siblings for half the night. I about mine, and he about his half. He is industriously occupied with a major poem in Spenserian metre.

And all
London's lions

It is Sunday in the park. After having run on ahead in order to sniff round the next corner like a dog let off its lead, this story now returns to its master, chronology. Mr Cohn, Mrs Lisbeth and Eric Watson are still sitting there at the café table, Mr Cohn with a broken chair slat at his back. They are sitting in silence, almost diffident. The rhythm of their conversation is beginning to fail as all the other tables begin to fill up. This is the time when everything is shut in England, and hungry and thirsty trippers who have miscalculated their meals catch sight of an open-air café. Suddenly car after car stops on the park road and people arrive from other directions in boots, rolled-down socks and with walking sticks. Mr Cohn, Mrs Lisbeth and Eric Watson have been there longest of all. In all modesty, that gives them rôles as gods in a play from Antiquity. They silently observe face after face, manner and behaviour. They gather strength and renewal of their own dialogue by eavesdropping on that of others. They study people who are just as unaware of their parasitic gazes as the people on a stage in Antiquity are of gods perched in the scenery.

Someone wipes the back of his neck with a handkerchief, another puts her curls in order, polite children offer half of something to their small brothers and sisters. One child starts expectantly and threateningly sliding off her chair to offer herself as a playmate to a boy in a tie and pullover, whose only reply is an annihilating look. The variations extend in concentric circles until all the tables are occupied.

'What a hot day it has become,' says Eric Watson. 'No thunderstorm around?'

Later, Mrs Lisbeth said: 'Mr Cohn, what you told us about the thunderstorm in Hastings and the inkblot on the Muse, is all that true?'

'The inkblot has been substantiated.'

'Mm ... but all the rest can't be. You can't ...' She stopped. 'Emotions can't be *substantiated*. You translate your own memory into someone else's situation. They can never really match. I think that's what I was thinking.'

'What Mrs Lisbeth means,' said Eric Watson, wilfully interpreting, 'is that you're starting abruptly in the middle of Byron's and Augusta's love story. Or rather towards the end of it. She would like to know how and why it began and what their childhood was like. Take this opportunity, Joel. She's your first audience.'

'I was just coming to that,' said Mr Cohn.

*

One day in June, 1813, Augusta saw her brother as an adult for the very first time.

They were alone in London in August, apart from the millions who don't leave the city between seasons.

Those millions provided the senses with – undercurrents.

When once later on she mentioned how strongly she felt the presence of overcrowded London – that she would always be fond of him, 'the dearest, the warmest, the best among people' – because of all the nightwatchmen, fights and burning rubbish, he simply answered, 'Yes.'

But alone together are two people who are tired of each other. People with eyes for no one except each other stare into the backwater. 'Lovers are observant', you know. Love opens people not only to each other. One can measure love with the range of emotions. Memories, he smiled.

He maintained you talk about love best by describing a horizon – not emotions. What chance agents of love do together could be called 'beautiful' or sinful or tragic or comical, but, like everything compulsory, outwardly it resembles a joke between men. How could insight ever understand the seriousness of desire?

Memories of love are nevertheless bound to words. They are about how something seemed to be *at the time* – snowflakes falling, the endless distance to a lighted window and the closeness of the moon;

77

the climate that always satisfies lovers, either roasting them or drowning them or making them lose each other in the mist . . .

'I've never been able to live without something to love. Even when I was a boy of seven I was – yes, it confirms my hindsight – very seriously in love. The harrow and the carding comb drew through me internally, tearing up blood and making sight and hearing more acute, a wealth of inventiveness as well. She was my cousin and was called Mary. The memory of her . . . it is hillsides of rust-red bilberry scrub, mountain peaks behind, streams of smeltwater, roses, the broom and heather over, and the fourth corps of the Cameron Highlanders.'

'But,' said Augusta. She had been thinking, not of the nature of emotions, but of certain definite days in life, when their passage ran through the largest city in the world, roaming in pairs, like the tracks of a rabbit.

Society had begun to leave London to be reunited in Cheltenham, Bath or Brighton. He was also always on the point of leaving, but, as so often, his dislike of departure kept him there.

Social life still went on in some houses. One evening they went together to Lady Davy's soirée for Mme de Staël.

In surroundings long familiar to Byron alone, Augusta alone, they were now like two drops of water on a waxed surface, all surface tension and like twins. They stood far apart from each other, and when they sought each other's eyes, they saw other people. They thought they were then seeing real faces beneath the social ones, as their eyes were adjusted to events below the skin. They were that conceited for a few days. She was wondering what he really saw in her. She didn't ask aloud and she answered herself: when two people of an ordinary kind, used to the actions of love, meet without reservations and lengthily embrace, their hands fumble on out of habit and then it has happened. No damage has been done, for no damage is done that does not damage someone. She listened to his declaration of love, which amounted to them understanding each other 'in a special way'. In fun and in silence, without the pompous life-and-death solemnity love usually produces. That was true.

It was during these summer days that they felt their common origins to be an asset, not a problem. It weighed heavily that everything that might mean anything seemed to be just as obvious to them. Anyhow, he laid almost supernatural weight on their common parent, Jack

Byron; on that they had common aunts and cousins to gossip about; each other to tease; each other to imitate and inveigle into an old childhood language and memories that went so far back in time, he was almost 'Baby Byron'.

Augusta thought it all might be due to the fact that he had no other close relative. The thought did not disturb her.

Byron had a strangely ungovernable temper. His worst quality was his immediate anger. Unpredictable, it was, too – he could take insults with equanimity, but minor accidents sent him into a rage. Then there were changes of mood and long purple darknesses. She soon learnt that you could not reason him out of his mood, but had to coax and wheedle and amuse the corners of his mouth upwards. He liked being treated as a child. As a child, he defamed himself, maintaining he was so hardened nowadays, he seldom put himself out so far as to be truthful and genuine. That applied to his poetry as well as his love affairs. Then he at once regretted his unguarded words and angrily started denying that he dissembled to real friends or to Her! Then he said he would be sure to ruin her life! It had not yet happened that someone had come to him with a pure heart without having it crushed!

She laughed at his pretentiousness. 'Then I can destroy my own life myself, dearest B,' she said, and, quietly: 'Though I'm relying on you to say nothing?'

He couldn't do that. Although at the time he didn't even deign to answer such a question.

On their way home from Lady Davy's, he made a peculiar speech about linings. It all began with Augusta showing him the way her coat was patched on the inside. He looked with interest at the darns and patches of different coloured cloth. But instead of promising her a new one, he pouted his lower lip and said that what you see of people is the hardest shell they've ever been! This is what he said:

Inside that shell are the old remains of shells the core has grown out of, like a kind of lining of rags. At first there's no lining at all. The newborn soul is a hard sphere. Shaped like an O. That O screams, loudly, loudly, not yet dissolved by anything. Then come the years of childhood when you try to wrap your defences round you, but they are insufficient and burst out from your growth. The result is patterns on patterns, rag on rag.

'Yes, indeed, for I rely on you to be discreet,' Augusta emphasised, to make sure. 'Because you know, dearest B, that people who have nothing better & more sensible to do than gossip & natter & insinuate themselves in half-truths which they then make whole & they turn the pure nature of God into fly-spots & you know what I mean. Although it is not a serious matter – hmmmmppph – peculiar notions may arise, and, or, what.' At which she spat on her handkerchief because she had found a spot of soot on her glove.

He said a poet cannot be a good poet and write from his own lining until he has become the hardest shell he can possibly be. Before that, he is not *sensitive* enough to understand his own secrets.

He said it as if with heavy certainty, he had swung his way through his sleep.

Poor B smiled at her with sparkling eyes. Augusta felt something. She wasn't sure whether the mussel pie had been altogether all right.

'Music and drama are different,' he went on, continuing his lecture. 'Only the word is ordinary in the *material* of those arts. (Damned if Fletcher hasn't forgotten to heat the water for my bath again. I can't sleep if I don't have a hot bath!) And then they have their instruments, the symbols on the score, the actors. I have nothing but words . . . so here we have William Shakespeare and Edmund Kean on the same stage. One has cobbled together *Richard III*. The other performs him. Shakespeare has written this great drama. Kean is so great and self-confident that he unhesitatingly *plunges* into every rôle, like a pearl fisher who knows what depths to go to and how quickly to come up, and who has already found the best and at best can double that. He alters Shakespeare with *Shakespeare's* words and *his own* pauses. He charges the words with his own silences. Then he extracts his pieces of lining – ten, fifteen at once – and in *silence* can imply a thousand words.'

He sighed.

Augusta put her handkerchief away. Sometimes it was impossible for her to remember whether she were thinking when she kept quiet. For the most part, she was assembling her duties, calculating and calculating what she should do next. If she didn't note down a list of the results of what she was brooding over, there was a considerable risk of forgetting it all. But she did not remain silent for the sake of peace. She shrugged her shoulders. Instead of starting up the slope again, they stopped. She was sitting fluffed up like a bird in the rain. Silent and mute like a bird in the rain. Byron had not changed her at all. She

80

couldn't imagine anyone who could change her. But he had scraped on her and thinned her eyelids; it shone through as she slept. She saw moon-pale faces fluttering along Piccadilly. Women in green. The pane in the carriage door captured one after another, two and two. The glass sliced out a piece of life and *shook* it, for the surface of the street was uneven. Augusta listened to Byron's talk as her intuition ran on at its own pace, embodied in an intelligence of its own. It started sweeping and purring over the whole of her life like a black coat, a cloak, and suddenly a pale astonished face rushed past the carriage crying out why she was very cold. The coat had no lining. She listened to his talk and squeezed his hand. As every other finger had a ring on it, he winced with pain – that answer was more dear than words.

Probably all was well, she said, but she herself had practically no secrets, and no depths, as far as she could make out. Or 'lining' for that matter. One probably gets what one deserves (if one is lucky) and he needed his secrets and she needed a great deal of money, which she hoped she would receive some time. Otherwise there was little to say. She was always the same, the only one-stringed Augusta, unfortunately.

She fell silent again, weighing up whether it was a shortcoming to be simple when so much of the best is double. But instead, a great deal is ambiguous. Her hand diverted itself by pulling off his rings and threading them on to her own forefinger. There was a very large gold diamond she would like to have. Yellow as a lemon or urine, with a matt appearance. Her eyes rested on the pane, which sliced out first a parrying woman, then a woman in flight, two men in the first stages of a fist-fight and finally two running nightwatchmen. Her intuition continued its horrible leech-like movement inwards and found that it was she who was a shortcoming, though not the kind that causes pain: what she discovered instead was a muteness in her disposition, an insensitive swollen place she had never known was there, but which was clearly sensitive all the same, for when the thought bumped into it, the tears began to well.

She was very surprised, for she cried only when the occasion was there: when someone had departed, a tear also for the pup trampled by a cow, when Janet sings a sad song or when Leigh begs forgiveness so handsomely for having gambled away sums absolutely necessary to the household. Nor did these tears follow the usual alleviating route; they were strange ulcerous tears, breaking new channels until her whole body was full of inconsolable eyes which Augusta's main eyes looked down upon. What was running out of them was Augusta herself. Sometimes she felt unborn, as if she had never been born.

For her mother had died a few weeks after her birth and instead of lying in bed like a real mother, she had said: 'Poof, I'm no silly goose' and 'Convalescence will make me ill,' so she had mounted a horse to join in the hunt. She had got hiccoughs, of course, and died when Augusta was three weeks old. The goodwill of reluctant relatives – in bringing her up they had separated her from the memory of a will of her own and into a life where young women are never heard of again. They had never denied her things people need and ought to have. They had never tempted her to long for anything more than what she could have. Easy. What is easy to acquire is so hard to keep, or to prize and take away. One day, 'you, dearest B', will be as heavy as lead. She knew that.

He looked at her without participating in this sudden emotional storm. He preferred it when she laughed and that her laughter was sufficiently melancholy. Interplay at different levels is an art that finally shapes the pattern of character. One is shaped by the intellectual opportunity with which one has the courage to comply, and if they had only permitted her one single level and very little courage, he would ensure there was also enough for her, soft tender sister. The carriage turned down into St James's Street as he – with the inside and outside of his hands – dried her tears. He turned his hands over her hot face and over all other eyes: the curved inside, the hard outside and the eight spaces in between the fingers.

Three times a day, the mail brought new details of the plan for a duel to which he felt obliged. What idiocy, tittered Augusta, and how foolishly old-fashioned. That men should shoot themselves and each other – and bits of innocent tree trunks off . . . for irresolute females & racing bets & because they definitely consider one should think this and that about things on which one certainly cannot have definite views, etc., etc. Look at our old William, condemned after having slashed old Chaworth with his sword. Bah! So what's the aim, what purpose would it serve and what the point is is beyond me, & I consider it is as if one had to understand and bear in mind that . . . yes, and so on.

Otherwise they were on their own and at peace in the cramped room with their singular provisional furnishings of curved legs, divans, jars and packing cases.

But Fletcher was with them and knew everything.

At the back of the house, swallows and pigeons were nesting, the pigeons simmering slowly, sounding like a pan of marrow bones from dawn to dusk. They were safely resident indoors, in the attic, ironically preening their wings as smoke and crashes came from Byron's pair of pistols. She asked why he didn't kill a single pigeon to frighten off the rest. He replied that he would never again shoot a bird, whether wild or semi-wild. 'The last bird I shot was an eagle in Lepanto Bay in Greece. I don't remember whether it was from thoughtlessness or by mistake. I only winged it and tried to save its life. It had such bright eyes, but it was suffering and it died within a few days. I've never done it again and will never again try to kill a bird.'

The swallows' nests adhered like clay wombs round windows and ornaments: in the evenings, a colony of lyres chasing their silhouettes against the swarms of mosquitoes from the ebb of the Thames. It was almost like down south, he said. There was a hawthorn hedge down in the courtyard. Birds in cages singing inside it and on the other side, they sometimes saw a mother grieving for the son she had lost in some stray dishonourable mock romp between the French and British in Spain. Presumably *fallen in battle*, but hitherto reported missing, Fletcher gestured discreetly, when he came back after having ascertained the circumstances from a pink-and-white maidenly face through the hawthorn. If you ask me, there's little hope. Please note – if you ask *me*. But who does that . . . who ever asks any of us before they start their wars?.

'No private person wants war, my good Fletcher,' said Augusta sternly. 'We're not often private persons!'

They watched the robbed mother airing a young man's clothes. She threw fits which hurled her to the ground with the coat in her arms, spasms turning her face raw red. She was visited by two fortune-tellers who had *seen* him on a deserted island to which the English fleet was on its way. And so could sing softly and Irishly while she waited and fed her birds, and suddenly stood still. Her lips white. The first pains again. 'Do you think she really loved him, the way she's letting herself go?' whispered Augusta, as small as an anxious animal as the woman raged.

He boxed at Jackson's boxing studio. He fenced. He swam in the Thames, contracted a fever from it, then rested his head in the lazy warmth of the hollow of her neck, and he laughed like the puffin far away in his burrow. He maintained their mothers had parted them 'out of the same womb' and that ever since then, they had yearned to be reunited 'in the same womb'. Him, anyhow. 'But, my Byron,' said Augusta silently. 'Such foolish words.'

He said one loves strangers. People want to love without estrangement. But it is strangers who love. When they have come close to each other, they no longer love, but are affectionate, the next best glow always the best. The best is too ardent. And if one nevertheless chooses it, it is expensive. 'Perversions, you know.'

Augusta disliked the word. His voice contained a note that buzzed in his head and vibrated in her breast, where it set in motion a thought about her husband: My dear girl, he used to say, her husband, looking into her eyes, his gaze flickering, seeking his own. But he was a horseman. He could in no way make himself be like a woman, as Byron could, half-sitting under her lamplight and suddenly leaning his warm face back in such insolent, scared, commanding submission.

He didn't want her sleeping in his house. He wanted to be captured and free, and every evening when the carriage was to take her back to the sooty black building where Henry VIII had held court, he came behind it, stopped it and made the homeward journey again into a nightly outing. Sometimes there, sometimes here, sometimes nowhere. One night where the river narrows. They went through Chiswick and stood for a moment on the bank.

They stood where the Thames began to narrow and the towpaths wound their way along the banks to the north-west. The Thames swelled with the tide like the casing of a fish sausage. The smell of seaweed and salt broke out towards the outflow and everything trembled, lapping over the banks. The mass of London enclosed the Thames a few bends further east. It was extending outwards like all cities. But also inwards, where the hills round about – despite prohibitions – crept closer and closer to the city limits, stealthily melting into London.

Here, in the river's third loop, nightingales still sang their odes and small patchwork fields emerged in and out of the ditches. The houses on the banks were on high ground because of spring floods and autumn storms. They got out of the carriage there and walked for a while, an evening promenade. He said they had begun to build larger docks within the quays, because the merchant fleet had been afflicted with three times as many bandit attacks since the war veterans had returned from their heroic deeds in Europe . . . With its water-mass, the moon pumped ships into the mouth of the river and let them sink out in the empty ocean when dawn came. It stood still in the sky, trembling in delicate ripples on the black surface of the Thames.

The veterans kept to their colonies on the opposite shore. Augusta had browsed over them in the newspaper. Someone (Burdett, Burkitt?) had lamented over the fate of those who had served their king and were now too ragged for war or country, as well as for their own families. They had lost an arm or two, a leg, a pair of eyes, coughed up their lungs: they were what they had become by seeing themselves in the horror on other people's faces. The soul sealed in a raw clod. They burnt their rubbish, with dignity, on their river bank. While on *hers*, she and he strolled regarding their misfortune. Augusta said that 'one is always seeing so much sadness'. He said those people have not the slightest belief left in the task of life being to compensate for misfortune.

The evening was so quiet they could hear the rushing of the river through the sluice gates far far away. 'But has life such a task?' she asked. He replied that they themselves presumed fortune was capable of compensating. She knew that quite recently he had begun to send money to the grieving mother on the other side of the hawthorn hedge, since Fletcher had passed on the pink maiden-face's information that 'one' couldn't pay one's bills. Indeed, Byron couldn't pay his. But they were so large. The neighbour's expenditure could be contained in the framework of his purse. The humble letter following his gift was richly bespattered with 'allow one who has himself experienced Grief in the greatest measure' and 'so as not to allow Your Sorrow to be embittered by privation'. He really did have a moment when he threw his eyes up! 'Now, now,' protested Augusta mildly on behalf of the sick old king. 'It's no one's fault that he, the one calling himself the Emperor of France . . .'

Another night he got it into his head that they should go to Skinner Street and visit 'a philosopher with the longest nose and best head in London', who was said to be 'host to a deposed vice-president of the

United States of America who had tried to make himself into *emperor* of those states and also was said to be lawlessly *allied* to his own *daughter*!' All these descriptions. They swarmed. So that she never remembered any names. And nor did they reach that street, either, for it was among the typhus alleys, where Byron's carriage soon stuck and they had to back out. They roamed about, got lost and drove round and round as if in a labyrinth, houses rising above and inside each other, like bridges between each other, like shacks under bridges, digging themselves into the abutments and spewing smoky grease out of holes in the walls, their shadow slanting and black. One had to breathe with a handkerchief to one's nose.

Dandelions growing there never became more than stalks, just as unseen people remained stalks, with no stability for their heavy bald heads. An autumn-like stillness reigned in spite of the labyrinth being full of people: the street was like one great room with intestines up in every open window, those who lived in there and outside striding around on their nightly errands. Or sitting on steps and looking, or leaning on corners, themselves as mouldable as drifts.

Byron jumped down and walked a short way to look for a way out. He stepped over a dog lying on its side as the life oozed out of its entrails. Children up late appeared from between the paving stones to imitate his way of walking. They hadn't much hair. Diphtheria had just been there and gone again with its heavy load, leaving behind a few downy dandelion heads. A little boy imitated better than the others, but then he was lame himself. 'You see,' said Augusta angrily. 'And you warm to people like that.' 'You don't have to like the people you speak for,' he replied. 'You love those you love.'

The carriage rumbled on, lost over gravel and stones and iron barrel hoops outside inns, Augusta no longer worrying about forgetting the name of the philosopher with a long nose and the vice-president wanting to be an emperor. She simply wanted to get away from there. And anyhow it's the long nose and the treachery you remember about people whose names you also remember. A basket of brilliant – strawberries rose for sale out of this rat-brown summer night: the child lacked both hair and nails. 'Do you want to die?' he asked temptingly, he asked, Byron, as she bought it off the child. He tried to take the basket away from her and give it back. 'No, you can't do that,' she said, resisting because she wanted some strawberries. 'He's selling them for a living and you can't feed him with them, either.' 'He'll sell them again. And are you going to put into your mouth what he's had in his hand. Mother of three children!'

The end of the alley sloped downwards. At midnight, a fiery red aura of all this hot tallow lay above it, fumes the gulls snapped at. They stood still several times, in the sealed city, seeing stalks shaped like drifts propping up the houses. The drunken, the childish, the night birds, they did everything under the bare sky – not high – the only roof to their lives. Every stretch of street resembled the next and when they were again lost, they arrived at the same indifference as that which creates slums. Only Byron again became agitated by a couple having each other on a barge. In the fleeting moment as she herself turned her eyes away from it, Augusta saw a dark woman, calculatingly looking down along the man and opening her coat. But Byron twisted his neck and knelt down to see her quickly sweep her coat over him, spit a pip out over his shoulder and look away: to see the bodies billowing under the coat and finding each other upright, slotting in and thrusting mechanically, to see him jerking almost at once for a few seconds. Disgusted and tempted to *die*, he twisted his neck so that it creaked and she had to take him by the head and laugh him out of it. And then he was silent for a long while, first to maintain the woman resembled someone he had known as a child, then to make her believe that on his part desire contained greyness and tears and sorrow. Finally to pronounce his silent melancholy: 'When my mother gave birth to me, she closed her *legs*.' But Augusta knew him and knew that they were all the excuses of a sinner. She put a strawberry in his mouth and just as every child's scream ends in it sucking, his talk was drowned in munching. If it does not harm anyone, then no harm's done, she used to say, confidently. Housewife who once butchered herself. With closed, kissed, forgetful mouth. Smile.

Every fourth hour, London's clocks struck in a gust of time from east to west; and all London's lions, of marble, of granite and oak, of jade, of ivory and gold-leaf, yawned and changed position.

Debts and
money

'Why do you let it have so much to do with love?' said Mrs Lisbeth. 'Actually, it's all about love.'

She studied the two men with that stupid unaffected expression Mr Cohn found Eric Watson's attraction to so unfathomable. Both men were holding mugs of tea in their hands. Mr Cohn glanced down into the remains of his cold dregs and oriental leaves. Eric Watson looked back at her, raised the mug to his lips and moistened them.

'I didn't mean to criticise,' she hastened to say. 'Not criticism, I mean. I wanted to . . .' She laughed suddenly, her mouth large and wide open, at the same time shivering and swiftly clamping her upper arms against her chest. Mr Cohn looked up and caught a glimpse of swollen tonsils. She was swallowing with some difficulty: 'I don't think love is all that interesting. It's too much the same for everyone. It's almost democratic. Ha ha. They're always saying Byron lived such an eventful life. What's happened so far is less eventful than mine. Much less eventful. You say nothing about his poetry. What do you think of his poetry, Mr Cohn?'

Eric Watson and Mr Cohn looked at each other and smiled as if they'd heard an unintentional joke. 'You anticipate me,' said Mr Cohn. 'I was just going to mention something about the universal image. But a universal image must be analysed according to the way one has chosen. It's nothing in itself, Mrs Lisbeth, and I've chosen to relate this slightly inappropriate love between siblings . . . The other day I imagined a situation in which Byron frightens the pious Augusta by saying an Islamic evening prayer. I don't know whether you've witnessed such a thing, Mrs Lisbeth, but imagine a dark closed face –

88

an Arab – at night revealing the blue fire in his eyes and a rectangle of clenched teeth. It is like when the lights are put on in a house and you're standing outside wondering about the sound: a calm but intense invocation. In your churches, Mrs Lisbeth, if you're a Lutheran (one of the religions furthest away from religion), the priests hitch their voices up on elastic braces and pray. It's a formality. The Arab prayer is not fair-haired but erotic. Not erotic as in religious revival, but as in calm. Not that I understand Islam, and I doubt Byron did, either, but if you idealise – which he surely did – you find that the Arab singing prayer expresses physical desire for divinity. The same desire applies to all life wherever that divinity manifests itself. The desire for a woman (for instance) is pure. The song to God is coloured by desire for woman, the earth, the sea, as everything is unity, and one and the same, and body and soul. That is to say . . .' Mr Cohn stopped to listen to a faint roll of thunder in the east, then he saw a magnesium click as short as an explosion in a street lamp. '. . . the way of loving is equally characteristic of a person's politics as the way of working.'

She shrugged her shoulders:

'He walks and stands and travels by carriage. Even the incest is passive. Seems mostly homely: "hands used to loving easily fumble further and then it's happened". Yes, indeed. You make no use of the heavens round your hero. You make everything too .,. .'

'Provincial?' Mr Cohn attempted, after she had stammered between words for a while.

'But, dear Mrs Lisbeth. Society, the circles – he moved in during the period we're describing – are the most provincial in existence.' Eric Watson flung the dregs of his tea in a glittering curve over the grass, at which his labrador tensed his muscles in expectation of a firm object or a scent of urine before returning to resting position with a sigh. 'Look at our real provincial life! Every day, Mr and Mrs Cohn meet a mixture of known, and *unknown* people who may bring an atonal resonance to their day.' (You do go on, Watson.) 'I myself have a whole region to get to know, again and again, daily meeting strangers and often passing fields of newly released bullocks. The other day, I spent two hours at a crossroads discussing life in general with a farmer whose name I don't know and who doesn't know mine. After a quarter of an hour, I switched off the engine, but he stayed on his bicycle all the time, both feet on the pedals, leaning against the car roof. I started by asking the way and I wonder whether we weren't into the Synod in Antioch before we got on to the difficulties of keeping sheep out all winter and how pathetic it is to see a sick ewe taken away in a wheelbarrow. In between, we discussed local as well as international politics, and got annoyed with each other, because he considered that some elimination of people who disturbed the general good was surely in keeping with the Creator's view, as he saw it, close to the earth. We even spoke of sulphurising fruit wine and *Lawrence* – yes, Mrs Lisbeth, he had seen him and talked to him long before he had known the man wrote "such things".

'And now we're sitting here talking about Byron with a delightful foreign lady who's chosen to come and live in our little provincial town. Do you think that such opportunities arise in society circles? Oh no, in them, the same boring bunch of dullards see no one else, and are quite definitely satisfied with each other. That's where the real collective is. There's no worse provincialism than the limitations of praise – the talk is either about money or genius or lineage. Voices are raised for those outside to hear, but reasoning is on the same principle as when a wave lifts a flock of ducks. The slope looks huge, but they are all affected equally and not one changes position. *We* are Bohemians compared with that!'

Jokes Eric Watson, letting his dog loose in the garden, pretending not to see the old lady picking marigolds and parsley, then going into his house, saying axiom tictac quasi veritas felix? And is answered patiens singsong. Four eyes meet like four dusty nickel spheres. Strangers make each other's eyes come to life. At home they are like mist at sea – emotion's cataract – but not hostile. Somehow, they also see each other. Suddenly they notice a floral pattern on the kitchen curtain, cornflower, and remember how they bought it.

Mr Cohn saw Mrs Lisbeth tipping her chair and leaning towards the sun, now with a wrinkle of poisonous purple from the thundercloud on the other side of the landscape. She rubbed the goose-pimples off her bare arms and her hair began to curl in the mist leaking up from the grass, out of the moss-green pond with a single pelican in it; no one could remember how old it was. He knew she would soon accompany Eric Watson on an outing in his car, into the countryside, it usually was. Mr Cohn had in his possession the undesired knowledge of the way it usually was. He could have told her how embarrassingly quickly it usually began and ended, but she would have taken in as little of that as a sparrow's song in the shadow of an oncoming express train. Advance information is seldom comprehensible until afterwards. It is meaningless intuition from the start: he looked at her. She knew everything from the start and that made her intractable and impatient.

To console her, he asked about her husband, and she looked delighted. Oh, yes, Larry (never was the German accent stronger than when she pronounced the name 'Lerri') was a construction engineer with a firm in Nottingham just planning a large station building. He had been lucky to get such interesting work, as he had returned almost as a kind of foreigner to England. But for his part, he was so hardworking and – in contrast to his English colleagues – wasn't used to things like working hours and 'weekends, which for some here seemed to entail half the week!' Lerri and she had wanted to live in Europe, for a while, anyhow, during the period when they had thought the children would be born and go to school. He hadn't liked Germany because – Mrs Lisbeth looked at Mr Cohn and dusk suddenly fell, hiding her eyes in the shadow of the sockets – of the foreign language. After two months, they'd had enough of London, such a *dirty* city. She breathed deeply twice in order to leave no doubt about what she meant.

'What do you think? What's our position regarding Byron's verse? What shall we reply to the lady?' Eric Watson smiled again at the unintended joke. 'It's admirable.'

'It's wonderful,' replied Mr Cohn, immediately, as if in a music hall duologue.

'Though you're always being surprised again and again by its qualities as you read it, for it's not profoundly moving like so much of the less good verse you read.'

'It's sensitive and it's fun and at its best it's both at once.'

'All versifiers are really more unfathomable than the words they manage to achieve.'

'My dear Mrs Lisbeth, he was only thirty-six. He'd been dead for almost fifteen years when he was my age, and I'm sure if I were to versify, I would have several years left until I reached the "clarity in which words and truth meet", whoever said that.'

'One of his best poems,' said Eric Watson, 'is "Darkness". Its theme is from the countryside round about here, but that wasn't what I wanted to say. It's a short little *modern* exercise that arose during what we call the Diodati summer. Byron and Shelley and dear Mrs Shelley spent a whole summer by Lake Geneva with a few others, and on a very famous thunderstorm night' (Good heavens, isn't that hail! Come on, come on! and chairs tipped over in that abandoned late summer way. Corners of white tablecloths fluttered, a xylophone of great hailstones played on copper, glass, dishes and a pair of forgotten spectacles: human traces alone rose out of the grass; human eyes peered out from below the fringe of the awning) 'the company decided that everyone was to write a ghost story – or a horror story. Mrs Shelley wrote her little classic of Gothic horror, *Frankenstein*. Byron gradually produced this poem, which is not about bloody fangs or constructed monsters, but about earth without life. Yes, Mrs Lisbeth' (said Eric Watson), 'it foresees, not least, Verdun. And neither it nor I blame any particular nation for Verdun, for in an evil world, it is the naive who govern, because they are the only people who manage to place the burden of guilt on to others. And I say this despite the fact that my younger brother was killed there, at nineteen. "I had a dream, which was not all a dream", it starts, then goes on with a cool enchanted enumeration of dearth, expressed in pure words of dearth. The sky is birdless, sunless, starless, the tree leafless and the earth plantless. A desolate land, that poem is. That far, Byron's poetry reaches.'

The hailstorm turns to pelting rain. A whole group of people fall silent under the awning, childishly caught out at aggravating the weather: the treetops angrily whipped about by wind and water, vapour of its own water swirling out of the dust round ropes of rain, the grass becoming soaking wet. Those who have umbrellas dance with them, twisting and straggling along the road. The others go inside and sit round a cast-iron coal stove, the heat from which is actually the eye of the maelstrom of draughts. Mrs Lisbeth is very cold and soon finds herself enveloped in Eric Watson's jacket, listening to a long and numbing conversation on something quite different, to which she is quite indifferent.

Mrs Lisbeth dozed.

Mrs Lisbeth was dozing against the wall nearest to the stovepipe, the slits of her eyes glossy black and moving heavily between Mr Cohn and Eric Watson, heat-sensitive from voice to voice, without listening. To Mr Cohn, it was like the larvae of the privet moth crawling over his cheek. He was suddenly very, very irritated indeed by her apparent attention, which had the pretension, apparently, of seeing through him. He rose to his feet and said goodbye without explanation, before setting off the short way home, stepping over puddles that often turned out to be a trifle longer than his legs. He began to jump. He jumped, but all the same got his feet wet.

*

(This is Mr Cohn's second attempt to begin at the beginning. So – 'One day in June in 1813, Augusta saw her brother for the first time as an adult.')

For a while Augusta became one of the ladies-in-waiting to the Queen. Her husband had quarrelled with the Prince of Wales and lost both salary and position. Someone had helped her into the court instead – one of the brothers on her mother's side, perhaps. Her rôle entailed a few irregular duties in return for an annual income of her own and rooms in St James's Palace. She seldom saw her employer. She was not even sure she would recognise her face without its surroundings of pomp: the worn old lady, whose public fates were the same as the secrets within her. For the face retained an expression of nothing – she who shows no reaction nevertheless keeps something for herself.

The echo of emptiness rolled through the state rooms of the palace, climbed up into the dark oak hammer-beam roof, went on through halls, galleries, stables, apartments and right into the cramped room where Augusta, on the first of these June days, was preparing to see Byron again after eight years. She took no notice of the emptiness or the sea-grass of dust flowing from the cracks in the ceiling. The size and furnishings of the room meant nothing to her. Her own home was cluttered disorder, and in every other respect, she was free of avarice. The Palace was for her two private rooms, from which, undisturbed, she could plan certain errands in town; which also entailed selling what one had to sell in order to find money to settle the most pressing debts.

She sat in front of, looking into, the mirror. Sometimes seeing, mostly unseeing, in order to find, beyond the door that was her own pair of eyes, the right daydream – the room where problems solve themselves. With her forefinger, she poked in a stew of small jewellery she could sell, but not even the whole lot would cover a single debt. She looked at her eyes, called 'sapphires' by wealthy gentlemen. All that Bordeaux, all that hock. Rubicund men took 'sapphires' as pledges, but had forgotten everything when they faded. Oh, well. Those who harm no one, do no harm, thought Augusta the next morning.

Her older brothers, the rich ones on her mother's side, gave her small pieces of jewellery and presents for the children. But when she asked for help, they lectured her on her choice of husband and refused to fork out a penny more to pay off his gambling debts, pennies they knew from experience would go to creating new debts instead of paying off the old ones. Augusta found it impossible to differentiate between gambling debts and the necessities of life. During all her married life, they had been associated with each other, and one evening, when one of her rich brothers-in-law had spoken at length about his new racehorse Medora and his many years of bad luck at gambling, she protested. Surprised, he replied: 'But Gus, I can afford to be in debt.' About her husband, they said it would be best if you could ship that, what's his name now, Trevanion, Dallas, yes, of course, Leigh, off to the United States of America and be rid of him, what, haw haw?

She looked into the mirror, past herself, but came to no daydream, only a reflection of emptiness, where money troubles welled up in wave after wave for each and every thing she could remember. The first of them did not fade before the last, but they crowded together with her in that little room until her anguish and shortness of breath gasped back at her out of every corner. Remaining was her younger brother, on her father's side, 'Baby Byron', whose soft animal one-year-old head she remembered. Before his first year had gone by, they had been separated, she to her maternal grandmother, he to his mother. They seldom met as children, only for brief days and even briefer summer weeks: the eyes of a coquettish sad little boy so attached to Augusta in the garden swing, as she pushed off with one foot, steering the air with the other and eating an apple.

In his last year at school, she had visited him on Speech Day. He had recited from *Lear*. (Augusta, alone at the mirror, looked into her

94

large protruding eyes and saw through time into his almost identical ones, set in a round, no, to be honest, fat and boneless face.) What had he read from *Lear*? Like every other 'theory', that had long since sunk to the bottom layer of amnesia where Augusta managed to mix up most things she was told and learnt.

But one thing she did remember. As she stops to get her breath back on the hill up to Harrow, a group of youths appear on their way down. They really are youths, Augusta thinks irritably, trying to pollute as much as possible of the world with their voices in the way young dogs do. One of them is fat and red and – rather than limping – making a gliding movement with his foot. Augusta prays to her God not to let him start running when he catches sight of her. The moment the thought is complete, she rejects it. She knows it's an error – she has forgotten him. When Byron caught sight of her, he stopped.

He stopped and turned pale, leaving rust-red freckles behind. The sight of yearned-for Augusta made him blind to her. And hostile. He saw himself with her eyes. ('One of them had gorged himself on pork and cream in his day and rather than limped – foundered with his foot.') The moment lasted. The other boys streamed past, like waters avoiding a dam. Then they were alone.

He and she stood looking at each other, breathing in the air in small scared gulps, embarrassed like children finding themselves playing when they're too old to do so. Then with almost insolent exaggeration he folded her glove over his hot hand and brought it so close to his face that she could feel its grill-hot radiance. He started calling her 'ma'am' and 'my dearest Augusta'.

They looked at large families all day. Sometimes at each other – turning their eyes away self-consciously. Were they alone in being lonely? Should they help each other out of it? Or despise each other for it?

In the twilight green – of dusk – their eyes were more able to bear each other, for open black pupils make the eye more impersonal and easier to talk through. He told her how proud he was of her, to be able to show off his sister and prove that after all he possessed one sensible person in the world! He was also proud of the traditions of his school, the respect of his masters, the friendship of his friends and the sympathy of his headmaster.

Before she left, he called his schooldays 'a miracle'.

She couldn't think anything else but those words about miracles being a defence. So much of what was said was only defences. In the green twilight, their eyes tolerated each other. So much that happened is only looks, and what is involuntary, what sounds when you say too much. Then you send in the right words that straighten things out and smooth over things and eyes that have burned have water poured over them, rendering them harmless.

He looked at her with an expression she couldn't interpret: formal and appealing, fascinated and tormented – and his cheeks flared like roses: 'Nothing will ever be so easy and pure of heart as being a boy here. That you came! You coming here confirms everything and makes it even more precious to me. My dearest Augusta, ma'am.'

And with this breathless cordiality, something honest flowing through it, he parted from her and danced away out of her mind, which soon let itself be taken up with her dowry; her new home; as wife on the crossroads between Newark and Cambridge; with the children that were born and the money that fled from her hands as she reached out for it, forever ending up in some stable pursued by ill-luck. Outside her house, the world blew headlong at human striving, she knew. People sat up and hurried off to help, to make themselves a name. Cousins fell, made money in the war. He, the younger brother, travelled far and wide, and of him she heard from friends, no, not the *eternal* friendships of school, but the new ones.

But eight years had now gone by and Augusta was putting a jewelled pin into the bow on her left shoulder. She pinned another brooch on to her bodice and licked her teeth in front of the mirror. Then she stepped out to a hired carriage that was to take her the short stretch up St James's Street. Was to have taken her. A large crowd and two carriages barred the street by Mr Brooks's club for gentlemen and Boodle's gambling rooms opposite. The driver asked and Augusta answered: yes, take another way. She had also thought of asking if he knew the reason for the crowd. As no answer would be forthcoming without causing trouble, she allowed herself to forget it all. That was not difficult.

These days, if she walked past two people talking to each other, she kept hearing time and time again 'a very unexpected French offensive', which confirmed her anxiety that the world would after all go under. She craned her neck; a few gentlemen slunk back into Brooks's stern façade, others hurried up the street towards Piccadilly. The Emperor of France was building a tunnel to England. The Emperor of France had a queen ant which gave birth to them all complete with rank, musket and victory-skins, the soldiers. The whole army had frozen to death in Russia, but it had no mothers, except this one, which could replace every man with a new one in a single year!

All in good time, in spite of everything, they would come crawling through the tunnel to England and build new walls right across the country and she and her children would be sure to be on opposite sides of an insurmountable wall.

Augusta dreamt, looking out at the Mall, the leafy plane trees, the park, a group of pelicans slowly plodding. The sky opened right out of the sunlight and started raining; small impulses swayed out of the emptiness and spat dust from the street. The panes wept. Limes, blossom, leaves turned deep green with moisture and people took shelter in entrances. Two kinds of drops drummed notes on the hood, on the coachman's hat. She pressed her cheek against glass to see the weather and saw one single square cloud, the rest of the sky carelessly put together, clouds of all colours rushing high up above this one calm cloud. And a rainbow. And the colours of the clouds playing on the walls. A smell of newly mown grass. She liked the city, with its solitude and her two small rooms. London in the summer is – just sitting on grass somewhere, smelling the sluggish water. The eye has a line right across, its own horizon. The underside sees in the dark. Hears people and birds chatting in the darkness – quietly, not importantly, richly.

Bennet Street was a stump of road between St James's and Arlington Street. The carriage stood outside the corner house, herself in one corner, small, curled up, gathering courage for a cheerful, light-hearted prayer for money. Two voices were making a quarrel public to the whole street, the quarrel fairly one-sided . . . 'and to make night into day is not granted to many. Making day into night is worse – a sin, to say it right out. If Our Lord has also sinned against me, then it's in my nature to be grateful for his few small gifts, one of which is that he has given us light for half the day. And those who do as His Grace does, for the sake of peace, not only have the pleasure of making me curse with annoyance. He will ruin his eyes by just looking at light

97

and never at daylight. Just look in the mirror! He already looks like a rabbit.'

'But . . .' came diffidently from a point slightly higher up.

'But! But! It's as I say. I deliver coal and do you that service in the daytime. The fact that coal makes a noise when it's to go down the coal-hole is as it is. Or am I to carry it down one piece at a time! So as not to disturb his sleep! Eh!'

'Now, now . . .' replied the male voice before being interrupted again.

'Fletcher has said His Grace has said "more at a time but fewer times". That's what he thinks, "more at a time and fewer times"! So perhaps I can carry three times my own weight so that he can snore undisturbed until dusk? Now when I haven't got a single man to help me, I suppose I can well lift three times my own weight. Not that it's all that great. But what people pay and all . . .' the cracked voice went on complaining, now sufficiently low that the male voice managed to get in a ' . . . there, there . . .' before she went on: 'And as far as his health is concerned, then he'd sleep better at night if he didn't take a bath every day and use up all the coal on bath water. I've never heard of a grown man lying in the bath like an idiot day after day like that,' shouted the old woman, now departing. A cart creaked past in unison with her voice: 'His colour is unhealthy and the whites of his eyes are like a mole's. And if he doesn't look out, he'll soon start losing all . . .'

Augusta took one step down the carriage flap and then a long step to a flat stone to avoid soiling in the damp dust. Byron was standing watching her from the top of the steps.

She searched along the doors and windows, ignoring her first recognition. There was something special about her actual delaying; at first she saw him immediately, then she began to search and found him again. It was the kind of thing that never happens with mutual clarity. But it became one of the strongest memories of her life and she knew it the moment it happened. It was dream-like, meaningless and inexplicable, and led to everything else.

He stood at the top of the steps, his shoulder against the doorpost, looking at her as she resisted recognising him: because she had not expected to see him there – because he, too, had changed. He was smiling strangely, neither friendly nor courteous, something prickly surrounding him; whether it was his hair that had curled in the rain, or his left eye apparently protruding, making him peer. The details fastened in her searching looks and went with them, like points.

As she sought for traces of the man standing there, he found the time had come. He started weaving himself into her consciousness, thrusting a dark and biting thread through her pattern, each time he ran through, turning abruptly and pressing back, filling her with a sense of *cress*, dark green, water . . . bitter. All this as he stood quite still as if reflected in water, looking at her. All this in the course of two or three blinks, then the membrane burst. Recognition and estrangement washed over each other. Everything she knew about him was at once confirmed by this alien man on the steps. But as she greeted him, that first powerful impression of him remained. In tension and loss.

She took two or three steps towards him and held out both hands, surprising herself as she did so, for that might have been her gesture to the port-wine men who called her eyes sapphires. Anyhow, he grasped them and pressed them to his chest. Perhaps she had expected more, but no, there was a reserve. He wanted distance – didn't want it – and held her hands firmly against him, letting them receive the heavy, porous beats falling against his ribs.

'I didn't expect', she said shyly, 'you to receive me on the steps.'

'Neither did I,' he said, smiling gravely. 'I was standing here to be scolded by Mrs M.'

'Is she allowed to speak to you like that?'

'She alone. Only she has permission to say exactly what's on her mind. The old soul wishes me well.'

Later he said: 'You know, both her surviving sons are . . . Johnny I hardly knew ye . . . cripples. Her husband went off many years ago. Alone – she supports wrecks and – wreckage, five grandchildren! Most people aren't brave, you know. They're compelled. She has a fine sense of humour. She's got a good eye for *me*, after a glass of gin, which she keeps taking because it makes her feel better. Though she does go too far occasionally,' he added. 'Tell me, do you also think I've begun to lose . . .'

The carriage rolled away, leaving the street empty. She looked up at his hair-line, but it was still thick and even. It had darkened since the last time, the reddish colour still there but like watermarks on the surface. Between his eyebrows he had the perpendicular lines of an offended person. Further down, similar irretrievable lines of laughter and grimaces leapt from eyes and lips. He was no longer fat, but rather thin, and the skin that had contracted had darkened and taken on a colour that reminded her of the last remnants of a bruise. Yes, he was slim now. And there was that reserve.

They closed the door behind them and went into the house. Up the stairs. In through another door and closed it. In the depths of an open window moved the silhouette of a man. It was Fletcher.

They sat for a moment listening to birdsong, in silence, to find a reciprocal note. Cats crept in the grass. A terrier raced barking round rabbit holes. The words of this thin darkened Byron came as easily as the drought-song of the thrush; just as it swung up in trills, he used Italian phrases and told her about Greece:

Dolce far niente and *mia cara sorella*.

So interesting.

'The Mediterranean is a sea of creation. The divine myths are no mere chance. Between blueness stabs – fresh cheese. Everything there is thousands of years old. There, everything is about managing to live a human life – to accomplish it within a human lifetime. There, one senses that this short insect life we live *disturbs*, as one eagerly scrambles up on to timelessness, and right across it, and down from it. Only sky and sea are young, between them a hairless earth, olive trees with leaves with their eyes closed, goats which live off nothing, and women – a single spasm of youth before they become withered earth mothers. I don't know what kind of life is happy or unhappy. One day I'll tell you all about the rest. But now I must say that what lured me home (apart from being short of money) was a more vapid deity in nature, one that offers humanity the chance of rising and living in a faith that governs creation, at least *its* creation. That is northern Europe. Thought and people. And now I yearn for the south in order to yearn for England. That is what I'm like.'

So interesting.

'One is as one is created.' Augusta hears her own voice: in her thoughts again with one foot on the carriage step and the other on its way to meet a flat stone in the street. The stride opened her, the hope, the anxiety over making a false step moving her blood and clarifying her gaze.

At that moment the coal woman dropped the shafts of the cart she was pulling and looked round at a grand lady in a pale yellow silk gown, corkscrew curls under her hat, cape, parasol and barely covered breasts.

Byron said that life would be worthless if one didn't become more than what one was 'created for'. 'Then you're lucky,' said Augusta, changing the subject, and for a moment they had great fun talking about their aunts and cousins, but in the middle of a tirade about Aunt Julia, she heard herself saying that she herself had never succeeded in becoming anything more than she had meagrely been created for – enviably! sigh, at the moment, I am nothing but an anxiety which is terrible, oh, Byron, bills are overdue & distraint threatens & Leigh is opposed in higher places as you must know, not that I want to say anything against anyone and particularly not the Prince of Wales, who has troubles enough of his own, poor man, but they don't agree now, Leigh who is so outspoken and demanding. My siblings won't help us any longer, everything's upset and paltry and I don't know myself, don't want to know, don't want think about – to what extremes I've gone to get money . . .'

'*I!*' said Byron, 'am your sibling!' But she had to wait until late that evening.

He told her how he had tried to have his family seat sold, the old abbey, the derelict church, the old mansion in ruins, scarcely habitable and surrounded by cleared woodlands.

This house obviously required the *right buyer*, she must see that? And yet he had great hopes of this purchaser, in fact thought he already had him – a certain Mr Claughton, with whom the lawyers were negotiating. Without hope, he would otherwise not have been able to incur debts himself as nobly as he had done, she must see that? The perspective of patience is long and obscure, but seldom wholly unrewarded. Within a few years, he would be financially independent and that would include her.

He looked at her to test out the effect of his words, but Augusta's face had simply stiffened into the grateful grimace that admits a charitable deed in view, while the present hurts with every heartbeat.

Then he turned morose and said he was truly heartbroken at having to leave Newstead Abbey, which had been in his family for two hundred and fifty years. Not only that. The melancholy of the place, its sunken abandonment, had attracted him at once the very first time he had gone there with his mother, when he was ten.

*

And mirth raced through his body as he thought how quickly that day had sunk in dignity, from Mamma's young lord to lost little beast, as she wandered round the house and became aware of the extent of its decay. He shouldn't trample there! Or touch there! His clothes! . . . Has a mother ever before had to endure . . . ?

The drawing-room she had expected so much of was a ruin. A relative had told her the ceiling was ornamented with 'hundreds of cameos'. But only a few rows of plaster profiles remained. The rest had collapsed, with parts of the ceiling, one stormy night. And that catastrophe was intact – a hole in the sky. The windows grinned out into the night, but – as the horrified faithful servant Murray tried to console her – moonlight anyhow glittered in their teeth (you've chosen a good evening to come here) and between the roof beams they could see the constellation of the Harp?

'What! Are you trying to make fun of me, man!' shrieked Mrs Byron, her proud flesh beginning to ripple over her body like waves in choppy seas. At the time she was a few years over thirty. She actually died at just over forty, and since then he had loved women of forty, but his memory of that night was crystal clear and included an ageing, disappointed woman, disintegrated, helpless, raging, 'Poor Mamma, worthy of so much respect and compassion, but incapable of arousing either. One also has to be loveable.'

Wise from much hurt, Mamma's young lord slipped out of her grasp in order to avoid any further inspection. At his arrival (as she was still cleaning up after the spell in the housekeeper's room, having taken the keys into her possession and thus over enchanted territory), he had scampered round alone to view his heritage, and stopped, chastened when confronted by the solemn, pathetic destruction. Parts of the building were on the verge of collapse, not dangerously, more like when a badly maintained woodland runs wild. Nearly all the walls had had smallpox, the murals leprosy, the fireplaces for some reason bricked up, while other holes had been made. Panelling had fallen off and been chopped up for firewood.

He was still at an age when you feel the best in you comes to life when faced with a huge pile of scrap. A boy of ten feels his creative force when he can build himself small nests out of what is apparently unusable. In him, in himself, a quality appeared, tempted by half disintegrated figures, such as those remaining on the old murals, the remains of city walls, bodyless colonnades: while life and use declines, the expression of it becomes strong and active; the spirit of craftsmanship is not destroyed by destruction, but becomes something else, something airy. And that air blended with his own imagination and drew him with it into history . . .

So he fled from his mother's anger with distaste and contempt (feelings which unfortunately were not rare in his dealings with her) and continued on through passages, crypts and grottos until her voice was sufficiently far behind enough twists and turns.

Then he was in the Great Hall, where he sat down on the second step of the stairs. It was a room, or rather a space, rosy with leaded glass below the ceiling that hovered sea-grey on layers of beams of vaulted oak. Several goats were lying in the straw on the floor, thoroughly ruminating over his regard before again resorting to being real mothers, maternally. Females with horns, he thought, and looked into their eyes as they looked back at him, squarely. That was how it came to him, that great wonderful feeling of ownership. Various instincts somersaulted in each other's grasp – one cannot describe just how such things happen, because development is movement rather than character, and language is character rather than movement. One unbuttons and buttons up vision, in the same way as weather shifts a landscape, a leaden sea becoming a lake of glass . . . 'But it's water all the time,' said Augusta. 'Yes, but the *similarity*, which helps us from this truth to the truth in the experience, is a larger step in the history of mankind than being able to stick your thumb into the lake and say "water".'

Four goats looked at him, peacefully, yellow and kindly, and handed his heritage over to him, such as it really was, not just house and grounds, but six hundred years the future of which he at once embodied like the eye of a comet. Later – with a little more education – he learnt something about the goat as the Mother of Destiny: it was a myth, stemming from the primaeval gaze of the goat, in its stillness setting the imagination in motion, then demanding the fantasies back again for its myth. But now he had to hurry on as Mrs Byron's voice 'and goats in the hall, what a stench, oh, ah!' welled out of the passage and 'Byronne, where is the boy! Has any mother ever had to endure . . .' This time he escaped unseen as far as the outer steps and sat down on the second step from the top, almost at the height of the

August moon hanging red in the dimness. It swelled and dusted the sleeping greenish-grey sweep of Nottinghamshire, returning out of flat melancholy lakes which metallically diluted its colour over the surface. Two miniature forts stood opposite each other on the shores of one of the lakes, spiky with authentic details. They were larger than ordinary houses and constructed like real military forts – they had told him that the recently deceased old man, the fifth Lord Byron, had built them to play at war on the palace ponds, and he and Murray had until recently sunk each other's model ships with toy cannons. That was unworthy of a boy! He would launch small flat sailboats on the lake, and if the company mentioned the forts – which was inevitable – it would be time to say something about insanity in the family.

Insanity. The moonlight played on the only remaining wall of the abbey, its face, its entrance to nothing upright like a pointed Gothic instrument and letting the wind of light aim dissonances through arches that had once glittered with glass. The space, the negative nothing that had once been nave, chapel, altar, filled his eyes with phantoms. One of them freed itself with sudden buoyancy out of the shadows and ran off with its neck curved like a sea-horse, not stopping until it got to the first lake, then wildly wiping its head with its hands. Meanwhile, it was transformed.

Byron thought for a while before describing to Augusta the way the transformation had occurred. He was sitting on a short sofa, his best leg outstretched over the lid of a chest, tossing an ornamental silver and wood dagger between his hands, sometimes looking over in her direction. The taste of cress came back over and over again. New sounds scrambled over each other against the four walls, as if something were slowly approaching. It was evening. The clock in St James's struck the quarter and drew her eyes to the pendulum clock that always struck half a minute later. The neighbouring Blue Posts began to fill with customers and increasingly, drifts of fumes from crackling cauldrons floated up from the kitchen, drifted across the courtyard and up and into the sky where they melted the moon, which at that moment was providing a faint reflection of the story: that of the August glow above Newstead.

The phantom was a girl. Their maid, May Gray – at that moment he saw an indestructible picture of her, her long waist, her body, every day carrying out the same movement of lifting two full pails of potatoes or water or slops. She had within her a gaunt and patient *jerk*, which made her strong enough to lift anything. When visiting ladies came, she served them their tea, but with cracked hands, with black earth and blood in the cracks, with hot whisky as she breathed out. Mamma then took her outside to scold her, but she scolded even louder, so that it sounded like a fight between two fat tomcats in the bushes. He was very frightened of her. She loved wrapping him up and he was afraid of what she might do, and she did . . . But then she was afraid of bats. So she broke away from the shadows of the church and was a phantom, a deformed creature with a head like a sea-horse. For every step away from the church, she increased her pace to shake herself free, but her patch of warmth stayed in her tracks, tough and mobile. His own senses created the rest. His eyes blinked and the distance increased even more. May's tail tried to catch up with her, but the longer the distance between them, the more lonely became the horse-head and the shadow-cloak and finally the connection was broken and it was invisible.

Then May was alone, rubbing her head free of the feeling of cobwebs and bats. Transformed, step by step, within him, from a creature into someone else. He had been just as convinced that she was what she seemed to be outside the church, that she was what he recognised by the lake. Anything was the truth at the moment he saw it. And time was a truth potion that changed the world before one's eyes.

May cleaned round her ears once or twice, then looked into the lake and bent down to examine something under the water. Ten foot or fathoms of wind came wriggling through grass, reached the lake, spoilt the view; she bent lower and started back.

Her legs were very long, her knees sharp. What was feminine, a thin soft summer dress, clung to them, unpleasantly, as if she were disguised as a woman. She strode across the path, over the low wall and placed herself to stare at the well with its sculptured lions, twins, spitting images. They stared back out of eyes that were sterner, created by a god older than hers. They had kept still for a very long time. The wandering of the moon gave them a slow facial gesture, outwardly.

From the well she went over to a tree, from the tree to a window to look in, from the window she wandered on rather timidly, like a goldfish when released into a drawing-room bowl and the infinity in all directions turns out to be glass.

Then she caught sight of him up on the steps and came and threw back her head. 'Boy,' she said in a thick voice. She had been forbidden by Mamma to call him George, but laughed at the idea of using the title to 'the little lad'. 'There's something dead on the edge of the water,' she tempted him. 'A lamb, I think. The eye you can see is a great ball of scum and peculiar things are swimming round it, munching on it.' May's gaze was fixed in the air, just behind him, as always. Long afterwards he still remembered this as hot ashes, as when you take a lump of ashes in your fingers and let it fall apart and feel that it is glowing and sending pain from finger to the end of the finger-nerves in your back. What May had said did indeed interest him. But he had already had enough, he said. Everything here belonged to *him* and he thrust out his chin at her, ill-disposed for all the times she had frightened him into silence when she had wanted him to go to sleep. 'My dear May, your imagination is surely playing tricks on you again, my dear May. I wish it hadn't done that so often in my *childhood*, my dear, my night's sleep would have been more peaceful, you know. It's probably nothing but a piece of leached wood, my dear May.'

She didn't even wash properly, either, or at all, her smell climbing up to him and giving him a great sense of nausea when he realised that he had always taken it to be the smell of food. She had run, she had been afraid, small beads of sweat running, and she scratched them away between her eyes, between her thin breasts, absent-mindedly between her legs. A scoffing smile demonstrated what she thought of his arrogant answer. She still had a stick, hard enough to hit back whatever he threw at her. 'Of course, you'll have to wait ten years before this becomes yours more than in name,' she muttered with satisfaction. 'I've heard that and I've listened. Until then you have to resign yourself. And obey. And behave properly. You don't become free that easily in this life.'

Ten years went by. Then five years. 'Augusta,' he said, revealing that his thoughts were busy elsewhere as he spoke. 'I know how to get hold of a sum for you. (All may be well, my girl. You can button up your buttons. Leigh can start afresh.)'

'But my poor dearest B!' cried Augusta, letting the words gush as reaction slowly set in. 'I am shamelessly grateful. Mais cela fera un désastre pour vous! I can't really allow it & now when I know your own straitened circumstances & I thought perhaps when I dared come, that your finances (you know) were largely speaking decent, with that poem read and bought by everyone and all. For I met Sir Walter Scott (Scott, that is) at the house of Lady (whoever it was) and people say he'll be *copiously* rich on literature itself (though they say that his gall bladder troubles him), but he also has a large family and is said to be a wonderful family man so of course the money simply *flows* out, as it does for us all . . . & I'm shameless enough to thank you for your offer & assure you, my very dearest B, that if you are serious about this, then you will never regret it & I'll sign anything now, for the situation is desperate for us & could be worse & no doubt my brothers will come to life now that they know how unselfishly you have stepped in . . .'

Her relief made its appearance without questions or security. She trusted his word and felt as if she had suddenly been showered with water. But he sat in silence. He sat in silence looking at her after she had fallen silent and, with an expression of bliss, was breathing in the wonderful air of postponement. He bit fiercely on a nail and brooded, brooding on a blister until it burst.

'This is my responsibility,' he said morosely. 'Stop all that about "my brothers". I don't want to hear any mention of them. Your family! Ha! They've never handed me anything else but the tip of their cold finger when I could have done with some support. My only condition for lending or giving you money is that I don't have to hear "your brothers" mentioned. When I look at you' – and he did so with an unpleasant expression in the semi-darkness – 'I see' – his voice became full of air – 'the only person I have in the world. All else is conditional when it comes to – friendship. But we are *siblings*! How could you forget it . . .' and now his voice broke and began to rise. 'Why didn't you come to meeeee?' it went on whining and hissing – 'when I neeeeded you sooooo, oh, ah . . .' She got up. He got up. 'I begged you to – in vain, like everyone else. No one came, although I said I was in *despair*. No one. Death struck all around me. My mother lay dead in my house, one of my best friends drowned in a ditch. From London came a message saying . . . So absolutely fearfully sad, old boy, said those who called themselves my friends. But I have accepted a shoot in Essex. What damned bad luck, old friend, but all flesh is hay etcetera and unfortunately I have promised to escort my mother and my sisters round the Bond Street shops on Wednesday. Another time, old boy, if things get you down again, eh? That's friendship for you. And you . . . you didn't even write a line except about that you had problems with some damned *wetnurse* . . .'

His face was so red, she was frightened. A strange pulse was beating in one of his eyes, like glowing coal in a dying fire, striking. Augusta tried to steer her thoughts back to the moment he was talking about, but just as suddenly as she had been showered with water, she was stranded. The suddenness blunted her memory, all her strength now drawn into the present, as he stood there right up against her with shaking hands and twitching eye. It's true what they say, she thought. He is a little mad. A wave of faint sound went through the room, an umbrella being taken out of an umbrella stand, a door closing.

What she had felt all the time as reserve on his part was now shattered into reasons. As she watched him shrinking – the sum of money shrinking away – she felt a certain cold admiration for his way of dealing out punishment and reward in the wrong order. She herself nurtured every day and her instinct was first to correct a little girl, then solve her problem. In that way, for a moment you enclosed its core, every day round its fruit; to continue was always to start again. But Byron exploded the solution in her hand as she received it. It hurt. That was surely to be a more intelligent way and perhaps more modern, more improving, but in everyday life with small children, it was impossible.

With imperceptible movements, slightly shyly, she started pulling herself together in order to leave, but he noticed and seized her by her upper arms. He went on talking, fast and incoherently and incomprehensibly, but he had apparently now gone over from reproaches to self-reproaches.

He spoke grandly about debts and feelings of guilt. He talked on and on about his guilt, about his debts. About people to whom he was indebted.

It is an inertia, this business of not knowing each other and yet being related. What kind of procession was going through his head? What was it thundering out with head held high in his head? His voice reached her in patches. The grip of his hands was almost in her armpits. She glanced, and with lowered head, saw a drop of sweat run over his thumb, then another. The intimacy of this was so minute, so involuntary and unexpected, that the weight with no name made a lurch inside her. She put her head on one side and started to laugh.

Began to coo. Began to laugh, slowly, as he stood there lining up his miseries like jars of preserves, with 'Byron' on every label. As he stood there grasping ten stems without flowers in his hand. As they stood there, daughters of all the unhappiness in the world. Like everyone. These threads go through everyone. Only the poets tie knots in them.

'Why didn't I come?' she laughed, so much, she grew out of breath. 'Ah, dearest B . . . the wetnurse had milk-fever and a high temperature. I couldn't find another. I had no milk to give. The little one was starving and could take neither cow's nor goat's milk, nor honey-water, nor tea with milk, either, nothing. Leigh had no money to gamble with and was at home, getting in the way, as unoccupied men do . . . yes, I had no security for the smallest loan. I couldn't get him out of the house and became pregnant again. At the last moment, I found another wetnurse. Nature, you know, has in truth impaled woman on the palings. At that moment, I couldn't imagine any worse troubles than my own.'

She laughed even more, and more happily; he looked at her, with receding drama. 'Well, that was a long excuse for a minor misdemeanour.' Augusta burst out laughing again.

In its very greatness, everything is a little foolish. Now everything was forgiven. The fingerprints on her arms faded. The evening put sheet after sheet of darkish glass between them. The choir of the city mumbled as the wind blew their way. Of the dead, she said later: 'It does no one harm, what no one is harmed by. Those who are dead don't need your indebtedness. They are with God and wish you well.'

Truth and
truthfulness

'Knowledge over and above a certain limit,' said Mr Hazell, 'tempts people into research, not mediation. The happy dilettante is the best teacher, as far as I can make out. His knowledge is building blocks that are easy to move. The next best teacher is the retired professor with an enormous knowledge of detail he has managed to re-establish into building blocks to the same extent that he has mastered his doubts about simplification. He doesn't just live in the present. He knows he is the result of simplification.'

Twice a month, Mr Hazell went to Nottingham to lecture at a working men's institute. He was paid his travelling expenses, given a cup of tea on his arrival and a present at the New Year. This activity was idealistic, the course fees symbolic. There was a great demand for lectures on Jack London, Zola, Maxim Gorki and, for some reason, Oscar Wilde, but not for Dickens. Among the individuals – but also collectively – there was utterly predictable interest combined with unfathomable yearning. Otherwise it would all have been meaningless.

He used to say just that to his 'pupils', of whom the majority were men over fifty, the rest men and women round about twenty – none from the middle generations: he used to say that just as in any bunch of listeners you find predictable interest combined with unfathomable yearning, you also find in every writer of note (he nearly always used the word writer, in protest against the public concept of 'author', a flatly constructed word meaning nothing), just as you find in every writer of note the compulsory form expected by the spirit of the day and the reader, combined with genuine talent.

Most of all among the younger women (who to Mr Hazell's irritation, tried to show their profiles of opinion by cutting their hair in the shape of chamber-pots and framing them in greyish brown collars), protests against the concept of timelessness then arose, despite the fact that he compared the timelessness of talent with something as modest as an ancient grain of dust. One becomes wise from wounds inflicted. Some years earlier, he would have made use of a more glamorous image.

The same young ladies (that expression was also prohibited) raised objections to his taking up some contemporary Italian prose writers, as there might be some doubt as to whether their socialism were solid and where it had begun to rot against fascism. The girls sat with trembling nostrils awaiting the approaching name of d'Annunzio.

Even frostier were the young of both sexes when he spoke on the 'lake-poets' of English Romanticism, of whom the brothers-in-law Southey and Coleridge in their youthful radicalism (as he put it) experimented with Utopian cell societies. It turned out that his young listeners disapproved of Utopianism; anyhow the forms that arose before Karl Marx (God save his soul) provided the whole matter with a scientific basis. Unscientific Utopianism was called bourgeois individualism, well-meaning, misguided, social narcissism and so on.

Youth has no measure of stature, thought Mr Hazell, sometimes also when he looked at his own son Rupert. Stature to them is a measure of their own height and scope. What I consider stature to be is according to them a form of muscular laxity. The older listeners possessed tolerance of stature towards Joyce and Yeats as well. They had to laugh at a girl (they defended the greater aggressiveness of the girls as they, being the most active, were always at a more elevated starting point in their reasoning) – had to laugh at a girl who thought that as early as in the second chapter of *Ulysses*, Joyce had flirted with pure anti-semitism, camouflaged behind artistic affectations, by describing a greasy Jew shitting offal. Then she had on her part set it aside . . . the old men had laughed with her a little, and then laughed her out of court, because everyone likes a lightly fried kidney and nothing makes one so light-hearted as a really good motion.

They took in and followed everything that became rather sensitive when Mr Hazell tried to portray the vertiginous tragicomedy of life with the help of Byron's *Don Juan*. He suggested that they shouldn't deny themselves the sin of talking about national peculiarities. Even if the publisher of the poem was the seducer from Seville, and even if the *ottava rima* verse form were Italian, an Englishman was necessary to invent the combination. *Invent* the combination. Only an Englishman is capable of giving his lofty idealism, his great love or his indignation an intensifying blow with a joke. Look – how sparingly humour unmasks a discourse heading straight for the sentimental or the grandiose or the diluted. Feel – the way this interruption with a laugh in actual fact intensifies the discourse within you; its observation has ceased to be obvious, you have become divided between its serious and comical aspects and you now have to strive for synthesis yourselves.

'Dialectic?' suggested Mr Hazell shyly. He noticed from their faces that he had been far too theoretical. Not many in the group read poetry. He looked up his *Don Juan* and leafed through it feverishly without finding the given example. Eventually he came to Juan's departure from Seville and started reading aloud at the point where the young man is standing on deck, thinking with melancholy of the great love he is leaving behind, a love coloured by, caught unawares by and obliterated by seasickness. 'Passion endures seasickness,' said Mr Hazell, 'but the through and through forgetful affection for a feeling – the unilateral – is made foolish by life, which is always changing mood.' And he went on reading aloud. The ageing, mildly amused faces were pervaded with something very well known to themselves as he quoted Byron's comments concerning the ailments to which love is able to and not able to give shelter (with particularly bad marks for catching colds); he saw those faces affirm scepticism, of everything written really, as he went on reading, from the seasickness to the shipwreck, from the tragicomedy of life to its cynicism – the terrible scenes on the overcrowded life-raft, death, desperation, cannibalism inserted into the merciless rhythm of the verse with cruel niches for comedy. 'Like – er, life . . .' he mumbled uncertainly, as he felt his verse-foot slipping on his listeners' attention.

'Anecdotes, anecdotes – ' cried the younger generation and a youth said with a certainty that shook Mr Hazell that 'humour' is a talent and also a class matter. Only at a lofty distance can one see the comical in the tragic – or for that matter the tragedy at all. Life is no combination of -isms, but facts one interprets according to the circumstances. The younger generation preferred Shelley (about whom they also knew nothing), just like the Victorians.

They considered that joking and pulling people's legs, instead of describing a dialectic (or even dualistic) process, broke it up into sequences and anecdotes and that satire (which could be magnificent if it chose a worthy purpose) among universal phenomena (if such things exist) degenerates into foolish insults.

He collided with them on a point at which he maintained that what is universal is the breeding ground for 'worthy purposes', while they considered that our actions in the material reality of the day are the breeding ground for the universality of the future, and Mr Hazell realised that he had allowed himself to be drawn into the threadbare discussion of the chicken and the egg when he had really meant to talk about the advantages of breach of style.

He detested Shelley. Very much delayed, he was fortunate enough to catch a delayed bus and went on squabbling with his semi-profile reflected in a dusty, rain-wet, dusty window, grey and middle-aged. These young communists, by God, had not read Shelley! Had anyone really done so? Who can read a cold-blooded beast of abstract ecstasy, who not only gives his poems titles that bring to mind gastric medicine, but also somehow seems to have composed them like an apothecary! They had talked about what Shelley thought about the Peterloo massacre. They had counted up all his *not*s, directed against their own objects of persecution: marriage, the church, school, upbringing, God, market forces, ownership, so-called morality and so forth. No, they hadn't read Shelley's poetry. Some people took with them greater values into the afterworld through the gravity of their faces rather than the ink in their pens. And yet they presumed the poem harmonised round what was unambiguous and introverted in his standpoints, as all (and again they showed their unanimity with the Victorians) *good* poetry does. Yet again, Mr Hazell stood there with his (or Byron's) breach of style, which yet again was a sign of the confusion of an unredeemed person – when he himself knew they were the triumph of harmony: overcoming your faith is a larger step than putting your doubts in order of preference.

These creatures thought, of course, that Shelley was a man ahead of his time, only because he happened to have the same opinions as they had now – the world's most cherished misapprehension. He tucked Shelley under his belt by telling them how the man's lifetime of insensitive tourism could be illustrated by his touristic existence in

Italy. The only Italians he could stand were classical statues. The Italian he preferred was Latin and he despised all Italian smells, manners and women.

When the increasingly heated discussion came to the core – that Byron had actually made a contribution to world affairs and died as a volunteer in a war of liberation (not without satisfaction, Mr Hazell brought up the heritage of Englishmen at that moment in Spain), they replied that Shelley would have done the same if he had lived. 'Absolutely!' cried Mr Hazell. 'And he would have got in everyone's way and got entangled in everyone's legs and given illiterates Plato to read and cut his leg on a wooden sword and invited all his upright friends from Hampstead with wives, children and nursemaids to wage war and arranged regattas on the Missolonghi lagoon and alone marched against a troop of Turks to philosophise with them and would have been accidentally shot in the head and become a martyr and left the flock of whining Englishmen – who had no business there in the first place – for Byron to look after, just as he had done in Italy.'

He felt he had gone somewhat astray in details unknown to them, and his argument (or whatever you could call it) skidded off and fell flat on the ground. In addition, it is the peculiarity of radicalism, he thought, looking at his moustache in the bus window, not to accept argument once one has taken a stand. That could lead to breach of style. He smiled, he smiled at the moustache and wondered whether it assembled his face or dispersed it. Reflected, it suddenly made him think of pubic hair.

The slow vehicle that kept stopping and starting with a jerk and emptying and filling with people, dripping wet or only slightly, crawled to the north-west, and the safe, damp boredom gave him the idea; what if one really could liberate Byron from the ignorance of the present? (Our story has now, in its capricious way, gone back to January 1937.) A week before this journey of Mr Hazell's to Nottingham, the members of the newly formed committee for the Byron anniversary had appointed themselves with the same generosity they had availed themselves of at the New Year. He knew that some of them had a fairly decent knowledge of the subject. Why not ask them to make brief statements during the anniversary day and he himself would contribute the story of the rivalry (to the main characters quite unknown) between Byron and Shelley.

Schedule!

Shelley: man born Innocent and corrupted by Society. If one liberates him from 'upbringing' and education, which is nothing but dross from evaluations that have come about through the victory of the strong over the Weak, he will remain spontaneously innocent and act according to beautiful norms, aptitudes for which today one finds only in Children still undestroyed. Only with Purity as a weapon can one fight evil. The struggle for existence is not the natural way to live.

Byron: man born innocent, Man born as innocent as the fly that wishes to buzz round your nose and be killed if it doesn't succeed in taking itself off into freedom. Man born as an innocent egoist who thinks about nothing but his own satisfaction and guilelessly persuades himself there is any amount of satisfaction to be had. One of man's satisfactions is other people. The other human satisfaction is integrity. He outrages people and outrages his integrity if he adheres to his original Innocence. Adaptability is required here. One learns more about the world by knowing how one threatens it than by thinking one makes it happy with one's very existence.

That was how Mr Hazell drew up his schedule during his bus trip home, and took notes. He parried the movements of the bus and finally jabbed at the paper with a full stop that became a blot.

Innocence! Innocence! Innocence! Mr Hazell grew angry with three debaters who kept him back at the end of the lecture and he asked them, with what he thought was a brainwave: 'How do you motivate your innocence?' They had been heading in quite a different direction and turned only half way back to show that they didn't understand. '*What is the basis of your innocence?*' 'Innocence? What innocence?' said the youth with a grimace. 'You dedicate yourselves to damning everything except your own standpoint and call everything else villainous. The opposite of being villainous is being free of guilt' (maintained Mr Hazell rashly). 'Well, what is the basis of your innocence? Tell me that and don't try to avoid the question by confessing sins of omission or points on which you are not as well up as you ought to be or that you are suffering from a depraved desire for tea in the student room!'

Several surprised laughs appeared on otherwise laughter-free faces. They also came out into the air as untrained tittering sounds.

'Innocence! Innocence!' cried Mr Hazell. 'Innocence is nothing else but *inexperience*, which insists on keeping on its own course regardless of what happens and which tramples on everything it doesn't consider itself duty bound to observe. How do you motivate your innocence? How have you *earned* it?'

'Knowledge over and above a certain limit,' said Mr Hazell nine months later, but without as yet having produced a contribution of his own to the anniversary, 'tempts people into research. Not mediation. How has the summer been for you, my friends? Too short? As far as our Rupert is concerned, he seems to be writing. A novel.' They all smiled, one a trifle caught out. 'I've seen the piles of paper. As long as your arm. Let's not have unreasonable expectations of Rupert. He has his term, and when he is here he has a lot to do. You understand. He's coming a little later. After practice.'

Rupert had just finished practice. He was standing absolutely still, with the instinct that holds out the prospect of invisibility as long as you don't move, and measuring the distance to an open lighted window. She had her room up in the attic. Slanting walls formed a black-and-white pattern with the beams. Over these walls leant the shadow, projected by the lamp in the window, reinforced by the lamp in the room. The shadow that was Brenda herself, dancing with herself. She snapped off in the middle – one shadow half danced over a straighter wall, the other over a slanting one. A few steps to the left and they were united again. She splayed out long shadow fingers and changed the grip on her hip to dance more closely. From her other hand came a shadow of another kind, a coiling transparent daughter of Brenda's shadow, cigarette smoke.

Rupert changed his position roughly, shifting his weight from his left leg to the right, and again stood stock still, the leather melon clamped like another head between shoulder and neck. He was covered with mud from head to foot, in great lumps that someone might have thrown, though naturally he had not been exposed to such brutality, but bore the marks of a grass field no longer covered with grass, but ploughed up by bodies and tortured by craters. The powerful thighs under his knee-length shorts, his calves, buttocks, arms, back and even the right side of his face prepared him with pleasing pain for the evening's commendation and the next day's bruises.

The music was not coming from Brenda's portable gramophone but from Brenda's wireless. Heavenly meshes, gas bulbs, glass locks, interference treating the notes like rubber bands, from sender to receiver: released, they rushed over to the window and leant out their muted horns; caught up, they tried to stretch themselves so far; thin and pale from stretching, they rubbed themselves against a saw of radio scales. Straight into them sticks the thermometer Brenda plants there to open an inlet of flesh. Out comes a velvet voice, which pussyfoots down the scale, and clips up scar, stitch by stitch. Brenda sighs – from her hips and up through the vase with no handle that forms the shadow of her torso, the bubble of air moves. She doesn't stop dancing. Indolently, leisurely, syncopated, doesn't stop dancing, embraced by the representation of herself and someone else, somewhere else, with a cigarette which is smoking itself against her hip.

Rupert often felt amazingly old. His mother called it growing pains and anaemia and 'always-with-your-head-in-a-book-half-the-night' and stuffed him with calves'-liver and small doses of port-wine. He tried in vain to tell her that it was nothing to do with physical decay . . . Every morning, he woke up twenty-two years old and during the day passed his father who was unsuspectingly inclining over the invariable of middle age – and towards evening encountered a spiritual exhaustion he was scarcely able to hide. He sat in silence with thoughtful friends, or alone, and thought. Thinking went well. It was worse saying what he thought, for the constructions that built themselves up had no desire to come out into everyday speech. Something peculiar had happened. He had been thinking with one part of himself and answering taciturnly with another. If he truly wished to express what was going on inside himself, he first had to formulate the words silently to himself, otherwise something else came out, not quite corresponding. This was a development he recognised from his father's father. Grandfather had forgotten the difference between thinking and speaking and grew angry when people didn't hear his thoughts. Rupert wished he could occasionally forget for a month or two that he had a family. If he could occasionally forget them, he needn't wish for their demise in between. When he was away from home for months at university, he ought to have been able to forget them, but they hung round his neck like a string of shrunken heads and were certainly not his trophies: he was theirs. It was wonderfully liberating to lift one's whole body up in expectation, to catch the ball and blindly parry everyone's attacks and together with them plump down on to the field, its short coat of grass and hide of peat slowly breaking up into green shards and exposed mud that struck back with a drenching smack in the face. A fellow-player or an opponent landed on top of you out of the recklessness that was all part of serious games, sinking his knee and four knuckles deep into Rupert's thigh, where numerous blood vessels burst and soon tried to close in painful healing. That was nothing. Some kind of pain is liberating, with some kind of mortal dread – swift – one reaches that level of life so hard to achieve.

When Brenda was walking in the street, wearing a suit on her way to work at a firm of solicitors, or a summer dress when shopping for her mother on a Saturday, she was nothing in his eyes. A rather pretty girl with such slim ankles that all shoes looked too big for her. It was now, in the anonymity of her shadow, divided over several slanting walls, with American music lapping round her, that she achieved *her* level of life. The hardness in the picture. Rupert still found himself on the extreme exterior of his skin, where it was cold, wet, ultra-sensitive and bleeding. During the evening, he was to age inside a pocket of himself. He wondered about his father, and his mother – the one with the calves'-liver – and his grandmother, his mother's mother (who nervously interfered with everything in the cause of generously being interested in everything), and his elder sister with her milk-heavy breasts and her husband reaching their levels of life in one single orgasm. Rupert had had a relationship with a girl of his own age since he was sixteen and knew that love extremely seldom . . . His relatives seemed to be perfectly satisfied with layers of water and starch.

A woman over thirty shouldn't wear her hair long, his elder sister said, forestalling her mother's and grandmother's suggestions, and having her naturally long golden fair hair cut and permed into small curls, forming a greyish-brown dry structure. Rupert shouted with rage as an indifferent custom castrated this wealth of varied beauty. These people drove around their layers of starch and water with energy in the core of their beings, but never allowed themselves to confront air and light. Like long black hair, the shadow of Brenda and smoke glided over walls and ceiling. Quicker now. Brenda was pussyfooting faster and shaking with her arms outstretched so that everything released in her was dancing in soft counterpoise. Rupert thrust the ball under his arm.

'Evening,' he said curtly to the other Byronists sitting fingering their glasses of mineral water in his father's study. His mother had had hot water ready and he had thoroughly washed his face and arms and dug a surprising amount of mud out of his ears. He had used a flannel and sponge to wash down his legs and feet. He had sniffed his armpits, but that would have to wait until tomorrow morning. For a long spell, he had stood flapping the metallic wind off his own body. That depressed him faintly, as if an early warning had resounded unheard.

'Time is passing,' said Link the dentist, impatiently slapping a heap of manuscript on the arm of his chair.

'My life is passing from spending time on you,' said Eric Watson. (Rupert had heard Eric Watson using language to his own advantage as far back as he could remember.) 'But it might pass quickly if only you would open up to the suggestion for a start and wait until afterwards to reject it. Well, this lady has seen the world and met its inhabitants to a far greater extent than any of us have. She has trodden ground that is just as trodden and just as untouched as Greece and Albania were in Byron's day. She has now become so interested in our little project, or rather in what she has heard Joel and me tell her about the poet, that she has handed in two small contributions of her own. One is only a couple of pages and is a story of an elephant that wears itself out at the Arsenal in Venice, in the spring of 1819, I think. You remember that it happened on one of those days when Byron had begun to court Teresa Guiccioli. The other is rather strange and is about a kind of woman she met in the Balkan mountains. Ersatz-men, to be more precise, called virginesca. They're quite simply disguised women, she says, who in times of a shortage of men take over the rôle of head of household. Friendly but as incorruptible as Islam and the Inquisition, she says. They are needed, so exist, she says. How many centuries it's gone on, she doesn't know, and one can't subject them to a Lamarckian investigation to judge their physical adaptation to the need. They namely do not propagate themselves.'

'Watson has dug up a sixth wheel to our wagon,' mumbled Mr Cohn, to put Rupert into the picture. 'A German lady who knows very little about our subject, but who he thinks might fall in love sufficiently quickly' (brief blink) 'with it to reduce our lead.'

Rupert shrugged his shoulders and replied with no rhyme or reason: 'What worries me is that I have no idea what Byron looked like. That hinders me. How do you imagine a person's way of moving and thinking if you don't even know his contours?'

The room filled with dark brown murmuring and, with polite distaste, Rupert looked at the glass of port-wine Mr Cohn had just handed him. On top of what his mother had just portioned out, he began to feel as if they were secretly trying to build up his placenta. He held the glass by its stem with two fingers and started twirling it round so that the liquid kissed the rim and was in danger of spilling as he went on:

'. . . there are paintings of him, of course, but even if they all show that florid arrogance, they're all still only interpretations, aren't they? With a little luck, they might have made a daguerrotype of him, and however blurred that had been, we would have known more about his exterior. The descriptions are also only interpretations. Have any of you ever taken part in that awful party game in which one person goes out and the others agree on someone they will describe, then he has to guess who it is? No? I have to tell you that those *closest* to you appear so alien, you simply can't believe your own ears.

'Then I saw something when we were up at his publisher's, Murray's in Albemarle Street, where they keep masses of Byron relics: his small white wedding gloves. Small, I said. Yes, small, incredibly small, truly maidenly gloves. Have they shrunk? I asked, but the publisher smiled at my question, because everyone asks it.

'And everyone has his own information on the way he limped. Someone saw the shadow of lameness. Trelawny – mendacious and unreliable, true – said he stumbled into a room in order to set the laws of gravity in motion and that after a hundred steps on a walk, he squatted down with his veins swollen and taut as ropes. All this just won't do. I want to know *something*. Facts, facts.'

'And how is it all to be done?' said Link. 'Should I, so to speak, give my lecture and somewhere in western Greece step aside and allow your Mrs S to come forward in a duet and deliver what she has about that virgin and so on? My dear Watson, the more modest the performance, the greater the demand for simple dignity.'

The murmur yellowed as the voices rose in argument. Mr Cohn said in a quiet voice: 'How should it be done?'

'Wouldn't you also like to know about his contours and shape? There's something so generous and magnificent about his words, and God, how *small* those gloves were!'

Mr Cohn suddenly met two eyes directly, glowing with the insanity of youth, the insanity that takes the world back and forth and sideways simultaneously. Rupert also coloured his lips red with Portuguese sweetness before he said what he had said once before. 'He was embalmed.'

'Good gracious, you morbid oaf,' laughed Mr Cohn. 'Haven't you grasped that we don't share your leanings. Opening coffins, good gracious! Very Gothic, certainly. But information actually exists on his height, which happens to be the same as mine – ' Mr Cohn rose to his five-foot-six-inches to demonstrate – 'and as far as his weight is concerned, it varied between fourteen and nine stone, mainly slim after he was eighteen, thin in his last years. You wouldn't see even that on a hundred-year-old corpse. You can't judge a prostrate creature's upright height.'

'But I mean it,' said Rupert angrily, then fell silent, retreating into his stubbornness, where he could still hear the echo of an hour-old well-being: the grass splintering like glass, the fragrant smack in the face from the mud, the slow, surprised grimace as knee and knuckle plough into his taut thigh muscle. The shadow of dancing. The hand swiftly in and out of his pocket. 'I *mean* it.'

'I also mean,' said his father, who had just crept up behind his back to pull the reading lamp out for Eric Watson, 'that I think it's rather original that our first reading should be by an outsider. And a dilettante, comparatively. Maybe the happy dilettante is the best teacher?'

(elephant at the
Arsenal)

An elephant was running amok at the Arsenal.

What is a town landscape to an elephant? The same as small communities in the marshes round Venice are to man as he goes round with his shotgun after birds; to the extent that he is not particularly observant of nesting places and leaves his tracks in anonymous mud.

The owner of the elephant excused himself by saying the elephant was 'in love'. In the Countess Albrizzi's gondola, they used that word, smiled and peeled almonds as the craft struggled against the waters to reach this unannounced spectacle.

Those who had seen everything from the beginning said the elephant snapped off its foot-shackle with one single jerk, as if it had never been captive except in its keeper's eyes, and the wise Italians laughed at the way man thinks he has captured things and tamed them. When the pressure rises in the cauldron, metal acquires wings. A rutting elephant – quite a lot. He overturned a vegetable stall with his right foreleg, then picked up another in his trunk and flung it down on to the stone street. Splinters flew and vegetable juices spurted in clouds of red, yellow and green drops. A growing crowd fell silent as the trader behind the great stall of melons dared to defy the creature. Dark and humble, they all understood that his urge to defend the fruits of his labours might be equally savage. The elephant stopped, tensed, and for a moment seemed to take in the sight of the little man holding two wooden trestles directed up at it. Two eyes peered out of the mass of ancient drooping grey hide, observing. Their gaze touched on the melon-man, weakening what was primitive in his courage. The next moment, he fled and the next moment his stall sagged, tipped over and green and purple melons rolled all over the Arsenal area.

The marble lions sat crouching and reclining by the wall, regarding the ugly lumbering old beast crushing melons with its footless legs. White in the first rays of sunlight, they peered across the shady market square, watching it slowly turning the colour of a bloodbath. Rumours spread all over Venice. Dozens dead, hideously massacred heads! But it was a consciously false assertion – all who heard it noticed the agitation was pre-arranged. If the melons really had been heads, the Venetians would have stayed at home, but now they came running, every one of them with his stick.

It was one day in May. Long before morning, he had woken the sleeping gondolier at Zobenigo and ordered him to paddle to Mocenigo. Low pressure in his head. The promise of marriage still on his bitten-off tongue. *Non più andrai* . . . etcetera. All things can be done once too often. And if you then do it once more just to establish whether past boredom was owing to her – your nose gets rubbed into it. He hurriedly leaps out of the craft to land on the canal steps, but fails to notice the low high-tide has been in and lapped at the layer of algae. Like a 'cursing Neptune', he squelches in a swampy watery layer where a gondola is sleeping on its side in the dry, a number of bodies waken and raise their heads from the benches fixed to the wall. Bellowing, he summons his twenty-four servants, who in their drowsy nervousness trip him up several times as they help him out of his wet clothes. 'Fletcher!!' he roars, for the twenty-fifth, and the whole house becomes a jungle as the child wakes and starts screaming in chorus with monkeys imitating, dogs barking, birds cackling and cats fighting.

So the water has risen during the night, not much, but enough to leave puddles the next morning, now slowly evaporating and altering the echo. Shoes clatter against the stones. The whole city veers to the north-east.

Tita, the huge bearded gondolier, was striding back and forth alongside his newly tarred and still fragrant gondola. With a hand on the wall. With three slaps of the palm of his hand against a wall, his feet shoved the prow or the stern out of a narrow canal intersection. His passengers were quite comfortable. He slid the boat between the decaying houses, their tired eyelids of sunken blinds, their fringe of rusty grilles, their steps of dead maidenhair. Their ruins, the light passing through a vacuum towards the water in a network of dusty rays. Through these rays glided Tita, standing inside the last wag of the gondola's tail.

What makes an elephant behave like that? His owner assured everyone there was not the slightest scent of a female before Ravenna. The word female went round. 'What are they saying?' Byron called to Tita, who leant down and repeated it. 'Ah . . .' They swayed up and down in the watery garlands from other gondolas, then soon hove to at the closed gates to the canals inside the Arsenal wall. 'I don't think he needs any scent, although he's wild. Every wretch fortifies himself internally. The longing is there, with no object. And there's violence,' added Byron as the animal swung his head and trunk, taking with it the ruins of yet another stall, flinging it up in the air and when it landed, trampling it to sawdust. 'Look at him,' said Byron to the girl sitting beside him, resolutely brushing his arm with her loose reddish-blond hair. 'He's surrounded by water and surrounded by people gaping at him, yet he still thinks he has fought his way free in Venice.'

Free in Venice! Yet he has to sit with his head on one side like the others, waiting for the pain and the will to be reincarnated with each and every one of the elephant's outbursts. They could see him from every direction, now that he had almost cleared the place of vegetable stalls. A lion was pointing into his book, another grinning toothlessly. The elephant walked round on his great treetrunks, morose, the crowd billowing calmly away from him, the crowd now the beast, a great mouthing movement round the elephant. As he raised his trunk, revealing his tusks, the great mouth trembled with greed mixed with terror. The mouth spoke vividly in thousands of voices, regarding this amazing animal in its outsize hide. 'The monster' so badly shaped in a lump, a monstrosity out of a marl-pit, with hanging folds of hide, flapping ears and small expressionless eyes. Expressive eyes. Again, someone was meeting the poignant solemn gaze ('human') residing in that uncharacteristic body and regretting that he was there and laughing.

The elephant picked up a melon, slapped it against the stony ground until the flesh was bared, and ate. As he spat out pips, they all laughed. How everything created is like the next! He mournfully made water, as if ten vats of wine had burst all at once. And they all became mournful, for he seemed to have spilled some emphasis in his urge and would soon become amenable. He shook his great head and flung up his trunk again, his tusks glimmering like two sword sheaths, then set off at a sagging trot towards the canal running on into the Arsenal. The crowd divided almost exactly in two, only one or two running back and forth between its halves to be on the same side as a friend or mother. The elephant breezily swept aside people, turning violent and sailing against them on his ears, trumpeting – no one knows what caused the surge of waves that made all the gondolas swing sideways and a lip of green water thin out over the market place, diluting the melon blood and cooling the elephant piss. The ruins of vegetable stalls stood crippled and silent with figs, tomatoes and dandelion leaves. He filled his trunk out of the canal, lifted it and squirted powerfully. 'Bravo, bravo . . .' 'Magdalena, run home quickly. Your mother needs some help with the mangle!'

*

'Jeremy Bentham sits there stuffed, in a hall somewhere in London,' said Rupert. 'And anyone who wants to can look at him. What is macabre in this context is only that it's so unusual. But anyone desiring some concept of his ideas and also some impression of his body can do so.'

'*Mr* Bentham,' replied Mr Cohn irritably, because he had wished to listen properly to Eric Watson's reading. 'He himself demanded that a taxidermist should indulge in his remains and rig them up somewhere in portrait-like lustre. He left the part of himself that one finally best relinquishes – doesn't one? – to the afterworld and allowed it to be stuffed. The worst of it is that the face isn't his, but has been replaced by a porcelain doll's face. And all this from a philosopher! I know no one who has even been so stupid as to stuff his domestic animal. When souls have fled, every position you give them is nothing but random imitation.'

As for Link, he had followed the reading while busily leafing through a book, and by the time Eric Watson had finished, he had found the model for Mrs Lisbeth's story in one of Byron's letters from May, 1919. 'Listen to this,' he said, and started to compare: 'In the second piece, the light-hearted attitude of the "authoress" to facts appears. The elephant did not break its shackle, but killed its keeper. It did not knock down vegetable stalls, but half a house.' Link found examples and read them aloud, not noticing in his eagerness that he had inadvertently gone on to the next sequence in the letter – 'a young man in Bologna came upon his sister as she was diverting herself with a Bologna sausage, and said nothing about it, but when he found it on the table, he rose and greeted his brother-in-law . . .' (?????!!!!) Er, a thousand apologies . . . Crudely. 'Could one make a limerick out of it, do you think?' said Eric Watson, smiling, as a trio of distinguished faces told him they were certainly not prudish, but some things do seem, however, to be more pointless in speech than in writing. Had Byron really been so pointlessly tasteless? Eric Watson smiled to help Link out of his embarrassment and back into the main furrow. He himself was not offended by crudities. When a man gains experience from talking to strangers at forks in the road, bubbles of methane gas sometimes erupt and become pointless jokes which have to be forgiven. 'But to be serious, my dear Link, why should she choose what is most dramatic? What would she say about Byron, or anything, by choosing the most dramatic truth? Why death and ruin to a house when it spoils the description? I always finish reading a book that opens its mouth wide and screams on the very first page. Why? Because I feel hard-boiled as I leaf on from the tragedy at the beginning in order to enjoy the flow in the immediate continuation. The old novelists, Dumas and Balzac and so on, always start with three chapters of genealogy and economic prehistory before the plot takes over. And the plot begins with acclimatisation. Today one is often given a shock at the beginning of a novel, and as only Nature herself can build on endless horrors without being ridiculous, the modern author's graph sinks from page two onwards and the reader becomes hard-boiled as he willingly forgets the powerful effect which had originally lured him into the story.'

'May I repeat,' said Link calmly, 'that this is no novel. It's a statement. Facts. Truth.'

As Eric Watson and Link allowed themselves to drift away into an amiable dispute on 'truth' and 'Truth', with Eric Watson championing the latter alternative, Mr Cohn hissed: 'For my part, I would not be present at an exhumation. I have never heard the likes of such tasteless and absurd ideas. They would come from a person like yourself. If you start your studies by poking at human arms and legs and taking faces off people, you can't be all that sensitive, I suppose.'

'I began with a rabbit liver, Mr Cohn,' replied Rupert. 'I don't understand what you're alluding to. I don't see dead people as objects. My interest is more . . . how can I explain it? Last summer, we stayed overnight in a cottage on the west coast and, late in the evening, I was sitting out in the privy with the door open, watching shooting stars. Then I saw the starry sky reflected some little way into the bushes. I could see it from headquarters, but couldn't really see what it was. It looked like ten to fifteen Pleiades, but the ground wasn't wet, so it couldn't have been a reflection. It could have been dew glittering in the moonlight, or the moon itself trickling its light through the leaves, or a conference of glow-worms. It was as meaningless as Byron's present stature and contours. Nevertheless I sat there, my attention almost sending me to sleep. In addition, a brisk north-east wind was blowing below me. When I later went over to check the matter, it turned out to be nothing but spots of paint. They had painted the privy white a few days before and flung the last drops into the bushes in order to use the tin to soak the brushes. Do you understand?'

'Yes, indeed. Precisely. "Check", you said – that's precisely what I have against it. Check!'

The time had come for Mr Hazell to interrupt the free discussion. Eric Watson and Link could have harped on about truth and Truth half the night, but now enough was enough. 'This is our sixth meeting,' he said. 'Hitherto we've acquainted ourselves with two small pieces by a German lady (how she came into the picture to start with, I still do not understand), and also heard several great plans and a considerable amount of bickering. Link here is all ready to read out his contribution. Let him do so before he wearies and goes home. Gentlemen, take the opportunity to listen.' Eric Watson applauded, seconded and moved his reading lamp closer to Link, who at that moment turned shy.

'Hm, yes,' he said. 'I don't know.' He leafed through his handwritten pages, reminding Rupert of his own acquisition.

'I've got a Remington Noiseless,' he whispered to Mr Cohn.

'Quiet!' said Mr Hazell.

'I also think that a "statement", an essay, comes to life from the speculations that come in between already established facts,' said Link. 'Why do you think I'm a fact-fanatic, Eric? Writing essays about real people is archaeology. One reconstructs by reconstructing. But one makes use of at least the shards and stones one finds, for they give some indication of the proportions.

'My stones and shards come from Hobhouse's diary. What I'm going to read tonight is the account of Byron's and Hobhouse's travels in Greece and Albania from 1809 to 1810. I have kept to Hobhouse's chronology and his strikingly detailed descriptions which we are incapable of imagining. Without him, we wouldn't have known that Byron amused himself capturing boats in the Gulf of Patras, for instance. I've found no reason to turn that into anything else. I think it's fun as it stands.

'What precedes the young men's Grand Tour – concerning friendship and all that – I'll pass over. Hobhouse was perhaps the best friend Byron ever had, that unglamorous kind who helps, preaches, corrects and takes on all kinds of thankless tasks. They met at Cambridge, where both were at Trinity College. When Byron first went there, he was an excitable fat young man trying to make an impression on the other noble young gentlemen by spending just as much money on debauchery as they did. This led to his being sent down from the university and moving back with his mother within a year. When he got back to Trinity, he had been through his famous slimming cure, one slice of beef per day and otherwise nothing but green tea, plus sweaty cricket practice wearing eighteen layers of thick wool. I don't know whether appearance had anything to do with it, though perhaps temperament also changes when you lose weight. Anyhow, he found his way into more intellectual circles. Byron was, after all, a very widely-read man, but in a totally unsystematic way. In school he was already reading truth as sagas – like so many children – and nourishing his imagination with history, Latin and Greek. He never acquired structure to his knowledge from a curriculum, but from the sheer breadth of his reading and from inspiring friends. Not because his new coterie in Cambridge were bookworms and men of pure living. Sometimes they went on raids to Brighton and London. Occasionally they went with Byron to Newstead Abbey, where they helped him enjoy the delights of country living with late nights and mornings, wine and country lasses. That far, Hobhouse's diary (anyhow the *published* part I have read) is very succinct. It doesn't seriously begin until the two friends have taken their degrees, and complete their education by going on their Grand Tour of classical and exotic places, which at that time was considered appropriate for all young men of good family.'

Grand Tour
1809–1810

Byron and I left England on June 26th, and arrived after a rough passage, at Lisbon. We put up at the Buenos Ayres Hotel, where a Mr Bulkeley charged us 13 per cent to change our money.

In the evenings we go to the theatres, where the audiences are much addicted to Iberian dances of a lascivious nature.

The earthquake could well have occurred yesterday, or last year, rather than fifty years ago. Organisation, hygiene, building. All is chaos. The city is a natural for beauty and prosperity – lying in an angle of the steep hills at the mouth of the Tagus. The river is very wide, at least twice as wide as the Thames. From its source in Castille, it winds its way round the fortress in Toledo and across the sun-scorched sandy plain of Estremadura, then becomes Portuguese and spreads a belt of greenery around it. The last thing it leaves is a sandbank in the Atlantic, where the ebb and flow of the tide meet. The tidal water is brackish, says Byron, who swam across one morning at the widest place. He says one can master the powerful currents by making oneself pliable. Anyone struggling against them becomes submerged. The exchange of water between the colder sea and the warm river creates small determined whirlpools and on one occasion he had rotated several times down below the surface before he had found a flatfish to flee with.

Perhaps it's the war that lies behind the many ruins? Mr Bulkeley says that most of them certainly stem from the earthquakes and – if we look closer – we will find people still living in the remains. Pieces of boarding and other easily handled building material are propped against the holes in these permanently makeshift arrangements.

Inside, the matrona cook their bread soup and people play cards. Mr Bulkeley says the Portuguese seldom have a government and so have learnt that a government is not necessary. For the moment, however, the English govern the country. The French before that. Portugal is governed by whoever has taken her as spoils of war and used her as their theatre of operations. No good can come of this.

However, religion is what has become the main enemy of this backward people. Everything else is brought in and taken out, but religion remains constant. Out of a population of two million, three hundred thousand are monks, a shabby flock of wolves, with no lairs, it seems. They drift about the city, shameless in every way, supporting themselves by begging from the poor. The other day I saw some of them in church pulling about a woman, while close by another was praying at a shrine. Begging is their only source of income and they exercise it with a stubborn physical intensity that unfortunately brings blowflies to mind. Depraved, they are, untrustworthy, impersonal and against all their vows, a menace to the entire female sex.

The Inquisition still exists despite Bonaparte. Last month they dumped about a thousand unfortunates into their torture pits.

Dead bodies are exposed in the churches with a plate on them, and are not buried until sufficient money is collected to pay the priest! Not for the first time, one wonders about the kind of adherents the Creator has attracted, but earlier impressions fade in comparison. The Revolution and Napoleon Bonaparte – perhaps they do shoot the stucco off national buildings, but that probably also entails a kind of lawful cleansing as they advance?

Lots, quantities, hordes of dogs roam round Lisbon. When the French were in power, they shot ten thousand of them, to the eternal resentment of the Portuguese, for dogs are the only cleansers of the streets of Lisbon, good ratcatchers to the extent that their pups survive the rats, which are as large as half-grown dogs.

Service in the army does not appear to be popular. It is recruited by surrounding the public gardens from time to time and taking for service persons who are found inside and are unmarried. Transport is provided by seizing equipages, both of the nobility and other people, and sending them off to the army, paying for them with worthless paper money.

We climbed out of all this horror and the smell of fish up to the hill with its mediaeval fortress. From there, we could hear Lisbon's cocks crowing in the triplets of their colourful tail feathers. A sudden response out of the bushes revealed the whole park to be a huge bird's nest. Noble birds, from the now distant colonies, gone wild, were nesting among noble trees also gone wild. A peacock immediately displayed its tail, as if it had long been waiting for paying spectators. There is something greedily reserved about such remnants of days of glory. I had bread in my pocket. We devoted ourselves to speculations on how these birds came to be alive instead of simmering in the stewpots of the town.

The Portuguese flora is astoundingly beautiful, but to me nameless. I wish I had a book which would tell me what I am looking at. One forgets what one does not name. Byron loved a tree with blue flowers. It is indescribably beautiful. The trunk branches out much as a fruit tree does. No leaves, but a veil of blue flowers. The blue of them is like darkly shaded eyes, like many blue eyes crinkled by sternness, and when it is outlined against the greener bluish tone of the sky, he is regularly struck dumb by its beauty. He has found out their local name, 'Woman between nights', and is enraptured now by daily confrontations with her.

In his baggage, he preserves a scarlet uniform, with no rank, abode or model. I suspect he has created it himself in consultation with his romantic tailor. He is thinking of using it as 'court dress'. Indispensable when you're on your travels. When we got to Lisbon, he said: 'This is undoubtedly the most beautiful city in the world.' It was the first we saw outside England. When he got to the other city, Cintra, he said: 'This is undoubtedly the most beautiful city in the world.' He is also a true democrat when it comes to female beauty. None can escape feeling chosen.

On July 22nd, we crossed the border to Spain and bathed in the little border stream. We enjoyed its shallow glass, cold, our feet on pebbles. Roundabout blossomed fields of flax, hardly visible in the parasitic abundance of poppies. My friend sympathises with the flower I call a parasite and tries to fasten one between two stones, in memory of opium, in memory of his body. The running water immediately tears off its petals, one by one, and carries them with it downstream. The flax flower I threw in after it stays whole in the water.

The heat tremendous, not streaked with wind or mitigated by the green as in the countryside in England, but total. We rode in the sizzling light of the plain, on shadows of horses quadrupled in length – their legs darkly shimmering like those of spidery flamingoes, herons. The soil red, pink, lilac. Footbridges help us over the 'rios', but we didn't see the water in them, for all the plants of the plain had climbed down and the resultant leafy river meandered, wound its way and curved round a single bright red berry looking upwards. Far, insuperably far away, was a human dwelling place – the village, a sleeping head in the angle of an arm. The remains of Moorish fortresses as well as Castilian lay in collapsed piles of bricks and crumbling rock. We came up and saw on every church tower a stork's nest. Fletcher on the verge of sunstroke. We crept into a mill and found a little cool on the damp earth floor, particularly as we had thought of drenching our shirts with wine and putting them on wet. We were fuddled by the fumes, but didn't dare use water, which appears to be in short supply here. For the rest of the afternoon we were in the saddle, so sluggish from the heat and wine that the landscape starting swimming before our eyes, like a dream of which the only basis of reality was the actual feeling of riding in our calves, thighs, buttocks and the small of our backs. The path ran along the edge of red ridges separating the sandy olive groves in the north from a precipice and a chasm on the south side: ears of corn shimmering bronze as they swept away from the wind. A wide river was amazingly calm, the water resting. Green and clear, it floated on its sandy bed – with no banks it must surely overflow quite undramatically in the spring and irrigate the crops, to return to being these three tree-covered silken ribbons when the corn ripens. Or withers. Three black pigs were rootling below an oak. I picked some mistletoe out of the fork of a tree. Byron said that would bring bad luck and for once his servant Fletcher agreed with him. The afternoon heat was considerably worse than at midday. It rolled over our heads and steamed up from the ground, concentrating its qualities from all corners of the compass. Below us ladies were harvesting flax – the women's harvest becomes blouses – working at a pace in keeping with the heat. Hats of straw, veils of white rags protecting them from the sun and completing the sense of a dream as the brims floated through, over, the whispering blood-red of poppies.

The holy Catholic church of Spain has provided its flock with an unlimited number of very much revered saints, thus also handing out excuses for feasts and sins in all Spanish towns. Wherever one goes, fireworks are being prepared. That evening, we rode into a desert-yellow square and slowly circled it. It was surrounded by four-storey houses, all the shutters closed. The sandy wind slid over the roofs and down into a hot swirl that danced in the dust of the square, scorched, settled. Fletcher's horse was frightened. When it slipped on a stone (polished by feet as pebbles are by the waves), its rider fell off. In the evening, the blind windows of all the arcades became seeing, sounds rushing out of the urns of silence. We were there. The dance commenced.

They dance their Iberian dances along the street, actually on the streets, stamping in the dust and looking round as they extend their bodies. They stand and look at each other, a man and a woman. Her innocent face grows hard. The couple stand face to face, stamping like deer and circling as if fastened to each other with the short cord of desire for battle. They raise their arms in a double bow and splay finger horns behind their ears. They wind their arms back along their bodies and display tail-feathers of fingers. They twirl in submission and superiority with an arm raised, another lowered, and she submits with her posture, although she grimaces dryly, absently. Never, on any occasion, do they touch each other. When the man puts his arm round the woman's waist, there are nevertheless several handbreadths of air in between. In that spirit in particular, the girl's face hardens, not so that the sinful movement makes it sinful, but instead it takes on a mask of chaste passion. They dance in ancient colours of eight, a leg sweeping the billowing spots of her flounces inwards.

At night, the whole thing ends in Chinese pyrotechnics, the pieces shooting up from the banks of the river, roaming and gasping over the Roman bridge, rising slowly over two merged cathedrals, and are annihilated, in always equally satisfactory wheels, suns, ice princesses and yet greater miracles. The miracle is actually the storks. The shattered sky drives them out of their nests on the cathedral roof. The silhouettes of great birds chatter and swarm like huge insects in purple smoke. And underneath, the silhouette of Salamanca.

On July 25th, we came to Seville, which lies on the plain above the delta of the Guadalquivir. For the time being, the Spanish junta had their headquarters in town, which meant all the hotels and posadas were full, the number of inhabitants trebled. In the end we were accommodated by Josepha Beltram and her sister, who own six houses in Seville. These were the cleanest quarters we had hitherto encountered, although not all that comfortable. A white house in a whitewashed alley close to the Moorish palace. In a small tiled inner courtyard, the sisters kept caged birds, the kind of birds that fly freely at home. They twittered and the spring water fell, and the little windows on the two floors of the house looked down on a dead sparrow floating on its side in the well. Josepha Beltram was very captivating, though not young. To be sure, my friend was also attentive to the sister. Our departure (after three days!) was *melancholy* and locks of hair changed hands. Josepha's was a yard long and Byron sent it home to his mother.

Along the banks of the Guadalquivir, a long line of Women between Nights spread their transparent indigo shadows, across a channel, which with much labour was transporting its silt towards the delta. The whole town was boiling in blue light and running people. All the eating places were full to bursting, very – incredibly – small women rushing between tables with their arms holding out tureens rippling with bread and eggs. Their faces were the actual colour of hard-boiled yolks, they breathed out negative oil as they pointed: we're full up. Their pores, open and black. We roamed around for hours without acquiring any food. In the end, we fell asleep without dinner or supper, all four of us in one small room.

I dreamt about painted eyes in the cathedral. 'Is the contrast true?' asked Byron. 'Does it say anything real?'

We had first viewed the Moorish palace with its modest material, so exquisitely sculptured – like a filigree of grey meringue or a jewel made from a wasp's nest. And yet it was stone! Someone had treated it as air, or paper, or liquid silver. The proportions of the rooms were harmonious; here we have the symbol for that expression – spatial harmony. One feels peace and relief, as if everything about the room had been measured with yardsticks corresponding to a human being's ability to sustain a note on a little flute.

We stepped into the darkness the Catholic kings manifested in their victory over the Moors. To achieve that, they had needed Mexico and Peru. They had needed the ghostly clusters of the armadas on the dawn sea. Had needed the plague, needed unharmonious scales indefatigably running and chasing in the bass of the organ.

At first we could see nothing as we went in from the midday light, only blackness and the procession of saints disappearing into it like a shooting star into the surface of well water. Then the blackness turned brown, then bronze, for the quantity of gold constituted a glow. We shuffled uneasily through the gigantic hall that looked black and scorched, although it was also a Catholic bazaar, chapel after chapel calling out their gaudy specialities. The citadel in the middle exceeded everything I had hitherto seen of gold in burdened masses. The darkness gave its gold a dusty touch of bronze, but it was certainly always gold, all the gold found in Peru, and it was like looking at music: the anguished runs of the organ in the bass. And yet they say Seville was not one of the strongholds of the Inquisition.

Medio augusti – Sardinia. We have had a pleasant sea voyage from Gibraltar, where to everyone else's surprise we once again saw the luggage we had shipped by sea from Lisbon. We were appalled at their surprise but grateful for our previous ignorance of the risks, as it would have been unendurable to ride across Spain with the caravan of our household goods. One should travel light!

Now and again I meet the Royal Family. Byron, coming back from a ride in the country, describes it as neither agreeable nor attractive, having seen nothing worthy of notice but three heads nailed to a gallows. People of the lower sort are in leathern garments with broad leathern belt, into which is usually stuck a knife. The village people throw over this a short piece of black shaggy goatskin, with two holes for the arms. The whole country is still in a state of uncivilisation. The gentry will often steal their neighbours' flocks or shoot their horses, and no man travels outside a town without being armed. One gentleman the other day, after being convicted of sixteen murders, cut the throat of the son of a neighbour in whose house he had been brought up as a child, and on being outlawed for this crime was seen arm-in-arm with one of the Queen's equerries.

The army is in a deplorable state – officers sufficient for at least 30,000 men, and yet only 4,000 privates. Money is as scarce as provisions are cheap – beef twopence a pound, and a bushel of grapes for a dollar. Bread, which is exceedingly fine, is one third the price in England.

*

135

We were in quarantine in Malta and left her with her colours crumbling in our eyes.

September 23rd – We got our first sight of Ancient Greece from the Channel betwixt Cephalonia and Zante.

On the morning of the 24th, as we were entering the Gulf of Corinth, we fell in with, chased and captured, a small boat laden with currants, and, fitting her out as a privateer with a spare two-pounder, we went off in her with the surgeon, Mr Swann, a midshipman, Mr Barker, and ten men.

The next day we fell in with a Turkish vessel of about 70 tons, to which we immediately gave chase. She fired upon us in return, one of our crew sitting next to me being shot, and another bullet passing within an inch of my ear. Eventually, the wind dropping, we pulled alongside, and, jumping aboard, her crew at once surrendered. We brought her into Patras the next day. We stayed but an hour or two, and went on to Prevesa. That evening we captured a boat from Ithaca, and a Turkish ship from Dulcigno. Lord Byron rummaged her, but found nothing save some worthless arms.

All through October, we travelled in northern Greece and Albania. Ali Pasha's domains. Extract from a letter home:

Dear Matthews,

We've now been out for three and a half months without having stayed in the same place for more than a week at a time. It's easy travelling with Lord Byron, because he's an opportunist for good or evil: he accepts the local morality – however repulsive it may seem – and adapts to local comforts better than I do. We do have camp beds with us – because of bugs and rats – not to mention innumerable household articles, but none of them comes into use. On the way to Ioannina, we ran into a storm and had to take shelter in a wretched hut for *three days* together with a troop of Albanian soldiers.

This is a primitive country, only held together as a nation by the despot. In reality, people live a tribal existence and are neither Albanians nor Hellenes, but, for instance, Suliots who refuse to profess adherence to *any* capital. So the villages are small fortresses, all high up, some clinging to the mountainsides. The nights are full of dogs and fleas. When the one bites, the other

136

barks. It's never quiet, although all the conditions ought to exist among these mountains of snow, conifers and cool, intelligent downwinds. Sheep bleat for miles around, their bells clanging in the wide silence, frogs croaking.

The houses in Greece are Turkish in character. The ground floor is occupied by animals and tools, a gallery leading up to and around the dwelling house. They have no fireplaces and the food is cooked out of doors. In winter they just have to endure it.

All the men go round heavily armed and incidents occur all the time. Weapons seem to speak their own language when there are far too many of them. I took a walk in a village and looked over a fence where a feast was going on inside. A man just put his wine cup down and stabbed his brother-in-law in the neck. His wife brought vinegar and bandages. Then the party went on. All under a roof of vine leaves and ceanothus.

Albania pays a tenth to the government, of which Ali Pasha keeps a quarter for himself. In addition, he squeezes a lot out of the country people as compensation for his 'protection'. His soldiers can shake down wherever they like and take up quarters among the inhabitants for unlimited lengths of time as long as they content themselves with living off them and not stealing their money or their wives.

Despite all Ali's taxes, on the whole one has to say that the country does better under his rule than it did before. He builds bridges and clears the countryside of all robbers except himself. His country is a peculiar hotchpotch of Christian and Muslim. The Mussulmen do predominate, but sometimes wear Christian amulets round their necks and they trade in *wine*, which they thin out with water, strengthen with pine-needle oil and flavour with lemon and resin. Not to be recommended for European stomachs. Not this either: outside Ioannina, we saw a side and an arm hung up in a tree. In the sunlight, with a whole lot of vegetable stalls below. We thought at first it was for sale, for a butcher had his stall quite near. And almost fainted when we realised what it *was*. A quarter of a Greek patriot, who had been tortured for three months beforehand. And people were walking round, laughing and crying – at other things. I can't really describe my feelings at such expression of cruelty and barbarity.

Any more than I can explain the taste of the strange food (Greek cuisine is not up to much), alien customs and ways of expressing themselves. All this is taken in by the senses as a picture fully completed in every detail. It is no longer altogether alien to me, but will never be part of me. Byron says about this alienation that it is a good strategy for life at home as well as away. He's working on a long epic poem in Spenserian metre. The main character is called Harold and is *not* himself, although he says everyone will think he is. He says people are idiots always looking for the real truth about the writer in his *works*, while for his part he is seeking the real truth about *them*, and the world around us. He still likes tumbling round ha'penny half-truths like that. He writes industriously. And he was the one to maintain he was finished with all scribbling . . .

October 28th – After a three day ride, we caught the first glimpse of gilding and knew we were approaching Tepaleni, Ali Pasha's capital. The guide said the town was rich with trophies of war. He considered the Vizier a good ruler (turned up his eyes when he said this and appeared almost to be beholding his own brain) and a good *son*: in a town to the east, many years ago, infamous violence had been inflicted on his mother and sisters. When the fortunes of war favoured the Vizier twenty-five years later, he succeeded in taking that town and executing the inhabitants. All precious metals were melted down and taken to Tepaleni to gild and silver the town.

It was nothing shameful to entertain a certain unease at meeting such a formidable ruler. Byron put on his 'court dress', I my actual if not so magnificent uniform. The Vizier's adjutant said they had long been looking forward to meeting important representatives of the English Crown, and Byron and I exchanged a bleak half-smile.

We were received in a hall with a marble floor, blue tiles and a spring splashing in the well in the middle of the floor, surrounded by a large number of purple ottomans. Ali Pasha received us standing, a very great honour from a Mussulman prince. He took Byron round the waist (my friend blushed) and pulled him down at his right side. He studied him searchingly which gave me an opportunity to study him. At this time, Ali Pasha was a man of about seventy, but at the first possible opportunity, he emphasised his youthfulness by letting it be known that two of his younger wives were with child. His hair was white and cut short, though it was not possible to make out its quantity, because as a good Mussulman he wore headgear. His beard was also white, but untrimmed and fanning out over his kaftan chest like an old-fashioned collar. His eyes might appear dulled and tragic, but little animals ran about inside them, lighting torches of cunning or irony, as when he smiled at my friend, flattering his vanity: he was sure Byron was a man of good family, a conclusion he had drawn from his ears, his curly hair and small white hands. He bade Byron look upon him as a father, and during the following few days behaved like a father to a child – at least twenty times sending small gifts in the form of filigree bowls containing almonds, sherbet, fruit and *sweets*. In return, Byron sent over an English rifle inlaid with ivory and silver.

I asked the Vizier if he had had any personal encounters with his previous ally, the Emperor. He pulled half his moustache along with his smile as he said: 'When you say the Emperor, don't you reckon with the presence of an Emperor in Russia and one in Austria and one in China?' I replied that to me a kingdom was hereditary and a true empire self-created. He reflected on this for thirty seconds, then said that Napoleon was a terribly impatient man, who never seemed to be quite aware of what time of day he found himself in at any moment. It was possible that Bonaparte considered he could ignore the time, which on the other hand had reciprocated his lack of regularity with hideously bad breath. Bonaparte had confided in the Vizier that the fact that he had never learnt to tolerate the sea was a great shame to him. Ali Pasha had given him a herb considered in those parts to prevent seasickness. As an ally, the Emperor was as unreliable as any man with 'a higher purpose'. For such people, treaties apply only to the other party. 'And such people always cause their own downfall. Thus impatient people destroy themselves before anyone else has time to do it.'

When he spoke in this way, I found it hard to see him as a 'Mussulman', a stranger, another way of thinking. The little animals in his eyes shone like cat's eyes when confronted with light in the dark, and their expression was in total accord with my own thoughts.

On November 7th, we sailed through the bay where the battle of Actium had been fought. The wings of history were quite still. Everything else seemed to grow through the centuries. Historical places – one imagines them again from the dimensions of one's own day – therefore seem so *small*! This bay would not be big enough for the manoeuvres of two of our modern frigates! We went ashore and boarded another boat that was to take us to Patras. It had a crew of forty men and was armed with four guns.

Today we got on board a galliot of forty men and four guns, and sailed for Patras. In spite of a squall, we insisted on starting. The waves grew, the rocks came closer, the sails jammed. The sailors at once ran below while the Captain wrung his hands and wept, and Byron swore. The ship would probably have been lost had it not been for the services of two or three Greeks who eventually brought us to the Bay of Phanari. Fletcher shrieked for his wife and feared a 'watery' grave. We lay down on deck and advised each other to be fatalists – for what use are tears and laments in a situation of this kind?

*

'Such arrogance!' said Mr Cohn. 'I'd quite forgotten that. That they actually risked the lives of fifty men without even adhering to a timetable.'

'All of them are dead now, anyway,' said Rupert.

'My dear Joel, great adventures and *les grands tours* do not cover their own expenses,' said Mr Hazell with a laugh. Amused by the delayed indignation.

*

The ship would certainly have been lost if it hadn't been for one or two Greeks in the crew. Characteristic of their native island, Ithaka, they navigated through the narrow space 'between Scylla and Charybdis', and finally steered us safely into harbour in the Gulf of Phanari.

November 15th – Utraique. It's beginning to be cold and raw. The air, the smell is full of decayed seaweed and blackened seagrass. It stinks of soldiers' latrines here and you get used to it.

Fifteen days ago, some brigands carried off a Turk and a Greek from the Customs House, the former they shot, and the latter was stoned to death. Our party, augmented, as a precaution, by some forty soldiers, took their dinner *al fresco*. The Albanians assembled in four parties round as many fires, dancing and singing, most of the songs turning on the exploits of robbers. One began thus:

140

When we set sail
A band of thieves from Parga
We were in number sixty-two

The most polished of them, Bolu Pasha, had only four years ago been a
formidable local brigand, commanding something like two hundred
men in the mountains of Hepacto. Byron says that in some natures
there are wolves and in some cultures robbers. I just hope the wolf
instinct is not aroused to life in our dogs while we are asleep . . .

(We continue through mountain and valley. Sometimes a long
sloping golden plain, pondered on by a Greek, a Turk or an Albanian
on the edge of the picture. His long skirt, his sliding stockings and
pointed slippers, his sleeves flowing in the wind, long leather waistcoat
over – curls. Flowing in the wind, the pointed twisted cap above.
Ammunition low on his hips, pipe like a signal out of the black crevice
of his mouth. He stands with his friend on the edge of the plain, its gold
and green sweeping in a circle at his feet, and straight out of its sea
level rises a snow-clad mountain. The shapes of the earth are
unfathomable and therefore also the face looking at them, and
therefore his music.

We rode through the narrowest enchanted Ossian ravines, cliffs on
either side and trees with their roots half exposed, all grey foliage,
fresh water we blasted out of the ravine, out into an ocean of light of flat
land, salt marshland lost in a mist of infinity where before one might
just perceive the end of the world, long before it was made round.)

Via Machalas, Prodomos and Natalico we came to Missolonghi,
which lies by the lagoon – on a peninsula between swamp and marsh.
The first thing we saw was a dog running over a grave. The town has
about five thousand inhabitants, who live well off what the sea has to
offer in the great fishing grounds of the Gulf of Lepanto. They have
even been able to afford to pave several of the larger streets, and yet the
chickens are but legs beneath clouds of flies. They are *caked* with flies
and slaughter must be a relief to them. Every other kind of insect also
creeps and crawls. All night, the shores laugh with sea birds. The
British Consul here took Byron for the new Ambassador and insisted
on speaking French to him and heaping solicitudes on to us; but when
persistent rain held us up for a day longer than we had thought, his
hospitality rapidly evaporated.

Byron is deep in one of his melancholies. He's angry with Fletcher, who has written home to Mrs Byron complaining about his distress. Byron has preached a sermon to his faithful servant on the theme that he is suffering from no more than cold, heat and lice, something a traveller in foreign countries and wildernesses must be prepared for and which he himself, 'as well as Mr Hobhouse and his servant endure without complaint'.

The real reason for Byron's gloom is once again absent letters, a feeling of not being missed in England. I am quite familiar with that feeling. I myself have also sent three letters to the same address without receiving an answer. And yet, I am the one who has to make concessions to his mood with the consolation of an unreliable postal service.

We made our way across the bay to Patras, the largest town in Peloponnesus, the trading centre for currants, oranges, olives and cotton from Lepanto. The forts supposed to guard the town are a treat to the eye, the largest of them serving as a sheep fold. Is it courage to be unguarded? Are the Turks indolent or do they consider they have their subject people the Greeks in the palms of their hands? For how long, one may well ask.

For in Vostiza, we lived in the house of Gogia Pasha, son of Veli Pasha's prime minister. This young man (very well educated, speaks ancient Greek and modern Greek and reads Herodotus in the original) gave us a detailed account of the rebel Riga's attempt to start a national uprising against the Turks twenty years ago. The subject filled him with great enthusiasm, which seems remarkable in a man employed by the Turks . . . When we pointed this contradiction out, he said a people's freedom is its face. He said that after a few months in Greece, we would see how this country consisted of one eye here, a lip there, but nothing that could mirror itself or recognise itself. He said a country becomes desolate and broken when foreigners paraded there, the people growing false and indifferent, with no morality when a stranger takes over all power and responsibility. A symptom of such decay is all these squabbling tribes and their robber chieftains – were they to be the heirs to the kings of Sparta and Argos and Corinth? I said they might be in my opinion, as classical Greece had constantly been involved in civil wars, but he retorted that a logical consequence of classical Greece would be a nation, not a 'shattered bandit oligarchy'.

He added that when a country is not strengthened into a nation, it becomes wide open to an advancing world around it. If the Turks had not come from the east, the Bulgarians and Russians would have come from the north. For Byzantine imperial dreams had many adherents in Greece as well, and the meeting between north and east might still transform Greece into a battleground for war between two alien armies. 'In the west we have Napoleon Bonaparte, at sea we have the English and everyone wants his share. Without the foundation of nationhood, Greek history will finally be torn to shreds and fall to the lot of various interests.'

This speech had made Byron's melancholy lift like a kind of morning mist, in the exaltation of which he unfortunately happened to wing a bird of prey, an eagle, or was perhaps the bird which had so calmly outlined its wingtips against the greyness between sea and precipice and sky only a hawk? He wouldn't allow me to give it the *coup de grâce*, but tried to nurse it back to health, but a day later it nevertheless died, and it had suffered.

December 14th – At midnight we came to Salona; we decided to ride through the night and reached Delphi when it was still early morning. The clouds loosened their roots from thousands of thorns and pine-needles, but had to leave behind some vapour. Which became water. And the needles glistened with it, dripping with the sound of scattered rain, though the sky was very deep and green. Below us there were also clouds: Delphi is – was – situated on one side of the slope of a valley in the form we in England would call a ravine. But it's infinitely larger than a ravine. At the bottom, the cloud mass was lapping around in a colour like the North Sea and it was not until later in the day that we saw that it wasn't a bay, but a valley.

Practically nothing is left of the old cult place. The fact is, you can't imagine marble, gold and statues of the good Apollo in this rugged wilderness. 'Perhaps it was granite at first and the cruel Apollo (whom I trust), before the Athenians came here and dressed it up,' said my wise friend, as he put the tip of a needle into a flame, then stuck it into a boil on his arm, where a few days earlier he had tried to twist out a tick, but without extracting its head. We argued about this and agreed that everyone had misunderstood the Greece of Antiquity. There must have been ancient mountains and morning mist and boils and spruces and it couldn't have borne the remotest resemblance to Racine and his pure view!

Discussions on the right way to travel: should one do so armed with my normal thirst for knowledge? Or with pistols and an indolent interest in everything and anything, which is his model.

Byron is a dear friend and an outstanding young person, whose moments of perfidiousness are richly weighed against his lustre, generosity and *joie-de-vivre* (thoroughly marbled with melancholy). He willingly allows me to change his mind when that is required. He listens seriously to my motivation. He persuades me with original, brilliant arguments. He does not allow his lameness to get in the way of anything he wants to do and suffers it bravely – even when climbing on boulder-strewn ridges. Though occasionally he gets on my nerves! He peers over my shoulder when I've made some find and tries to identify it with the aid of books and instruments I've brought with me. But he never makes any himself, or he never makes any effort to do so, anyhow, but relies on chance. Instead he lets me read spiteful things he's written about me to our friends – smiling that he does not wish to go behind my back:

'On Parnassus, on our way to the spring in Castri, I saw twelve eagles (Hobhouse says they were vultures – at least he says that conversationally) and I took them as an Omen. The day before I had written a few lines about this mountain and when I saw the birds, I hoped that Apollo had accepted my mark of respect. I cheat in poetry during my poetic period of life – whether that is lasting remains to be seen – but I have at least worshipped this divinity and I have been to His well and I am grateful for what He does for me.

'What else is there to say about this place? Why should I say more? Isn't everything thoroughly described in the Boke of Gell? Isn't Hobby keeping a diary? Yes, he is indeed keeping a diary. And he trots around with maps and compasses of both kinds, and Greek dictionaries and keys to ancient inscriptions, measuring stones and surfaces and accepting the old wives' tales of the local inhabitants as truth and reading aloud to us about Pindarus, Parnes and Parnassus. I myself get on to (another) donkey and ride to the top of respective mountain and lie down in the heather. Up there fly eagles and hawks, the true descendants of Antiquity, quite unmoved by the fact that times change.'

December 25th – The last few days our horses have galloped and we have stopped them only for absolutely necessary rests. The magnet of Athens grows stronger with every mile we put behind us. On the twentieth we were in Thebes, a modern city, which despite all my efforts, refused to part with a single sign of its ancient origins. Anyhow, we bathed in Dirce's spring outside the city.

Then we rode on across the long flat plain in front of the mountains, downpour after downpour riding behind us and overcoming us. Christmas Eve in a stable at Skourta, a miserable and deserted village.

We got our first view of Athens from Chasia, where Signor Strani advised us to make our half-way halt. My breast was in turmoil, I have no hesitation in admitting that shapeless, unformed emotions were swirling round inside me trying to get the better of each other. There was the rock of Athens, like a great ship on the bronze yellow plain. Behind her the Attic mountains. So much dignity. But the actual temple was like a white grid round a mosque. And the ship was pouring white smoke out of innumerable chimneys, for the sanctuary was inhabited by Turkish soldiers and their families, and they were cooking food.

The surrounding countryside was very romantic, but we looked on it with our eyes directed on Athens and were moving in that stumbling way – with no feeling of riding slowly or fast – that applies when one is aiming for one particular goal. The road ran along below the wall of an old fortress. A forest. A dell, with herds of cows emerging swaying through the twilight mists. The steep hills opposite dressed with vines and olives, the last red rays of the sun against the blue cupola of a mosque. More and more people on the road, Jews, Greeks, Turks and then us, now beginning to resemble them, for the wide trousers, long jackets, boots against the mud, cap against sun and rain, and unshaven faces for the sake of comfort, suit the wholeness of being here. It was Christmas Day as we slowly rode into Athens. We gave each other a gift of an orange each, stolen from a cart in the crowd.

January 7th – We have taken lodgings with Madame Theodora Mayne. She has three silly daughters, all under fifteen. Byron is already brooding over whether it would be indelicate to pay his respects to just two of them. The two eldest unfortunately have the beginnings of a shadow on their upper lips, as clear as in contemporary boys! Neither do the ladies hesitate to show hair under their arms!

Indoors they wear only an embroidered waistcoat with gauze sleeves and they also conceal their legs only scantily with gauze. They lie on the sofa eating confectionary and candied fruit, so their facial colour is not what I would call healthy and their figures are not what I would call trim. Byron says Spanish ladies smell of strong scent and olive oil and Greek girls smell of olive oil and some herb used for de-worming dogs. English girls, he says, smell of bread and butter. The old goat takes a great interest in the thirteen-year-old Teresa, with neither proud flesh nor moustache. He played with the thought, with her, of taking her back to England. The mother, listening to all this, said she would have no objections for thirty thousand piastres. He has written a lovely naive ode to the object. We have decided to keep some distance between us during our stay in Athens. So we have rented two houses next door to each other and have only knocked out a passage in the dividing wall. The owner wept but calmed down after a pile of our piastres, the rate for which is excellently low against pounds and dollars. Thank you, dear Lord, for a little private life and comfort.

January 8th – We sent the customary gifts of tea and sugar up to the Disdar, the Turkish Commandant on the Acropolis, and so were allowed in to view it all. 'It all' today is a confused mixture of still extant remains from classical times, and Turkish buildings: mosques, office buildings, military installations and dwellings. One side of the temple of Athena has collapsed after gunfire. One short side is also seriously damaged and the age of the building becomes more evident almost daily: suddenly a rumble can be heard all over the city when yet another marble section totters over and crashes straight – at best – to the ground. The Disdar implied that the destruction quite often crushed both living and dead things on its way. In his opinion, it would be wisest to pull down the columns before anyone else is injured, but he was awaiting politically calmer times, as agitators would otherwise regard such a measure as evidence of Turkish misrule, regardless of the reason for it.

Some remnants of the frieze actually remain on the Parthenon. Byron walks round cursing Lord Elgin because the man had plundered this plundered people of their last national treasures by taking down most of the frieze and dispatching it to England, implying, so to speak, it will be safe there, cared for and preserved, while here it would have faced a very uncertain fate. The latter objection, however, has no effect on my friend's indignation. On the other hand, he (we) mix with great amiability with Signor Lusieri, who advised Elgin to take down the marbles and in addition served as initiator, expert, advisor and supervisor as far as the actual work was concerned. Behind every Lord there is assuredly an ordinary man of common sense . . .

Inside the yellowish-white marble temple, we could now see at close quarters the little shacks where the Turk hides away from his subjects. Poor children with dirty faces stared at us. The victors. We soon found the losers when afterwards we wandered round the actual rock and saw smoke rising out of a chimney pipe sticking out between two blocks of stone. Under them, a cave mouth and inside many pairs of Greek eyes shining in equally dirty faces.

On our way there we had been insulted by a renegade Spaniard, of whom we complained to the Waiwode on our return. Our Spanish friend thereupon was bastinadoed with about fifty strokes on his feet, in Fletcher's presence. Whatever I think of it at home, autocracy has its advantages.

Spring has already come to Greece. We have made the most of it by visiting the sights of Attica. From bays and promontories, we have gazed across the Aegean Sea. It arches towards us, though doesn't take us, and breaks on the shore. When one stares out over the sea, it's as if the eye were seeking a focus, although everyone knows that humanly speaking the sea has just as many voids as focal points.

We had a horrible adventure; we were half way up the Parnes mountain when we caught sight of – and remembered – the famous caves there. An old fellow from the locality offered to be our guide. After fumbling our way along the first dim part, we lit torches and proceeded to explore the interior, which contained an innumerable number of subsidiary chambers running in apparently endless ribbons in towards the core of the mountain.

When one goes into dark spaces carrying several burning torches, one becomes disturbed by one's own shadow. It is so multifold that one starts spinning round on one's own axis to ward off its persistent attacks. When one starts spinning like that, the grotesqueness of the shadow is reinforced. In small caves, it crept up close, on to the wall, like a smiling fish. In the big caves, it expanded hugely into distorted spiritual beings, idiotically exaggerating the slightest move. What it was like for the others I don't know, but I couldn't stand seeing so many versions of myself and became out of breath, losing all sense of direction. Byron said Plato probably alluded to this roving nightmare; 'Why should he in particular be the only Greek without humour free of illusions?'

I didn't listen to what he was saying so much as to his voice: he spoke first and laughed afterwards; the first words clanged from roof height, then we came to a narrow passage which swallowed his voice, and his laughter swelled out into the next cave, which then increased its echo into an anguished hissing sound. It blew out a torch.

The torch went out. As we fumbled our way on, we suddenly noticed all the torches were beginning to lose their power. Their strength began to fade. Quite terrifyingly! We turned back towards the entrance, the exit, but the torches were quicker to die – the fire diminished down the handles, where it bubbled and spat itself out. We started running, but not in panic. A thumbnail of light showed us the cave mouth just as the last torch went out. How many times has chance not saved my life. I've often saved it myself, as when a fly flits back and forth away from the lashing of a handkerchief. But more frequently, I haven't even been aware of the danger until I've realised salvation has already arrived, like a kind of tender amused miracle. With postponement of only a few seconds, we might all have died in there. No one except the guide had the slightest idea of the geography of the caves, and he seemed paralysed with terror when he saw our torches fading.

March 8th – We said adieu to Athens on the 5th, and went by the *Pylades* to Smyrna. It was hot. Indolent, high winds all the time. The water gilded by spring light greasing and oiling our keel all the way east. We saw Naxos. We saw Delos. The water turned turquoise and received sweaty bodies like a refreshing crystal bowl.

Darwin said that the shoals in the Gulf of Smyrna have all appeared within the last few years, and that there is every reason to suspect that in time the Gulf will be entirely filled up. We are to stay at Smyrna with Mr Werry.

In the evening, we both, with Captain Ferguson and Mr Darwin, went to call on pretty Miss Maraschini. When they reached the drawing-room door, Byron and Darwin ran downstairs, leaving Captain Ferguson and me to pay our call alone – a most unusual trait on Byron's part.

Rain has not fallen for a long time and all classes have been praying for rain – three days being assigned to the Turks, three to the Greeks, and three to the slaves; and they have even contrived, by separating the lambs from the sheep, to make the former bleat while the orthodox Mussulmans are also imploring for rain. All religions appealing to their separate gods; in that way, everyone is praying for the same thing, the same heavens, without muddling confessions.

March 11th – Mrs Werry actually cut off a lock of Byron's hair on parting from him today, and shed a good many tears. Pretty well for fifty-six at least.

May 3rd – We left in the *Salsette* frigate, Captain Bathurst, and went by Mytilene to the Dardanelles. Byron and Mr Ekenhead swam across the Hellespont today. Ekenhead performed this feat in an hour and five minutes. They set off two miles above Europe Castle, and came out *at least a mile* below the Dardanelles.

May 14th – We landed at Constantinople, being towed against the strong current to a point under the walls of the Seraglio garden. In the evening we crossed to Pera, a crescent moon transfixing the apex of a minaret in the velvety night: again the tender irony of Providence; a salvation of the tourist's ardent dreams this time. After having sampled the sight and its swift transitoriness, we put up at an excellent inn where we treated ourselves to the best dinner we had had since we left London.

May 28th – Today a problem arose concerning Byron's possible appearance in the official procession to the government building. As Mr Canning refused to walk behind him, Byron went home. The rest of us set out, preceded by about one hundred officers in two rows, twenty of our own marines headed by Mr Lloyd, and Mr Ekenhead on horseback; a dozen servants in yellow and gold, eight or ten pages in red, with fur caps, immediately preceded Mr Adair, who was on horseback, Mr Canning, Captain Bathurst, Mr Morier, the Consul, and myself, with several gentlemen of the Levant Company. We eventually arrived at Top-Kaneh.

It took Byron quite three days to get over this trivial contretemps, days during which he trudged around on his own, his nose either in the air or pointing to the ground. What redeems him is nevertheless that all matters of dignity sooner or later tickle his sense of humour, also when applied to himself. In an evaluation of his fellow human beings, he says that in the long run he can only live with people he can laugh with. Despite everything, that is the true Byron – origin and sum total. He may be permitted to sacrifice some of his youth to religious self-dedication, 'try everything' (as he calls it) transforming all worlds into his own body and submitting the *destruction* to it. On the other hand, manhood is balancing between all inclinations (the practical as well) and providing surprising precedents between them – then withdrawing them – in and out of the mysterious conglomerate which is personality. And laughter is the actual sense of balance.

July 14th – Byron and I left Constantinople in the *Salsette* frigate, coming to anchor the next day just above the Castle of the Dardanelles. A great dispute arose between frigate and the fort as to which should salute first. The difference was adjusted by Mr Adair going on shore the following morning to visit the Pasha, the frigate saluting him as he left the ship. Diplomacy sometimes appears to be the most time-consuming of cockfights – but – anything – as long as the spurs are not brought into use unnecessarily. The Governor of the town, a very Falstaffian person – asked us how we liked the Sultan's palace in Constantinople. We replied that so much of it we saw we liked. 'Ah,' he said, 'for fifteen years I swept it out.'

July 17th – We arrived at the port of Kea. Two ships were waiting there, the one that was to take me back to England and his boat back to Athens. Before I went aboard, I took leave – *non sine lacrymis* – of this singular young person, on a little stone terrace at the end of the bay, dividing with him a little nosegay of flowers; the last thing perhaps that I shall ever divide with him.

An emotional
outing

On a beautiful evening in October, Gwendolyn, the maid at the inn in Pen-y-Bont on the boundary between Shropshire and Wales, carried Mr and Mrs Eric Watson's bags upstairs. The gentleman had in fact wished to carry them up himself. The room was two floors up and he had not been able to resist a discreet look or two, as he thought, at Gwendolyn's left leg. She noticed the looks emerging from beneath his eyelashes, fished them out and responded to them, then seized the two small suitcases. The more furtive the looks, the more telling to Gwendolyn herself. If her leg were tender from something, it was unwelcome attention. But it was her job to carry up the guests' luggage, show them the room, and in the interests of the house, ascertain what ought to be known about them. One thing she had managed to ascertain immediately.

Looks.

(Looks.

With a single look, you capture a creature. With the same look, you put it down into the Lilliput of your own experience.

At the same time, you preserve the health of your soul by never grasping the way the other person's look re-shapes yourself. People never think they are seen as they see themselves. She wants to be seen as she sees herself, dreams about herself, and actually lives on the assumption that this desire to some extent agrees with reality. Anything else would be unendurable.

So you remain innocent about yourself and the impression you give. Sensitive to that – over-sensitive – when you think about it, but otherwise innocent.)

In a mirror, Gwendolyn saw 'Mr and Mrs' Eric Watson following her up the stairs. The lady had taken off her hat with its pheasant feather as if it had been a disguise, wonderful to be rid of. Her hair hung over one shoulder in a thick plait. She was looking contented, like a smiling mussel, not a middle-aged woman. In Gwendolyn's case, it wasn't her look that was furtive, but her smile. But that couldn't be caught by Mr and 'Mrs' Eric Watson because she was professional enough to show them the back of her neck.

They were sinning and they were innocent. Totally innocent as far as gossip back home was concerned. Mrs Lisbeth was, anyhow. How could anyone have seen what she hadn't shown? They had both been very considerate and *very* careful to obliterate their tracks behind their – plans. Mrs Lisbeth's husband had gone to an industrial fair in Brussels and was to be away for a fortnight. (To the extent that her conscience managed to make itself heard through the storm of emotions, it complained less about Lisbeth's actions than about Larry's naivety.) Eric Watson had never needed to account for his travels back at home. He had taken the train to Wolverhampton the night before Mrs Lisbeth had got into her car and set off westwards. 'I'm going to take this opportunity to see *England*,' she energetically told everyone she met. 'Now I'm going to see Stratford,' she confided to her bewildered baker. 'Oxford,' she told her astonished milkman. 'Cambridge' to the greengrocer, who shook his head, 'Durham and York.' That was also true, for in the interests of discretion, they had agreed that she would stay away a whole week, while he was to return home at the weekend.

Who minded? Her words and energy were in vain, as everyone's looks had long since been fixed on the indolent silence. While Mrs Lisbeth swept and cleaned, experienced looks blew away dust and fumes that had gathered on the tracks. No one saw what she arranged for them to see. They saw her arranging. They smiled behind her back. Some smiles were good-humoured, others contemptuous.

'The bathroom's the one with the noughts,' said Gwendolyn, pointing. 'Dinner will be served in three quarters of an hour,' she went on, 'if you can be ready by then. Thank you very much, sir.' She smiled almost to the nape of her neck as she stumbled over the implication in 'if you can be ready . . .' Mrs Lisbeth had already noticed it, for now she spoke in a clear official voice: 'I must have a bath, my dear. It's been a long day. Would you please let Cass out of the car and take her for a little walk. She's hardly been out today.' 'Neither have I,' said the tall gentleman unconcernedly. 'Can I have the bathroom first?'

They both came down a short while later. In the pantry, where she was folding table-napkins, Gwendolyn opened the door a crack. Mrs Eric Watson had clearly changed her mind about that bath. 'Dogs,' she said, distinctly, as if to an idiot. 'I see that you allow dogs in the rooms. May I bring her into the dining-room? She's very civilised and doesn't beg.'

From the pantry – where there's a half-blind window because of the chimney wall, resembling spectacles for a child with a squint – Gwendolyn observes the couple as they walk along the stream and stop to speak to an angler. The three of them are silhouetted, the angler pin-like with his rod and line. The dog sits on the bank looking into the water.

From that level, spirals of life wander upwards in wide circles over the harvested, newly sown fields, over the sheep fences and velvety green pastures, from where the white black-faced sheep climb further up into the heather, where the hilltops darken and meet the clear air, colours mingling with twilit pale nuances.

No angler catches fish in the evening. He catches colours. He looks at the time and hauls in his line. The dog gets up and wags its tail as the little ripple from the line approaches the bank, the sensitive glimmer of the float at the point of the V. Gwendolyn smooths out the same table-napkin, folds it and smooths it out. She is envious and stays with the feeling in order to localise it. Every feeling has a physical point of pain – she knows – if you find it, you can learn to breathe to enable you to control it. She envies the angler because he is peaceably packing up his things and chatting with the couple without envying them. She envies them. They are seeing all this beauty for the first time, together, and their heads are like royal silhouettes against the light, still fiery from the sunset. It is spinach-green, pink as salmon and yellow as apricots, still an utterly light light, but the earth lies in the shadow.

'Tourists . . .' says Gwendolyn.

'What did you say, Gwen?' Little Noreen from Drogheda is the inn's other maid.

'I'm saying those two aren't married. Not to each other, anyhow.'

Noreen spoons jelly from a large jar into small quartered bowls for jelly and pickles, and soon abandons her task.

The angler sees them as he comes striding along below the house. In the one-eyed window, two girls' heads can be seen like uneven pupils. One round, one sharp. They are looking beyond him. The royal light is sinking very fast now, Mrs Lisbeth and Eric Watson no longer silhouetted against it. They are pale shadows in the darkening countryside and are walking with their arms round each other. She frees herself and bends down to look at something on the roadside. He waits, observing her from behind, from above. Gwendolyn doesn't think Noreen can take in the significance of a position, a way of seeing, a gesture. She is seventeen and has never even been to the cinema.

As the woman stands up again, she meets the man's observant eyes and starts back, almost imperceptibly, but anyhow. Then he takes hold of a *button* on her jacket and pulls her to him. It's very delicate. His persuasion is minimal. Its strength is the weak thread with which the button is fastened to the cloth. He kisses her lightly. Her response is far too loud. She throws her arms round him and they meet from top to toe and kiss again, as far as she can judge – *deeply*.

'Ooooooh,' says Noreen in disgust, turning away and stamping her little foot once as the scarlet flush fills her hands and almost flows over them. She is so easily hurt, it becomes almost a game to offend her. So soft, you can poke hollows all over her.

Gwendolyn thinks 'you have to be tested in the hard school of life' to learn to resist insults. So she makes sure it is her little Irish friend who serves at the illegitimate couple's table. Noreen asks nicely to be excused. But in exchange, Gwendolyn offers to make their bed and clean their room, which is considered greater and worse.

As Noreen does her duty, quickly and shyly, her answers in whispers only, Gwendolyn devotes special care and repartee to two professors of mathematics who come here to go fishing the same week every year. They are her friends. Almost every morning, she cooks their fish breakfast, that is, if they have succeeded in catching anything when casting at dawn. Eric Watson looks up when she makes them laugh. (One of them says: 'You seem to be in your element this evening, Gwen. Has something special happened?') Then his eyes also darken and become questioning before changing to a smile, the secret interest in it – with no obligation to anything – filling her with great bitterness. He doesn't see what he is sowing. He doesn't see what he is *sowing*. He turns all his interest back to his partner, who is making an effort to listen to Noreen whispering: 'Would you like cheese and biscuits or ambrosia soufflé for afterwards, Madam? And you, sir?'

'Afterwards,' hisses Gwendolyn as they collide on their way out to the kitchen, each with a demolished dish of duck. 'It's not "afterwards" but "afters". You silly!' Noreen straightens up and becomes a little taller than Gwendolyn. She looks round without listening, unseeing, slightly shattered, her cheeks scarlet. Mr Eric Watson finds her irresistible as she serves him a helping of soft ambrosia soufflé, which she has involuntarily decorated with one of her rusty curly hairs. He thinks she is curvacious all over but has an artful waist. That's how he expressed it a few hours later as he watches Mrs Lisbeth taking off her petticoat.

People go to bed early at the inn in Pen-y-Bont. Most of the guests come to fish in the stream. The others go on day trips in the surrounding hills. A dome of that deceptive sleepiness induced by digestion after a day in the open air descends after dinner. Sleeping off dinner is not healthy and as everyone knows, a way of inviting nightmares of truth. So everyone tries to clutch on to life for an hour or two. They have each other for distraction. That soon wears off. There is also a pile of old natural history magazines and a piano with no lid. As Eric Watson sits down at it and plays 'After the Dance', 'A Nightingale Sang in Berkeley Square', 'Stardust' and 'Alabama Shuffle', Mrs Lisbeth can stand and look down into the instrument, where small felt-covered hammers touch dusty wires. Some hammers don't reach, but just jerk at his touch. Then there is no note. She glances from the innards of the piano to Eric Watson's fingers on the keys. The connection is slightly mad, as if the framework of the hammers were playing on its own.

People go to bed early at the inn in Pen-y-Bont. For distraction they have each other and that soon wears off. Sleeping pills are the stream rippling past all night, a sound composed of thousands, each one worth listening to. Water hurrying, not hurrying past, but always hurrying, outside your window, always an opportunity – opportunity after opportunity. It is also the tempting playful way that runs by itself. And it is your first conscious awareness when you wake without being woken.

The next evening, Eric Watson deserted the piano. After Noreen had taken away the coffee, he opened an old knapsack he had had under his chair and put several books on the table. Mrs Lisbeth took one of them and riffled through it to cool her cheeks, now glowing from the Indian summer sun. Gwendolyn saw her gaze above that accordion of book pages. But he did not respond to it, for he had put on the spectacles he wore for reading. When he looked up, he resembled a nocturnal animal with enormous permanently wide-awake eyes, shaded by something feather-like. The stream rippled by, but he had locked his hearing and sight inside those absurd spectacles to read and write.

Poems without words

'Apple!' he said, biting her cheek hard.

It began with expectation. With his hands, emerging from the sleeves and setting about renewing their acquaintance, stroking with the fur and against it with his wonderful rough talent: writing streaks of nakedness on sleeping skin and returning to obliterate the distrust in a young girl's desire . . . like flax in a field of poppies, like poppies in a field of flax. Shapeless elders mingled inside her eyelids, glowing, indifferent to crops or weeds. The sound of fire: caused only by the winter outside. North-east to south-west, it blew, the flames rushing out of the fireplace to go with it, soon becoming the same chill, some sparks remaining in slow careful tracks through the dark, like poems without words.

On the mantelpiece were still miniatures of her as a child – of the lovely artless child Annabella – a miniature of the dog she had had as a child; she had no siblings; and urns of pale green jasper with white silhouettes in glaze on the porcelain's velvety surface. Two sprigs of vine in a glass vase. The feathery draught of soot in the hearth and – far away – tinkling delicate sounds of table lay thyself.

Other sounds were their breathing, for long spells following each other like the breathing of two animals as they run, flying along side by side. They drifted apart and became the echo of each other, more and more remote, until the distance had gone full circle and again merged them together into one. She had lost her shoe. He took her foot in his hand, limb, soon let it go, superstitious. It continued. With expectation.

Her stockings bore traces of loose stitching, all the way from top to toe, opening and closing as they ran hot beneath his hand. It silenced her. As mute, as silent, as always!

Ever since the first time he had shaken hers in greeting. And made her language turn numb and float up to the surface of an intimate inner silence. When she went back to her room that evening, she at once sat down and listed his qualities on a quarter of a page. She had now actually met him. The good on the left (not arrogant but more understanding when faced with seriously meant criticism. Respectful to people who respect him); the disturbing on the right (self-absorbed and often preoccupied to other people. Dramatic or histrionic). Between these qualities, she then drew lines which showed how the same character expresses itself in advantages and disadvantages. The diagram clarified her memory of him and she realised quite clearly that she was not drawn to him.

But once she made him burst out laughing without her understanding how and he held out his left hand and managed to give her arm a squeeze – warm and cool, swift and vanishing – before she had time for much more than awkwardly beginning to miss it.

She was confused when her aunt came a few months later to convey his proposal. She was also disappointed. Well . . . not that she hadn't expected this in the long run. But the haste. All that farsighted rhythm in his presence was disturbed by something resembling an impulse. She regarded Lady Melbourne gravely, noting that the affectionate, hard, frivolous lady was making peculiar shakings of her head. She was shaking and pleading his cause as her features simultaneously expressed a series of reservations, which all quite obviously concerned her, Annabelle's, suitability. She stared sullenly at Lady Melbourne's mouth as it linked together the intended party's two names and heaped weight and securities on each side. After a short pause, the mouth smiled slightly crookedly and said: 'and of course, my dear, he loves you.'

Annabella retreated. Some jewels in Lady Melbourne's brooch burnt through her eye. Under no circumstances was she going to enter a relationship with a man, she said, who was not sufficiently familiar with her thoughts and qualities to have the right motive for a liaison. One doesn't appreciate a person after chance meetings, she said with emphasis. What would come of that? An enquiry of this kind could have been directed at anyone.

Her aunt smiled and bent down to pick a feather off her dress. 'Why do you never understand that many contemporaneous things also go on in heads that concern themselves with you?'

She was careful to decline his 'enquiry while retaining friendship'. As a reason she mentioned: another man.

For two years, she fulfilled the process he had attempted to circumvent with his thoughtless proposal. Annabella couldn't bear conversations being interrupted by the intellectual laziness of the speaker and turning to chatter or impulsive whims. An idea must lead to its logical conclusion. In that lay the adventure.

They did not see each other. But she wrote herself closer – an experiment – she worked the words straight to get there, honestly. When they saw each other again, they were actually betrothed, and he teased her about this long spell of pen and paper and 'learnèd references and instruction'. 'I don't know what you mean,' she said. 'I was joking,' he said. 'Oh, yes . . . but jokes also have some significance and I don't understand it.' The hand came out of the sleeve and silenced her.

That was those two weeks in October, folding over like yellow pancakes round melting contents: Indian summer days of sun, through mist, over ripeness and decay in the fields.

He was a guest in her parents' house, so that the two betrothed could get to know each other before the wedding. Why? She sensed the same wise question in him. She herself found she loved him most at a distance, in the same way she was to love him when she knew him well. It was this awkward situation of semi-friendship, semi-alienation that risked everything. He was unreachable when he was there. On the other hand, she had possessed him in the exact wording of her own letters; in expectation of his: in the *memory* of their few encounters that permitted long undisturbed nightly interpretations of looks and words.

His actual person swept crookedly through her home, incapable of honouring its routines. She was aware that her father had a tendency to long anecdotes. She knew social life was full of gentlemen of that kind and that Byron otherwise knew how to respect them: you just continue in their mood, but here he made no attempt to. He sat in an artificial listening pose and refused to react. Annabella had a strong sense he did not at all appreciate her mother. At table – below the bridge of her parents' conversation – he might let his gaze rest on one of them, then give her a half-smile. If childhood is a sojourn in dappled shade under tall trees; if the rest of your time is tree-felling and planting, then this was where he wielded the axe. He offered her his face, which she had to have, but demanded in exchange that she united with him against the elders. Then she tried to raise his eyes to a level common with theirs, but he pulled hers back to one common to them. Thus fell the tree that gave the richest shade. She suddenly realised the greatest choices in life are not moral but personal choices, that that is the prevailing order and you therefore plan and conjure up the unsurveyable. A satisfied safe feeling inside her burst and at once became a scar. Then she killed his look.

One day she saw him captivated by her mother, who was telling him a little story about a match that had recently occurred in her immediate surroundings, between a young lady of good family and an artist whose name it was unnecessary to mention. What had confused everyone was that this artist – during his bachelor days renowned for his exaggerated generosity to temporary lady acquaintances (both when it came to gifts and dedications) – did not present his bride with as much as a fragrant bouquet or a lock of his hair. Could he understand such a thing?

She avoided him as much as possible, every third day staying in her room with minor discomforts, some ailment. If he were left alone with her parents for a day, there was always the hope that everything would have been transformed by the time she came down. If she discreetly managed to keep him at a distance, her inner picture of him need not be destroyed until he again corresponded to it. Oh, yes, she knew all right: he would not correspond until she had adjusted it a trifle, but he had asked her to change him and make him into a better person and she had promised, although she knew that such prayers and promises are to a great extent illusory.

They climbed among the rocks on the shore, with their hands and feet, with sandy soles that could find no foothold on the rock. They climbed to the top, offering each other their hands, pursuing each other with breathless laughter. There they stood, slightly above the sun, looking down on to the surface of the North Sea, floating opaque veils of mist like a meadow on a summer's evening. It had been calm for days, the only movement of the water a wave far below the surface; the shifting level always and everywhere forcing an encounter between two masses, thrusting against and thrusting away and meeting, its back to another, never stopping, shaping itself in the plasma of the eye and continuing into the brain, hypnotically: the sea hard as stone and flowing. When Annabella was free and went there alone, she spat into the sea or threw stones, right into the middle of the circles they made. These paltry but thoughtful indications saved her from becoming a 'hermit. A hermit with no purpose or soul, only suspended in the elements' like a salted ham on a ship's mast. When she made a hole in this perfection between heaven and sea, the illusion of being dissolved in its greatness vanished and she reverted to her own self with a simultaneously painful and enjoyable sense of owning herself.

She turned round with these words on her tongue... but suppressed them and instead smoothed down her hair. Not only because she was shy, but mostly for that reason. He had sat down on a flat boulder with his back to a grassy slope, his eyes closed against the sun, like a fox in a slit of a window. His upper lip twitched, moved to laughter. Annabella flushed because she had almost let out her secret to him, and she still had it on her tongue. It was not just shyness, but also such uncertainty about him!

Sometimes he could put himself in other people's places and interpret their feelings from their words, but he often dismissed anything earnest and serious in a hard voice, and she could already imagine his comments: my dear Bell, you describe the feelings of every lion and tiger which makes the world its own space and a stream of piss or two. With regard to your tendency to minor ailments, I think a shower from above would equally quickly reduce you from a part of the universe to dear Bell, careering back to the hearth.

She clenched her teeth. He opened his eyes. He was troubled. He searched for her features against the light. Words piled up and wouldn't go beyond her lips. She looked out across the North Sea again. Small patches of shadow from the clouds were adding layer upon layer. She remembered 'his' comment even more clearly. She tried to resist it, but was devoured by disgust. Disgust at being a woman and never having the last word. Disgust over how impossible it is to get close to or keep away from what is great. And men. Paltry! Life was summed up in that spat-out word. Self-control speaks:

'They say we English talk about the weather.' Annabella heard herself sublimating it all into a usable remark. She admired her voice, as if it had been someone else's. 'That weather ritual, at least in my opinion, is our way of humbly joining something great and eternal. Faced with what is really great, we can't be anything else but minor rituals. It is only people's deeds that can make them varied and magnificent. Isn't that true?'

'You're a clever girl,' he replied, then added something.

'Oh,' she mumbled wearily. Wearily, staring at the man who never understood what she wanted to have said. What she said and meant by what she said. 'The future,' she said, thinking of a pair of scissors with loose blades that wouldn't cut. He was not as people thought. He was often dismissive and moderately intelligent and idiotically pleased to raise a 'laugh'. Laugh? He never attempted to gain her aspirations, only her yearning. And when he touched her, he knew she would be *quiet*. He pulled her over him on the slope of small thistles, colourless dried flowers and grass. And it was bewitching, as he first pulled her resisting weight closer and then received it. Something cunning, a sleepy irony came into his face when – without changing grip – he first made her fall and then stopped her falling.

That intuitive shift of his muscles, his awareness of it, was bewitching. A man. Was for Annabelle a melodious obscurity, never changing, but slowly gliding out of key into key.

He said things – and set her in motion, obstinately, as when one tips over a boulder by giving it a hundred gentle shoves and making it rock.

Lady Byron suddenly gets up and it turns out that when standing she is short compared with when seated. She looks down at herself from a slanting reflecting ceiling mirror. She looks up at the mirror. The train shakes and she sits down again. The steward rushes up to offer assistance. She asks: is it much further?

Several times in her long life she has been forced into the formal settlement of accounts of other people's lives. Her uncle, her mother, her father. That business of giving away articles of clothing and memories, consulting lawyers, sorting all the pieces of paper which ought to have been burnt by the person in question. You didn't want to see them. Papers in which you suddenly saunter and meet yourself, slantingly reflected or half turned away, as you are bound to be in someone else's description. When her aunt, Lady Melbourne, died, Annabella had been married for three years, but separated for two of them.

The cousins Caroline Lamb and Anne Isabella Byron were sitting on a sofa, sorting the dead woman's correspondence. There was a great deal of it. Caro's gilt ring flashed as she handed over a bundle from Byron.

They smelt of camphor and something else. Annabella hesitated. Caro smiled encouragingly. Annabella inwardly consulted her weak point, but it said it loved pain.

And so she encountered herself – as she seemed in his letters to her aunt. Cut out of her life, she floated in from the right, from the left, cut, cut to pieces, she staggered through time and touched herself with a series of gentle stinging slaps in the face.

1. 'This morning I am going to see my – betrothed. I don't know what will come of this story. I am not in love, but there is no reason for me not to be, as I happen to be the most susceptible creature on earth. Caro says I will never be able to keep up with a philosophical woman with a bad figure, but I don't think anything is beyond the bounds of possibility. In addition, I have a great longing to overcome all my other urges: to get away from all this love and loving and exhaustion.'

2. 'Our A is almost too perfect. Although from the very first moment I have been prepared to be her obedient, second-rate B, she is never quite satisfied. She has a system of judging people and is in full agreement with my flattery being superior to my way of *tolerating* people ... Also, there is endless talk here about *emotions* and *feeling*! Ugh. Mademoiselle is highly emotional and often runs away to hide her tears. Every other or every third day, she is absent, the pretext ailments, which deeply disturbs her devoted Mamma, but does not convince anyone else, for seldom have I seen so many signs of an iron constitution. All this is profoundly disturbing. The last thing I need in this world is an irrational woman behind a façade of algebra and geometry. I fear that she will not be able to manage me. All those wise letters breathing peace and gentle humour and discipline ... can it be that in my flight from mad women I have landed with the worst of them all?'

3. 'I have now found a way to mitigate these emotional outbursts – the commonest of them all . . . it's marvellous. She is naively passionate. She is like a child in all these matters. She is dumbfounded and embarrassed, but nevertheless submits to the treatment with confused enthusiasm. However, this has brought with it new dissonances and another level of tears. She becomes nervous. I observe restraint. An English aristocrat must have a chaste bride. I believe less and less in this marriage and have offered her all kinds of respite and freedom. But she does not wish to hear with that ear. Nor do financial troubles (and there will be *troubles*) worry her in theory. Nor does a husband afflicted with financial troubles, in theory . . . But I have given my word, and if anyone is to stop any further development of this, then only she can.'

Annabella sniffed at the last of the letters, devoutly. It still had a faint smell of tobacco smoke that had once been inside him. When they were married, he didn't smoke, but he had started again after she left him. Out of the affectionate letters which at last were her lot when he had lost her, the smell of tobacco smoke had risen like a genie, brown and harsh and intimate from the corner of his pocket, bringing with it the memory of his chest, his tongue, lips and touching her with an infinitely greater sense of loss than the written words. It reminded her of what it was like sitting on his knee or feeling his chin along her parting as he read over her shoulder.

He didn't smoke when they were married, perhaps because she had said she liked the smell of cigars. Lady Melbourne's bundle from that year had memories of camphor only. Most stemmed from the first week of that year: their 'treaclemoon', as he liked to joke:

4. 'Honey or treacle? I've never liked either. Sweet as sweet. Though one is supposed to be good for you, the other your undoing . . . But hitherto I have nothing but good to report and we have already been married for five days. Marriage is probably an excellent institution, considering how many take to it (at least as a guise) for the continuation of fortunes and families. Bell is the embodiment of perfection. At this moment she is lying in the corner of a sofa, sleeping sweetly. I believe the step we took to be

the right one. Though time by degrees recasts belief into knowledge. So I shall not declare our happiness all too hastily . . .'

Apple!

Out of the tangle of contemporaneousness the memory provides, Lady Byron once again draws out her wedding night, that winter night, the green jasper urns, the man who pulled by the hands so that she would fall and then – when she fell – with his intuitive shift of muscles received her.

Why had he gossiped about her? Why had he felt he had to gossip? All movements in the world recall each other and he ought to have known that a fierce current out from the object sooner or later drifts back, like musty bathwater. Gossip takes a sweep through the world and is mechanically changed. Then it reaches the ear and eye of the object. Lady Melbourne had been told everything from the very beginning. The secret had existed between Byron and her aunt – hopes, doubts and confidences. Between Byron and his wife there was something physical, the kind familiar to everyone. And yet it remains secret by being kept secret. No one knows what two people are together – provided one of them doesn't gossip. When that happens the membrane breaks and everything runs out.

After some years, the mechanism of gossip had brought home an old memory to Lady Byron. The friend in the house, Hobhouse, had been told that Lord Byron had 'had' Lady Byron on the sofa before the wedding dinner.

When Annabella went into dinner on her wedding night, she couldn't have had any idea that this precious memory had already begun to be hollowed out by his mind's preparedness to denominate, to tell. She went in behind him. 'I love you,' she thought. Her hands felt rough, red and hot. 'I love you,' she thought.

They had made one corner of the dining-room grand for them. Napery and porcelain and hothouse flowers. Annabella caught hold of a hand. It belonged to her old nurse, who had returned to service status just for her honeymoon (treaclemoon!). She put the hand to her cheek and smiled a tearful thank-you for it. The woman put her other hand against her girl's red cheek and looked straight across the table at Lord Byron, who had introduced himself an hour or two ago by leaping out of the carriage and walking out into the woods without any greeting. The bride had been left standing alone and with some effort lightly explained. Yet it had created great dejection in the house.

He seemed collected now – not 'shy' either, as Miss Annabelle had excused him. Collected now, but she nevertheless gave him a warning glance as she bent down to touch her girl's hair. 'All well?' she mumbled. 'Your cheeks feel so terribly hot.'

Annabella let out the tiniest chirping laugh. She tried to draw breath, and finding her breast full, blurted out: 'Everything! Everything's *perfect*! Everything . . .'

In the silence that followed her words, she herself took them in, allowing them to be coloured by the latest hour in her life. They became true. The truth spread all over her body and became a deep smile.

He responded bleakly, like a half-truth for the general public. Chilled, she tried conspiring with her gaze, but it slipped into his, with no resistance, like a flabby handshake. Still eye to eye, he snatched up his table-napkin and stifled a sneeze. Uttered – 'Of course everything's perfect if you disregard the fact that *I* am getting a cold. Damn it! That's what happens when you dash round the countryside in the middle of winter.' (Sneeze.) 'Ugh, if only we hadn't banished the Romans, England today would have been part of Italy and we would have escaped this damned climate.' (Cough cough cough.) 'I want a large tankard of hot red wine (any wretched kind will do), slightly sweetened, in half an hour. Later on, you can bring hot grogs, a lot of water and a little rum (I have my duties to consider). I presume you're well supplied with soda-water round here, as I must have large quantities of Epsom salts! I also want a hot water bottle in bed, as I've noticed a considerable draught along the floor. I have a *terror* of damp bedclothes, which often cause me ailments unmentionable in the presence of ladies. I have a hot bath daily. And under no circumstances do I wish to be woken in the morning, as I have late working habits. That's all, I think. My servant is familiar with the details.'

Silence reigned while the nurse left the room. 'I don't think she has the slightest intention of waking us early tomorrow morning,' Annabella laughed quietly. 'My poor Byron. Why do you try to destroy atmospheres which have never had time to arise?' She laughed more loudly. 'I'm a strong woman, you know. I can bear my happiness, even if you think it's difficult.'

His response was again silence. Then he caressed her with his look, took her hand and looked at the clock. It was repeating itself, repeating itself.

He thought, the friendship of friends would be the perfect marriage. Friendship is a framework of civilisation. People are weights flung against each other. Within the framework, they miraculously stop to examine each other. What is love? It's not civilisation. I know that. It's damage.

'Poor thing.'

The clock repeated itself, repeated itself. Annabella hoisted one shoulder and rested her head on it. She looked at her husband. He looked happier, more lively when he could talk about the past than when he was reminded of the future.

'I was rather fat at the time,' he said then. 'I had to submit to rigorous methods to achieve a reduction.'

Annabella interlaced her fingers and rested her chin on them, her pale heart-shape losing itself in the shadows from the fire.

'The last time I heard him sing an adoramus, I was sitting up in the alcove of a window. When I tried to jump down, the hasp caught in my new gown costing three pounds and slowly tore it in half, and in the process, your husband also split his new trousers and caused a scandal in the chapel. When my friend finished singing, his voice had broken.'

Annabella hung her head, but was startled out of semi-slumber when a large cat emerged from the darkness, slid up to the window and stared in. She loathed cats, their snake-like movements, sinuous habits and yellow-eyed cynicism. Small pattering heart-beats ran out between her fingers. Byron said then: 'My God! Student life is a Monotony of Endless Variation.'

He saw her propping her elbows on the table, exhausted, unused to being up so late. She had pressed the palms of her hands against each other and was resting her cheek like an angel. She was very pale. He thought – but life separates you from your friends. I wish I didn't know that. You part and meet again in surface friendship, hostility at having been so close to each other. You want to have his memories of you back. But with memories intact, you look harshly at each other, just because you've become strangers – in all innocence. Meanwhile, the cock crowed 'but your cheeks are nevertheless round like crab-apples. I would like to bite them.'

*

That night she woke from dreaming about a hot heavy bumble-bee. The first breath dispersed the summer, the second the day, the third the daylight. Oh, all the way to tomorrow remained, she realised with a movement that had to be stopped for the sake of the other body. It was very warm in the room, bouncing light and fluffy against her mouth from breathing. She thought, I must breathe to live, and at once it grew difficult and panicky. The air was not right for her.

Fires were burning in two fireplaces, a flame dancing up out of a lump of resin, dancing and trembling and leaping, amber-coloured, to the eye the same all the time but in reality reborn, and like all life, chasing after its flight. Yellow. White and blue in its bed, the fire burned and washed over the red draperies round the bed with its wanderings. He woke from her wakefulness, then was wide awake from her panicky breathing, which soon faded when she no longer need lie without moving. He flew up and stared like a witch at the shadows of the fire: 'I'm in *hell*!'

She looked at his back and its wandering muscles. The play of shadows from the flames on coarse red rep was licking up it. From the material, a third image of fire fell enlarged over the walls and opened them, uniting all the particular fields of picture, wallpaper, door, into a single gas, red. A fourth image came back into the bed, pink tongues pushing each other ahead; also up his back. All these flames could have made good warmth, heat – . To him they instilled the horror of being burnt alive. The colour of the bed draperies, however, had been especially chosen. Her mother had gone to all that trouble; which also applied to bed linen, of silk.

Then he remembered where he was; he looked down and scooped his hands into the cold water of consciousness. And moved cautiously before lying down to rest, first with his eyes closed, then with them open, turned towards her. He was not looking at her. Where the firelight chirped in his eyes a vision grows, an arena. A perfectly round whitewashed hole lies in the eye. A stork rises off its nest. It lengthily extends itself to its full length, huge bird, flaps, wings. Down and small feathers float hesitantly – all day – outside the church tower. It looks round. It takes off and with its white wing span embraces the sky, which is so deep, so blue, so blue that the stork starts to be sucked quickly into it – powerfully. Of this master-bird, all that remains is a headlong white dot. Then it is swallowed up. But at the same moment as this happens, it careens round and once again becomes itself on one side or the other of the sky. The heat of the plateau arches below its body as it glides swimming on. It rises, it falls with the wind and its shadow races over the dark red earth, over hills of vines, fields of flax.

It follows the river, no water flowing up the bed, a muddy channel perhaps. Everything has been sucked up in a zone of healthy leaves curling up in the drought.

The stork catches a frog and perches on the Roman bridge. Cruelly thoughtful, like all predators when they have caught their prey but not yet killed it, it lets the frog wriggle in its beak, disposed to pleasure by the tickling. The bridge crosses a river resembling a delta, flat and sandy. On the right is the town on a cliff. The cliff is of sandstone. Ochre yellow, grain after grain collapses down into the bed of the river and creates its delta. Out there among the sand banks are the circular gypsy tents, steam billowing out of a wash boiler, and no one can forbid the smoke from taking the direction it has to, white and musty, in towards the cliff. Low houses of stacked rubble climb up the mountain, leaning against the mountain, supporting it. On the top, the houses are of ochre yellow sandstone. And at the very top soars a cathedral with a stork's nest on its tower.

On the left of the bridge, the ground slopes slowly up out of the river channel and away over towards the horizon, its surface brick red. A sparse regular spread of oaks covers the whole landscape. The shadow is black, rising, horned, and whipping its tail, shaking its testicles as the three mounted men from the horizon try to occupy it. Cruelly thoughtful, serious and free of triumph, they prise it round them without breaking it and draw it and its resistance behind them across the bridge.

To the arena, to the arena, then the most primitive of buildings. Abandoned in the midday heat, the most abandoned of buildings. The wall – one single one and circular – is thick and leans inwards. Everything is rounded off and whitewashed over and over again, the wall growing out of the ground, sloping inwards, in the midday sun its whiteness so strong that it yellows, grows grey. And in the well basin next to it floats a grey sparrow, dead days ago. The hours pass.

The drumfire of light on the wall softens. Suddenly spots and unevennesses are outlined, a number floating together into a blue edging along the foundations and round the gateway, which is arched and the same beseeching blue. It opens. And in stride the men, deliberately, in a long thoughtful line. Rich and poor alike slap the dust from their sleeves and take their places.

With heavy eyes, they contemplate strange music. The bull is large, but when it boldly fumbles into the circle, it resembles a dog on ice. Black as its shadow, it stands with its legs splayed and glares at its shadow, then spins round it. From three directions, three figures step towards it with their arms held high. They encounter the primaeval angles of the stork shadows flying across the sky and chasing across the floor of sawdust and sand. The four birds hinder one another and the music ceases.

A man steps out of the barrier with one arm hanging. With the other on his sword, he awaits the high point of the silence. He minces like a woman, alternately curtseying and pulling himself up temperamentally round the bull, tempting it, making it hang with him, its nose in his armpit, in his loins. In seconds of unity, the man stretches, opens himself as if he had just sensed the first grass-green wind on his limbs after months in prison. He strokes the bull the wrong way over its neck, then turns his back on it. Listless, his shoes flopping, he walks back to the barrier. The four birds free themselves from each other. The stork climbs up against the wind to reach its nest. The three figures thrust and tease and leap. From the bull's neck, blood wells unnecessarily and the bull makes sideways attacks at a horse, ripping up its belly. The horse neighs, just neighs and tramples on its entrails. Someone shouts.

In bed, the bridal couple quarrelled about what is natural and what is unnatural and she said she would submit to anything that pleased him so long as it was not an *abomination*. And he said there was no worse abomination than loving submission. And she was a pattern of chastity! And that was all the same to him!

*

From Pen-y-Bont, Eric Watson and Mrs Lisbeth went on to the real Wales, her car easing its way unobtrusively between the hedges. All the roads were lined with a blaze of yellow briar hedges. They could make out from the colour of the sky what kind of landscape they were travelling through, but the direct view was hidden by hedgerows. It was like motoring in a labyrinth, and yet it was beautiful. Guessing is peaceful.

Far further west, near Aberystwyth, the hedges came to an end. From the road, they could see a little river crawling out across the ebb of a ford bed and cows with heavy udders wading out to drink from the brackish pools.

And began to swell. They swelled, they became porous, dissolving and swelling in the misty distortions of vision. They became more and more dissolved, softer, part of everything else. And when everything had flowed together into one, the mist hovered across the road, swept up the hillside, smelling of onions, sea, dandelions and cowhide.

It was an obstacle. Instead of continuing along the coast, they turned back. The next evening, Rupert saw Eric Watson dancing with a large woman he suspected was 'the German lady'. If not, it would not have been extraordinary.

'Who's that handsome boy staring at us?' Mrs Lisbeth said.

'Who's that couple who keep looking in our direction? Do you know them? *Do* you know them? They look as if they knew you. I wish. I wish I could do that dance. Can't we learn it? It looks so easy, the way they work together in the steps. As if by instinct – rather than having to learn it. I wish I could dance from inspiration, from eroticism. It looks as if they could. It always looks as if good dancers dance from eroticism. Though everyone says that inspiration is an award for proven industry. Look at that! Look how they move like cocoa and cream.'

The girl was stroking Rupert with her nails between his fingers as she talked, a putative sensual touch, the effect on him a whinny he was only just able to restrain. It would not have been extraordinary if time and place had not been dusk and very popular tea rooms in Cambridge. The further away from home the cat strays, the more assiduous the philandering, Rupert's grandmother used to say to give verbal weight to the most shifting relationships. It was full house, as it was most evenings except Sunday. Between the tables were baskets, innumerable bags containing books, parcels, rolls of paper, leeks, bottles of whisky and gloves. The waitresses in black and white requested in invariably friendly tones that these objects should be moved so that they could get past with their trays.

At the entrance, the cashier sat in her booth, yellow curls on her forehead and a brooch in her dress, her fingers clinking on the keys, remarkably small and slender to be able to get the machine to the degree of shuddering sighing clatter at which a pink receipt could emerge. Another couple came in; with rain and mist on their glasses, they tried to follow the direction of her gesture towards vacant seats.

They put their coats over the backs of the chairs. Damp coats and woollen scarves. Mixing their smell with clicking castanets, colonial drinks and the fragrance of buns and cakes straight from the oven.

Anyone looking in sees sharp sounds of a hundred young people who never lack for subjects of conversation. They talk all the time, prodigiously; anyone temporarily unable to make himself heard stands and waits with his mouth open and the words on his tongue. Not only the volume of sound but also the pitch climbs in the competition until it reaches the same pale yellow colour as the glitter in the Waterford glass chandeliers.

Anyone on the other hand looking out sees the sooty fog swaying through the street, sees himself and the whole room reflected in the window pane. The window reflects the tea rooms all the way into the real mirrors fixed to the walls and there – in the middle of an optical exchange of wall mirror and window mirror – he sees the oval of his own face.

In the mirror corner, the ensemble played, their fronts the audience-front, smiling at the dancers or devoting themselves to the music. The leader had turned-up hanging moustaches (ready to hang the Christmas tree balls on, thought Rupert). But the mirrors also made a circular panorama of these gentlemen. From behind, three of them showed bare scalp instead of swirls of hair, the bass-player's jacket tight across his back, the pianist made up. The mirror profiles showed how unconscious of themselves people are and have to be. Their mouths open, they turned their noses up towards the clouds. One on the right. One on the left. Both know only their own apparent merging, what you yourself control when you switch on the light above the mirror. Rupert rescued his hand from the girl's irritating attentions and clenched both fists under his cheekbones, leaning his elbows on the table.

'Handsome . . . ?' replied Eric Watson in surprise. 'That great lump?'

That was his view of Rupert, an athletic young man with a large square head and already deep bays in his reddish hair. His face was haughty and expressionless, his eyes glittering from critical slits, or staring at you flatly as if you were a peculiarity he regretted. His whole being expressed control and enjoyment of controlling. Eric Watson knew practically nothing about him – and he told Mrs Lisbeth so – but Rupert reminded him of unbreakable glass, the kind with a surface tension making it impervious from the outside, though it could explode from an internal blemish.

'Handsome,' she maintained. She was smoking slowly, studying the youth slowly, in the shelter of her cigarette. 'He has,' she brooded, 'a third eye.' She touched herself on the Cyclops place on her forehead. 'His face has very attractive lines of strength, or passion.'

'If it attracts you sufficiently, perhaps you can persuade him to forget he has seen us,' said Eric Watson, not jealous, but slightly ill-at-ease. Rupert saw them. He saw them stretch out a bare, very white and plump arm and a jacket sleeve. They stretched them out parallel in front of them and angled the other round each other. With a peculiar curling movement, they dropped this bowsprit and started walking round each other in gentle backing attacks. A couple of turns. Some shuffling steps forward; at the next syncope the couple stood like two sheets of cardboard, two-dimensional, untouchably close together. Then they began to propel themselves over each other's surface, vis-à-vis. Without taking their eyes off each other, they slid away sideways, but turned their heads after a few steps as far as you can turn a head and hang it. Hung them but held them strictly parallel. Rupert saw them. Solemnity. Not the melancholy of the music, nor the happy parody of passion of the students when they danced. But solemnity.

Well, this led him to turn to look at the girl, his girl friend. She was busy at that moment poking at the inner shell, the membrane, the skin off a chestnut, rubbing on a pat of butter and starting to munch. He watched her scraping and poking to get the skin off and the way her face expressed a certain irritable unease at not succeeding and not getting her titbit. He looked at her. Pity she would never again be a stranger. She was just alien, in the sense that she was guarding spiritual barriers no one would pass – anyhow, not him. Perhaps because he wasn't sufficiently interested in what might be gained behind them. Everything they permitted each other was predictable. There was nothing left of the estrangement you conquer swiftly, almost indiscriminately.

173

He switched his attention to Eric Watson and the German lady – they were probably doing it from eroticism. For now the couple were revealing flaws if you looked closely enough and disregarded their solemnity. The lady had large buttocks; so undisciplined by intended garments, they climbed cloven in the dress's floral folds as she swayed away from the immediate vicinity of her partner's loins (thought Rupert). Eric Watson tossed his head and wagged his elbows, making every turn just too sweeping. As if he were commenting on his solemnity in ironic asides to the audience.

(faun unveiling a
woman)

The bridegroom had now stopped laughing at his bride. 'It doesn't matter,' he repeated calmly. He lay down in the same position as before and looked at Annabella. He looked at her and closed his eyes. He opened his eyes. They smiled. Flecks of gold and black floated in their blue – lakes breaking the light and washing over land. She leant forward when she saw an arrow between his eyelids. A hair? A boat rowing across the lake? The water's counter-movement makes it appear to cover the whole distance with one single delicate shudder – shooting over the surface, always slightly ahead of itself and eager to stay in the lead, its shadow creeping along the bed of the lake. The water laughs against the prow and the eleven children in the boat cry out.

The craft lands on a grassy shore. Two of the eldest children immediately leap ashore as if the bump had propelled them. They pull on the ropes to salvage their small brothers and sisters dry-shod, but they refuse to be protected and scramble over the side and plop into the water. The sandy bottom is marshy, the children of all sizes shrieking, splashing, toiling and squabbling in mud. The older ones rescue the smallest, now bawling through wide-open funnels another disappointment over the world always responding to their actions but not their desires. The medium-sized children remain seated, fascinated, letting themselves be enclosed by something that gives way, cold-warm and buttery, spurting in spirals between squeezing fingers, tenderly absorbing them in lovely excrement.

The eldest girl hoists her skirt up round her waist and strides out into the water to bring back the most obstinate of the boys.

The eye with sun-spots goes closer and sees her, from behind, the

175

way she approaches the boy, shifting her balance between one long leg and another. Her hat has fallen down her back. Ribbons glide out of ringlets of chestnut hair and float on the water, before it washes over them on the edge of the shore. Charlotte's white legs lower into the dark lake, light reflections striking between them, striking under her arm and round the boy's face, now with a grimace warding off her attentions. Clouds of drops blow up from the surface, the clipped water hissing through the air and enveloping the chastisement; she tugs his hair hard, she pulls his ears and hauls at his arms and collar; he thrashes about and grabs and spits, all without being able to hit back with a single blow; finally she has a grip on the back of his neck that makes little brother amenable, and tractable, blind as a baby animal, as he hangs in her hands (teeth). Charlotte turns back to the shore. 'Lottie, Lottie,' cry her brothers and sisters. Her face turns broad from the sunlight. Behind her collar bone a chasm sighs as she lifts and drags.

A yolk of lustre just above each knee, for every step. 'Lottie, Lottie, let me go, I'll be good,' the boy demonstrates with persuasive gestures and rushes – released – straight back into the mud. When she has captured him for the second time, she clamps him firmly between her legs and pulls down his trousers. Thoughtfully, she regards two bare buttocks, stiff and streaked with resistance. They are personal, they are pitiful, like all parts of the body in themselves when naked and trembling beneath the severity of a look. Where was the head belonging to them, really? 'Lottie, Lottie,' cries the children's mother. Her voice comes from the grass and carries calmly down slope and shore meadow to the girl, who then gives each buttock a hard smack and sees the redness of her hand appear on the skin, the fingers apart. 'One should keep one's fingers together when one smacks,' she thinks. 'The smacks are better then.'

The children's mother is cutting up bread for them, her lover spreading the butter. He stops with butter on the knife. The sun melts from the sky, sluggish drops fall on his shoe and dry white. Charlotte is sitting down by the shore. She is eleven, a miniature of a grown woman, no, no longer miniature, only a few degrees before the definitive contour. He drops the knife on the edge of the table, and as it falls to the grass, he goes down the slope towards the meadow, very lightly as the thought has already gone the whole way and is only drawing his body with it.

She sits still, drawing lines in the layers of mud on her calves. The slant in her eyes glitters up towards him. A leech has fastened itself on the inside of her foot, behind the ankle where she already has several mosquito bites. He starts back when she shows it to him; he loathes those living things. It extends itself, it makes itself compact from satisfied dog-hunger, thirst. The shiny black snake wriggles in his hand. He shudders, she shudders as he knocks away her hands in order to jerk at the leech himself. One of her eyes has dark spots, the iris marked like a clock. The clock hand goes round once or twice. She is breathing a little with her mouth, a great deal with her body, which is emitting waves of childish warmth and a peculiar acrid smell. When he looks for its source, he finds a pearl of lapis lazuli in her ear.

A stream of blood comes out of the disconnected mouth of the leech and another out of the mosquito bite it had opened. Not suddenly, but at once it is hanging there, curling like a silken thread between mouth and mouth. It bursts and becomes a rivulet in her wrinkled skin. It is thin, it is touching, it is red. A taboo glides in under the sun, thin and almost invisible like those feathery clouds. The sounds of the light-shadow fade and the depths come to the surface. He, she looks up. The slant in her eyes is defiant; as the sun penetrates through sparse feathers, something happens: its yellow sparkles come racing through to perch in the foliage, one at a time; their bodies a tautening, their faces a smile. They never come down to the ground but melt from one mass of leaves to the next. He, she looks up. The earth itself grey and mute. He sits with the girl's foot in his hand, taken by surprise, slightly repelled, sitting with the girl half in his arms, the feathery clouds hastening into each other to stop the summer's most exaggerated rays attempting to lure his zest for life into encroaching on life. But he already knows that if what is spontaneous is to be more than an easily chastised caprice, then it has to be upheld 'consciously'. Whims emerging from the secrets in his being, habit and custom soon trying to overcome them, only to be upheld consciously and laboriously. Never in the dreamt-of spontaneity that first evokes them. Breaking the laws, the Law, following the spiral on his fingertip *in*, is no game. One offends against customs in their own shallow light.

A siskin alights on the top of the nearest bush, its presence swaying graciously in stillness. It looks back with its beak propped against its neck. The hand of the clock in Lottie's eye makes yet another

177

revolution. He goes on holding her firmly, just that, she is content with that. The gold speck in her lapis is about to fall slowly asleep, slumbering. She speaks French, a language she knows he has not mastered, and calls the Duke of Wellington 'le coq du village'.

The children's mother walks in the grass, strong and stately above a swaying skirt. The brim of her hat prances about as it catches the wind and out of the skirt fall innumerable round-headed children, like baby goats following in her lee. The eldest finds a pair of scissors in the pocket of her dress and stretches up to cut a lock off Mama's lover. He is holding firmly on to her, though on his knee, letting go so that she can start getting up and forcing her down the moment she tries to. She laughs loudly every time she has her will broken and pulls out the scissors again to snip like a swallow round his head. 'There, there,' he whispers. 'You know you mustn't get excited.' She snips on until he takes the scissors away from her and sighs and threads them on two fingers and cuts. He cuts a long strand of hair at the back, right at the nape of her neck when the hair parts as she bends her head forward to be kissed. There.

The children's mother lies naked in her room at night. She exercises her long parson's-daughter feet as she reads by the light and stretches with pleasure whenever she comes to a passage that causes her to agree with Rousseau or Tom Paine or if she is reading Crawford. The open window wafts out – mint. Outside, the crickets saw away, the rhythm in itself uniting all rhythms – ardently, it hurts and thrusts and boils: tight, indefatigable as a Turkish fiddler on his fourth rosin hour. Above it, the silence rests, and above that sounds move far far away, sheep, the jay, the larvae in the bark. The lady's spouse has gone to his bedroom. Her children are asleep in four chambers. Her lover is seated at a table finishing his letter. With a slow hand, with an effort, with reluctance – the other hand scratching from his knee up over his thigh. He turns his head and says a number of gloomy words about exchanging feelings being the same as 'shaking hands, being at your service. When I was unmoved by her and acting interested, she perceived me as most sympathetic of all. If she said she was happy, I could only answer her with a general perception, for one never really knows what happiness is, or unhappiness, if one doesn't at least live in the resonance of it oneself. If I were happy, I myself, her face contorted with distaste and she thought me egotistical. If our happinesses infected each other and we were simultaneously united, we – obscured each other, you know.'

Lady Oxford looks up from her book, peering shortsightedly. Disturbed at her reading, she replies, 'Yes, yes, yes,' and tries to remember whether he is talking about any particular woman or perhaps even his mother? Or whether he is just going on building on some youthful idea of universal incompatibility. Anyhow, it doesn't really concern her. Why is so much of the insufficient strength in the world devoted to establishing the hopeless when so much can be helped? she thinks. 'Why so much *dies irae* when the Day of Wrath . . .' She goes on reading, but stops again at the memory of the evening's musical event in the pavilion, where she finds a subject to tease: 'Just think, dearest B, despite the drama in her part, the soprano went on sounding like a hopeful early vegetable, because nature had endowed her with that particular voice. And we talked about the tenor making a sound like a barrel hoop outside an inn when he was grieving for his shepherdess. Only our baritone sounded human and had an expressive voice. Nature has her doings and sounds, which we can't change with liberty, equality and fraternity. On the other hand, liberty, equality and fraternity are the only things we can achieve . . .' His upper lip now twitches scornfully: 'But could we really achieve *that*?'

His upper lip now twitches. What a woman, to be radical with examples from distractions in her own palace pavilion. Cautiously, his head starts swimming. He leans it against his hand and looks at her stomach, where until a week ago he thought he had sown the twelfth child. She is approaching the end of her fertility at a time that reminds her of the start, with its irregularity and anxiety over illness, children and the anxiety within her. But she reads her book. It annoys him that she prunes everything trying to grow wild. Her book reduces all anxiety. She tells him to be sensible and not let his strength run out into humbug. 'My dearest B! If I had your opportunities. Or only the sturdy opportunities every man has at his disposal . . . but I have the impression that all young men with insight and influence abrogate responsibility for the history of our time and allow reality to shape itself, while they shape an "inner" reality . . . well.'

Well, he is perhaps fifteen years younger than she is, and perhaps he is seeking out his own seriousness. She tries to smooth things over. He describes the nature of matter and loses himself in it. She strikes the bedpost with her book. The blow reduces confusion to clarity. He is searching for grasses in a crevice of opinion, doesn't she see, not through a conscious will, but because his thoughts draw him there. She respects those who categorise species of grass in the west of England, but not him. The idea is namely to submit the will, and the will sets limits to what is possible and meaningful for man, or rather, for mankind! His head, heavy on his hand, swims: he shares her standpoint! Why devote so much time to the hopeless when so much can be helped? But he is not driven by his will, which agrees more with her 'good sense'; he is driven by a roaming light of which he is also only a part. So it does actually help each time she reduces his singular nameless curiosity to 'your youth, dearest B' and laughs at his anxiety which is nevertheless so much less significant than anxieties! Political! Well, it's obvious, isn't it, and while he looks at her, her nakedness seems wholly closed and buttoned and dressed.

She follows the lines in her book with half-open shiny black eyes and runs her fingers through her hair, which is still largely soft, though here and there are stiff grey straws. Sometimes she reads aloud. He looks at her stomach; it is naked but dressed. He looks at her face: nothing is so chaste as certainty in belief. It reproduces itself, has eleven children. Doubts couple incessantly, run on in bastards, miscarriages and shame. He scratches his leg as he writes: 'And believe me, Caro, in this case I am in agreement with your mother. It is necessary that this deplorable affair remains over. Nothing you say or do can change that. So take your Mama's advice and go with her to Ireland and let us never see each other again except in the atmosphere of knowing better, which the years and distance at last give us. I am grateful to you for returning my letters (I intend to do the same to yours as soon as I get to London) and enclose the lock of hair you request. I would have had them make a ring of it if there had been more time.' He scratches on as he writes 'I remain, Lady Caroline, Your Humble etc. etc. etc. Byron', his finger beginning to run round the contours of some scissors. Insects create a network of tracks round the lamp, a ball of thread round deadly light flinging their shadows sprawling and playing on the wall. With her expression of having seen everything, Lady O does not see them; with the same expression, she observes him cutting a lock from her pudenda, where the hair parts when she wants to be kissed, then tying the lock with a piece of red silk and enclosing it in the letter he has just finished writing. They laugh maliciously together. Oh, well. Innocence has its seductive silk. Experience its hardiness.

Annabella flew out of her slumbers and opened her eyes. He opened his. They lay there, each in a different position. Eye to eye, as if to watch over and guard even in sleep. Like children, when the dream of a huge flood over the fire in the centre of the body arouses them to sensual pleasure, soon only to freeze in fear of having wet the bed, to finish dryly, the almost disappointing experience of now being able to do everything internally and to yourself, with no visible result. Sometime during the small hours, they had superficially fallen asleep again, so lightly that they at once wake each other with their wakefulness. Neither wants to be caught sleeping here!

An early sound had penetrated the silence and lay there inside it. She didn't know if she had been woken by it or by a relic from childhood: the expectation just before its clang, and then – the bell. A long since forgotten rhythm of the day seized her. She lay there in what had been Mama's bed, in her room, in her childhood home (God knows whether she was born in that bed) and woke with a sense of childishness over the torrent in the core of her body: a childhood memory connected with a sound – and now it came again and the words that had triggered it off – 'morning milk'. Morning milk, the hand grasped the cord again, two small bells swung in the great darkness of the house. The taste of boiled milk on her palate forced her up, making her swallow and swallow to be rid of it. She found herself sitting with her hands round her knees, one cheek against her shoulder. Wide-awake eyes. Then the walls of the house opened and she looked through the rooms, down into the kitchen, where an unwashed tangled head of hair came round the door, then a hand to take delivery of morning milk. She slowly grew cold, seeing several figures shuffling into the kitchen with shawls over their nightclothes, to rake out the stove and relight it, to pump water to heat. 'The advantage of a lot of servants,' she thought wearily as they crisscrossed past without bumping into each other, 'is that they have each other.' She pondered on this as she saw them starting the day without washing, mouths black from the night, not speaking. 'That makes things easier for them. What about Fanny Elphin, who has only a housekeeper, apart from the old woman cleaner and the ladies who come in to sew? Mrs Elphin's housekeeper has too much work to do on her own. Heavens, you would never have time to do anything properly if you always had to think about keeping warm.'

Her cheek against her own shoulder was the tenderest feeling that night. A mirror, a moon. The moon showed itself in the gap between the curtains, North Sea moon. Salt water clouds in dull colours adhered round it, now leaden green, then white in a reddish mist. Then it lay still, to steal, collect the light of the coming day. In the half-light, she recognised her own reflection from the side, her dark hair ruffled, her face obscure and blurred. But. She smiled gravely at herself. She caressed her cheek with her shoulder, her shoulder with her cheek, and everything was brought back into everything else and everything was lost.

It was good for the servants to be many. They served each other and had time for other things. She didn't like Byron's servant, Fletcher. He was more conspiratorial than to hand. She would arrange life. She would have it in protected forms. Marriage was not primarily a combination of souls and bodies – at first, yes – but in the long term a combination of habits and household, which, in the long run, says much more about people than their words and expressions of tenderness.

In the weight of this, love finds peace. In the cultivated state of love, that was impossible. She tried to extend her real self to touch her husband without using her hands. He sweated at his hairline. She wasn't a hundredth so worried about his hair growth as *he* liked to suppose. It was really quite terrible: nearly everyone takes great pains over the first impression they make. They smooth and polish the façade and then there's no money left over for joists or sound flooring. From which one can draw the conclusion that most people wish to please most people (thought Annabella), and then they grieve because that makes them lonely. Nature had created hair to protect the body, its bare skin judged to be weak and nameless. But Byron was no great man, no great thinker, and no great poet, either. Not really discerning. He was an attractive poet, but not great. He was no great man, but attractive, and she had never intended to be so *shortsighted*. She was not attracted by his reputation or his face or his often banal (emotionally banal) verse which frowned on the craziness of the world while kissing that world all over its body. She would like, would be able to work for that kissing, sipping talent – and its somewhat more than superficial beauty – perhaps to fall inwards and allow itself to drown in a gravity that transformed it into something 'rich and singular'. Like the love her parents had, whose kisses fell inwards, long before her own arrival, and were elevated to a musical score that didn't need kisses to live on.

She also could write verse. *He* destroyed himself in his own verse and kissed himself all over his body. He was so dazzled by himself, he repeated himself and failed in the rhythm. Her sonnets were considerably purer than his forms. She never thought of disguising an iamb as a dactyl just to save herself the trouble of fundamentally thinking out a verse again. She would rather write a little less, but correctly. She always fulfilled her intentions once she had begun something, and was already endeavouring to avoid regretting her youth in the future. Why did everyone take it for granted that at forty you *tolerate* your youth? Youth. You are born a character, and might just as well work on it as misuse it, even if you happen to be young. As far as her – husband was concerned, he would never carry out anything completely. His whims and self-absorption would never allow any weightier ideas to circulate in his words and mature. Everything remained thorny preliminary studies, occasionally beautiful, but what is beauty on the third inspection? She had warned him about this the very first time they had met. But his capacity to accept criticism was not magnificent. Criticism irritated him. But she loved him. And she did. Yes.

She slowly grew cold. Her eyes became accustomed to the half-darkness, her reflection still distorted by the ruffled hair, which she plaited away to bring out the cameo face. Then she looked out of it, into it, out of it, into it with that listless regular exchange that can be the dream-cradle of the soul. But then his shadow rose. His face. When he pressed it to her hair, his face constantly appeared in the mirror. He was reversed, she the right way round. He allowed himself to be caught out by this phenomenon experienced almost every day. Essentially, it was like seeing him for the first time, truly. The faulty eye was smaller than the other one, his smile colder as it examined her the other way round, with access to a key to her face she had never possessed. You are reversed, I am the right way round, the smile said, craftily. She withdrew. And caught another glimpse of the double-face, hers the right way round, his reversed.

Whatever was an amusement to him was dust to her. No real problem, no genuine symbol but a dust she had to perceive wholly in order to free herself from it. He looked directly at her with his reversed eyes and a key to her face she herself did not possess. She looked at them both, mediating through glass.

She looked at him in the mirror, tenderly. It was the early morning after a sleepless night, both their faces rested. She wished she could put her head down on his chest and listen to his heart beating. Then he looked at her abruptly. 'Apple!' he said and bit her cheek hard. At first his hand was friendly, then began to manipulate again. A prickling pleasurable pain. It rose like a V and before she had warded it all off, the pain sank away, leaving the desire behind, childish, high and brushed with gold. She would have been capable of rearing up backwards over his shoulder and gliding over it like a slippery fish, in one single movement, then falling into the pool.

But her mirror-face was looking at her. And saw his profile looking officious. So she avoided him again and answered all his questions and assurances with silence. 'This is ridiculous,' he said, starting again. Yes, it was ridiculous. They were wrestling in bed. Laughing at first, then angry. He pushed her away with a coarse remark. Then he said: 'One day you're sure to save my life as well.' She shivered with cold. It was loathsome to be looked at, minute after minute, by those alien snake-like eyes. With a cry, she wound her arms round her head and heard him asking whether her mother used to hit her on the fingers. What a question!

'No one has ever tried using violence on me until now,' she replied calmly, her head half hidden in her arms, still hidden. An image of white bandage fluttered through her memory and tied itself neatly round her hands before bedtime. She could help pack the left hand herself. But that was all. Was it chicken-pox? Measles? Nettle-rash?

It grew quiet. She took away her arms. He was lying on his side. Head bent, nape of neck exposed. He was mortal, he was human.

'Though I'm rather offended by you, dearest Byron,' she said sadly to her cameo face. 'I would have liked to be acquainted with Augusta and her little ones before the wedding. I don't understand why you keep me away from your family. Am I so terrifying? We have so few close relations between us, we ought to take pains with those we have.'

The invisible man in the bed replied: 'Time enough for you to *experience* her.' Annabella saw her face thinking:

Also, all the themes in his verse were broken up, broken to pieces. He had used defiance and melancholy as a means of avoiding logic. Not only was the framework broken, but the content also ran out of the words. His writing represented little more than a feeling for the moment. Here and there a reflection was born – that is, a reflection of something else – but died of its own accord after a line or two. A few atmospheric lines on what longing is. Never a whole poem on a completed idea, definitive, freed from the darkness of everyday language, with the power of symbols and the magical excess of rhythm. Never. But she had to admit he listened to her views without interrupting her or getting agitated. Except one evening when she found on his table a verse from 'Hebrew Melodies':

> My soul is dark – Oh! quickly string
>   The harp I yet can brook to hear;
> And let thy gentle fingers fling
>   Its melting murmurs o'er mine ear.
> If in this heart a hope be dear,
>   That sound shall charm it forth again:
> If in these eyes there lurk a tear,
>   T'will flow, and cease to burn my brain.

And so on with that regal desperation. So sentimental, she had said. Beautifully thought, but fairly banal. Is this the other side of you gentlemen (she had been unable to resist teasing), who are said to be so fearfully cynical in St James's. Well, why not – banalities and cynicisms are probably extremes that balance one another.

He was usually so reasonable when she appraised his individual lines of verse, but then he suddenly started hotly and angrily defending this one. The words were only to accompany Mr Isaac Nathan's music and they were about Saul the Hebrew. How could she just dismiss things as banalities on the grounds that she daily washed behind her ears. Her banality might be someone else's dirty reality and 'who knows whether a circumcised culture does not perceive your *circumscribed* culture as absolute, comical, cosmic *melodrama.*'

At heart, he naturally knew that this was a poor argument. How would she be able to start out from someone else's basis of judgement when she proffered her opinion. At heart, he naturally knew his verse was bad and banal, because he made excessive efforts to include her impression of it in innumerable examples of what she, 'a girl from the country', couldn't 'understand' before she travelled in 'the world'. Languages, for instance. Had she any idea that the equivalent words in two languages were never equivalent to each other. Not to mention how six words in modern Greek gradate one single equivalent in English and that as soon as you take Italian on your tongue, you became another *person*, a changed creature – no less.

And yet . . . what she also ought to learn to 'understand' was that in all cultures there is a secret agreement between what is religious and what everyday, and that this agreement leads to the 'good-humoured compromise in which people of all faiths and colours can put their hands into each other's pockets'.

She had looked on while he talked this way and that about Moorish and Jewish and Spanish and Turkish. She let him talk and listened to what he said. Finally he fell silent. Then she replied: 'But my dearest Byron. Fundamentally, one can experience everything here at home in England.'

Kean Byron
Bonaparte

Meanwhile Link the dentist was following his own chronology. Several evenings a week, he sat absorbed in an old censored diary with the aim of extracting some material for his theme: 'Kean, Byron, Napoleon – The Romantic Connection'.

It is fun reading diaries. What is typical of the day is obvious in them. Historical discourses describe what is typical of the day as something deceptive or superficial – if it's described at all. Fashions, ways of speech, manners are fleeting facts that can produce various responses at several checks. But in a diary they are solid; historical genuineness rests on them. They surge, they bolster up, and readers of today are offered the third dimension of lesser culture beyond bald facts.

It's boring reading diaries. So many inessentials, so many winks at yourself, all those unanswered laments. You search for sympathy in yourself by being both sender and recipient. It's impossible.

Reading censored diaries both stimulates and inhibits the imagination. It's mixed. One evening, Link remembered Henry James, who was given the chance to read uncensored letters and other Byroniana and said that it had given him stomach-ache. His puritanical soul had been unable to get out of the box of letters quickly enough, but shrieked as it pinched him.

Link was also a puritan. We all are, more or less. But he was curious, all right, and wanted to know what the unspeakably shocking consisted of. In the literature on Byron, here and there were mysterious lines about the poet and his friends having a 'system' of debauchery. Byron's own letters, those of his friends, his poems, all revealed nothing worse than erotic quantity (cheerful) as compensation for idealistic love

187

(sad). Link considered the other attraction of Byronism was the search for the dark point where reputation and individual falls. That point was nowhere to be found, was found again and again, but still didn't exist.

Like so many loving lovable people, Byron acquired a demonic reputation. Far too much yearning, desire, love directed at the same point, is demonology, is what creates the light and shimmer of demonology. Is lovableness in itself demonic, as it tempts out so much that cannot be reciprocated?

Link was grateful to the censor of the diaries, for a pair of trousers let down makes it such an effort to look people in the eye. The writer of the diary actually never let down any trousers: John Cam Hobhouse was no demon. He was over forty before he dared propose to a lady. He was political, a Radical Whig in his youth, rather less radical after a period in the House of Commons, and Tory after that. At a mature age, he was ennobled to Lord Broughton. Byron would have laughed had he been alive. That was how their friendship was established: Byron laughed; Hobhouse worried, and after Byron's death did everything to keep his reputation clean for posterity. He was political and rational and saw his friend with the rather miserly eyes of friendship – affectionate, protective, offended and sceptical.

On alternate evenings, Link reads the diaries and on the other evening does something else. He 'writes' Hobhouse's diaries by letting Hobhouse's facts and his own interpretations merge on a fifty-fifty basis. His chronology is nevertheless somewhat in arrears. While Mr Cohn and Eric Watson have already covered the time before the Napoleonic Wars, Link was only just starting.

*

July 6th, 1811 – Visit my father in Richmond Park. After a walk round the roses, we start harping on my future. He won't hear of an academic career, and nothing political until I've acquired 'military insight'. I reply that I have no *thought* of gaining such qualifications in alliance with the worst despots in Europe, against Napoleon, who despite everything produces modern themes. My response turns him grey with annoyance. Dejected, we agree that I shall try to win my spurs in his old Irish regiment. I do not look forward to a year by the misty Liffey, surrounded by Celts occasionally behaving as if they had nothing to sacrifice but their lives.

The dispute has raised our voices. My sisters come in with strawberries and their needlework, then lie like cool weightless meringue over and around, smoothing things out. My father reads aloud from my brother Benjamin's latest letter, in which he accounts for his regiment's movements in the battle of Albuera. 'I wish he would write about the countryside and people for once,' my younger middle sister says. 'The whole world seems to become his battlefield. I really do love Benjamin, but his whole world has become a battlefield and supply lines. He writes like Caesar, and for my part I must say it does not reduce my anxiety.'

My youngest sister replies: 'But you know perfectly well, dearest, that it is part of man's nature not to allow himself to be distracted when everything is at stake! We women, on the other hand, are constantly dilettantish.' Then all four of them laugh. In the company of women, you are often a joke you don't understand.

They went into battle 527 rank and file, 1 lieut.-colonel, 1 major, 7 captains, 18 subalterns. They fought four hours, and then drew up behind a hill to count numbers. They were 118 rank and file and six subalterns. Benjamin and another officer were the only ones without a hole in their clothes. (My father exchanges a look with me, for the sake of my sisters. Something grows under their hands as they listen to the subject of losses, simple monograms and in one case double.)

The brigade went out of the field commanded by a junior captain and the regiment commanded by a junior lieutenant. Benjamin first commanded the light company, and then held the colours, through which were eighteen shot-holes.

July 8th – Mr Kean in *Richard*. He was extremely happy; and is a very short man with piercing black eyes which he often turns on the Prince of Wales' box, where he had found a helpless admirer. 'Off with his head; so much for Buckingham,' was given thus: The instant he received the news of Buckingham being prisoner he said quickly, 'Off with his head!' and then, advancing to the front of the stage added with a savage smile, 'so much for Buckingham.' With the same walking gait, he limps up to the footlights, his smile growing with the insight of what he has done and reaching a climax at the footlights, where the light turns up and sullies his face into Satan: 'so much for Buckingham'.

The Prince of Wales has by chance just purchased Buckingham House on the Mall. Kean pauses for the suppressed amusement in the auditorium. It could have been fatal, but instead this political interruption made his part more intact. It is said that no one has ever acted like Kean. He declaims, not standing, but running, lying, *living*. He has shed all the rules of acting. He weeps real tears and wipes his nose on the curtains, roaring with fury. He gave the part an exhilarating savagery I think it needs. His scene with Lady Anne was highly finished. His expostulation with Stanley in the north, 'What do they so in the north?' with a loud, shrill taunting interrogatory, had an extraordinary effect; and lastly, his combat with Richmond was surprising. He continued pushing with his hand after he received his wound, and dropped his sword as if he had not lost his weapon and showed by his vacant stare that he was struggling with the effect of the fatal blow. Only with its suddenness was death able to seize him, then he fell flat backwards at once.

It is said that Kean and the Prince have fallen out because His Highness has seduced and betrayed one of Kean's best players, a red-haired donna, Elvira, who has found herself locked in an apartment in Knightsbridge ever since.

Kean is a simple man. Kinnaird told me that he sent his wife to Pascoe Grenfell, his patron, to ask him if he thought it would be any presumption or impropriety in his now keeping a horse. Grenfell said no, and his partner Williams sent him one that cost eighty guineas. Kean, so Lord John Russell told me, was going to drown himself when he had been in London a short time and had been refused by manager Harris, who told him he was too short for any character. He thought, however, of his wife and child, and that stopped him. But he was prepared to return to the market places, where he had previously practised his art (performed his tricks!).

We shared his supper after the performance, laid out in the theatre green room. His taste in food is also simple: cold mutton, oysters, thin wine, sweet cakes, coffee, toddy. He drank a glass after every sentence. Said you sweat a lot during a performance. We were allowed to be his audience while he undressed Richard – stepped out of crown, deformity and leather with a tender care that was poignant.

A draught has a route through that green room. Swift candle flames follow it directly: it provides the heavy draperies with a rhythm of their own, listlessly, hesitantly – fiery-nosed, meeting in small black holes. Meanwhile Kean tells us anecdotes about himself. One was that in a single evening in Stroud, Gloucestershire, he had played Shylock, danced on a tightrope, sung a popular song called 'Tempest', sparred with Mendoza and finally led a game of blackjack at a party. An excellent foundation for an actor, he considered. Anyone beginning and ending with character parts never learns to bring to the art anything but soulfulness. It becomes a vicious circle between writer and actor if no breach of style comes in between, he said: one learns to understand an audience, its sensuality, its intelligence, its generosity, by demonstrating the width and breadth, the highs and lows of one's talents. A pure character doesn't exist, he said, even less so pure art which is also good art. The art is wonderfully impressionable and influenced by accidental circumstances! One evening in Leicester, for instance, he had forgotten his lines and had recited Milton's 'L'Allegro' three times instead, one after another, while his body went on acting Othello. The audience hadn't noticed anything, but the uncertainty had made him bold in his acting, and as he spoke his final words, they stood up and shouted their approval.

Dreaming, his mouth wet with wine, Kean said: He experiences. He learns. Perceives a part so much more when he has a very beautiful woman to play against. We assured him we had all experienced something similar . . . Kinnaird explained that for his part he could talk endlessly to lovely women who didn't know how to spell, while he sat mute with plain ones, who in themselves could have enriched any conversation with their brilliance.

I remember that more draughts and yet more continued their folding games with candles and curtains. One of them was so persistent, it started nosing smokily against the plush. Kean put the candle out with saliva, but it left a hole in the cloth surrounded by sparks, and went out as when tears dry on your eyelashes. The whole theatre risked catching fire!

At two in the morning, we separated, very pleased with each other.

July 15th – Letter from Byron in Malta! Also on his way home at last. And he was going stay in Greece until the day of his death! Letter sent in May says 'health bad, temper worse, for my body is infested with what Mistress Quickly in *Henry V* maliciously calls "burning quotidian tertian". It finished off Falstaff and possibly me. I came across it last summer in the Morea and almost died, and then it came like a kind of reprisal as soon as we dropped anchor in this hellish oven.

The attacks come regularly every other day, sprouting out of ague and working themselves up into Vesuvian marrow-melting fevers, then abating into a soaking entailing man and horse having to free me from my sheets.'

The letter says he is going home temporarily to solve some obscurities with his banker: the man refuses to sell assets Byron wants to sell, while toiling away like one possessed to dispose of Byron's dearest possessions.

My friend happens to be on his way home on the same ship as yet another piece of the Parthenon frieze, and would certainly have holed her between Scylla and Charybdis if it had only been a question of annoying Lord Elgin. On the other hand, he also has many marble pieces with him for me which ought not to be destroyed. And his own harvest is 'two manuscripts. Partly the long verse in Spenserian metre that you know about, which is intended for my *private* archives, and partly an imitation of Horatius' "De Arte Poetica" which I consider to be publishable. As far as my *fantastic adventures* are concerned, I am saving those for a personal meeting with you, Matthews and an unspecified number of bottles of champagne. Meet me in London in July.'

July 17th – We met at Sittingbourne. Yesterday and today I have seen my dear friend again after a year's separation. We have spent these two days in and around Canterbury. Wherever we rode or walked round in circles outside the town, apexes of gentle golden brown cathedral shadow have reached us and urged us to go back to the stone bench where the talk is serious. I said it was high time for me to change my life. He says it is high time he changed his. I said he seemed changed. He replies that I should have seen him with a *moustache*. He looks ironic, which is often the case with people who have just regained their health after much fever and many feverish dreams. A wholly unconscious irony; as if the cool and country air against his eyes were only too audible.

His face is brown, his lips also burnt, which you can see as he licks them with the pale pink tip of his tongue. He is thin and parched and ironic in that absent-minded way which arouses your – hostility.

On the periphery of the town, he tells tales about the French and English colony in Athens. They had left Greece on the same boat as he had, all with chills on their sexual organs, dripping with the same gonorrhoea – they have all been moving in the same circle of shepherdesses. He tells me a secret. Anyone testing the innocence of pure emotion easily lands in a mess.

One morning in Piraeus, Byron saw some soldiers riding along with a large knobbly sack, elbows, fingers, heels, the ample cleft of a female backside revealing the contents to be human. He stopped the convoy, which, however, said nothing until the first coin changed hands. Then he found that their burden was a whore plus a large stone. Until recently, she had been the chaste sister of four brothers and intended for a certain official (with morphine-dreamy eyes, whose dreams could no longer be fulfilled by his twenty-year-old minor queen). The girl's mother and sisters had examined her one evening when she came in smiling behind her hand, and thus had established that she had lost her asset. The punishment for that was to be lowered into the sea, like a litter of puppies of undesired mongrel breed.

As he told me this . . .

My eyes become hot and misty as the memory of Greece rises up to them, populated by, among others, my friend: the dry, the slanting, dark glass-yellow sun that gives the mainland mountains their weary colour. Beyond the first sound, the mountains continue black, island after island after island. The deep-throated taste of the Mediterranean, the prickly keen-scented smell of thyme. The freshness of the morning. A woman in a sack. My friend is an Englishman and he has a pouch of money. At first he argues, but that is pointless. A Turkish officer of lowest but one rank cannot risk it for nothing, particularly when surrounded by witnesses. Talking is useless – across the border of absolute ways of thinking, all meetings become parallel. He puts his money-shod hand into an officer's pocket. The weight of the one pouch meets the other and a quality arises, a thought. The wrong thought but it will do. Out of it comes a bonus: it turns out that the officer also feels compassion for the girl who had loved so unwisely.

The sack falls in the dust. As the soldiers ride away, the contents quieten, or stiffen, all ears and hope, against all sense. My friend tells Fletcher to untie the knot. Why must there be so much senseless unhappiness in such a good climate? A lizard looks on, then scuttles away, long stretches with imperceptible leg movements, up a wall, up a mountain. The sun is dark and glass-yellow. Fletcher is forced to use his knife to open the seal. Then the sack falls apart and there lies the girl, semi-naked and almost dead with terror. My friend almost faints with horror. He is the one who knows why she hid her laugh behind her hand. And they had only met in the way young people do. Jupiter and Mars had been almost united in the sky that night and the gentle mumbling and tittering of the young people had twisted a rope into this egg with a red yolk. All softness revealed tempts *steel*. Like being woken by a *blow*.

Byron and I sat on our stone bench and watched the cathedral cat amusing itself with a mouse trying to get away by scuttling into cracks below the foundations. He said he had set up seven points of argument for a new alignment of his life:

1. I am twenty-three years old and can reckon on the best moments of my life being behind me, while the bitter moments will double their frequency in future.
2. I have seen humanity in its various national guises and find it equally insufferable everywhere. If anything, the balance falls to the Turks, who don't talk all the time.
3. I am *désolé*. My worst compromises go unpunished. Beautiful and loving actions lead to ruin for those they are intended to favour.
4. I am lame in one leg, so have a physical disadvantage which increases with the years and will mean my old age will be more discontented and less bearable than it would otherwise have been. In my next life, I am counting on two – if not four – legs in compensation.
5. I have become a damned selfish misanthrope.
6. My affairs are in a terrible state.
7. I have survived all my appetites and most of my conceits, even the vanity of writing.

He looked gravely at me: my views on this delivery? I paid:

Meus pater wishes me to disappear into the damned *militia*. At a time when his other sons are already risking their lives at sea and on land. Everything I see of him confirms my opinion of old people. They are self-righteous and blunted. I'm sick to death of *le beau monde* in London. If I had an annual income of five thousand pounds sterling, I would fall in love and then life might be slightly bearable.

I have lost all my delight in books, and they have been my only joy for a long time. What's the point of writing and reading? You struggle and struggle and then you die without having acquired the slightest advantage from your labours. And for the advantages you acquire for others, you never receive the slightest acknowledgement. No more than one little word of gratitude is needed for me to be happy. Though what use is acknowledgement? It makes me neither a wiser nor a better person. When it comes down to it, it is nevertheless only one man's view of another, and the person expressing it usually does so more out of sheer self-interest than from a pure heart. Does his praise make me richer or more imposing? Does it stop me rotting partly above ground and in penury below it? Does it change the fact that my disappearance will be of less weight than that of a drop of water evaporating off the surface of the ocean?

With a crunching sound, the cat gives the mouse the *coup de grâce* with its molars.

This private antiphon of misanthropes bored us after having barely consoled us. Without noticing how it happened, we had returned to familiar tracts where our vitality stems from problems that are general, in a philosophical way. There we agreed that man *is* originality, but *creates* effectiveness. He says this striving is the basis of all human greatness and the certain downfall of humanity.

I reply that it is also the mother of all the contradictions in our lives, so therefore the only thing worth writing about.

He says: 'Ah.'

I say that everything *created* by man – from religion to the loom – describes his perception of chaos.

He says in parenthesis that isn't it fantastic that people nevertheless create religion before the loom? Worth thinking about for those who refuse to believe the spirit is the equivalent of materia. (Man's soul is greater than his principles!) Primitive folk-art with its staring eyes and insolent proportions, its crocodiles and bellies and pricks are safe and familiar with chaos.

We are agreed that an internally very chaotic person has to re-shape his character to something more protestant – like a sonnet. The savage sea can express itself in the heavy boldness of the hexameter. But Shakespeare turned his perception of chaos into the rolling chaos of blank verse. Byron says it's 'incredibly great to make chaos into chaos without simultaneously making the writing meaningless. There'll never again be a writer like Shakespeare.'

Then I interject that the fewer roads there are in the desert, the sterner is the god of the desert as far as rules of the road and tolls are concerned. On the other hand, the mother and time released lure out desert gods. At first, freedom is the god of freedom. Later, not.

And so on. Nothing cheers us up so much as a little abstraction! Every window glittered than evening. We had a large dish of small roast birds for dinner.

*

'But how will people know which are original thoughts and which are words you put into the mouth of the poet?'

Two people in the room laughed at what they at first took to be a deliberate joke. But Link took the spectacle arms off his ears to be free of his reading glasses and see Mr Cohn's face. It was small and innocent, recovering from the confusion of having caused laughter, and was looking at Link with the expectation of one who had at last asked the question on his conscience.

'I think I've already answered that several times: you *don't* know.' Mr Cohn's face had become somewhat dismayed, registering that Link's hand was trembling very obviously as his glasses hung from it. Strangely enough, the dismay grew into a more harmonious expression as the face observed the grey inside of the trembling hand throwing a reflection of the same colour as Link's forehead.

Those who liked Mr Cohn first noticed his swift timid facial expressions. He was not young, but his face still contained a brook of rapid perceptions, racing from source to mouth, bubbling and splashing without deepening its channel. His face was not young, but smooth. 'You don't know,' Link said again.

Later that evening, he confided in Mr Cohn that the trembling of his hands was not a personal symptom but a professional ailment, an affliction of those who had to deal with certain poisons every day. That was sure to calm the trout stream, for common suffering is never as melancholy as an individual one. 'You don't know . . .'

'I saw you in Cambridge two weeks ago,' said Rupert.

'Come over to the window,' said Eric Watson. The top window rattled against the lower one, the wind sending an arrow of draught towards the fire as Rupert parted the curtains and glanced out at the high vaulted starry night, the only divergence apparently the lights from his house.

196

Eric Watson ran silky soft fingers over Rupert's forehead. 'What are you *doing*?' whispered Rupert, but just as abruptly followed those fingers with a sullen caressing movement of his head. Both stopped. Hand and head. 'Yes, I saw you, too,' mumbled Eric Watson. 'In pleasant company, it seemed, but certainly less socially risky than mine . . . I touched you on your "third eye",' he added with another touch. Small muscles are so expressive, he had no need to say another word. Rupert understood who had seen and said something about a third eye.

'Discretion a matter of honour?' implied Eric Watson, half aloud. 'Not for my sake, you understand, for hers . . .' Rupert is already saying nothing. Silence is the only possible answer when someone asks you to keep his secret and is afraid to insult you with the anxiety that you will sweep it aside.

'Have you ever' (Eric Watson seemed to change the subject and titter at the small annoyances of life) 'flirted with a relatively unknown party and in the introductory verbal course of events discovered an unwelcome pressure from Mother Nature? And not really known what to say, because certain situations are far too awkward in the light of each other. And finally you're in such a state, you almost pee in your pants. And from this inner pressure, the outer pressure increases in your declarations of love, semi-hysterical from false passion and genuine desperation?'

Rupert looks at him in surprise. He often has an audacious way of looking surprised, unmoved and surprised like a princess spoken to by a swineherd. 'No, not as far as I can remember,' he says coolly. It would have been an advantage if he had been able to maintain that sophisticated attitude in his answer. But unfortunately his tongue couldn't resist moving from answer to question: 'What was the outcome, Mr Watson?'

'I'll tell you "the outcome" at your stag party, for instance. It will provide so much more happiness there, like "the outcome". I really don't know why I'm talking like this at all. I must be nervous. That's supposed to be some kind of explanation for why I'm sitting here scratching your forehead.'

'That's not necessary. Do go on.' Rupert was looking steadily at him, but with no surprise, looking at him with his slanting eyes and staring at him with the large shiny lobes of his forehead, never quite closing his eyes. 'You have no reason to hide anything from me. I don't look on you in that way.'

A gust of wind made all the windows in the house rattle. Mr Hazell reminded himself yet again that he ought to have nailed new insulation strips to the windows. The very thought of such a task bored him to the edge of depression. A houseowner is a bird flying against the wind, against all the instincts of its moral laxity. For a moment, the other conversations ceased for the privilege of commenting on the weather forecast. They were listening for more signs of the forecast storm and thinking about running under an inside-out umbrella. Mr Hazell excused himself, closing a sliding door behind him. In the kitchen, his daughters were busy damping and drawing sheets. The youngest was bare-armed and bare-legged apart from a pair of thick woollen socks serving as slippers. They were his socks and there would in all certainty be holes in both heels when he got them back. She was also wearing his pullover, and his shirt, for that matter. 'I'd be grateful if you'd leave me my *shirts*,' he said. 'But Daddy,' laughed the girl. 'All my blouses are in the wash. Do you want me to go naked?'

He stayed for a while.

He listened for a while to their chatter: it was without pauses, without reflection. He tried to imagine a corresponding conversation in the two other languages he knew – French and Spanish. But no. The Latins argue rapidly, but they don't keep the conversation flowing like a perpetual motion machine. When his daughters chattered, seven words out of ten in a sentence were padding, a speech-song that was essential only in the sense that people talked to each other. It was English.

Presumably, thought Mr Hazell, people talk as they eat. There must be a considerable difference between people who eat a solid breakfast with a lot of milk, fat, sausages and marmalade, and people who breakfast standing up on a gulp of black coffee and a cigarette.

'Do you know if we've any insulating tape in the house?' he said, after having gone through the kitchen drawer where they kept broken curtain rings and key rings, a towel-ring, a charred kettle holder, three electric plugs, several rusty padlocks, an extension lead with a two foot long cable plus an assortment of odd nails, tacks, nuts and bolts.

'No, but we know Mummy's been asking you to buy some more ever since the spring!'

The cat was lying on a wooden chair the girls had thoughtfully covered with an old cot blanket and pulled right up to the stove. It had curled up into a ball and turned its chin up, purring in its sleep. Mr Hazell could not bring himself to touch it, for it would then immediately wake and turn its head round the right way, and he would no longer be able to see the delicate nostrils (how can you breathe through anything so small?) and the cat-smile that was the shape of its upper lip. At that particular moment, the elder girl happened to slip and spilt the ironing water, which shot a fountain on to the stove. The stove hissed, the cat leapt up, scaring the father. The father placed himself obliquely behind his body and smiled quietly at the usual battlefield painting of kitchen and young daughters, an ironing board almost tipping over, a father, a cat stretching first its front then its hind legs. And steam. And country china on the walls. And shoving. And affectionate hands on napes of necks, of which he distributes the most.

Cold and wide-awake, he passes the dining-room, where the curtains are actually billowing out from the draught. Damn it! Rupert could have done the insulation in the summer. The girls helped their mother, but did that young rogue ever do a hand's turn in the house? No, he certainly didn't. The wind was breathing out through cold teeth and it was still only November. The rogue!

In his study, Mr Hazell tentatively pulled the third desk drawer open a fraction and at once closed it. No, he did not wish to open it. He did not wish to flay his eyes with the sight of the three pages he had written and read into shreds: 'We left Montalègre at half-past two on June the twenty-third. The sea was calm and after rowing for three hours, we came to Hermance, a lovely little village with the ruin of a tower the villagers say stems from the days of Julius Caesar.' That was an echo from Percy Shelley.

Mr Hazell willingly shifted to another object of interest. He noted a roughness in the desk drawer and energetically started jerking it in and out to smooth off the unevenness. Or could it have been to bring disorder to its contents?

Some kind of disorder often turns out to be a kind of order, which Mr Hazell could appreciate but would never be able to create. He admires the order of disorder. Great contemporary artists create disorder. They imitate magnificent chance, not human organisation.

Mr Hazell modestly wishes that chance would mix up his notes and provide a result that would give him the end of the thread of this assignment.

The committee has four members who can complete assignments with the shameless ease of the curly tail of a pig. Mr Hazell has the wild ambition of someone who wants to straighten out a curl. That could be so simple. On the bus, in the car, at work, among all those duties preventing him from writing, this ambition takes the shape of ideas, words, words that evaporate when he has 'peace and quiet', words that curl, go wrong, heavy, the weight of the tongue – yes, that's what happens the moment he has the 'peace and quiet' to work in, a kind of organised measured restlessness.

Essentially, neither does he really know what he wants. His friends happily tumble on with their plans without a thought for the final form and rounding off of the project. They appear to be relying on the effect of quantity; seem to think – like most people – that an interesting subject spontaneously provides interesting results. Talent spontaneously providing talented conclusions. What Mr Hazell would like is poetry . . .

'Neither is documentary description', says Link (just as Mr Hazell comes back), 'anything more than an interpretation. If the truth is the sun and we are the earth, then our perception of light is that of the sunlit planet. Our naked eyes cannot tolerate looking at the sun. Should they do so, they would still be unable to describe what they see. On the other hand, we can perfectly well look at and describe what gets in the way of the rays of the sun – some kind of silent shadows of light are our actual sight. I am using these authentic diaries because they show me the strength of details and because they teach me to manufacture details. They don't take me an inch closer to the sun.'

'The only truth about this "sun",' muttered Rupert to Eric Watson, 'is the content of the baron's coffin, nowadays. And I don't understand what you've all got against taking a peek. He will look like any old mummy and I for one would find it useful to see his length and contours at the end of his life, because that's the time I'm writing about.'

'Are we to rig him up?'

'What?'

'You know as well as I do that if you want to know his height then you'll be misled by his *prostrate* figure. The dead look taller lying than standing. A ruler does, too. A mile, too. And sanctimoniousness! Have you no respect for the dead, you oaf? Have you no sense of respect?'

'Respect, respect, I don't know about respect. One can do anything in a sensitive way and one can be insulting with piffling trifles. Only by *living* do you offend!' (Rupert: a youth after all.) 'Uniting people who otherwise would have no need to have anything to do with each other. Through my parents, I have two cousins who are the scum of the earth and with whom I am nevertheless forced to have some kind of relationship. Through a certain lady, you become intimately related with her husband in a way that would deeply offend you if it had been direct. And as for her . . .'

'Rupert,' said Eric Watson solemnly. 'After all, you're still a child.' So much was gained by this statement that he sat in silence for a long spell, enjoying how you feel when a rash statement gives you a sense of advantage. Then he added: 'Yes! Respect. The very action of digging up a hundred-year-old corpse to measure it shows lack of respect, even if it happens clinically and in a spirit of discretion. The very action of refusing to is respectful, although *that* happens because the thought itself gives you the creeps. If you doubt these norms and think that I'm the one to have laid them down, then you're wrong. Custom is always far stronger and more *intelligent* than rebellion against it. That's true. Mutual intelligence, in my opinion, is far superior to the most brilliant philosophical theory. How could it be otherwise?'

*

London, February 19th, 1812 – Today, Byron (*Lord* Byron) made his maiden speech in the House of Lords, on the penalties for the frame-breakers in the weavers' rebellion in Nottinghamshire. No one is said to have been surprised that he demands leniency. We have both seen what the Luddite rebellion entails. The introduction of machine looms, each of which does the work of seven men, has consequently left six of the seven without a living. Starvation prevails in Nottingham. Who then can be surprised by some smashed looms and assaulted officers of the law? Yes, quite a number are surprised, as the majority of members of the House are in favour of capital punishment.

Earlier in the day, I found my friend flat on his face on the sofa in his room in St James's Street, recovering from a kidney-stone attack, a misery which seems to recur with a certain regularity. He was exhausted after being bled, enemas, emetics, and other aches and pains, though particularly after the pain, which he says is unfathomable. You want to take the sharpest thing you possess, he says, and stick it right into the centre of it. You long for a worse torment, anything, as long as it takes your mind off the stone. The stone, however, is as minimal as its effect is enormous: you would surmise a forceful clink in the chamber-pot (before that the spectacle of a snake swallowing a rabbit) when the obstacle has run its course, but in fact it is scarcely visible, he says.

His speech in the House of Lords was being copied by the secretaries at that moment. He showed me a letter with the same content, addressed to Lord Holland.

He told Lord H that he had grown up in Nottinghamshire and had seen with his own eyes the result of the progress of the 'monopolists'. The weavers in Nottingham had been good artisans. They had not lived in affluence, but had supported their families and made cloths of excellent and durable quality. Now one saw emaciated children, sullen and violent people on the roads, because they had been evicted from their homes.

Byron maintained that he was as opposed to violence as anyone else, but the weavers were now faced with the same situation as a nation whose harbours have been locked. Bewilderment nourishes violence. The Luddites *fought* against the machines, because that was their *last remaining* possibility. 'Therefore I consider one should minimise the penal aspect. They are a severely afflicted group sacrificed for a number of tradesmen to enrich themselves with methods that have stolen the weavers' work and lowered the quality of the produce so that it can only be sold abroad. Guaranteeing the working man his livelihood and welfare ought to be a more important task than backing up a small number of wealthy monopolists.'

'This quality business,' I interjected, 'may well be so that it is a matter of deliberate decline. Lowering of quality must have a kind of quadratic or cubic relation to sales: as the life-span of the product is reduced. The plan may be that in time they will again employ the weavers to satisfy the demand for goods that don't – hm – last.'

Byron sat up, groaning, his hand pressed to the side of his belly – 'My dear Hobhouse, stop it! Don't complicate the issue for me. That is rhetoric. If I include too many components, my indignation turns to brooding, musing, truth-seeking, and then the House falls asleep. The first duty of a parliamentarian is to keep his fellow-members awake. And anyhow, in politics' (said the man of experience) 'it's not a matter of "on the one hand or the other" but of demagogues meeting and rubbing and (he swept his free hand out) grinding out some kind of sparks between them.'

Which he also did. Still divinely pale, in full mourning for his mother, he showed great self-confidence in his new rôle (maybe because it was half a game to him) and spoke in rhythmical passionate sentences: slipping in his modest insolence occasionally, being outrageous to his opponents and annoying the Lord Chancellor.

March 20th – Byron suddenly became a famous poet yesterday. *Childe Harold's Pilgrimage* the work is called.

April 21st – Dinner at Reilly's – Baillie with me. Stayed up all night at the House of Lords. Debate on the Catholic question. As full citizen's rights for Catholics would include several million Irish, there are more opponents than in other matters of liberal reform. Soon after midnight, Lord Byron swept in, refreshed by a ball at Almack's, boundless attention and praise in general. I have never seen anyone more at home with his success. He acts himself all the time. Sensitive to what people take him for, he *is* that. In the drawing-rooms – among ladies – he starves his soul with melancholy. Among his old friends, he is sometimes far too much of a good thing, but mostly coolly happy. He had the House of Lords in paroxysms of laughter over the Catholic question. Lord Grenville, however, was more effective in his reasoning, as was Lord Wellesley, who maintained the Papal Nuncio provided the first resistance to Bonaparte in Cadiz.

May 11th – I heard at half-past six that Perceval had been shot on the steps going into the House of Commons, by a man who stepped up to him and said, 'I am John James Bellingham, a merchant of Liverpool,' and shot him through the heart. W. Smith was there, and said, 'Who has got a pistol among us?' At that moment a man, whom he took to be Wilberforce, reeled up to him and fell at his feet, just calling out 'Murder'. Smith picked him up and took him into the Vote Office, where he died in two minutes. The crowd of spectators stood there just as indifferently from the moment the shot was fired until the police took away the murderer, who had meanwhile been strolling around with his hands in his pockets, chatting with people round about. It is said that his motive was not political but rage over Prime Minister Perceval failing to answer his letter, or something of the kind. How can you protect yourself against such people? Smith said that a very dramatic event like this is part and parcel of so much ordinariness and the usual waste of time, that witnesses can scarcely be *historically* aware of what is happening at that moment.

June 13th – Back in London again after a week's delirium. We set off on the fourth, Byron, his cousin George Anson Byron and I. Half way we stopped at a milestone I particularly remember, because our dead friend, Matthews, and I stopped overnight by it once when we were walking home from Newstead Abbey. We stood in memory of Matthews, who died barely a year ago, trapped by water weeds when swimming in the Cam. It was a bad moment. Matthews was my best friend. Byron said he was the essence of something of which we were only the juice. He consoled me by saying that Matthews and I had for ever made an impression on the place, in the thousand-year-old eyes of the milestone, together with all the others who had rested there. We splashed wine on to it, spices, rosewater and perhaps a few tears.

We got to Newstead the next night in the middle of the light June night. The air was mild, but the wind poisonous, whistling in the ruins. I was too tired from emotion to keep the cousins company. The outline of the mansion, those strange little forts by the pools – my eyes sought in vain for memories of when we were all young there. Well, we were still young, but nonetheless so old that two of us are now conclusively young, the rest of us surviving them and no longer able to feel the same innocence in innocent enjoyments.

I looked on for a while while my friend and his cousin got drunk. George mixed all kinds of things in a jug and drank it with the corners of his mouth as drainpipes. Byron stuck to red wine, but his 'skull-goblet' holds one and a half bottles at a time and he tried to empty it in one go. 'Good gracious,' said Fletcher. 'If you wish to see His Grace moving like a larva, then await what is to come.' (The goblet is the skull of a monk my friend had once found when digging in the potato field. He had it set in silver and the skull-goblet is known all over London now that he's a famous poet.) He drank out of his skull-goblet and became incoherent. I said goodnight. I was thinking about Matthews, who had drowned and had drunk out of the same bone.

Why should he sink to this level now? It was not good for him. He has a cursed tendency to lure demons out of his seething store and is then terrified to death when they come trampling out. The white night had begun to turn to pink and green as I was woken by one lighter and one heavier step on the floor. I automatically made room for him.

But idiotically, in a naive voice, he told me that his Mamma was under his bed complaining so loudly, it was impossible to sleep. I muttered 'yes, yes' and moved over nearer my edge. His breath was like vinegar as he told me that he hadn't gone to Mrs Byron's funeral. I turned over and looked him in the eyes. He nodded. It was true. He had stayed here and practised boxing with his page as the funeral procession made its way to the church in Hucknall Torkard. He couldn't endure an event in which everyone had to be in the same mood. He had stayed at home and boxed with Robert Rushton instead (he smiled suddenly like wet lightning in the dawn light). I said to him that under those circumstances, I would have also haunted him. He drunkenly defended himself: indeed he had wept over her corpse all through the previous night! Alcohol makes people elementary – so they drink more than they want to. His quivering body was a gentle mechanism in my bed. I said: 'Yes, yes, go to sleep now.'

My friend is apt to complain about insomnia, and all those nights we spent back to back in Spain, in Albanian cabins and Greek huts, I have survived him. This time, too. He abruptly fell asleep, heavy with wine, and while dreaming, made room for himself at my expense.

I spent all the morning in semi-slumber, eye to eye with the freckles on the back of his upper arm. They began moving, slowly, lengthily forming whorls increasing in speed, and kept on increasing, then tumbled down into their own eye and – in the actual collapse, they exploded again into their original pattern. Every explosion woke me up completely, and each time the freckle began to be sucked into its shell-whorl, I dreamt ourselves – in another, wordless, differently coloured context – somewhere secretly living on a freckle, where mind and emotion were different from here, and someone else was dreaming us.

Sailors must be what people say they are. When I got up the next morning, I found George with egg-yolk on his moustache, busy at a hideous breakfast table. He told me you clear alcohol out of your body with a sturdy meal and then a sturdy shit or two. Later, after having put the latter behind him, we inspected house and grounds on horseback and on foot and by boat. One or two pheasants rose off the ground and rushed away. George laughed at the pheasants' course along a horizontal line. We didn't see any legs but the body moved forward like a wooden decoy borne by a steady hand along the horizontal line. Grouse also raced up before the horses' hooves. And hares with long shanks.

George took the oars of a leaky rowing boat, I bailing astern. My work was harder than his. He spat out chewing tobacco to see if we could seal the cracks with spit and tobacco. All knowledge can be of value on occasions. He looked up and his eyes turned pale grey – quite alien. I followed his gaze and saw the house. Light, grey, quite alien in the remarkable sun-mist.

I couldn't find words for what I was thinking when George's eyes were invaded by this alien look until I got back to London. I was thinking somewhat abstractly. Roughly this:

When I say 'I live in London' I have a feeling of unreality. As if I didn't exist, as if the city didn't exist. When I say I Live In London, London disappears and I disappear. My self and my city fall apart and are dissolved by that positive explanation. We are united in the same sentence to be dissolved, as if it were a deadly sin to define myself and my city so clearly. With inner blindness, nature strikes the person who defines himself. A laugh and a penalty comes from within and annihilates the mutual self and city. Something seems to be breathing me out.

Inside the house, we studied what Byron calls his sensual solaces. Tortoises, all brought back from Athens, a hedgehog, a bulldog etcetera. The tortoises had laid eggs in the spring and a broody hen had been hired to sit on them, but with no success. Perhaps there's a decisive difference between cold-blooded and warm-blooded warmth. That also applies to the greatest extent to the kindness of the harem. Some of the maidservants are rustics – to put it in a friendly way. Others are so shy, it's a torment having anything to do with them. And yet cold-blooded rites are carried out at Newstead Abbey. The following days I was as elementary as anyone.

July 22nd – Went to Drury Lane and saw Kean as Othello. Byron found us a box near the oboeist. Two and a half acts were tame, but from the phrase 'not a jot' he started to demonstrate his Art and – as Byron put it – threw a kind of Levantine rage into his acting and his *face*, which we orientalists in particular understood and appreciated. Kean's way of stabbing himself with the dagger is masterly. The audience in an uproar of tears and jubilation. We went into the green-room, to which Byron has access since he became a member of the theatre board. Kean came in after a while, now in a Scottish pepper-and-salt suit, but still with the remains of make-up on his face, which was otherwise pale and unshaven. When I asked why he hadn't used a darker tone for his stage face, he replied that the reality in between is to enliven theatre tradition. Othello was no Negro, but just dark in the sense that he lacked the British freckled skin and pale beard. Othello was the *Moor*, that is, an Arab or a Berber. So his own – Kean's – appearance was in itself Moorish enough. But he had preferred to add two or three nuances of brown as a concession to the expectations of the audience.

He told us that his desire to act had really arisen out of his desire to crush calcified mannerisms, 'organs which retain the form they had when the blood streamed through them, but whose body was now no longer muscle but cartilage'. He thought he had now gone as far as an actor can go as far as acting 'naturally' on the stage was concerned, but that he often saw ahead the possibility of something 'supernatural', in which the actor lets his vitality and life-force replace the scenery, declamations and other stage forms: shows his real face, speaks without theatrical dissimulation, exposing the raw genius, exposing himself. But he also knew that a sudden change of theatrical style brings down an iron curtain in front of the majority of the audience.

'You know as well as I do, My Lord,' he said to his only rival for the favours of the London audience. 'Just by circumventing obsolete forms, you can't achieve what is called higher truth. The truth is forms. We are all receptacles that life has dipped into and the real person is reconciled with his form, *is* his form. We can only discover and see forms. Then we can see whether they are living or dead. But the actual difference – life – we can never see, or say what it is. That is why the form, the rewriting, is our only way of portraying life and so we must respect the traditional ways of doing it, while trying to change them.'

Byron said that reminded him of Rousseau, followed by the Reign of Terror, relieved by Code Napoléon. I said it sounded like my friend Q, who ran away with a theatre company, leaving behind him a letter in which he cursed his father, his name and his university. He failed as an actor and suddenly – one morning after he had drunk his last shilling in some harbour – he found himself on board a warship, a considerable way out to sea. Fortunately, he says, according to superior example, he lost an arm at Trafalgar and was able to return home. What he lost was his right arm, the one he had written the curses with, so all was forgotten and now he has inherited his father's estate, which flourishes along the lines of modest renewal in the spirit of tradition.

All three of us laughed at my story. Then we took Kean with us to one of those places which cure his 'stage dust thirst' and he drank deeply after every sentence. He told us he was in love again. Byron is also in love. Only I am never in love. I do not allow myself . . .

July 29th – Went to Byron's house, 8, St James's Street, with the view of taking him with me to Harrow. In London, the rumour is going round that today is the intended day for his escape with Caroline Lamb. Who does he think he is? Romeo?

When I arrived, there was already a large crowd in the street staring at the creature in the carriage. She had dressed herself up in some way, rather more than less conspicuously. When she saw me, she struck the inside of the carriage a few thunderous blows, at which the coachman set his pair off up towards Piccadilly. I went into the house via Lock's shop and ordered a new hat from Mr Dollman. He said her carriage had been outside for two hours and every single soul in the house knew what it was all about.

Byron was sitting in the drawing-room with his head in his hands. 'I know what you're going to say,' he said. 'But it's no use. If this woman is going to be my destruction, then I welcome it, as I would welcome every other destruction.' I replied we were not going to have any destruction that particular day, and then started arguing in the way he had initially rejected. After a while he started to realise the apparently simple truth that one does not *die* of running away with a crazy woman, but one is forced to live with her. This insight aroused him completely. Sometimes I wonder whether he is stupid. Then he begged me for help and advice. He said he daren't break his promise to her, for then she would take him for a rogue.

I replied that he would be behaving like a rogue if he carried out his plan and anyhow he needn't worry about his reputation, as the whole of London knew she had made a dead set at him from the very first moment. I said the whole of her life was social life. That milieu is the prerequisite for her charm and for your attraction to her. Without it, a passion that has taken nourishment partly from the curiosity of others – dies. That's obvious, isn't it?

He was incensed by my denigrating it all, and also by a few more things I had to say about Lady Caroline Lamb. To convince me that this was a matter of 'love', he handed me a letter she had written. I waved it away, but he insisted, so I read the kind of romantic rubbish we all produce on given occasions of lofty self-deception. It seems to me that people are never more similar than when they experience sexual passion. Not when they hunger, nor when they mourn or when their legs are amputated, but when they suffer agonies of desire. They all express themselves in the same banal words. But I presume that banality is relevant when one knows what they are expressing. Byron's expression told me that he was expecting feeling and understanding on my part. Lovers are also insufferably self-absorbed.

He went back into the other room with the letter. Then I heard her carriage again. I went to the window and saw her getting out, heavily veiled and with her overnight case in her hand. She also came in via Lock's shop. I heard steps on the stairs, light but menacing. The sound of her feet receded dreamily, like the echo of a slow clock. Byron appeared with his travelling coat on and a tear on his eyelash. He's so sentimental, my friend. All his life, we've had to save him from himself. I was forced to be the boulder in the current and ordered him to go into his bedroom. He obeyed immediately.

The creature came, observed me indifferently, sat down close to the fire and shivered. She looked at me again after she had warmed herself for a while. Her heavy smile started rolling out of her eyes and at once became a tragic grimace. She twisted her hands and sunned herself in the warmth from the fire. I was talking to her all the time, but she was listening for my friend wandering about sighing behind the bedroom door. 'Listen to him,' she said contemptuously, but when she looked at me, her eyes flared with determination. I asked her to be calm and wait there, after which I went in to him. He was now in a kind of panic at the thought of spending his life with any woman, particularly a 'wild one' like this. He started lecturing me on how marriage ought to be based on friendship and suitability, not on 'hatred and desire', and so on and so forth. But then he had peeped at her through the crack in the door and changed his mind again.

Well . . . I followed his gaze. There she was, leaning back by the hearth, legs stretched out and parted and her disguise in a heap on the floor. Underneath she had on knee-breeches and silk stockings and velvet green livery with gold buttons which winked in the firelight, the reflections chasing the movements of the flames through her honey-blonde curls, leaving there the memory of sparkling red. Slowly, licking, she was smoking a slim cigar and letting it burn between her gloved fingers.

My friend has no concept of adjusting. Instead of compromising, he shifts his desires and satisfies them all. During the discussion that followed, the lady at first became agitated, then wild and cried out: 'Then blood will flow!' She snatched up a dagger lying on the back of the sofa. Byron leapt forward and stopped her from using it on herself. The discussion continued. I was its draught horse. With a rope on each shoulder, I dragged them in the direction of a decision and they danced like blind elves at the end of each rope. One can be furious when people let their sexual passion push aside all other considerations, just as if it were impossible to control – or for that matter at all *important* – they fling it around so that everyone round about is struck by its distended bladder. What did I get for all these labours?

I walked to and fro between them – and what use was it trying to do something for people who come hell or high water want to tread the path of damnation! She sat there with her knees apart licking another cigar. All my suggestions fell like dust around her – that she should take the carriage to my rooms in Duke Street, and later have it fetch her, or be fetched by friends in whom she had confidence. She replied that she would go there if Byron would keep her company. She interrupted my protests against this with a laugh and at once a stream of honey flowed off her lips.

'Truly, if I understand you, Mr Hobhouse. Are you jealous of me or of him or just of what exists between us? I must tell you that I found him not in the slightest tempting when I first saw him. With those bitten nails and other things . . . in the carriage that first evening, he begged to be allowed to kiss my mouth. I refused! For one or two reasons. I have always presumed people will lose interest in me. I often change my clothes. People can shift their attention from one thing to another and still retain the same person.'

She yawned desperately.

'Oh, how it revolts me. He's not interested in the future. He's utterly indifferent to the England of the future. Do you know, theoretically I'm very interested in the future. I wish I could be active in politics. That would suit my temperament. While *his* view is that politics should not touch on natural courses of events, but leave as much as possible as it is. He's told me that.

'Tsss. In our circles, women aren't allowed to do anything properly. Only in conversation and in their beds can you influence men of action. It's so terribly dull and exhausting to be at an advantage with people who don't try to be that in return. You can penetrate through men's lack of interest only by challenging them or by saying something that captivates them against their will. Life's so tedious. Two of my teeth ache and taste of blood. He begged to be allowed to kiss my mouth and I gave in, and now everything's too late. We must stay with each other, Mr Hobhouse, can't you see that, everyone knows what we've done. I've told everyone. You can't have him back. Are you jealous of him or of me? He and I. He and I. We don't like each other, but we must perish together. And it's certainly right that we perish. Anything else would be unendurable. Isn't that obvious?'

Went on and on chattering and whispering and licking, she did, the cigar glued between her lips as she talked and small chunks of ash floating down her page-boy breast and plump trousered thighs. With another indulgent laugh, she dismissed my suggestion to let her come to my rooms in Duke Street ('why, why do you want forthwith to save two people who don't understand how to save themselves') but when by chance I touched her arm, she rose abruptly and was prepared to go with me. In my first astonishment, I didn't know how to exploit the situation. It was like listening to a bolting musical box, then suddenly picking up its cool immobility and holding it in your hand. While the explosive mechanism is still working, you close your fingers round it and find it calm. That evening I noted that touching is of great value. It seems obvious, but what is self-evident can be very surprising.

So Caroline Lamb's body marched submissively down the stairs two steps behind me. The spiritual half went on protesting.

'You must see that you can't influence anything, Mr Hobhouse . . . oh, you're so comical. We're created to destroy one another. Nature is arranged like that, and it arranged it that way for B and me. One can never break the laws of nature, although one can be mistaken, because it is so easy to break the laws of God. When I married, I was illiterate. They say William married me because I was illiterate. I couldn't read books. I could hardly write. Ignorance is like a chastity belt. My mother is wise. She knew she could have let me out on the street naked and got me back ignorant and pure in mind as long as I couldn't read. The moment I learnt to read, I realised that even I am Dr Faustus! Knowledge is an invitation to great sins, of which the worst is to feel yourself chosen. When that moment comes, one begins to recreate the world.'

Said Lady Caroline Lamb: 'As you hear, I'm only quoting God.'

The shallows
drown before
the depths

As early as the beginning of December, Mr Cohn noticed the very first signs of flagging in his friend's affairs of the heart. The most infallible among them was that he lost the desire for any project that had arisen in unanimity with his erotic fantasy, the flames now subsiding.

The previous time, the object had been a red-haired teacher and the project the construction of an air-raid shelter for five households, including Eric Watson's own. After two weeks of industrious designing, acquiring materials and digging, however, the initiative-taker realised it was all meaningless, for

'. . . there won't be war on this side of Europe this time,'
or
'. . . shelters are useless in modern warfare,'
or
. . . he, Eric Watson, had no desire whatsoever to survive a war fought with modern arms techniques and the enormous development of fighter and bomber planes.

At the time, Mr Cohn had pondered on the over-simplification of the subconscious. The *symbol*, the shelter, had been ready since the spring and the other participants considered Eric Watson had done his full share during two weeks of hectic full-blooded enthusiasm.

They had now agreed to meet in the pub just 'for a chat'. Another sure sign. Eric Watson started talking about his labrador, which, confronted with approaching winter, seemed to be finally adjusting to old age. Eric Watson said his escapades in the old days – those outings on his own that had led to angry owners of bitches reporting him to the police – well, they'd stopped some years ago. All that remained now was a little pottering about in the garden looking for last year's bones. Once or twice he'd tried running after some interesting scent, but had immediately come lolloping back at a whistle. No one ever becomes that obedient. It must be the internal clock slowing down . . .

Home and old habits now offered the only temptations, the very lack of excitement itself acquiring a desirable quality. 'It's the residual surprise when sensations have come to an end' (muttered Eric Watson, tenderly running the toe of his shoe along the dog's spine). 'The old boy's over twelve. It must be three or four years since his escapades started getting shorter and less sure. And his messages first started getting those pleasant human nuances when he took to sofa habits rather than wild dog habits. Though now we can see the beginning of the end and can envisage the end in the middle, unfortunately. What do you think? Ought we to relieve him of his coming degradation?'

The clear greenish-grey eyes swiftly passed Mr Cohn, pursued by a suicidal glint, the look running out of the corners of his eyes and hiding at the back of the globe, while the familiar face resumed its familiar expression. 'Good gracious!' protested Mr Cohn. 'I wouldn't say anything if you needed a working dog, but he's a pet, or whatever you call it. If he feels at home being a sofa dog, then let him go on as long as he likes. I can't understand people having their domestic animals put down when they're no longer on top form. Sooner or later, my friend, we'll all become more domestic than animal . . .'

He looked at the labrador vegetating at their feet, his coat still good, but his eyes a little dull as he raised his head and thumped his tail in response to the sound of his name – in connection with being put down. Mr Cohn often wondered whether animals realised they had names. He swallowed a lump in his throat. He shivered. He flushed: don't go putting your dog down because of another matter.

Then the talk became general. And then it came. Eric Watson began to dispose of his project. The blurred smile Mr Cohn detested spread across his face while logic – so essential to reasoning and so inessential to life – ran along his lips. He said he had woken up the other night and used both hands to count on his fingers the number of reliable, well-substantiated volumes already dealing with the destiny and works of Byron. Then he had got up to do something about the cold in the room that had woken him, and with soot and ash on his hands he had managed to accumulate six more titles. Then it had been quite clear to him how impossible this game was, for although it was rather entertaining and although he considered the labours of his friends – as well as his own – worthy, he couldn't understand how in sober moments anyone could dream of making them public, 'if only in such modest forms'.

'So, shall we stop?' said Mr Cohn.

Eric Watson grimaced with distaste at such large words as 'stop'. 'Start'. 'Stop, start, stop, start. Don't give the matter such dignity, as if it were a question of starting or stopping. Let it remain at us having had some pleasant evenings,' said Eric Watson. 'And why shouldn't we go on with them? Though shouldn't we perhaps then give our friend from town something for his petrol expenses?'

'And I have expenses for our refreshments,' added Mr Cohn, noticing that blurred smile becoming superficial.

A wave of bad atmosphere slowly made its way between them as they still went on looking at each other. Mr Cohn turned his eyes away, flinging his attention round at random in order to be dismissive. Conversations were going on in ten different groups on the premises and he would have liked to join in on any of them rather than listen to this serious 'talk'. The barmaid was standing at the bar counter with her grey dishcloth pressed between her hands, listening wide-eyed to another girl whose back was visible to Mr Cohn. Her head and hat were inside or on the other side of a lampshade with brown fringes, but he could see the light from the lamp on the barmaid's face, in her eyes, drinking in invisible words and then suddenly answering: 'But Brenda, it's not worth it!' In response, her friend stood on tiptoe out of her shoes and Mr Cohn caught a glimpse of two discs of pink heel where the thin woollen stockings had worn through. 'It's not *worth* it, Brenda,' repeated the barmaid. But her heels climbed in and out of her shoes to give emphasis to an argument. The headless girl's back was thin, her shoulders a clothes-hanger in her jacket, her bottom two bare plums.

Mr Cohn heard her light asthmatic voice. Then he heard the barmaid's answer: 'Of course, money means almost everything in the world and you shouldn't hesitate to do almost anything to get it, but you know as well as I do that it doesn't make up for something else. It provides lots of joy, but doesn't replace any other joy. It's simply not *compensation*, say what you like, and quite often money is even a joyless asset if there's something (Someone!) else you're really missing.'

At that she snapped briskly at a regular customer trying to butt in on the conversation. She flicked her evil-smelling rag at him and when he changed rôles and ordered another round, she pressed porter out of the pump with an angry 'you could have said that straight away instead of standing there eavesdropping on a private conversation . . . Eh? . . . I'll do my job if you mind your own business, Alf. Psst. Listen, think it over, Brenda, before you decide. It can't be worth it. He could be your father. And London, London . . . what's the use, if within six months you start making yourself ill with longing for (Him!). Of course you will. What's young is somehow *healthy*' (her eyes met Mr Cohn's without seeing them, held them, then saw them, after which, a trifle put out, she added) 'anyhow for anyone who is young herself.'

Behind Eric Watson's back three strangers were staging the Battle of Waterloo with the help of the table top, a crack in it, two wallets, some glasses, a bottle being rolled back and forth and a hand now and again scattering round glasses and wallets to represent trees.

Here's Brussels, one of them said, pointing far off the table in the direction of Eric Watson's glass of mild. Napoleon was heading there that evening. His Old Guard had their parade uniforms packed in their knapsacks in preparation for the triumphal march. Napoleon and his staff were here (again pointing quite a long way away off the table) – in the village of Rossomme a few kilometres outside Waterloo – for most of the battle. Why, people have asked themselves. In all his campaigns, he had always been part of all the hue and cry and had surveyed battles from high positions. Why didn't he vouchsafe Waterloo even a glance until the battle was almost lost towards the afternoon? Everyone knows that on June 18th, 1815, Napoleon was suffering from severe haemorrhoids as well as inflammation of the bladder. Both these ailments must seem particularly unattractive on horseback, for we all know horses never stand still, even if they look as if they do. On the other hand, both the one and the other had been part of the imperial anatomy for many years. Haemorrhoids in particular seemed to have been a malaise between the 1700s and the 1800s more than any other, afflicting old and young, poor and rich. The other ailment was not uncommon among cavalrymen, who had to sit for days on soaking saddles. That June was a wet one, so Napoleon's sufferings must also have been shared by many of his soldiers.

Here (a hand closed over a wallet) we have the La Belle Alliance inn and behind here we have a low hill and a marsh where in the morning Wellington lined up his rheumaticky soaking-wet troops, who had been trying to sleep in the muddy field as it rained throughout the night. During all the years he and Napoleon's marshals had been chasing each other across the Iberian peninsula, he had learnt one essential and that was not to expose his men unnecessarily. At the time, the fashion was still to puff yourself up for battle, showing your massed troops on the horizon and advancing, rolling in one weighty line after another. This frightened the enemy, and you were no more vulnerable, for the accuracy of the artillery was not much to boast about, not working on the principle of hitting its target, but firing in a given direction and what it hit or whether it slaughtered friend or foe was a matter of chance. In Spain, the Duke had realised that from a military point of view, the mighty strike the weak, until the weak have found the weak points of the mighty, after which, might becomes synonymous with ungainliness. Armoured knights once experienced the same thing, floundering and croaking like stag beetles on their backs if they fell off their horses. So the Duke's tactics were to find landscape formations where he could semi-conceal his forces, allowing them to be glimpsed, but keeping them fairly well out of the way of the enemy support artillery. Here! a finger ran down the crack in the table.

This is the sun now, said speaker number one, slowly raising an instructive whisky and soda in a cloudy pale parabola above the table and stopping just before midday height, then leaning forward to take a gulp. New listeners had left the bar and, with sceptical interest, joined the history lesson. Their laughter made Eric Watson turn round. The sun had almost reached its zenith and the Battle of Waterloo had not even started yet. Wellington was striding round on his hillock, Lord Uxbridge riding around the battlefield talking to his friends, which he otherwise did gradually in the heat of battle. Orderlies rushed off to urge on Marshal Blücher, who was coming up with Prussian reinforcements. Far away, half a day's march away, the French reserve brigades were sitting among cherry trees eating chicken. Meanwhile, the Emperor was sitting with his head in his hands on a tree stump in Rossomme saying nothing whatsoever.

On the battlefield were – and are – three strategic fixed points that had to be dominated to keep the route to Brussels open. Nowadays the art of war is of course a product of civilisation but fairly independent of civilised areas. In those days armies were still wholly dependent on houses and roads, though on the other hand, arms technology was way behind civilian technology. As a soldier, man was most effective with cut-and-thrust weapons, as in the Middle Ages.

The English were swarming in and around the 'castle' of Hougoumont and La Haye Sainte farm, between which thenceforth the French infantry, the cavalry and finally the Imperial Guard were to direct their fire after thrusts towards the line of defence.

The first thing that happened in the battle – apart from the usual sniping – was that the French attacked Hougoumont at midday. It was only a little subsidiary battle, but from there, wave movements ran towards the two listless armies glaring at each other, and during the afternoon and evening, alternately producing a whispered *cri-de-coeur* from their losses. Eye-witness accounts from Hougoumont tell of the cackle of feathered creatures, barricaded gates and locks shattered by the methodical thumping from tree trunks plus arm muscles. People died inside and outside the walls. Enemies chased each other through stables and brewhouses, slipping in each other's blood, crossing themselves briefly in the chapel before diving behind a pillar and aiming at their pursuers. They ran through the bedrooms of maidens, tiptoeing suddenly in muddy boots at the sight of an abandoned flowered blue wash basin and jug. They pursued each other in the orchard and pressed themselves invisibly behind a tree for the opportunity to filch some unripe apples, for they had had nothing to eat for two days.

Then the French infantry began to muster for the attack. The Emperor had muttered some contradictory orders from his tree stump and Marshal Ney led the battle. The fact is that the Battle of Waterloo was an affair between the Duke of Wellington – with his hands free – and Marshal Ney – with his tied. If Ney had been allowed to use his forces in the way he wished to, the French would have won. But he was distrusted by Napoleon – understandably enough – because during the latter's exile in Elba, Ney had temporarily switched loyalties. On this day, it is said, he fought more loyally than any private soldier, remaining at the centre of battle from start to finish, which can be seen in that he had no fewer than six horses shot from beneath him. (Said the speaker with admiration in his voice. Another in the company continued:)

The French infantry now came charging against the English lines. Here we have La Belle Alliance (one wallet), here La Haye Sainte (an inverted glass) and here Hougoumont (an inverted glass adorned with an indiarubber and two nuts). Here comes the infantry (the bottle rolls and rumbles over the table) preceded by drums, drumming their triumphant salvo from Wagram, Friedland, Jena, Austerlitz, and frightening their frozen, soaked opponents. The French army was still organised according to the ideal of might. La Grande Armée was dead, but Napoleon Bonaparte nevertheless believed that an invitation to fight had to be responded to with something overwhelming. And it *was* an overwhelming sight: those monstrous Roman foot columns shaking the muddy ground as they advanced, sixty men abreast and God knows how long, the one level with the next, one after another, resembling an invincible natural disaster, so terrifying that Wellington's army peering over the hill must have had a crisis of nerves. Rrrrram, tam rrrratata tam. Imagine it yourselves, the sense of the Day of Judgement! The inevitability of the situation. Dismal destinies in hats reminding you of the prow of a ship breaking the stormy waves of the North Sea. Terrible human machines –

But this, as has been mentioned before, was their weakness. For a reasonably well-placed artillery, the columns turned out to be arranged like dominoes. When the English had got their sweaty fists round the loaders and flintlocks and bullets and powder-pouches, and fired off the first hundred salvoes against the natural disaster, it started to stagger, tremble and collapse. In gunpowder smoke and mist, you can't see the full effect of your actions, but what happened was that the columns became prisoners of their cores, and the core was everything except those four or five in the lead or outermost or farthest back. When the first line fell at the cannonade, the next generation tripped over them and in their turn were trampled on by those behind them. The rear panicked as it suddenly found itself up against a barrier of dead and wounded, and like slow-worms, every grouping into casualties or disorderly retreats was sliced in half. The gist of it turned out to be huge losses on both sides, but the English, Scots and Irish (we mustn't forget the Gordon and Cameron Highlanders and the

Inniskilling Dragoons, without whom Britannia would not have survived the day) had managed to hold the Duke's hill-marsh.

The hands now started rapidly moving among the matchboxes, crumpled sandwich paper, railway tickets, glasses and cigarettes to provide the crowd of interested sceptics with a picture of the way the battle went in the pause before the next onslaught – a skirmish here, a suicidal raid there, an attempt to join up a broken line, the efforts of the medical orderlies to clear away the less hopeless cases to the hospital tents, where the doctors were mainly working with saws. Listeners rescued glasses they had put down, so that their drinks would not be spilt in the heat of the battle.

What happened then is a classic in the history of military desperation. There was Marshal Ney galloping around, clearly aware that it is always the attacker who has *time* as well as the enemy to fight against. And there sat the Emperor on his tree stump, crippled by unmentionable ailments, giving no orders, dismissing the real commanding officer's suggestions. Ney's suggestions were massive cavalry charges supported by fresh foot soldiers – in other words, the Imperial Guard. But the Emperor refused to let them go. They were his élite troops and were to march into Brussels that evening, whole, clean and intact. Helplessly, Ney ordered cavalry charges all the same. Wave after wave (three bottles rolled after each other between 'Hougoumont' and 'La Haye Sainte') stormed up towards the Wellington line and created the same effect of massive terror in the British and suffered the same massive defeat as the previous infantry. The Duke himself uttered a much-quoted phrase (an example of the sophistication of English arrogance) when he saw the whole of the French cavalry riding with maximum vulnerability but no infantry support.

'Pooh, a woman could piss it out?' suggested one of the interested sceptics.

No, no, that's what the Lord Mayor of London said when they woke him one morning in 1666 because the city was on fire. Wellington, polishing a nail on his tunic, said haughtily: 'So the man was only a clodhopper after all.' The cavalry suffered hideous losses, not least on the part of the four-legged, and without horses, cavalry is, so to speak, no longer cavalry.

But the British line of defence was also a bloody inferno in which the British, the Belgians, the French and horses merged their sighs and cries. War was intimate in those days, as can be seen in the paintings, everything happening within small squares: at the bottom lie the dead and wounded, medical orderlies bending over them, and over *them* step the infantry with lowered bayonets. With brushed moustaches and calm eyes, they advance, so to speak. Some waving 'Vive l'Empereur', some falling with the regimental colours, so slowly that someone else manages to catch them – for we have little idea today of the importance of the colours at that time. Over them, or almost on them, climb the mounted officers, protuberances from the throng, exposed.

Half way up on the hillock, and yet on the periphery of the actual battle: the staff, all in their peacocks' uniforms, except Napoleon – the refinement of the autocrat to dress up his subordinates and himself act the sparrow. On a white horse. On the hillock opposite, Wellington paces round in the same uniform as his staff, the royal uniform, Wellington also a symbol, but of its successful rôle in a long tradition. Napoleon is a symbol of himself, banal in his eagerness to be that.

Let us not try to hide that the British force yields under the fury of Marshal Ney's assaults. They try to rest as the cavalry charge abates, not looking at the enemy then, but in the direction where the Prussians are expected. On the other side of the battlefield, a rumour is going round that Grouchy's reserves are on their way to relieve them, so the French looks are directed towards Ligny – where, however, Grouchy is still eating chicken in the cherry orchard and musically evaluating the sound of gunfire in the distance. This appears to be a battle that cannot be won by existing forces, but by the side which first gets help. Or? Is it Napoleon's old luck rising through the battle-strewn evening, like a lone surge beneath the silky surface of the sea?

My friends! Tides are running through the pursuits of mankind, but the Emperor's time was now the final ebb in which such a tiny roll of water is the farewell wave of fate. Below the Duke's hill-marsh, the enemy lay higgledy-piggledy in a mess, the poor wretches dying glance by glance, though glad to see each other as their comrades retired in each direction in an attempt to cobble together with rubber bands and sewing silk the illusion of an upright *line*. And in this position we are weaker than they are. Defeat guffawed, as they say, in our faces, the Belgians cautiously beginning to practise 'Vive l'Empereur' again and the grin growing when the adjutant arrived, foaming, with the message that the French had taken the La Haye Sainte farm, while simultaneously they could all see the roof of Hougoumont now ablaze. This sense of tides prevailing, Napoleon Bonaparte rose off his tree stump, seated himself on his white horse, his wet saddle and his haemorrhoids and decided to let his old favourites – the Imperial Guard – go.

On the battlefield, they were all immediately aware of the grey sparrow among the peacocks, approaching in slow gliding flight and landing roughly here (oh, yes, that was the symbolic function of the other wallet). It is said that at first the Emperor plunged into the whirl of battle, tugged the moustaches of some of his 'old boys', which was his affectionate habit, and yelled *avancez braves hommes* or whatever you say in such situations. This was what he usually did, and so it aroused some wonder and surprise when on the advice of anxious officers, he soon withdrew to shelter among them. His own brother, Jérôme, said: 'Why protect himself now? So stupid. If he wants to die *well*, this is his last chance to get it done . . .'

Later on that evening, Napoleon had to abandon his carriage bolting south and flee on horseback into the forest. Inquisitive enemy troops were soon swarming round the huge caparison containing every conceivable and inconceivable comfort for a soldier's life: camp bed and desk, gold plates, silver wash basin and commode. It also contained his medals and a great wealth of jewels. For the first time, he seemed to have seriously reckoned on losing; you defend your desperation for victory by providing for yourself in the event of misfortune. There was also a proclamation of victory in print that was to be read out at this very moment. But for the soldiers who could just spell their way through it, it was as ghostly as yesterday's newspaper.

The short-lived success of my enemies separated you briefly from my Empire: from my exile on a rock in the sea, I heard your laments. The God of War has come to a decision on the fate of your beautiful provinces: Napoleon is among you. You are worthy of being Frenchmen. Arise now, all of you, and join my invincible phalanxes in order to annihilate the last pockets of the barbarity that is your enemy and mine: they are already in flight, their hearts filled with rage and hopelessness.

Napoleon

Even later that evening, old Marshal Blücher sat down and laboriously penned a letter to his old wife: My dear Wife. You remember what I promised and now I have kept my promise. Superior numbers forced me to retreat on the 17th but today – the 18th – I have together with my friend Wellington put a definite end to Bonaparte's future dances. P.S. I had two horses shot from beneath me!

(Sometimes one has the impression that there was no greater insignium of bravery in an officer than to have as many vulvas as possible massacred, so to speak, between his legs.)

A few hours later that evening, the wind having dispersed the worst of the gunpowder smoke and the British forces having watched with delight and disbelief as the Imperial Guard fled in panic from them, the Duke of Wellington closed his telescope and waved his hat as a sign that the day's work was done. As he inspected the lines on his way to the recaptured La Haye Sainte, he was bombarded by Prussian artillery happily continuing to fire in the original direction, severely afflicting their allies. The fact is that the Battle of Waterloo was concluded with a couple of hours' skirmishing between 'friends', and many lives were lost either by mistake or owing to the real hatred that grows within associations of convenience. Alliances contain, as we know, only half or a quarter of the heart, negatively united *against*some third, whose destruction frees those partners from each other.

On the other hand, Wellington, irritably fending off the Prussian fire with his elbow, asked a passing officer in a very muddy uniform about some matter and received the reply: *Je suis désolé, monsieur le Duc, mais je ne parle pas un mot d'anglais*, at which the officer galloped after his fleeing comrades, southwards. Then Lord Uxbridge came rushing up yelling, Damn me, Sir, you're exposing yourself far too much. You're actually riding in the worst thick of it. At that moment, a bullet smashed Uxbridge's knee. By God, sir, he said, there went my leg. Wellington looked: By God, so it seems.

Or:

A shell from a cannon bounces up and smashes Uxbridge's knee. Wellington looks at it: By God, sir, there went your leg. Uxbridge looks down: Indeed, sir, you're right.

That's what the writing of history after Waterloo is like.

'Brenda, it isn't worth it, Brenda,' said the barmaid.

We, said the first speaker, 'we' won the Battle of Waterloo because 'our' allies arrived in time, while the impatiently awaited French reserve brigades were still lying in their hammocks watching the light June day with its cotton wool clouds going by in an emerald green evening. It can also be like that. For a man lying in the grass feeling buttercups nodding heavily against his head – all the noise, smells, breathlessness, fear and haste and exploding bullets and slashing into spongy resistance, all in the name of some kind of nameless sluggishness – are impossible to imagine. But a man simply fighting can easily imagine a quiet summer's day.

But we were also victorious over an untried illusion: the Imperial Guard, that unusually tall élite, veterans from classic battles, the pride of the Emperor. Their reputation was based on history which time had coated with a shimmer of moiré. They were to be thrown in at crucial moments, silent, mustachioed nursemaids to the already worked out victory. But their reputation turned out to be untried. They had quite simply lived all too well, like a sow with no obligation to farrow or provide pork chops. Confronted with the fierce artillery fire from the other side of the hill, the guards' enamel cracked. In huge columns, they marched towards the crucial point, terrible and magnificent to behold, at first courageous, but the columns folded like butterflies as the rain of bullets hammered holes in their midst and – *sauve qui peut* – hastened the way of collapse.

'Nothing is of value except what one values oneself,' said Mr Cohn.

And so the shroud of night sank, and in the light of the moon lay forty thousand men, wounded and dead, on prime arable land, among the heads and legs. Our earth is covered with species of soil shot with red, but the earth of Flanders is inextinguishably blood-red. This stage, a sight that soon also saw hope and faith bleed to death, was to return again a hundred years later: the new disputes driving out the Waterloo tourists of the past.

Night came after the victory, 'the victory'. If Waterloo is known for anything else but the fall of Napoleon, it is that the command forgot to clean up afterwards. No orders came to bury the dead, look after the wounded. Departure. With no silence. The last artillery pieces were exploding like a fireworks display, and then out of the silence rose a cloud that grew into a storm of lament. The battlefield was about two thousand yards by eighteen hundred, and apart from forty thousand wounded and dead, ten thousand horses lay there, dead or half dead, and innumerable comparatively healthy soldiers in anguish-filled bivouacs. It was a jungle night of infamy and plunder, soldiers murdering their helpless comrades to rob them of a few trifles of value. Some people say that one 'shouldn't condemn them or be surprised, for on a junior scale, they are behaving on the same principle as senior gentlemen do on a large scale'. But that's not particularly clever reasoning, for the actual scale of senior gentlemen's misdeeds makes them abstract to themselves. Meanwhile the powerless torment each other in a way that is direct and obvious to all. If they are given the right to do so and we excuse them instead of being indignant, they are freed from the obligation of exercising morality and reason – truly not inborn qualities. The majority of the bivouacked soldiers thought just like that, for they protected each other, lying in circles with frightened glances at the sparse pale-blue group creeping round with small bags, filling them with medallions of loved ones, rings, badges of rank, then teeth and then clothes. As early as the very next morning, the first tourists arrived from Brussels to share the queen's nectar of sensation.

That was the end for the young men of Europe dreaming of a premature death, romantically – they said to each other as they cleared their table of artillery, cavalry, buildings and dukes. One may wonder why that young Bonaparte in particular will always embody youth. Revolution meant youth only in a sensible way. He stood for the other half. Napoleon was a death of the century and a birth of the century. He was the immoderately personal success and failure. Romanticism and eroticism and violence – everything youth has always valued. At least, until they have experienced it . . .

'. . . . it's not worth it, Brenda,' said the barmaid.

And now the pub was full of smoke and fumes, the windows misted over with sweat, laughter and loud cries drowning each other, as when a boy flings himself on to a heap of boys on the grass to join in the fight to find out the reason for it. Mr Cohn's short-sighted eyes saw them as spots, hot faces, male forearms. They saw a yellow patch of light reflected in an oil painting of a potentate on horseback (probably the duke the pub was named after). 'Nothing's of value that one does not value oneself,' he mumbled to Eric Watson. The yellow patch went out for a moment, and then burst out anew even more brightly, and Mr Cohn rose in terror of the lightning, the explosive sound. Somebody had absent-mindedly lit his pipe and put the glowing match back into the box. Everything started burning, the gentleman's trouser pocket, or the handkerchief he had in vain dragged out as a white flag, the glass of rum, which cracked and led four tongues of light-blue alcohol flames towards the edge of the table. There is something demonic about fire.

The barmaid came round the bar with her bucket and old rag and started eloquently dabbing up charred ash. Brenda had turned round to look. With her elbows loosely on the bar, she was twirling an artificial emerald and observing what her friend called stupid 'little boy' pranks. She let her hands dangle, but twisted her artificial emerald round her finger. She was looking scornful. She suddenly gave Mr Cohn a glance out of the icy corner of her eye. She was slightly exalted, not by the fire, but by what she had been discussing with her friend. The fire confirmed it.

Eric Watson soon came back with his dog. It had dramatised the fire and so gone in for co-operation with a hitherto unnoticed pekinese. The hysteria had been great in both bass and descant. The little dog had run home, but a power struggle was going on between Eric Watson and the labrador. Mr Cohn thought it unnecessary. That hard hand on the scruff of the dog's neck, and the trembling sniffing face of the dog. Brenda then drew a quick line behind her friend's feet with the toe of her shoe as she delivered yet another bewildering look in the direction of Mr Cohn.

Everything calmed down and became normal. Someone loudly ordered a ham sandwich.

'I must tell you,' said Mr Cohn – and fell silent.

The evening, life swimming though a darkness. For every hold he took, Mr Cohn was moving through a substance of profound silence. It was all round him, hooking itself firmly in his elbows, and he dragged it with him – old, soft cobwebs, like the skin on milk. 'Nothing's of value that one doesn't value oneself!'

The more he swam, the more he dragged with him. The dog was persuaded to lie down. Brenda leant over the bar and gave the barmaid a hectic girlfriend-kiss on her cheek. Then she went out, but left behind the memory of a slow, slow wave.

At the Waterloo table, they had moved on to private military memories, and Eric Watson's eyes appeared out of their network of ironic wrinkles to listen at last. 'The thing is that you yourself value the interest which makes what you're doing into something worthwhile,' said Mr Cohn. 'It doesn't matter if it's old and familiar or new. An interest you don't value doesn't exist – from an interest point of view. On the other hand, any old rubbish is worth something because you value it. I value my molar tooth because I need it.'

Eric Watson blew the head off another beer as he sat down. Mr Cohn had seen the barmaid wash that particular glass in a bowl of soapy water with the same rag she had just used for the floor. Then she had dried it with a slightly cleaner cloth until it was shiny, improving the effect by breathing on it several times. She had placed it on the shelf and then taken it down, her tongue quivering in the corner of her mouth as she pumped beer into it and measured the quantity of liquid against the quantity of head. Mr Cohn saw Eric Watson's lips pout to blow, then close round the edge. Mr Cohn smiled. That dirty kiss seemed to inspire everything with a kind of justice.

A gulp, two gulps, three, half the glass. His eyes had still not shrunk back into his irony – no, Eric Watson was listening. He nodded at all that about value and valuing. He was quiet for a while, playing with his glass, then said: 'I couldn't get back to sleep that night when I was counting up titles, you know. One's never more content in separate bedrooms than when one can't sleep. I counted sheep. I counted girls and whatever else you can think up. In the end all I could do was to get up and do something sleep-inducing. I chose to play with my Annabella scenario.' The ugly blurred smile appeared again, but immediately vanished.

'One should never really do something one "values" in the small hours. It's a mystery about Lady Byron. Fletcher used to say that any woman could cope with Lord Byron – except Lady Byron. Some of all those books I counted up to myself during the night try to work out why. None has succeeded. All they do is to take the side of morality, as opposed to immorality – or, if you prefer, the cheerfully irrational way of life as opposed to prudery and principles.

'I found that was just what I was doing. Taking sides. But who knows what goes on between two other people?

'I sat there in the cold, trying to be objective. Trying to extract the mystery out of their conflict, instead of out of her personality. First I looked at their correspondence.

'As everyone knows, she abandoned him without giving him the slightest idea of her intentions. She took the child with her and went to her parents, and while he was wrestling with his finances in London, a letter thumped down telling him their marriage was over. In the exchange of letters that followed (his emotional, hers authoritative), in a purely political manner, they adopt opposite standpoints. He says that during their time together, hardly a day went by when she didn't sit on his knee and listen to his loving chatter. She says that hardly a day went by without him communicating his displeasure, disguised as criticism of marriage as an institution.

'At that point, I couldn't go on. His letters, of course, were more convincing because they were more descriptive.

'Nor is there any evidence to show that she knew the nature of Byron's connection with Augusta before well-meaning friends arrived to add fuel to the divorce campaign. I read his *Epistles to Augusta*. There is no clue in them. They are fraternal verses.

'Then I looked up *Don Juan*, in which Lady Byron is implanted in Donna Inez, to see how he regarded her when he loathed her.

> His mother was a learned lady, famed
>   For every branch of every science known –
> In every Christian language ever named,
>   With virtues equall'd by her wit alone:
> She made the cleverest people quite ashamed,
>   And even the good with inward envy groan,
> Finding themselves so very much exceeded
> In their own way by all the things that she did.

Then he goes into more detailed contempt for her pretensions.

> Her favourite science was the mathematical,
>   Her noblest virtue was her magnanimity;
> Her wit (she sometimes tried at wit) was Attic all,
>   Her serious sayings darken'd to sublimity;

Not to mention directly.

> Her thoughts were theorems, her words a problem,
> As if she deem'd that mystery would ennoble 'em.

And then he was insensitive enough to describe how this inner being of hers showed to her disadvantage.

> Some women use their tongues – she *look'd* a lecture
> Each eye a sermon, and her brow a homily,

The gist.

> Perfect she was, but as perfection is
>   Insipid in this naughty world of ours,
> Where our first parents never learn'd to kiss
>   Till they were exiled from their earlier bowers,
> Where all was peace, and innocence, and bliss
>   (I wonder how they got through the twelve hours),
> Don Jóse, like a lineal son of Eve,
> Went plucking various fruit without her leave.

Jóse is of course Inez's husband and Byron's euphemism for himself.

> He was a mortal of the careless kind,
>   With no great love for learning, or the learn'd,
> Who chose to go where'er he had a mind,
>   And never dream'd his lady was concern'd;
> The world, as usual, wickedly inclined
>   To see a kingdom or a house o'erturned,
> Whisper'd he had a mistress, some said *two*,
> But for domestic quarrels *one* will do.

This is how it ends.

> Don Jóse and the Donna Inez led
>   For some time an unhappy sort of life,
> Wishing each other, not divorced, but dead;
>   They lived respectably as man and wife,
> Their conduct was exceedingly well-bred,
>   And gave no outward signs of inward strife,
> Until at length the smother'd fire broke out,
> And put the business past all kind of doubt.

'But that's not the truth, either,' Eric Watson went on. 'It is evident he nourished a hope – even stronger towards the end of his life – that she would put a time limit on the punishment and that sometime they would be able to live respectably and age together.

'I have, of course, a theory about Lady Byron,' said Eric Watson. 'But it's just as biased. So you're the only one I'm going to tell it to.' He looked at the girl Brenda, who had suddenly come back and was now gathering the barmaid's hands in hers and squeezing them, the artificial emerald spattering grass-green reflections over the zinc. She stood on tiptoe, her heels shimmering pink and symmetrical through the holes in her stockings.

'I have a theory, but I don't know whether I can evaluate it.

'As with all new circumstances, this little Byron marriage probably limped along. As is usual, both parties had terrifying glimpses into an alien soul. What is incredible, what is miraculous about all tendencies, passion or tender goodwill, is that this offers deferment. You have the terrifying glimpse into an alien psyche and allow it to rest. Let it snow, thaw and snow again. Then that's how it would probably have gone on if the couple's poor finances had not forced Byron to wind up their residence in Piccadilly, and Lady Byron to go back to her parents with their month-old child Ada, to wait until he was ready.

'She left one cold morning, sent a tender letter on the way and yet another on her arrival, which occurred in time for dinner the next day.

'But what was it they really sat and talked about at that dinner table – that splendid Milbanke family? I have a theory. I think Annabella made a slip of the tongue and took her mother into her confidence. I think it was like this: Annabella offered a couple of light-hearted confidences and was totally bewildered when her mother suddenly responded by shrieking *You must never go back to that man!* I think it was like this – '

The newly fledged mother drank a couple of glasses of champagne too much to calm herself after the journey. She suddenly confused jargons. It is childish to use the wrong jargon in the wrong company, but she was not much more than a child. She started expressing herself in London style, letting drop some audacious slippery Byron-formulations. Ah me! – in London she had little success with such things. There they found her stern and prudish. But nonetheless this had become part of her and it seemed natural to give her parents some idea that she had changed – roughly like paying the interest on a loan. Perhaps like a hallucination, she imagined her parents were two contemporaries (that belief is also childish) and, misled by their confidence, she allowed the whole of her youth to swarm into it.

Suddenly she saw what was in front of her – knife, fork, table-napkin, remains of food – rear up at her face. At the same time, she heard someone giggle, felt her body strain with laughter like spewing mild milk, and found herself supported by Mama's and Papa's arms over to the sofa and *there* – wonderfully indolent, her hand on her lap – she spoke to her mother in a way that offended that woman's most profound images of her. For a few minutes, not a single one of the household's safety rules were observed, all safety catches off. She told them about a few interiors from an artistic marriage – she must have appeared proud of her experiences – the devil's wife. Poor Annabella – too prudish in London, too sinful for Mama.

A very controlled person can do nothing but take revenge if someone has done something causing her suddenly to overflow. Like a pan of porridge pouring over the stove and continuing in slimy garlands down towards the floor, Lady Byron received a shock and feebly tried to clean up around her. Drunk and indecent, she was, and forced to think quickly, for there was Mama with the child in her arms, delivering two alternatives:

One was Byron's way. That entailed all kinds of risks and no certainties, an attack on her person and ideas of faith. Worst of all, he who made her abandon all customary rules and guarantees, himself guaranteed nothing in return. She would be wholly at the mercy of herself.

The other way was her self-respect, her inviolability, the childhood way, predictable and safe.

A young mother. An old daughter must have guarantees.

Byron was her only love.

She loved him and would never be parted from him. But she couldn't live with him, and in revenge because she couldn't, she divorced him in a way that indissolubly bound him to wonder. No explanations, no quarrels, no solution, just abrupt absence – they never saw each other alive again. He could never forget, or be unmoved by her, or lukewarm. She bound him to her much more

231

firmly than she could have done if they had gone on living together. She reckoned that out. After submitting herself to her decision, half against her will, she found one could bind someone's thoughts more securely with one's absence than with one's presence.

*

Shortly after this, Mrs Lisbeth became Mr Cohn's friend instead, in all decency and quite platonically. (That expression is misleading. There was no question of love and, as friendship, it was not platonic.) She became his Thursday wine-friend. That became most Thursdays, in the afternoon when not so many people came into the shop and they could talk about wine. That was the day and the time when there were fewest customers: in the autumn darkness they could light a cellar candle and taste deliveries.

Outside the cave of his office, where it smelt of mice and kidneys, the bottles glimmered upright in the shop and horizontal in the store. Outside the house, the street sloped gently. Outside the built-up area, Nottinghamshire swept in wave after wave beneath the mist – earthly graphics – ditches and pastures. Numerous pit villages: around pit-cages and slag heaps, rows of miners' houses, never-ending, ugly, like a queue of refugees, said Mrs Lisbeth.

Mr Cohn filled in a pile of forms and listened to her. As she talked about her admired D. H. Lawrence, he transferred completed forms from one pile to the other, his mind at the same time occupied by something else: he was listening to Mrs Lisbeth's careful English and translating some words back into German. He also did that kind of thing when he read translated books, extracting small bits of the translation and raking out the original from underneath. Then for a while he switched his dark eyes back and forth between translation and original. He was almost inscrutable to himself. A young couple, said Mrs Lisbeth (*ein Pärchen*), the great danger of love (*die Lebensgefahr der Liebe*) and an almost artificial pot-plant (*von einer fast nachgemachten Topfblume*).

Outside, the mining villages and rolling countryside under the sunken vault of the mist. The roads run between hedges, small square cars driving hither and thither across them, eating up distance and binding it all together, all of it.

A bottle glimmered, upright here, horizontal there, and Mr Cohn's office was a cupboard in which a discarded armchair and a footstool constituted comfort, and a telephone, a table and a desk-stool represented usefulness. When Mrs Lisbeth sat down in the armchair for the first time, the broken springs said boiinngg and stuck their tops into her bottom, at which Mr Cohn flushed right down to his stomach.

It all began one appalling Thursday when the sun had apparently never risen and the wind was driving the icy mist ahead of it. He was trying to stocktake between customers and could hardly bring himself to be polite when people came in with slush on their boots. Each one made roughly the same meteorological remark. The people were chilled and weary, like himself, and he detested it when they came in and disturbed him, bringing with them cold temperatures and slush on their boots. The other work, work Mr Cohn had done until ten years ago, had often demanded a brusque tone of voice and a dismissive manner. He missed that sometimes now, as his right.

Outside in the street, Mrs Lisbeth was trudging back and forth with harassed steps, although it was obvious she was trying to break her own indecisiveness, not the time.

The first time he noticed her was when she came out of the baker's and clumped a few turns up and down in front of his shop window. When she caught his eye through the streaks of rain, she ran straight across the street into the grocer's shop and soon emerged again with a small parcel (Stilton, Mr Cohn presumed, as he had heard her confess to her insatiability when it came to that type). She took her cheese for a walk. He began – almost reluctantly – to keep an eye on her with some inkling of what was to come. She took a trip to the greengrocer's and came out again, puzzled by her purchase: a cabbage apparently as heavy as lead. Then she set off again, bareheaded, shooting looks in Mr Cohn's direction.

He was wishing something nice would happen to him today. But he also knew that days proceed in consensus with yourself – the day you get a pleasant letter, you get several. The day you put your foot in the chamberpot and get burnt porridge at breakfast is also a day for abstract spiritual pain.

It's this business of mining districts. Some days, the shirts come in off the clothes-line with streaks of dirt from top to bottom. Days like that cause dust which – as he tried to remove it as he was doing now – collects into greasy spheres which can't be gathered into a handy pile of dirt but smear over the wiped surface. Poor Mrs Lisbeth came out of one entrance with a cotton reel in her hand, looked in confusion at it and put into her pocket. Then she carried out some reloading manoeuvres with the cabbage, a packet of tobacco, the bread, the little parcel of cheese and a few other things, and steered her way here, there, nowhere before venturing into the wine merchant's.

He climbed down the ladder as she came in. He listened, immediately filtering out the clumsy remarks she made with the intention of arriving at the state of confession to which her dispirited wanderings had brought her. Have you anything that makes me *forget*, she blared. Mister Cohn, you could have *warned* me! she thundered. I wish him in *hell*, she rumbled. Plus other clods of clumsy remarks Mr Cohn's ears chose to filter out. He didn't like it when people shrieked and flung out coarse words, especially when it came to women, whose shallow voices try to be deep, but only rage superficially. It sounds so silly when great rage tries to act itself. He retreated a step up the ladder and watched her face, now quite pale with embarrassment as she kept on wailing. 'Be quiet!' he said. Her face was wet and grey with rain and at that moment possessed as little control as a tooth is able to wrinkle its skin. 'Be quiet!' he said. He was feeling sorry for her, not because she felt betrayed in love, but because she had lost control over herself in the first place. If you do that, you also have to be secretive and proud, Mr Cohn thought, and as his thoughts continued, they came upon Eric Watson once saying '*words* were like *the dog*', friendships. He thought about friendships and about this appalling woman, standing there rooted to the floor in order to breathe in a whole mass of air that did not belong to her!

Then the wind turned, a smattering of rain against his windows.

Mr Cohn felt the tears rising in his eyes and turned scarlet, like an English face beneath its dignified mask: 'Be quiet!' he cried. 'This is incredible! Who do you think you are! What a tone of voice to use! You come here from somewhere else and demand that *you* should be warned about close friends almost the first time you appear. For that matter, it was certainly too late to warn you the very first time I spoke to you, because it was already all too obvious what you had in mind. You were in such an inexplicable hurry to do what you're now regretting. Why do it if you're going to regret it, and why – at your age – force yourself on to complete strangers with your "regret" if you simply had to do it. No one had time to give you a word of warning, even if they'd been interested in saving you. Why should anyone want to save you? You've been shameless. Why warn a woman who is only too willing to lie on her back and part her legs for a man with nothing to lose if he makes the most of the opportunity? Why should I warn you, an undiscriminating woman I don't know, against a friend I have known for decades? You're supposed to be a woman of the world, yet you're so naive, you immediately fall for a man with the most obvious charm, whom every schoolgirl in the district for the last twenty years has fallen for. So naive! You should be ashamed of yourself. If you were even slightly a woman of the world, then you should save what can be saved and in secret enjoy the details of this adventure of yours you haven't yet made public. It's loathsome to see a grown woman being dragged around by her emotions, then running here and babbling and blubbing, you're incredible, first you want to be warned and then you want to be consoled for your stupidity. You infuriate me. And what about my feelings . . . ?'

At that moment a customer came in. He was not naive. One glance at the situation – which he probably misinterpreted in one or several ways – made him turn his back and look at them indirectly through reflections in bottles. Mr Cohn had unconsciously climbed the ladder again. He knew the customer had heard the end of the harangue, though not how much. The corner of the man's eye was fixed somewhere between him and Mrs Lisbeth, whose serpentine strands of hair now had *mouths* of rivers funnelling channels of water over her coat. It had become very quiet. The customer croaked discreetly, pointing to his throat, then to a bottle of rum. That was discreet. Discreet. Mr Cohn got down the ladder. Mrs Lisbeth let out the 'muffled sound' expected of her and ran out.

Half an hour later, she was back again. 'I really wanted four bottles of Bordeaux,' she muttered. Her gaze on him was considering full hostilities, but she seemed to realise that would have been too childish. Instead she started listing the desirable qualities in the wine.

'Are you trying to impress me?' he said sourly. 'If that's what you want,' she said, 'then my brother is coming to stay with us and he had vineyards in Franken, if you must know!' 'Frankenwein ist Krankenwein,' said Mr Cohn, then went on: 'I presume he's called *Horst* and weighs fifteen stone and has a square head!' (When

235

Englishmen once let down their barriers, there is absolutely no stopping them.) 'Lend me a basket,' she cried furiously. 'I damned well can't carry everything!'

Then the brother came. And left. A small man with black hair and a patch over one eye, stiff-legged from a bullet wound. Mr Cohn was ashamed. He was always prepared to be ashamed and he was ashamed all the week Mrs Lisbeth was in Ireland with her brother, who had gone there to introduce the German discovery of fish sausages (Eric Watson maintained).

He was so ashamed of his words about the crippled brother, he felt obliged to be almost amiable to her on her return. In itself, he couldn't make out what drew her to his shop time and time again. If she as much as caught sight of him, she came rushing in to exchange a few words about the sun and wind. There was neither need nor reason for such visits. The first time she came in to show him her new Irish tweed coat, a rust-red ulster which in her stupid unreserved way she had to show was 'reversible. Look at the quality and look at this emerald-green moss-green colour, isn't it *beautiful!*' He was weighing or measuring something.

'And what did you think of the country and the people?' he asked indifferently as he measured out the next portion. She sat down, uninvited. 'They're still waiting for the man from Spain, though they have De Valera nowadays,' she said with an important expression, as if she'd just served up the entrée at a large meal. When he didn't react at all, she tried listening to what she herself had said, and her face split into that huge smile which showed her pharynx and always reminded him of a dark-red glass cave. 'Did you hear what I said?' she said. 'It sounded like a password: they're-still-waiting-for-the-man-from-Spain . . .'

'It is a password,' replied Mr Cohn, even more dryly. 'For those who know it. It sounds like a password for those who don't know it.' He went on weighing and measuring. Muttered: 'The Irish are not particularly coherent in their wishes. For a while they thought it was a man from Corsica who was their Spaniard. Half of their precious treasury of song from "the Middle Ages" consists, as far as I know, of tributes to Bonaparte. And now some of them have decided that a gentleman from Linz (whom you know very well) will save them – is it from there he will be coming? – your Austrian, for they say he isn't

German. Thank goodness, for I myself love German culture, as you will understand!'

'Thank you,' she said, closing her cave and turning pale. Mr Cohn weighed and measured, weighed and measured, sneaking a look at her. After all, it's voluptuous to flatten the smile of an undesired woman into a thin line. Though it hurt him somewhere, because there was a promising glimpse between that smile and line. He wanted to apologise, but she forestalled him by mumbling, 'You've more prejudices than I have.' Then she raised her eyes and stared at Mr Cohn's face as if he'd been a miniature and she were shortsighted. She imprinted him. He felt imprinted. His heart fluttered.

Every course of events has a number of elements that create literary gaps in the novel that is being written at this moment. And in a gap of that kind, Mrs Lisbeth and Mr Cohn began to sip wine from small glass cups, entrenched in his little office cave, where at most a ragged feather might contemplate the idea of violating Mrs Lisbeth.

He told her about a company in the textile trade where he had been head clerk before it went bust, and he told her how in his youthful innocence, he had ordered – and been given – Sauternes and pork sausage at a spa on the north coast of France. She told him about teachers at the girls' school she'd been at. She told him about the Australian climate, which he couldn't imagine. She said Australia was a continent entirely without culture but with great vitality. Mr Cohn replied that if she thought she had said something contradictory then she was wrong. Then she told him about her father's vineyards. And her brother's. And about some wonderful mountains just south of the Dolomites. And Greek mountains and the Massif Central. They found they both had the same childish taste in Wine. They wanted it light and fruity and with sweetness. Neither of them understood the terribly costly dark château wines praised by the experts. She said – but one can only enjoy a lack of education when one is sufficiently well educated to understand that . . .

The day before Christmas Eve, she brought some iced fruit cake her mother had sent her from Germany. Mr Cohn took down a bottle whose contents reminded him of what the man in Deauville or Trouville had cheated him with. She smelt it. It was an act of friendship – they looked in each other's eyes and appraised the symbol, not too much, not too little. Quietly, he twisted wine out of the bottle, an almost arrack-yellow liquid swimming up in the glasses. It didn't taste at all bad taken with the cake. He had no weakness for sweet things, but it didn't taste at all bad.

She was a sloppy woman. When they finished their slices of cake, she smoothed out the crumby greasy paper she had brought them in. She smoothed it out and rustled it and munched and went on talking about something else. But then she turned it over and pushed it over to Mr Cohn. He looked at it and started searching for his spectacles.

'It's Byron's voice,' she said.

'It's his own voice,' she said.

He found his spectacles and at once recognised the voice, the voice of a conqueror, though one obedient and willing to learn.

'I found them yesterday and they are so full of charm,' said Mrs Lisbeth. 'Have you ever thought, Mr Cohn, that his own voice says more about him than all the analyses? Look here, and here. I began to think about everything you will soon be telling people on his birthday. But they won't know what his voice was like. And if they don't know that, they won't understand why he was loved, why you devote so much time and trouble to him. If people could hear these letters, they would understand his voice.' Mrs Lisbeth went to the lavatory. She was four months pregnant. She hadn't known that when she'd first met Eric Watson. Though she had known since – meanwhile. Mr Cohn couldn't bring himself to be indignant. In some way she was too clumsy to be rebuked.

The letters were from the autumn of 1813. Byron was staying in the country with Webster, his school-friend. He had fallen in love with the latter's wife and reported day by day to his confidante, Lady Melbourne. It was Lady Melbourne who was told everything about everything. Her kindly understanding was the protected corner in Byron's life.

(faun unveiling
a woman)

Let's go to the opera together, then you'll see my wife *weep*, said the
madman, looking as if he were offering a swig from the Holy Grail.
She was tall, fair and rather too Germanic for my liking, when I was
finally allowed to fix my eyes on her. Hohenzollern or Sachsen-
Coburg lower lip, but it wasn't at the opera but in the country, at their
home, to which he had invited me without further ado, despite the fact
that to all appearances I got on his nerves.

We sit there, round mealtime paraphernalia, her sister, her husband
(my old friend) and me. *He* wants to pair me off with the sister, whom
he lusts after. The sister was only too apparent.

When we met She was cool. Her expression told me she knew what
kind of person I was – She said so aloud, for that matter – quite a
number of hints. I didn't think she liked me at all. But by God, she
became more and more talkative and confidential, her husband more
and more despondent. Apart from the sister and me, they have two
guests in the house, a Mr W, very handsome but stupid, and a Mr A, as
ugly as sin but entertaining. The whole company went on a carriage
outing but I declined. Carriage parties should be duets, and sitting
bouncing between two or more of your acquaintances is unendurable.
He started harbouring suspicions because of her and my nonchalance
towards each other. Now he suspects our friendliness. Why does he
harbour suspicions at all? It must be something about the way she
behaves to him when they're alone. Women with something else on
their minds are suddenly different in moments of passion. They are
more indifferent or exaggeratedly ardent, as if while weeping they
were wringing out a cloth behind your back. Now he's angry about my

239

Italian books (Dante and Alfieri and other similarly harmless authors) and is demanding that *sa femme* shouldn't see them – for, by God, this is a language that does great damage!

When I asked him about a mutual acquaintance, he exclaimed: do you ask mutual acquaintances about my wife when you talk to them? I've never known anything like it. My virtue seems to be quite wasted here, as is hers, for I've not seen a single sign in her that would encourage my less good self. She's pretty in her way, but not for the life of me can I imagine anything inappropriate behind that pure forehead. I myself am consequently equally pure, as it would never occur to me to make a thrust forward without being met beforehand, so to speak, half way. She collaborates much more with her other two guests, but then it is me and my nonchalance he suspects. Or friendliness . . . He must have haemorrhoids in his imagination and a mania for scratching them, for he is absolutely determined that I shall stay, although my presence gets on his nerves.

In accordance with the pattern-making of his imagination, my host has become more and more unpleasant to me and in that way brings about what would otherwise have been avoided: his spouse compensates by being more and more friendly. Let us call her Ph. I am in love again . . . and if I'm to have confidence in words – for we've hitherto stopped at the verbal – she is a participating party . . . The place for our great declaration was a billiard room! I did not fall to my knees in the middle of the room, but made a speech instead. Just beforehand, we had slid into very friendly tones and she had asked the question 'how a woman who likes a man can get him to realise that, when he himself hasn't discovered it'.

We went on playing billiards without scoring, I presuming that as my thoughts were not entirely occupied by this distraction, then neither were hers. Not entirely, but fairly pleased with my progress, I then did a very incautious thing – with pen and paper – in tender and moderately well formulated prose (no poetry, not even when I'm serious) and here there was indeed some risk: first how do you convey it and then how will it be received. However, it was received and was deposited not far from the heart I wished it to reach – then, who should choose *just* that moment to make an entrance if not *just* that person who ought to be in the Red Sea if Satan had any manners at all – but she kept a straight face and kept the paper and I kept up appearances as best I could.

Here is a risk. Everything would be lost should I have failed. But there is so much more to gain should she be receptive, and one always takes great risks to have something worth having. My note blossomed – more than that. My (I've just been interrupted by il Marito and am writing this just opposite to him – he has come with a political pamphlet he wants me to decipher and applaud – I'll content myself with the latter, ah, now he's gone again) note produced an *answer* – very decorous, by the way – though rather too much about virtue and the deepening of affection into some kind of ethereal process in which primarily the soul is involved, which I don't understand particularly well as I am a useless metaphysician – but generally it all begins and ends in platonism, and as my new proselyte is twenty, there's plenty of time for materialisation.

Anyhow, I hope that this spiritual system won't last long, and whatever happens I must be bold enough to carry out an experiment. I remember that my previous case was the other way round: 'first we fought, then we produced explanations'. Well, that's the state of things at present – an abundance of mutual goodwill, masses of melancholy – which unfortunately I have to say aroused 'the Moor's' attention, and as many conditions of tenderness that time, place and circumstances allow.

This is all Webster's own fault. If only he didn't despise his wife and run after every little country girl he lays eyes on, and on top of that boast about his little conquests, then he wouldn't be surprised if others value what is too good for him.

In addition, he has quite literally provoked me to such a pass by exercising something that is not at all unlike brusque coercion – indirectly, of course – but quite clearly. He was namely going to do this or going to do that should any man dare etc. etc. etc., while at the same time every woman is expecting him to assert his interest in her and be guilty of 'a misappropriation'. Oh, dear me, just who is this extraordinary monopolist? It really is remarkable that when it comes to other subjects, he is like other people, but in this area he really seems obsessed. I am not considering quarrelling with him if that can be avoided, but a couple of his statements have turned my heart's blood black and made the honey of my mind crystallise.

P.S. It is six o'clock. This story risks becoming serious and I think the platonic is in danger. We have almost had a scene, almost hysterical and truly without reason, for I behaved (for me) almost annoyingly with great decorum – her way of expressing herself surprised me, so young and so cool she had at first seemed. But all this illusory stuff must come to an end, as such things usually do, and that would already have happened had the opportunity not been lacking. Had anyone entered in the middle of tears and accompanying consolation, everything would have been spoilt. We must be more careful, or alternatively less tear-soaked.

P.S. number two: It's ten o'clock. I'm writing after just having evaded an orgy of red wine and rhetoric about God knows which pamphlet that idiot was aiming at. My host is a strange gentleman . . . he has just made a suggestion to me: a bet, that he puts a given sum on that he manages to win whatever woman the challenger suggests. Any woman. Thus he is offering rivalry with anyone of the male sex, including friends and acquaintances present here. I declined from humble respect for him and the rest of the company. Isn't this the perfect comedy?

Newstead Abbey, October 10th

I am writing to you from my ancestors' melancholy residence, where you find me equally grey and dismal as the first deceased among them. I loathe the thought of what is irretrievable and am not going to be emotional now. Webster came with me here alone and is now sitting opposite me, and between us are red and white champagne, Burgundy, two kinds of Bordeaux and lighter wines, all relics of the cellar of my youth, which is still quite formidable in quantity and in excellent order. But I leave the wine to him, preferring a sober conversation with you. Ah, if only you knew what a quiet Mussulman (apart from the wine) life I once lived here. But don't let us think about that. Yesterday I sent you a long letter and now I must revert to the same subject uppermost in my mind. At the beginning of last week a change occurred in my desires, my hopes, my perception – my everything – and it will all provide you with new evidence of my weakness. My guest (ex- host) has just congratulated himself on possessing a partner with *passion*. I don't know and cannot yet say with any certainty, but I have never before seen more definite preliminary symptoms.

I am inclined to take people at their word when I receive an answer. If she is faint-hearted, I can never extract better evidence of its condition than what her own admissions provide. Instead of exercising pressure, I told her I wanted to be hers on her own conditions. I said this without any incisiveness and think she first took it all with calm and seriousness, but in the middle of our mutual declarations, or – to use her expression – 'more than mutual', she collapsed into painful tears and this at a time and in a place which made it all very dangerous for us both. Her sister was in the next room and nor was Webster far away.

Naturally I said and did what for the moment was appropriate, and we fortunately restored the sunshine in time to stop anyone observing the clouds darkening our horizon. She says she is sure my declaration of love came exclusively because I first noticed *her* inclination. As I mentioned to you earlier, I have no expectations or observations whatsoever in that way. (Oh, that one could show a beloved creature the speculative gossip one writes about her to one's understanding Friend.) Her behaviour when we are together with the others is as official and cool as before. No less successful is she in giving me a note and herself receiving one, plus a ring, more or less under Webster's nose, without his seeing it! And yet she is cleverly pious, says her prayers morning and night, as well as taking measurements for a new bible every three months. The only worrying thing is Webster's complaints about her aversions when it comes to participating in his interest in increasing the population – if this is her inflexible maxim I will have striven in vain. But I think her looks at me, her way of changing colour, her trembling hands and, most of all, her devotion, all speak another language. Between the one and the other, my mind is in a state of chaotic inactivity, but you won't pity me and I deserve no compassion – has there ever existed a worse slave to impulses than your admiring friend?

But I cannot live without someone to love. You probably laugh at my eternal changes, but just think about the circumstances that broke off my last three amours, and then you'll find that you can't really blame their ends on whims.

Newstead Abbey, October 17th
The whole company has come here, and now to my report.

But first I must say I'm feeling rather ill as a result of my stupidity last night. Around midnight, after drinking deeply and sleepily, I took it into my head that I should empty my skull-goblet *in one draught* – it holds pretty well a whole bottle of Bordeaux – and then almost died Alexander's death, something I shall do with pleasure the day I have made his conquests. Sufficient sense remained with me that I realised that I was in no state to join the ladies, and went to bed – where Fletcher tells me I first had convulsions and then lay so immobile that he thought 'Goodnight Marmion'. I don't understand how I could consider doing such a foolish thing, but I think that one of my guests was boasting and 'company, bad company became my ruin'. I generally loathe drinking and apologise for this excess and will not be *able* to do so any more. Back to my theme. You are right, I have been much too sanguine – as far as the *solution* is concerned – but listen:

One day when we were left entirely on our own was almost fatal. Another victory like that and Pyrrhus would have been lost. This is what happened: 'I'm wholly and fully at your mercy – I admit it – I give myself to you – I am not *cold* – whatever others may think – but I know I won't be able to endure the thought afterwards – don't think that these are just words – I am telling the truth – do as you have to now.' Did I do wrong? I spared her. There was something so tremendously strange in her manner – a kind of gentle determination – no scenes – not even a struggle, but I still don't know what it was that convinced me that she was serious – it wasn't that little 'no' that I've heard forty times and always in the same tone of voice – but her *tone* and her expression, and yet I sacrificed a great deal; it was two in the morning – be off; the devil whispered that it was only words etc. etc., but I don't know if I ought to change my mind. She seemed so very grateful for my patience – evidence after all that she was not acting the usual chaste hesitation which can be so tiresome on occasions such as these.

You ask if I can consider going to any lengths. If by 'to any lengths' you mean duel and divorce, I have to answer yes. I love her – if I hadn't done and in addition very much, I would have been more selfish on the occasion I've just described. I have offered to go away with her and she has replied that she is refusing 'for my sake'. Meanwhile everyone is as unhappy as is possible – *he* quarrels because of unfounded melancholy. The sister is suspicious, but rather amused, the friend in the house also suspicious (I don't know why) and not at all amused – Il Marito, full of motivated but unthinking jealousy, building up a martial physiognomy – strolling with an ally, swearing at all the servants – preaching to both sisters and purchasing sheep. But he doesn't leave her side now, so we are beside ourselves. I am very feverish, restless and silent, a condition which seems to be the mute agreement of all, by the way – briefly, I cannot predict anything and perhaps it will all end in nothingness.

So here we have half a dozen people all in a great brown study, and two, if not three, finding themselves in a state of great confusion, and as far as I can judge we must continue in this way. She doesn't *live* with him and nor does she want to, and they have been 'separated' for a long time, so I am not responsible for anything in that sense. Poor girl. She is either the most sophisticated person of that age I have ever met, or the least. She *agrees to* so much and constantly says: 'rather than you should be angry' or 'rather than you should like someone else, I'll do as you wish'. She delivers herself over or seems to deliver herself so completely over to my instructions in all respects that it quite disarms me, but I really am unhappy over the constant conflict within myself. Her health is so poor – she is thin and pale and seems to have quite lost her appetite, that I doubt she will exist much longer. That's also her own opinion, but these fantasies are on the other hand common to everyone who is not particularly happy.

If only she were my wife, or if there were possibilities for the future, our first refuge would be a warm climate where she could recover. What is most bewildering – and yet I cannot bring myself to stop them – are her caresses. They seem completely childish and, I think, innocent, but they astonish the Scipio in me and *I* limit myself to the praiseworthy part of these testimonies of affection. What a hellish situation I have got myself into. *Potiphar* asked me a foolish question the other evening and I answered it by saying I admired the *sister* more, and what does he do if not tell her that, and his wife, too – who rather too suddenly asked if he was *mad*, which started off a lecture on that a man shouldn't be asked the question of whether he were mad just because he said that his wife's sister was a beautiful woman: he continued on this subject for his customary spell of time. I hope he got a sore throat.

I am trying to remember a quotation (Mme de Staël quoted it, I think) from some Teutonic sophist on architecture. 'Architecture,' says this Macaronico Tedescho, 'reminds me of frozen music.'

The end of our youth

(And this is Mr Cohn's last contribution:)

Augusta has got off the train, thinking about her own attempts as marriage counsellor, encouraging girls with private incomes to put themselves out slightly for poor B. Happy young women with city sense, who could have laughed off his stupidities instead of weighing them up as Annabella had, investigating them and setting about reforms. Cheerful, clever girls, who had been friends of Annabella's from the start and would have known how to deal with him.

What a stupid little misfortune their meeting had been. Married people must be separate people (Augusta considers), not a rock to which a yellow horned poppy (is that the kind of thing she's thinking about?) fastens. What a misfortune that her B, not at all suited to marriage as the *Bible* ordained, found himself with a poppy. Or a rock.

Augusta is now on firm ground, but her body is still responding to the shaking of the train more violently than when she was on it. She fumbles beneath hat and veil up to her forehead, but where skin should have met skin there is a barrier of glove-leather. The semi-blind smile comes back. The spot of sunlight. She lifts her wrist to her left eye, the best one, and sees three small leather buttons she can't undo on her own. Resignation swiftly descends, is always there. A submission. It takes a long time to ask for help. Sometimes she thinks about her relatives, who would mourn their own deaths if they knew, and they knew this was her position without them.

Modestly she lifts the same hand once again. Perhaps after all the fever can be felt through leather. She remarks that she has had a touch

247

of the ague. For the man standing nearest to her, it sounds as if she had said 'mmmi, mmmmi'. Don't mutter. Said poor B. I wish you'd learn to speak clearly and speak out. How can you ever get what you want if no one knows what you're saying!

They were in his carriage. Uphill, downhill, round corners of Nottinghamshire beneath its thin cover of melting night frost resembling silk with small ripples of wind billowing below it. They swung round a cliff with a diadem of pines, a farm where they saw bullocks peacefully butting each other, and then the road had given way to thousand-year-old oaks, split in two and hollow, but alive.

They had already been through the city of Nottingham and stopped at various places for him to demonstrate his history. The house where he had lived as a child. The road from the inn to the quack where they had sought correction for his foot.

With long fingers, he described the city's attempts to climb out of its depressed hollow and raise chimneys through the fog. Another child drew its heel along the inside of Augusta's stomach, she following it with three fingers. He lectured on. I and the Mater lived in those oppressive small rooms. The maid was always drunk. The spiders in the ceiling were the primaeval spiders of the district, gigantic mothers of everything with eight legs. It always smelt of cabbage. Though I like cabbage, and the smell. I even wore underclothes – you laugh – and had toothbrushes and tooth-powder, for I was equipping myself for the future. The more ignorant and naked one is under one's clothes, the more one lives in the present, Augusta! We even tried to cure a disability which for someone really poor could have been a welcome source of income.

The city really did make great efforts to climb out of its hollow by driving brick chimneys up through the fog, the landscape the huge robber forest. She was naturally more impatient than he was. She wanted them to go on. She leant against him, but he went on peering back into time, silently, thinking or not thinking, with a dog-like ability to let time pass: without thinking, but as if he were thinking, without seeing, but as if he were looking. The stillness in this was deceptive. He was listless with all the vehemence of one who is active.

They talked about no longer knowing anyone in Nottingham. Augusta knew no one in the country towns and everyone lived either in London or in the country. 'Well, what can one do here *pour s'amuser,*' she sighed. He felt to see if her hand were still in his, and squeezed it. Nottingham fought its way up into the January light. 'Stockings!' he exclaimed. 'You certainly know nothing about anything except family news.' The carriage wheels clattered as paved streets gave way to wet gravel, and he turned his hand over in hers with that tender relish he devoted to her ignorance and achieved the small brother-sister kisses in the curve of the palm as he polished her thumb with his.

Then she remembered a story about weavers in Nottingham who destroyed their looms, or possibly someone else's looms. And police, or troops, had been called out for that reason. It had happened here, hadn't it? But a long time ago. Or two or three years ago? Or a year? It had also been political in some way. As Byron rubbed her thumb, he was rubbing images into view: what was political was a law on the punishment of weavers, and her B had personally opposed that law in the House of Lords, delivered a fiery speech about poor lords, or weavers, and those who heard him said he was a real Demesth . . . er . . . Demeter? That he had spoken well, and that he had gripped his audience, entertained it, and that he was an idiot. Out of this compôte of thumbs now rose the word 'Luddite'. One of her other brothers had talked about rebellious rabble and certain people encouraging the rabble to fight against all progress and machines which are good for *them*, and for *costs* and *production*, and for '*us*'. Into the bargain came a formula she now opened her mouth and uttered:

'You can't halt development, dearest B.'

'Why not?' he said almost simultaneously, then added suspiciously: 'Who says so?'

'Well . . . everyone, our dear Percy.'

'Good, good. You could never have thought up such hollow drivel yourself. As far as you're concerned, you could halt *time* without noticing it. So you're on *my* side, don't forget. If Percy says you can't halt development, that's because he thinks he steers it. That statement always comes from people who think they steer development.'

She shrugged her shoulders, her back resisting the direction in which they were travelling – it was very noticeable that Nottingham-shire was leaning up against its interior. The ground crackled beneath the wheels from scattered acorns. The cook's boy had taught her to play cocks with the acorn-holders. He taught them to lengthen the tip with seed-cases of ash. Beech-cocks. She hoped the fourth child would be a boy. That would please poor Leigh. She traced her finger over the boy's heel inside her.

*

So in every course of events there are elements that are chronologically real but which become voids in a literary context, and so we shall resist going deeper into the quiet sober tasting of wines that came to create the foundation of Mr Cohn's and Mrs Lisbeth's equally moderate friendship.

Let us simply mark time by mentioning that one Thursday Mr Cohn talked about different ways he had seen of drying hay. He maintained you can get to know the popular culture of countries and rural areas by observing their way of drying hay. In certain counties they raised haycocks like Hungarian bee-hives, in others you could find emaciated sugar loaves. In France they naturally had stern and hard-packed racks, in Bavaria huge boastful stacks. In mountainous districts they spread their hay sparsely over forked gables. The longest he had seen had been in Norway, where nothing less than a precipice sets the limits. Between mountain and fjord, pastures were striped golden with long drying racks. Mr Cohn said something about 'gathering together and spreading out'.

Another Thursday he asked her to describe in detail an opera performance he wished he could have seen himself. He loved *Don Carlos*, but had never seen it performed on stage. 'When I was young,' he said, 'it was nothing but Mozart and Wagner. The Italians were too beautiful and emotional for my taste. Unfortunately, you don't learn to appreciate emotions until you're old and easily moved to tears. Do you understand modern music, Mrs Lisbeth? I mean music of this century. I think it heaves and sprawls, then chops off its head and kicks it ahead of it. Or hangs itself to death on a barbed wire fence. I can't believe what is ugly cuts any deeper than what is beautiful. Don't you think?'

On a third Thursday, they tried to describe to each other how their respective home towns had been affected by the runaway economy after the war. Mr Cohn revealed – and even after all these years he couldn't control the shame of what had happened to him – what it had been like to be unemployed at the age of thirty-eight, with three young children, and dependent on a mother from whom he had distanced himself twenty years earlier. He had felt like a living limb on a dead

250

body. He had worked and grown up in the same firm ever since he had left school; stupidly and desperately he had rooted himself in a cold machine as if it had been his own land. He stopped abruptly, for the shame had turned his cheeks red and his voice thick: 'Don't let's talk about such gloomy things. Everything sorted itself out and we're more secure now than ever before.'

'Yes, let's talk about it. You can't conjure it away with silence. Everything you're afraid of comes one day. What you long for comes only sometimes, but everything you fear comes, not just once, but several times. You *may* encounter the same thing once again,' whispered Mrs Lisbeth, as if a loud voice would tempt out the catastrophe immediately. 'One has to live contentedly. In safety.'

'That's true, Mrs Lisbeth, but you have no children . . . yet,' he corrected himself shyly. 'When you have children, you can't do more than forget the risks of life, either. You can't get rid of risks. Children can even die for you. Everything's very insecure. You know, many young men here were quite apathetic when they became dependent on their poverty-stricken mothers. And the way they had swaggered around with bared arms before! Some of them became vagabonds. You wouldn't believe me if I described the equipment they scrounged to become tramps. Roller-skates and sticks, hooking on to lorries with the handles to go up the hills. Ho ho . . . it sounds like Hollywood. No one will remember now everyone's secure again.'

Mrs Lisbeth brooded.

'They say we women survive catastrophes. They say we never see a pile of useless rubbish, only decent boxes and a floral cloth. So we cut the dirty edges off the cloth and set the table on the box. But I saw a lot who had given up. I was very surprised by the *authorities*. I had always thought authorities lived off the people without giving anything back. Then I saw them organising so that every individual had something to live off, through their solicitude. They were like Jesus in Sunday School – they didn't forget a single lamb, as long as it came bleating. Perhaps I'm telling you wrong again. But that was what I saw, because the solicitude was a *shock* to me.'

One Thursday, Mr Cohn handed over the shop to his younger son, who was staying with them. He found himself seated on the left of Mrs Lisbeth in her old Ford, the back seat removed, sandwich papers on the floor and a strong smell of dog and manure. When he felt

251

something under his seat, he pulled out a blue and grey diagonally striped tie.

Mr Cohn was to show her Newstead Abbey in winter garb. He considered the mansion was at its most suggestive when the trees had lost their leaves and grey mist climbed over the ruin.

Mr Cohn was disappointed. 1938 had already slid into the last week of January. How quickly time consumed an endless year and yet nothing manages to get done. At this year's traditional New Year reception at the Hazells' he had experienced yet another of his childhood echoes, remembering the occasion when he had been the last person they could amuse with an outgrown game. He remembers the vast fruitless labour to extract vanished concentration in friends, who, for the sake of his childishness, had pretended to want to play, while between themselves they grinned and alluded to competing at masturbation and suchlike.

On some occasion on New Year's Eve, what is now called 'the so-called Byron Committee' were standing in a corner toasting each other round a tray-table, the top of which was a relief of a horribly ugly pigeon. Eric Watson simply repeated what he had said to Mr Cohn a few weeks before, that he had grown tired of the project. His statement produced resonances in all the others. Link agreed it seemed pointless to fill in the already coloured picture, and made helpless gestures over an imagined box stuffed with notes on Hobhouse's meeting with 'Byron, Kean, Napoleon and others'.

Mr Hazell said that babblers can be just as puzzling as the silent. Byron had already said everything about himself, but nevertheless remained inaccessible. He said he had tried to describe the Byron–Shelley theme, but it was drowning in Lake Geneva. Rupert said he was drowning in the Missolonghi swamp, partly because his studies in anatomy offered far too much competition. Mr Cohn's eyes caught his at the word 'anatomy' and as they met, Rupert began to remember and gleam, repeating that he would have no objection to making the acquaintance of Byron's anatomy. Suddenly he made a Mark Antony-like speech in favour of exhumation.

'Just as suddenly, the rest of them came to think it was a good idea,' Mr Cohn complained to Mrs Lisbeth. She was a patient woman and didn't interrupt his monologue, which had already begun as she held the car door open for him. They had applied for permission to open

Byron's tomb – by chance it was the second application. The first had come the week before and had arisen from an argument in London on Byron's position in the family tomb. So the matter was settled.

Who was Mr Cohn to resist a passive herd choosing to rush out into the wilderness just because the entrance into the pasture was too narrow for them all at once. The road lapped up dismal wasted light from Mrs Lisbeth's headlights. It wasn't raining, but it was wet.

'Goodness me, then don't,' she said mechanically.

'I'm not afraid,' said Mr Cohn. 'No one believes me when I say I have no fear, but I do have respect. I have an instinct for respect! When something is dead, I give it a look of farewell . . . leave it in peace from me and all seeing eyes. The dead must be left in peace. A corpse as an object of curiosity – mummies, Lenin – is an incomparable barbarity. I just don't even want to imagine the crude minds which think up such primitive things.'

'Are you going to stay at home then?'

'My dear,' replied Mr Cohn jamming his feet in terror against the front as she braked hard for some sheep zig-zagging in front of the car and offendedly looking sideways at them. 'It's not that simple.' (jamming his feet). 'I'm in one of those situations when you regret whatever you choose. You must see that.' (She drove well, but fast.) Then they arrived at the gates, passed the lodge gate cottage and started winding their way up the drive towards the Abbey.

*

They passed a village. Byron looked away when the church where his family tomb had been blasted into the wall came into sight. He disliked seeing his tomb. But Augusta was looking at the squared shapes of the church and an almost doubled-up old man by one wall. With his stick, he was hitting something running around on the ground, then it rose on its hind legs and snapped back.

At last they were on their way together to their Heritage. Great acres of ruined woodlands. From one hillock among hillocks, they surveyed the wastes of scrub and saplings living briefly and pointlessly in order to destroy each other.

It was growth devoured by parasites and harmful insects, choked by dry summers and rotted by wet and yet never ceasing to continue living off its surplus of waste.

253

Stumps of the past still protruded after all those years, overgrown and rounded off by the black moss that corrodes trees to dust. Roots sent out shoots, a felled lime becoming a rattling lime bush, long shoots crowding and splaying away from each other, though all in the same direction, their efforts to reach highest towards light and air weakening each and every one, so none had the strength to branch out, all of them growing wildly from the top until they started dying at the roots.

The thinning achieved in this way still did no good, for the dead branches remained there among the living, choking them or forcing them up into preposterous growth striving up to the sky. Nor was it the right time of year to decide through a carriage window what was alive and what was dead; everything was clinging lifelessly to everything else.

'No, I no longer notice it,' replied Byron. 'I've never seen it any different. Worse, more likely. When I inherited it, everything here was already a fact. No money,' he said, 'ah me!'

He was remembering. 'When I was fifteen, my greatest wish was to be allowed to lie under a tree here with Mary and suck the lobe of her ear. But Mary didn't want to have me. I have to sell it. Now. That's the only solution. To sell the whole lot. Then – abroad! Venezuela!'

Venezuela! Names inspire Byron. Names are loud songs he shouts out aloud in this forest with no forest echo. Forest with no forest, the sound striking directly into the cloud cover. Augusta looked round and found they were going downhill again, the road a velvet ribbon in the clearing's undergrowth. It swung, twisted, then took a turn round the church, thus recalling yet again the last way back for the Byron family. When she thought about the tomb that was filled up just along this road, she told him what ought to be done.

'For *money?*' he said, looking at her with a wickedly pleased expression.

'Yes! It's a brilliant starting point for tenderer feelings & I know just the right lady & you would both gradually experience a richness in the match & won't you consider the matter, dearest B?'

He went on looking at her. Suddenly his eyes seemed to devour themselves, pouring inwards like sludge when pressure in a hole in the earth gives way.

'Now, now, dearest B, be serious. It'd be a solution for all parties, and The One I Am Thinking Of is sufficiently lovely and sufficiently rich and sufficiently easy-going for you to be able to laugh with her & you know that if only you can laugh at the same things then The Tenderer Feeling will come sooner or later.'

'Venezuela!' he cried, and was so inspired that he had to scribble on a piece of paper: the law of gravity is no law. Sometimes the hopeful flyer whose wings have already begun melting is helped by him who has just thrown himself off a cliff.

A last bend, and they came in to the drive up to Newstead Abbey. It was a warm day for January. Wild narcissi in the grass, but only a few, as if scattered from a handful, their gaze the faithful gaze year by year. Held hers, while the mansion unfolded its wings behind.

A sparrow suddenly becomes interesting against the background of a peacock. You are embarrassed by the grandeur and look at the sparrow. Yes, everything was embarrassing and she at once turned very shy. The house was rejecting her, tempting her. Or she was rejecting it, and catching it bit by bit with swift glances. Byron and she driving up the drive. The pupil in the corner of her eye – bit by bit grew into a whole: a grey building, steps hovering in glass oriels, the ruin of the church on the right, the Abbey kitchen on the left, behind it the shadow of yet another darkened wing.

Her shyness was a kind of distance. She presumed the cause of it was the same as the cause of the irony when you first meet someone's boasted-about lover. This was a gloomy, desolate silhouette. She waited, troubled that she might be asked to issue a judgement, but Byron was not in the mood for asking questions. His eyes had filled again, heavy with smile. He was like a child! As soon as he was at his house, he had forgotten how prepared he had been to sell it. His eyes were full of a smile, not full of joy, nor wholly possessive – all light-heartedness gone – the weight of a burden he preferred to bear.

'For money?' he said musingly. 'Is she an ordinary person you're thinking of? I wonder . . . I believe that whatever you undertake in life, you shouldn't do it for passion or for money.'

Augusta frowned and asked him to be serious. He replied that his ideal wife would be Vicar Primrose's wife. 'He chose her on the same principle as she chose her wedding dress; not for its surface gloss, but for its robust qualities'. She asked if he meant the Vicar of Hucknall. A half smile: 'Hm, no. He lives over in Wakefield.' He followed her gaze roaming over the silhouette of the chimneys, black against a bulging spread of golden clouds. The sun glowed through gaps, its rays repeated in their faces, throwing a bucket of light on to the grass, and several daffodils began to open up out of their crêpe pupae.

'As you see, it's a spacious house. I could enter into a marriage of convenience and she could live in one wing with her interests and I in another with mine, then we wouldn't need – ' *Abruptly* the carriage stopped with a double jerk at the steps. He swore as he only just managed to save Augusta, heavy with child, from falling.

That aroused his fury, so in her turn she had to save him from striking and abusing the driver, who sullenly blamed the potholes in the drive, though Augusta had learnt that no excuses helped when this mood of his fended everything off. He was the kind of person who became angrier and angrier from being angry. So she wasn't even allowed to look round on the steps, but he dragged her behind him, making her stumble away from 'the deliberate insults THEY bestow on me . . . THEY hide their grins behind explanations . . . THEY go behind your back!' He hurried her impatiently through the Great Hall where surprised servants looked on as they ran towards the end wall, lame little gentleman and round little doña straight at a cruel wall full of bullet holes – before brusquely turning and shooing her up one lot of stairs, then another and into a little room, where, once inside, he hurled the door shut. The key fell out of the lock on the other side and hit the floor with an innocent little tinkle. Augusta hid her laughter in her muff. He was shouting about all those insults you had to take from people pretending incompetence for the fun of being insolent. Burnt food! Mouldy mattresses! Avalanches of soot when you leant into the fireplace to see why the fire wouldn't burn! Scalding hot water when you put your foot in the bath. Iron marks on your shirtfront and the seat of your trousers: and always *deliberate*, so THEY felt compelled to mock HIM! 'What are you laughing at?' he shouted.

She wiped her eyes on her little muff and tried to *bite* off her gloves. They seemed to be welded on, the tops already bitten, for her hands had been swelling for months. Every new foetus found an appropriate way to deform her differently: this one was pumping out water into its mother's hands and feet. People's ridicule was only another minor bout of the empty scorn nature bestows on us all from the beginning. That was why you were angry, and was this anything to be so angry about? She noticed she had forgotten to unfasten the buttons at her wrist and at last got the gloves off her burning hands. Relieved, the laughter sank back into her and was at peace, dull as unpolished pearls.

'By all means,' she said, continuing to tidy herself up, 'if one can't be cheerful, then . . . but if he'd really meant to offend, he could have shaken us so that the cork had flown out long ago & all their tittle-tattle when you bring your only sister here for the first time and rush her like some infection through the house without even letting her look or greet them & into a windowless room with her. What are they supposed to think?'

She loosened her fur collar and busied herself with her own comfort. In a mirror, she could see a door ajar and his dead mother staring out, rigid-eyed like a pig with rage over a length of wallpaper. You could also see she was screaming, her chin pressed against her throat, emitting what must be a terrible noise. Augusta nodded in greeting. He turned that way then turned away. 'It's not windowless,' he said. There was a knock on the door. Yes, now she could see rips in the curtains. Augusta went across and looked out over the lake. There was a very quiet knock on the door.

They went walking in the park. Here were the only trees, figures detaching themselves from them and running away in the twilight. Augusta touched a place a figure had just left, expecting body warmth, but it was cold wet bark, not a memory. Winter, the calendar said. He picked a stalk of parsley and chewed slowly on it, then spat it out. By the dog's tomb, he picked last summer's flowering rose, and everywhere this year's daffodils were out on short stunted stalks. But neither flowers nor Byron could disperse the brooding greyness in the atmosphere round about.

She touched the skin of it and felt that it lived there and not even the loveliest summer's day could change that. It was not a question of decay, nor of ruin, nor a splinter in her eye she thought – which made the grass grow grey out of the grey soil and gave the narcissi an autumn drowsiness, like dusty bees. An arch above ground, a vein below, she sought a pivot for all this melancholy, looked at his face, looked at the lake.

'Do you want to go for a row?' he said. A small wooden boat lay drawn up by the fort. Creatures rested against tree trunks and ran away as they came closer. Augusta placed herself like one of them under the

257

leafless treetops and tried to measure the circumference of the trunk, but her stomach got in the way. Byron helped her by meeting her hands from the other side. Just what everyone did, and so pleasant to do it for the first time.

They pushed out the boat. It at once began to sweat and take on water. 'Oh, not so bad,' he said. 'We can bail it out. You row and I'll bail.' She took a step towards a board in the middle of the boat and turned round enough to lose her balance and thump down on to it. The oars were to be fixed into oarlocks on the side. Before she had managed to work it out, she helplessly scraped oars against boat while he looked on. He was still standing at the side of the boat, looking on. When she finally understood how to fasten the oars (with a giggle), he put his knee against it and slowly and hesitantly pushed out from the shore, then sat down on the side and started bailing.

Augusta followed the drops with her eyes as they left the scoop and passed through the air in glittering tracks of colour. He looked up. She dipped the oar in like a ladle and moved in various directions to get straight. The boat crashed into the reeds and he stretched out a leg to push it off again. She tried using both oars nearer the surface and then got the craft to wriggle a little way away from the shore, first with one oar, then the other, and finally got so near the surface that the oar blade flicked a great scoop of water on to him. Giggles assailed her. She still had to look at her rings to make quite sure which was right and which left. Amazing that all her life she had been unable to learn something her daughters learnt in a week.

He went on sitting on the side, watching her trying to straighten course with first one oar then the other, with deep, but light strokes, and wobbling, swaying up and down on the spot, gusts of laughter all the while fighting past all resistance and forcing its way up her mouth. He looked on. He looked at her like a doctor, defending himself only slightly against splashes of water, and that in its turn tickled her inwardly so that she had to laugh even more, leaning forward, leaning backwards. When she had stopped laughing, when she managed to stop, she was clean internally as if a brush had gone through her and scrubbed about in all pockets. She rested on the right hand oar and let the left one drag in the water. A bird on a protruding branch gently drooped one wing and preened it with its beak.

'You must admit, dearest B,' said Augusta – the violence of her

258

laughter one more undertone in her voice – 'that I do handle certain other things with both talent and skill . . . ?'

He was sitting with his back to the west, to the red flush of the evening, shading himself. The strip of smooth water the boat left behind it suddenly turned lilac from small waves, the background increasingly changing, the wind coming out of the grass, the sun sinking through jagged rips in the clouds and colouring the surface of the water with reflected lustre, crinkled by the wind. It grew darker and lighter and reddened and clashed, all natural things moving towards each other and dissolving in the encounter, the response tumbling in reverse deep down in the water. She grew anxious. He was getting up. Finally he leant forward, took a step or two and grasped her hands on the oars, angling them low and deep, evenly, trying to imprint on her the efficient rhythm with both hands moving simultaneously, apart from the faintly scrolled difference created by the water's resistance, emphasised by him preventing the oar handles from colliding. He let go, but remained leaning forward, watching her completing a few strokes before it all went awry again and she began splashing. He dug water with warm hands round hers. Behind him, the sky grew larger and uneasy, a purple cloud splitting into two and the sun thrusting wildly out of it. Like a volcano, she thought, fire in ash. All the outer edges feathered and lights went on in the windows of the house, casting lacework through the ruins. She said to him she was – 'look here!' – hardly three months from having a child and he mysteriously replied in that case it could also apply to him, but that was no reason for not being able to *row*. She told him not to be silly.

Byron looked over his shoulder to turn the boat towards the shore. A few long raindrops came flying, and for a brief spell all was embodied in her closed hand feeling him rowing. He turned the boat half way round. She was cold. The sky raced, then the sun went into cloud again, its colour-script running across his face. He turned the boat round fully and stood to the west, stood moving back and forth with the strokes of the oars. She looked down at their hands and together they propelled the little oval which grew according to the oars into a larger and larger oval of air and water. A sufficiently long oar – from within the same hand movement – would be capable of rowing round the world if all hands folded over one another, thought Augusta without emotion. In itself, the thought was unimportant, but all the same, perhaps that was what lay in the depths of this agitation in Nottingham about looms and what Percy had said about Development. The thought reverted from the dripping blade without becoming an argument, becoming flesh. Nearest to her body, a slight irregular circular movement was repeated, in which the one pair of hands forestalled the other, so as not to collide at the next turn. In that little movement lay the intelligence, greater than the extended mechanism. She loved his face when it was preoccupied, now, as he looked round for the shore's edge, when he thought about her by not thinking about her . . . 'You're silly,' she whispered. He stepped past her – the boat bumped into the shore reeds – and helped her ashore before dragging it up.

Between the lake and the house the wind flew freely, the rain running. One of the dogs was howling round at the back – or as if it were a miserable wild dog! They had lit candles in the Great Hall as well as in the second of the two apartments nearest to the ruin of the church. She wanted to hasten in, for she was cold and had been frightened by the howling of the wild dog? But he wanted to keep her there for a while and put his arm round her waist to quieten her and listen. He wanted her to hear with eye, ear, hand. 'Eye, ear, hand':

Over there, for instance, where the road for a moment becomes a span over a waterfall, there the one lake runs down into the other, and the road goes on, disappearing behind the trees beyond the smaller fort; that's where the way back comes, tempted by a memory. It comes like a yellow lapping river of light, closer, and starts pouring past: dexterous finger-fluent piano music by a beautiful amateur. The warmth rises with the fumes from burning candles. The scent rises out of jars of potpourri: roses, lavender, cummin, failing to hide the stale smell of urine, of assiduously stimulated, unrequited boy-love.

The girl stands behind her barred window dabbing her piano fingers against her lips. They are over-sensitive or numb from swelling, the lips or the fingertips. Her throat swings deeply down into her dress and comes to a fork where it parts into one, two breasts, where the boy stands on tiptoe, anguishedly pressed against the wall. She smiles and he thinks her wide slightly mad eyes can see him. But she sees nothing, for her eyes are vacant, blind to everything outside the soft barrier she has raised all round her. That barrier will soon harden and turn her really mad, but up to now it is still only slender innocence, and it amuses her to know that he's standing there flattening himself like a beaver's tail! 'Everything here's extremely cosy,' says the boy with red cheeks and a sweaty nose. 'It's so light and warm and *intimate* here: and Mary's music: you couldn't imagine it ever being different here with you, could you, Mr Chaworth? I would also like to be part of this, *for ever*.' 'You can stay the night,' the girl's father offers dryly. 'It's too late for you to ride home now.'

The river becomes fast, darkening, as if it had glided in under a shadow. A stray boat is drifting in the middle of it, the girl Mary and the boy lying in the bottom of it, side by side, holding their breath with hollow chests so that stalactites from the roof of the cave shall not reach down and draw names on them. Her eyes are also empty, for she has abandoned them. Her mouth is contented, her body opening and closing itself, searching for his longing, which is indeed the right kind, but not what she herself is longing for. It's not sufficiently dangerous. He glances sideways at her with inexpressible feelings. It is so cramped they have to touch each other along their whole length, but he doesn't dare loosen the smallest finger of his hand with the intention of touching her hand. They wash along with the river and lie towards the mouth of it, before they get there, the image rolling up like a carpet of crushed glass.

Byron started just before the noise came from the kitchen where buttery hands three times managed to catch and lose grip on the bowl before it finally smashed to pieces on the stone floor. He sighed. The bowl was neither expensive nor exceptional, not at all, but beloved. It was of yellow glass and had been with them over all the years for desserts of preserved fruit. His mother had bought it. It had been beautiful when they had had no money for things people call exquisite. It had been one of the few objects in his childhood that insignificantly, tenderly, had spun a memory of the atmosphere of life at the time.

A wave.

A wave of painful movement emanated from the fragments which could now be neither mended nor crushed. From fear of starting to weep if he resisted it, he didn't resist it, but rose to where it took him, drawing Augusta with him. He smiled. He renewed his hold on her waist. In the tomb lay a dog, several others lying buried there in the ground where they had run freely and behaved badly. Chased pregnant game and so on: his dogs. He could certainly point out most of the places. The very first of his dogs, for instance, lay over there. He sees something faded golden and blurred, flying coat and forgetfulness. He hears his own voice tracking back in time and breaking into a falsetto: Woolly, it says very matter-of-factly. Woolly, you've done so and so. Woolly, you're going to *die*. What's this now? Has he killed a dog? No, now the voice comes back to announce: Woolly, you're after all a sweet and affectionate little dog. If you're unmanageable that's because you've been badly *brought up*, but we'll soon cure that. I'm going to spare your life, but then you must obey my slightest *wish* from now on. Wish, it echoes lovingly. Wish, it reminds him cautiously, the word wish suddenly broadening the whole episode at that faded place, except the fact that Woolly had eventually offended.

It was sitting straight in front of him seeing the boy's little pistol pointing at it; it didn't run away but made a motion with its head to one side – appealing, dignified submission. It sees he is a child but doesn't know whether that knowledge will help. In the child, sluggish hot fluids are reshaping themselves. One is the capricious right of ownership, a sentimentality. A longing to squash softness hard between his fingers makes the child doughy with desire and clench his teeth. He bends down to stroke, his hand deep inside the warmth of the scruff of the neck, becoming so emotional he has to wipe his cheeks and nose on his sleeve. Tears relieve, but weeping makes tears bitter. All the time, he is shooting a message of love and cruelty at the dog and receiving it back differently, not influenced by the dog's feeling but by its body. They look into each other's eyes without understanding each other. And yet everything encountered with the look is extinguished. The hedgehog in the tall grass which looks up as you come too close with the scythe, you yourself being careful of it. Ah, Woolly, I know, sobs the boy, and the dog – released from the peculiar lead that is not visible – rushes away across the yard, pirouetting and laughingly chasing tails and shadows, snapping at outstretched hands. The boy also laughs, his twittering voice losing height and slowly sinking through the years to land by the dog tomb. 'Yes, that's Woolly's grave over there,' said Byron. 'Only Boatswain lies here, as you know. He lived a life of his own.

'Oh, the things he got up to. Full of parables like Jesus. Animals make themselves understood with parables. Don't take any notice of the epitaph on the stone. It's not mine, but Hobhouse's. He's a cold cynic.' Augusta read most of the crazily dignified verses all the same. There was a great academic vacuum between them and Byron's words.

No, an intervening space. It wasn't a vacuum. An echo of male voices comes walking into it, nearer and nearer and more and more intimately embedded in the furnishings. They stop. They all talk at once. The night passes. Finally there's only one of them who has anything to say. He raises a glass of water and tilts it first to one eye, then the other; he examines the water for gravel. Then he wipes his eyelashes, long and adhering to each other like on a recently weeping child, and says:

A fly has nothing, seeks no home, but flies everywhere *comme chez elle.*

Then he says:

From the almost chaste uniting that once made me – how far have I not strayed from my parents' bed. Twenty-five years. Decay – history is decay.

The others have been overcome by hangovers in the middle of their intoxication, but are still not so far gone that they try to repair the overlap. It's almost morning. Worn out like older men after a day's work – yes, they actually take on an expression of that kind – they get up to go to bed. Extra young maidservants who are just getting up to start their day's work hold tight to each other when they hear student voices swearing with bad temper and clumping around lost in the passages.

The day swings half way and they are up again, fresh as canonised saints after having swung down into the air cushion under the water for a while. They shoot at targets on the short wall of the Great Hall. Someone is reading, some fencing and some boxing with swift extended but solemn gestures, the bear chained to the staircase looking inscrutably on. Two cats observe it all from the balustrade on a carved half-wall and now and again absent-mindedly rub up against each other. A man who is afraid of women – Augusta sees that they all are – tries to overcome himself by arrogantly treating a country girl like a duchess. He kisses her hand with icy licked lips – not without distaste – and talks nonsense. She doesn't dare laugh at him until she is back again with the other girls in the pantry.

Matthews has equipped the little boat with mast and sheet. He swings round so unskilfully that he sweeps the surface of the water with his back and almost capsizes. Astonished, he wipes his eyes with a wet hand, and Byron, who dives up out of the sheet, sees his eyelashes clinging like on a newly bathed child. 'Welcome to the harem!' he says. Most of them have stayed on the edge, afraid of the servant girls and the endless black water. They are in a cellar simply converted into a bathing pool. The smell of old stone and earth is tomb-like and unpleasant. They quickly scramble out of the water, which is very cold and has an inky black undercurrent. Only Matthews stays with him, a great swimmer like him and rational, easy to convince that the depth is a fair ten foot and underneath it no mouth but stone.

They move in the water, in the meagre torchlight, white like the underneath of something, sparring with a resistance, and Matthews – who is smoking a large cigar – is saying, 'You'll soon find when you travel out into the world that England is a victorious colonial power because there's nearly always a worse one even closer for most countries. When in our own interests we oppose the claims of minor or temporary despots on new territory, in the eyes of those territories we acquire a quality of what is objective and lasting, which essentially seems to agree with their own truth. It is not so, but they take it like that, as the mind would spin if there were no great power as contour and protector above all minor troubles.'

Byron shakes his head. Napoleon Bonaparte is in league with the Czar of Russia and owns the world, on his way to Russia. Matthews puts his cigar down on the edge and dives, for he has lost a trouser button. Byron follows. It becomes a long long trip and afterwards they have to withdraw their arms, cleaving the water and keeping them alongside their bodies, instead letting their heads and shoulders come first, wriggling and fumbling for following currents. It is dark, phosphorus streaks streaming behind them as they breathe out and providing them with a guiding light. Stalactites hang right down to the surface of the water, sometimes penetrating right through and making the omega of the cave into a set of sharp polished teeth. They are careful and dive deeper. Then it grows lighter from the mouth of the cave, fingers of sun playing on the river water, as in a pale green pool, and they are both drawn up to the surface by their lungs bellowing in air.

They come up under the mathematical bridge across the River Cam. The reflection of it moves its trigonometry into a dance which pushes itself dead straight within itself. And Matthews compares it to music, 'but not Mozart, not Mozart'.

Upwards, swimming on their backs against the deep river basins, they look back at Cambridge's sandy grey, mildly blasted façades. The architecture is wonderful but not first-class, Matthews thinks. It lacks the final sharpness of real originality, but on the other hand, it's not the style of the English to be too original. Even Wren hides the claws in his kid gloves and has created a brilliant discretion. And yet it's beautiful, especially this stone in Cambridge, grey but with the whole scale of blue and red in its greyness. You can weep in King's College chapel on Sundays, when the sun shines through the windows, the colours melting the stone walls into a flood of glass. And the arena of pews heading forward on a sea of music. Made of *voices*. Green, quasi-feminine voices of boys soaring high under the protection of the bearded.

Mown lawns and windless meadows. Flowers growing between willows, on the river banks lilies, dead nettles and globeflowers. From the surface of the water, they see everything twice as high, floating and gleaming in unreal proportions. A flock of crow-like boys in black, in top hats, strangling collars, pushing and stumbling about each other's feet. They are pretending to chase each other, pretending to hit each other and fall heavily against each other when they are pushed. Their singing voices break out to and fro above breaking point as they shriek. The choirmaster would take out his cane if he heard them.

One of them is sitting alone on the river bank with a bunch of globeflowers in his hand, his hat gleaming alongside. The great choir is down in the ship of pews as a silver solo rises, a voice so needle-fine and delicate that they all hold their breath. Lightly, carefully, the boy strikes the yellow globeflowers against his thigh, the reflected sun in his shoe-buckle dazzling his eyes. Four knobbly fingers, the only thing that exposes him, run through his fringe, before it falls forward again and swings its blond feathers over his face, as it turns, used to flirting. Two deep eyes follow them, but Matthews actually wants to find his trouser button now.

On the outskirts of the town, the timber-framed houses creep closely along the river and are reflected, transforming their swimming strokes into climbing in black and white beams. They glide out of them, back into the water, where they roll on their sides, backs, fronts and cease thinking about it. Past the timber-framed houses stretching a floor over the water, past houses sucking up grass into their foundations, past pastoral pastures levelling out the shore and taking them up into a garden, behind farmhouses and muck heaps, they swim rolling on their backs, fronts and sides and think nothing of it. Finally they come to one of those river pools where they once swam every day and dived for coins. It still glints down at the bottom.

But when they try to grasp it, they see it become air and shimmering towards the surface, as their fingers twist round in the mud. Slowly, strangely, with the grazing sensitivity of fish, they fumble their way along the bottom and then suddenly into a forest of water weeds. The light trickles. Gentle and dark green, it penetrates down into the closeness. A foot, a hand against a weed, receding and endlessly reproducing the movement. When it can no longer be seen under the water, it comes back to the surface to lap up its tracks.

Every plant is covered by plants and then by lower species protected by their slime, and they like sticking to each other. One captures Byron's arm, another his leg and winds an indolent grip round him. He tears them up by the roots, but his prayers lie only between his hands, which he holds in front of his chin as he shoots to the surface for air. Matthews' head is also floating on a floating carpet of water weed. He has found something. He has clamped a pewter coin in one eye and maliciously distorted his face to keep it there. But he hasn't found his trouser button. He looks round with his seeing eye. The dull landscape round Cambridge, the flat calm fields of sheep, an angry girl riding astride with her skirt tucked up to her stomach and preparing to leap over one of the hedges. The seeing eye fills with friendship and winks 'Come!' But Byron is not yet like that. It fills itself with friendship and reminds him of all the occasions when 'do you remember and do you remember', reminds him of all advice given and the first time it tactfully corrected his friend's attitude. It contains a small world of meals in a mill, raids in Brighton, good behaviour in face of the magnificent beams in the roof of Trinity's dining hall. The singing note of words follows the images, but they don't matter: the eye tells how they have contributed to his friend's soul, through moments of influence, as explanations never explain. And do you remember. And do you remember. Then it ends and Matthews dives again.

The water weed lets him through with an artificial cry, as if he had penetrated it, though in fact it has made itself slippery and hollow and suffers slight agonies in the effort to straighten up. But his current attracts a back-suction and into that surge stalks and heads. Curious, it passes in under his feet with a soft brush and lets him through. Suddenly, what he is looking for is there.

When he has taken what he wants, he returns the same way, but then it's impossible, for the plants are interwoven. 'It's your own fault,' they sway. 'You caused this disorder, now try to straighten it out.' Now with his foot, now with his hand, now with both and all four. And now with a violence that stiffens the interweaving. Everything bounces back while awaiting.

A ray of light races up to the surface, where the surplus of water weed rests like a well-woven mat.

'Cunning?' it says as with a gentle nudge he makes his way into the thicker weed. Small strips of water waves transmit the message in the beat of his heart, as when a lighthouse takes a bearing on the depths of the night. Ah, oh . . . they thump out into the River Cam, in the abandoned swimming pool, on the edge of which his cigar slowly smokes itself, in a water-spider grazing on the lowest form of life on water weed, in his mother's head far away. It moves distrustfully in the direction in which her son is dying, they say.

Now the water weed has caught him by the elbows and the backs of his knees. He has let go what he had been seeking and found, throws his weight against his shackles and pulls them back. A new strand winds itself round his waist, another links round his neck, one on his wrist and all are helplessly lost in each other; the more they entangle themselves together, the higher they lift him in a taut net, and when he is dead they fail to spit out his slack figure as they want to, but are caught in it through each other, in each other through it.

Byron sees his friend in his helplessness, calm now, except for the dead hands clutching and grasping at his rib-cage. Quiet now. He gives him a last look before taking the much quicker way home. He gets out of the pool. He sweeps water off his arms and smokes the last puff of a cigar someone has left on the edge. Then he goes out into the park. It is autumn. The sun has no eyes left, only the mouth smiling and melting the contours of the world, and with a sense of the flexibility of watercolours, mixing them all. Dust swirls ahead on the path, swirling up, forming an equipage of golden grey. The rider hangs wearily down from the ridden, sidesaddle, the face against the horse's neck. Nothing happens. Hands grasp the sundial and twist. There are the hours of the day, the compass points of the seasons, imprinted in a sphere of bronze ribbons. The hands twist the dial off its plinth and *fling* . . . the ball bounces in light long arcs over Nottinghamshire. Someone opens his eye wide, where a hollow of time flares up. The ball rushes into it and the eye closes.

It started to snow. It snowed over Newstead for days. It snowed so heavily that the first semi-thaw remained and laid the foundations for a smooth world. Bushes, hedges, plinths disappeared into the sweep. Augusta ran her hand over her bulging belly which smoothed out the round sharp details a human being is; which also showed the calm of the storm the coming into existence of a human being is. With that whispered analogy, they settled down in peace.

That lasted a week. All sounds that live in the silence exploded from the inside and did not reach out. It was as silent as before the wave movement of the world. She looked out of the window. Snowed-up footprints fumbled away along the road, but returned, frightened by their own depth. No one could remember such snowfall in Nottinghamshire. But war winters are cold, the warmth not spread evenly over the country as protection against the cold, but crowded together into warmth in some places, they said. Augusta sat on the floor inside the great fireplace and stared into the fire that had become her neighbour. On the fourth day, they had thought of leaving, but then the snow fell like weightless rain, only occasionally in a curve away from the wind. In a dark corridor of the house, he took her in his arms from behind and they rocked and lullabied and said that in this way their prayers for a short moment of eternity together had been heard.

Part Two

With brief
interruptions
for peace

My dear Byron,

So what did you get? instead of experiencing history – and
sharing your experience with me, your oldest friend? Instead you
had complications of the heart. You would have gained everything by leaving that flock of hens to its fate and coming with me.
You find yourself by forgetting yourself. If you wallow in your
own troubles you may simply drown in them. But we've always
had different views on the way a gentleman should best proceed
with his so-called emotional ties . . . mine is as before: tie knots in
them to remind you of possible future needs.

I have seen Europe during Bonaparte's retreat. Not as an
individual soldier sees it, but as cohorts and brigades would have
seen it if they could have been combined into a single pair of eyes.
The continent is bleeding and coagulating itself. We who were
once Bonapartists – and still hide his picture at the bottom of the
box – live divided, approving and despairing. Not even the
Frenchmen I meet want their Emperor back in his full glory of
victory from before Moscow. On the other hand, the alternative is
terrible: the Allies wish to re-establish the days *before* Napoleon.

The idealists say that every living creature irrevocably changes
the world. A reconstruction of the past is therefore impossible
and against nature. It could be nothing else but a perversion – like
trying to stage a night-time dream in daylight. Or like moving
back to your father's house after having failed in the world. Royal

houses leapt off the earth at the sharpness of Bonaparte's ploughshare. So they're thinking of reconstructing them. In all their incestuous warpedness, those creatures of the past are despots who will take revenge on their people because they willingly accepted liberation in their triumphal march. But *status quo ante bellum* seems to be the unconditional plan of the Allies for Europe. And for that matter, liberation soon became oppression. All royalty is an abomination. It was a flaw in Napoleon's character to seek legitimacy in titles. He was more of a realist when he was the leader of a bandit dynasty from a Mediterranean island. They say the Emperor denies the statement that he had an illegal connection with his sister Paulina Borghese. They say his motive was not morality but 'Corsican' doubts – whatever they are – and people who have shared their sisters' childhood and youth, in his opinion, could want to fuck them, however beautiful they were. But now to my account:

After much fuss and running about at the Home Office, I got my courier passport at the end of May, 1813, and some despatches to the crown of Sweden, and sailed in June from Harwich to Gothenburg. I went on through Scania and arrived at Helsingborg, where I took another boat to Stralsund. Bernadotte, Crown Prince of Sweden, was there in command of the Swedish army, and after delivering my despatches to him I was desired to dine with him. When I told him that the Danes had declared war on him, he smiled and said: '*Nous leur rendrons tout cela*' – we will give them as they bring. I remarked nothing particular about him, except that when I first saw him his hair was in curl papers, and that at his Court dinner the salt-cellar next to him was secured by a lock and key. On remarking this to my next neighbour, he said: 'I suppose you know what happened to a late Crown Prince?' I did not know, but was afterwards told that he was generally supposed to have been poisoned.

Leaving Stralsund, I passed by Strelitz, and delivered despatches to the Duke of Cumberland. This was at two o'clock in the morning. I was shown into his room, and he jumped out of bed to receive them. A more magnificent frame of a man was never seen. His Royal Highness asked me to stay a day or two at Strelitz, but I went on, without stopping, to Berlin.

At Berlin I formed an acquaintance with the Princess Louisa of

Prussia, married to Prince Radzivil. She was a highly accomplished and most amiable Princess, much beloved by her family and those whom she honoured with her notice. The English in those days were favourably received in Germany, particularly at Berlin, and I was permitted on more than one occasion to join her small circle at the tea-table of Her Royal Highness.

As the cease-fire from the fourth of June was still in force, I could travel fairly freely and continued via Breslau to the Russian headquarters. I was also introduced to the handsome but somewhat juvenile Czar Alexander in the camp at Peterswalden. One evening I dined with Potemkin and his officers. I also dined together with Lord Cathcart, in whose camp I made the acquaintance of Sir Hudson Lowe . . .

*

'My dear Link,' said Eric Watson without attempting to hide his irritation. 'This is beginning to sound like the genealogy in the Book of Moses. If you're really going to list all his dining companions on an eight-month journey, you'll arrive at a number well over two hundred and forty.'

'Sorry. My intention was just to demonstrate this very human contrast between royal obeisance and republican speech. It was so typical of the circles round our hero. And of the time,' mumbled Link. He looked up, apologetically, then leafed on through pages of his notes and tried to lower his voice in the desolate premises.

'The intention was apparent.'

Three pairs of eyes went through each other.

This was their first meeting after the exhumation. It was April, over a month since they had been confronted by the sight of the mummified Byron, and what troubles them most is not that Mr Hazell is ill in bed, still feverish after influenza, which has forced them to find alien premises – a dismal café where they served Ovaltine – no, the sad thing is that Mr Cohn has stayed away and has not even wanted to meet Eric Watson for a whole month.

The last thing that happened between them was that the two friends had met in the street, at which Mr Cohn had told Eric Watson about Mr Hazell's 'flu. He was quite dramatic about it. At first, Eric Watson thought this was owing to that sister of Mr Cohn's, who fell victim

273

to Spanish 'flu. But after a while – a while that became more and more speechless – he realised that the constantly repeated word 'infection' implied something Mr Cohn thought had come from the opened coffin.

Eric Watson laughed for almost quarter of an hour. Meanwhile Mr Cohn tried to modify the impression of superstition, trying to modify what was superstitious and quasi-scientific and speculative in what he had just said, and when that didn't help and Eric Watson went on sending up cascades of cheerfulness into the March twilight and towards Venus, who smiled back, then he changed tack and became aggressive, emphasising the vulgarity and the inability to leave things alone in opening Byron's tomb 'on the whim of a stripling'. He couldn't accept that there were people he'd known and laughed with for years who could suddenly take out a pair of scissors and cut the hair off a cadaver in which the object of their admiration had actually rested. He had found it indescribably vile to listen to their comments on parts of the body Byron had wished to keep secret, and about things *everyone* wants to keep secret. How could they be so lacking in respect? It was just what Mr Cohn had objected to from the very beginning. Without secret respect, without the secret, no self-respect. Now you know what is secret, so what? You've just satisfied your *curiosity* and are stupider than ever!

But there were still two minutes left of the quarter of an hour Eric Watson had to laugh in. When he had stopped laughing, he wiped his eyes and said: 'If your infection-theory is true, Joel, then we'd better start digging up leeches. Heehee . . .'

So now they were only three. If they'd been quite certain that would be so, they would never have met, for between them they lack the companionable ability to bind people together.

Two people can talk to one another, find each other, enjoy and amuse each other on what they call each other's 'wave length'. But very often the harmony arises only in the shelter of a third person. Perhaps a taciturn person, who somehow distributes and controls the atmosphere. That's what it's like when Messrs Cohn and Hazell are present. But now they are absent.

Anyhow, they don't understand why Mr Cohn should be so offended. Partly because he usually has a sense of humour and partly because Byron hadn't been all that horrible to look at.

Rather beautiful, in fact. A brittle nut-shell of a long since departed life.

'Sorry,' says Link. 'I capitulate in the face of your arguments. I'll recapitulate past all dinners and meetings and names if you like.

'After having completed his duties as telegraph boy of his day between commanders, Hobhouse continued to Fiume on the Adriatic coast – you know, that town d'Annunzio occupied twenty years ago when Italy was not given it at the Treaty of Versailles. Serbia? I think. Croatia? Wherever Hobhouse goes, he lives – as we would call it – journalistically. He is an observer, a tourist among historical events which he will later describe in various books at the final stages of the Napoleonic era. For that matter, they eventually received a friendly judgement from St Helena: "Well caught," said the Emperor. "I was captured." ' (Ha ha, said Eric Watson.) 'So he is a tourist of history hoping to intervene much like d'Annunzio. He makes no demands for comfort, but naturally he is in the very best company. That is also why we name his dining companions. They were noble and aristocratic travellers, travelling for pleasure, and they became the predecessors of scientific travellers such as Burton and Speke, the immediate predecessors of Rhodes and other traders, I presume. The connecting link between the one and the other is Disraeli. When he was young, he worshipped Byron and travelled in his footsteps through the Levant. His father had taken over Tita, Byron's gondolier, as his servant after the poet's death, so Benjamin's adoration had a quality beyond the usual. He wrote a Byron–Shelley novel called *Venetia* which is not good. When Disraeli became Queen Victoria's prime minister, he sent England herself on a Grand Tour across the continents. Imperialism is when the representatives of a whole nation do what individuals of that nation did before.

'Let us return to Hobhouse, a very early tourist. So here are early tourists sitting in caves, asking each other to pass the salt and pouring out "just a couple of drops, thanks" in the muddy field. In a mud hut, they talk about fox-hunting and the translation of the Bible. They could be anywhere, under any circumstances whatsoever, but are quite unaffected. They are Englishmen, are Englishmen. We island people are borne to our island – like Lohengrin on the swan of the saga – to the ocean edge of a foreign country.'

*

275

I spent all autumn travelling back and forth through Germany and Austria, following every war from one battlefield to the next. Everywhere, people have buried their dead, dragged away the wounded, doctoring the tussocky hills as best they can. The miracle of re-growth appears on the plains and hills. The foliage recovered. The barn burnt. Replace. But that immensity always returns with its great boots and tramps right through. It needn't be war. Needn't be anyone's fault – if you don't believe weather curses, for several times hailstorms have swept through Bavarian valleys and cropped the corn right down to the ground only a few days before the real harvest. I have never before seen fields have such late crop failures. It was all accompanied by incessant thunderstorms and one farmer had his stock bull killed by lightning. Otherwise war comes trampling along just as you have got used to a few months of local peace. There's always something breaking up the good habit just as it turns warm. People aren't changed by the break-through. Their characters never recover. Human beings are like that, either recovering or going under.

Everywhere you hear stories *de la guerre*: in Dresden I had a brief chat with the French Ambassador's valet, who told me that one night, with much hanky-panky and secretiveness, he had been given the task of taking care of the Emperor himself. NB turned up at two o'clock in the morning, his face was sunk in a fur cap; it was black with cold and dirt, and a grimy beard. 'I had the honour,' said our valet, 'of washing his feet with eau-de-Cologne.' The attendants who sat on the seat behind the carriage in the open air were in a wretched plight: one was a Pole; he had lost the use of both his legs above the knee, and four fingers of each hand had been cut off. The Frenchman had lost all the toes of his right foot. Our informant attended Napoleon during his stay, except when he was closeted with the King of Saxony. Napoleon went to bed for two or three hours, but did not sleep; at half-past seven he rose, took a cup of coffee, and started for Erfurt.

The day before Christmas I found myself in Leipzig. It was a strangely calm day. A monastery bell tolled every half an hour and on the hour in the immediate proximity of the inn. The landlord said it wasn't a monastery but a workhouse for orphaned and crippled children and the bell summoned them to their duties.

I took a solitary walk, and in the suburbs came to an enclosed garden. I strolled about for some time, picking my way amongst fragments of cloaks, gaiters, belts, pieces of paper, covers of books, and other articles, denoting that this had been one of the scenes of the recent mortal strife. These were more thickly strewn by the side of a small stream about one-third as wide as the Avon at Bath. Seeing on the bank a monument freshly erected and set around with newly planted shrubs, I stopped to look at the inscription on the stone; so this was the chaotic remains of the mortal combat that had taken place two months ago, only two months.

Hic
In undis Elstri
Josephus Poniatowski
Princeps
Summus Exercitus Polonorum Praefectus
Imperii Gallici Mareschallus, Tribus Vulneribus
Letiferis Affectus Ultimus Ex Acie Discedeus
Dum Receptum Magni Gallorum Exercitus Tuetur
Vita Gloriae Et Patriae Sacrata Functus Est
Die Octobris XIX – A. 1813
Anno Aetatis Completo LII
Popularis puulari Miles Duci
Hoc Monumentum Lacrimis Suis Irrigatum
Posuit
Alexander Rozznechi

Walking a little farther, I came to a field beyond the banks of the Elster, more thickly strewn with signs of the days of slaughter. But there were other and more painful tokens of the great uprising of the oppressed races against the conqueror. A pestilence had broken out in the city whilst in the occupation of the French, and from the effects of it, as well as the four days' fighting, the churches, and every available receptacle, were filled with sick and wounded. It was computed, as I learnt from good authority, that no less than seventy thousand corpses had been buried in three months, in the city and the immediate neighbourhood of Leipzig, and, considering the enormous amount of the armies engaged, the mortality does not appear at all incredible.

That's what it was like. The whole plain was in itself a monument to this European war, its tragedy and cheerfulness, its multiplicity and stupidity and heroic sacrifices. Leipzig was one of Europe's thousands, tens of thousands of towns, a place in itself and in its own development, temporarily visited by total warfare and then permanently marked by this great, perfidious, travelling war. The remains of the battle were a monument to this. But the final remains of the remains were to be a false obelisk and wall containing that inscription.

I continued on to Weimar. By the ducal statue lies a crushed hat full of bullet holes in memory of the fallen hereditary prince. We are getting nearer and nearer to the war in our straggling little coach. In Leipzig, it was three months ahead of us, in Weimar one and a half. Soon we will be a week behind, four days, two days, one night. It is drawing to the west like a storm. Travelling in Europe is like following behind an extended storm and hearing its terminal eddies, while you yourself walk in silence and see the grass rising again. They who rise.

We passed the battlefield at Hanau. It was still raw, covered with dead horses – some of them half-buried, their legs sticking up like frozen poles, and the postillion had to excel in his skill at driving to worm his terrified horses between horse cadavers without landing in the ditch. Which happened occasionally. The next day we were in Frankfurt, one day behind the fighting, for the whole town was engaged in transports of joy in their immediate – and certainly temporary – freedom between the departure of the French and the real beginning of exercise of power by the victors. The hotels in Frankfurt were enormous constructions, as are the city's public buildings. As far as the kind of comforts concerning health, hygiene and decency, the standard was below all criticism! As far as the Opera is concerned, on the gentlemen's part the wall alongside the street was placed at their disposal, where passers-by of both sexes could witness it. Where the ladies on the same errand were, fortunately I have no idea. And this in a city that not only prides itself on its Culture, but also from its size and crowded buildings must be extremely susceptible to epidemics.

I struggled across flat countryside, across rivers, Flanders, and the Dutch canals in increasing winter war, constantly getting stuck in the snow, repeatedly stuck for lengthy periods, the whole carriage twice overturning into a snow-filled ditch. It took us hours to retrieve it and sort out the baggage, carry out repairs, ending up weeping with exhaustion. We stopped overnight in a deathly cold deserted house, soon so used to the weirdness of war that we no longer reflected on the thought that we were occupying a family home, a family's ex-home or an ex-family's home. In time and place, the whole world is a mixture of war and peace. Some villages look as if the passage of war has forgotten them. Everything is cherry wine and corpulence. The next village can be an appendage to a battlefield, contorted by frozen corpses, neat pyramid-shaped heaps of gathered cannon balls – of the non-explosive kind – and shrapnel. The whole of Europe is a widespread sparse battlefield, war the primary industry and everything else serving this hulk.

Tonight, after eight months' travelling, I returned to England, and remained at anchor outside the harbour. A long time, because of the storm.

*

On his way home to Nottingham, Link felt the car beginning to jerk fitfully again, the same fitful jerks as a month ago. At the north road into the town, he turned off the engine so as not to wake the good citizens with bangs and fumes; an almost invisible downhill slope continued all the way to his house. He steered cautiously with his brakes round a few sharp bends. That went well. A car, like a child, always gets its old complaints back again. Inflammation of the ear or a defective regulator – damn it.

A short rest and then he got up. The rest blew away some of his bad temper. During the trip home – with the taste of bad tea still washing round his teeth – he had feared that the whole atmosphere of that miserable café, with soured Eric Watson and indifferent Rupert, would also infect his drawer of Byroniana. But when he got up, sat down at his desk and opened what he had previously closed, the delight came up through his fingers. The process of inspiration had at last turned. Link was an experienced amateur researcher. His past included a period of research into the planets, into plants in small fast-moving water courses, the history of costume, Ben Jonson and examples of European ships.

In most cases, he had found that when his work had filled up the subject he had staked out, then that contribution had turned and come back, like a fruit of himself. Inspiration was the word. 'Inspiration' was the protection. It was the moment when, after having achieved a certain maturity, an organism makes itself immune to earlier dangers.

279

It continues to develop and challenge its medium – its mother and narrator – to give it what it has to have.

And in precisely this way, his drawer was fruitful. It received him now like a benevolent animal always prepared to join him. The matter had become something rather like a walk at night. The house slept. Link the dentist wrote.

*

February 10th, 1814 – I went to a performance at Covent Garden. Full to bursting. Sweat and perfumes. Shoulders and bosoms. Hot as a mirage and far away out there in front floated the stage. The footlights, almost blue like lightning, masked actors outside the mask, giving them a third face of chalk-like cruelty. I saw my friend Byron again in a private box. It's a long time since I was so happy. I went with him to his house in Bennet Street and stayed there until four in the morning. He showed me some original letters from Robert Burns he had acquired. He gave me one of them, in which Burns says he is going to cease farming and devote himself instead entirely to his work as tax collector. It's striking to read such explanations from a poet who in people's minds is linked with a life of idleness, roses and whisky. But this was his plan for life and I now have written evidence that no one can read his own destiny. Byron showed me some personal letters from his 'erotic anthology'. He indicated obscurely that I had been away for eight months, a space of time when staying at home provided time to start something that has almost terminated itself . . .

February 22nd – Napoleon has defeated the Allies and made them retreat some way away from Paris. Dinner at Holland House. Seething with delight. We are all old Bonapartists and cannot restrain our exaltation when He shows his youthful paces, even if we wish he would soon be made to give up. Naturally . . .

February 23rd – I dined with Byron and bet him a guinea for two that the Allies are this day at Paris. Sat with him at home hearing his *confessions*.

March 12th – Went to Drury Lane with Byron and saw Kean as Hamlet. A strange play. Enticing and impossible, in our day far too often interpreted as a Werther drama. In my opinion, Kean succeeded excellently, best in his first speech to Rosencrantz and Guildenstern, also in his confused speech to Ophelia, whose hand he held and kissed with wonderful effect as they parted. In the to-be-or-not-to-be soliloquy he was on a knife-edge of strain, electrifying the house. Like all actors, he loses his grip in the latter part of the rôle. His fencing ability, however, was superb – what else from a man who can dance on a tightrope. As he fell, the stalls and the whole auditorium gave him a standing ovation for several minutes. People have different opinions about Kean's Hamlet. Most consider it inferior to his Richard, or Othello.

What is happening to our great artists? Certainly I have sought forgetfulness in gin. And crawled on hands and knees through the tunnel of intoxication. And at the end of it found regret: 'nothing changed'. And finally admitted relief of *soberly* wearing down the unbearable to the level of the tolerable.

We waited for Kean in the greenroom, where a half-dressed Mademoiselle B was having a hysterical scene because Madame R had driven her to move during the corpse-scene by tickling her with a bunch of dried flowers. Anyone visiting the greenroom at Drury Lane (and probably London's – the world's – other theatres) realises that every theatre performance balances on the edge of a precipice. A play within the play seems to be the actors' internal envy tempting them to sabotage each other's lines, to overcome the sabotage and watch for the right moment for revenge.

Kean was waiting for us in the alley, standing with his back against a wall, calm and pale. Then he drank as if drinking were hard work. His actual method seemed to aim at keeping a drunken balance. Too little, too much, risked failing in one direction or the other. He has an ideal with his gin. Not oblivion, or *joie de vivre*, or stupidity, but a dangerous ideal.

Byron rendered – with as good as authentic voices – Mademoiselle B's and Madame R's duet. Kean said that actors live as if in a litter in which everyone wants to grow up but most are sacrificed to foxes and wolves. The one first to find a tit pushes aside his brother from the next. He said the theatre is the only place where adult people weep loudly and shamelessly over other people's successes. You learn to live with this. You get used to it. All ways of life have a balancing point (said Kean taking a very well-balanced mouthful of gin) that outsiders cannot fathom because their own is so different. You! – for the first time ever Kean raised his black eyes and looked first at me, then at Byron, as if able to see right through us – you have 'your circles round a singular centre'.

A lovely smile. An equally painstaking gulp of gin. A glance at the glass. A humble prayer for more. I am one of the greatest artists of our day, said Kean. He said: I have done the art of acting a service or a disservice by making it more direct. I am the one who has done that. And worn myself out. I have made it *young*. That's exhausting. To be an old-fashioned declaimer is not easy. It is a craft and you have to master it. Empathy is a killer. Every time you rob yourself. You steal from your own life when in an exalted form you project the emotions you have learnt. It's not that remarkable. Most people rob themselves. Don't do anything else.

When we parted, it was in the same alley as we had met in. Faint criss-crossed rays of light. The alley was so narrow, it rescued him in his Balance, where a wider street would have let him go on the rocks as he cruised and careened.

March 21st – Spring has come. Long walk in Richmond Park. Yes, truly spring, I noticed in my father's way of slashing with his stick as we walked and sank into the long leafy undulations round the river and pools. The air is thin, everything increasing in pace. I feel exalted, on the thin border of despair. Beauty is brittle. In London, salutes for Wellington's victory at Adour. In the evening, a small dinner of only 150 people. They say they are pleased to see me, but I feel myself undesired, unloved, intimate circles enclosing me in their dirt and cleanliness without allowing me entrée. What do people think of me? Do they think I don't want them?

Lord Byron, whom I like more and more every day, not for his fame but for his fondness (not dubious, I think) for me, introduced me to Lady Melbourne at her request. Whether it is a peculiarity of hers, I do not know, but she trembled as we talked. In truth she owes me a *bad* deed, she says, because I stopped her son disposing of a bad wife, when I steered away Byron's escape with Caroline Lamb. I replied that each of us ought to take care of *his* lamb, which was rewarded with a small smile from a great one-time beauty. She treats Byron like a favourite object. He says he is her lover in all but love, 'which is a bagatelle'. What a lot one has to listen to!

April 8th – Cambridge. This morning Scrope Davies came into my room with the most recent issue of the *Star* and a cheerfully desolate cry: all is over, Hobhouse. Bonaparte has been deposed.

April 10th – News that Napoleon, after some struggle for favour, has abdicated the thrones of France and Italy, for himself and heirs, and has chosen for a retreat the Island of Elba, which was offered to him at the instigation of the Emperor Alexander, with a pension of £250,000 yearly, thus closing with the most extraordinary of all his actions the most extraordinary of human careers. It appears he said on hearing of the sum assigned to him, 'It is too much for a soldier like me.' Thus recurring to his darling and first choice of life. I cannot help feeling affected at this speech.

I feel I must see France before all traces of the Napoleon era are obliterated. At five o'clock, I set off for London, on horseback to save time. I had my bay mare, which by half-past one in the morning had carried me all the way to Wade's Mill, where I woke the innkeeper with noise and words of abuse and had breakfast for an hour and a half. I sought out Byron as soon as I got to London. He decided to come with me to Paris. Louis XVIII is to leave immediately. I sought out Hamilton, Second Secretary at the Foreign Office, and after tramping around in the waiting room for an hour, I was told that the government was not issuing immediate passports to France. Dined with Byron at the Cocoa Tree (my reward dinner). At midnight we went with Kinnaird down St James's to see the illuminations. Carlton House was radiant, *Vivent les Bourbons* on the façade and a transparent on the roof showing the triumph of the lily.

April 12th – Byron is not coming with me to Paris. He is a difficult person to live with! Instead he has written an Ode to Napoleon Bonaparte and offered to dedicate it to me. I'll have to make do with that.

April 16th – Get my passport, requested to go to the Home Office, where I will be given despatches for Lord Castlereagh and a courier's passport. I shut up my rooms, pay the servants, stay the night at the Angel Inn and take the eight o'clock mail coach to Dover.

April 17th – Easy crossing. Spring tide in Dover, so we rode on wet men's shoulders to the gangway. Arrived in Paris on the 19th.

May 1st – One parade after another in this beautiful city. First Louis XVIII comes back and arrives at the Tuileries with great pomp. The streets of Paris vibrating with a quiet lack of enthusiasm. In the evening, the fireworks explode in front of the palace. All the balconies of the city are hung with strips of cloth, mats, flags. Huge crowds had despite everything collected outside the palace. The façades of the

Palais du Corps Législatif were illuminated with green lamps, standing there like a fairy-tale palace. When the fireworks on Pont Louis XVI started detonating, the Seine looked like a river of fire.

The day after the King's entry, I witnessed a more imposing ceremony – the passage of a portion of the victorious armies before the Court of France and the allied Sovereigns. The troops marched along the Quay, and the above august personages were at a window opposite to the Pont des Arts. The King was sitting in an armchair, and the Duchesse d'Angoulême sitting opposite him. Standing between them, a little behind, was the Emperor of Russia: immediately behind Louis XVIII stood the Emperor of Austria; behind the Duchess, Monsieur, le Duc de Berri, and others not distinguishable, at least not by me, although I was immediately opposite to the window. The troops that defiled were about thirty thousand, composed of horse, foot and artillery; they were principally Russians. I remember that almost all the officers of the Russian Guards appeared exceedingly young. The Czar was pointing out interesting details to the Duchess. It was like an autocratic family photograph. Minus the white sheep. As I looked round for it, a number of shots were fired in the air and I heard cries of *Vivent les alliés* mixed with a few subdued *Vive le Roi*.

And there was the white sheep – most remarkable of all – our own Wellington, on a white horse, in a simple blue cloak, with a white neckcloth and round hat, riding between General Stewart and Lord Castlereagh. As soon as his presence was known, there was much crowding and a storm of whispers. A friend of mine sitting in the window with the royalty later told me that to a man they all craned their necks. For my part, I felt a boundless desire to see the great man who had renewed the art of war itself along the thorny plateau boundaries of Spain. I took a considerable risk of being trampled and crushed in my eagerness to get close to him. Two other Englishmen next to me showed equal eagerness and pushed past with the words: 'Oh, for God's sake, let me see him! – I'm sure, sir, you will show me indulgence, but I absolutely must see him!'

And in June, the great victory celebrations are to move to London. The autocrats of Europe are on tour (Kean said), like a company of actors in a successful melodrama. He himself had appeared in a less successful performance of *Macbeth*.

His own dagger-and-murder and regrets-and-anguish scenes very

very good. But Mrs Bartlett's Lady Macbeth was unbearably beyond all the demands of the rôle . . . Kean is not drinking. Something is oppressing him. He said he had met a man who had met a seaman from the crew that had taken Bonaparte from the Italian mainland to Portoferraio on Elba. He had said Boney had been jovial for the whole of the crossing, talking and laughing and saying the world had made a great mistake when it had taken him for a genius; he had been like everyone else. Which anyone else ought to have been able to interpret by the type of successes and failures he had had.

June 11th – Went to the Opera. House packed – they say over two thousand people got in free because of the crush at the entrance. All the boxes as full as lifeboats on a sinking ship. People were suffocating and tried to steal air from each other. Open all the doors, someone shrieked. Outside, the summer night was thick with London's organic cries. Inside, the air was as warm as *skin*, moving like an incessant and constant touching of alien human skin, and breathing was like breathing in out of other people's mouths. Panic created waves through all those heads, and what was all the more remarkable, it all managed to quieten down by ten o'clock when royalty arrived. The ovations made use of the energy of panic and thus were able to continue for quarter of an hour or more. That matter is quite clear. I would prefer a thousand times to freeze to death than to suffocate from heat! The orchestra played 'God Save the King', everyone stood up, and I've never seen a more grandiose sight than that row upon row of ladies in magnificent creations. From Lady Tavistock's box, I had full view of the royals. With the exception of the King of Prussia, everything but everything was a flame of red. For his part, he was wearing blue. The Czar sat on one side of our fat Prince of Wales, the King of Prussia on the other. The King and the Czar were wearing the Order of the Garter, the Prince lamentable in sickly obesity between those austere monarchs radiant with health. The performance was of an operatic melodrama called *A Girl from the Country*.

June 27th – My birthday. Have broken all my good resolutions of last year, but henceforth am starting afresh.

August 11th – Met Byron and his sister. What can one say about her? She looks like a newly planted plum tree, knowing she is perfectly capable of standing upright on her own roots, but letting the dead straight support pole seem to wind itself protectively among her branches as she exchanges an ironic look of understanding with the spectator – me.

September 30th – Lord Byron – I hear – is to marry Miss Milbanke.

October 1st – Sent my congratulations to Byron . . . (?)

October 19th – Found a letter from Byron, in which he asks me to be his best man.

December 2nd – Dinner with Kinnaird. Present: Byron and Kean. I wish I could get to know Kean. But his very being prohibits it and raises its barrier with gin. There are such people, very open, simple and comprehensible and at the same time totally hermetic. Diagonal lines run through their faces. You don't know which side of them they are at the time. Kean is like that. Very communicative and doggedly mute. He said: You talk about people. I am people.

A few flakes of snow fell. We lit our cigars and I started reading out selected pieces from an account from my friend Macnamara that had come in my mail only two days earlier. Macnamara wrote that – in the name of truth – he had forced himself on the Emperor on Elba. He had quite simply stood in Napoleon's way as the latter was riding from Portoferraio to his villa. He had doffed his hat and waved it when the Emperor had made as if to pass. The Emperor's horse had spat at him and the Emperor held it in and asked Bertrand or Drouot, still riding: 'Who is that?' Reply: 'Don't know. Probably a stranger.' Said Napoleon to Macnamara: 'Who are you?'

'I'm an Englishman,' replied M.

'Aha. Are you a military man?'

'No.'

'In that case you must be a gentleman. Why are you here?'

'Only to see you.'

'Hm. When did you get here?'

'This morning. We had a storm last night and thought we'd founder.'

'Really. And where do you come from?'

'From Paris.'

'When?'

'I left there fourteen days ago.'

'That was a quick journey. Which way did you take?'

'Via Turin.'

'Have you news for me from Paris?'

'Not much. They have arrested thirty or so people and doubled the guard.'

'Have they now?'

Macnamara repeated what he had said. Napoleon ordered a horse to be given to him. One of the attendants dismounted and gave his horse to M. Napoleon turned to Bertrand, and said, 'Have you heard this?' Bertrand answered, 'No sire.' 'You shall ride with me,' said Napoleon to M., and they rode side by side for a short time, until Bertrand remarked, 'This is the road, sire.' Napoleon replied, '*No*; I will go to San Martino' (his country house), and thither they rode. On the road Napoleon said, 'What do you think of the state of France?' 'Empereur,' replied M., for so he always called him, 'we had a storm last night; now there is no wind, but the sea is agitated.' 'Well answered,' said Napoleon. Arrived at San Martino, Napoleon took M. into a small room, and shut the door. 'Now we are alone,' he said, 'you can ask what you wish. I shall answer you.' The conversation that followed lasted for more than two hours, and a most singular talk it was. My friend was not embarrassed by any modesty, false or otherwise, and took full advantage of the permission given him to ask questions.

He said: 'Why did you stay so long at Moscow?'

Napoleon replied, 'I looked over the meteorological tables for thirty years, and never but once had the winter set in so early by five weeks as it did in 1812. I could not foresee that. I made mistakes, as every man does, in the many years that I have been in public life and a soldier – perhaps ten a day.'

M: 'What, ten a day!'

N: 'Yes, ten a day. I made a mistake about England in trying to conquer it. The English are a brave nation. I have always said there are only two nations, the English and the French; and I made the French. What would you have done if I had landed in England?'

M: 'Risen against you to a man. I myself, with all my admiration for you, would have poisoned you. I would have sent you a dozen bottles of drugged wine, anything to get rid of you.'

N: 'Well, you are right. Then you do not think the English would bear being governed by me?'

M: 'No.'

287

N: 'No! Why not?'

M: 'They admire your abilities, but there are two or three things which you have done, and which they cannot bear.'

N: 'What are they?'

M: 'You would not like to hear them.'

N: 'Yes, I shall – speak.'

M: 'Well, then, the death of the Duc d'Enghien.'

N: 'Bah! such childishness.'

M: 'What childishness? Killing a man like that!'

N: 'Yes; what business had he to plot with Pichegru and Georges within five miles of France? Why could he not go elsewhere? He was tried and condemned by a council of war. He was not shot in the night, he was shot in the morning. I was told I must put him to death.'

M: 'I am glad you have cleared yourself of that.'

N: 'Well, what else?'

M: 'Poisoned your sick.'

N: 'That's not true. There were fourteen or sixteen ill of the plague. I assembled a medical board – they said the sick would die in twenty-four hours. I determined to wait that time rather than leave them to the Turks, who would cut off their noses and ears. At the end of the time only one or two were alive, and they were dying when my army marched. No, that charge is not true.'

M: 'The massacre of two thousand Turks at Jaffa.'

N: 'They were three thousand. Well, I had a right. They had been my prisoners. I released them. I knew they were in Jaffa. I sent a captain with a flag of truce to warn them to get away before the town was taken, as, if they were retaken, I should be obliged to shoot them. They killed my messenger, cut off his head and put it on a pike. The town was taken by assault, and the men were shot. I had a right. Mr Robert Wilson and Sydney Smith, who blamed me, would have done the same; besides, there were not provisions enough for French and Turks – one of them must go to the wall. I did not hesitate. I did not waver.'

M: 'How did you escape from Egypt?'

N: 'Nothing was more easy; but if Sydney Smith, instead of playing the politician with the Pasha of Egypt, had been attending to his professional duties, and cruising before Alexandria, I could not have got away.'

M: 'Did you not bring away three or four Mamelukes with you?'

N: 'Yes.'

M: 'We had a foolish story in England.'

N: 'What is that?'

M: 'You will be *fâché*.'

N: 'No. What is it?'

M: 'Why, they said you had fallen asleep, and one of your Mamelukes having some of your papers by accident in his hand, you took up a pistol and shot him dead.'

N: 'No; this hand is innocent of blood – innocent as yours. No; I never did this; it is nonsense. My Mameluke never slept in the same room with me; he had a chamber apart.'

M: 'Is it true that your Mameluke offered to cut off your head at Fontainebleau last year, and that pistols were left in your room for you to shoot yourself?'

Napoleon laughed heartily at this story. 'No, that's ridiculous – what! kill myself? Had I nothing better to do than this – like a miserable bankrupt, who, because he has lost his goods, determines to lose his life? No. Napoleon is always Napoleon, and always will know how to be content and bear any fortune. It must be confessed that I am in a better plight now than when I was a lieutenant of artillery.'

'Bravo, Empereur!'

During the conversation Napoleon said, 'Mon rôle est fini.' He added that he was writing his history. M. said, 'The writing of history will be a great triumvirate – Alexander, Caesar and Napoleon.'

Napoleon looked steadfastly at him without speaking, and M. told me he thought he saw the Emperor's eyes moistened. At last N. said, 'You would have been right if a bullet had struck me at the battle of Mojaisk; but my last reverses wiped out all the greatness of my earlier years.' Saying this, he walked away to the end of the room, and paused for some time in silence. M. next told him that Italy was in a turbulent state, and hinted that Napoleon might do something there.

N: 'Not there.'

M: 'Perhaps you think that country not large enough for you; but recollect the Romans gave laws to the whole world.'

Napoleon then said that Louis XVIII was a 'brave man, too good for the French. And so was I. I was too good for them.'

M: 'What? Too good?'

N: 'Yes, too good and they finally betrayed me.'

Napoleon said he could not think of Marmonth 'sans rougir', a man whom he had brought up from the age of sixteen, and who, only the night before he went over to the allies, had, at a secret interview close to Paris, sworn fidelity to him. He insisted that his last movements upon Paris would have succeeded if Marmonth had remained faithful. The allies might have had one gate of Paris, he the other. They would have been obliged to leave 300,000 men in the city, and then he should have beaten them; the treachery of Marmonth decided the business. 'Not one of the French marshals was worth that,' said Napoleon. He (N.) could make a French army bear and do anything.

N. continued: 'Wellington was a brave man'; he would sooner trust him with 100,000 men than any of his own Generals, even Soult; but it was very foolish to send him (W.) to the Court of France to face those whom he had humbled.

M: 'Why do the French Generals talk so slightingly of him?'

N: 'Because he has humbled them one after another. How did the English like the Bourbons?'

M: 'They thought little of them; they did not like the Duc de Berri, he was too debauched.'

N: 'Debauched! what do you mean – that he loved women?'

M: 'No, not that; he . . . and that is not liked in England.'

N: 'Neither is it liked here in France any longer.'

M: 'Did the Empress Maria Louisa like you?'

N: 'Oh, poor woman, if she *didn't* love me!'

M: 'What sort of boy is the King of Rome? Is he a fine boy?'

N: 'Well, I have seen very little of him. I was at the war. I know practically nothing about him.'

N. talked with much indifference of the child, and of the Austrian alliance. He said: 'It was a funeral marriage'. Napoleon asked repeatedly about the Princess Charlotte, and whether she was not a person of spirit and character. Of the Prince of Orange he said that he had intercepted a letter from him to his father, in which the Prince had abused the Prince Regent of England violently. 'This,' said N., 'was wrong, and I had a good mind to publish the letter in the *Moniteur*, but I did not. As to Belgium, the French will have it, or Louis lose his crown in a year – nay, in three: put that down in your tablets,' he said (tapping M. on the shoulder), 'and say Napoleon told you so. How is the old king? I know he never liked me; did he abuse me?'

M: 'He followed the bent of Ministers. However, he praised you for one thing.'

N: 'What was that?'

M: 'I don't like to tell you.'

N: 'Speak out.'

M: 'Well then, when you divorced Josephine and married the Archduchess, he said he wished he could change his wife too.'

Here Napoleon laughed violently; indeed he did so frequently during the conversation.

M: 'Is it true that you said that the Emperor of Russia was a bête sans le savoir, and the King of Prussia a savant bête?'

N: 'No; it is not true: the Emperor of Russia is a brave homme; but the King of Prussia the greatest bête I ever knew: he kept me half an hour talking to me of my uniform and my buttons and laid hold of my coat, so that at last I said, "You must ask my tailor." '

M: 'The next time you invade Russia you should have an alliance with England.'

N: 'Ay, ay, I committed a fault there.'

M: 'Is it true, sire, that at council you used to cut the chairs, and even your throne, with a penknife?'

N: 'Non, non, that's ridiculous. Where do such things come from? Do people think I've nothing better to do than such idiocies?'

M: 'You are fortunate in having such good health.'

N: 'Yes; I never was ill in my life.'

M: 'Yet our foolish newspapers and storytellers made out that you had all sorts of disorders, and one of a peculiar character.'

N: 'Ah! what was that?'

M: 'I do not like to say.'

N: 'Nay, speak out; I shall not be angry.'

M: 'They say that in Fontainebleau you were infected with . . .'

N: 'Ah, non; I've never had an illness of that kind in my life, or any other for that matter.'

He smiled, but said this seriously. Napoleon said Lord Castlereagh was a 'mauvais politique'.

M: 'It was because of him you had to abdicate.'

N: 'No, it was treason.'

M. asked Napoleon what he thought of Colonel Campbell.

N: 'I know little of him, this gentlemen. But why was he so often with me?'

M: 'To watch you, sire.'

N: 'Judging from the English whom I have seen, I should say that they know very little what I have done, yet they are anxious to know what I shall do.'

Napoleon said he liked Frederick Douglas best of all the English he had seen, adding: 'Though he is only twenty-five, he looks like a man of forty-five,' which is true enough. Napoleon spoke slightingly of the King of Naples, and called him a 'magnifico lazzaroni'. He said that Murat was the first to desert him. He repeated his question about Paris; and when he heard that his symbols and Ns were defaced, he said: 'Ah, that's a bagatelle, and perhaps I ought never to have put those Ns on buildings.' M. asked him if it was true that he placed money in any foreign funds. Napoleon seemed hurt at this, and replied: 'No, never: how could you believe it? I did everything I could to destroy your funds. Talleyrand might have bought into your funds: I never did; no, not a penny.'

M. asked him what orders he wore on his coat. Napoleon said that one was the Legion of Honour, which he would never part with; the other the Iron Crown of Italy. M. remarked that troops of all nations would be proud to serve under him if wanted. Napoleon said that he had no money to pay them; he had been obliged to borrow, having given the soldiers with him all the money he had. Napoleon asked M. where he lived, and being told at the Aigle Noir, said, 'Very well, I will send for you again.'

Perceiving that M. frequently rubbed his eyes during the conversation, he asked the reason for it.

'Why,' replied M., 'I can scarcely believe my eyes that I am alone talking with you.'

This pleased him, and when M. talked of his delight and the fear he had of taking up too much of his time, Napoleon said, 'I can assure you I am as glad to talk to you as you can be to talk to me; a stranger is a great entertainment for me.'

M. asked if he was not afraid of being assassinated.

'Not by the English,' said Napoleon; 'they are not assassins. I am obliged to be cautious in regard to some others, especially the Corsicans, some of whom have a strong feeling against me.'

I made a note of this conversation, at least as much as I remembered of it, on the same day that I heard it from my friend, who also told me that on quitting Napoleon he was accosted by Bertrand, who said, 'So you've had a long conversation with the Emperor; he must have told you a great deal.' M. said, 'The Emperor was very condescending; he must be a very good-humoured man and never in a passion.'

At this Bertrand smiled, and said, 'I know him a little better than you.'

Fever (1824/1816)

In an interval between the first painful days of influenza and his convalescence, Mr Hazell floated up into a state of feverish activity. He tossed from right to left, raised his head from the pillow and lowered it again. Once or twice he raised it to see who was standing there looking at him. 'Claire,' he said with embarrassment to his youngest daughter. 'Can you ask your mother to come.'

The girl's long hair fell forward of its own weight as she leant over him and put her hand on his forehead. He could feel each of her fingers, each joint on each one of her four cool fingers, the thumb separately. That gave him the confidence to leave behind him such a fine robust girl. Life wouldn't end as long as she was still there. She made the kind of remark that had always annoyed him, then said: 'Your temperature's over a hundred, Daddy! I'll get Dr Segal again.'

'Just call your mother . . .'

'Why Mummy? I'm here, aren't I? Mummy's out shopping. I can do anything.'

'Oh,' said Mr Hazell, shy in his need. 'Can you ask Rupert to come.'

'Daddy!' Claire plumped sternly down on the edge of the bed. 'Your son Rupert isn't here either. He's in the middle of term. And if there's anyone prudish in this house, it's Rupert.'

'Prudish?' said Mr Hazell in surprise. 'Prudish, prudish . . .' He twisted from right to left. He raised and lowered his head. A pocket-watch was tucked into a fold of skin below his ear. When he pressed his finger against the watch-case, he could feel his pulse racing. A second no longer had any value whatsoever, no lasting quality. 'I miss the slower time,' he confided in his daughter. But how could she understand that? She straightened up. 'Now listen,' she said, far too soberly. 'Ssh,' he urged. 'Daddy, if you're really as muddled as you sound, then I must get the doctor. I must. Now please tell me if you're joking,' she whispered. 'Can you hear what I'm saying?'

Mr Hazell smiled and wound (unconsciously erotically) a strand of her rust-red mane of hair round his hand and smelt it. 'You don't know life,' he said. 'At my grandfather's death-bed – I was your age – I was also convinced he was joking. He usually was.'

There had been another thread to this thought as he first began to put it into words, but the look in the girl's eyes stopped him. He searched for it: 'Those irretrievable things. Or . . .'

Claire helped him. So he was content and looked at the butterflies on the ceiling, then abandoned them, for they probably weren't of substance to him. Mr Hazell was perfectly aware of where he was – in his sober marital bedroom. But that knowledge did not stop the walls floating and beginning to show films of an aquarium. This happened regularly, like breathing, and must have had something to do with the rhythm of his fever. Nothing surprised him. The remarkable thing was that the flowing fluttering surfaces caused him to be collected and systematic. What the doctor later called 'mild hallucinations – take those flowers out, they give him no pleasure' – entailed a conscious fantasising. How many times had he lain staring at those flat yellowish-white walls? The place for the inhibitions of his imagination – for the first time he found it abandoned. And this, in his marital bedroom.

Art, thought Mr Hazell, absorbed in the long wall with three windows. A great-tit was perched outside the glass pecking putty off the window frame. It looked at him and pecked and pecked away, and looked at him. It tossed its head and changed eyes to look at Mr Hazell.

However, there had been no eyes. The eyelids had been glued together, almost grown together. Otherwise Byron hadn't been horrible to look at, fairly intact, if you disregarded the fact that someone had sawn off the aggravating right foot. A fragment of a jar beside the fallen column. Anyhow, Byron was not lame in death. He would have approved of that. He was not horrible, but 'a life long since fled the nutshell'.

Who had said that? In a consoling tone of voice to Joel Cohn, who hadn't wanted to look at all, pleading to the very last that it was an enormity to break the taboo, and that together they had anticipated the ruthlessness of a new, almost unimaginable era. Yes, it was his own son. It was his son, recently capable of opening his mouth and expressing himself like a wise man. A life long since fled the nutshell. Mr Hazell sat up with a vague panic-stricken suspicion of infection. He forgot it. The great-tit flew away. The wall closed.

The wall closes and the wall opens. He realised he would never write about Byron and Shelley on a closed wall, on the straight wall. He wouldn't write. He was the only one of the five who could write, but he wouldn't, for that wall in particular had to be open, and draw him with it into the generous – loss! – of the third dimension, where nonetheless most of the intelligence of mankind flows, mixes and tumbles on without ever being fastened to paper (of all materials). And with this realisation, it all began slowly to go backwards:

It all goes backwards.

Mr Hazell closes the coffin with its eyeless poet, who, in purely Old Testament fashion, has rid himself of his lameness. He seals it. He groans with the effort and groans a little more as he manages to heave it all up into the hearse. Six weeping horses back away to London.

On the Edgware Road, the equipage stops abruptly at an invisible wall. It was time. It turns. And then it all starts moving forward instead. Clippety-clop, clippety-clop.

*

The spectators are tightly packed along the Edgware Road on that lovely June day in 1824, between them a funeral procession in which not one single distinguished guest is participating.

'Look at that! You ought to have died twelve years ago. The greatest and the best glowing with their absence despite your fresh status as a hero. You can't expect them to dare to honour a man who has scattered doubtful rumours around himself. Incest is one thing, but it was very stupid of you to boast to Caroline Lamb of your visits to Turkish baths, "those marble palaces of sherbet and sodomy".'

'So what,' snaps the poet. 'Who has asked for this? I've lain here splashing around in spirits all the way from Missolonghi to London. Bury me on the spot, I said to the poor wretches, without all the pomp and fuss customary in my circles. And *no* autopsy. And *no* embalming. And what did they do – apart from arranging a whole lot of disputes about when, where and how I was to be buried? They cut and hacked and sewed and prepared until I looked like something out of Victor Frankenstein's production.'

Apropos of that . . . apropos of that . . .

The sun is shining, the pollen floating down through the airy early-summer day. No, not pollen. Dandruff.

The spectators in the windows along the funeral route are mute. In strata. One of them contains a woman combing out her hair, long shiny dark-blonde hair, and she is just combing out the very last of her widow's veil, as well as her housewifely hairpins, and then she lets her hair swing like independent guitar strings.

She is sitting sideways, half inside, half leaning gracefully over the windowsill, gathering a long tail of hair in her hand and grooming fiercely. She shakes her hair out over horse and carriage, regarding it all, but stubbornly holding on to life. Then she takes the guitar in her arms to honour her dead friend a trifle –

> So we'll go no more a roving
> So late into the night,
> Though the heart be still as loving,
> And the moon be still as bright.
>
> For the sword outwears its sheath,
> And the soul wears out the breast,
> And the heart must pause to breathe

she attempts.

'But Jane . . .' says the other woman with mild reproach. The one standing out of sight. The one with the veil forever burnt into her hair – all of it held together in a dusty bow. Jane strikes a false chord to make fun of formal and possibly false expressions of grief. She says people should mourn according to their natures. Their Own Natures. You weep for this man by letting down your hair and letting your fingers twist among strings! Mary Shelley listens, looking gravely at her, making some effort to take in the words, but naturally finally misunderstanding them and thinking she is right to *desecrate* the passenger down there:

'Ha ha. Yesterday I went down George Street to look at the coffin and met Fletcher, who looked dreadful and was crying, describing in

297

heart-rending terms his master's last moments, like an actor who gets more drama out of the melodrama the more often he acts it out. I couldn't help remembering the way he went on about Byron's meanness and heartlessness less than a year ago.'

Jane sighs with boredom. *Finita la vendetta! Basta!* Not one single time more does she want to hear Mary's 'unvarnished opinion' of 'the great Lord Byron'. She doesn't want to hear another word about all the ways in which His Grace could be said to have betrayed the memory of Shelley, his widow, his ideals, his furniture, his friends . . .

To Mary, Byron seems to have been a kind of embodiment of the cruelty of *chance*. It's all the same to Jane. She is not part of the conflict. And Mary needs someone to loathe. When chance afflicts her, making her Shelley's widow, the surviving mother of three dead children, she has to be allowed to hate someone who with his friendly lack of interest may resemble the deity one is not expected to believe in, and so she cannot curse it. The more friendly, the more cruel. Who needs friendliness? Jane tunes her guitar, her hair fluttering in the wind.

Mary notices she has spoken without listening. Anger is tone deaf. Here come the six horses. Then the hearse, with *croquenbouche* décor, tassels and fringes. Poor Albé, all the same. What a journey home. They ought to have made a pyre for him down there, as they had done for Shelley – poor creature, they could have done that. 'Albé gone?' she cries in astonishment when she looks into the hearse and is overwhelmed. The actual coffin seems to have acquired that closed, indifferent face. Albé . . . dear capricious fascinating Albé. Now everything is gone. Now we're all gone!

'Not "we", surely!' says Jane, going over to her bureau and writing a letter. Mary stays where she is so that she can recognise faces in the procession, then see the people disperse, then see the wind dispersing the kind of things a crowd leaves behind it, stains, footprints, rubbish.

The whole story reverses eight more years. The scene lightens. Another, younger wind disperses the remains of Easter 1816. Two crows are flapping through Hyde Park. It has been a terrible winter. The temperature dropped, the barometer falling as if bottomless. The crows had not understood the way people complain about such weather, so they had hacked at the barometer and made it fall even further. In February, all hollow trees crashed. Icy pains in bad teeth. Now it is April, but although the trees have started to come out, the winter winds return – half and half, as regularly as faded memories of terror, and in one of these the crows take each other by the arm. Not affectionately.

As always they are dressed in black silk gowns, black capes and small bonnets. Black is economical, saves labour and is unfussy. Beneath each hem, small black shoes with holes in their soles peep alternately. The fairer one also has carefully darned gloves. The dark one – the one hurrying them both on, eagerly, carried away – has trimmed the ragged tops of hers and is showing off the display of ten small skin-roses. Jointly they use their strength against the north-easter, although the fairer one, Mary, would have preferred to follow the wind home. It is the first time. Previously, they have always enjoyed walking into the wind together. But now Mary has a living child; she would have preferred to stay at home with her baby, the lovely snuffling 'Willmouse', and is afraid the others do not understand how to relieve his breathing. If only Clara would stop chattering all the time. The wind whips the words out of Clara's mouth and distributes them round the park, a small fraction only reaching Mary's ears, the rest to strangers and into the ear of emptiness. This is what it sounds like: '. . . . and have persuaded Albé that a free woman has quite different claims from a Wife tied by traditional commitments . . . have made him understand that my desire is our mutual freedom. Freedom effected through Each Other . . . not dependent . . . without significance . . . The Special Importance of the Moment rather than the measured time of contract . . . freedom to create other emotional ties.'

Naturally it is possible that Mary's ear construes the conjunctions and leaves the inner sense to fly across the Serpentine. In that case, it doesn't matter, for she has heard Clara's whole argument before, not once but many times: Albé has experienced what the traditional marriage can bring with it and he says he's had enough of it. Oh, Mary. Our life would be very very perfect. I'm no silly goose. You know that I don't strive for two people's happiness. No, I'm thinking of us all. It's as a foursome that we can create undivided perfection . . . know perfectly well Albé will understand Shelley's unique goodness and his genius . . . he'll at once see you as you are . . . the most delicate, the strongest of all . . . chatters the stupid girl day after hectic night. As far as Clara herself is concerned, she has 'never been so happy'!

Mary writes in her diary: 'My happiness would be undisturbed would I but experience two things – that Shelley regained his full health and absentia Clara.' She finds it painful to have to meet Lord Byron under circumstances such as these. She is not at all convinced by Clara's assurances that he, 'Albé', is expecting them. She has seen him once, here in this very park, riding alongside the carriage in which his wife was concealed, again and again leaning down to speak through the window, and each time straightening up laughing. She would now like to obey the stubborn attacks of the wind and have it at the back of her skirt in order to flap home, to the south-west and her little William. She never trusts anyone or anything. It is more than likely that neither Shelley nor Hogg nor the nursemaid understands to hold his little head so that he is not choked by his cold. But Clara has her in a firm grip. Clara always grasps things in a steady but faulty grip. A week or two ago she had shown Mary a letter she was to send to Lord Byron.

This is how she had expressed herself: *If a woman, whose reputation has yet remained unstained; if without either guardian or husband to control her, she should throw herself upon your mercy, if with beating heart she should confess the love she has borne you for many years . . . could you betray her, or would you be silent as the grave?*

Very sophisticated. Very naive. And sophisticated. Offering – as its own demand – the secretiveness and togetherness without obligations attached which every comfort-loving man desires from the woman he does not love. Sophisticated. Very naive. As if you could gain something by not demanding anything. As usual, Clara had her philosophy all wrong when she came to put freedom into practice. The falseness of the honest.

'Why do you call him Albé?' says Mary trivially, in amongst these great declamations. That's the only thing Clara hasn't explained. Clara turns out to be a trifle abashed.

'Oh, that . . . you see, he didn't like being called George. Nor does his *wife* or his sister call him that. That's because practically all his cousins are also called George, he says, and he says he would feel exposed in their presence if I called out George.'

(Called out George . . . it is Mary who grins. She grins in the shelter of the wind. Perhaps the poet also puts his lace handkerchief over the girl's face when she 'calls out'?)

'And he doesn't want me to call him Byron. That's a comradely form of address between men, he says. The fact is, hm, Mary, between you and me, he's somewhat proud of his birth. There seem to be a number of 'established facts' in his understanding of life and one of them is the value of a title. He can certainly be freed from this with a minimum of argument. In addition, I have to forgive it, because what can be the reason except that he has been a poor boy who has no particular wish to deprive himself of the compensations of his elevation?'

(A small thought in large clothes, Mary thinks.)

'He prefers me to call him My Lord or Lord Byron, in syntactically given circumstances. L.B. is the compromise I use to myself, and admit that pronounced, the initials produce irresistible resemblances to the Light of Dawn. Naturally I shouldn't call him Albé. One shouldn't flatter people with nicknames.'

'Marvellous!' says Mary in astonishment, and soon took over the name. Behind Byron's back, they generally said Albé. Until everything came to an end.

The moment they step inside number 13, Piccadilly Terrace, she smells the familiar scent of catastrophe. It agitates her, almost panics her, then affects her physically, for this is truly very familiar to her. Clara has not described it. Perhaps she doesn't smell it. She certainly doesn't smell it, for what she has described is a magnificent household in a state of stylish collapse, inhabited by a gentleman indifferent to objects and relieved by his wife's absence. So, a Man After Clara's Heart, sworn off all such dependencies that cannot be given a higher abstract meaning.

However, Mary sees a man with his hair plastered over his temples, apparently stunned, robbed of his earthly goods, amputated from his earthly ties with the same dull confusion as anyone else. In the smell of catastrophe, Mary senses the icy nuance of distraint. He was listing the number of particularly valuable books which had been auctioned, and she almost felt she had to cry, for in her home they had at least managed to keep their books each time.

'I hear you're the daughter of William Godwin,' said His Grace, 'in my opinion, the only philosopher of rank in England since . . . since. Greater than everyone in the same league, Bentham, for instance. Have you seen his Panopticon? – such stupidities. Naturally I have read your father's book with that interminable title summarised into *Political Justice*, but nowadays I'm so far gone in years I can no longer comprehend his ideas. He says man can only show his just face when he has been freed of the oppression of institutions. I should be the obvious example, but I don't think I *have* a face since I was "freed" from the institutions of marriage and fatherhood . . . In my opinion, there is no such thing as the genuinely human (particularly not in the sense of goodness), but what the individual human being *is* is part of a colossal vitality that settles in layers on the institutions.

'I consider institutions are the skin formed by the body of society – our *appearance*, I mean – and as you know, it is not always what we wish for. But what can *one* do about that? Despite surface differences, people are covered with skin and hair in more or less the same way all over the world. And institutions are fairly alike everywhere except in the ideals of idealists (where they are usually even worse). Your father is a great philosopher, Miss Godwin, the greatest since . . . er, since. But then I'm too old.'

Mary answered briefly: 'He is older.'

Byron showed approval with a very fleeting smile and then repeated – really like an absent-minded old man: 'I hear you are the daughter of William Godwin?'

'And Mary Wollstonecraft,' said Mary. That was the first time that day (the first of many times during their acquaintanceship) that she was all too ready and willing. She always held out her hand to him for longer than he requested, and he took it coolly and with surprise.

'Hm, yes,' babbled Albé absently. 'I don't think much of female literati. They do what they think they have to do, but that's nonetheless unnecessary. Your mother is said to have lived by her learning, tragically, and should thus have elevated her scribbling to real life, which is more than can be said of most of us. Drowned, was she?'

'No,' said Mary, her eyes hot with irritation. 'She died of fever at my birth.' His great eyes – on the other hand – began a slow widening, as if this were the first he'd heard of puerperal fever. 'Unfortunately,' she added. Albé's eyes were now as wide open as if he were about to give birth to them; Mary knew she had again been too informative. She regarded those eye-globes glistening and shifting in all nuances of grey, and then had regrets. Why did she tell him things? Why not let such a discourteous person remain ignorant of one's circumstances?

302

It's a meaningful punishment: to withhold yourself; also from people who are not important.

'How terrible!' The enormous eyes had acquired a mawkish lustre. He had large eyes, a large nose and large curved lips. Suddenly, fatally, all that became small and shrank into the middle of his face. There was a smell of catastrophe there. She looked round, saw the empty rooms and took a step from the right nearer to her own centre, then a step from the left nearer to her own centre, so that she became almost half her own width. He followed her manoeuvre with his eyes, as if recognising it. His hair was wet and he had recently changed, in the middle of the day, like an infant.

'Please sit down,' he said politely, 'presuming you can find a comfortable place to sit. You probably know everything about me, Miss Godwin. Everyone does. None of the world's great catastrophes arouses enthusiasm in the press even approximately corresponding to what is released by a wife's antagonism to her husband. You can scarcely believe your eyes. Miss Clairmont has told you that you will be stepping into the ruins of a life. Unfortunately, they lack the patina of age. By that time, I will probably have learnt to live among them. In contrast to your parents, I have no learning to survive and so nothing to excuse my actions. So my misfortunes are just as hopeless as an infant who has lost his mother. I still don't understand a day of the past year (and a half). I did not wish to marry. I was married and did not wish to divorce. I was divorced.'

(Meanwhile Clara talks and tries to interrupt the conversation to introduce the speakers to each other, with the aid of a few painful civilities. She talks far too much and sweetly about Shelley, who is not hers. Laughing, she disguises herself in an exotic costume she finds flung into a corner. He never listens to her. He snaps in reply. Mary despises him a little, because he despises Clara, who has given herself to him. His sin is worse. He has given himself to her without wanting to have her. No man would understand such a description, least of all a man who says to Mary Wollstonecraft's daughter 'I loathe literary women'.

But she couldn't disregard his 'how terrible' and the emotional glisten in his eyes.) When Clara began to run round the house to demonstrate how familiar she was with it, he said quietly: 'You're not in the slightest like your sister.' Mary replied promptly: 'We are neither sisters nor half-sisters,' raging at herself for revealing herself again, and Claire as well. Far too eager not to be linked by blood to her stepmother's daughter, she had put out the whole of her warm hand into his cool one yet again. Angrily, she went further: 'My real sister is Fanny.' After that she heard herself saying: 'Her father is American . . .'

For the second time, she had to move her two sides closer to the middle so that she almost obliterated herself into one long streak of aversion. Lord Byron looked her up and down, down and up, neither contemptuously nor appreciatively, but said helplessly: 'Miss Godwin, do you really think I could love your sister?' Mary lowered her eyes and shook her head, in order at least to avoid audible disloyalty.

Byron, Albé, went on: 'I do not love your sister or your non-sister Miss Claire Clairmont. She refuses to understand crude hints and continues to come trotting and warbling to my door at all times. I haven't *time* for her. The first time, she came with a peculiar letter, in which she bade me be as silent as the grave, something I soon complied with by not receiving her. Then she came back, and yes. In contrast to the experience of a wife disappearing without a word of warning or explanation, softening your heart in order to crush it, at the same time trying to involve everyone I value and making them share her loathing . . . in contrast, a little admiration did appear good. I do not wish to embarrass you or torment you, and I am not usually as open-hearted as this. It makes it much easier for me that Miss Clairmont is not your sister. I would not address you in this way if I hadn't some hope that you could help me put an end to all this. In itself, it will die of its own accord, as I am leaving the country within a few weeks. But nonetheless, I wonder whether you would help me convey my situation and my motives to her understanding, so that cruelty can be avoided. Can you?

'I shall tell you what my situation is. I do not fit in with any dreams. Least of all Miss Clairmont's. She seems to imagine me as a counterpart of a certain Mr Shelley, father of your children, as far as I know? Judging from her expositions, it appears that we four would constitute a commune of spirituality and radicalism in a dying England. Very free. Unprejudiced. It makes my head ache. Miss Godwin, could you possibly imagine sharing your sister with me in a commune and allowing her to take little samples of Mr Shelley? Such things *happen*, but it is insane as a *programme*. Programmes, in my opinion, have to be strictly conservative and lacking in detail. Inside them and in secret, sin will be committed, but never sanctioned in the programme, because then it loses its purpose.'

'What is the purpose of this "sin"?' smiled Mary, but Byron was in a monologue, not a conversation.

'Miss Godwin, to avoid cruelty to your sister, I need your help to explain my situation to her. I am not free. I have never been less free than I am at this moment. Breaks are infinitely stronger chains than ties. Do you understand?'

Mary had to avert her eyes from him to be able to hear. One of the cats took a huge lithe leap, visibly rising into the air and landing like a snowflake on the very narrow banister.

'I did not want to marry. I did not love the woman I married. Nor did she have money, which some people consider appropriate to maintain now. Between us, our finances were equally good and bad, so it was neither a question of a "good match" nor of the ordinary emotional storm (obsession). I simply married a creature free-standing from me, who inspired mixed feelings in me.

'So we lived together as most people do, and reasoned and judged people we knew, and quarrelled and were reconciled and I still didn't love her, but after a while it was only her presence that could console me for that lack . . .'

Mary understood at once what he meant, but he seemed to imagine that he had served up an obscure paradox, so sat in silence for a long while before his unnecessary clarification:

'When she was installed in my life, and the more she fortified her position, the more the flatness of her topography appeared in my ideas of "happiness" . . . or what. And out of this flatness, details detached themselves which became so *intimate*, they entailed greater consolation for what she had deprived me of than what a reconquering of my stormy past could have achieved. You look bewildered.' (She did *not*.) 'Let me say it again: she herself was the best medicine for what she had inflicted on me. Gradually, the medicine became food. I tried just once to compensate for this lack of passion, but what I . . . used to . . . do, left me more or less unmoved. You are sure to have experienced something similar. As you grow up, you lose the taste for certain irresistible things and miss them, while at the same time you develop a taste for such things as previously seemed uninteresting.

'Now you see, "love" had arisen. "Love", whatever that is. It was a love I had never wanted to have; neither the object of it, nor the sort was to my taste – everything bore the musty colour of dullness. It was bread and it was butter.'

The cat processed along the banister with small firm steps, turned snake-like straight through itself and tripped back with a balance so self-evident, it was as if she were relying on her ability to fly.

'Why is it,' said Byron, 'that lovers first all confide their sorrows to each other, secret sorrows? I have sat here for these two months and between curses and appeals tried to work out what love "is" – an idiotic mode of thinking, Miss Godwin, but you are consoled by the knowledge like an antidote (though it's a poison, all antidotes are also poisons). Meanwhile interrupted by your non-sister, confound her, there she is, twittering along the corridor again, no, she's going past, poor Fletcher . . . a totally idiotic way of thinking, as the result is entirely dependent on your mood and so changes from day to day. Where I am at present is this:

'Love is to burden someone with your *weight* – like a *gift*, and have it accepted as a gift. It's a damned miracle! Ordinarily, you survive people's company by giving them doses of some kind of lightness. But what you at first desire overwhelms you with its sorrow, for only with it can you describe your ability to feel. Honestly.

'When you speak of your Sorrow, you tempt with the contents of your heart and lips. The strange thing is' (Elby slid down into hindsight, like a goldfish plopping back into the bowl after you've changed the water. Mary accompanied him. She smiled at him through a large lens of yellow floating dust. He had been caught by his ordinariness, for certainly Shelley and she had made love on her Mother's Grave.) '. . . the strange thing is that as desire decreases, sorrows fade. Passion gives everything its vitality. Love is the joy of life, is the end of the glow-worm, sorrow a mask, the mask a mask . . .

'I think I am on the point of coming to the point, Miss Godwin.' Byron smiled with his mouth closed, just like the cat looking at them, measuring its leap. 'This bread and this butter – this woman who was the only one with the ability to console me for what she had done to me – with her very presence drew out of me a thirty-foot tape-worm. If I previously succeeded in depriving people with my sorrow and debility, she set about hauling out the wasting element. She took me much more seriously than I – can take seriously. Marriage seems to be an intimacy of souls that you live through, so lost to yourself that you come out on the other side like dazed strangers to each other.' Again Mary saw that he distrusted her ability to grasp his paradox.

'What more can I say? I have already said too much. We were associated with each other. The whole question of love came to a level where it was inaccessible to passion. So Miss Clairmont must leave this house before she makes herself unhappy. She must see to her own interests. We have spent on each other whatever insignificance we had to give and I have neither illusions nor desire for more. I am associated – with uncommon respect – with a woman whom I did not love.'

'Aha,' said Mary, intellectually interested.

With constant
interruptions
for peace

March 13th, 1815 – My father wakes me with the news that Napoleon has fled from Elba. They say he left the island on February 28th with about eleven hundred men gathered from Elba, Corsica, Italy and – to some small extent – France. His ship tried to go into harbour at Antibes, but became involved in an exchange of fire with the fortress. Instead, he went ashore at Cannes on March 1st, with four guns in the advance guard. They abandoned the guns at the first town gate, the men deserting. Two or three sections of the troops were dispatched to the same number of forts, equipped mainly with grandiose words, and were disarmed by force, by superior numbers and – as far as words are concerned – by mocking laughter.

March 15th – Napoleon Bonaparte has been outlawed and there are a hundred thousand *louis d'or* on his head. The same applies to all his adherents and instigators. When he is captured, he will be court-martialled immediately by the first military commission. I am preparing for departure to France.

March 17th – Letter from Cockburn – fears that all is over in France. General Marchand has been killed by his own men, who then went over to Napoleon. This occurred during the retreat from Lyons, which is said to have welcomed the Emperor with open arms. Soult is leaving the War Department, Clarke taking it over. Monsieur cannot trust his troops, nor can Masséna, who is said to be holding on to the Bourbons. They are starting to take some measures to defend Paris. It is maintained that Napoleon is a hundred and fifty miles from the capital. Grenoble taken with twenty-four guns. Embargo on French ports.

Yesterday's early post confirms that Murat has deployed in north Italy and that on February 28th he made a joint proclamation from him and Napoleon, THE EMPEROR OF FRANCE AND THE KING OF ITALY, promising Italy unification and independence. Everything seems to have happened in a conspiracy between these two: the fact that no one has guarded against that possibility is unfathomable. Napoleon, for instance, had an agent in Naples, while we even lack a minister there. Murat has an army of eighty thousand men and seems to intend to use them against the Pope. His hyperbolic proclamations when he joined the Allies, his ambiguities just beforehand, the way he has been treated since then – all nourished the suspicion that the King of Naples would join his brother-in-law, Napoleon, at the first opportunity. The Austrians are boundlessly unpopular in Italy. They say the Milanese and the Veronese have already taken the opportunity to massacre twenty thousand of them. Even Switzerland has taken up arms against the allied liberators of Europe – eighteen thousand foot soldiers to assist the Emperor. So the time has come to see what our own government can do.

I soon receive a letter from the Congress of Vienna which helps me with that information: Lord Castlereagh has divided Saxony, given Poland to Russia, Italy to Austria, and is now on his way home to be praised by a satisfied Parliament.

More information from the Congress of Vienna: the Czar of Russia and Countess Wierbord had a dressing competition. They met and on a given signal left the room through separate doors. The Countess returned completely changed a minute and twenty-five seconds later, the Czar achieving this in one minute fifty seconds. General Czernichef and Sophie Zichy had a similar competition. While these farces are taking place, Napoleon sets foot on French soil and says: *Le Congrès est dissous!*

March 23rd – Reports of the King being at Calais, others of his being in Belgium; certainly he has fled from Paris, and according to all conjecture Napoleon must have entered Paris on Tuesday. The army at Melun gave up like every other corps and melted away before the Conqueror. The news of Napoleon's landing at Cannes arrived in London on Thursday, March 9th; in thirteen days we learn he is in Paris; in twenty days he traverses the whole extent of the country, which would take a common traveller with ladies a longer time, waiting by the way three or four days to give balls, and reviews at Lyons. We do not know that a shot has been fired.

England wears a melancholy air. All is to be done over again; we have lived in vain for twenty-five years; we are bankrupt as it were of power, and must recommence our struggle for life. And now come friends who had the good fortune to get to Paris before the embargo. They have with them even more confusing details. I stand staring at a pan of boiling soup and see fragments of vegetables and noodles swirling round in a never-ceasing new pattern. Now the macaronis come home and tell of their swirling. Desperate Paris laments round one single thought: it was insane to allow Talleyrand to go to the Congress of Vienna – had he remained in Paris, the Napoleonic conspiracy would have been discovered.

An old woman in Paris stands in the street stirring her chestnuts and crying: Vive le Roi. A man beside her replies: Vive l'Empereur, and she hits him with her ladle. That seems to have been the only battle for Paris. And perhaps Paris is already pacified by stories from the countryside. Such as this one: Napoleon advances towards Grenoble. The city defenders prepare to fire. The Emperor dismounts and strides up to a grenadier, pulls his moustache and says: 'And you, old moustache, I remember you from Austerlitz.' The soldier lowers his weapon and cries, 'Vive l'Empereur!'

March 27th – Rode to London to prepare for my journey to France. No letters from my newly married friend, Lord Byron – vaguely worried. Now a letter has come by the midday post. All my suspicions seem to be groundless.

April 1st – Before I left London, I visited my friend at his new 'headquarters', 13, Piccadilly Terrace. I expressed surprise that he had chosen a house numbered thirteen. He sighed and took my joke seriously – as expected, his superstition is unshakeable. Lady Byron came in and shook my hand in thanks for an autograph I had sent for her collection. She looked well but rather pale. When she had left and I cautiously made some remark about her state of health, my friend smiled that meaningful smile that is expected, or rather a shadow ran across his face. From that I came to the conclusion that he is to add a generation to the Byron family tree, despite all those cheerful predictions to the contrary. As I bade him farewell, he clutched my hand and said he wished he could come with me. He urgently advised me 'not to enter into matrimony', which he said was the most unnatural of lives 'although I have the best of all wives!'

April 2nd – Dover was a mass of rumours, a sulphurous hole. We saw ship after ship swinging up the Channel. We thought we could almost see the way they lowered the lilies and hoisted the tricolour on the other side. The *Duke of Wellington* set sail at four. Got up after nine, and found we were at anchor a mile from the harbour of Ostend, the tide being out, and the sandbank, which is daily encroaching, preventing us from coming in. However, we went in boats, I having no difficulty as to passports or Custom House. The harbour was full of English transports, and they were landing some horses of the 11th Dragoons. The town appeared in military occupation, swarming with red coats. I took the opportunity to inspect it. It lies on a flat tongue of sand and has a long narrow harbour. I climbed up on the fortifications and wandered about. No English officer disturbed me, but a soldier of the Prussian army forced me off the parapet. That is what German discipline is like. No individuality is permitted.

April 12th – I arrived at Paris in the rain at half past seven. We trudged round rue St-Honoré searching for a hotel supposedly called The Prince Regent, but only succeeded in finding a wretched inn we were deceived into deciding on when we saw the name Hotel Great Britain.

I spent the following days largely with other Englishmen and with Frenchmen who liked, disliked, worshipped, hated the Emperor, and was plied with so many anecdotes altogether that I could have written five novels on the spot. Yes, these days, Napoleon was the greatest of novel heroes, well-sold, on everyone's lips. Not just stories circulating, but rumours to a greater and greater extent. Most of the French want to stop time. Napoleon as Emperor, the grandiose atmosphere of the Empire back again and the oligarchy gone. But status quo presumes peace. If you capture the moment, it can produce a sense of peace – while the war keeps growing beneath the surface of peace.

April 16th – We went to the Tuileries, I and Latour Maubourg, who had heard that I had come to France with the intention of seeing Napoleon. We left our horses at the gate to the Tuileries Gardens and I took Madame Souza's arm. First we went into Queen Hortense's state room on the ground floor, with arcades out into the courtyard. We met a company of people and I noticed a lovely gentle-eyed woman who turned out to be the Duchess of Vicenza. She spoke to me and told me she usually prayed for peace with England.

The square began to be filling with the National Guard, who filed in without number. Thirty thousand were to be reviewed; twelve legions, forty-eight battalions. The Duchess told me a hundred cannons were to be fired to-day for the reduction of Marseilles and the general peace of the Empire, and she mistook drums for guns. In other instances she showed her anxiety. She said she did not fear the military, but was frightened at the men in plain clothes standing near the entrance of the palace, where the Emperor was to mount. Latour Maubourg said, 'I am under no alarm,' to which she replied, 'I own willingly that you are braver than I am.' Indeed, this day has long been fixed as a day on which some great blow was to be struck by the Jacobins or others. Some said a woman was to do the deed.

The place continued filling with troops; several led horses, of which two or three were white, and were led under our windows. Suddenly we heard a shout of *'Vive l'Empereur'*, and I ran through the rooms to the gate of entrance. Napoleon had mounted and was gone off the left of the line. In a short time, however, the cries of *'Vive l'Empereur'* came towards us again, and an officer galloped by waving his sword to the line. Shortly after followed Napoleon himself with his *cortège*, and distinguished from them all by being in a plain cocked hat, without tassels or feathers, but ornamented only with the small tricoloured cockade. His hat was placed square on his head; his uniform was that of a Colonel of the National Guards, with one star and a small cross hanging from his button. He went past on a canter, and suddenly drew up. An old soldier near me said, 'See there how he stops to read the petition of the meanest of his army.' I could not help waving my hat and joining in the cry.

I caught repeated glances of the Emperor as he cantered down the lines. He seemed to stop at the end between each line, and his approach and progress were always announced by shouts of *'Vive'*.

Went to the gate again. The regiments moved nearer the palace, and the gates of the triumphal arch being opened the remainder of the Guards, the 24th battalion, came in from the Place de Carrousel. There was a crowd of officers about the gates of the palace, and I got in amongst them. A space was made between the palace and the arch halfway, and a large body of officers of the National Guard quitting the ranks came towards Napoleon, who with his staff drawn round him addressed them shortly in a speech, every now and again interrupted with shouts. I was close behind his generals but could not hear a word; the press was great, and the gendarmerie on horseback rude. We waited then in a throng some time, until movements took place in the troops, who prepared to march by in columns of companies, being pressed up under the windows of the palace.

I suddenly heard the *Vives*, and the Emperor passed close by me. He wheeled round, and, coming into an open space, just before the palace gates, put himself in front of his staff to review. He was on a lean-looking white horse. Two officers, who knew from Maubourg of my pilgrimage, pushed me forward, and I got within ten paces in front of his right hand. Scarcely a regiment had passed before he suddenly threw his foot out of the stirrup, and came with a sort of lumpish tread upon his feet, and put himself in front. His horse was led off, an aide-de-camp rushed forward to take hold of the stirrup, but was too late. Some of his staff dismounted, but a General with a red ribbon always stood on horseback on his left. There was a press of officers and a very few men in plain clothes, and women on each side. Maubourg and myself were the only gentlemen in plain.

I had for some time a most complete opportunity of contemplating this extraordinary being. His face is the very counterpart of Sir James Craufurd the runaway, and when he speaks he has the same retraction of his lips as that worthy baronet. His face is deadly pale, his jaws overhanging, but not so much as I had heard. His hair is short, of a dark, dusky brown. The lady in the Tuileries told me the soldiers called him *notre petit tondu*. He generally stood with his hands knit behind him or folded before him, three or four times took snuff out of a plain brown box. Once looked at his watch, which, by the way, had a gold face, and, I think, a brown hair chain, like an English one. His teeth seemed regular, but not clean. He very seldom spoke, but when he did, smiled in some sort agreeably. He looked about him, not knitting, but joining his eyebrows. He caught my eye, and soon withdrew his gaze, naturally enough the first. I have only him to look at, he having some thirty thousand.

As the front of each regiment passed he put up the first finger of his left hand quickly to his hat to salute, but did not move his head or hat. He had an air of sedate impatience. As the regiments came by they shouted, some loudly, some feebly, '*Vive l'Empereur,*' and many ran out of their ranks with petitions, which were taken by the grenadier on the left. Once or twice the petitioner was nearly losing his opportunity, when Napoleon pointed to the grenadier to go and take his paper. A little child, in true French taste, tricked out, and marched before one of the regiments. A general laugh ensued. Napoleon contrived to talk to someone behind him that none of the ridicule might reach him. A second child, however, dressed out with a beard like a pioneer, marched in front of another regiment directly up to him, with a petition on a battle-axe, which he took and read very complacently. An ill-looking fellow ran from the crowd, I believe, towards him in an old regimental with a sword by his side. The grenadier and another stepped forward and collared him, but Napoleon, unstartled, motioned them to loose him, and the poor fellow talked close to him some time with eager gestures, and with his hand on his heart. I did not see Napoleon equally well at all times, but stood, during the whole of the review, close to him, gazing at him through hats and a musket or two on tip-toe.

I positively found my eyes moistened at the sight of the world's wonder – the same admiration of great actions which has often made me cry at a trait of Greek or Roman virtue caused this weakness; but I do not know that if Napoleon had not then stood before me as the man against whom all Europe was rising, and as the single individual to dethrone whom, or rather to destroy, a million of men were rising to arms from the banks of the Tanaid to the Thames, that I should have felt such a sensation. No; there was something of pity, which made me look upon him with such gratification and melancholy delight. Add besides the reflection of his recent exploit, the most wonderful of all his actions, and I am not astonished or ashamed at having experienced such feelings at the sight of the man who has played the most extraordinary, gigantic part of any human being in ancient and modern times.

The last regiment of the National Guard was followed up by boys of the Imperial Lyceum, who came rushing by shouting, and many of them running out of ranks with petitions. Then, for the first time, Napoleon seemed delighted. He opened his mouth almost to a laugh, and turned round to his attendants right and left, with every expression of pleasure. I did not catch the sound of his voice. I should say that

Flahaut brought Lady Kinnaird into the *cortège* behind him, which making some bustle, he turned round, and on Lady Kinnaird blushing and dropping several curtsies, made, I believe, an obeisance. The people by me said, 'Ah, it is *la petite Anglaise.*'

After the boys went by he went into the palace. I followed with the crowd, and found him sitting on the steps speaking to someone. I pressed up within two paces of him; he passed quickly upstairs and received his Court, some of which shortly after came down.

Fanny Beauharnais was once a beauty. She was vastly civil to me, asked me how I liked the sight, and seemed pleased at my curiosity. She ended by saying, I believe, she hoped to see me again. She talked anxiously about peace. I always say what is true. I believe the people are for, the Ministers against it. A man I met when dining out replied in this way to my question why Parisians seem so unmoved by all these dreamlike courses of events: we do not value life as highly as you do. Nearly all have done service in the war and when you have run all risks and worse, nothing remains to fear, nothing is left except your life to lose. Only a life, yet another life.

May 29th – I couldn't help it, but went to yet another review of the troops. Sometimes Napoleon stood almost directly below my observation post in a window. He inspected his troops on foot this time. He moved among them. He marched in time with a column, in perfect time with it. I saw him go up to a grenadier and give him his flag and – after talking to him for a few minutes – pulling his nose. I also saw that when a middle-aged colonel leapt up to him, Napoleon broke off his speech and cuffed him smartly over the ear, which seemed to delight the colonel – he strode off smiling broadly and showed off his ear, which was red from the blow. I have never seen anything like it and was almost frightened when I saw Napoleon stretching out – for the colonel was a fine-looking man – and striking heartily, but a man in general's uniform standing beside me said calmly that this was a usual and much sought-after caress.

June 12th – Napoleon has left the capital. In his speech to the deputies he said: *I march tonight!*

When I think of Napoleon and his warriors as predecessors of the Cause of the People as opposed to the conspiracy of kings, I can't help hoping the French will have as much success as possible without my countrymen's honour being compromised. Yes, even if I myself would

315

have wished for the Cause of the People to be in cleaner hands. I am divided – as an Englishman, I do not wish to witness French triumphs; as a lover of freedom, I do not wish to experience the opposite. Tomorrow I shall also be leaving Paris. In the park I spoke to an invalid from La Grande Armée who had been given back his full pension on the Emperor's return. He said: 'Napoleon is a good man who knows something about the people, though he thinks rather too much about war.'

June 19th – On the roads all round Paris, I hear that three days ago the French army won a total and decisive victory over Marshal Blücher and the Duke of Wellington – near Brussels. I get out of the carriage and walk slowly behind my slowing carriage. The coachman tickles the air with his whip and sings a song. The deeper the evening, the warmer and more moist the air becomes. The moonlight traverses pale streaks of mist and pearls through the tops of the oaks and they meet in a glade of tall grass.

June 20th – There is a strange report in the corner of a column in today's *Moniteur*:

Beyond Ligny, June 16th, half-past eight in the evening.

The Emperor has just won a total victory over the united Prussian and English armies under the command of Lord Wellington and Marshal Blücher. At this moment, the French forces are advancing on to the town of Ligny, near Fleurus, to pursue the enemy.

June 25th – All is over. At St Albin, just as we were to journey on, a man stopped our carriage and asked whether we had heard the news. What news? Well, the bad news – *the Emperor had returned to Paris and abdicated.* We stopped in Sennecy for ten minutes and managed to get hold of a newspaper.

Napoleon seems to have won victories on the 16th and 17th. On the 18th, he attacked the English at Waterloo and had almost managed to break through the line to Brussels when – at about half-past eight in the evening – four battalions of the guards were afflicted with some kind of confusion and started fleeing in panic. The French army thought that the Old Guard had been thrown back. *La Vieille Garde est repoussée*, was the cry, and in that situation a traitor whispered '*sauve qui peut*', let him save himself who can, let him save himself who can echoed and the whole army started running. In vain the Old Guard tried to stop the panic, but was instead borne along with the size of the herd, even squadrons of the Emperor's own lifeguard being forced to retreat. They all rushed to the communication points and it ended in utter defeat. Poor Europa, you will have to pay the penalty for that under your bone-white despots and their rows of grinning teeth. French guns, gun-carriages, the whole range of artillery, all the army equipment left behind and taken by the enemy on the battlefield. The Emperor had to flee through Belgium and return to Paris.

The people round the post office where we were reading the newspaper did not want to believe us, but the postmaster confirmed it: *C'est vrai, il a été complètement battu.* There seems to have been some impatience at the core of the guards that caused the catastrophe. There was no longer any reason to doubt what had happened at Waterloo. But nonetheless we could not believe it or take it in . . .

July 6th – Paris capitulates again to the collected armies of Europe. This evening I rode out to the city gates to see the English troops on the hills.

July 7th – I hired a horse and rode out to try to gain information on a matter that has occupied the whole of my inner self, but which to tell the truth I have taken lightly after having seen the lists of dead and wounded. I thought luck had been on our side. I shall spare myself the trouble of an account of the way I heard how badly mistaken I was. An indelible wound has been made in my heart. I have lost the most affectionate, the bravest and the most honourable of brothers – he was the flower in our unhappy family. The enormous losses suffered by the English Army in this fatal victory have for me been concentrated into one soldier.

My brother fell at Quatre Bras. The last time I saw him, he was on horseback in Brussels and I pointed out to him that he had a bullet hole in his cap. 'Yes,' he said. 'I got that in Bergen-op-Zoom. Next time it'll hit lower down.' And that is what happened. He was on horseback, serving as aide-de-camp to General Halkett, and found himself in front of the line as the French troops advanced. He fell at one of the first bursts of firing. Got a bullet in his throat and died immediately.

My father wrote to say he had sent the letter with the account of his son's death to a very prominent member of parliament. This man's reply ended with: 'Oh, how I envy your son.' A few days later, my father's correspondent committed suicide.

July 27th – Met Lord and Lady Byron in London, and our friend

Douglas Kinnaird. She says a number of beautiful and wise things about life and death and how personal loss clouds the jewel of peace. Meanwhile she rests her hand on mine and looks objective. She already has a curve of proverbial blessing beneath her dress. He says that he can't help feeling blunted in the relief over every misfortune that does not afflict him in particular. He says this with a weary look.

February 25th, 1816 – Riding from Richmond Park to London in twenty below zero when I get a message from Kinnaird to say Byron's suicide is now probably very near. My father advises me against intervening between spouses. He says reconciliation usually afflicts the intermediary. I take my servant with me and whatever else is needed for a few weeks in strange houses. We set off. The first minutes are an intoxicatingly fresh experience. It is easy to breathe in the cold air. It is beautiful – the sky a deep blue with thin veils of chimney smoke. The bare trees glow in all the colours of the spectrum, in dripping formations of mist the cold has burnt on to the bark. But suddenly your nostrils freeze and a stiffness becomes perceptible in your respiratory organs. You see peculiar distortions of light when your tears turn to ice. My horse has a beard of icicles and slows its pace instinctively to avoid sweating and becoming chilled.

My servant, riding diagonally behind me, throws his shadow in front of me, tormented, in long boots, his wife's woollen shawl wrapped round the brim of his hat, most of his face, shoulders, upper arms and chest. In that simple way of the people, he holds his hand over his crotch, having no idea, not indicating there might be something inappropriate in the gesture. Alone, we gradually make our way down Piccadilly. London is a deserted city. I and my servant in long boots, on horses icing up like boats.

Mrs Leigh received me. She said that 'poor B had fallen asleep after three or four days & nights without any'. She gave me a cup of red-wine soup with sugar and cinnamon. She said 'if you can help poor B then in truth you will be succeeding in doing the impossible. This whole business is a terrible attack on his reason & have you seen the all too unambiguous signs that his liver is failing, Mr Hobhouse, his mood is the reason why poor A has taken this step, which *sans doute* she will regret, for never before have I ever seen a woman so attached to her husband – aha *perhaps she was forced to leave him because he has a way of being absent even in his presence*,' said Mrs Leigh with her special type of clearsightedness in all her disarray – 'such things exist, Mr Hobhouse & the world is full of all the peculiarities that defy our interpretation, though perhaps she longs quite simply to be able to make him really unhappy by prohibiting him from anything to do with Ada & he worships that girl as you yourself have seen & I have written to poor A and asked why she does not equally well put a pistol barrel to his forehead & pull the trigger & that would on the whole be more merciful than this torture . . .'

I gave myself permission to flee this avalanche of opinion. I went to my friend's bedroom, so that he would see a familiar face at the moment of waking. He was sleeping very soundly, a dreamless drugged sleep with the aid of some poison from the arsenal his apothecary was so generous with, a green light dispersing his superstitions and the darkness. When you sit and look at a face, you learn the features by heart, but the text is always changing and the face finally becomes very alien. I thought about those who had touched it – a snakepit of tongues between those lips – and yet innocently. Lady Byron's cheek grown together with his, now parted by a surgical incision – for I do not doubt that down to the last dot, Miss Milbanke is following a plan she has established and will never share her doubts with anyone else. My friend is the one who is the publicly shifting wind.

He did not wake. It was too dark to read in the room. Then the pistols on his bedside table caught my attention. Mrs Leigh had prepared me in that she had not interfered with his habit of having them within reach – she said that such a conspicuous gesture as to 'appropriate the pistols might call his attention to *the way out* in question . . .' I went closer to look at those familiar objects, but saw them in the way one sees reflections of light at the bottom of a dark well. There seemed to be an infinite distance between my eyes and those pistols, from my eyes to my hands playing with them. My eyes swelled and glowed and at the same time looked at his – covered by the green shimmering blindness of eyelids. I had taken out my right hand and from that a finger that swung one of the pistols round its barrel and left it aimed at him. My mind played with it at an infinite distance from my feeling. My eyes glowed at his, which did not turn away but stared back with blind shimmering green surprise.

I turned back to my chair and banished my vigil with daydreams and by recapitulating the main points in my defence of Byron. Half London was suddenly using his name as abuse and imagining hideous depravities that were to have driven Lady Byron to leave their home for her own safety. I daydreamed for a moment about the red-haired M.E., who had shaken her curls and said 'he should have married me instead. I am both rich and tolerant', daydreaming about her on my own behalf in the name of honesty.

My daydream was interrupted by his dream – a word from his bed, in his sleep! 'Some . . .' he remarked matter-of-factly.

Scarcely a year had gone by since we started our journey north, his journey to his marital project. It was Christmas Eve. Miss Milbanke had waited a week or two. I stopped the night in Cambridge, he at Six Mile Bottom to celebrate Christmas with his sister. We were to continue the next day, but he didn't appear until about three the following day. We set off and dawdled with three long stops to Wansford. I couldn't remember ever seeing a lover in less of a hurry.

The next day we got up late and dragged ourselves as far as nearby Newark, where we arrived early and spent the whole afternoon and evening reading in front of the fire. The bridegroom seemed less and less eager to reach his goal. The next day we travelled a short bit and slept at Ferrybridge, and the following day we actually managed to get all the way to Thirsk.

No wonder I felt like an idiot when we arrived at Seaham on the evening of the 30th and tried to explain our delay, Byron affectionate, but impersonal in his understanding of *their* agitated feelings. I found Miss Milbanke in slight disarray outwardly, not beautiful but pleasing. She attracted a kind of interest of the sort that can be misinterpreted as love. She showed all the signs of being fond of Byron and he seemed to love her – anyhow when she was present . . .

What had happened since then? For my part, I was abroad most of the time. Their façade was quite neat and tidy – no disharmony apparent to Byron's friends. He spent a lot of time at home, too much, in my opinion. When they were seen out together, he hung around her all the time, proffering small attentions such as cups of tea, fans and shawls.

A month or two ago, he told me that his finances were such that they would drive him insane and that she did not understand anything about that. He said that no one could imagine what he had had to go through and no man should marry – it doubled his unhappiness and halved his well-being. 'My wife,' he said, 'is perfection itself – the best creature breathing; but, mind what I say – *don't marry*!'

The fact was that during their marriage, this splendid woman tried to manipulate his inclinations away from his friends. This embodiment of perfection never understood to treasure a custom such as amicable loyalty. She could not grasp that people have an ability to be firm in their principles without embracing her way of thinking. A total inability to understand irony and humour caused her to be offended and irritated by the tone of conversation between us. She functioned with Virtue as her starting point. This was marked, despite her educated and well-formulated manner. She could not see morality and principles in any other way of life except her own. She could have separated in another and calmer way, but her dramatic flight and the consequent petrification had a definite aim – to give the world the impression that Lord Byron was a monster. One who had committed such horrors that his wife was not able to endure even a single minute in his company.

Mrs Leigh had confirmation of this when she was called to the hotel in London where Byron's mother-in-law was staying and from the lady in question heard the most violent condemnation of him. When Mrs Leigh realised that the Milbanke household was implacable and intended to go through with a divorce, she requested a postponement by passing this on to her brother. She implied that Lady Byron's decision might lead to his taking his own life. To which his mother-in-law replied: 'All the better! Such men shouldn't be allowed to live.'

To me, childishness is a mixture of naivety on your own part and calculated coldness towards those around you. The only explanation Lady Byron gave was that for a long time she had wanted to believe her husband was insane, but that after her return home to her parents, she had realised he was just evil and base. How she had come to this conclusion, she did not explain. Mrs Leigh did tell me how Lady Byron's suspicions towards my friend had made her go up to the attic – repeatedly during the autumn – and unlock his boxes of private papers, letters and diaries to make a thorough study of his pre-history and secret self. She had found among his belongings a small bottle of laudanum and some obscene books he had bought in the Orient. Lady Byron had then consulted her medical dictionary and, to judge by the symptoms, she had assumed Byron must have water on the brain . . .

He turned his head a minute fraction of a fraction under the green light, which dispersed superstition, which dispersed the darkness. How could he be so unhappy over the loss of this severe child?

While I tried to make my impressions whirl to rest, whirl to rest, time and time again I kept getting up to wake Byron to demand the missing piece. There was a piece out of this story, something missing. Either it had been carved out of Lady Byron's sense and reason, or he himself had withheld it. I looked at his sleeping face and searched for openings, but could find no place to mark the gash. Standing over his bed, I experienced – perhaps every other time – the same distance, the same well-depths as previously, though once or twice the opposite as well – a suffocating closeness in which he seemed already dead.

I took his pistols. The missing piece contained death. All the rest – the accusations and counter-accusations, serenade and rejection, and the increasing *publicity* in all this (which would have driven anyone out of his mind. When the newspapers get hold of such things, they lack all mercy and take every rumour to be the truth, then improve on the truth and let someone be pilloried by it – in this case Byron) – things of that kind are unbearable but they pass. Something in this story was incurable and I was unable to grasp what.

Fletcher came in. I know that if anyone is in possession of a missing piece, then he is the one – perhaps he would even give it to me . . . oh, what a thought – every day, the world is a newly healed place which would be turned into a meaningless bloodbath if everyone possessing knowledge were provoked into letting it out. Strict regulations for the way truth is turned into silence are the only security of individual life! And if a man like Fletcher possesses the key to a truth about a man like Byron, it would still not be certain that he knows what he possesses or what it might lead to.

Fever (1816 – the Diodati summer)

Mary Shelley needs no more fodder for her thoughts.

Square windows are a peculiar idea. The soul looks out on to the world through shapes resembling splinters of glass; triangles with small curved sides. Two splinters had stood polished and open the moment she was born. They gave her the first glimpse of what was to be her ultimate weather. When she was born, dawn had happened to be at dusk. A strange sky arches over Mary's life. It is going to take a lifetime to fathom it out.

Clara and Shelley. And Albé and then Maria Gisborne and Teresa Guiccioli and Trelawny and Jane Williams and all the others. All of them travelled and rested, travelled and rested. Mary wished she could be allowed to stay still. But she herself collaborated in that they took her with them on their travels and rests, travels and rests. Of which the rests caused more trouble and pain.

'You ought to have lived in an English village and never had to leave it,' said Albé, with his terrible blunt intuition. Mary detested intuition. It understands far too immediately, but on the other hand never understands to express things with the same finesse as it understands.

'With friends,' he went on, 'whom you shouldn't have to let into your life like this. And who shouldn't let you into themselves, nor should they let you out into *awful* freedom. You should have been slightly churchy. You should have listened to a stream all day long. You should see your children playing in the meadows, and harbour ordinary worries about snakes and wasps. There should be a balance' (balsam, stammers Byron) 'for the cold that comes swirling through your warm heart. The drama, these Alps, drugs, courts are wasted on you. They are an abundance you are incapable of safeguarding. Mary, do you want . . . do you want me to . . . No. No.'

Tears poured out of Mary's eyes. She had been intoxicated with black drops. Who, who? Clara? Mary's eyes tried to turn up in her head. She gasped them down with a great effort and tears poured out of her eyes and nose. Albé wiped them away with goodwill and the back of his hand. Lampreys, the eye on a water stem. Came upright on its tail and shone in the dark corridor, moving totally out of step. Shelley? No, he was probably out in the dark with Clara, helping to blow wind on her bark boat. In Madness, we must all be very strong and sensible and organised. Albé, for instance, went on wiping away tears and snot with the back of his hand and goodwill. Her round mouth – only one part of her body seemed to keep itself outside this intoxicated chaos – gently protested.

'You should have lived in an English village,' repeated Byron, continuing to devote himself to her face. 'You would have had all the opportunities to improve your French and your Latin and learn to read Petrarch and Tasso in Italian. And Dante . . . of course, you're the kind of person who would wonder what you would owe the devil. It's not necessary to travel abroad. Under any circumstances, it is uncomfortable for a woman. Particularly for a woman like you. You have no need for drama. Everything is already clear to you; without illustrations . . . no, let me do it! – why do you resist? – washing and wiping is absolutely innocent! This is the first time I have seen you anything but superior and prudish. Mary. You have chosen to live an immoral life, superior and prudish, and people should live according to their choice. Who has *intoxicated* you so? Not Shelley? Even if you live in sin with him and Miss Clairmont, it is not necessarily as liberated as he wishes. Liberation is a cruel ideal. (Believe me.) Be superior, be cold and prudish! Do you want . . . do you want me to . . . No, no!' Albé pressed against her, questioningly and exceedingly briefly. No, no.

'They say that you *think* all the time. Not about something else or someone else – just murdering your brain and frowning over an insoluble problem as you allow yourself to be loved. He says you can only be diverted from your thoughts by means of *trivialities*. They maintain that you can be happy and free only with things that do not move you. What a sorrowful fate trying to move You' (Albé laughs at it

324

all by once again – promisingly but just as exceedingly swiftly – pressing against her. Sampling her. Then he added) 'a sorrowful fate for Mary, too, but perhaps worth the sorrow, for *Frankenstein* is an outstanding book to have been written by an eighteen-year-old chit of a girl. She,' he said, knocking on her genius, on her head, on the monster-seams where she was put together, thirsting for love, loveless. 'How did it begin?'

How it began? How it began? Well, as he knew perfectly well, it began a few months ago, when the crows in Hyde Park went to Switzerland because Clara had to see her lover again. This is how it began: Mary Godwin, Mary Shelley, rolls back the month of June. She rolls up half of August, then July, then the month of June – the dark reflection of the Jura mountains in Leman. The peaks of the Savoys with their contours of cream and fire from the sinking sun. The evening when it began, the lake bottom of an Alpine shaft and Mary, Shelley, Clara at the bottom of the bottom of the shaft. The silence sighs and sleeps . . . An ear. An oar. A splash behind the spit of land. A glimpse of a prow and its reflection, soon visible, spreading a veil of swell, a soft moustache slowly dividing from shore to shore.

Three dusk-coloured figures are standing on the grass below the Hôtel d'Angleterre in Secheron, strangely, unusually silent, watching the two people on the lake, where daylight still persists – the boat full of red, golden and purple colours, like a lunch-box of leftover festive food. The one rowing is singing on the water. Columns of sun now come straight up out of the lake – the beauty of it cannot be retained, for in its transitoriness it is at its most frightening. Columns of air and light and water decompose at a single splash, becoming smoke curling down. Lord Byron is rowing and Polidori talking.

Then the boat floats up on to the green patch above a sandbank and Albé laughs in the same green colour, light-heartedly unconscious of what is to come. Mary hears a dragging sound of the bottom of the boat. Why is she standing there waiting? Mary Shelley Clara? Because no one can understand how totally uninteresting she can be to someone who interests her.

Shelley has listened to Clara, obeyed her and financed this journey to Switzerland. He has seen that Clara is in love, and as he himself is a good compliant man when people seek him out, he thinks all good feelings (like 'love') must be well received by the recipient, regardless of everything. He has never understood power-loving love or unhappy love. To him, love is love and its complications only a fruit of the oppressive norms of society. Mary Godwin has heard him discuss the subject in absolute harmony with her father. They were in full agreement round the theme that inclination is elementary (unfailing) trust which can only fail to achieve its goal by being met by a normative distortion.

So Shelley could not have done anything but help Clara to Switzerland. Mary had not had the patience to explain how L.B. was to rebuff Clara, from motives not normatively distorted. Mary was the only one – between lake and land like this – who could predict the coming minutes. She smiled, an unintentional smile, roughly the same shape as the shoreline between the naivety of the land and the ignorance of the lake. Oh – absentia Clara! Absentia Clara!

Well, so they had arrived at Secheron, impatiently hustled on by Clara, who feared her lover would have time to come and go. In actual fact, they had arrived a good two weeks before him.

The hotel was expensive, in every way better suited to a peer in purple and scarlet than a young family of three adults, a baby and a nurse.

Clara examined the guest book every day. Every new arrival was questioned by this indiscreet girl: had they by any chance observed Lord Byron on their way? Yes. They had seen him booking in at a hotel in Brussels, had seen him riding on the battlefield at Waterloo with the British military commander as guide; yes, they had seen him floating along the Rhine and writing sketches about Drachenfels; they had seen him gazing at a waterfall here and there; had seen his eyes widening as he crossed the border to stunningly fat and sumptuous Switzerland.

Meanwhile the three of them went on daily outings in the boat. Clara and Shelley boldly, without reflection, Mary with sheer fantasies of images of death.

Life colours Clara's and Shelley's cheeks red as they stand poling their way out. Mary chose to keep them company, for the sake of the sport but with no oars; took her eyes off the lake bottom, not finding it. If she had to drown, she wanted to drown in shallow water rather than deep. She wouldn't want to go on sinking towards eternal darkness and be sucked in under a rocky ledge at the bottom of Leman. She wanted to die in daylight.

Late one night, the colossal wheels of Byron's Napoleonic carriage rattled over the gravel in front of Hôtel d'Angleterre. That night, Shelley used sharp words to stop the silly girl from running through the corridors of the hotel with triumphant lure-calls to warn her lover of her presence. The next morning, she found his slanting signature in the guest book. He had given his age as a hundred. Clara hurried to compose a note which ran as follows: 'Dearest, I would have guessed two hundred, considering the *time* it has taken you.' Then she waited in and around the lounge all day, but the note received no reply. Nor on the next day, nor the next. Nor did Lord Byron put in an appearance. Mary wondered whether he had climbed out of the window to avoid Clara – late in the afternoon, she saw him walking a dog along the shore. At that moment Clara was at her post indoors. For she did not give up. She was never aware enough to give up, and Shelley strengthened her obstinate courage by taking his hammer and trying to nail down that 'good and true feelings bear a conviction which is irresistible'. He and Clara stood upright in the boat and poled away with red cheeks. Mary sat as far down as she could get, dragging her hand in the water like a cool current that made her fingers transparent, in spite of it being only the outermost skin of those horrible depths. Meanwhile, Shelley and Clara poled and strove and tried to get out to the point furthest away from all shores.

On her lonely walks, Mary ran into Clara standing in corners. Ready to go. For the second time, prepared to capture Albé and conquer him with obstinacy.

Byron weakened when he caught sight of her on the shore and at once gave up. Saying not a word to Polidori, he leapt over the side of the boat down into the water's edge and trudged despondently over to the three expectant young people standing close together in a fellowship of head, hand and arm, like three links in a plait of hair.

In the middle a very tall overgrown boy, his exterior indicating he had not got around to visiting his tailor since the last four inches had been added to his stature. Shoulders were splitting sleeves which were ragged quite a way above the wrists, and the length of his trousers was compensated for by bootlegs, but that did not conceal the indecent smallness of an outgrown pair of trousers in relation to what they were expected to contain . . . Shelley's hair stood on end above his knobbly face. But this face possessed a wise and inquisitive pulse, holding Lord Byron's looks and turning them into something in exchange. In contrast to most faces Lord Byron had come across on his journey, this one did not stare at him to console itself, but from delicate hunger.

On the right side of this youth huddled the little Godwin, scarcely coming up to his armpit, and there made little movements as if settling herself into her nest. On his left was that person who insisted on running after him with wide open loins. It was insufferable. It was inappropriate and repulsive and she was an utterly insufferable girl, like adhesive, like fish glue. She was bewildering, not in an attractive way but more from her appearance and resourcefulness than many he had come across – but unable to combine these advantages with beauty or intelligence. Among all the women he had known, she was the only one to arouse aversion even before it had happened. Diffuse feelings of shame on his own part; that over-ripe, semi-rotten dream you dream just when you wake up feeling sick.

Lord Byron said 'Ah, Miss Godwin,' and solemnly shook hands with her. Wearily, he shook hands with Claire Clairmont – giving her three fingers and a mute bow. At that moment, Clara tried to free herself from Shelley and lean over towards her lover, but tripped mawkishly over her skirt, and if Dr Polidori, who had tied up the boat and was on his way past Lord Byron, had not mechanically stretched out an arm, she would have fallen flat on her face.

In this dark confusion, Lord Byron said, 'Ah, Mr Shelley. I've heard about you from' (he listed three names without mentioning Shelley's women). 'I've read your "Queen Mab" and – I appreciated it . . .' He looked anxiously at this beanpole to see what effect 'appreciated' had. From experience, he knew that the simplest expression of appreciation can also confirm the most complicated creations. Expressed more clearly – a little praise is enough. What did this giant think? Yes, the corners of his mouth twitched with delight and he turned his eyes up so that the water-green clouds coloured them with happiness. Poor fool, thought Lord Byron. No audience. It's a torment to write for emptiness and not readers.

'This is . . .' He introduced Dr Polidori, his physician, who was standing on a high tussock behind Shelley to measure his own minuscule height, plus *something*, against this lanky youth.

'Are you a *real* doctor?' The voice was light and metallic.

'Of course. Do you think I use a toy one?' said Lord Byron with a laugh. 'He may well be a trifle young, but he can both cut and saw. Apart from writing verse, it turned out. Had he revealed *that* talent during our negotiations, I would never have appointed him.'

'Do you know the *anatomy* of the human body?' said Shelley, cutting straight through the 'conversation'.

'Yes,' replied Polidori, giving the company a contemptuous glance.

'Would you – for a reasonable return – teach me the basics?' asked Shelley.

'One learns the basics on the actual material,' replied Polidori, with yet another degree of contempt. 'I doubt you could acquire such a thing. On the other hand, although the illustration plates are idealised, I can certainly show you some and explain them. Though not for – hm – what you mentioned. My duties include some hospitality. Diversions, as far as it is within my limited abilities,' said Dr Polidori, bowing offendedly from one lady to the other and walking away.

The rest of the company stayed where it was, wavering like slender plants in the wind.

After a while, Lord Byron said: 'I think our doctor was offended by something. But don't worry. Firstly, I am his permanent stumbling block. Secondly, a day has never gone by since he came into my employ when he hasn't been offended, insulted or deeply wounded on at least seven occasions. But he's a very young man, with a young man's lack of expertise, and he says he has left his lonely old mother for my sake! I wish people would stop sacrificing things for my sake (or saying that they do). I am quite nonplussed by so much benevolence and can never think of a just sacrifice in return.'

Lord Byron was twisting a belt or a cord extremely impatiently between his fingers. He would have liked to raise his cap to Shelley, Godwin and la Clairmont, with a noncommittal phrase about meeting again, but these three strangers reeked strangely of *legitimate* expectation. Why legitimate? In that case, the mortgaged party was himself, for the other three were standing very still, staring like so many fillies at the manger when they see the stable boy coming with replenishment.

They were silent. He made another effort to leave, but instead chose the next concession to polite conversation.

'I have decided to rent a villa for the summer. We've just been looking over two that can be rented for a singularly reasonable price. Staying in hotels in Switzerland is far too expensive! And there are far too many English tourists here. Clap your hands and a hundred flap up out of the bushes. And they all stare at you and scrutinise you and write home about whom you've met and which acacia tree your dog has cocked its leg against. Tell me, are you staying here because of the comfort? You can get private servants much more cheaply than service. I don't understand why you haven't sought alternative accommodation yourselves.'

Said Lord Byron, in complete innocence. Shelley looked embarrassed. Claire protested: 'But this was where *you said we could meet, dearest.*'

A hideous grimace crossed Lord Byron's face: Mary thought the God of primitive rage had come pumping up from its hiding-place in his body and had briefly shown its vile smile. Every muscle in her body turned weak and every vein went cold at the sight. It was not a grimace, but a black calloused mask with empty eyes. She had no time to grasp how he got rid of it, for he was soon as smooth as the lake, and his voice was as smooth as the lake as he described some of the houses he had viewed: the romantic one Dr Polidori had preferred and the lighter, more modern villa he himself had signed a contract for that very afternoon: Villa Diodati . . .

The Diodati summer! – in later years, spells of time are put in order of precedence. Mary counted the summer of 1816 as her happiest. Could it be said to be a high point . . . in a balance that according to all their silent agreement was to be a summer, then cease?

In the most exquisite manner, everything synchronised with everything else.

Six years later, Albé declared that for his part, that summer had been the unhappiest of his life! He had just been through some of his 'difficult and heart-rending separations', his 'name was defiled', his 'finances in ruins' and his 'country had spewed him out'. Mary loathed him for those words. She pursed up her mouth, but not until she had opened it for a cheap comment: 'If unhappiness was what made you into such a thoughtful friend, such a magnificent poet and incomparable host, then I wish you plenty of it!'

For Shelley and she had been unhappy for exactly the same reasons.

But from the start, they had the sense to observe – preserve – the amazing sweetness of the constellation of that Diodati summer, a sweetness that temporarily transformed misfortunes into vexations. And vexations are something a man can with philosophy easily dismiss to the level of trivialities. Days and nights were like one long day, a day that veered exaltedly, and they spoke like minor gods.

At first, Albé moved in at Diodati and, shortly afterwards, they chose for themselves a little house at the foot of the vineyards running down from his grass. The path between the houses was industriously trampled, running between vines and in air that was like music – as such, it healed Shelley's chest and baby William's lovely but delicate self. Never had he flourished so – never again was he to flourish as when the vines bloomed at Leman. The undramatic, exquisite fragrance was also what William was, and when you agree with the air you breathe – then you are secure.

Clara was not 'absentia' but nonetheless absent, owing to a disturbance of temperament. Albé had spoken to her alone. She was an obstinate girl and reacted with only one day on her sick-bed. Albé had a serious conversation with Shelley and when Shelley repeated in a subdued voice the contents of the conversation to Mary, she was triumphant: 'And you heard those exact words from my lips two months ago, dearest Shelley, when I met him at Piccadilly Terrace. But instead you chose to bolster Clara's hopes, although you ought to know now' (said Mary spitefully) 'that she always constructed truths out of her own illusions. We can't condemn him, for Clara admits he was *not* her seducer – in that she is a free woman. And we've always agreed not to condemn anyone who does not love. He has made it quite clear to her and to me and to you that he does not love. And here we are,' said Mary.

They were Four, all reservations between them established and understood, inner boundaries carefully marked out. The third eye that could be open at night was always closed in the morning. Everyone considers the Diodati summer a scandal between two poets and two girls. That's not true.

In the morning, the third eye was closed. Most nights, Lord Byron churned out poetry in the way an opened vein pumps out blood. Mary and Clara went back and forth between the vines with originals and copies of the third canto of *Harold*, as well as of shorter poems. They copied some in his drawing-room. Others in their own little parlour. With their own eyes, they saw the careless sloping handwriting on his pages (which they transformed into neat handwriting on theirs) shaping the finest of verses. He opened up for nature. Everything that had been cramped and egoistical – or far too stiff and cramped and egoistical – in the first cantos swept away in face of the winds of insight that come from a longer life. Shelley said that the first part of Lord Byron's *Harold* stuck out with as much *ego* as a curled up hedgehog has prickles. Shelley said that the shape of adulthood is not height but breadth, and that Albé's experiences of possession and loss made him more generous in his way of accepting impressions. In his early youth he had *circumscribed* his perception in order to adapt it to a sterile misanthropy. Albé himself has said that his misfortunes had taught him to enjoy without possessing. When misfortunes afflicted him, he realised misanthropy was a state for the inexperienced – not for the particularly experienced, as one likes to think when one is young.

Mary heard all this and much more at second hand. Conversations about life, art, politics carried on between two poets and a young misanthropic doctor at sea. The doctor could nevertheless be heard all the way ashore. He listened to three words of anyone's argument, closed his eyes and made a dismissive gesture with his hand. Then, loudly and passionately, he started championing an opinion on the periphery of the common subject of conversation. If they tried to bring him back to the central theme, he hauled and tugged at this solidity in his foolish despairing desire to be back on his periphery. All the time, all that summer, he was very unhappy at finding himself not in the centre and that the centre could not be shifted to his own chosen periphery.

On the other hand, the two poets circled round the same centre, agreeing and disagreeing like dogs playing round the same stick. Shelley came home and said: 'Albé is an extraordinarily interesting person. Just because of that, it's appalling that he should be a slave to the worst and most vulgar prejudices and is also as mad as a hatter':

– together they had laughed at the hypocrisy of Englishmen but – Albé considered at the same time society had to have rules and norms against which measures are taken from *above*.

– together they had condemned marriage – which, however, Albé considered a necessary evil.

– in unison, they had condemned the church and royalty and the educational system and landowners and industrialists – but, point by point, Albé deviated from the *consequences* and with regard to religion was able to say he didn't *prefer* any of them but with hindsight *preferred* them all to profane philosophies which 'refuse to be changed, by reality, or by being used'.

– he was willing to bring in a republic the following day.

– he couldn't 'love man' more than any other creation. He was not prepared to give man a special place in creation. He considered human genius a well-intentioned copy of what the cruel chances of nature put together. What Shelley called 'intellectual beauty' was to him a pale imitation of a higher intelligence, which he would like to call God if that would annoy Shelley.

– regarding upbringing, they had a colossal dispute which for a few days threatened their Diodati summer. Lord Byron said he detested children with no manners. He said that badly brought up children were an abomination not only for humanity in general but also for their misled parents and themselves. He said that all badly brought up children he had come across had been profoundly unhappy creatures, lost in their freedom like blindworms, which are at once trampled on when they crawl out of the flower-bed. He said that all nature brings up its offspring and initiates upbringing by creating a basic framework, if necessary with a juicy talking-to or two. He said that badly brought up children really are unhappy worms.

Shelley calmly tried to protest that L.B. had misunderstood the matter, if he thought freedom from traditional and oppressive upbringing entailed allowing the child to run wild. The task of parents (yes, of all adults, for the Child was a common task) was to observe pliably the essence and talents and needs of the Child and carefully assist it in its labours towards completion. 'One should always be around for one's Child.' Morality? – but that's there from the very beginning. It is upbringing that deforms the Child's natural sense of justice, for upbringing as we know it teaches the Child to see to its own interests, and to interests that are extensions of its 'ego' – the nation, royalty, privileges . . . While *Rousseau* teaches that you have to incorporate the Child with its own real essence, the extension of which is humanity, man and nature – the sublime ideas.

'Rousseau!' mocked Albé, 'flowers and leaves. Café rococo! And

333

sent his own offspring to a children's home. There we have a perfect example of a half-baked profane idea. Who has ever come across a child who can be brought up with such courteous discretion (like the head waiter at a club who with small hand gestures of recommendations invites one's guest to sit down at one's table). Bah! The world is full of walls and children run their noses flat against them if you don't at first act as a wall yourself. Or do you prefer to ignore the world, my dear Shelley?' said Lord Byron with a grimace. 'Or perhaps you intend to bring up *your* children for the better world that hitherto exists only *beyond this life!*

(As those words pass along the ribbon of memory . . . Mary knows that it was a tactlessness before its time . . . the only dead child was the one who had only just started to live. William was still alive and little Clara was neither born nor dead. Yet. But the three children, particularly William, also pass along the memory ribbon and have passed . . . It happens more and more often that Mary thinks 'grief' and does not feel.)

'Maman-maîtresse,' said Albé.

It was a few days after the great thunderstorm – the one everyone thinks he knows about. The one when they were all standing in the Diodati drawing-room looking out at several thunderstorms – in actual fact only one – rushing backwards and forwards across the lake and using the whole night for its immense collapse. They say that the zinc-white fire and the black jittery shadows of lightning gave rise to a mutual writing of ghost stories. The tall rags of rain striding across the water – they gave rise to Mary's *Frankenstein*. Rubbish. Everything apart from that gave rise to her idea of Victor Frankenstein's idea of manufacturing a human being from other people's (best) parts. How could a banal thunderstorm possibly bring about the thought that a combination of the best leads to something unhappy, unfinished and monstrous. *Maman-maîtresse* . . .

It was true that Clara suggested a manifestation of the Diodati summer by all of them, all four of them radiating out from this terror-filled romantic scene of nature they had shared, each into a romantic horror story?

Clara was also the first to start walking round with a creative appearance. However, they very soon realised that it was something

334

quite different from a horror story that was creating itself inside Clara . . . Shelley never took her idea seriously. Neither did Albé bother about the thunderstorm, but wrote his singular poem, 'Darkness', about a world without life, or a mind without life. Poor Polidori wrote an idiotic vampire story, which he later tried to publish under Byron's name. He said that 'great writing by a little man finds justice only if it is published in the shelter of previous praise. The world is that cynical!' Then he committed suicide.

A few days after this, Byron spoke of Rousseau's famous novel *Julie, or The New Héloïse*. Although he had recently said 'café rococo' about Rousseau, he now spoke with wide-open eyes and sincerity, starting out from that everyone had read it. None had. So he continued all evening telling its story of free and natural love – so chastised love. This touched them all, for they had all been punished for their freedom. He told them how Julie overcomes conventions by maturing above them and above the established forms of love. He enthused over her way of following the moral messages of her tender love and breaking with 'morality', and over her ability, after her death, to live on in the affection for each other of her husband and her lover.

No wonder Shelley looked suspicious. Byron's lecture flung hook after hook into his thirsting eyes: that novel seemed to be a confirmation of his – Shelley's – dreams. As far as Albé was concerned, it was just like him to be so fascinated by a novel without daring to embrace its theories.

'*Maman-maîtresse*,' he said to Shelley, who was quite taken aback by the expression. Mary had been out for a while and thought Albé was talking about Rousseau's foster-mother, whom he later called his '*maman-maîtresse*'. She couldn't understand Shelley's expression. She folded her hands in her lap. Claire folded her hands in her lap. A look passed between Shelley and Byron which came from the same original words. They fired it at each other. No one wanted to keep it. It disintegrated in each look and they then distanced themselves from each other with the speed of lightning.

In the second week of June, the poets made a plan to sail round Leman, landing at all the places where *Julie* was set. Dr Polidori tried to force his way into their company, almost flinging himself to the ground in despair, throwing himself into the shallows with his massive foolish despair over not being invited. When the boat set out

335

like an arrowhead with a wash straight at the dark Jura mountains, he stood hidden, semivisible from the lake. Mary saw him, too, his sobbing shoulders. A man (she judged) so compacted in the centre of his own attention, he is incapable of living.

When Shelley was happily back, she was given a minutely detailed account of all his adventures and every emotion he felt as he had faced each and every one of them. It started: 'We left Montalègre at half-past two on June 23rd' and ended: 'On Saturday, June 29th, we left Ouchy, and after two days' pleasant sailing, we arrived on Sunday evening at Montalègre.' In between, he seemed to have enjoyed the Swiss countryside, which was only surpassed by Rousseau's brilliance at describing it. He had indescribably enjoyed the tears he had shed when he read his way past wooded overhangs, through rocky bays, along grassy slopes and through the swirls of silt from the Rhône where it meets the Leman. Everywhere they went ashore, *man* had left his tracks. The death-grin of civilisation. The profaning by religion of everything that is sacred. They had visited the mediaeval castle of Chillon and seen what sophisticated death machines the despots had made out of nothing but a dungeon. They had been to Montreux and walked on the terrace of the house where Gibbon had finished writing *The Rise and Fall of the Roman Empire*, with its view over Mont Blanc. Byron had broken off and kept an acacia twig, but he himself had felt nothing but indifference for a man who judges the past, compared with one who creates the future and the New Man, such as Rousseau.

He might well have died. Albé related this quite briskly. They had run into bad weather with unstable boats incapable of withstanding the waves and which threatened to be smashed on the rocks. He had taken off his coat and told Shelley to do the same, which he did. In the tumult that followed, he realised that Shelley couldn't swim. Then he had told him what to do when he was towing him ashore, should they end up in the water. Shelley had instead clung to the boat like a fox to its prey. He had said that under no circumstances would he allow himself to be saved. Under no circumstances whatsoever was he going to allow his life to burden another life, risk another life. If the lack of a certain accomplishment was to be paid for with death, then he was prepared to suffer for his inability to swim.

'Damned arrogant, eh?'

Yes, very arrogant, very humble, simple and even worse, arrogant.

336

Dr Polidori was the opposite. When the boat was first out of earshot, she saw him sobbing on the shore. When it began to move out of sight, like an arrow towards the black reflection of the Jura mountains in the lake, he said:

'You must understand. My bitterness is not a whim of the moment. I left my lonely and aged mother in the care of distant relations in order to accompany Lord Byron to Europe. It seemed to me to be a worthy task to devote my care and attention to his welfare, not just physically, for as you know I am richly endowed with both education and talents within various fields in which he could delight and benefit from qualified company. I was at his side at Dover. I rode with him across the battlefield of Waterloo. We sailed together down the Rhine and were inseparable. I was his best friend and he could not have found anyone more faithful! I have never been happier than during these two weeks when I have been allowed to be of indispensable delight to a great man who is suffering.'

On Mary's memory ribbon, Polidori is speaking Italian, because of his name, his black hair, his blindly black eyes and his way of jutting out his chin and chest at the person he was speaking to, as if that person were an opponent. He made himself out to be so embittered that it was impossible to be curious about him. How can you be interested in a creature who all the time cruises backwards ahead of you on the road to get into the right position to be correctly seen? In that way, he caused himself to remain unknown. Didn't he die in Italy? But of course he was an Englishman. He hissed disappointed English sh-sounds over her:

'Naturally I understand that I'm only a poor *employee* and Mr Shelley is a nobleman, a Published Poet, who has been to Eton and Oxford. And it's an established convention – which however I hoped a poet and peer of the realm could have overcome – that the relationship between a wage slave and his employer could not be as free as between two gentlemen with private incomes. And yet, Miss Godwin, I cannot begrudge either my rightful disappointment or my secret tears. I know you are able to understand. You have such bitter eyes.'

This last information she worked on in the following weeks. With her eyes half-closed, glossily veiled, she received the seafarers and started preparing a special celebration for Shelley's birthday.

She decided on the theme one day when she saw him raking dried hay, and like a sparrow taking a flying bath in it: he took the rake full of hay and flung it up in the air, from where it returned over him, glittering and golden it was, and had, like him, come from the earth, and was to be taken back by the earth. And the sum of being and returning is in the end a few remains of unfathomable lustre.

For two weeks, Mary and Clara sat making kites. Every time Shelley went over to call on Villa Diodati – every day – they took out needle and thread and cloth and hastened, lengthening the stitches to be ready in time. Two months of the summer had gone by. Unnoticed, the water had also become Mary's primary element. Every time she stepped into the boat, it was with relief, freed of landlock, obstacles and inertia. Fear of the depths was like a poison – the kind you first spew up and then have to have. In love with fear, she stood in the boat, moving with the directions of the current. And all through that birthday, they sailed with kites as sails. Shelley, Mary, Clara, Albé and Polidori. They had one each, and at first they held them low and rigid in a billowing display of colours. Then first Clara's arms straightened and she gave her green kite all its string. 'No, you know what,' shrieked Dr Polidori, 'that was a waste! Do you know how high it'll go, and at the slightest movement it'll fall splash into the water. You have to give way only when you feel total resistance.' Shrieked Dr Polidori, stamping with little running steps in the boat as the kite was about to lift him up into the air. He gave it three turns of string and was almost jerked overboard. Albé did as Claire had done, let the whole reel run, and a purplish red kite made love to a green one, nudging and pushing in her armpit and getting tangled in her tail. Mary was full of laughter as she let go of hers – yellow and brown like a wise bee – but almost lost it to the wrong wind; it lay horizontally above the water, flopping pitifully. Mary herself lay down in the boat to find the strength to save it. It was instinct, and she knew not why, but the whole of the stretched top-heavy string began to rise, like a willow sapling after a jab from a horn. Then the actual body of the kite whirled and started playing with the other two.

'Bravo, bravo, Mary,' cried Shelley, who did not start winding in the string of his sky-blue kite until then. 'But let's try to keep them further apart. If we stand as close together as this, the slightest drop in the wind will make them tangle round each other and then everything will be ruined. We really ought to go in several boats and spread ourselves

338

out.' Shelley was always practical as far as aquatic enjoyments were concerned.

Their boats glided round each other all afternoon. Darting ahead arrow-swift. Then this slow curve of boat.

With constant
interruptions
for peace

April 23rd, 1816 – The great day. Melancholy, irretrievable, longed for. Byron shakes the dust off his feet and goes into exile – for ever, he says. For a while, I presume. Anyone living will see.

England has lost all her pink roses. For him, England has become synonymous with Milbanke. A climate of low pressure, but above a surface requiring sunshine . . . Miss Milbanke is his demon. The English are a race with rage in their souls, their worst hypocrisy hiding it beneath exquisitely civilised manners.

He says he will settle in Italy, where one can live in peace, and do no harm. In accordance with this, he has appointed a little physician with an Italian name. Dr Polidori is full of enthusiasms and wild looks but otherwise utterly English. 'Cheap,' says his employer, who is forced to think about pounds, shillings and pence.

April 24th – The north-east wind too high for the channel crossing. We passed the day as best we could and in the evening went to the church to see the grave of the poet Charles Churchill. It was very modest. An upright stone, a patch of grass. Byron lay down on the grave with, as he said, 'yet another one-season singer' and gave the caretaker money to improve the grass.

Polidori behaved oddly during the night. I warned my friend about the little doctor's disconcerting gaze, his raptures when praised, and the three tragedies he says he has written. He has already told me that if he had had the same advantages as Lord Byron, he would have been much more praised and esteemed today than he is. It is rather sad and very foolish, as well as a mystery why such creatures are always attracted to famous people and twice as small in their shadow.

April 25th – The captain said that he had no intention of waiting another minute. After some muddle and confusion, Byron took my arm under his and we walked down to the quay. He went on board just after nine. A great deal happens on board at the moment a boat casts off, and that kept him in a good mood, but he looked affected as the packet glided away. I ran to the end of the wooden pier, and as the vessel tossed by us through a rough sea and contrary wind, I saw him again: the dear fellow pulled off his cap and waved it to me. I gazed until I could no longer distinguish him. God bless him for a gallant spirit and a kind one.

May–June – Yes, well, I suppose it was the only thing to do to avoid the wagging tongues of London. It stinks. I try to speak for my friend and am glad he does not have to experience it directly. Those who discreetly sympathise with him try to stop me defending him, but tell me to attack his enemies. How does one attack a woman who loved foolishly and spread the consequences of that in the form of moral annihilation of her ex-beloved. Her family has gone so far as to blame Byron for his *lameness*.

Lord Holland requests me to react in private, not publicly. He says that some defences are the same as playing the attacker's game. He says that Byron will come out of this and that in Paris people in general condemn Lady Byron.

Lady Melbourne says her unfortunate daughter-in-law at last has a mission in life: Caroline Lamb is devoting all her time to revenge on Byron because he abandoned her in 1812. She has already written a novel with him in the rôle of Satan. She whispers about his 'unmentionable' sins and names them.

Lady Melbourne's opinion of it all: Mr Hobhouse, to me, when one has pronounced the words sodomy and incest out loud, the deed has lost its demonic value. As far as our friend is concerned – during certain years in youth one likes to improve on one's stories – to make an impression – what has eventually happened, Mr Hobhouse, is after all no more than a little piece of flesh gone astray – over and above that material a mind so sorrowful and affectionate that neither Satan nor evil can find room there. Don't you think?

In the summer, I decided to join him on yet another European journey.

*

341

July 29th – Left London together with my old friend Scrope Davies, his servant and my servant Poisson, then began another journey with no clear aim (as my father anxiously maintains). Early the next morning, the tide took us on its broad back and we arrived at Calais the same day. We met Beau Brummell, who lives in an inn there – inexpressively reduced from what he had once been. How many times have I not seen his elegant back through the bow window of White's club in St James's Street. That place was *his* in London, and he always sat with his back to the street with either an open newspaper or an admirer in front of him. If he took a step out into St James's, all the dandies rushed indoors to copy if possible an apparently absent-minded *innovation* in his garb that immediately became a must in taste, because he possesses the magical ability to quench a thirst that knows which confirmation it wants but not what it looks like. Brummell was bold in his position or indifferent to what might happen to him. When he quarrelled with the Prince of Wales, and met him together with a mutual friend, he asked the latter 'Who is your fat friend?' He had to flee his tailor, shoemaker and gambling debts when insulted Exalted Persons refused to give him further protection.

I actually could hardly believe my eyes when I saw this king among dandies sitting in a little French inn with his overcoat on indoors and a woollen scarf up to his nose, with a cold in the heat wave. He drank arrack with us. His fall is in its way just as great as Napoleon's. He takes it just as coldly. Scrope Davies bowed low to 'a pathfinder', knowing full well that his own gambling debts in their good time will force him into similar exile: he still has debts from our days at Cambridge and for the time being takes out loans *with his old debts as security*! he says. Everything of value is in exile. Napoleon on his island, Byron by his lake, Brummell in the attic of his inn, gazing at the coast of England – not missing his native country, but also not accepting his exile.

August 26th – Set off to Secheron, along the finest road in the world. Went on to Nyon and Coppet. Came over in a boat to the vineyard below the Villa Diodati. Went up and found Byron in a delightful house and spot.

In the house at the time was Miss Clairmont, a degenerate woman I have seen invading his house in London during the worst days of invasion. When I expressed my surprise to her, she said she was copying a newly written *Harold* canto. When I expressed my quiet surprise to him, he excused himself by saying she had followed him, and now, in addition, she had begun to produce a 'swelling, which – please note – dates from our first meeting . . .' The woman's brother-in-law is the famous Shelley, and a third person in the company is the latter's official concubine. All of quite good family. Shelley is the only son of Sir Timothy Shelley, who – after draining dry the bitter chalice of parenthood – had removed his hand from him. Shelley lacks all ability to take advantage of the advantages fate has dealt him. He might have modified his political opinions a trifle, at which Parliament would have opened its doors to him and he could have been of some use. Instead, he makes his opinions public with the aid of pretentious gestures. Well, that's all the same to me, but I am worried that my friend – who for the moment, for the sake of his reputation and his interests, ought to avoid notorious company – has joined up with a man who already made a bad name for himself at Eton and was sent down from Oxford. And about whom the whole of London talks because he abandoned his wife when she was in circumstances, to go instead to live with these *two* women – why in Byron's position I would put two question marks against the appearance of the 'swelling'.

Shelley turned out to be a swaying willowy figure. He is very tall and looks as if he were trying to hold up that length with no backbone. Which is why Byron calls him 'Snake' – though he says he got it from Goethe's *Faust*, of which Shelley has translated the first scenes for him, among others the one in which Mephistopheles alludes to '*meine Tante die Schlange*'. Shelley is in fact also pretentiously godless. He has a weakness for Wordsworth and tries to graft this alien species into the soul of my uncritical friend. If Byron were not such a morsel for all *interested parties* – as long as they show him the slightest friendship – the task would be easier for us, his real friends. He admits that Scrope and I improve the quality of the company to an inconceivable extent.

August 29th – Byron, S.B.D., Dr Polidori, and myself, set off in two carriages for Chamouni, with three servants. At starting, our postilion, who was a butcher, was found not to be able to ride. Byron and S.B.D. left the carriage, leaving the Doctor and me to our fate. My servant Joseph mounted and took the reins for a while and not until hills and bends levelled out did we dare entrust the matter to the butcher again.

343

Towards evening, we entered the Arve valley. Enclosed by its arms, we were swallowed up by another world, ambling along in a precipitous rust-red mountain shadow, all colours merging into the darkness. Then night fell. I walked beside the carriage without having to hurry. You could see nothing but shadows of shadows, hear nothing but the peculiarly subdued sound of carriage wheels, footsteps, hooves and breath against moss. Yes, you could hear the stream rushing and giggling below us, and late birds measuring the distance between mountains with their calls, but it was like patterns of silence. It smelt of pine needles, glowingly fresh. The road was a trifle rough, but not bad, and for a good coachman it would have been good, though our butcher almost succeeded in tipping both the Doctor and the landau into the Arve.

August 30th – Towards Chamouni in three country carriages. First a stretch of flat country, the Arve flowing on the right, flooded, green-swollen, foaming. High young alps passed us, with shorter and shorter gaps between them, until they became flocks. Some of them had snowcaps which in the morning light were the same colour as pale peaches.

We started climbing up the hills to the left. Strode and clambered and waded across a dark water course. Continued climbing upwards but lost a little height again when we came to a village. Dinner in the orchard outside the inn.

Finally walked over the Arve, which at this place hurtles down a very steep, magnificent wooded chasm. This is where our journey's Miracles began. We wound our way up a zigzag path for an hour. Then we saw below us our first glimpse of the Chamouni valley. Walking in the peaks is laborious, but it is much the same as walking long stretches, though covering three hundred yards upwards is qualitatively very different from doing so on the flat. The farms in Les Houches were scattered over yellow and green fields. Every step upwards increased the magnificence and passed through the astonished eye in conscious rapture. A surfeit of alpine peaks reached the clouds, penetrated through them and acquired their extreme lustre above. Sometimes bolsters of cloud and mist covered the lower mountains and made them highest, but from a path at cloud level, we soon saw the real Alps floating above, enormous and inaccessible, black as their own shadows, but the primaeval mountain white-hot with running fire as a trivial rivulet caught the rays of the sun. It was a cruel and matter-of-fact sight. 'Cruel' was also the impression we had when we saw our first avalanche fingering its way down with a tail of white powder. Then we saw the Bosson glacier, its eternal masses of blue ice fumbling all the way down to the lush warm valley – a miraculous rather than a romantic sight.

We decided we wanted to see this primaeval animal at close quarters, and from the village of Les Houches we had the guides take us up the spruce forest to the right of the glacier, a rather tortuous rise. We scrambled up the field of ice, hauling ourselves up to the surface by our arms for the last bit. There we had to balance over a number of wide cracks, the sources of the glacier echoing up from their depths, bubbling and rushing. Above us we had the alpine precipice; below the vertical broken-up mass of the glacier stretching all the way down to the fields of corn. Coming down on the other side later was dangerous, not a little, either, especially for Byron, who slipped on an icy edge and hurt himself; fortunately he escaped serious injury, and cleverly said that a bruise was the medal for the experience. We came back to our starting-point after having walked across the glacier in an hour and a quarter, which is a quarter of an hour less than the average visitor needs. Half an hour later we found ourselves in Chamouni, where we stayed at the Hôtel d'Angleterre.

After we had entered our names in the columns of the guest book, Byron ran his finger down the pages, pointing out familiar names such as Wordsworth and his sister (and their fox terrier). He also found Shelley and his women, who had done this trip a month before us (unfortunately). After his name, Shelley had scribbled in Greek what he considers his description: 'atheist and philanthropist'. Byron looked at me. I looked at him in amusement, for this was childish, without being wrong, and the kind of ingenuousness which – at best – you regret later; not because it is wrong, but because it is so immeasurably grandiose to give yourself a philosophical label in the light of the surrounding countryside. Foolish, then. 'Don't you think I should do Shelley the favour of erasing it?' he said, and did so with some care.

September 1st – Back by the lake. Byron has allowed me to read the new cantos of his *Harold*. Parts of it are very good, although it begins with a lament over a daughter he scarcely knows by sight. I don't know

345

whether I like it as much as the earlier cantos. They contain a note of mystery and metaphysics which is not in accord with my friend, but with Shelley, who has fortunately now returned to England, not least because the 'swelling' is to run its course where it belongs. Byron is already speculating about the child: he intends to acknowledge a son as his own and bring him up in the tradition of an English nobleman. According to custom, a possible daughter is to be brought up in the country he settles in, to marry a local worthy and become his – Byron's – consolation in his old age. The pregnant lady has declared her desire to present the 'father' with the child. To keep a hold on him, I presume!

I took on the unpleasant task of telling my friend how little metaphysics and mystery favoured his poetry. I reminded him that he is an heir to Pope. I told him that the immense mysteries of nature and the universe are only reduced through human speech. Let a creature like Shelley force his fussy attentions on the Alps, spattering multitudes of 'Lo!' and 'Hark!' on to their chaste untouched clarity. A great writer such as he should preserve this untouchability and be great on a human level. One day he will admit I am right, as usual, but for the moment he is sulking. I did not bother to read 'The Prisoner of Chillon'. I find it increasingly impossible to read the work of my friends or find any pleasure in it.

September 9th – Went out fishing in Byron's boat. Caught nothing and in addition received a degrading reprimand from a fellow in uniform because I was fishing inside the harbour area. Went into Geneva instead to read the newspapers.

Dinner with the increasingly insane Polidori. Our poor Doctor now spends most of his time locked in his room because he is 'not wanted in the illustrious company'. He is very disappointed over Byron not accepting him as a poet of equal merit. He also talks to the candle flame of his dead mother. Poor man, he forces himself on us like a bad smell. He is resigned over my destruction of his dreams of being first in Byron's heart since Shelley and company disappeared. Byron is the recipient of far too many yearning lunacies. People travel for days and nights to introduce their insanity to him as if it were a costly and exclusive gift. It is what comes of being a public figure. No good can come of it.

September 15th – Helped Dr Polidori to settle involved accounts with Lord Byron. He does not answer to Madame de Staël's definition of a happy man, whose capacities are squared with his inclinations. Took leave of him, poor fellow! He is anything but an amiable man, and has boundless ambition and inordinate vanity: the true ingredients of misery.

September 17th – I tried to write something, but could only boggle:

> It is not cowardice to fly,
>   From Tyranny's triumphant face;
> It is not banishment to die,
>   An exile only from disgrace.

This was the beginning of Byron's and my second walking tour in the mountains. Being lame in one foot is no obstacle to his climbing mountains, sliding across snow, ice and glaciers, striding across fields of boulders. Rather, he is remarkably sparing with complaints about the mutual inconveniences weather and wind give rise to. My friend detests physical compassion, for he considers that a very small number of people are capable of dispassionate compassion and most people use it only as compensation for their own misfortunes. A dreadful judgement of man's ability to feel, but not without a grain or two of truth.

Byron and I, with Berger, a guide, and a mule, and our two saddle-horses, set off to cross the Dent de Jaman, overlooking the level of the lake. Continued ascending among rich pastures on declivities till we passed Chainy, a small village in the mountains, part of which was lately burnt down. The sight did not tempt us to stop for rest and refreshment. I was sorry that chance had handed it to us like a stern hallmark of experiences to follow. Burnt-out houses and charred roof-beams are the most depressing sight I know. It is horrible. It paralyses you, and I admire simple people because they always manage to demolish their collapsed past and build up something new.

Instead of stopping at the inn (still upright), we went on upwards for an hour and chose a mossy slope to camp at midday for the fried fish and wine we had brought with us. The horses grazed sparingly at the grass round a pointed rock. The mule wanted nothing.

After a brief nap, we went on, alternately on foot or mounted. A long languorous waterfall called upon us to pass it as quickly as possible, as it often brought a stone with it in its cascades. Then we followed a staircase path up into the sky. It tormented my friend. He said nothing and naturally neither did I. But one manages the steepest path quickest, breathlessly, to be done with it, because one doesn't dare stop, stagger and look back. We were soon standing at the top of the pass on a stretch of clover where half a dozen outbarns lay scattered. Cowbells in all directions – clanging when the wind turned.

On one side, we now had a chain of very high, very green mountains, on the other side the Dent de Jaman, which soared up vertically out of this vista. We decided to climb and scrambled down into the glen to get at it from the best side. At that moment we heard a laugh from the opposite alp; happy cries rang out from a peak almost as high as the Dent. We looked up and saw a tall man with a cow at his side, which would have looked absolutely unnatural if one had painted it there and then – made a picture, art.

Climbing mountains is at the same time both timelessness and impatience. We made our way through a herd of fine but inquisitive cows. Berger let one of them lick salt sweat off his forehead, but I did not feel called upon to follow his example, as at that moment I saw another of them carrying on an unmentionable practice with a third . . . This was at a great height. We left horses and packs with a herdsman and started climbing. It remained green for a long time and cows were grazing even higher up, also above a great patch of snow the summer heat had in vain tried to melt. Finally, I crawled on mossy rock that was slippery from rain and melting snow. And yet it was not particularly difficult. I reached the top, where I could see Lake Geneva, the north shores in particular, the whole of the Canton of Vaud, both branches of the Rhône, the Savoy mountains and the Alps in the Canton of Bern. Berger came after me to the top, but Byron stayed fifteen yards below. Thin clouds floated below us, like gunpowder smoke – the comparison was Berger's.

Back at the clover meadow, we found the tall herdsman still there on his alp, his affectionate cow at his side. He waved, took out his pipe and started playing. We could hear the notes quite clearly, as rounded as pearls, for the air was pure. Berger called out to him to sing 'Ranz des Vaches', and soon that shrill song – or rather, a series of howls and grunting incantations – rolled through the corridors of mountains, only a minute later to be followed by a chorus of bellows, bleats and the alert barking of dogs.

This still life of lure-calls made our experience of life in the Alps even more engrossing. Byron said that the melancholy evening over these pastures was like a dream of altitudes – something far too rare and wild for the reality in which he and I allow our lives to pass by. He said it is a touching arrogance when people who *describe* and *judge* and try to *handle* the world at large think that they have it under better control than people who sow and tend their creatures and mind their own business. I was far too affected by my experiences to make any relevant objections. The cows are taken up to summer pastures on July 11th and brought down on October 11th. Many die when they fall off the crags.

September 23rd – Climbed up the bare green declivity of the Wengern Alp, where there were no herds, but a solitary flock of goats. In two hours we were just opposite the majestic Jungfrau and the two Eigers. We took the bridles off the horses, and put them to feed. Byron and I then ascended to the summit called Malinetha. We were fifty minutes getting up and when we arrived at the valley of Lauterbrunnen, and the sides of the Jungfrau and Eigers were enveloped in clouds, which dashed up like waves of foam from the measureless crater and gulphs below. For a minute, I felt like an angel above the first sea of creation. Every man thinks that such things come from his unique ability to experience. This quantity of exactly similar exclusivity says a great deal about the greatness of nature and the smallness of man. The two Eigers were soon cleared, and Grindelwald was a sunny track beneath, where frequent dark cottages looked like scattered flocks of goats. We lay down a short time contemplating the scene, and wrote our names on a bit of paper, which we hid under a small stone near a blue flower.

Fever (1817)

The one crow was already the shape of a fish, a large cod. It flopped. She gasped and leant one hand against a birch tree as she supported her back with the other. The fish bladder rises out of a movement of that kind. The black coat glides open. Underneath, the black silk dress shone like tight black skin. The dress was now far too short at the front. The cod had white paws. The other crow has a secret button inside her.

They are trudging carefully along a river. It reminds them of Flanders; the river is marvellously calm beneath its thin layer of ice. Ice rustles, turning the surface over in long swirls, as water does for a while before it starts boiling.

The alders, aspens and birches, all of them bare of leaves except a stunted beech that has kept its dead leaves on its branches and rustles them as the girls walk against the wind below it. Mary is thinking about Flanders, calm canals, straight avenues. She is thinking about seasickness, interrupted travels, interrupted stops and lack of sleep in Europe.

It's good to be in England. They live in a house that has a Name! It is dark and out of the way, but it has an English name. They have chosen it and they have chosen their guests. In front of the open fire in the kitchen, the cat is playing with its kitten. The nurse is giving little William his cold bath. (Shelley considers that promotes health.) Shelley writes a great many letters and coughs himself to sleep. (The few hours he sleeps.) He says he sleeps standing up like a horse and will die when he lies down. Mary is studying her Plato. Clara is hemming small sheets and impatiently puts them aside. She sews small blouses and napkins and throws them down, hungering outside Mary's Greek lesson. 'Come in, then,' says Mary. 'Come in . . .'

They stroll along this Flanderish river. But it is English, for it flows in England and the vegetation along the banks is lush and inhabited by hibernating water voles, delicate little snakes and frogs.

It is the first day of the year. The crows wish each other a happy 1817. It would be best if it embraced the previous year's fuchsia colour and drama, but excluded its disappointments. The crows laugh beak to beak. The nurse considers Clara should take to her bed and await her confinement, but Shelley has prescribed long walks and fresh air. He considers that apropos of giving life, a woman reaches her strongest and most triumphant levels: that she should then be allowed to give her greatness free outlet instead of lying flat like a pitiful object in the care of others. The midwife says the child may be born at any moment. Clara says that Byron's Son will come into the world on the twenty-second of January – and by coinciding his father's birthday with his own, will 'confirm and bind' their kinship 'for ever'. Shelley says that . . . Mary wishes she could keep all human beings in the world apart from each other. Then things might be calm. A woman's task in life is to keep those she gathers round her apart – so that there are no explosions and assembling would be impossible!

Neat little snowflakes fall on the fingers of Mary's darned gloves and on Clara's bare finger-flowers. Mary's melt slowly, Clara's immediately.

A formation of birds crosses the sky. But the arrow has gone mad, the whole system dissolved, as if cancer had brought disorder in the bird minds in the south.

They keep the same course and there are even the remains of the arrow shape, a tumbling, collapsing arrow. As far as can be seen, it is a struggle for the position of leader, not individuals seeking precedence; no, a very hesitant rebellion against the principle of arrows reigns there, and they fall, rise, swirl around each other as flakes of soot do when the roof has collapsed in a fire.

Clara clutches her heart. Mary longs for roast wild duck. She wants to shoot one for herself and eat its wings, because she has a bloodthirsty button inside her. If she doesn't give it what it needs, it will eat off her. And there is certainly not enough of her for a button to grow strong enough for the life it is to live outside her body. But

Shelley considers human beings should not eat corpses. When you live with a very moral man, you think he is right, but moral aspects do not steer life. Life is savage.

After watching the formation for a while, they also hear it. Clara says: 'I wish Shelley would write to him again. He doesn't answer my letters.'

Mary licks up a drop of snow and feels the tips of her fingers on her tongue. She smiles inwardly – at the button – but replies seriously: 'Dearest Clara. Think about Albé's impatient disposition. If Shelley wrote as often as you require him to, he would draw disfavour upon himself from The One who prefers to Address rather than be Addressed. Everything is now close to understanding, and the moment you have your Son, you also have an argument no individual with an ounce of normal feeling can resist.'

Clara: 'But Marie, in your excellence, you fail to see how the matter has a side that affects our whole household. If I give birth to this child without the true father agreeing that his name is named in connection with mine, the world will point out *Shelley* in his place.'

Mary: 'Dearest Claire, we have agreed on a story.'

They had agreed on a story. Claire will be given out as the child's aunt, the mother's sister. On its side, the child will be given out as an orphan. And that, Mary thinks, will be an ironic truth. It won't have a mother. Clara has decided (and Byron has accepted) that the Son will be brought up in his father's house. As Clara's hook-hold on that house . . . ah, Mary knows that it is a hook with no staple. Albé does not want to have anything to do with Clara. He has said that and repeated it. He has made it a condition of his fatherhood that it excludes the mother. He wants the mother to understand this. How can he expect Clara to understand such a thing? And what kind of father will he be? He, who feels himself so generous when he gives of his surplus . . .

Mary takes Clara by the arm and feels the temporary extra weight. She leans her head against 'your non-sister, Miss Clairmont' and says that Shelley and she were only too willing to put their own parenthood at the little one's disposal. Byron would have no objections. He has said that the child is Claire's and he will only look after it should she wish that. But – she leans her head even closer – they would be in some difficulties – simply from a time point of view – in explaining two infants within such a short spell of time, for . . .

Clara crying out and flapping her finger-flowers: 'Really! Is it true, dearest Marie? Ah, if we both had girls. If we kept them as two small sisters; Mary – I would call mine Mary and you yours Clara – for a highly ingenious exchange in the coming generation, as you see, and shared characteristics per face and name!'

Mary says 'Mmmmm' and hears Clara talking and sees the skein of birds coming back. They have just seen their reflections in a Flanderish canal and must now again confirm themselves in the English river. This time she hears the sound before she sees them. It is shrieking.

The actual sight howls and laughs as it resists the magnet, defying the system and the image of a formation provided by nature: there is no other way to fly than what exists. Everything else is careless. Cancer is careless. It disperses what should be collected and collects what should be dispersed and everything rises like soot above a fallen-in roof.

Mary says sceptically: 'Mmmmm.'

With constant
interruptions
for peace

October 13th, 1816 – Yesterday we arrived at Milan, the most exuberant and vigorous town I have seen, including London and Paris, which are both content to be London and Paris. Milan seems to make an effort to be Milan, and an effort is always preferable so long as it is not officious. Within three hours, we had a visit from Polidori. He told us he had crossed the Alps on foot without mishap. He considered that to be a far superior way of travelling and reminded us of his courage and manly strength. I told him that Byron – who was in his bath at the time – had been worried about seeing himself as the origin of a character in a novel called *The Vampire*, recently published in London, undoubtedly written by the little Doctor? 'Ah,' said Polidori, 'undoubtedly the name will provide the appropriate audience, after which I can reveal my identity.'

A moment later, Lord Byron came dripping into the room. He gave his ex-physician a long look from beneath lowered eyebrows, but said nothing.

We decided to go to the theatre, all three of us. Milan's theatre life is astonishingly cosmopolitan. People went in and out of the boxes, introductions succeeded one another, and after a summer of isolated experiences of nature, social life was quite captivating. The ballet was magnificent, well staged and excellently performed.

October 15th – We have continued visiting theatres, museums and churches. Byron also looked at pictures and studied them, although he has no understanding of visual art. On the other hand, he is in a state of ecstasy over a display in the Ambrosia Library. Lucrezia Borgia's letters to Cardinal Bembo are there. They were full of personal appreciation, or perhaps something more. 'Do you see the way she signs her letters?' he said, a tremor in his voice. He flushed with a kind of diffident ecstasy, looking guardedly at me, and his pulse shook him as if his heart had grown ten times its usual size. I looked. She had signed them with some crosses or plus signs. After having gone round the library, I returned to find him still reading them, with heavy eyes, eyes weighing up, floating with concentration and forgetfulness. There were also a few verses by her in Spanish. Byron went back several days in a row to read them again. There was also a long strand of her blonde hair. He tried to get a copy of a letter and was also given a semi-promise of it, but in the end no more. He took the hair instead.

At an evening conversation with new friends, he said something I noted down – that he could no more be dogmatic than he could be an atheist. His *sens intime* of divinity was – although he could not account for it – evidence of its origin; as sure as the compass has a magnetic pole which causes its reactions and responses.

October 16th – This night I wrote a letter for Polidori, who is going to try to make himself physician to the Princess of Wales. Poor thing, she must be mad. The Princess of Wales at an entertainment she gave, where was Count Boromeo, had an ass brought in to table, caressed it before the company and crowned it with roses. We have already had to rescue Polidori out of difficulties with the authorities, because he slapped a captain at the theatre. We saw it from our box, and if we had not hurried down and with a great many words and deeds made it clear the man was already headless, he might well have been so.

Byron and I made our entrée into the brain of Milanese society when we had dinner this evening with Monsieur de Breme in Casa Roma, a magnificent palace. Apart from us, a large number of young men in black was there. They had all come to see The Celebrated Poet, and even my own insignificance. They all knew my books on travels in Albania. They called Byron the New Petrarch. We blushed at each other, but accepted the hyperboles together with the wines.

A Monsieur de Beyle was also there, one of Napoleon's secretaries. Unfortunately, I talked so much with other people, I hardly had time to have a word with him.

Instead I was monopolised by a Colonel Finch, who hung sniffing over my chair and talked endlessly about his feelings, which are egocentric; about his opinions – which are confused. Anyhow, he is a democrat, and he is convinced that the Congress of Vienna is a 'conspiracy' against human rights. I dismiss all people who start talking about conspiracies almost before they have uttered the word. They are childish and cannot understand the world in any other way than that it is cunning: life is a conspiracy of parents against children; wind and waves a conspiracy against the shipwrecked. Finch confided to me that he aimed to return to England the day a certain member of his family had had the decency to die. He said: 'Mr Hobhouse, I am sorry that I am not at home in England at the moment and able to read your *Travels in Albania* . . .' I was just about to thank him and bow, when he added: 'Well, I'm not saying I would like it!'

October 23rd – Went to the Opera and again saw the interesting Beyle there, that ex-secretary to Napoleon, and he told us several interesting stories about the 1812 Russian expedition.

Beyle was waiting on Napoleon on the Russian expedition. After the affair of Maristudovitch, and when the cavalry was dismounted, Napoleon quite lost himself. He actually signed eight or ten decrees of advancements, or some such things, 'Pompey'; and when Beyle took the occasion afterwards to say, 'Your Majesty has made a slip of the pen here,' he looked with a horrid grimace, and said, 'Oh, yes,' and tore the decree and signed another.

He never would pronounce the word Kaluga, but called it sometimes Caligula, sometimes Salamanca. His attendants, who knew what he meant, went on writing or listening without making any remark.

During the retreat he was always dejected; his horse not being able to stand on account of the ice, he was obliged to get off and walk with a white staff. This is a French saying, 'When a man is in misfortune he takes the white stick.' One of the six or seven people close to him happened to say out loud, '*Ah, voilà l'Empereur qui marche avec le bâton blanc.*' Instead of taking this in good part, he said gloomily, '*Oui, messieurs, voilà les grandeurs humaines.*' M. de Beyle walked close to him for three hours then; he never spoke a word. It is not true that the army cried 'Down with the Emperor!' On the contrary. They all thought they were dependent on Napoleon to save them. They all kept their eyes on his face, to see what it might show in the way of hope. Once or twice, a few soldiers cried out, '*Ce malin nous fait tuer tous.*' He turned round and looked at them and the soldiers burst into tears. The army's troubles were so great that every man was half mad, many of them wholly so. Even the bravest hearts broke. Davoust cried like a child.

For a whole twenty-four hours, eighty-four brigadier generals and division commanders came to headquarters weeping and wailing: 'Oh, my division . . . oh, my brigade . . .' Dysentery was afflicting the army. All of forty-five thousand in Königsberg had been captured by the enemy, more or less without resistance . . . but the Russians showed mercy and let the French stay there for two weeks, thus having the opportunity to hear the opera *Clemenza di Tito* performed by an excellent company of singers and musicians.

The Russians showed less mercy and unfathomable carelessness at Tchitchagof, where the French army was expecting to be totally cut off from their retreat. There was a river there they had to cross and then twelve bridges over a marsh; if the Russians blew up one single bridge, all would have been lost. Beyle was riding at the head of the staff; there was only one Cossack looking on while the French crossed the river and marsh. Napoleon was slightly encouraged and managed to laugh at the Admiral's stupidity.

When Napoleon abandoned the army, Beyle became secretary to Murat for a while, as he was then considered in command. Murat sat weeping bitterly in bed. Beyle's life was saved by Marshal of the Court Duroc occasionally bringing him a cup of coffee, which made all the difference between life and death.

In Königsberg, medicine was arrack, of which Beyle drank a dozen tankards a day. The soldiers were so exhausted and so changed by their physical and spiritual experiences that close friends did not recognise each other. Nicolai, a collaborator of Beyle's, did not recognise him for two whole hours. Marshal Ney was the one to keep his head.

When Napoleon came back from Moscow, he found three letters in Paris from Foreign Minister Talleyrand addressed to Louis XVIII, beginning 'Sire'. The letters were read out at a council meeting with Beyle in the chair. General opinion seemed to be that Talleyrand had to be punished, and Napoleon himself agreed with the majority in the matter. Cambacérès said: 'What, more blood!' This saved Talleyrand's life and closed the discussion. Napoleon did not say another word. Beyle's opinion was that any impartial jury would have condemned Napoleon. Far from being too cruel, said Beyle, Napoleon

357

was not cruel enough. He had the Bourbons in his power but was unwilling to be rid of them. Beyle implied that there had been an opportunity. With poison.

I have every reason to believe that Beyle is telling the truth. But he has a grim way of speaking and appears to be – and is – a sensualist.

He tells us that the battle of Borodino was the happiest day of Napoleon's life. He sat on the ground between two dunes and banged on a drum. Every time anyone came to report losses, he suggested the man should go in place of those killed. When his head was cooler and he was no longer in the heat of the battle, he could show compassion. But during the battle of Wagram, for instance, Bernadotte sent adjutant after adjutant to demand reinforcements and report losses. In the end, Napoleon was furious and said, 'The idea is to take the batteries. He can send adjutants afterwards.' Then Bernadotte himself came and said he must have reinforcements. The alternative was to achieve his aim at the cost of hideous losses of men. Napoleon called him a whole series of fearful names, of which cowardly wretch was the mildest, then dispatched him to take the batteries even if he lost fifty thousand men. Which he did.

Bernadotte behaved in the same way to everyone and never curried favour with the Emperor, an indication of a common republican past the Emperor did not appreciate. When Napoleon heard that Ney and his army section – which had been missed on the plains of Russia – made their presence known, on the other hand, he leapt higher in his joy than Beyle had ever seen anyone leap. Though he did not make Ney a prince until later on in Paris, when in passing he said to an adjutant: 'Tell Ney he's a prince.'

November 9th – We roamed about all day in and around Vicenza, a lovely little town set in hills. I wanted to see the fresco paintings of Tiepolo and the Renaissance theatre, but no houses of tourism and beauty were open that day. Instead we were offered the sight of an enormous number of beggars. I have never seen anything like it before. It looked as if in some perverse way, Vicenza specialised in beggars, and also beggars with deformities of a hideousness nature could never have invented without the help of the demon of nightmares. I hastened to abandon the horrific thought that this rich presence might be because these creatures actually procure *offspring* between themselves! Some of them were in a condition one refuses to call human.

Byron protested that I should not take offence, for the poor wretches had not asked to be born monsters. His reprimand was so obvious and officious that I was beside myself. But as usual I controlled myself for his sake . . . He became philosophical in the middle of the throng: when the soul inhabits a body – is it then its opposite or its equivalent? He was looking at a woman with half a face and feet on her knees, apart from ten other defects.

We were standing in the middle of Vicenza talking about creatures shuffling up towards us or rolling along on small trolleys. The guide was looking with interest between us to catch what he could of our conversation in English, a language he wished to learn 'thoroughly and bottomlessly'.

Byron said that the struggle for life is to find a balance in which one 'for a long time and often is forgetful of oneself'.

He said he knew that, because a man who is lame in one leg finds it much more difficult to achieve balance and freedom and oblivion. A handsome and symmetrical ordinary person has that for nothing. But a man who is lame in one leg has to manufacture it for himself. First with compensations, 'and such things are always wretched to witness', then through finding the real point of balance 'for a creature like me'. And so he doubted that this hideous figure could possess forgetfulness. She needed genius to manufacture a balance from those conditions.

Our guide, who had enthusiastically misunderstood everything we had been talking about, replied that compassion is and has to be an exterminated quality in Vicenza, and we could not really even imagine the extent of the wretchedness until after nightfall, when those who were ashamed to show themselves in daylight appeared.

November 11th – This evening we left the mainland. A half-hearted offshore wind helped, pushing us on with waves and setting the shore lanterns swaying – they swung like melancholy oranges in the darkness. Three flat-bottomed curved boats pushed out. They call these waters *la laguna*, but as far as I could see, it was a flooded meadow of the same kind we have seen many of in northern Italy. Though the heart of the Venetian empire was supposed to be here in the middle of this brine, sand and an illusion of luscious glades of trees. As with all extinguished empires, a ghostly signal still remains. It no longer sends out its fleet all over the world, but allows its siren to sing and instead makes the world come to it. Just because of that, this salty meadow was a disappointment. She should have lain shining in the sea. Here she lay on a kind of tongue of land, even if flooded and sliced through by shallow canals. For that matter, one could not see her.

After hearing me complaining about the Venetian mainland's ugliness for quite a while, my friend told me to be quiet, keep my mouth shut, shut up shop. *He* had been captivated by the rocking of the gondola. He felt that at last he was on his way over the horizon to another world. In the silence, I felt the same – regarding *him*.

It struck me that this pubic-looking stretch of water, some tangled vegetation and a lot of mud, signified the final distance between him and England. Him and Miss Milbanke. Him and me. It was no longer a question of travelling but of settling, and only a short time remained before we would stop being each other's friends and begin to be each other's guests. At that moment, I grew hot with panic at the thought of myself continuing to be a traveller all my life. Then I cooled down, for the consequence of our separation was that my inner self was already preparing my own future, in accordance with the wishes of my father and my middle age: never again enchanted; progress; comfort; with any luck a suitable match. A circle with visiting points that grew for every visit. Roast beef and steamed puddings.

Behind us the sun went down, green all over. Italy swallowed it into her embrace and left us to the brackish sea. The boats gurgled towards the whirlpools of water in the tidal marsh. They were like beds and so uncomfortable to sit in, and like fish, they consumed their route. Sometimes we penetrated through canals between small islands of reeds and sand, with a single tree as stability, and we heard the sickly dragging of boats over mud. Islands stranded on wet mobile mud. Pudding. Silhouettes of mooring stakes and mysterious trees.

Then we came closer, and one realised that this was supposed to be Venice, but she was like a sleazy town by a river. Along the languid shore grew an embankment of rubbish that had been thrown into the sea but had yearned back home. Venice is not a magnificent experience until one has gone right into her, not really until one has passed through her and come out on the sea side of her – and turned round! (like my wife, says Byron). When we had got into the deep canal system, it was so late, the lights were already out. It was enchanting, like bad acting. I was greatly affected by the silence, by the dark silent houses, the soft swaying line of the gondolier, on an oar leaving no more sound than a fish on the surface of the water. The extinguished street light on the gable of a house outlined its filigree ironwork against a church bathed in moonlight. And the moon itself was reflected in water smothered in blackness – it drew the gondola, which carefully followed its yellow disc, but never rode over it.

Byron spoke softly like a lover in the darkness and actually made a promise for life: he said he was ashamed at the thought of the way the cripples in Vicenza had made him compose philosophical truths such as 'nothing is of merit in the *world*'. He was particularly ashamed of putting his own trifling suffering in the centre and as an example of these questions. He said that in Venice he would live like an honest man, never take up poses, listen to other people. And so on . . .

Later the echo of oars under a bridge woke us and the boat owner cried: 'Rialto.' Soon after that, he tied up at the Hotel Grand-Bretagne that lies on the Canal Grande, and there we were shown up a splendid staircase and into a room in which the gilded details and silk tapestries spoke of the house belonging to better people in better days.

November 12th – That it should be so cheap to stay in Venice is a truth I would beg to modify. It is the kind of reputation that arises wherever English tourists gush out. An army of beggars, stinking misery and established swindling is what all travellers can expect in this Mecca of travel.

A great number of houses are in the last stages of decay. I cannot see how this city can succeed in surviving the next fifty years! Green water weeds, almost a kind of green slime grows out of the canals and up the walls of the houses, moss grows down them, and abandoned swallows' nests adhere like stucco details on the walls.

Our 'lackey', provided by the hotel, informs us that there are nearly two thousand official gondolas. Private houses which in the past owned five or six boats now have one or none. In daylight, the city is not so gripping as at night. It resembles Cadiz or some other flooded beauty. Byron has already fallen in love with the green, grey and red decay which he says suits a divorced man's mood. He has returned to the same level – or bottom – in the curve of his despair from which I have already tried to save him ten or so times over the last six months. The difference is only that I have ceased understanding his grief, for he now talks in nothing but disparaging tones about Miss Milbanke. He knows nothing about his daughter. She was a month old the last time he saw her. He says that his greatest anguish is for Mrs Leigh. She is the defenceless kind, he says, because she never understands when she is being attacked. She is a 'lonely, lonely woman'.

As long as I have known him, he has despaired, as one does when one has lost what has been dearest to one's *innocence*.

January 7th 1818 – Soon after the latest contribution to my travel notes, I left Venice for Rome. This happened about a year ago. Between Byron and myself, an ennui had arisen that I related to my rôle as second in his battles. I do not know what he assigned it to. Our ways had already parted before my departure. He took up residence on the upper floor of the house of a coal merchant called Segati in Frezzeria, and within a few days had started up his rights as a gentleman over the coal merchant's wife. He said he was terribly in love with Marianna, who had gigantic black eyes without being directly cow-eyed, a pale gentle face and a neat figure enveloped in seven revealing veils. It was warm in the coal merchant's house.

On our last evening, we took dinner together, then went on to the Teatro di San Benedetto. He said apathetically that his life had now come to a climax in accordance with his conditions. He was happily in love with another man's wife and was writing light verse as a distraction. He was living in a city where he did not have to take a step if he didn't want to, and where it was cheap to live. I replied that it was probably even less of an effort to be dead. We made our farewells with our left hands.

In the spring, we saw each other again in Rome; he had struggled out of the degeneration of his mind and we met in our natural friendship that over so many years had been a subject of joy, a jewel in life, not unflawed, but who wants perfection? He rented a room in the house of a dentist opposite the Spanish Steps. I don't know if that was just chance. My friend's only fanaticism is the state of his teeth, their whiteness and sweet smell. He was neatly dressed. Almost every day, he went out along the Via Appia to sit on Cecilia Metella's grave and read Horace.

When summer came, I returned to Venice and spent most of my time at La Mira, my dearest friend's villa, which lies in healthy surroundings on the River Brenta. We worked in the daytime and rode around in the evenings, with not a few opportunities to ease a whole family's upkeep with a single dip into our pockets. He showed me sketches of several different works he had begun or planned. A narrative verse about Mazeppa, a short domestic farce in Venetian style in *ottava rima*, two or three ladies, 'reading-drama, Hobhouse. I can't write actable plays. Everything I write has one single voice!' – and an Armenian dictionary. For more than a year, my friend has been paying regular visits to the Armenian monks in the monastery on the island of San Lazzaro, which lies a few wet yards from the Lido. This is to exercise his brain with yet another foreign language and alphabet. He proudly showed me the results of his studies, of which one is that together with the monk who is his teacher, he is completing a dictionary. What joy to see an ambitious man and a gentleman once again after a year of sorrows.

So I was also willing to make a fair copy and attach notes to the fourth canto of *Childe Harold*, a unique test of his literature and a hundred steps forward from the far too exalted feeling for nature in part three – which he entrusted to Shelley. I will take this triumph with me in my luggage when I return to England. Byron has another daughter, by Shelley's other mistress. He told me this one evening, in the company of several Venetian Englishmen. He says that according to their agreement, Allegra (a Venetian name) is to be brought up in his house, and he asked whichever one of us first had the opportunity to visit this unusual family in England, to parcel Allegra up well and send her over on the first available boat.

During the autumn, I read the beginning of a novel by Byron. He himself is the model for *Don Julian*. Florian has also done a portrait of himself as a young Spaniard, though there is no similarity between the two works. I told him he might well find he has even greater success as a novelist than he has had as a poet. He replied – with great solemnity – that that would constitute a defeat. Poetry contains substance from what (more and more frequently) he calls *le grand peut-être*. Prose is totally subjected to the ordinary – a little of anything. And then he took out the poetic companion piece to *Don Julian*: *Don Juan*. A few verses he had captured when hunting the previous day:

Nothing so difficult as a beginning
   In poesy, unless perhaps the end;
For oftentimes when Pegasus seems winning
   The race, he sprains a wing, and down we tend,
Like Lucifer when hurl'd from heaven for sinning;
   Our sin the same, and hard as his to mend,
Being pride, which leads the mind to soar too far,
Till our own weakness shows us what we are.

But time, which brings all beings to their level,
   And sharp Adversity, will teach at last
Man, – and, as we would hope, – perhaps that devil,
   That neither of their intellects are vast:
While youth's hot wishes in our red veins revel,
   We know not this – the blood flows on too fast:
But as the torrent widens towards the ocean,
We ponder deeply on each past emotion.

And a little further on:

'Whom the gods love die young' was said of yore,
   And many deaths do they escape by this:
The death of friends, and that which slays even more –
   The death of friendship, love, youth, all that is,
Except mere breath; and since the silent shore
   Awaits at last even those who longest miss
The old archer's shafts, perhaps the early grave
Which men weep over may be meant to save.

So far, these words were of my flesh, but then he went on to his erotic
breathing again:

Juan and Haidée gazed upon each other
   With swimming looks of speechless tenderness,
Which mix'd all feelings, friend, child, lover, brother;
   All that the best can mingle and express
When two pure hearts are pour'd in one another,

And love too much, and yet cannot love less;
But almost sanctify the sweet excess
By the immortal wish and power to bless.

I handed his work back to him, a trifle moved by his fidelity, for the inspiration for these lines certainly did not stem from Signora Segati or any other Venetian, but from an English girl, a woman half overgrown by time and new ideals. Give her my love, he said, for today we are separated after a long and intense time together. He accompanied me to the boat, and when he let go my hand, he said that he had once been a person with strong feelings, but that had now been sucked up by life itself. I am prepared to take the first part of his statement quite literally. God bless him.

Fever (1818)

Between Verona and Venice, she gives up. Mary has had too much. From that moment on, all experiences seemed to become their own blinkers.

She looks out occasionally and observes: the hills, the groves, the sun-yellow light, dark eyes seeing her vanish.

The carriage is trundling along a road. The road is of the day everywhere. The carriage limits itself to trundling along. From extreme to extreme. It is always extreme somewhere – if only in between. They have had the road as their ideal, Shelley, Clara, Mary – everything was to be of the day. Then accidents happen.

The hills, the groves, dark eyes and baskets of freshly picked lemons. She sees it all, but the details protect themselves from her gaze. They protect her gaze from thoughts. The horses have blinkers preventing their walking imaginations from bolting. Mary – for her part – drags with her the surroundings like a mouse dragging with it a cobweb in its whiskers. It is a very hot summer's day, but not a spark of it sparkles in her heart.

Baby Clara has diarrhoea again. Mary feels the swift rattling passage of air and water in the parcel that is little Clara. Oh, this drains the strength from both of them. For a long long moment, Mary disregards the practical circumstance, staring straight ahead with eyes in which in a strange way grey goes into grey – the white and the iris. The baby is too apathetic to cry when it is soiled. Where does it all come from? Clara's stomach has been empty for more than twenty-four hours and yet it continues to empty itself.

Elise has William on her knee. He is fretting with heat and thirst.

366

Elise has harped and is still harping on: 'Rice and salt and water. A little boiled rice and herbal salt and a lot of water, Frau Schelli, was what we used for such conditions in my Familie.' But Mary knows that far too many small children have died from the experiments with medicines home-made by domestics.

If ever, she must now stand firm by Shelley's and her principle: fast for health. Which is confirmed by Clara's reactions: when Mary gives her a cup of fruit juice – milder than salt and water she would think! – it results immediately in vomitings giving more than they had taken.

If only it weren't so hot.

If only they weren't on the road and it was not so hot.

If only she herself were stronger to stand up against the will of others.

If only Mary could escape this poison of thoughts brewed on 'if only'. It is not even possible to daydream. Nothing in the daydream attracts you when you are in despair. Everything comes back to the brew of poison, where she lives, the taste of which she has in her mouth.

If only Claire hadn't been so immoveable, idiotically firmly determined to give her daughter to Lord Byron.

If only Shelley hadn't been so – to be quite honest – officious as to take charge of the transaction with the least possible trouble for *Lord Byron.*

With great trouble for the rest of us. If only Shelley had reserved for Mary's and his daughter Clara a small fraction of his feelings for Claire's and Byron's daughter Allegra.

They had come to Italy that spring. Shelley Mary Clara, and an even more delightful repeat of that constellation: William Clara Allegra. The boy was now three and a bit, Clara ten months, Allegra sixteen months. Clara was still an infant. William was a little individual, thoughtful and delicate but high-spirited, willingly allowing himself to be excited and led astray by Allegra, who was already rushing about on two fat little legs: up to mischief and coquettish, learning Italian words, shrieking and dominating, smiling at her own sweetness and weeping with self-pity.

When she did that, Mary searched in her eyes, but found them mute, preoccupied with herself. She told Shelley that Allegra had a sheer demonic strength, already reading the family's reactions to her little tricks and learning lessons and use from them.

367

Shelley replied at first with a strange silence. Then he was amazed. He reproached her and was amazed: our Allegra is a little *child*!

Mary replied irritably: 'And a little character, too. It wouldn't be all *that* surprising if she didn't take after her father to some little extent, would it?'

Shelley: 'My dear, we would ill reward her openness and innocence should we try to check these earliest expressions, would we not!?'

They were living by Lake Como then, in a lovely airy house. The days were fresh, the nights mild and lovely with vine blossom. They read and worked. Shelley's cough fell silent, while William's little voice and Allegra's big one grew, twirling round each other and laughing like small teeth among the pink, shore-polished stones.

Then they were to move. Claire became impatient. They moved closer to Venice. They lived here and there, closer and closer to Venice, to tempt Byron to come and see his child and its surroundings. But it proved impossible to shift Him from Venice. He refused even to discuss anything that might entail the risk of eye-contact with the child's mother. He wrote that Miss Clairmont is the tiresome sort of woman whom no man can relieve of her illusions about *him* without being cruel. If from this enforced cruelty she drew the conclusion that she herself should keep her daughter, then he considered that right and reasonable. But if she maintained that Allegra was to reside and spend her life in his house, this presumed guarantees of her own absence.

Mary smiled at his illusions. To think that Clara understood cruelty. If you amused yourself by slowly murdering her, she would make that into you finding her indispensable but having a nervous breakdown and seeking help for it in that way.

Not even the most ruthless cruelty could shake Clara's belief in her own persuasiveness. She thus finally persuaded Shelley to take Allegra under his arm and deliver her to the Palazzo Mocenigo in Venice. Shortly afterwards, she herself travelled in order to be in the vicinity when Byron needed her. A week or two went by before a message came from Shelley to Mary to say that she should pack up the household and come to Venice, where dear Albé had offered them all – Claire as well – the use of his country place for the summer and to have Allegra with them. Mary was reluctant. She liked Florence and had just put the final touch to a kind of installation worthy of the name home. William had recovered from a stomach ailment which had left him pale and emaciated. And finally, the balsam warmth of the Italian spring had wound itself up into a brutal breathless heat that neither she nor the children bore particularly well, even indoors. So they were to be on the move again? A mild admonition came from Shelley. Then another. Then an impatient one.

Apart from admonitions, the letters contained detailed accounts of the way things were going for Allegra, but no questions about their own children – only banal hopes about their health. Throwing small kisses.

He described how he had left his little favourite Allegra with Albé. Allegra's scrutiny of Him had been no less unvarnished than His of her. He had been utterly delighted with his beautiful child and hastened to find likenesses with himself – her hair, chin, her impudent expression – with Augusta and Augusta's children, his Aunt Julia, his cousin George and – even with Lady Byron! Allegra for her part had cried a little, but had nonetheless consoled herself with a kitten, and when he – Shelley – had sneaked away, Albé had been teaching her to say *'una gattina'*. At writing moments, Allegrina sat on Papa's knee sucking her thumb while he twisted her curls round the tip of his own nose and hers, making her laugh round her thumb. When she came in to him, she would say *'Bon di, Papa,'* scramble up on to his lap and give him *un bacina* or *bacinino* or whatever she said. The servants idled away half the day in wonder over the little countess and taught her Italian words as well as her own importance.

Dissonance. Dissonance. Then at last it had come. Claire's anguish. Shelley had helped her win the sympathy of the Hoppner couple, friends of Byron's who had small children themselves and so occasionally also looked after Allegra. For several days, she was with the child every day in the Hoppners' living room, where her loss dawned on her, and her despair had moved the friendly couple to offer her unlimited access to their home, presuming He was not to be told –

as they say he often expresses a veritable horror at the thought of Claire being in Venice, and says that would make him leave town immediately.

At three o'clock I went to see Albé. He was delighted to see me. Our conversation at first naturally concerned my reason for being there. (Claire's most recent request: to be allowed to have Allegra in Florence for three summer months.) My progress in these negotiations is uncertain, although he shows unexpected understanding for Claire's – and with that our – wishes. He says he does not want Allegra to go to Florence for such a long time, because the Venetians will then think that he has tired of her, and he already has a reputation for being capricious.

Then he said: And Claire will want to part from her just as little as she does now. It'll be another spell of love and another separation for them. But if you like, she can go to Claire in Padua for a week (I pretend that is where we are living). When it comes down to it, I have no right to the child, he said. If Claire wants to have her, then let her take her. I would – in contrast to many others – continue to support her. I won't abandon her. But Claire should be made aware of how incautious such a step would be on her part.

Well, my dear Mary. At this point, our conversation came to an end, for at that moment I could not see how I could pursue it any further, and I thought quite a lot had been gained by the good spirit and good humour that had prevailed during our conversation. He took me out in his gondola – to a great extent against my will, for Claire was waiting anxiously at the Hoppners' – out across the lagoon to a long island of sand that is Venice's defence against the Adriatic Sea. As we stepped ashore, his horses were waiting already saddled and we rode along the shore and chatted. Our conversation consisted of stories of his wounded feelings, questions about my circumstances, great protestations of friendship and respect for me. We spoke of literary matters – his fourth canto of *Harold*, which he says is very good. He actually quoted stanzas with real energy.

I hardly recognised *our* Albé. He is transformed into the liveliest and most cheerful person one can imagine. Venice . . .

There are two Italies. One is her green land and transparent sea, her majestic ruins, airy mountains and warm glowing atmosphere permeating everything. The other consists of Italians of today. The first is elevated and sweet perfection; the other is decay, repulsive and vile.

The fact is, Italian women are perhaps the most contemptible alive beneath the moon – the most ignorant, the most repulsive, the most bigoted, the dirtiest; countesses smell of garlic so no ordinary Englishman can go anywhere near them. Well, L.B. mixes with the lowest kind of these women, people his gondolier picks up off the street. He allows fathers and mothers to bargain with him over their daughters, and although this is usual enough among Italians, it is melancholy when an Englishmen encourages such nauseating sins.

He collaborates with monstrosities who have lost everything one might call human patterns of movement and ditto physiognomy, and who do not hesitate to practise behaviour that is not only unmentionable but also impossible to imagine in England.

He says he does not like it but endures it.

He is still not Italian and is profoundly and heartily dissatisfied with himself. When in the distorting mirror of his mind he regards human nature and the future, what can he then see but images of loathing and despair.

I think that his 'Words to the Sea' shows that he is a great poet. And he possesses a certain degree of honesty while one talks to him, but unfortunately, this does not survive one's departure. You can imagine how reluctantly I leave my little favourite Allegra in a situation in which she comes under his authority. I have tried argument and prayers, all in vain, and after this failure, I know that I have no further rights.

I do not doubt – and for his sake I should hope so – that his progress will soon come to a violent end, which in its turn ought to mean that we can renew our original bonds with Allegra.

Wrote Shelley. Mary packed. She dismissed and paid the Italian servants who were not to go with her. She took her belongings down off walls and racks, so the installation ceased to be home. Ha ha, oh yes, Shelley wished for a visit from the Great Reaper for Albé. Ha, a bitter satisfaction told her that man would not die of well-being but in virtue, at a great age. She wished that Shelley for once would say and write to him all the things in the way he said and wrote *about* him. Instead he kept on writing deferentially 'My Dear Lord Byron, Your genius . . .' 'My Dear Lord Byron, Your desires . . .' 'My Dear Lord Byron, Naturally . . .'

Mary happened to tear one of Shelley's lace collars as she was packing it. She unpacked her sewing box and started mending the tiny little hair-fine silk stitches. 'My Dear Lord Byron. I have no idea of the extent of the intellectual field it has become Your Destiny to fulfil. I know only that Your capacity is of surprising calibre and should be exploited to the fullest measure. Not that I would advise You to strive for praise. The motive for Your labours should be purer and simpler,' and so on; 'from some moment when a clarity in Your mind makes "the truth of matter" obvious to You – feel that You are a chosen one among men, in and for some higher intellectual enterprise: and that all Your efforts from that moment should strive towards this sole aim,' and so on and so forth. 'What this aim should be I am not qualified to say. In a more presumptuous atmosphere I would recommend The French Revolution as a theme containing images of everything that is best qualified to interest and instruct humanity.' Idiot! What artist wants to instruct and interest humanity! The lacemaker creates – from the joy of her fingers and the absent-mindedness of her mind. Mary's needle refuses to mend this collar; it catches, puckers, tears, making straight crooked and crooked straight. She cries out an embittered 'Aaaaah' and tugs at the thread so that it wrinkles up the collar into one single bunch, then breaks it off so that the whole thing becomes a rag.

'Frau Schelli,' says Elise. 'Our Clärchen has done bigs again. I think Master William must have infected her. She has done bigs four times in the last hour.'

'But she's not being sick any more,' says Mary, to calm her.

'No, no more, but she's as hot as a bun, Frau Schelli. I don't think we can travel.'

Mary looks at the nursemaid, who in contrast to herself seems to be quite present in what is happening. She does not act presence – her cheeks are round and also hot as buns, like little round buns in embers. Work is a stability in a woman's life. It is difficult to go to work and difficult to want it. But it is the only thing that neutralises the poison of family life. Now this must end, now all this roaming about must come to an *end*!

'Bah, we're going.'

On the way between Vicenza and Venice, Mary gets out of the carriage for a while. A stream winds its way alongside the road. She squats down to take up some water in her hand. Perhaps it's a ditch, an irrigation ditch, a drain. She smells the odour of latrines, but the water is clear. A frog is swimming in it, very like a human being in water. The lizards scuttle sideways up the furrows in the dry stony soil. Mary presses her hat down on her head. It is made of straw and she looks like a donkey. She stays in that position, feeling a slight breeze – for cruder beings there is no wind, but it cools her armpits a little, where her mourning dress is soaked. The carriage rocks slowly ahead in front of her. Inside it William frets, Elise consoles. The baby is too apathetic and is no longer whimpering.

Among all the awful things in life . . . Up until these last hours, Mary had thought that among all the awful things in life, the worst was when her sister emptied a whole bottle of laudanum in order to die unloved. Not because she thought she was unloved, but because she *was* unloved. Today there was no reason to beautify. Fanny was at best someone's fourth or fifth choice. That is what life is like: the illusion is that you *think* you're unloved. In reality you *are unloved*.

But nonetheless it is far far worse to see a baby age. During the journey, Clara has put a great parenthesis round what an old woman would count as the contents of her life. Clara has obliterated the content of the parenthesis. Mary daren't oppose her in this. She is now emaciated, a strangely satyric old person, whose hollow eyes show experience of life, experience of death, and this makes Mary into Clara's helpless child.

For long spells – while Mary and Clara silently look at each other – everything regulated by law ceases: who is mother and who child, who is helpless and who strong; who falls and who rises, who dies and who will live. They tumble with each other, safe in a darkness where all eyes see in darkness. Clara and Mary are light-heartedly in agreement that one of them is to die and the other later, and that they are swimming together in the relentless depths of the darkness, both very good swimmers. In the usual chasm, grief is nothing. But Time brakes with a tearing sound, and here Mary sits in her time and her surroundings, with her baby, who has just ended the parenthesis in which according to the laws of time it should have had the contents of its life. She will leave behind her memories like a bird, or an insect, or the frog swimming breaststroke in the ditch. When they left Florence she was a pale little child. Now she is a yellow stern old woman, who has lived her life without living it, but nonetheless with the immense experience of the end, the only thing finally of any value.

Time brakes with a tearing sound. And brings Mary back into the framework of time. She cannot tumble here, not with Clara. Clara is still there, Mary is appalled – that is how it is organised, without the compassion one deep down possesses.

There is nothing she can do about it. You could turn your back on it all. She turns her back on the carriage and walks backwards behind it, lifting both arms, and another faint breeze cools both armpits and the moist bodice of her dress. She still has Clara's dirty napkin in her hand, high above her head, and in a trance of rage lets herself be soaked by the wretched watery smell. She starts walking forwards instead of backwards. Twenty steps, or thirty. She flings the napkin into the stream. It opens, the contents run out, away like thin fibres, like unspun thread. The carriage rocks away. Then she hears William cry out. An ordinary, everyday cry. She doesn't hear the words, only his voice, which might be one among thousands.

She stands as if in a shower of understanding. The colours wash away. Look, Percy Bysshe Shelley, look what I have with me for you! An ancient child needs no mother!

But don't you see? William will be a child still for some time. His features, his mind, his eye, they are all still childish. You have some time left before he becomes a little old man. Has a small voice. Small voice. It is imprinted on Mary like one of her own facial features, but is a much beloved scar. The rain thickens to a storm of maternal feeling such as she has never known before; a blissful compassion, a shocking passion, greater than love, incredible. Stumbling, swearing, she follows the carriage. She catches up with it: her maternal feeling must be exercised with great respect and restraint. Come, William, come . . . she carefully takes his hand and carries him for a while. He is rather heavy, very sensitive to her.

But Shelley is sensitive to the skies. He meets them at the Straw Bridge in Venice. She sees him running and leaping along the canal, at least a head taller than all those around him. The sight of him does not bring her any relief, but a sense of yet more worries. She had sent an express message from Vicenza about Clara's state and now Percy Bysshe is racing about over there, look what I've got with me for you, head higher and face prickly. He finds it difficult to reach them. The whole city seems to be going in the opposite direction. Ten thousand Italians breathing garlic over him, light-hearted, talkative, chewing, rich and poor, unknowingly tinted red from a setting sun already dipping into the water, floating on it and running.

And the armada of gondolas over the whole width of the canal raising their prows towards theirs – they are lilac-coloured in the reflections of their shiny blackness. The sun reaches only the reflections, and the result becomes episcopal purple.

'*Ach, mein Gott!*' cries Elise, throwing her arms round William.

The whole city is heading in the other direction, the canal filled with everything that will float. All in brilliant colours, ruthlessly ornamented with colour, hurling back the reflections of the sun a thousandfold on to their lonely little craft with its two gondoliers. Mary calls to Shelley. He stops, shades his eyes, looking at her across the sea of people on foot, the sea of people in boats. She sees his eyes looking at her. Amazingly enough, she sees those small shaded spheres seeing, intimately and impersonally at such a distance and in the middle of all this violent physical counter-current. They don't represent the familiar but the distant. They stand still, hidden by oars, banners – gawping, shadows of everything moving – at first hidden, then visible, hovering and staring, intimately impersonal. Shelley! she cries again as with the vigour of their task her gondoliers penetrate into the compact mass of boats.

The next moment he has leapt down into a dinghy and is stepping from it on to a gondola, running across a handsome great gondola with sixteen oars, and is almost there. Mary! They meet; for an hour they are one great silence – in a flood of Italian utterances, hummings, laughs, cries, oaths and light chatter like lapping waves. Everything heading in the same direction except Mary and Shelley and their children. The great welter of colour almost makes Mary ill, the canal full of boats and festively decorated barges. After sunset, all the torches are lit, the palaces illuminated; the palaces start sailing, great boats themselves, and her head tosses in immense exhaustion. Shelley praises Byron's doctor, who has been sent for because of Clara. Mary doesn't catch the doctor's name, which sounds like garlic in Italian. Let Dr Garlic come and see what he can. Someone leans his green-shimmering face in and praises William's beauty. Time and time again, their gondola is pressed in below the edge of the canal, which is seething with people, and twice they receive an abrupt staggering visit from some stranger unable to withstand the pressure from up there. William screams loudly. Shelley names this festivity and says she is lucky her first impression of Venice is when the city happens to be showing some of its past glory. He says Dr Garlic is the most famous doctor in northern Italy and that he will cure little Clara *presto*. A high barge sails up, fountains of coloured water on board with men in black blindfolds dancing on their knees as they make patterns in the air by swinging short red veils. It seems very pointless. Allegrina has had quite a high temperature for three days, Albé was beside himself and had his horrible housekeeper, Signora Cogni, put a candle in every one of the temples of superstition in Venice. Neither goodwill nor ecclesiastics cured the little one but medical science in all its glory, as represented by Dr Garlic. The crowd rejoices and applauds human manoeuvres in which the red veils are emptied of small feather balls, which are then skilfully lifted up on the spouting water. Another layer of air comes between the earth and the dance, all elevated, totally meaningless . . .

Shelley points: 'Rialto!' Then Clara dies. Mary feels something, looks down at what she has in her arms, is mute, grimaces rigidly, but cannot help a kind of interest in the course of events. The dying Clara is lying there with her eyes closed. Her consciousness held her apart, to the very last the instincts of her muscles and sinews able to stretch out arms and legs, give her throat a function, hold her pupils together. Then Clara has abandoned her body and everything has collapsed. Her eyes are open, the pupils distended and her whole being fallen in towards the point of her annihilation. Mary tries to see the memory of consciousness in Clara's eyes, but they have become caves of darkness where before they had both tumbled together. Mary herself no longer has any knowledge of the entrance; Clara was the one to show the way when they were there. She shifts her hold on Clara so as not to drop her. Then the last of the air in those dead lungs escapes and the vocal cords close for the last time. They close a little and say 'heh'. To Mary, it is as if she had swallowed a lighted candle. The truth is given life by what has gone before. She envelops Clara to keep the secret to herself. What Shelley cannot grasp for himself he does not need to know. She meets someone's eyes. As they slowly sway past each other, she sees someone else looking from her to the shroud and back to her. A face like a dollar, turning in the air, flashing. Has gone. Feather balls and men in breeches are dancing on the barge. They take off their eyemasks and receive applause. Shelley is talking about the other Clara, about Allegra, about Albé, about Dr Garlic. He doesn't look at her, nor does he see that his own daughter is dead.

Byron is standing on the canal steps up to the Palazzo Mocenigo, spectator to the festival. For Allegra's sake. Naturally, she is sitting on his arm, half-asleep with her head against his neck, sucking her thumb. People peer out of the open door, from the balconies, are sitting at his feet. He has a whole milieu to help him look at the spectacular barges. A second of it sticks in Mary's memory even then. Torches, flames, some pale snake-spotted remains of sun and twenty to twenty-five faces stretching forward with parted lips, or closing them and turning away. (A dreamed trick as if painted by Cranach the Younger.) They look and look away and surge round his feet. Someone laughs from up on his roof. As if they all might have better things to do, but out of shame – with false gravity – are watching these *official* pleasures. Mary Shelley sees it surge, hears it laugh, sees the false gravity, sees the contented child, the comfortable father. The gondola sways in below the steps. She looks up, as if out of a well. He looks down. Starts smiling in welcome then . . . for the second time, that hideous grimace occurs, the grimace Claire had lured out of him at Leman. He is the god of rage. He is a medium for the God of Rage. It happens every time he catches sight of Clara. It abates. 'But Mary,' he says slowly. 'What have you got there . . . ?'

The god of the art of healing is a mouse.

All night, all day, it sits in a wardrobe grating bark. You wake, you watch. The innumerable other sounds in the Palazzo Mocenigo are irregular – irregular house sounds. At first they are disturbing. Then you hear . . . them shifting in their sleep, like night weather: someone coming in, someone is thrown out, someone quarrelling, someone making love? Someone dreams, and flees, his luck, his lapse. Grows –

But all through the night, the mouse sits in the wardrobe making its mouse-sounds as it grates bark on a grater of genuine apothecary silver. Bark of alder, of aspen and birch and plane, of cedar and oak of the house itself. Mary is awake. On the ceiling, she can see the famous reflections of moonlight on the water in the canal. That's better than the wallpaper and tapestries and the works of art on the walls, but like the art, seems to be re-used light. The moon provides the reflection of the sun, the canal setting the white stillness of the moon in motion. The ceiling fixes the movement into two dimensions. It disappears down into the drowned depths of the eye. Mary is awake. The eager little mouse-like silvery industry reminds her of someone she knows. But who? She ought to search further. She has already searched all over Venice. That first morning, Shelley said:

'You'd better go and look at the sights now that you're actually here.'

Shelley said:

'Our little Clara won't come back even if we shroud ourselves in the external pretension called mourning clothes, or sew curtains together as a sign that we are inaccessible in some kind of formal state. Death, my Mary, is part of the process of living and we survivors live most *sensibly* in that we unite the one with the other and again open ourselves to the multitude of impressions of the senses that has always been the only way human beings can reconcile themselves with their destinies.'

Mary said:

'Yes, my Shelley.'

And so they went out in search of the city of Venice.

The heat had increased even more. In the little walled garden on the land side of the palace, the few drops of the fountain splashed in mechanical circulation, the leaves winter-green, the flowers painted dark red. Her breasts were empty as she leant her forehead against the wall of a house and felt the dry stucco shuddering from the vibrations of the earth.

They strolled along the alleys. Mary would have got lost, but Shelley knew the way. Every time she peered down one alley from another – and along its long cramped perspective, where a black cat was brooding – he led her in the other direction and in the grey heat guided her to desolate places, where the same fountains continued the same mechanics; once again the same circular movement of silvery glittering individual drops. He found the way, but did not find Venice. He was able to show her the decay. In truth, simple people lived like bats here in town. Large families looked out of dark cavernous rooms at street level. The beggars were innumerable, the magnificence powerless. 'Bonaparte,' said Shelley, 'dissolved – let's see . . . in '97, the remains of the Doge's dominions. He considered the whole city was built as a feudal theatre, and in that he was right.' 'Perhaps not entirely, my Shelley,' said Mary. They looked at the palaces and the ruins of palaces, churches, ruins of churches. The swallows swooped like black nerves in the cone of the sun – yes, the cone of the sun in the singular, alone and intimate above a little canal, sometimes almost nothing but a tree, a Gothic shoelace when ornamental roof-edges were the only bastion of silence against the terrible heat.

Independent of everything else, a smile rose through Mary as she 'crossed the street' by going up and down the steps on a bridge. It never reached her face – a mute smile – and yet its unpredictable bubble hovered inside her.

Mary stopped in front of a picture of the festivities on the Canal Grande, composed round some swimming faded white corpses. It was interesting. The faded colours were interesting, she said, the fading of all things. The canal was full of boats – like the previous evening – the high, Venetian chimneys jabbing the sky with their capitals. People were staring at the middle and there were several bewildering corpses swimming. Shelley asked her to concentrate on something less close to them. In his opinion, harping on what lies close is a perversion. The bubble came up and Mary at last smiled. Men are weak. They have no idea that great theoretical interest can be found in what 'lies close'. Here at last she had a fragment of Venice – found with the help of little Clara. The swimming corpses, the mediaeval astonishment all round. She wanted to think, bind with her thoughts, for some strange long gauze bandages were also swimming there. Then all at once Shelley felt his foot hurting, his back hurting, he was breathless and had a headache. She found no more fragments that day. Nor anything relevant to the night mouse-sound. She leant her forehead against a wall and felt the earth moving. On their way home across the lagoon, she saw all the leaning towers of Venice. If they had been able to whistle, it would have been a wonderful silvery dissonance.

The ceiling reflects the canal reflecting the moon reflecting the sun . . . and who knows whether it stops there! As the light races through the universe, Mary lies nailed down by severe and simple pain –

on the world's most circumscribed place, for anyone who cannot swim or has no boat. The mouse scuttles across the floor on patent leather shoes for its night meal and to find another tree where it can harvest medicinal bark.

Albé comes across the floor on small patent leather hooves. He finds it difficult to keep his balance with the huge wooden dish in his arms. 'But what have you got in your arms, My Lord,' Mary asks. 'Bark, bark, Mary, bark, bark, treefuls of bark. You know, the swallows didn't come to Venice in April. And yet we stood waiting on the Lido the whole month. And what is the result? Invalids, invalids, tertian fever, the ague, malaria, sickly people abounding. Open up!' Mary opens her lips a little, but is far from sure that she is one of the sick. She cannot feel whether she is ill. A confusion may have arisen.

Albé leaps over the edge of the frame of his mirror and lands on two small patent leather hooves. He comes slanting across the moonlit floor, each time the leg dragging behind him becoming twice as long as the one he puts forward. Ah, all these props!

He takes the spoon full of bitter brown bark and measures: 'There we are! What does this look like, Miss Mary? Open up now!' She opens a little wider. He *rolls* in the spoon and at once spreads dust so fine that each individual grain becomes one with the glassy red cave wall that shudders, hardens, wants to spew out – accepts. He had been right. She certainly was ill. Considerably better, she now follows him to assist him with the dish. But still makes sure she takes shelter in his shadow. They trudge – small figures – through rooms built for Titans. High-ceilinged, elegant decay. Panelling, curves, beams, stucco. Silk wall coverings on the walls, abrupt exclamations of porphyry patterns on floors of black stone. The moon shines directly through the huge dusty windows down on to the floor, the reflection of the canal wriggling on the ceiling and reflecting – better than directly – the pulses and protuberances of the sun. In every corner, a mattress with someone sleeping on it, rising on an elbow and – gaping: a glassy red cave open, a wind blowing it clean of fever, with a sigh (so lovely), Albé spins in his bark spoon and every cave shudders, chokes, wants to spew it out, accepts – rejoices.

'I have often wondered,' says Albé to his assistant, who is now insisting on carrying the dish while he serves out portions, 'I have always wondered how people happened to think up something like this muck helping against the ague.' Albé is a matter-of-fact thinker when surrounded by panelling, curves, beams and stucco. 'You realise, Miss Mary, that it's a very much more remarkable event when ignorant people feel their way forward through the plant kingdom and the mechanics of materials than when apothecaries and architects build on foundations and know that knowledge is there to have, which the former did not know, though when the Russians cook wild mushrooms, they' (he adds confidentially) 'still put an onion into the pan and if the onion turns blue, that means the mushroom is poisonous.

'The Russians, Miss Mary, are people with no patience, but with all the time in the world. Otherwise they are uninterested in facts and matters of detail.'

Now a trifle bewildered, he bends down in order to look up at the cleft roof of a glass cave. A reversed ravine. They are suddenly right down on the canal level of the palace. As are Byron's protégés, who have huddled together on uncomfortable wall-benches or on the ground floor itself. A huge copy of a statue – Octavius with a Napoleon face – stares down at them. They have taken off their carnivalish cripple's guise, the one Shelley loathes and which is their beggar costume – spiritually – instead of the usual snoring, sleeping feverish cripples.

The night envelops the most hectic destinies in fellowship with sleep.

It is low tide. The entrance to the Canal Grande is open, only the grid in front, the surface of the water – the moon milk not only reflecting against the roof but all over the room, which constantly, again and again, plunges into green. And gravitationally, a gondola rises by, at the height of the floor, first the crest, then the neck and the slender body. Lastly, one with everything, the gondolier, riding upright and absolutely silent, his silhouette absorbed. Only the white water. Whitening up into small crests of waves, sparkling there. 'Do you speak *Italian* with that palate?' says Albé to the poor hare, hesitating for a moment with his bark spoon. The hare titters and replies with a soft rubbery sound. He has too high a head as well, and far too small crooked legs. His sex, large and handsome and packed in a red bag, points at his toes. Though no bored greedy laughter now. No grins and rolling eyes or slinking tongues. No upturned eyes and bulging humps or clamouring claw hands. It is closed for the night. It is low tide. All destinies enveloped in the fellowship of sleep. 'Oh well, as long as it doesn't sting in you,' warns Albé, twisting his spoon inside the hare's mouth. Which shudders, chokes and retches – accepts.

He forces a spoonful of bark into Fletcher's recalcitrant beard. It rustles and crackles like an angry fire while Fletcher insists he is as healthy as a fanfare. But he has to. Everyone has to: every man, servant . . . every woman to make sure. Lord Byron serves them bark by the tree!

Byron himself is in his study. He works best at night, and night is the time for work as long as 'my pen *stands* between my inkwells'. 'Ah, men and their little metaphors . . .' says Mary to Albé, who suddenly sought his way into her shadow, and there began to shrivel on his hooves. The bark dish shrivels, too.

Lord Byron sits in his dark dim red study, one leg tucked under him and his chin in his hand. He is dressed like the walls – in dark red velvet, his hair unbecomingly half-long, and he is staring concentratedly unseeing at the wall, from where the Mocenigo Doges stare back from their frames. No eyes meet – he is unseeing, because he is writing. Describing or creating? Mary goes across and leans over his shoulder to find out. In the light of a single candle.

> Mix'd in each other's arms, and heart in heart,
>   Why did they not then die? – their lives prolonged,
> Should an hour come to bid them breathe apart;
>   Years could but bring them cruel things or wrong.
> The world was not for them, nor the world's art
>   For beings passionate as Sappho's song;
> Love was born *with* them, *in* them, so intense,
> It was their very spirit – not a sense.

'Hmm, the fourth line isn't good,' says Mary as she wipes up the little mineral lake on the desk with her tear-stained handkerchief. 'That's a makeshift solution. It shows it's there for the sake of the rhythm. It breaks your stanza off in the middle, after which you have to start again on the fifth line and that doesn't fit in with the rhythm of *ottava rima*. You must re-write it and join the two halves of the stanza to each other.'

382

'Good heavens, then give me a rhyme for prolonged or wrong,' growls Lord Byron.

She fills his glass with more mineral water. 'Oh, prolonged! Why don't you put "too long"?'

'Mmmm, yes, but with those rather threadbare clues, you're asking me to fabricate a more indivisible whole, my dear Ariadne?'

'Chance, My Lord, is a common fantasy of humanity. Individually, not one of us can understand or steer it, but we can suddenly understand each other through its products, without being forced into long-winded interpretations and explanations. Chance is also fairer than the law. If you want to do something really magnificent, you must put your trust in it. Your last line isn't good, either. Wherever poetry contains an adjustment, the reader spots a makeshift rhyme.'

'Good heavens, Mary! What then does your Shelley say about your having such religious insight?'

Why did he have to ask just that question? It makes the whole house lean. The mineral water bottle tips over again. Mary can't take her little handkerchief to it this time, for it is already soaking wet, and anyway, would not suggest it, for the water rushes out as if from its source, as if out of bottomless desire. It simply refuses to stop, but rises instead. 'Jump!' says Lord Byron, sitting astride a stream with Mary on his lap – for she is unable to swim. Jump, jump . . . the stream rushes over thresholds and chair legs like the tip of a tongue over a row of teeth. Now they are further down in the Titan rooms and servants can be seen everywhere, mouths wide open for spoons of bark. It is as much as Mary can do to hold on to Byron's reins. The stream twists and turns and noses its way in and out of all the rooms.

They come to the Spartan corner, a room where the moon shines in through the east and south windows simultaneously. A heavy wave movement from Lord Byron's leg and they are on dry land. But the mouse has arrived there ahead of them. A little ahead. It has just reached the birch tree and has started nosing round the trunk with its pink finger-flower nose. It dithers and trembles and discards. The small pink feet scuttle and scramble on Shelley. The birch grows out of Shelley. Thin, of course, with wind-tortured posture. Pale as lead, swaying in the moon wind. The straddling silhouette hangs on to a corpse-white cupola diagonally across the canal.

At last Shelley is sleeping really soundly. It's not often he can be

383

caught doing that. His rest is usually *prepared*, his sleep as methodical as washing. He doesn't yearn for the sea of dreams. He yearns for the sea. He doesn't yearn for the voluptuousness of sleep. After death. The mouse has already sensed that. It climbs a little way up the trunk and sniffs, then munches at chaste birch bark. Can it be anything? No. No. Trees growing out of Shelley can't cure others. Trees growing out of Shelley cure no one. Ah, all these props.

One last look at the white room. The last but one door to open . . . the mouse soon runs right across the floor to the last one. Mary and Lord Byron fall to their knees. There is the little bed. In the bed, the little girl. In the girl's eyes a very small devil takes a leap up on to the bolster as she stops screwing up her eyes and opens them. 'Hehehe,' she says when Mary's long fingers start arranging the ruffle round the child's neck. Hehe. Mary is a mother. Mechanically she adjusts and arranges the clothing. Asks and grasps and turns and spits and rubs and examines and moistens – with reason and without. 'Teehee,' says Allegra.

She sits up and at once starts ranging her toys in front of her on the bolster. A sugar sifter of tarnished black silver, two small wooden dolls, a one-eyed dog and a very small devil. Then a dried red rose, two building blocks, a mouse with a silver grater, and a stuffed bird. Then she starts work, talking the astounding talk that comes to small children when they are playing, inventing a connection between their finds – the rubbishy silver, the beautiful craftsmanship of one's own handiwork, the dead with the living. A rivulet of absurd logic runs over Allegra's playing lips: and the tiny little mouse slipped out on to the great big staircase and went tippety-tappety into the hall and Papa *kiiiiills* it dead, splatch, with no head, no tail, *la mammina è una porca* and the mouse is *deeaaad*. Promises Allegra and sprinkles with her sugar sifter over the poor one-eyed dog.

Small curls grow round her face, which is concentrating on the game and nothing else. No distractions. The chubby fingers move round the sugar sifter, the dolls, the dog and the devil, then to the dried rose, the building blocks, the mouse and the stuffed bird – all during a stream of description from the little mouth, the little head with satisfaction adopting its own logic.

'Doesn't she speak better Venetian?' asks Mary. The devil notes that Allegra's eyes are open and leaps back in, which makes her say to 'Papa' something about *'fare pipi'*. *'Dio!'* cries Lord Byron in embarrassment, waving his arms. *'Presto, pronto, Margarita!* Why did you rouse a sense that is asleep, Mary? That is the only thing she can say in Venetian and what she says she has to do, *o Dio, Dio, Margarita, o, o, Margarita!'*

The last door opens with an impatient crash and in strides a tall lady only just managing to arrange her clothing as her feet patter across the parquet floor. 'Ch'è?' The lady has the hoarse voice of a boy acquired from scolding people in the alleys. 'Ch'è? Ha!' She snatches Allegra out of bed with the tender brutality children and animals tolerate, and with one single movement, *la Fornarina* takes the child under one arm, kicks open the balcony door, goes out and moves Allegra in under the other arm, looks for something, finds the watering can, shifts Allegra back, holds her out over the balcony railing and trickles water over her bare toes. 'Hehehe,' replies Allegra, beginning to piss in a long profile of light through the curved, misty house-hidden depths of the Canal Grande. Everything else darkness. The moon has gone behind the clouds. The wind flutters its profile three times. The poor spring water of Venice rises a trifle. 'Legs?' mutters *la Fornarina*, looking into Allegra's roguish eyes as she wipes her between her legs with her nightgown. She puts down the watering can and gathers the child up in both arms . . . she *hurries*. She spills one breast out of her dress as she hears the music from the half-open last door, hears Eboli singing, black as – ho, ho, the court harem. And that is the last door in Palazzo Mocenigo.

With constant interruptions for peace (last word)

May 14th, 1824 – This morning at a little after eight o'clock I was awakened by a loud tapping at my bedroom door, and on getting up had a packet of letters put into my hand, signed 'Sidney Osborne'. On the outside were the words 'By Express'; there was also a short note from Kinnaird.

I anticipated some dreadful news, and on opening Kinnaird's note found that Lord Byron was dead. In an agony of grief such as I have experienced only twice before in my life – once when I lost my dear friend, Charles Skinner Matthews, in 1811, and afterwards when at Paris I heard my brother Benjamin had been killed at Waterloo, Quatre Bras – I opened the dispatches, and there saw the details of the fatal event. Also there were four copies of a Greek proclamation by the Provisional Government of Missolonghi, with a translation annexed.

I read this proclamation over and over again, in order to find some consolation in the glorious conclusion of his life for the loss of such a man, but in vain. All our ancient and most familiar intercourse burst upon me and rendered me alive only to the deprivation I was now doomed to endure.

Afterwards I saw the account of his last illness by Fletcher in a letter to Mrs Leigh, which letter she copied for me. The reading of this letter tore my heart to pieces. It showed the boundless and tender attachment of all about him to my dear, dear friend. I shall keep it for ever.

When the first wave of my grief had sunk away, I decided I would lose no time preserving what remained of my friend – his good name and reputation.

I went to see Kinnaird. We had a melancholy evening, during which we recalled all the delightful things about our friend. I shall never forget this terrible day.

We could not avoid taking up the question of the 'Memoirs' in Lord Byron's hand which are the property of Tom Moore and which in his lack of judgement and his avarice he has sold to Murray for the extraordinary sum of two thousand guineas. I felt called upon to mention the matter earlier in the day, when I called on Mrs Leigh. She says none of his *real* friends and family could wish for the publishing of them. She was in an afflicting condition. She gave me Fletcher's letter to read, and I could not restrain my sorrow, but again burst out into uncontrollable lamentation. I thought right to engage Mrs Leigh not to communicate to any but the nearest friends one part of the letter, which mentioned that since Lord Byron's fit on February 15th he had placed on his breakfast table a Bible every morning. This circumstance, which pleased his valet Fletcher, I was afraid might be mistaken for cowardice or hypocrisy, and I was anxious that no idle stories to his discredit should get abroad. I daresay that the Bible was on his table. I have long recollected his having one near him; it was a volume given to him by his sister, and I remember well seeing it on his table at Pisa in 1822, but unless his mind was shaken by disease I am confident he made no superstitious use of it. That is to say, I am confident that although he might have a general belief in its contents, he was not overcome by any religious terrors.

He often said to me, 'It may be true. It is, as d'Alembert said, a *grand peut-être*'; but I own that I think he was rather inclined to take the opposite line of thinking when I saw him at Pisa, for when I remonstrated with him on the freedom of some of his latter writings in that respect, he said, 'What, are *you* canting?' He then protested that he would tell his opinions boldly, let what would be the consequence.

Mrs Leigh was in agreement with me that ambiguous and obscure points about her brother must be handled with discretion. Captain George Anson Byron – now unfortunately Lord Byron – went this evening to Beckenham in Kent in order considerately to inform Lady Byron and Ada. We had time to talk it over and agreed on the subject of the 'Memoirs', which he also promised not to mention to her.

May 15th – I had my first meeting with Moore up at Murray's. It is absurd. Moore maintains Byron would have wanted the 'Memoirs' published. He says that 'his friend' gave him them in Venice with definite instructions to publish them on a suitable occasion and 'for a devil of a lot of money'. Moore had not consulted 'his friend' on either the assignment or the devil of a sum, but had followed Byron's wish that he should take on the first and receive the second. He said he could not take the responsibility for suppressing anything a deceased person had wished to be published. I think I have good grounds for my suspicions that Moore did not wish to suppress the two thousand guineas Murray had already paid for the rights and which in that case Moore would be forced to hand over.

Murray himself – who stands to lose more money than Moore on a cancelled publication – on the other hand, was in full agreement with me. Tom Moore asked me to show him a single point in the manuscript in which Byron's account could damage any living person. I have not read the manuscript, but did not reveal that, as Moore attaches a strange prestige to his relations to 'his friend' and at this time in particular has taken a great deal of trouble to appear as his 'best' friend. Murray, who has read the manuscript, muttered that that made no difference, but people could be expected to read them according to a system of interpretation (an expectation) that might cause posthumous damage to Lord Byron, his family and his already published work.

May 16th – There has never been a person more loved by his friends. He had a mysterious and very rare ability to bind to him those close to him. Not with obligation and persistence, but with something wistful, or arousing yearning. No one could be in his presence without being conscious of his attraction. His manner was inviting but not obtrusive. He was never cheerful or serious in the wrong context and he always seemed created for just the company he happened to find himself in. There was a simultaneous gentleness and firmness in his address. He was free, open and unreserved with whomever it may be, but kept so much of himself to himself that he also showed his closest friends respect and distance. He was very susceptible, sensitive and perceptive, but he did not allow his emotions to lead him astray into the kind of hyperboles in which one betrays the best of oneself. I don't think anyone has ever lived who, with his essence, his style and his outward being, showed more inalienably that he was of good family and breeding.

May 21st – Met the new Lord Byron, who said the previous Lady Byron did not wish to see her name mentioned in the discussion, but that she was just as anxious as anyone that the publication of the 'Memoirs' should be stopped. We sought out Moore, who at first sent a message to say he was working, but half an hour later appeared in his slippers. He maintained with great obstinacy that Byron wanted to publish and Byron's wishes should determine the matter (+ his profit, I should think . . .). I told him that not a hundred but thousands of times I had convinced my friend of the destructiveness of his *wishes*, and in the long run had won his gratitude by changing his attitude.

Moore was terribly stubborn. He had no new arguments, but kept repeating the old ones. He is a terribly stubborn little man, who says we are not only robbing him but also the reading public and the hereafter, apart from insulting the memory of our friend by questioning his judgement, etc., etc. Byron seems to have *spilled* copies and parts of copies of these memoirs around to every Tom, Dick and Harry! Murray has the original. Moore has a complete copy which he has shown to anyone who wants to read it (and which he says will guarantee the inoffensiveness of the manuscript. For the devil, sin is virtue, and so on) and there appears to be at least half a copy somewhere in France. Scrope Davies says he received a fragment in his hand some time ago in which among other things, it stated, as I already knew, that Byron 'had' his wife on the sofa in the drawing-room before his wedding dinner. That information is enough for me.

May 27th – Another meeting with Moore. Today Mrs Leigh was also present. He said we could force him only because he had received money from Murray for the manuscript. If he had procured it honestly he would have been able to maintain the morality he even now had on his side, or the reason . . . if we preferred. Mrs Leigh and I then spoke of Byron's greatest failing being his need to surround everyone close to him with a kind of nimbus – with mystery: and then particularly those beneath him when it came to position in society and intelligence.

'Do you mean me?' said Tom Moore, who was eavesdropping on us. I would have replied yes, had I been the kind of person who honours poaching. His evasive manner, his slightly charming and hardly demanding qualities had brought out the worst in my friend. Mrs Leigh (who indeed could have been subjected to the same

389

criticism) mumbled and tripped and stammered out an embarrassed no to his question. Nonetheless, Moore was embittered. He said although Byron had not written his secrets in his memoirs, he had told them all to *him*, in the knowledge that he would not be handed moral homilies in exchange. In contrast to some other people, he had never treated Byron as if he had to be *looked after*, which had brought on him Byron's gratitude and unreserved confidence.

I had no desire to bring this appalling situation down to Mr Moore's level and so refrained from saying what *I* knew: that one of our friend's reasons for going to Greece was that he had no desire to become 'like Tom Moore, and sing at parties after forty'.

May 30th – 'If it were done when 'tis done, then 'twere well it were done quickly,' said the seventh Lord Byron, tearing up the first page. I must add that when I saw the familiar slanting handwriting, the oh, so intimate colour of ink – even smelt a faint Byron-smell from the paper – all my senses went into swift profound retreat, but after that first moment of weakness, I managed to remind myself that surgery is not murder. Allowing the infected branch to remain can infect the whole tree.

Yesterday we gathered at Murray's office in Albemarle Street. We went up to the drawing-room where John Murray had already started a fire in the open fireplace. We had the original and Moore's copy. Any eventual fragments adrift could always be denied if they came into the public eye. Lady Byron had herself maintained we could count on fictional versions on the market for a while. For us it was important that what was factual departed this world.

Moore was there looking on. He said he found it heart-rending. Who does not find it heart-rending to tear up and burn written words? I take the responsibility for my heart. After a while, it went better and finally one tears and burns with all the enthusiasm of the destructive. My only consolation is that I know I have thus done my friend a greater service than I ever did him in his lifetime.

June 19th – Today a letter came from Mr Barry, Byron's banker in Genoa:

You will excuse my mentioning to you rather a singular request that Lord Byron made me when he was on the point of sailing. The eccentricities of a man of genius may, I hope, be mentioned to a friend valued by him as you were without giving offence, or appearing childish or impertinent. He had kept for a long time three common geese, for which, he told me, he had a sort of affection, and particularly desired that I would take care of them, as it was his wish to have them at some future time, it being his intention to keep them as long as he or they lived. I will send them to England, if you please.

July 1st – The brig *Florida* with Byron's goods on board has been sighted from the Downs. In the evening, I went to Rochester, stayed overnight, and the next morning continued on to Standgate Creek, where she lay at anchor at ebbtide. Not much activity visible from the shore, the mast tops drawing circles in the summer clouds. I found a boat but no oarsman, so I rowed out myself; they had seen me, recognised me, and a ladder was lowered as I arrived. On board I found Colonel Leicester Stanhope, who had been the Anglo-Greek Committee's second-in-command under Byron in Missolonghi. Fletcher was also there, and Tita Falcieri from Venice, Dr Bruno (who when it came to youth and uneasy eyes could be seen as a natural successor to Dr Polidori!) and a number of other servants whom Byron had picked up here and there and who now felt lost and looked at me . . . Three dogs which had belonged to my friend were playing on deck, two Newfoundlands and Moretto the bulldog, which I remembered from Pisa. I could hardly bring myself to look at these animals, who had received so many caresses and bore the most uncomplicated memories of him. The thought of his hand in a white bushy ruff was suddenly very painful.

After an hour, the tide turned and the skipper wanted to take advantage of it to go on up the river to Gravesend. I cannot account for my feelings during this journey. I stood all the time by his coffin, supported by some stretched ropes, as if in a standing hammock; I was too weak to stand up by myself. I had been the last to bid him farewell when he left England for ever. I remember how he had waved his cap as the packet bore him on a wave from the pier in Dover. And now I was standing here, prepared to restore his remains to England.

Poor Fletcher burst into tears when he caught sight of me. He is the one who has been Byron's companion for twenty years – no one else. He related to me the whole course of the illness. I have read his letter and Pietro Gamba's at least a hundred times and had thought my tears would then be exhausted, but ah, they were but dammed up. As Fletcher spoke in what is for him a natural and for me an intimate flow of words, the picture opened itself to a wind which blew away the frame of the story and made everything real for the first time: his own loneliness in Missolonghi, his bewilderment, disconsolateness when my poor, poor friend dies, with twelve vile leeches like wings round his forehead, as the rain sweeps in over the flooded earth. 'What were his last words?' was all I could manage to say.

Colonel Stanhope reported:

'At intervals, Lord Byron expressed regret over having gone to Greece. He was angry with you and his other friends on the Greek Committee because you had made public his first enthusiastic letters about his desire to make a contribution in the Hellenic struggle for freedom. He said that by publishing his letters in the English press, you had obliged him to go there and rough it, while you yourselves devoted your backsides, beautiful words and toasts in champagne to the Cause. At less irritable moments, he said it was better to moulder away in Missolonghi than at the age of forty trudge round London drawing-rooms talking and singing like Tom Moore.' (I am pleased he contrasted those alternatives in particular in front of more than just myself.)

Stanhope says Byron could not be bothered to attack Lepanto although all the preparations had been made, victory was certain and everyone was waiting for marching orders. He never left Missolonghi if he could avoid it. He often quarrelled with Stanhope, but was also swift to reconciliation with a 'give me your honest right hand!'

Stanhope asked me if I had observed an amusing movement in Lord Byron's repertoire: he used to put his heel down on the floor and twirl round like a little girl. He, Stanhope, had often found it difficult to keep a straight face at this sight in the middle of a dispute about working methods in conditions of war and siege.

Pietro Gamba had another description of the way my friend shouldered the situation. He said that when they arrived at Missolonghi, everything was in a state of disintegration. Stanhope had arrived a month or two earlier and had not taken much interest in the military aspect, but was busy working on a project for general education and freedom of the press. (Good things in my opinion, but Gamba seemed indignant.)

392

For his part, the head of the provisional government, Prince Mavrocordatos, seems to mistrust his Greek units and rely on brigades of foreign volunteers, who cannot agree among themselves 'either'. The only person who could deal with the Greeks, primarily the Suliots, was apparently 'il caro Bairon'. Gamba told me about one occasion when a Suliot marched in in the middle of deliberations between Byron and Mavrocordatos and demanded to have a Turkish prisoner handed over for the purpose of cutting his throat. Byron said: 'No blood is to be unnecessarily shed here,' and asked Mavrocordatos to intervene with the man, who was still there. Mavrocordatos made an effort, in as much as he said some hard words, which had no effect on the Suliot, so Byron rose, pulled out his pistol and, holding it against the intruder's head, marched him out of the house.

For five or six hours, the *Florida* trailed in on the tide with little wind in her sails. Most of the time, I stood leaning in those ropes, or against his coffin. I could feel his presence. He was young when he died, leaving a large portion of the rest of his life to work itself out among those of us who had to remain behind. That was not horrible – it is forgetting which is horrible. On the contrary, his presence for brief moments seemed to be like a great promise, an equally great affirmation.

The flat banks of the Thames went by, slowly, like a thread of spinning wool. Memories:

The night we first arrived at Venice, my premonition was proved correct. The short trip across the lagoon became a parting of the ways between us, for we never became brothers on the same path again, but effectively moved away from each other. Then we maintained nothing more than the difficult art of Friendship, though with a touch of defiant loss, the defiance because the separation was so reasonable, and what is reasonable is a treacherous contradiction of everything youth values.

But there also arose estrangement between an Englishman and an Italian, with all that that entails in differences in codes of honour. For he *became* Italian. The last time I saw him in Pisa, he had gone so far as to adopt the manner of an *ageing* Italian: those measured movements, that sense of male worth perfected in age, withering and impotence.

But it was in the autumn of 1818, in Venice, that Byron and I ended our last time together as brothers. We parted on the slippery steps of Palazzo Mocenigo, a great barn on the Canal Grande that managed to house his wildly expanding household of twenty or so servants, terrorised and inspected by Margarita Cogni, the formidable wife of a baker, nineteen years old, who had run away from her husband to adopt Byron as her lover, which with his tolerant, indifferent Italian laughter he went along with. He said: 'In our youth, Hobby, we strive to keep our fellow human beings apart to avoid being caught up in their conflicts. Here in Venice, I have learnt to like a hellish noise. If they fight each other, or if I keep them apart . . . the result is nonetheless the same.'

About thirty or so domestic animals fought. He populated his world. In accordance with the 'real' life he said he was going to live, he had allowed 'reality' into the bottom of his house. In the dimness behind us were the homeless, the crippled, criminals and prostitutes, who had shelter there for that night. My friend was no fool. He did not invite them up on to his floor for a carnival with no masks. But he touched them like a blessing and protected the criminals among them from the gendarmes. He staged nothing, but he let everything be. At the time, this was his view of life. And into that life came Allegra Byron, who was delivered there by Shelley during the summer. Came and went. The little girl was eighteen months old. Sometimes my friend looked at the sweet little monkey, so like him in moments of uncontrolled rage, and came to his senses and hired her out to married couples who had better homes to offer a baby.

I saw all this as yet another act in his drama of life. Byron has tried a great many variations during our time together: the nerve track in all his dissipation was a line that was as straight and clear as mine, though my own did not provide such bewildering eruptions, but seemed straighter.

I returned to England firmly intending to follow it and give my life some stability, and in November I formally became a politician. On the 17th, a letter in Samuel Brook's own hand came from the Whig party committee meeting at the Crown & Anchor:

Resolution – that John Hobhouse, Esq., for his renowned talents and qualities of character can be considered as a suitable and right person to represent the City of Westminster in Parliament and that in accordance with this he has been nominated for the next election.

With that my life turned in a different direction from travels and education and fruitless authorship. I did lose my first election, but it was an expected defeat and did not appreciably disturb my plans.

At about the same time, Byron implemented his line when he sent home a parcel to Murray for printing and publication. In it was indeed his exquisite 'Ode to Venice' and *Mazeppa*, but first and foremost a Canto of *Don Juan*, of which he had shown me a small fraction in Venice. I read a copy together with Scrope Davies, who laughed happily and called DJ 'marvellous. *Our* Byron!' He has always been partial to what is indiscriminate in his friends. For my part, I had what was best for Byron in mind, so hesitated over whether the poem was suitable for publication. It had all of the sweetness, the natural aptitude for poetry in all respects that make Byron unique in our day and immortal for the future. But it also contains a wealth of blasphemy, attacks on a number of citizens of importance in English society, moral laxities, superficialities, sophisms, obscenities and defamations of Lady Byron (transparently hidden under the name Donna Inez). These stains were accomplished and ingrained. In my opinion, they ruined all the poetic harmony and consistency.

That was my opinion at the time, and I was not alone in this. The whole of London society was agreed that *Don Juan* should not be published.

Kinnaird, Murray and Moore all had to be persuaded for several hours before they realised that they must do what they could to stop him from wasting any more energies on DJ. We agreed – independently of each other – to impress upon him that an affair is an affair in Venice and quite another matter in London.

That was my honest opinion at the time. Since then I have changed my mind twice: May the following year saw DJ in print. The printed word is so much less direct and offensive than the handwritten word. When I read the poem then, I thought it was neither as good nor as bad as I had thought before, nor so unseemly, or so quick-witted. So now – I have re-read Cantos I–IV over the last week. An outstanding achievement, or rather a work that shows signs of outstanding capacity. Byron was a great humorist . . .

He was disappointed in my reaction.

I experienced my greatest disappointment with him in the spring of '20. In February, I was sentenced by the Tory majority in the House of

Commons and ended up in Newgate. This happened because I supported a reform of Parliament and wrote a pamphlet that gave emphasis to my views. It was said that I had been guilty of instigating rebellion because I had written that if Parliament were not guarded by soldiers, the people would have gone in and dragged members out by the ears. I was imprisoned without trial.

On February 28th, I was released and received at a dinner for 450 people at the Crown & Anchor, where I was also told that during my imprisonment, I had again been nominated for Parliament. On March 25th, I won my seat at the election. Only slight toothache reminded me of my mortality that day. But in April, I received a letter from Murray, containing a kind of 'ballad', in which Byron makes fun of my imprisonment. It was an appalling piece of verse and he had published it in the *Morning Post* with the signature 'Infidus Scurra', a name we used to call Scrope Davies.

There I was. With an inner reluctance to see and understand this evidence of his true nature. He wrote it when he thought I was still in prison. An idiotic verse with rhymes such as 'Hobby Oh' and 'lobby'o' and 'mobby'o'. He knew I had been subject to attacks from all political parties and most political pens. He decided to contribute with a personal kick, he, too. I realised that a tremendously strange misunderstanding must have played a part in it all. He must have got the nature of my prison sentence wrong and he couldn't really have grasped how close to my heart was representation of the people. But nonetheless. How can a man give way to his simplest urge to write and allow it to afflict a friend who has stood by him in all *his* battles and who has never denied him a single service? It is sad evidence of emotional coldness. Under any circumstances, it tore away the veil, the mirage through which I had hitherto regarded his singular person and I have never again been able to regard him in that light.

Some time later, I received two letters. One from a friend who had been to St Helena and was able to tell me that Napoleon had liked my book about his hundred days and was considering writing a commentary on it. The other from Byron, in which he exculpated himself for the 'ballad' and assumed a semi-ashamed profile. Otherwise very friendly and affectionate. I wrote in reply that he was a 'shabby fellow' and left it to him to digest the phrase with no accompanying comments from me. That same evening I was at Drury Lane to see Kean in

Lear. It is not his part and not until the storm scene did his youth manage to do justice to the old man's age. Nevertheless, the play's theme of treachery, understood treachery and misunderstood treachery, induced in me a mood of profound melancholy. I sat there hating friendship for long stretches of time, forming a family, circles of friends, all this network that catches more mud than fish and makes the mud the content of life. I tried to get hold of Kean for company after the performance, but he was off with two girls.

The last time I saw my friend alive, he regarded me with sorrow and said: 'You should never have come if you were to leave again . . .' I said, 'Why?' and he smiled, 'Yes, why?' Both of us knew perfectly well that you *have* to experience all separations you have no wish to lay yourself open to. Then we shook hands and managed a middle-aged, somewhat embarrassed embrace.

That was almost two years ago. I was on a pleasure trip with my brother Henry and two of our sisters. On the fifteenth of September we arrived at Pisa and I at once went to enquire after my friend. It was rumoured in town that he had left or was to leave for Geneva, but I found him in Palazzo Lanfranchi at Lung'Arno, a river quay of fashionable but melancholy architecture.

Before we had got any further than exchanging the awkward greetings following four years of separation and occasional disagreements by letter, we were joined by the poet Leigh Hunt, who excused himself by saying that a voice 'fresh from London' attracted him like a magnet. He was not a guest of my friend's, it turned out, but Byron had given him and his family (six, soon seven children!) houseroom on the ground floor. Not from friendship. They had known each other fleetingly in London, as contemporaries and poets roughly the same age often do. But that was some ten years ago and Hunt had had considerably fewer children.

No, Leigh Hunt had been persuaded by Percy Bysshe Shelley (who else?) to go to Italy and live in Byron's house at Byron's expense, under the 'protection' (whatever that might mean) of Shelley. Mr Shelley, however, had recently been drowned on a boat trip between Livorno and La Spezia and my friend regarded the Hunt family as a kind of inheritance from him.

397

It turned out that Hunt and Shelley had beforehand succeeded in including him in plans for a 'radical journal' devoted to 'shaving the ears of the British establishment'. I convinced him later – on our own – of the idiocy of such an enterprise. If he gave the nimbus of his name to a radical wing primarily distinguished by its lack of judgement and charm, all would be lost. Implied – he would be lost the day he wanted to return home. He laughed at me and said he loved my disposition to package his life so that it could be guarded against knocks. Then he said sorrowfully: 'What have I got to go home to, Hobhouse? Newstead has been sold . . .'

At this first meeting, Byron was clad in riding clothes and suggested I should accompany him out on to the campagna, but I already had an agreement with my brother and sisters. When we parted outside and in the daylight, I established that we had both been a trifle formal. And when I later tried out the fresh memory of him against the old ones, I found his face must have become rounder and that damaged its expression. Otherwise no great changes.

After dinner, I went back to Palazzo Lanfranchi. We played billiards for a while. I drank wine and he took a drink diluted almost to pure water. It was easy, easy – the long series of double-doors to youth opened one by one and ended in a room of intimacy that could have been in Bennet Street where we had so often talked about the old days and today, generalities and secrets.

But no secrets of an amorous nature this time. Byron had been monogamous 'for three years'! His lovely tyrant, Madame Guiccioli, came in briefly to greet me. She was a red-haired girl with a very determined face. I could read Madame Guiccioli's power in her firmly closed lips rather than her feminine delights – which were not conspicuous. He called her by her other name, Gaspara, because it rhymed with her ladies' academy – the Convent of St Clara, and Gaspara of St Clara had to hear fairly often how delightful her semi-learned discourses were. But he was no more than amiably ironical and was her *cavalier servente*, submitting himself to her will.

He told me about his activities in Ravenna, where he had been initiated into an armed brotherhood for Italy's freedom and unity, the Carbonari. He had looked after their arsenal of arms in his house, which for that matter was not his, but Countess Guiccioli's house – all three of them lived there at the time – I don't really know under what

398

circumstances. The countess's father and brother – the Counts Gamba – were Carbonari, so had been banished from Ravenna and Romagna, and she had annulled her marriage and followed them, and Byron had followed her, and so on . . . I was a trifle confused by this series of relatives and relationships, but Byron accepted them all as obviously as the veins in his body, the lightning-shaped form of which branches off all the way down to the smallness where everything is invisible.

When the Carbonari were dissolved in Romagna, he had acquired their archives and was now able to keep them under the protection of his nobility. The authorities could not get at him (he tasted those words with pleasure) in any other way except through assassination (romantic!) or by banishing the Counts Gamba from one state to the next, which then received Guiccioli plus Byron thrown in.

He gave me overdoses of Italian politics. And when he at first met me half way, he had sauntered slowly, dignified like an old Italian, constantly wiping his hands on a handkerchief and folding it up and flapping it in front of his mouth when he laughed. He even emphasised his limp in the same way as elderly established Italians bring out whatever is characteristic of them.

The next day we rode out on two horses which were not first class. They puffed and blew and pawed the ground as if they were the reluctant main characters. My friend did not seem to take much notice of this. My impression of this Italian on the whole was that the question of quality no longer worried him. 'Live and let live – *vivere e lasciare vivere,*' he said innumerable times during those few days, and laughed, and flapped away the laugh.

Byron said that society in Pisa detested him because he did not wish to mix with the professors at the university and refused to go to a ball before Christmas. 'Imagine me marching into a ballroom with Countess Guiccioli,' he laughed. 'She waddles like a duck, and I limp.'

We came out on to the campagna and everything soon became delightful, shade beneath groves of olives and oaks and the sun pouring its late summer light over the ripeness. Every sunflower smiled at the person looking at it. An old man and a donkey and a cat were sitting on the stony ground under an olive tree, their eyes all following me. Byron was right. One should live in Italy, the country that respects its seasons and the ages of man. We dismounted at a bodega and shot at targets, a sport prohibited within the boundaries of Pisa – to Byron's vexation, because he liked a little shooting before breakfast. He had improved his accuracy almost to perfection. Just as we set off for home, a storm broke over our heads, the skies opening as if in real pain and spewing out gas and flashes of lightning, the rain pouring down massively. We were forced to take shelter in a hut in a vineyard and had an adventure which did not enhance our opinions of the morality of the country.

The next day it went on raining and we stayed in the Palazzo Lanfranchi. So did the Hunt family, very audibly. Byron said they were always at home. On their arrival in the country, Mrs Hunt had declared that she did not think a great deal of Italy and the Italians, after which she declared that she had chosen *not* to learn the language. She had held out something rather like a dandelion head which turned out to be her youngest, evidently expecting of Byron expressions of ecstasy at the sight.

The first time he had dared protest about the ravages of the six little Hunts – referring to the fact that he only rented the house and was responsible for its state when he left – Mrs Hunt first had an attack of asthma and then an outburst on her principles.

The atmosphere did not become any better from the Hunts coming destitute to Italy and being totally dependent on him. They expected him to spare them the humiliation of asking for money by anticipating their needs and filling the hole with a discreet and anonymous hand. But he had not the slightest idea of the needs of a family of nine. He said that it was insufferable having to be patron against his will to people who despised him for that, amongst other things. He had offered to lend *him*, with whom he could still speak, money for the journey home. But Hunt's reply had been that he had 'no wish to trouble Lord Byron'.

He said that on her arrival in Italy, Mrs Hunt had thought she was dying, but turned out to be pregnant – which under the circumstances seemed to be a less happy alternative.

'Hobhouse,' he said. 'Once in a lifetime, one ought to make a contribution outside one's own interests that would be grandiose. At our age, one has to think of making contributions without thinking of the effect they have. When we were young, our contribution was a by-product of the effect, but now I need to lose myself in something substantial. It must be your plans for parliamentarianism. Although I don't believe in them, I respect their intentions. I would do anything to have a Task of value. I would give my life for it – whatever that's worth. I would give it in itself just to get out of this overpopulated corner. Don't you know anything I could think up? I would do anything just to be free, but it is actually true that for once in my life I would like to be useful. Ascetically, altruistically useful!'

July 6th – Went to George Street with Kinnaird. Byron's previous lawyer – Hanson – has just been to view him. He said he would not have known it was him if it hadn't been for the shape of the ears and the Foot. I followed Kinnaird into the room and – drawn by an irresistible longing – although I expected to break down – I went up to the coffin. Or rather crept, gradually, until I caught a glimpse of his face. It bore not even the remotest likeness to my dear friend. The mouth was twisted; half-open, showing those teeth – which the poor man was so proud of in his lifetime – discoloured by chemicals. His upper lip was shadowed by a red moustache, from which his face acquired a totally different character. His cheeks were long and sagging over his jawbone, the bridge of his nose protruding and sunken between his eyes – perhaps because the brain had been removed – his eyebrows dishevelled and lowered, his forehead marked – by incisions presumably – his eyelids closed and sunken – I assume that was because the eyes had been taken out at embalming – his skin was dirty yellow parchment.

So complete was the change that it did not appear to be Byron. I was not so moved by the sight as I had been by his handwriting or anything else I knew had been his. So that is the soul: visible only in the traces consciousness leaves behind. When the body ceases leaving such traces, one does not exist any longer in it. I have seen many corpses on the battlefields of Europe, but never before seen the way a dead body is a remnant agreeing to a single farewell and then sternly demanding to be separated from one's emotions.

July 12th – The funeral procession through London comprised forty-seven carriages. A huge crowd looked on and the windows along the route were full of people clad in mourning. After about an hour, the procession arrived on the northern edge of the city and most of the carriages turned back, but those in the lead continued on to Nottingham.

July 15th – On the way there, I experience a homecoming. Matthews and I went on foot from Newstead to London in the summer of 1809. Byron caught us up in a carriage. I remember him passing us on the road by the lodge-gate cottage and we gave him a great cheer. I am the survivor of the three of us – still not yet forty, I have survived my best friends. The future is an empty square with no shadows. Of the five of us who ate at Byron's table in Diodati – Polidori, Shelley, Byron, Scrope Davies and I – the first took his own life, the second was drowned, the third was killed by his doctors and the fourth is in exile!

July 16th – Nottingham was thronged, especially at the inn where the coffin stood. Our old friend Hodgson and Colonel Wildman, owner of Newstead, attended as mourners. The Mayor and Corporation of Nottingham joined the funeral procession. It extended about a quarter of a mile, and, moving very slowly, was five hours on the road to Hucknall. The view of it as it wound through the villages of Papplewick and Lindley excited sensations in me which will never be forgotten. As we passed under the hill of Annesley, 'crowned with the peculiar diadem of trees' immortalised by Byron, I called to mind a thousand particulars of my first visit to Newstead. It was dining at Annesley Park that I saw the first interview of Byron, after a long interval, with his early love, Mary Anne Chaworth.

The churchyard and the little church of Hucknall were so crowded that it was with difficulty we could follow the coffin up the aisle. The contrast between the gorgeous decorations of the coffin and the urn and the humble village church was very striking.

The first part of the service was carried out with the coffin in the aisle. Then it was moved to the chancel, the mourners following it. Black lace, black wrought iron. I saw them lowering it into the Byron vault. Then the service was concluded. When one has long been aware of one's irreplaceable loss, the confirming ceremony is no real experience. There was more body and soul when we buried his Newfoundland Boatswain in Newstead's garden many years earlier. We took a few spadefuls each, alternately digging and shaking ourselves into life after having seen death. No, the remains. Death never shows itself. We laughed and wept and talked. Now I felt dumb and incapable of lamenting. I stepped down into the vault to check where they had placed him. They said his coffin was on top of the previous Lord Byron's. I saw that just beside it was another coffin, mouldy but with a plaque indicating it was his mother's. I wanted them to move him there, but they said it would give way. So I did nothing more and climbed out of the vault and with one last glance at the coffin, I went out.

I was told afterwards that the place was crowded until a late hour in the evening, and that the vault was not closed until the next morning.

Fever (1822)

'Ooh, ooh, ooh,' said Albé, poking his little finger about in his purse. 'Ow, ow, ow – ' as if expenditure hurt that much. 'Oh, dear me.'

Said His Grace to Leigh Hunt: 'In that I have been forced to give up all other deadly sins, I compensate with *avarice*!'

And expects other people to laugh with him . . .

'His soul' (Leigh lowered his voice although the door was closed) 'is no soul of an Artist. It is incomprehensible the way a man with his pretensions thinks he can treat equals like supplicants because they do not possess his aristocratic privileges and consequent wealth. The fact that he addresses the undersigned like a beggar is bearable, if trying. But you, my dear Mary . . . he shows the bad taste to attire himself in some kind of mourning for Shelley without showing the slightest influence from That Best of Examples. To Shelley, generosity was not even an act of goodness of heart, but a matter of morality, of course. I never saw Shelley do anything else but share *equally* with anyone who needed his help. Not that he set aside half for his own comfort – which any other person would have done – and then shared out the rest. Of the total sum, he shared out according to the principle of need and never kept more for himself than what – sternly – he judged necessary. That is how artists live between them (entirely regardless of also being a political radical). God knows that chances steer the lives and progress of artists – even Byron's (beg your pardon, *Lord* Byron's). Most of us live like cows with empty udders, which are also obliged to milk themselves . . .'

'I know . . .' Mary let Leigh's litany run the full length of its line. She couldn't bring herself to react when people listed things that were so obvious. It is polite to say things that are obvious. One answers in the affirmative. Nothing burns up. Affirming. Yes, it was certainly a torment to ask Albé for a loan. Only the poor have the capacity to share unconditionally ... how did she come to think such a banal thought? The correct thought is that the poor live in a mutual economy and keep its low water moving between themselves, in order that it doesn't sink right down into the earth. Well, the result of a banal or a correct thought is probably roughly the same. Lord Byron was as rich as Croesus. His mother-in-law, about whom he used to say that she wouldn't have the wit to die in case someone might find pleasure in that – she had defied his predictions and left him a handsome inheritance. Added to that, all the rest. The money rose like lava from a crater, making the volcano higher and broader and wider, and the higher it became, the more worriedly he poked about with his little finger in his little purse.

Ah, Albé, what you were like that Diodati summer. Poor and manly. Magnificently in debt. Wild and friendly.

When she was forced to ask for money, he did indeed not ask 'what for?' He kept his counsel to the extent that he did not say 'what, again?' But that was also precisely where the boundary ran. Ooh, ooh, ow, ow, oh dear. 'How much?' he commanded, pen in hand, and with impertinent application, he guaranteed himself a repeat of the painful scene. Shelley had never asked people how much they needed. The fact that they had to ask for money at all was evidence to him that they needed any amount, anyhow more than he could give them. So he had handed over what he had and left it to their judgement to housekeep. Lord Byron's little purse swiftly snapped shut just short of a rectified embarrassment. As soon as another made itself felt, slowly, sighing, he had to coax it out again. Stinginess is its own punishment.

Prudery is its own punishment.

When Shelley was still alive, Pisa was a town of joy. No. No! – why so many banal thoughts today? – Pisa was a town of some joy to Mary. For the first time in her life she had found a circle of women friends. They went out in a carriage together and talked, undisturbed, unheard by men. What a surprisingly rich experience. Mary's earlier life had not provided her with any higher thoughts on women as bearers of Promethean fires. (She smiles glumly.) But here she found them cheekily juggling with small torches. Was it in the light of them she

405

grasped that Shelley's life from the very first moment had been shaped as a hysterical catastrophe? That she could only save herself from it by rendering that circumstance banal. Taking tea with women friends. Observing his flaring idealisms – which included everything from reading experiences to love affairs – without taking part in them as before. For the first time, Mary started acting. Rehearsing a little.

She lay down on the bed she had been ordered to. Trelawny came and sat on the edge of it, his weight lifting her. This is a rare sensation when the person is a stranger. His black curly hair, his slanting eyes, his olive skin – he could have been a Latin, an Arab as far as appearance was concerned. But oh, he was very very English. They looked at each other in silence. Trelawny moved closer and lifted Mary again. It was a peculiar feeling.

Albé limped up and down the stairs giving instructions to 'The Doge of Venice', to 'Cassio', 'Bianca' and 'Roderigo'. Everything – he said – was to be in 'the spirit of Kean'. When he wasn't pointing, waving his arms about and echoing in the stairwell of Palazzo Lanfranchi, he was rehearsing his own lines to a mouth in the mirror. Shelley was not there. He was still alive, but he found he had no need for this amateur spectacle. Shelley and need were two needing each other. From her bed, Mary saw layer upon layer, closest Trelawny's dark head, then a group of ladies in disguise. Then the stream of house servants pouring through – now perhaps forty in number, thirty of them largely unoccupied, a retinue rather than a staff. Then a couple of actors talking to each other, then a larger crowd. Like separate slices beyond each other. Painting time on their separate slices. At separate times. Furthest away, Lord Byron sauntered about trying out by heart:

> Rouse him: make after him, poison his delight,
> Proclaim him in the streets; incense her kinsmen,
> And, though he in a fertile climate dwell,
> Plague him with flies: though that his joy be joy
> Yet throw such changes of vexation on 't
> As it may lose some colour.

Tumptetum. He twisted his face into a cunning grimace. Wiped it away and became Arrogant Pride. Tried out Wounded Melancholy, shrugged his shoulders and started again with something more malevolent. Mary waited mechanically for the Clara-grimace. That was possible. She knew what his face was capable of. But – no. He couldn't do it consciously; it was not an expression put on but something that forces its way out. And Lord Byron was not all that outstanding an actor, despite inspiration from (she smiled glumly) Kean.

Trelawny made himself more comfortable. Mary's little head surged up on the pillow-case of exquisitely fine lace. Madame Guiccioli had put it there before the rehearsal. She had blown one side of it off and stroked across the other, mumbling a stock phrase and looking meaningfully at Mary and Trelawny. Now she was sitting on a stone bench with her red curls loose, embroidering something that caused her no more difficulty than that she could study the interplay between Mary and Trelawny at the same time. The bolsters beneath Mary responded to the movement. She followed it.

He asked darkly:

How do you, Desdemona?

Mary replied (as Albé had suggested: 'artlessly'):

Well, my good lord.

Trelawny:

Give me your hand. This hand is moist, my lady.

Mary felt her hand being moist. She fell out of the rôle and tried to take her hand away. Trelawny's grip tightened. In a flash, Mary was angry, then her reason enveloped her anger. Then the rôle came back and caught the whole parcel.

It yet hath felt no age nor known no sorrow.

She looked up at a shadow and found Albé at the foot of her bed. He thrust out his chin in a peculiar gesture of encouragement as she said: '. . . no age nor known no sorrow . . .' That was unnecessary. Trelawny tightened his calves and thighs into an aggressive jerk at the bed (one might wonder if he had also seen Kean), making Mary's body surge, bolster on bolster on bolster, and he breathed hotly on to her face – pepper, boxwood . . .

> This argues fruitfulness and liberal heart:
> Hot, hot, and moist. This hand of yours requires
> A sequester from liberty, fasting and prayer,
> Much castigation, exercise devout;
> For here's a young and sweating devil here,
> That commonly rebels. 'Tis a good hand,
> A frank one.

Mary mumbled her lines in reply. Teresa Guiccioli's blue eyes peered sharply in the angle of Trelawny's arm. Mary fell out of the rôle again and used the whole of her body as weight to free her hand. She laughed, half sat up in order to help with her other hand on Trelawny's wrist. His pulse was beating slowly, the whole cascade of blood through the whole system. Hers ticked on drop by drop. His rôle – Othello – looked into her eyes. They looked at each other with sudden short-sighted surprise and his hand made a freeing spasm. Then it tightened again.

> A liberal hand. The hearts of old gave hands;
> But our new heraldry is hands, not hearts.

He lets go, flicking the woman off him. Mary is flung, humiliatingly swallowed up by the bed of jealousy. She closes her eyes. She looks at Trelawny, who came down from the Alps a month or two ago. He has seen the whole world. He is strong. He has experienced the world. He came down from the Alps in black. Himself black, on a black horse. A black light in pale grey daylight above Pisa, greyest just where the Arno runs, flows. She can't bring herself to say the next line in accordance with Albé's wish for 'light voice, innocent clarity'. It suddenly strikes her that Desdemona was not innocent. No one is innocent except (she smiles glumly) Shelley. She twists on the bed, caught out by sudden awareness. This Desdemona has something on her conscience. Trelawny attacks her, half lying, pepper, boxwood – they look at each other.

With short-sighted surprise:

> Is 't possible?

Trelawny:

> 'Tis true. There's magic in the web of it.

They stare at each other.

> A sibyl that had numb'red in the world
> The sun to course two hundred compasses
> In her prophetic fury sew'd the work:
> The worms were hallowed that did breed the silk;

explains Trelawny without interest, letting his eyes follow the curve of her hairline,

> And it was dy'd in mummy which the skilful
> Conserv'd of maidens' hearts.

Teresa Guiccioli slowly rises, her eyes on them as she gestures to her obedient Albé. Surprisingly enough, she and Mary have become friends. They ride in a carriage through vineyards and Teresa tells her of her experiences of men. It is never mutual. Mary has no experiences – some dutiful infidelity perhaps, in order to offend rules of fidelity in society. But Teresa has a complicated and interesting index of sins, an atmosphere corresponding to the bed. Green light, an inner compulsion. Not logical. Not enlightened. In Ravenna she says – they all lived together and she deceived her husband with Byron and Byron with her husband and out of this betrayal grew tenderness as a mean inner compulsion. Green light, naked thighs, the waking sleep. Trelawny's hands wander up Mary's arms as she evades his questions –

> Wherefore? Is 't lost? Is 't gone? Speak.
> Is it out o' the way? How? Fetch 't, let me see 't.

– and sees Teresa whispering to Albé – the little red friend and her astonished Lord: 'But my lovely, they're playacting, *Othello*,

Shakespeare, *poeta inglese! Il spettacolo* demands this boudoir scene. The marital couple! *Sposatissimo.* A marital bed is a sacred place. And anyhow an excellent place for murder, for the victim has already taken on a favourable position. He is going to murder his beloved, you see.'

'Ach, Bairon, amuse yourself by all means by treating me like an ignorant goose, but I am after all a Woman and see what I see and this must stop. *Subito! Basta!* they're acting two plays – you know that perfectly well and can see – one by Shekspeer and one by themselves about their own private concerns, secrets of their own, of the heart. If you let it go on – in the way it's already progressed over a whole week – it may end in horror and grief. I've said so!'

'Ho, hm, ah,' replies Albé. 'Is that what you think? As far as I know, it was to be in agreement with their principles, my lovely. They do not see the concept of fornication as sin but as more elevated decency', but he hesitates and Madame Guiccioli burrows her square little hand into his: 'Well, yes, my Bairon. What do they say you are? *Sensitivo delle donne?* This Mary is not to chastise o! Don't you see what a shallow little lake her feeling is? So easily dirtied. So easily stirred up, so easily destroyed. Look then at this great billy-goat you allow to stand astride her! No, no, certain women must be spared. At this moment, she doesn't know what is best for her and that is when I intervene! Yes! This spectacle must be suppressed immediately. Look at her! What does this Mary want? I don't know, but at this moment with the goat astride her she is thinking one can be helped out of one's cold destiny by a warm, warm destiny' (*destino freddo, destino caldo caldo*, Mary notes). 'My intuition, Bairon, my intuition.' Teresa wagged a forefinger under his nose, like a wife exhorting her husband not to eat snails with garlic. Lord Byron looks at Mary and Trelawny, looks past them, a shadow of them fluttering on the wall and there they are already a beast with two backs. An idea has united them.

He looks even more hesitant. '*La vita di Mary*', la Guiccioli goes chattering on, judging and condemning, '*è una.* Collected. A man, a task, a system. Oh, honestly, honestly I understand the desire of her heart, for *il Tre* is beautiful and green-eyed and apparently *un destino caldo*. Life is so cruel when it tempts with temptations one can reach, but which are impossible.'

Will you come to bed, my lord?

Have you pray'd to-night, Desdemona?

Why not me, why not me . . . protests Mary. Alone cold among all these warm destinies. Like the future. The cold. Why not?

Six months later!

Why not me?

Mary is sitting on the hill outside Casa Magni. She is not looking out any more, but she sees. To the north a curve of sunlit cliffs. To the south the slope down to the sea. The shore. The sea is green, it is blue and no longer pounding. There is no swell, the abscess subsided: no people fermenting below the surface, the storm has done, the poet has gone ashore. A ray-fish has been washed up on the shore.

In the sand below the line of tide water, some fishermen are standing looking at a huge flatfish with a tail like a thunderbolt. The eye of the fish reflects the midday heat like a dull jewel, an open oyster. Some of the men take a turn. Nearly each and every one of them takes a turn, then returns to the passive flock standing with their hands inside their waistbands, scratching the backs of their heads and measuring a little with their bare toes. It's as if it were unable to die. Its eye is a sundial measuring the whole of this endless afternoon. They can't leave it until the full circle is complete and the sea takes it back.

Far away down there in the south, she sees Trelawny getting down from his black stallion. The two of them, the two of them. He puts out his cigar and picks up something that looks like a grill and walks with it under his arm. The path he is walking on leads to her. It winds back and forth, round hills, up and down, a dusty ribbon where the shadows of Trelawny and his stallion fall directly below them, the sun at its zenith. It is unusual to see him on foot. She has recently seen him only as a figure represented by a swelling silhouette of the *Bolivar*, Lord Byron's schooner, which Trelawny has been sailing back and forth between Livorno and La Spezia to find traces, or news, of the brig *Ariel*, of Williams and Shelley. Now he has found something and has to walk on his own two feet. The abscess has subsided. No men fermenting under the surface. It is quite amazing how people at a great distance can see they are looking at each other. Small, small are their eyes, but their vision is always clear. Trelawny looks at her and sees she is looking at him.

The three children are playing in the shade under a tree. Jane Williams is trying to tune her guitar, the one Shelley had given her. She is nervous. The strings twang. Have you seen anything? Can you see anything? Mary sees Trelawny but says nothing. She comes closer. A man is taking a turn on the shore and returns to the fish. The jewel starts wrinkling in the heat. He takes a lighted straw and carries it to the eye. Mary gets up. The fire can't be seen, only the heat. He does nothing. The sea is quite smooth. Almost silent. Faint sobs in the caves weeping their way through windy nights. Gruesome. Now the sea is utterly smooth. The day before yesterday it was festering.

Part Three

The night they
open Byron's
grave

'Nothing so difficult as a beginning in poetry.' Rupert remembers this as he puts the full stop with a feeling that nothing is so sudden as the natural end of a poem.

His student friend, Joseph Szymaniak, has a skeleton of a small woman whose left hip-bone warns the afterworld – in curly silver writing – to *carpe diem*. A student-like joke.

A student-like principle which in a worrying way has begun to take over Szymaniak. Fat, sprawling on a divan – he said the future is not happening. You are hauled in on the line of your general plan, but the future is nothing but an alien milieu to which you go. Rupert thought it was a quote.

Szymaniak said the future is a milieu you plan to experience. On the other hand, eyes straight ahead, you learn very little about the life going on, which should be an exercise for the future. *Carpe diem*. On the whole – Szymaniak excused himself, after yet another of his many neglects the future was an uncertain factor. People in Europe seem to have gone mad. Could you really talk about dictatorship . . . when people so terribly *wanted* to believe and be led into 'the future'. For a Pole, the future is just as doubtful as the past (said Szymaniak). Poland keeps on *not* existing – regularly. So logically there are no Poles. Consequently he doesn't exist. He just exists as something self-created, programme-less, feeling, thinking . . .

He's like Oscar Wilde, Rupert thinks, after a year's acquaintance, during which Szymaniak has put on four stone and wasted a number of bons mots.

Carpe diem – Rupert was matter-of-fact about death as such. He had almost at once shed the first feelings of unpleasantness when faced with cadavers. Several of his friends had dreaded the anatomy theatre and had almost given up after their first student visit to the post-mortem room.

Rupert often sat with terminally ill patients, feeling the way he was carried forward by unrhythmical blood. It was restful, he was capable, here was routine, observance and jargon. But there was also compassion, dignity and foreboding constantly escaping back to the same distrust: could it be possible that Rupert was to die? Isn't a person who is young and capable the machinist at the channel of life, along which other people pass? Youth passes by so unnoticeably.

When later on he spoke to the deceased's relatives, he realised no plan for life was ever fulfilled, nothing completed or rounded off. A person often passes his life's twelve o'clock and goes on to both one and two without being able to enjoy a single minute. But when death finally comes, even there you perceive a kind of abrupt end – a hand raised and stopped. And then all the others. Only recruits die young. All kinds were found there – ileus and cancer, burst appendix, accidents – and the professor's rage at his failure with abandoned bodies after suicides, 'whose loathing consisted of the sheer inability to appreciate the value of what comes to us for nothing'.

Like this March night, for instance. Spring-like but frosty, yellow with forsythia, yellow with daffodils. A moon, a Venus. Also yellow. Otherwise a hive of feminine colours. Rupert screwed back the top of his fountain pen, which made him think about how he had screwed on a little gold ear-ring for his grandmother that morning. She hadn't been entirely clean behind the ears, and in a somewhat suggestive way he had found himself in the shadow of the lobe of an ear. He looked at the time. He hadn't finished what he had thought of writing. But he had finished, either because he was lazy, or because nothing is so sudden as the natural ending of a poem.

'Nonetheless, nothing is as sudden as the natural ending of life,' a relative had said to Rupert when thanking him. Some people have nothing at all to say as they leave a deathbed. Others talk restlessly – chatter. Some organise this into tidy formulations. It is impossible to say which of them feels the most – they probably all feel the same, but are different. This one belongs in the latter category. He produced universal explanations to reassure the young candidate that everything was under control. For a brief while, they sat opposite each other, in the strange expectation in which a much-travelled worldly-wise man weighs up whether he ought to tip the young man who has watched over his wife. His face was streaky with tears, one of them still glistening under the lower eyelid. He was probably thinking the last half hour had been the culmination of grief and now everything would at last be easier. But Rupert knew he had as yet experienced only the festival of grief, which would go on for a few days or weeks, perhaps months. Then *la tristesse de la tristesse* faded, as a nurse had explained to him one day in the lift going up or down.

'For of course, illness is a natural ending,' the man analysed, in another attempt to raise himself out of the category, out of the anonymity of a mourner. 'I've never thought in this way before.' 'One always thinks differently for a while when things are like this,' said Rupert consolingly, youthfully, shyly, the machinist at the channel of life. He was nonplussed. A support.

Far away from the clinic, far away from the university, temporarily at home in Nottinghamshire, Rupert screwed back the top of his fountain pen. He had just decided he could write no more.

Something peculiar and unexpected had happened. He had come to the end of the story without having told it all. Any reasonably good writer would have been able to tell him this *is* the natural end of the story. You have to end it in an intuitive certainty about the end, instead of struggling round the whole time-plan of the story. But Rupert was no writer, only a sporadic reader – and on that side of the barrier, the story appeared to fulfil a plan and every word to follow a conscious intention. So he went on brooding, dissatisfied and self-critical:

– there was a sentence on carp and days. It had crept out of his mind and put itself down on the paper, a peculiar sentence – it meant nothing. He had just described a course of events, an emotional course, and suddenly the sentence was there like an illogical consequence. Then he had thought of starting on a new piece, but it didn't want to. Something had been finally exhaled by the sentence – a phenomenon you don't expect, but soon recognise as definitive.

It had interrupted his story about half way through, he knew that, and the remaining half was the important half. It was stupid, like going off the rails. Byron's deathbed should have been the high point of his account. At Byron's deathbed all the loose threads of his life were to be

417

gathered, spun together and dispersed again. He had been aiming at this deathbed all the time. Rupert. Perhaps Byron, too.

There lay a pilgrim with no faith, a man with no fanaticism who had joined in a war of liberation and devoted himself to its most inglorious everyday ordinariness. There, the hero died on this deathbed, half-murdered by four well-meaning doctors, who had a great deal of mud thrown at them by the hereafter, but certainly did whatever medical science of the day was capable of. And in such a place, the greyness of Missolonghi gorged with rain and disappointment, flowing over the world and meeting people's eyes, then being turned by them into a shimmering, flooding magnificence.

It is not tragic when a man, implicit in his faith, falls to a bullet in what is for him a holy war. That is logical. But in the mind of a doubter, there is no inbuilt logic. It is fatal when he goes to war with clear eyes, and then that shatters for reasons just as complicated as his choice. Anyone can be moved by such things. It is not tragic when 'it is accomplished'. What is not completed, on the other hand, gives honest striving a sense of eternity and a touch of tragedy.

For Lord Byron's part, the holy struggle became an inconsolable and persistent effort to get the rival factions of the Greeks to unite. Over four hundred years as an occupied country, Greece had become a tribal society. Europe was in the process of moving into the era of national states and Greece was to be one of the first manifestations. But the material was a tribal society with no national feeling.

He stayed there in Missolonghi and persisted. His sickbed was made little of and became his deathbed. At least three pints of blood were drawn from his thin anaemic body. In between, he was given purgatives and enemas. The poet wrote requisitions for supplies and letters to banks. Nothing came of it . . . unreconciled with all the dramas of life, he was reconciled with death. That must have been what is so gripping. Could one hop over it?

But the very thought of taking up his pen enfeebled Rupert's hand. He propped his head against it. Inside was a sleeping point where his mind had previously shaped fantasy. For someone like Rupert, there was only one image for this. The carp – the day was a stop-ball that died before he could return it. It was Szymaniak's fault. Him and his *carpe diem*.

418

Rupert leafed through his notes for the second half of the story to see if he could use them as they were.

After his epileptic attack in February, Lord Byron changed considerably. He was considered an insufferable hypochondriac, depressive and sinister, as if all his old joy in small things had left him entirely, and with that his joy in life – which consists of small things. He started talking about nothing but great things, about determining and scathing things, and he seemed to be under the influence of some obscure process within himself. Outwardly, he went on following the agreed plan for assembling the rival forces of free Greece into a common front. Every day, he took fresh air and physical exercise as medicine. Went riding with no joy, only for utilitarian reasons.

The last manifestation
He dresses up his staff and his Suliot guards for a show of strength to the inhabitants of Missolonghi. It is one of the first days in April. The town has been threatened with invasion or rebellion or a combination of both, all staged by some tribal chieftain with a sufficient number of relatives inside the walls to be able to infiltrate. The rebellion does not happen, of course. Nothing happens. But nevertheless, it may be a good idea to demonstrate your presence to bring consolation to the dispirited and induce fear in the treacherous. At first some lines of Suliots run with flapping fustanellas, then some foreign gentlemen in handsome uniforms ride past, and then – on his own – a thin grey little man absently poking at the flanks of his horse with a dog-whip.

The last reverse
A Turkish brig goes aground at Missolonghi. It had come laden with arms, spoils at last in sight, but before sufficient forces could be assembled – and this in a garrison town – the crew manage to escape after having set fire to their ship. All night, the members of Missolonghi's international brigade stand on the muddy shore and see this deliberate waste of bullets and grenades and rockets – and the gunpowder itself – flying wasted into the air in suns, clouds of fire and showers of sparks.

The last ten days
April 9th
They go riding as usual. When they have been out for half an hour, they are surprised by a downpour of rain. They usually dismount at the gates of Missolonghi and have the neighbour row them home in the fresh brackish air between the blank surface of the water and the bank of clouds. The others want to refuse today because they are soaked through, but Byron wants things to be as usual. They dismount and then sit for half an hour listening to each other's shivers behind the rhythm of sleepy, elliptical splashing of waves. Two hours later, Byron is lying on the sofa with a fever, rheumatic pains and a headache.

April 10th
The next day he feels better and tries to chase away his weakness by sweating it out on horseback. On his arrival home he is seen abusing his stableman for saddling his horse with yesterday's wet saddle. The rest of the day he spends on the sofa again, with new ailments stemming from sitting on a wet saddle. He thinks aloud about the fortune-teller in Scotland many years ago warning him to 'Beware your thirty-seventh year'. He does not call on his physician, Dr Bruno, until late that evening, and he orders castor oil and a hot bath.

April 11th
Worse. Feverish ague, persistent cough and shooting stabbing pains. He is also dispirited and raises no objections when his staff start taking measures to move him to the island of Zante, where there are better medical services (English), but –

April 13th
– the terrible weather worsens, the winds rising to a hurricane during the night. It is dark in the middle of the day and the rain hurtles out of all the holes in the sky. Putting a boat out to sea is inconceivable, even more so putting the sick man into an open boat. Dr Bruno gives him antimony powders for his fever. Byron still finds the energy to oppose the blood-letting and leeches. A new doctor, Dr Millingen, is called in and he also suggests blood-letting, though he recommends postponement in the light of the patient's opposition.

April 14th

Could it be a premonition? Byron panics and wants to go out, out of doors and riding. It is not difficult to oppose him for he is weak and still has a headache, those pains flashing along nerve tracks all over his body. Mild force keeps him in bed, but the panic rises past their caring hands. His eyes are wild. They don't understand him. Only fresh air will help. They barricade him inside his illness. Parry, a member of his staff, notices peculiar words which make him suspect that Byron is delirious. Later on, he says that his heart bled when panic in those large eyes turned into insight and resignation. The doctors want Parry out of the way, for he is in favour of the resistance to blood-letting and instead suggests brandy as medicine. As a compromise, more purgatives are chosen.

April 15th

A bad night. Byron nonetheless gets up now and again to read letters that have come in. He discusses plans for a conference in Salona, which he means to attend as soon as he is well enough. Finally, he falls shuddering and shivering with cold on to his bed. In the morning, he is very dazed and lies stock still in the dismal room where strangers and servants and soldiers stroll in and out. Dr Bruno and Dr Millingen look at him, look and come back with leeches and scalpels. Byron protests again. Blood-letting from a weakened patient is like loosening the strings of an instrument, the notes of which are already false because the strings are too loosely strung.

He asks Millingen to find a witch who can ward off the Evil Eye. They are all a trifle perplexed. No one really knows what to say, but in the end members of the staff go off on a witch-hunt and actually find three. By then, Byron has forgotten his ingenious suggestion. The rain persists. In the afternoon, it is quite clear that the plague has broken out in Missolonghi. In the evening, Parry begins to see what until then no one else had wanted to know; Byron is seriously ill. No one else wanted to know. It would be far too uncomfortable, far too inappropriate – no one could choose this moment to be ill. The doctors don't want to know the risk. They don't feel they are up to it. Total chaos continues to reign in the sickroom, everyone coming and going at will, complaining to Byron about diverse discords, the doors standing open so that it grows too cold, the stove red hot, causing draughts of hot-and-cold air. Unease becomes noticeable among the servants and they disturb the patient with their tears and prayers that he shall get better for their sake. During the hours before midnight, Dr Bruno comes back and threatens with his scalpel. Byron is so agitated, he has an attack of coughing and vomiting, then, exhausted, promises to give his blood the next day, provided he is not better by then.

April 16th

Then the doctors come to collect the debt promised last night. But he doesn't want to stick by it and lets fly with accusations. Dr Bruno starts talking about how he has left his old mother alone in Italy just to serve Lord Byron – and this is the way he is rewarded. Dr Millingen threatens him by saying his illness – for the moment diagnosed as brain fever – may drive him insane, mentally disturbed for the rest of his life, if he doesn't submit himself to blood-letting. What is said has an effect. Byron is always receptive to the thought that he owes a debt of gratitude, and he fears madness more than he fears death.

'Come; you are, I see, a damned set of butchers. Take away as much as you will; but have done with it.'

The blood-letting did not produce the hoped-for results.

His recovery did not correspond to their hopes.

Two hours later they took their second pound of flesh.

For a short while Byron became less hectic, less feverish and slept a little. But when he woke, Parry was sitting by his bed and at once saw that his patient was mortally ill. His face was white, he could only glimpse what he was looking at, and he was delirious, talking ceaselessly, alternately in English and Italian. Parry called for Dr Bruno, who made the observation that Byron's face had gone rigid and his fingers bloodless. He sent Parry out and when Parry had gone, he carried out another blood-letting.

April 17th

Now everyone knows. And everyone knows the doctors' methods of treatment have failed. That does not stop them from going on. Sometimes Byron is woken by the weeping of the servants, and then he resists any more blood-letting. Instead he is given more laxatives and enemas. Then he dozes off and then they take a little more blood. His body is constantly pounded with losses. Clean out, say the doctors, clean out, and they gradually clean out spine, skeleton, mind and soul. In all their Hippocratic certainty, they start being gnawed by doubts and call in two colleagues – Ali Pasha's physician, Loukas Vaya, and the medical officer of the German volunteer corps, Enrico Treiber. After this examination, no one except Dr Bruno is in favour of any more blood-letting. The patient is in a state of shock. They agree to give him bark, wine and water, and to put two blistering plasters on his thighs.

April 18th

It is the last day. It is Easter Sunday. The inhabitants of Missolonghi usually celebrate it with unconventional salutes from morning to night. All those capable of bearing arms run round the streets firing their guns into the air or after a few sacks of resinous wine – as scare-tactics against each other. Byron is extremely delirious, dozes off, hallucinates, sometimes looking up with fever-free, pain-free, as if quite unbound eyes, and then they know he is conscious and that he is indifferent to them. The town guards walk around town grasping their rifle barrels, saying that Colonel Viron is in extremis and mustn't be disturbed in his labours at crossing over. People promise to be quiet. The international volunteer brigade, the local tribal soldiers, all of whom during recent months have quarrelled and together defied all description when it comes to trouble, rebellion and defiance – all sit in silence that day. Sullenly adult.

But inside the house, dissolution has set in. Dr Bruno has started to despair. What is happening? Certainly death had been included in their calculations, but not in this way. The plan has slid down into tracks leading into alleys not marked on the map. In his despair, he returns to his only medicine. He asks for the consent of the other doctors and fastens twelve leeches to Byron's temples. They take two pounds of blood. Then Byron also understands what is happening.

'Your efforts to save my life will be in vain. I must die. I feel it. I do not grieve over losing my life. I came here to Greece to put an end to my painful existence. My fortune, my abilities I have given to the cause. Well, now it can have my life. Let me request one thing. I do not want my body to be hacked about or sent back to England. Let my bones rot here. Put me in the first corner you can find with no pomp or foolishness.'

He has a peaceful moment as he says this. Smiles, too, a little, at the assembled household standing by his bed or hiding their tears at the back of the room. People run out to hide their weeping. But Tita the gondolier can't get out, because Byron is holding his hand. Byron looks at Tita weeping, at Fletcher who has also stayed – also weeping. He smiles again, not without a kind of satisfaction, and says quietly: '*O questa è una bella scena.*'

He is soon delirious again. Parry remains by the bed and gives the patient bark. Together with Tita, he rubs the icy hands. When he wants to do the same with the feet, Fletcher stops his hand, with nothing but a look explaining that no one may touch that foot, that damned sacred limb. Byron groans and grinds his teeth with pain. Parry loosens the blood-stained bandages wound tightly round his head to stem the blood after the leeches' feast, and Byron weeps with relief and sighs, 'Ah, Christi.' 'That's right, My Lord,' says Parry encouragingly. 'Let your tears fall, then the fever will go down and you can sleep.' 'Yes, I think I can sleep now,' says B. He says 'goodnight' and really does seem to sleep for a moment. His breathing is calm and the irritating, menacing rain is suddenly peaceful, regular and rhythmical water like the slow wave of the lagoon faithfully and audibly breaking against the shore. But then those eyes are open again. They have been open for three days, sometimes wild, mostly confused, sometimes mild. Now they are filled with anguish: 'Why didn't I understand this before! Now I must leave everything, and do so unprepared. Why didn't I go home before I came here,' he cries, rattles. Then – quietly, overcome: '*Io lascio qualche cosa di caro nel mondo.*'

He now wants them all round him, because he has much to see to. He is delirious for long spells, and he seems to be doing this service to his sick mind with the greatest impatience. He works himself up out of his madness, towards the lucid moments, and hurries there to tell everyone how they are to find their future livelihoods, how he has made provision for them in his will and to whom they are to turn to be given what is due to them. Then he calls on Fletcher to come closer and takes his hand. 'I'll now say my last wish,' he mumbles, pulling down Fletcher's head. It was to be delicate, it was to be secret and private. But no one can bring himself to leave the room. 'Go to Lady Byron and tell her . . .' says Lord Byron, lowering his voice again. 'Go to my sister and tell her . . .' Fletcher puts his ear close to his master's mouth, and for a long spell, all grounds for anxiety flow, everything that never became said, all too late insights between these two close points. Then Lord Byron breathed out and a faint, faint colouring of relief appears on his cheeks; an inkling, an inkling of his old humour on his lips. 'Now I've said everything, and do what I told you now, otherwise I will torment you.' 'But My Lord, I never heard a word.' Byron stares. But he can do no more. It will have to remain unexplained. All explanations have returned into the dying body and will never again come out. 'Then it's too late.'

The doctors have given him yet another purgative, a mixture of senna, Epsom salts and castor oil. This forces him out of bed at six in the evening, half-supported, half-carried by Fletcher and Tita. He mutters: 'The damned doctors have drained me of all my blood. I can't stand.'

When he gets back to the bed, he says: 'I want to sleep now.' Those were his last words. The doctors fix new leeches to his temples and let the blood flow all evening.

Irony of ironies. For four months Byron has been waiting in Missolonghi. For money, for arms, the hasteners and abstract takers of responsibility for the project. It has rained. He has waited, one day after another dragging the earth round in the mists of the skies. But not until despondency has become illness does the brig *Florida* sail into Greek waters with arms, money and medical supplies on board, and also a letter from the member of the Greek Committee, John Cam Hobhouse:

and as long as you have your health, then I cannot see what worldly assets you could wish for that you do not already have. The cause you are devoting your powers to is the most honourable a man can ever have undertaken. Campbell said the other day that he envies you in what you are now doing (and you must believe him, for he is a very envious man) even more than he envies you all your laurels in full bloom.

That night a violent thunderstorm exploded, lightning flickering into

425

the sickroom. Equally white, Byron lay in a coma. In its white flickerings the doctors could be seen quarrelling – weeping – taking up one position after another. The next morning, spring began. A stranger, sunrise, intoned its silence and then started melting up out of the lagoon, flinging rays in all directions, one of them striking *Florida*'s rigging just as it appeared over the horizon. Byron's eyes were closed. He closed his eyes. But just before he died, he did what the dying do: opened his eyes and took a last glance at the world.

*

Rupert patted these pages neatly together, his face betraying neither approval nor criticism. He stuffed them right at the back of a large envelope already containing the other hundred and one pages. After brooding for a brief while, he wrote on the outside '*O questa è una bella scena*'.

Then he looked at the time again, changed his shoes for boots and put on his jacket, winding his scarf loosely twice round his neck. He pumped up the front tyre of his bicycle, swung his leg over – delaying as long as he could in that balancing position as the wheels ploughed into the cold gravel.

Rupert cycles slowly on. The saddle is low, for one of his sisters has let it down in his absence. But that doesn't matter. He wobbles indolently from right to left, the evening chill combing through the roots of his hair. Sheep bleat their evening bleating. They bleat for hours, particularly when their lambs are six months old. One of them stands bleating on a rise, another on another, extending their necks and calling to each other without having to move from the spot.

This village hasn't ever changed on a large scale. It's like cycling through an Alpine village with farming crouching by the wayside. A cow lows in a cowshed, hitches herself up and her lowing rises to a kind of donkey's bray. There is a smell of cows. Rupert knows what cows smell like and he doesn't confuse it with the more virulent smell of a pigsty. And on the low hillocks, the sheep bleat with responses as lodestars, the earth bathed in the cool of a high pure vault of sky. Rupert's hair curls.

'For Sale' says a notice by the path leading to an isolated house. For the time being, the German woman and her husband are living there, but they have already bought another house on the outskirts of

Nottingham. The lights are on in the small windows. Inside, for the fourth time in eighteen months Mrs Lisbeth is still unable to decide whether she lives in the here and now or whether she is already in the future in another home. Packing up what has recently been unpacked is a dismal business.

The lights are on in all the windows. And in the church now. Rupert sees Eric Watson taking the short cut across the grass and creeping with long strides in and out of the moon-shadows of the trees. Then he brakes in the bicycle, because he doesn't want to catch up with Eric Watson and keep him company, talking alone with him. As long as he can, he stops, balancing crookedly, his leg high over the frame. Gas lamps, the moon reflect the sight in several fragmented shadows meeting and parting but unable to congeal into a whole. His front wheel ploughs into a wheel track. Rupert hurries to jump off before two snub-nosed boys coming in the other direction find some reason to laugh at him. A man stumbles out of the pub to get some fresh air.

It doesn't do him any good. He looks round for blind sympathy and almost reaches the heap of earth before he starts throwing up. The little boys, who might well have been thought to laugh, become extremely serious and hasten their steps like little girls.

The man has finished vomiting, perhaps. He is sitting with his legs apart on the ground. They look at each other for a moment, silently and yet in some way communicating, he and Rupert. There isn't much to say, nor much to look at, but there is something to hold on to. The man's eyes cloud, glistening like wet coal, and after a while he dares to get up, like a cow, lurching up on all fours, his backside first. 'Me stomach,' he indicates with a grimace and a pat towards his pancreas. 'An old story, comes back now and again. It's not the drink. Hardly ever touch the stuff, no, never anything stronger than beer or gin.'

'Er, no,' says Rupert. He waits until the pub door closes behind the man and then goes on pushing his bike, although Eric Watson is out of sight. Darkness falls quickly, the moon paler and smaller than a moment ago, and Venus has vanished.

Above 'Wines, Spirits & Finest Liqueurs', the whole row of windows is alight. One is open and Rupert is startled, for leaning against the window seat is Mrs Cohn, looking at him in silence with her crackling blue eyes. He sees them right through the darkness and despite the fact that the light is behind her. There is a strange taciturn

427

melancholy in her attitude, still an expectation of spring in her position. 'Good evening, young Rupert,' she says in the slightly affected way appropriate for some women who had known him since he was a child.

'Mm, g'evening . . .'

'Out to take possession of your prey?'

'What?'

'Can't imagine how you got permission to dig up the poor bard. Joel has just left. With mixed feelings, I should add.'

'Permission', replied Rupert coolly, 'was granted because there is said to be a dispute over whether Byron genuinely is in the coffin. The vicar has been asked to check the matter and we are to assist him.'

'Oh, go on with you! I know perfectly well how you've persisted with this.'

Mrs Cohn then sits there in silence for a while. That melancholy attitude. Light, her eyes smoky sharp at the same time, her arms folded on the window sill and her bust above, like a Czech matron selling caraway pretzels. 'How does it feel?' she says quietly. Rupert doesn't like her lowering her voice, making a secret of things. 'What?' 'How does it feel, of course, being on your way to meet Byron, of course.' Rupert politely feels around, but can't find an answer to her question except 'effective'. He is indeed on his way to the long discussed disinterment, but his 'feeling' is not the shudder she expects, but satisfaction at having succeeded in convincing the others – except Mr Cohn. He doesn't feel anything in particular. He doesn't reply. He looks at her. 'Oh, well,' she says finally. 'As long as you mess about with futile things, perhaps you'll keep off unnecessary stupidities . . .' And she abruptly jerks down the window. Rupert mutters an unseemly reply.

At first he pushes his bike, then he puts his right foot on the left pedal and scoots away – singing quietly, whistling. It's a popular song everyone is singing and it soon echoes out of an open window. But if the melody in Rupert's mouth is a rough trunk, the echo is a leafy rustling tree, encircled by saxophone climbers and violin rambler roses and birds' nests full of flutes:

Brenda is dancing with herself again. He's never seen a girl so disposed to dancing with herself. Brenda's shadow is half-sitting on a high stool and has its legs stretched far out in front of it. It turns itself half round and turns back again with a whiskery stick in its hand. She stretches out the fingers of her other hand and draws the stick a couple of times over each nail. The shadow takes the cigarette out of its mouth and spews the light shadow of smoke like a wave over the wet nails, plays with them, puts its head on one side, gets up and takes itself into its arms again.

Rupert puts down his toes, stubs them twice before letting the toe-iron scrape the rest of the speed out of the wheels. He props his hip against the saddle and the saddle against his hip and stands staring at Brenda as he usually does, her thin spine lizard-like as she bends down to turn the record over. It rasps promisingly. Rupert peers. It goes on rasping.

And goes on. Brenda looks down from her position of herself and partner. She disperses her dreams and sees that the needle has stuck in the music. Adjusts and takes up her position again, with both arms round her waist. The shadow of the smoking cigarette sifts upwards, alongside her black shadow streaming down into the magnetic field of the earth. She stands stock still, her head listening sideways as the singer sings the verses that end with 'tell me, who is the shepherd of this lost lamb?'

It's a new singer called Frank Sinatra. As he goes on with the refrain, he fetches his voice up from the depths, so fresh that there is still a little sand in it. 'There's a somebody I'm longing to see . . .' he tempts, freeing Brenda from her frozen pose. She billows like corn, she turns over like water in a wind-blown spring. 'Someone is watching over me,' the singer coaxes out, cautiously. Someone pokes beneath Rupert's elbow. 'Er, hmm, I think I'd better make my presence known. So I don't frighten you when you find me.'

Rupert's heart shifts from sixty to a hundred and twenty beats a minute. 'What the hell are you doing here!'

Mr Cohn is not offended. Yes, he is rather: 'It's not out of interest in the young lady, if that's what you're thinking.' Rupert calms down. 'I was interested,' explains Mr Cohn, 'in that shadow play. Did you see that it takes place on several straight and slanting walls at the same time? It looks fantastic when she dances, doesn't it? Like stirring an open fire.' Brenda sticks the cigarette into her mouth, lifts her hair at the back and makes ten jerky movements with her thin hips. Mr Cohn flushes, but it is dark. 'You scared me, that's why I was angry. I mean.

I'm not angry,' mutters Rupert. Automatically, they conceal themselves even deeper in the bushes and go on staring at the girl, four-eyed.

She takes the opportunity in the middle of the dance to grab a jumper and wriggle her body into it. Then she sticks her hand inside first the one then the other cup of her brassière and gives her delights a lift. Mr Cohn and Rupert lean slightly on each other and wipe their eyes at this ingenuous comedy. But is it so ingenuous? They neigh quietly like two schoolboys in a girls' cloakroom and Mr Cohn says it's much more fun than the cinema, but then abruptly turns serious. Rupert, too. Brenda tries to button up her skirt, finding it difficult to get it to go round her waist.

She lights another cigarette. The girl seems to chain-smoke, more or less. The record has come to an end and is rasping again. Brenda is in profile – presumably in front of a mirror – pulling at her waistband and standing with her feet astride, and she succeeds in uniting button and buttonhole. After that, she studies the result. She runs her forefinger over a swelling. She moves the waistband up and gives her belly space under it. The forefinger stops, hovers between her ribs. There it starts drawing circles, as if a sign of resignation. After a while, she takes the brush and sets about her hair with amazing brutality. She grooms herself so that strands and hairs swirl round her head. 'My dear,' mumbled Mr Cohn. 'It can't be that bad, can it?'

Animals can combine intimacy with publicity, definite in their appreciation of themselves. But with people it is different. 'Steady on, now,' says Rupert. 'I've done it before, this. I think she knows it. I wonder if she understands she can be seen. I mean that lamp, and that one. They give a perfect exposure on those two walls. And then a special angle on that one. She must see it herself.'

'Do you mean to say she is some kind of sophisticated exhibitionist?'

'Hey . . . we must make sure we don't expose ourselves as voyeurs.' Rupert pulls Mr Cohn with him into deeper retreat among the bushes, though the bicycle is lying in the grass.

Brenda's shadow has grown on the wall, becoming grotesque and dead. Suddenly it is she herself who can be seen. She has come past one lamp and is leaning out through the window to clean the hairs out of her brush. Hair floats down in small balls. She meets Rupert's eyes. Perhaps without seeing him.

After a while, she puts down the brush and straightens up on straight arms against the window sill and looks at the sky, breathing in its wholeness, breathing out some of it. There is a rustle in the bushes. It rustles when the earth is tormented by two people imperceptibly rocking in their efforts to stand still. Suddenly she stretches out her hand – the false emerald flashes on her middle finger – and turns out the lamp. At the same moment, a sphere of tiny little stars surrounding her house light up. They become hesitantly visible, as the hard-of-hearing sense crickets, dazzled by the buzzing of the ear, the trembling, now this side, now beyond the line of vision.

Mr Cohn and Rupert are forced to look at the stars. They don't know whether she sees them. They don't know what she sees. With the other lamp behind her, she is a shadow again, but not two-dimensional. Now the black contour is full and has senses. And suspicions: 'Is anyone there? Hullooo? Freddy, is that you?'

Yes, someone is there. The thousand eyes of daisies round their feet also glance up at Brenda. A thousand sober eyes, closed for the night.

A chubby little car on the road from Nottingham, chugging violently over the last stretch. It sounds like oxy-hydrogen gas, smells like it, too. The driver swears and changes down and accelerates but can do no more than just go with it. By the time Link the dentist rolls up to Hucknall Torkard church with a couple of final farts from the exhaust pipe, he gets out with the diagnosis clear – dirt in the carburettor.

'Well, er, no, er, no, I'm not so sure. Two weeks ago I had something like it and it turned out they had given me the wrong mix of petrol, boat fuel or whatever it was. The carburettor sooted up, boat fuel, I think.'

'Could also be something wrong with the fuel supply,' interjects the mechanically-minded vicar, who has already started lifting the bonnet.

Soon a vicar's backside, a surveyor's backside and a dentist's backside can be seen sensitively registering hands and eyes fumbling in the inner organs of the engine. Inquisitively, Eric Watson's backside rises: 'No, look at that! It's made of stainless steel. I've never seen that before.' 'Let me see, let me see!' cries the vicar. 'Yes, look at that! And crafted. Is it a spare part?' 'Spare part! There's plenty of stainless steel in this model. That's why I bought it.' 'Where's the battery? Oh, yes, there. Funny place to have it. Have you got another torch? I can see a few drops here. No here. Here.' 'Give me a bit of cotton waste, and we can see where it comes from.' 'What is it?' 'Ow!' 'What is it? Did you burn yourself, is it acid from the battery?' 'No, it's just hot.' 'Is it oil?' . . . and so on. Mr Hazell is standing on the steps and sees those three backsides like moon faces shiny with worn cheviot, flannel and wool. Fervour for the car. Fervour for the car.

'A spanner. I must have a spanner. No, no. That's a pipe wrench. An ordinary spanner. Haven't you got an ordinary spanner in the car? But . . . can we repair this if you haven't got a spanner? Have you any adhesive tape, then we could do a temporary job? No adhesive tape either!'

'*Uno momento*,' cries the vicar. 'I think I've got a spanner in the chest in the vestry. Wait a moment!' And flaps past Mr Hazell, who catches a glimpse of starched collar, a glowing look and the creator's, the preserver's delight. He hears a lid flung up and the vicar mumbling 'as long as it's not a pair of pincers', as he shifts his attention back to the car. Link is standing with his torso inside the engine. But it is Eric Watson who has found the fault and is smiling with his arm in the depths, for as usual he has his finger on the sensitive spot.

The path crunches as Rupert and Mr Cohn arrive with the bicycle between them. It is the night of borrowed shoes. Eric Watson has on those police boots, size twelve, Mr Cohn his youngest son's Wellington boots, Rupert his grandfather's winter boots, handmade in the nineteenth century and with wooden heels. The vicar comes waving his spanner. Mr Hazell sees his son's eyes register the open bonnet, the spanner, three moonlit backsides and eyes full of fervour for the car. Fervour for the car. He drops the bicycle down on the ground with a crash, and is soon with the other men shouting about a regulator.

That was how it began, that evening fifty years ago, when some people took a hammer and chisel and opened the vault in the country church of Hucknall Torkard. One of them waved a hand about to disperse the dust which had loosened from the walls as the hammer worked on them from outside. He switched on his torch and started fetching up the space from its hundred year old darkness. Their eyes and minds dim as they apprehend the first firm evidence of an existence they have occasionally thought they had dreamt.

That same night, the vicar wrote down his account: 'Reverently, reverently, I lifted the lid off the coffin.'

And then came Rupert's story.

O questa è una bella scena

I

When evening came, Lord Byron took my arm, we left the house and started down the steps towards harbour level.

The very last hours of the year were glimmering, a following wind sweeping the sky clean. I could well have mentioned this, but we did not speak. We were absent-minded and silent. As ten conceivable ways out of uncertain waiting are soon to be limited to one, you are not talkative. You hold your breath, nourishing yourself on a cup of lung and saving the rest, dark and still.

We hadn't locked up. The house was empty. After we had taken twenty steps or so, a gust of wind blew open the door and flung it back against the wall, so suddenly that two sounds were released from my memory. One was the death of my relative by his own hand. He had hidden his pistol hand inside Mother's musquash muff. All the faces talking about him turned naked. I had remembered this nakedness over the years, but had forgotten the reason. The other was the swan frozen fast in our pond one morning. We couldn't release it, and it had also gnawed off one of its feet. Then it lay still, but dead leaves shuffled across the ice. The next day we had it on the table.

The door went on swinging now that it was open. Nor was I wholly without experience.

The stars were brilliant such as they never are in England. On the planet Jupiter, they were sailing after six moons, a weightless moment reigning on earth – the kind that arises when people are on the way from thought to action, and for a moment are in between. Our hearts thumped as we placed our steps one after another. At every other one, my side received the gentle nudge of his lameness. I felt him making an effort to mask it for the sake of the stillness which requires equilibrium.

As we walked, our gaze ran up and down the village road below us, a long stairway that twisted, with level spaces, a moon street of lime on the black rock. The houses were in darkness, moonlight streaking lime between them, particularly along the winding climbing road from mountain to sea. That was our very nearest future. What lay beyond it we did not wish to see at that moment, although the back of the eye was already imprinted with it after five months in Cephalonia.

From an island, the eye makes clean incisions between sky and sea, searching in the direction of the unknown and indicating the way for a wave of longing, usually out to sea, but here towards land. For five months, we had looked out for the contours of the Morea, a three-pronged peninsula my books called the Peloponnese. I had still not been there, but he had. Several times. The Morea was a mirage for us in the scarcely visible blue distance. We had stared past its shore, towards the mountains, and lost ourselves in thoughts of the mainland, where everything was to happen. He had told me about his ramblings there as a twenty-two-year-old. 'I travelled with no map or sextant or compass or what the devil. Some people never know the smell of beehives, their noses are so full of bookworms.' He had told me about the climate nourishing almost nothing except vermin, and that 'death in the form of yellow malaria' had sat by his tent for three days.

We had gone on gazing nonetheless. Nature alternates between us and our goal, which was not the Morea but northern Greece, below the Albanian mountain range. A mild winter followed the summer. When the morning mist lifted, the island lay like teeth on the surface of the water, not quite clenched with their reflections. On still evenings, sea and sky floated together into a copper lustre. If it were stormy, the clouds became a splendour of burning rags. In vain had we tried to identify the line of ships billowing up in the wind. Was it the Greek fleet from Hydra at last? Or was it the Turkish blockade?

But now we kept our gaze at home, looking with nothing but a cup of eye and saving the rest, dark and still.

Was I anxious? Did I show unease, nerves, just because of a door swinging? A shudder went down my whole arm as I nonetheless caught a glimpse of the edges of the sea, of the harbour, where our reluctant horses were boarding the large boat, the one they called bombarda. The shudder recurred again and again, a hot-cold current from my armpit to my middle finger. A reply came after a while, from the arm round mine.

His three dogs were with us. The great Newfoundlands ran ahead beneath their mats of billowing fur. They came back to gather us up, then ran down again, probably doing the trip at least ten times. But Moretto, Lord Byron's bulldog, kept close to us, slowing us down because he wanted to go first and set the pace. He snuffled and slowly let himself down from step to step, the weight of his head forcing him to stay on his forelegs until his hind legs were well planted. He didn't dare a free fall even between two steps, but one step could not contain his length, so he had to curl up his rump like a caterpillar so as not to get stuck between levels. It was comical. I wanted to laugh, but couldn't, for when the framework is dark it sets off the leaden weight of life, particularly in a foolish movement.

Directly below Moretto, the road cut to the right, the precipice on the left. By looking down on the dog, we had a sea-view, smoothly black, spent breakers foaming round the bottom, the forces heaving each other through these depths, more collected, infinitely greater than all the wars of the world, greater even than the war that was our goal.

I dismissed the matter from my mind and drew my gaze back home: Moretto's lion-yellow testicles stared up at me as he stood there between levels. He had no idea he was comical, nor had the other dogs. They nosed at each other as they ran past: the initial stage of the almost invisible greeting they had in common: an acknowledgement with whiskers, a glimpse of a smile and finally a bark. Moretto's was the deepest, a tiger bark that woke every dog on the mountainside. 'Hey, Moretto!' said Lord Byron. 'Hoy, Lyon . . .'

Then we were almost down. There was a lighthouse on the breakwater the English had built furthest out in the harbour entrance, marking the place where you had to change course to east-south-east. Its tongue of light lay yellow on the water in the harbour, clipped and lapped by small waves. Sometimes a dinghy stopped in it, lying still with the balance and water-sense of a fish, revealing some of the islanders who had come down to witness our departure. On land and in small boats by the quay, they crowded round offering contradictory advice about loading. Those who really were going to leave occasionally listened to their advice and wasted time by moving packs from bombarda to mistico, from mistico to bombarda, then disagreeing all over again.

Human heads protruded out of the land darkness. Dark themselves, they were outlined against the water like buoys. The feeling of weightlessness left us, me, a weight that left us when the haste at harbour level found use for me and for him. He looked at me in his particular way and nodded. He had often told me that people who have only themselves in mind waste their lives and drift around without imprinting their features in any clay *at all*. 'Look at me . . .' he occasionally warned. 'Get married,' he might say, 'and obey your wife and stay with her.'

He said that kind of thing to provoke me when I was impatient about sitting in British neutral Cephalonia, waiting, month after month, while everything was happening on the Greek mainland. Other volunteers crossed the sound without delay. But we had to wait. Our group officially represented the Greek Committee in London – pounds and pathos and parliamentarianism – so we couldn't go to Greece on a chance hunt for acts of warfare, but had to find an equivalent to the dignity in our assignment. A rudiment of that was the 'constitutional army' under the command of Prince Mavrocordatos. Among eastern and western Greek factions, tribal armies and robber bands, he promised a kind of constancy and political ambition. But he had lost a bloody battle against the Turks at Peta and was still keeping out of the way in Hydra.

'I have come to partake for a nation – not a faction,' said Lord Byron in capital letters when the Suliot chieftains Photomar, Giavella and Drako came to his house on their regular errand to demand more money. They shrugged their shoulders and listened to their own thoughts as they heard his. 'My experience hitherto is limited to the Greek hawkers wanting to change dollars into piastres on shameless terms. And leaders of factions intriguing to get their hands on the remains of our money and use it to murder each other.'

In his haste, he dictated a number of letters to me. I remember the one that ended – 'and I also have with me a dovecote full of adventurers already tormented by this waiting. They think there's no other starting-point but the present. Now and again I have to open the hatch for one of them.'

437

The written word has a deceptive purity. When he opened the 'dovecote' and let out Trelawny and Browne as emissaries to the provisional government – knowing full well Trelawny would not come back – the impurity of the spoken word arose.

Trelawny hooked his forefinger with its black-and-blue nail into my buttonhole and muttered, 'Don't let him imagine anything. Factions are never *united* by goodwill, but are forced into it when one of them knows the way to defeat the others! Other variations are *unknown*! Byron always finds excuses . . . if they fight among themselves, there ought to be a reason for *us* to join the *noblest* faction. If you want to make a *name* for yourself in this, then *don't* stay with Byron. I've known him at close quarters for years. We are intimate friends (we've shared a mistress, an English girl) and he's as helpless as a child when it comes to *action*. If he can dream and dally and idle, then he does so. Preferably in the greatest comfort and God help us if he doesn't get his bath! And a constant change of underclothes. Goodbye, soldier! I have no intention of taking a *secondary rôle* in all this.'

Neither had I. I retreated and went around on my own for a few days. Other people's words are empty words if they don't match your own unsolved thoughts. That's what it was like when Lord Byron exhorted me to get married . . . and so on.

But now, having got right down to sea-level, I looked at him and he looked at me, those words clarified. In confirmation, the weightlessness fell from me as soon as I was occupied arranging for loads to be divided on to two boats. One part of that feeling simply disappeared – another took on the character of crates that had to go on board. He picked one up and immediately put it down again, smiling at the sound of tuned brass. It was the fanfare of trumpets from the Greek Committee, intended to announce battles for which hitherto they had forgotten to send arms. Our travelling companions, Englishmen, Italians and Greeks, said hey-ho in all their languages as they manhandled on board the printing press from the Greek Committee, which was also to go to war . . .

Our travelling companions – Englishmen, Italians, Greeks and a Negro, all shadowy grey in the dimness that remained of daylight. Colour is light. I saw that as Pietro Gamba ran through the crowd under the lantern of the bombarda. He was still holding the telescope in one hand, his saddle under his other arm, his eyelashes reddish-blond against his black hair, and he flushes when he replied to a question from Lord Byron: *Si una roba rossa!*'

I listened to what people were saying – a red dress. It was all wonderfully incoherent, like the flow of backward sounds when swimming under water. I took eight thousand dollars on board the bombarda, and one snuffling bulldog, listening to the languages, the way they mixed with each other, halved by bilingual speech in various directions. It sounded like bagpipes playing. I was no patriot. If I had been old enough to fight for England against Bonaparte ten years earlier, then I would have done so, but with mixed feelings and a fear of death. For a struggling Cause, on the other hand, I was able to feel the equivalent of patriotism. What is your native country if not a habit inculcated by the same kind of light waking you every morning, with the same sort of pale oblong words. The self-taught habit of giving yourself to something of your own choice. A nation whose borders run in your mind, must be more valuable, *seemed* to me more valuable this New Year's night in '23. Among clashing languages and unknown people, I felt at home, wholly and indivisibly resolved, with no thoughts of death. He laughed at me: you are your own herbal cure for your fever. You'll find clarification in application. He had found clarification. A memory from Cephalonia rustled in my pocket, a letter in his handwriting, unfinished but typical: while we others wrote home about our plans and hopes, he sent his friends the same eternal trivial list of demands: 'Please send me Epsom Salts, magnesia, Waite's tooth-powder, Smith's toothbrushes, Acton's Corn rubbers, soda powders and all the good novels you can lay your hands on.'

The crew hoisted sail, a salty vapour following the wind out of the folds, then the sails began to flap like sheets hanging out to dry. They crashed and banged, creaked and thumped, the water we were cleaving through sounding like an endless stream of happy bubbles. Our mistico was rigged astern with a mizzenmast and two lateen sails. It was an island boat, hardly that, I should think; no English boatbuilder had dared acknowledge it as his. It lay smooth on the water, shallow and quite open, with the exception of a small covered area reserved for Lord Byron and his papers. The other boat lay alongside, above us, relatively as high as a palace and lit up, with stamping horses in its belly. Its area of sail was larger, but so was its

439

resistance. We floated alongside it, listening to its weight: our laughing bubbles grew into clenched fists against the bombarda's stern: from child to youth; soon the water would be even older.

The neutral flag of Iona hung half-unfurled in the sterns of the boats. The wash astern gathered moonlight where the swirls of surface water simmered to repair what we had cloven. Far behind us, the tracks were wide and smooth, like a thoughtless past. I was the one to think 'a thoughtless past'. Or it thought itself inside me. Thin veils of vapour shifted round each other above the water and took on the colour of our lanterns – they looked like sounds, like bagpipes. Now that I was at last on my way from the protection of the British Crown and my parents' rights over my body and soul, all of that seemed to take me from behind by the waist and try once again to begin its tender domineering embrace. I had managed to escape my family and its unreasonable expectations of its sons, with no time for explanations. Sometimes I felt I ought to have written a letter to them about my plans in order to be able to make them real. The fact that I didn't know the risks I was exposing myself to meant that I myself took the risks less seriously. I knew that. People say that a past not clarified hollows out the future.

I sat with my back to that future and looked at waving islanders following us to the harbour entrance, singing patriotic songs and the boat crews joining in. We who were to liberate Greece did not know the songs. I saw Lord Byron reading the captain's lips and smiling. He was in a radiant mood. My own mood . . . no one but myself was aware how alone each and every one of us was. Sometimes I received an inner lift from the reality of all this, as if at last I had penetrated inside the frame of the picture and reached the painting. But when I tried to look around in it, I saw nothing and found not one point for the purpose of our journey, only distance and darkness in all directions. The others saw each other. The person playing the bagpipes doesn't blow the tune, but constantly fills his leather bag: old breath trickles out in notes, not the same thought that goes in and out. The others looked at each other without noticing their loneliness. I swallowed a great gulp of night. It was spattered with the barking of dogs.

Lyon the Newfoundland was crawling along the bombarda's rail, trying to get down to us. The Negro and Tita Falcieri grabbed his head, hind paws and tail, while he emitted bloodcurdling howls which did not cease until Lord Byron shouted: 'Well, let him go then!' and dog swirled into sky. He reached the side of the mistico with his forepaws and we could hear the woodwork scrabbled by rushing dog claws, then a splash between the boats. Loukas Chalandritsanos was first there to the rescue, then me. We hauled Lyon up half-drowned and tangled, then fended him off with an oar and a boathook when he tried to throw himself soaking wet into his master's arms. He tried to get away, tried to overcome the obstacles, stopping to shake the water out of his coat, then again and once again. 'Cheated!' he barked at us, shaking off another helping of water. The other dogs replied from the bombarda. At the same time, small boats in the harbour started shooting off pistol salutes, for they could see we were just about to circle the lighthouse.

The senses do not require much more to be satiated. A little sound and light in the lowest circle of an empty night. All the dogs barked. Hundreds of muzzle flames fired off and splashed against the land mass like fireflies. The smell of our answering salute singed the hairs of our nostrils, the laughter reflex born there and growing above the waves. The songs fell silent, began again more absently, less promising. And I looked at the lighthouse: such a little tower for such a long tongue.

Lyon at last got underneath Loukas' boathook so that he could put his head on Lord Byron's lap. They looked at each other for a while. Lord Byron bent down and kissed Lyon on the forehead, dragging his hands against the lie of his coat over his neck until his ears stuck upright and listened. '. . . . but you never thought about that. You could have been crushed, too. A shark might have nipped off your tail, or worse . . . You could have become the first casualty of this campaign. And thrashed us all in the race for heroics!'

Lighthouses shrink to small houses when you get close to them, then grow into lighthouses as you sail away from them. I was standing to starboard looking up at this one on its rock. Every stone had a faint curve for the common circle. As we glided past under its light, we ourselves lit up the tower with our lanterns. Every stone came alive, in a slow spread over the irregularities, a fleeting reddening, a row of lanterns drawing across the walled rows and making a face. Neither eyes, nose nor mouth, but a face all the same. I looked at it until it dazzled me when we had again risen sufficiently high on the sea.

For we were out at sea now, still under the protective wing of

Cephalonia, which was naturally deceptive, for we had to avoid its shallows as long as we were sailing along the south side.

The sea was full of personal shapes which at night you can only grasp with the experience of a seaman. My own eyes and ears extended towards them, my inner self rising at a purple lament that soon turned out to be the shifting of the elements in a cave open to the water line. I sat still and became used to it.

Something had stabilised itself in the movement eastwards. The wind was not on the surface of the water but at sail height, and the smattering and slapping had now ceased, both sails billowing forward like pale breasts in the darkness, nothing but fingers and ticklings on the inside. Between them, the captain's son was at the rudder, his eyes like cubes: observing, predicting, he rode with us along the side of an endless wave. He let us rest half way up out of a valley, vapour coming from the depths of it as the warmer sea became steam in colder air. There was a smell of salt, a taste of salt. I looked round – everywhere the mist was being wiped off the surface of the water and appearing again, a dance, statues of mist appearing all round, then becoming mist closer to land. In the south, they spun and wove round Zante, its contour blacker than the Morea's and outlining its own mountainous island self. Far away in the east, they played at the throat into Greece, round the mouth of the Gulf of Patras.

We could feel the mistico was a swift sailer. The bombarda was heavy and in some way full of resistance to its own shape and area of sail. Becoming separated happens quickly at sea. The play of the waves, currents and drifting create movements that can only be parried to some extent. Let your attention go and you are at once somewhere else. Still in the lee of the island, we drifted apart and after that the distance increased with every wave. I can't describe how it feels. We were lying on the water line. They were high up and looking down on us. Every time they passed one of the side screens of darkness, we sharpened our eyes and looked through it, then they passed yet another. It broke and turned cold when the connection between us could no longer be extended. At the same time, we found something of the sweetness of adventure as we extended a handful of water to the outstretched hands. We said last words, Lord Byron calling to Pietro Gamba in Italian. Something about destroying. We yelled into the echo which is so singularly like being in a room and lay

442

between sky and sea ... *giorno ... domani ... ascolta mi*, came the reply at first, but the more waves that came between, the fewer shreds of words ... *sic ... rema ... voi ...* came the complaint, and then the quiet grew against our ears and went on growing after everything was brimming. The world grew. We saw its curve between us. Then we took out our pistols again and made as much noise as we could, shouting: 'Tomorrow in Missolonghi!' Their New Year fireworks replied, insanely like ten pop- guns, and the wind tore our cries apart ... *ani ... is ... i.*

We were now glad of our shallow seat in the sea. The flag of neutrality was by no means a guarantee against warships. During our five months in Cephalonia, we had observed that the Turks certainly did not keep watch over their waters, but appeared and disappeared with great suddenness, never either conquered or conquering. There was something strange about the Turks. I had thought of their occupying force as a dough rising over Greece, right down to the water line. Instead it was fleeting and scattered. (Lord Byron said it was firmly rooted – like a bandage stuck to a wound – partly inseparable from what today is called Greek.) Various parts of the mainland were sometimes occupied, sometimes liberated by some of the factions. The Turk liked shooting sitting birds. With indifference and vengeful actions, he held his riddled borders. Anyone could pass, anything could cross them. But then he suddenly turned round, as if half asleep, and massacred whole populations, like that of Chios a few years earlier.

Our telescopes from Cephalonia had observed sporadic patrols of Turkish fleets, or individual ships. Craft that had none of the glory of Ottoman I had expected. No damask sails with broad pink and green stripes. No burning-glass in the stern. Nor any of the mystery of invulnerability I had always feared superior forces must have, which makes it slightly tempting – not just necessary – to challenge them.

In command of two ships from the Hydra fleet, Mavrocordatos had recently chased a Turk up to Ithaca, run him aground and pursued the crew across the island. Those who witnessed it said that it had been a question of man to man, the one man with about the same proficiency and fare as the other. The British commander had protested at Mavrocordatos' action. Odysseus' island was an *English* possession, won in honest battle with Napoleon Bonaparte. In skirmishes between

443

Turks and Greeks, England had chosen to remain neutral, thank you. The Greek struggle for independence was praiseworthy, but only to the extent that it took place on land occupied by Turkey! Lord Byron, himself in the habit of roaring with rage over bagatelles, burst out laughing at this hypocrisy. He put his hand over my mouth.

He assured me that such blind neutralistic arguments also filled him with distaste, but in wartime, neutral ground was a place for whisperings and not empty talk. He said neutral islands bring the war 'with itself' in its own way: everyone can go there and wave a miniature of his own flag. 'No one dies,' instead the 'infection' and dirty tidemarks of intrigue are tolerated while the rest of the world suffers and acts holy. 'The neutrals are vital for the idealists. Spleens are needed.'

Hero. I looked into his eyes: the laughter at it all. He peered with one eye, the one that protruded on some days. A taste of cress in the air. He took the Cause seriously, he took it on himself – as we know, he gave everything (Everything, 'everything'?) in the end. But the many moments when he was overcome, he laughed at it all and said that he believed what he believed because you had to believe something if you didn't want to be a blackguard and a vandal. He really had nothing against the Turks. He had smoked many a pipe with a Turk. 'Etcetera.' Turks and Greeks were in fact very similar in mind, ways and disposition, 'though likeness is the actual cause of all trouble. Alien natures have no idea what to quarrel about!'

But – he repeated – when one man enslaves another, at best he turns him into a rebel, at worst into a slavish character and destroys his soul and future. That was worth fighting. Though a sacred Cause supported by decrepit creatures who promptly have to adopt its sacredness, individually and mutually become hypocrites – then he has to laugh. He laughed wearily the day the Suliot chieftain Giavella came to his house to demand more money without even bothering to concoct a pretext. The next day, Giavella was dead in a Turkish ambush. It was totally silent in that ravine. On the third day, Giavella's wife came with her four-year-old son dragging along his father's sword and raging with his grand words.

So Lord Byron laughed at what he had seriously devoted his life to. Whether it hollowed out his gravity, or whether it strengthened his realism, I do not know. Only that a person who avoids the seduction of extremes was more difficult to capture than a blunt fanatic.

444

Only one thing would make him maintain seriousness: the only thing that makes us all into geniuses is a compelling *rhythm*.

The captain's son sailed as if the sea were a muscle, its individual contractions lasting a human lifetime, a long muscle into which song after song falls and ceases. Each and every one who has ever been to Greece knows. The islands are not only islands but wild mountains smelling of drought, their feet washed in green light, of sand or phosphorescence? High up there, where they spread their knees, lay a mist that did not settle. They stretched out their legs and the mist climbed down. We lay in free fall in the darkness, the pale breasts driving us ahead, moving away and back to each other, slowly, as if the boat were dreaming it was running. I dreamt I was dreaming. The open and closed striking of the waves against the side circled round within us, in our own weapons, the waves striking high and chasing foam over the edge. I tried to change mood, as I had done all evening, striking a blow at weightlessness, another at Missolonghi, another at my mother's musquash muff, another at the freedom and loneliness I had at last realised under the command of Lord Byron! But my mood meant nothing, for we had good winds all the time and shot eastwards with no delaying manoeuvres.

Somewhere in the boat, a conversation was going on between Dr Bruno, a young doctor from Genoa who had also left his mother, and Lord Byron's servant, Fletcher. Dr Bruno had found out that Fletcher had already been in Lord Byron's service during his previous journey to Greece, fifteen years earlier. So he asked questions with the assurance that the servant would give him credible answers when it came to practical circumstances. I noted Fletcher's cold in the nose – worried about being infected – and I heard his dreadful habit of combing his beard with his fingers and snapping hairs as if they were lice. He said:

'When I was in Greece, the Turks were rulers and they licked the Greeks and Albanians into shape. The landscape is not much to look at. The country is all stones and rogues. The latter live in caves in the rocks and emerge like foxes. We had to have a heavily armed escort to be able to get from one place to another. If you want to live with the Greeks in their own way, you have to live like a dog. They eat goat meat and rice, sitting on the floor of some wretched hut. They all eat out of the same dirty bowl and tear the meat to pieces with their fingers. No knives, no forks, only a couple of horn spoons. They drink some muck they call wine, but it tastes more of turpentine than grapes, and they carry it around in a stinking goatskin and everyone drinks from the same vessel. Then they have coffee they pound to a powder, and they drink it grounds and all, with no sugar. When they're not sleeping, they're smoking. They sleep on the floor in their clothes and shoes, never undress and never wash, except the tips of their fingers. They are covered with lice and fleas. The Turks were the only respectable people in the country. If they go, Greece will be like an opened lunatic asylum. It's a country of flies and lice and thieves. It's quite beyond me what business My Lord has there. And he can't deny that everything I have told you is true.'

'Bah,' came angrily from Lord Byron, far in front in the creaking dimness. 'Anyone looking at things through a toad's eyes sees toads. What Fletcher says may be right, but I didn't notice it. I've come here because I was tired of being in Italy, and because I liked Greece last time I was here, and because the Committee in London said I could be useful here.' After a while, he added: 'They didn't say what kind of useful, however, and neither do I know. I know as much about siege tactics as goodwill knows about the art of healing.'

But that was the only time that night he was heard to speak in tones of despondency. Soon afterwards, he entertained us with one of his old stories of Greece. It was about a storm in roughly the same place as we were then in. They had all thought they were lost – the sails jammed, the rudder useless, the jagged shallows, the crew all praying to God and Allah. He lay down flat on deck and felt long shudders, tremors from below: a boat does not co-operate with itself in the water. It is trying to fall to pieces!

As he spoke, the walls of the mainland came closer and closer. We went closer to them and started to distinguish the lower contours in front of the skyline of the mountains, where the reflection of the moon lay on hillsides of olives. You could see only the silvery light, not yet the way the trees grew, or the treetops, or the ancient trunks which look like bunches of deformed and petrified hemp. I anticipated the shape of an olive in my mouth. I bit. A splash of salt hit me in the face as craft and water collided in a faulty manoeuvre. I swallowed the stone. It began to grow. So I went to sleep. Just when I was most wide awake, I caught myself waking up. This hadn't happened since I was a small child and I now blinked my eyes like a child.

It was all even more vexing than the time lost was obvious: I had missed the moment we had entered the real Greece and now we were already in her arms. To the south ran the Morea, to the north the Aetolian barrier of rocks, and behind them the lagoons that made marshlands of the shores of northern Greece.

Our course was to the north-east, the flow of the tide making the mistico sway and roll in the heavy swell. The captain's son pumped her stem against the slope of the wave, then let her straighten up in a slow swan movement over the crest of the wave. The tenth or twentieth time, Dr Bruno yawned. He had just said he would never forget this night. The first words I heard after my nap were '*mai dimenticare questa notte*'. Lord Byron watched the next yawn out of the corner of his eye, and the hand that went to the liver. 'Neither will I,' he said. He sat in silence for a moment, following the movement of the water with his legs opening and closing. 'But we'll have to contract the distances,' he added. 'There's never much flat land in the memory . . . as long as it's not the memory of great loneliness. Then it's a mountain in its own right.'

In the middle of all this, they talked about headaches. He was worried about Ada, his daughter. The last letter about her had described regular attacks, followed by anger, irritability and melancholy. 'Too early,' he muttered. 'She's only eight, you know. I started having those when I was twelve or thirteen. I would wish she hadn't inherited my disposition . . . my mother died of an attack, you know, apoplexy, I think. I wish Ada didn't have to have our disposition.' He listened for a moment to Dr Bruno's newly formed theories on headaches, let some go past, thought over some, wrinkled his nose and shuddered whenever he heard mention of leeches as a healing method, but made no comment, then carried on his own train of thought: 'Though I don't know why she should take after us when she lives so close to her mother. Her life ought to be quiet and regular. They live in the country, you know, and I think my Ada is being brought up with all the country virtues. That's good. London destroys a person's character, especially a young girl's. If she lives in the country with her mother, that ought to counteract my blood. I can't believe her *head* is damaged? Lady Byron was delivered by the very best doctors and she allowed them to do their work, for she believed more in science than prudery when it came to it.' He smiled his half-smile. 'That my

447

mother caused me damage is quite certain,' he sighed, gesturing with his hand in front of his eye and half his forehead. 'At that moment, she chose to be shy. When my mother gave birth to me, she closed her legs.'

The waters subsided. 'Really!' exclaimed Dr Bruno with interest, soon remembering several cases of ignorant peasant women in severe pain and beyond the help of the midwife, who in their need pressed out an embarrassed laugh and crossed their legs at him. 'Yes, just like a simple-minded peasant mother,' said Lord Byron. 'And yet she was of good family,' he remembered to add.

Dr Bruno began a new address, this time on how cramped and confined it was for a soft little head on the way from foetus to human being, and how insignificant a pair of legs would be in that context. As a child, I had some sense of past experience. But adults had no memories of an earlier life and their example rapidly rid me of mine. Upbringing seemed to mean teaching your children to absorb themselves in the present. If I had said that aloud perhaps Lord Byron would have reformulated the thought some time in the belief that it was his own. But at that moment, Dr Bruno asked him how he could know such a detail about his birth. He laughed it off at first, then swept it round himself: 'How could I – not know?'

The conversation died away. Then it so happened that we once again lay just below the bombarda, her illuminated outline appearing out of the night behind an islet. There she was. We couldn't understand how she had got there in a trice. We had got half way to our feet to call out and make ourselves known, then an echo out there seemed to float in to us and take the words out of our mouths. All sounds on the way from one boat to another fell back into us and echoed. We thought 'Ahoy' and the night air shot in with it, cold and sober. Light reached there, too. No one saw us, but we saw ourselves in a difficult situation in hostile waters, straddling the waves. A current of cold air drew the depths of the night and – inside them – four people rose half way to their feet to call out.

It was quiet on board now, the sails filtering like the quills on a flying gull, their roots creaking like the gull's sinews. The happy bubbles ran up into our echoes and fell silent there. In my echo, in Lord Byron's echo, in Loukas Chalandritsanos' and Dr Bruno's. Fletcher had gone to lie down in the covered space, so knew nothing, but by chance was lying quiet and still. Lyon was pointing at the great boat, his nose and plumed tail level with each other, but he did not bark, just whistled, very quietly, turning round with a cunning expression to hide behind the pile of cork. The captain's son was manoeuvring like a shadow, his tools responding to him equally soundlessly, like shadows of tools, making us swing a few degrees: a wave helped us on, over the threshold away from the immediate proximity of what his experience had taught him to recognise at first glance.

Slowly, the bombarda changed shape before our very eyes and grew in length. She unfurled her Turkish flag, opened portholes amidships and looked one-eyed out into the darkness. She found voice, two voices speaking a language which in my terror, I listened to – for the first time. Since then I have heard tell of our adventure, mostly from people who were not there. They describe excitement. You glide into a rumbling cloud, submitting in secret to its shadow and secretly escape. It wasn't like that at all.

Only the boat had a course, a curve. We inside it, followed, we were silent, according to laws of common intuition we scarcely understood. Disorder took possession of me. As we saw the bombarda transformed into a Turkish frigate, somehow I went on being her friend. A man is not a clock; if he were, he would go fast or slow. An enemy with no idea you are there is flesh and blood. He has not bent down for his sword; it is lying beside him. One of them spoke as if his mouth were full of butter, the other as if through a beard. They were gossiping and laughing. I was about to laugh with them. Naturally I did not, but I thought of it and felt the same desire, as if faced with some physical release. It was that never-satisfied curiosity, what really happens when everything breaks.

After we had retreated by a few laborious lengths, I dared to sit down, totally exhausted, the sweat pouring, perpendicularly, ice-cold down my sides. It must have been a sign of 'terror', but I was much too exhausted to recognise fear. Dr Bruno was lying in the bottom of the boat. In the first stage of danger, Lord Byron had clasped Loukas to him, and did not let him go until the boy with an unmoved – or even chilly – gesture, freed himself. Then I saw Byron pushing back his pistol with a trembling hand. I saw the short barrel glint and knew the bullet had been for Loukas, who would be better dead than captured on a Turkish ship. It struck me that with our arms, suicide

449

would be the most effective way out, on the whole. We had only four guns on board, two shotguns and two small pistols for target shooting. Where was the Greek fleet that was supposed to occupy the bay? Where in God's name was it?

We rose on the water and set off at speed towards the rocky barrier to the north. The sails were high and my cap blew off into the water. As I turned round for it, it was already floating far away, the wind parting the back of my head and my hair whipping in my eyes.

Morning came.

The first of January, 1824. I ate a piece of bread and listened to its uneasy way through my empty intestines. Honour and danger were bubbling inside me, and bread. It was a cloudy morning. At dawn, we had at last been able to see the bombarda, but what we saw was her being chased towards Patras by a Turk, the two fully rigged ships cruising round each other like male pigeons in mating battles. And where was the Greek fleet?

We lay at anchor in the shelter of some cliffs separating deep sea from lagoon, the stern anchor drifting, in spite of the Greeks hanging over the edge, fishing for resistance. From where I was sitting, I could see the deep blue waves on the right and more Turkish warships, on my left fishermen from Aetolia poling ahead their long narrow lagoon boats with staves and sails. They were fishing with spears. The boats were called monoxylons, or so it sounded. They looked like carved instruments against shallow green water.

Despite the clouds, sun-powder, or sun-dust, lay over the lagoon. The water was brackish, the dust combining with the surface into a milky membrane edged with banks of reeds extending into infinity, this way and that, looking like dams in this delta of rice cultivation. A membrane of reeds over the sea, a measured smile the night had already told us of now closer, though diminishing. What was it? It couldn't be insects.

The dog had flopped into the sea and scrambled up on to a rock, where it ran around sniffing the ground, as unmoved as if it had been at home. Lord Byron also floated in the water, his head bobbing black far away in the waves. The boat turned her stern squarely to the north, where another layer of mist was bleaching. You could no longer see where the water ended and the land began. Reeds and marshland merged into each other and as far as I could see continued right to the foot of a line of bare stony mountains. With my eyes, I slowly became familiar with the most inhospitable tracts of Greece.

For four days, we lay alone, blockaded between obstacles. The mistico sailed too low in the water to risk going further into the reeds and quicksands the Greeks talked about, and the Turks were swarming outside, their ships patrolling the bay, large and small, sometimes one of them creeping along the other side of the cliff, and then so close we could smell their shadow. They were looking for us.

Naturally there were attempts to break out under cover of darkness. But each and every one of them ended with a retreat, and each retreat was carried out with the same swaggering anguish as when an animal tries to back out of its body to escape the lead. Manoeuvres such as these resulted in our getting further and further away from Missolonghi every day – you always flee a little further than back to the starting point. When we had reached almost as far as Dragomestri, several of us, including the captain's son, suggested the land route as a better alternative. Lord Byron gave us others the freedom to choose, but for his part he was going to stay on board, not just because of his shortcomings as a walker, but also because of some packages difficult to transport which he was responsible for, the Committee's sixteen thousand dollars, to mention but one.

Just as he had managed to persuade us to abandon the idea, it took hold of him. On the third day, he put ashore the youngest of us, the one most familiar with the countryside. Loukas was fifteen or sixteen years old – it is hard to tell in the Levant, where life is divided into a very short childhood and a long period of duty and responsibility – not really into ages. He was Lord Byron's 'page'. He was one of the children of the Chalandritsanos family from Zante. Lord Byron had found them in need and had undertaken to support them. In this way, he was able to satisfy his longing also to 'make provision for' someone when he found himself innumerable miles away from his own kin. He had a peculiar urge to 'make provision for', to busy himself with household matters of a financial nature. He could afford to. He moved cats from out in the rain into the house. They gave him presents of mice. The Chalandritsanos family gave him Loukas as a page. Who needs a *page* in the wild world? When we first saw Loukas running along the path to Missolonghi, Lord Byron said: 'For you know what his fate would have been on board a Turkish warship . . .'

He watched the boy go with all his immense empathy in his thoughts which occasionally could be his own 'fate'. And his eyes turned blank. Loukas ran, got a stitch, half-ran bent double and walked with the careless jerky steps of a boy. The ground is mute and hard after days at sea. We saw every stone, every unevenness drifting up into dreamy speculations in his face. Soon he was flickering behind curtains of reeds, which soon became denser. We hoped he would hurry. He had a letter with him to Colonel Stanhope in Missolonghi containing a detailed description as to where we were.

Every evening arrived with the resounding of the tide in the lagoon. No waves, only a swelling noticed as the boat began to sigh, gently tugging at its mooring. We looked at each other. It was swelling beneath us as in a lock, the boat's movements soft and from that our movements becoming soft as if we had infinitely long supple necks.

Then came the feeling of hovering, for the sun sank simultaneously: just as the first flood-tide movement makes us pay attention, the cloud cover also splits, and strong light precipitates nuances of copper, floating metal dazzling between the black strings of reeds. The crookedest of the sun's rays rub out the lines where things meet, *rub* against each other. Where the contour lines had been is just air, reflections between contours of kisses: a boat on the horizon as the sun goes down does not plough any waters but steps across a narrow mirage. And these are not just words, but every man can convince himself of it. In the evening we hovered lightly above the swelling of the tide, not captured by the water now, but voluntarily there. The boat nodded. With his legs over the side, Lord Byron sat looking towards land.

He was a dark figure nodding with the boat, as if cut out of black paper. The sight filled my eyes: he nodded back and forth, through time, while the tide lifted the boat away and the moorings took it home.

His silhouette contained all my views of him, finely concealed in black. When you first get to know a person, and then get to know him . . . everything changes, then is changed again, back to the memory of the first meeting, then he grows and steps over that memory in order to adapt in another way. In the end, the first impression is a place you will never return to, but which you credit with the importance of the origin.

We had first met six months ago.

My eldest brother had written a letter of introduction of the kind you like to have with you on your first journey abroad. It was addressed to the poet Leigh Hunt, whom my brother had got to know in England, but who now seemed to have a journalistic collaboration with Lord Byron in Italy, in Pisa and possibly in Genoa.

Genoa, to be more precise. It was a lovely June evening with ripe oranges and orange blossom on the trees. The driver had pretended he knew the address, but had gone astray several times and went into an inn to ask the way, then stayed there for longer and longer. I didn't bother to make a fuss, partly because my Italian was too poor for a quarrel and partly because I enjoyed the trip as long as it lasted.

This was the first time I had ever seen orange trees. Orange windfalls! I didn't think such things existed. In itself, the actual smell of the blossom reminded me of English orangeries, but I would never have imagined orange trees could form a perpetual avenue along the curve and, so to speak, besiege the track up towards the outskirts of Genoa. This usefulness surprised me – yes, I was dumb and stupid; for me the cultivation of the south still seemed to be décor. After the gallery of the trees, the mountainside fell through vineyard after vineyard, the whole mountain shorn 'as with closely cut curls', I wrote to an equally romantic woman friend. What did I know then about too much rain and too little sun, or the other way round. A vineyard is not a potato field. There is sweetness already in its very form. Its fruits are like coral ear-pendants, and while they are still clusters of flowers, they spread pollen in golden clouds, so lovely that they themselves are lured into taking back and drinking their own fragrant dust.

The treetops dropped windfalls that split against jagged edging stones and at the same moment scattered sparks of dark yellow juice. It all murmured, beyond it tumbling the great emptiness that is suddenly limited by a distant sight and becomes a view. Genoa's stairway lay washed by sea. The pink houses were dry-plastered according to Italian custom, so were full of hollows and cracks patched in divergent colours, like everything else in this remarkable country. The Mediterranean brings its waves of deep turquoise, the exchange of water swift and heavy for anyone walking along the shore,

453

though when I looked at it from above, the whole movement seemed superficial, as if frozen. The most extreme edge of it supported the breakers, the white ribbon of foam round the bay.

From the inn I heard the language, 'that sweet bastard Latin', and the driver appeared again, wiping his moustache with his forefinger and assuring me for the third time that we would soon be there. Then he turned the carriage round and drove back a long way, during which he first let out a sound of satisfied gorging of wine, then arranged for a loss of it as he relieved himself behind a bush. He finally found the right turning. I didn't bother to haggle outside the house. His eyes laughed with a kind of fatherly superiority as he cheated me of my money, and I smiled after him as he left.

I was at once criticised for this by Hunt, who met me on the steps and asked what I had paid. He was a man with an unjustly cheerful face in relation to his character. 'The Italians!' he exclaimed, then went on with a harangue I had heard with boredom from a number of English ladies, who feared sunburn more than anything else. 'I don't see anything terrible in a poor man taking extra tolls from someone who looks rich!' I had prepared those words with some care, as I had expected the harangue. Though not from Leigh Hunt, who was a known radical. 'Good heavens,' he muttered when he heard my phrases, 'after two weeks you'll have scraped off the icing, my dear young friend.' He was right, of course, and today I understand that the only way to be rid of your prejudices is to look them in the eye from the start and give them free rein.

As I followed him into his house a minute later, I also beheld fertile soil – hearth for misanthropy.

What was the first thing I noticed in that most crowded of rooms? As I was defending myself against the fantastic noise eight children can achieve in a kitchen with a stone floor, I watched a bee struggling up the ray of light from an open window, but which again and again fell back under its load of pollen. We were in a southern kitchen which was not large, but immeasurably cluttered. The eight children began with a very small infant and ended with a pimply troubled youth, who tried to tidy up a little when I came in. There were stacks of dirty dishes and the remains of several meals and Leigh Hunt carried on conversing through the sounds of battle. 'Yes, this is what it's like for *us*,' he said, accusingly. Regarding his other statements, I could only

454

mobilise a dutiful expression, for at the very most I caught only every third word. The older children fought with the younger ones, who were then treacherously nasty to the smallest, in their turn also maltreated by banging themselves against table edges and stove corners. At the very bottom crawled a dog with that capacity to attract everyone's rage prevalent in those who live in fear of a thrashing. When someone trod on it, it drowned all shrieks and clatter, and then the adults at last grew impatient.

Marianne Hunt sat on a chair beneath the rays of light, the bee constantly on the point of being caught in her curly hair. She sat there as if she would never rise again, a matron, her soul crumbling away when faced with all this anguish suffered from giving birth.

I was given my first first-hand story about Lord Byron.

'He sings little arias by Rossini, rather out of tune,' smiled Hunt.

'When we lived in Pisa, he constantly complained about the Children,' complained Marianne Hunt. 'You wouldn't have thought a poet and a peer of the realm would be so petty. But if any Child raised its voice, then His Grace would promptly appear on the stairs to ensure the child was chased back into our rooms. He was beside himself if there was a stain on the wall and never hesitated to let us know that our Poverty put us in a position of dependency on him.'

'He strolls around the garden warbling his Rossini arias,' interjected Hunt, a glint of torment in his voice. 'Naturally I'm glad he hasn't chosen a greater artist to profane. But all the same . . . Rossini! Doesn't that say quite a lot about his taste?'

'He's the meanest person we've had the honour to be with,' said Marianne Hunt. 'In our circles, it has always been quite self-evident that whoever has means opens his purse to whoever hasn't, and not as a gift, either, but boundlessly, until both are poor, after which it is established that whoever has means is the focus of the circle's finances for the time being. But his Ungrace deals out small *temporary loans*, always so small, you shortly have to ask again and are made to listen to his oh, yes, oh, yes, oh, dear.'

The tormented look again replaced the smile in Hunt's eyes.

'He rode on my rocking-horse,' said the eldest, who had come and stood close to me with one of the smallest children in his arms – a little fair-haired boy who, in contrast to the others, was fairly clean.

'Yes, he did,' laughed Hunt. 'He came to see me in prison a few times, and when I was released, he came to our home in London. He showed no sign whatsoever of avoiding our friendship then. On the contrary, he never seemed to want to go, and used to sit astride the rocking-horse, talking. He was healthier and fatter at the time. He was married then. Lady Byron once came in a carriage to fetch him and he sent for her several times, but she preferred to stay outside for as long as an hour instead of doing Mrs Hunt the honour. The good Byron was probably very embarrassed.'

At that moment, I had an explanation for the little blond boy's cleanliness, for his mother came down from upstairs. She was the famous Shelley's widow and took her 'darling Percy Florence' with her upstairs to give him a bath and a goodnight song. The Hunt children were given neither, but they had freedom. When they were to go to bed – as when soldiers interrupt the battle in order to die for a while – they were carried off by their father, whose face had fixed into a vaguely painful wonder, in common with almost all men whose shots in the dark all too often hit their target.

Suddenly conversation became possible, but then we had nothing to say and the longed-for silence became painful. Leigh Hunt asked indifferently about my travel plans and my brother's work for the Greek Committee, and I replied with anxious looks at Marianne Hunt, who appeared to detest the topic of conversation. A greedy silence – perhaps even hungrier – I found in the Shelley widow, who had come back and started cleaning up. She did it in a pleasant almost hospitable way, with no clatter of plates and cutlery. Her reproach lay in her absent-minded reply when Marianne Hunt said it could be left until morning. After that, I simply had to help. While I wiped, she didn't once look straight at me. It wasn't that she was discourteous, or that she was shy. I looked at her face and saw she was so distrait, she needed all her concentration to remember she was washing up. She might have fallen asleep with boredom. A fine network of veins round her eyes was raised like the nerves on a hairy nettle.

Later on in the evening, however, she took part in the first-hand story round the table. It had now become less fragmentary, but because of that also less understandable to me. They probably saw I was a young person who had read *The Corsair* and heard great rumours about Lord Byron, and while they detested being part of the temptation he exercised, they still found the rôle irresistible. They talked about their circle and immediately became so entranced by its exclusiveness that they also excluded me from the conversation. Nicknames, taunts, implied events and contexts were laid out in a star which expanded just to make a fool of me. They themselves were not happy. Gossip is like that. Adult people work themselves up into a mystique of names which isn't there. They talked and talked, hectically and mechanically, using a name I had never heard before. 'Albé,' said Shelley's widow, 'tried to play Iago with Kean as prototype. Trelawny did Othello with himself as prototype, ha, ha, every dramatic situation obvious to our Tre. He really *has* the ability to believe he is the person he is performing. So it was *me* he loved and almost strangled. I still have a mark.'

All I could do was to raise a vague smile when she named Jane Williams and poor Clara and *Bolivar* and *Ariel* and Allegra. She did so with a challenging briskness, as if refusing to know me in case I didn't know them. Since then I have heard those names so often, they have also become symbols to me. 'One day,' she nudged on along the row of anecdotes, 'when I was going up the road to Diodati with something I had copied for Albé, he and Polidori were standing on the terrace watching me coming. Albé said to his unhappy physician that he could not do such a thing with sufficient dignity, but he considered no man should stand staring at a woman struggling up a hill, but should go down and offer her his arm. Polidori accepted the challenge as usual, like catching a cannonball in his hand. With tremendous haste, he leapt down from the terrace, which turned out to be a considerable distance, landed in a briar bush and sprained his ankle. Albé was neither repentant nor surprised, only mild and friendly in the way he is when he has tempted people to do something stupid and thinks he has shown them their right selves.' A smile twitched in the nettle-down, but did not reach her mouth, which remained as much in mourning as Mary herself. 'They say Polidori is dead, he, too.'

Such a small tower for such a long tongue. A man spends his whole life in his own dimension, regardless of reputation, lays his flame over the sea, although only a little spark spatters out. The next morning, I met him myself. He came walking in his garden and I was so occupied noting the exotic species growing there, at first I didn't notice the thin little figure in ill-fitting clothes. Leigh Hunt touched my elbow.

I have described the way ships separated by the night lose each other

457

by seeing each other again beyond new layers of darkness. It is possible to meet in daylight in that way. I think what you determine with expectation changes shape all the time. Gate after gate swings open, and each time he is furthest away and starts approaching, but never comes right up to me. My heart thumps as if it were gigantic. Sometimes he seems to be in reverse, then the right way round, changing colour beneath the various lights of the light and shadows of the trees. What is a dream anyhow, compared with the somersaults of waking senses faced with something utterly special?

When we were introduced to each other, I hurried to mention our point of contact and confused him with it. In July '22, the leftist liberals in London had started a club for those involved in the cause of Greek liberation. John Cam Hobhouse was a fiery spirit in this ('Do you know Hobby?'), my brother belonged and was a subscriber ('Do I know your brother?'). Jeremy Bentham became the patron of the movement. ('Have you *de facto* seen the old phantom? If I'm to accomplish Benthamism in Greece, then I'll feel like some kind of colony of the ghost.') In January '23, they had formed the Greek Committee and Hobhouse had written to Lord Byron and recommended he should go out and 'make himself useful' there. ('What is it they expect of me?') The movement's practical leader, Blaquière, went ahead and studied the situation. ('They've allotted me the task of going to Missolonghi, said to be the place within the liberated area most threatened by the Turks.')

He looked at me, as far as I could make out still with the false notion that I had a part to play in the Greek Committee, because he said doubtingly: 'You look young?' I wondered what I really looked like at the back of his needle-fine pupils. I tried to get out of it all with the help of my interest in the outdoor world and pointed at a 'mulberry tree'. His great eyes followed the direction of my finger. He walked along the path. He stood in front of me, thirty-five years old now, and saw my expectations sliding on to him. 'And pine trees, palm trees and plane trees,' he replied. 'All of them grow at home in England, you know.'

Lord Byron's shadow glided together with the boat's across the surface of the water, purple colours following the sun over the horizon towards Italy, the darkness coming from the east, enclosing the moon, still large but not round, more like a stony white mosaic. The shadow fell from the water to the bottom. Our fish-shape slipped easily through the lagoon and fluttered across ripples of sand. Slowly, the yellow laughter returned, first one bird, then another, then whole colonies joining in measured laughter that went on all night, and then every night at Missolonghi, smelling of decay, laughing in yellow, and yet cleanliness and loneliness were also there. Nature was a glass tube, fingers running along its nerve. I was here now, instead of on my way home, and out of his silhouette emerged the next picture:

'Get married then. And obey your wife and *stay* with her,' he said when we were ready to leave Genoa. 'I intend (as an example . . .) to return home to mine! I shall do so barefoot and with my head bare and will make her listen to me, and I myself will be forced into absolute concessions. But it's worth it. Because – you see – hardly even the charnel house remains after so much roaming about and so much "love". It is worthless to live with no home or homeland and never be allowed to see your child. Anyone maintaining it's a good life is still a child himself. The man who is free and international – I have met them all – has pale cold hands.'

I looked at his bitten nails, two on each hand. Most of the furniture had already been stored, awaiting shipping to England, incredible numbers of letters and papers in sealed chests to be deposited in the bank during his absence. The menagerie at Casa Saluzzo was being dispersed round strange households. The dogs were to go with him, but monkeys, goats, cats, cranes, tortoises, ravens and I don't know what else he had collected over his years in Italy – they all needed new homes. His collecting mania was beyond reason: just as he was getting rid of his flock, he bought another parrot in the market (because he had never before seen such an emerald green) and invited a sixth cat out of the gutter. Ten or so species quarrelled and leapt and climbed the stairs that evening in Casa Saluzzo in Genoa, as Lord Byron made his bequests, examined his will and squared his accounts by correcting faults in the household books, his secretly thin scalp hairs lit through by lamplight and his pen spattering ink. '253 + 114 doesn't come to 467, does it?' he sighed, striking out his treasurer's results with a shower of ink. He made no effort to tempt me to go with him, or *not* go with him, to Greece. He had assembled a human menagerie for the journey. He had Trelawny, who had stopped off with him on his way somewhere. He had Tita Falcieri, once his gondolier in Venice, and

Lega Zambelli, once a useless treasurer in Count Guiccioli's house before – like the Count's wife – following Byron. He had had Fletcher for innumerable years and he had the constantly additional contributions and the constant drain from people around him. He had Teresa Guiccioli's brother Pietro Gamba. And now he had me, who had walked past his house and stayed.

He dissuaded me from all my ambitions that evening. He told me to *marry* when the campaign was over. About that he said: 'You must remember that reformers more than any other pound on a private demon of discontent, with the help of "good deeds". But that doesn't matter. Good deeds are needed. As long as they're not entirely steered by demons . . . Sometimes I think *demons* steer all good and make it into the first stage of evil. But that doesn't matter. This has got to be done!'

We had to leave Genoa twice. The first time the *Hercules* had hardly left harbour when a Tyrrenian storm broke out, driving large and small craft, struggling against the tide, back into safety, like animals in a forest fire – rabbits and foxes, pigeons and deer. There were high seas in the harbour, too, and men being seasick at anchor, but no one wanted to go ashore. For some that meant bad luck, for others just reluctance at the thought of a second farewell. Lord Byron said he did not want to see Teresa Guiccioli again to renew the pain of departure. Perhaps he did not want to take on any more pain he could not reciprocate. He just wanted to get away. Farewells, they wear out in the blue shadow of dawn where no one can move at all.

But when Fletcher had been up to the house and reported that She had already left for Bologna with her father, Lord Byron and Her brother Pietro Gamba went back up to Casa Saluzzo and stayed there until promise of better winds.

I stayed on board and helped Trelawny mend the stalls the horses had kicked to pieces in defiance and panic during the storm. I enjoyed his presence. He was convinced of everything he did and would do – a beneficial counterweight to my uncertainty and Pietro Gamba's theatrical enthusiasm, as well as Lord Byron's eternal hesitation and doubts. I liked Trelawny's way of working as we handed in planks and reinforced them with coarse nails. Every finger had a personality of its own, a history of working life of its own. I perceived with pleasure the smell of sweat and his calm before the journey. Apprehensions surprised him. When it came to his enormous experience of travelling – sailing, on horseback and on foot all round the world several times, he had lived in the *real* east ('as opposed to Byron, who had never dared move outside civilisation') and at twenty had lost his *second* wife (a *Mussulman*!) and cremated her remains on a shore in Morocco.

When Trelawny first appeared on the quay dressed for the journey, my earliest ideas about Lord Byron seemed to have taken shape. I had, of course, seen him up at the house in the daytime; now towards the end, when Lord Byron had begun to regret the whole Greece project, Trelawny saw to it that we got away.

But here on the quay, Trelawny came striding along in another lustre, handsome, with reins over his shoulder, sun and wind over black curly hair and beard and slanting bird-of-prey eyes, his Negro behind him in red livery, the sea-chests on a cart, a framework for Trelawny. Trelawny looked as if he could *carry* his stallion up the gangway, a long cigar glowing half-smoked in his mouth. He had very little baggage apart from his beloved ammunition. He studied our baggage and smiled without making a fuss when Lord Byron produced three Homeric helmets which he had had made for himself, Trelawny and Pietro Gamba to wear on the landing in Hellas.

'I refuse to have anything to do with that,' he announced. 'What in the name of heaven made you spend money on such baubles!' The helmets were shiny gold and silver with red plumes.

Lord Byron looked at them with the expression of a man wandering in the forest and suddenly finding himself up to his waist out in a current. 'Hm,' he said. The helmets on blue velvet bedding lay between us, but we were all looking at each other, Trelawny in a leather waistcoat and shirt, brown skin and black hair protruding from it, Lord Byron in his worn little Gordon tartan jacket with gold buttons and I in my German hunting coat. And hair and hide; to the extent that we had not masked ourselves into personalities, life had done so. The vacuum is filled in, the meaninglessness becoming a quality. But disguise has a limit.

At our next attempt, our departure was successful. On the third day, the *Hercules* was towed out of Genoa harbour, slanting sun glowing in the windows on the long tongues of land, behind them the black mountains looming up to the still storm-worn skies. The waves struck us and I was uneasy, but Trelawny said conditions were almost perfect.

While the two boats were towing us out, we saw a little rowing boat flapping in our wash. Something that looked like prisoners in a cage was also flapping. We saw a silhouette rise, stagger and almost lose an oar. He shouted: 'I'll forward the letters . . . hullo?' Then he threw out his hands and yelled: 'But what do I do with the geese? The geese . . .'

With small manoeuvres, we followed the channel closest to the coast where a stretch of shore swings in and out under the protective wall of the Apennines. It was a July night and fishing boats were moving slowly in the heat like glow-worms over the fishing grounds, their stern lanterns forming a well of light, and the fish nosing there were speared. They catch everything in the Mediterranean, not just particularly tasty species as we do, but small fish that are hardly a mouthful and so aren't gutted before grilling, and they triumphantly hold up for sale abominable molluscs wriggling in their own slime!

We could also see colonies of lights on land. During the hottest time of year, people stay up far into the night to do what they haven't the energy to do in the daytime. Or live. Warning beacons were burning on peninsulas and further inland the changing of the guard on the fortress tower was taking place by torchlight. Last summer Trelawny had sailed up and down this stretch of coast on the yacht *Bolivar* and with nothing but darkness for guidance was able to point out Portofino and Viareggio, and more private places for recollection. 'Pah,' muttered Lord Byron, hidden on the other side of the tall figure. 'I built the *Bolivar* on your advice much too *expensively* (all those unique details you were to have, and cannons and copper keel), then sold it for a song. Never have I made such a bad bargain! I never set foot on the damned hulk myself, except four or five times, and of those twice when I used it as a bathing raft.' He leant round Trelawny and caught my eye with an amazingly jealous expression: 'Our Tre here is a great sailor (he says, anyhow) and an even greater duper. Don't forget that! He persuaded me I wanted to play with boats in the summer. And got himself a boat to play with.'

It was not good-humoured. I was embarrassed but Trelawny smiled like a beloved child who has just been flattered. 'I'm a poor man in much too good company,' he smiled round his dying cigar so that it rose, the glow drawing two lines through the darkness; as it rose and sank again, the tip of the cigar glistened as he polished it with his tongue.

La Spezia. *La Notte.* Snow, my mind said as I opened my eyes and saw sand, limestone and salt shining where the waves were breaking. It soon changed its mind and leant eye to ear: 'Tell me, Tre, this stretch of coast – has it never struck you that in itself, it is sad and sorrowful?'

'Nature is never sorrowful, Milord. That is the spectator, reminded of something and colouring the area with his mood, and then every time he returns to it, *that*'s what he sees first.'

'What you say is wise but not true . . .' Lord Byron studied a drink Trelawny had mixed for him. 'Is this just water?' 'That's why you're so moderate, Milord.' Trelawny checked him, gently.

My attention went on wandering between these friends who could have exchanged bodies or souls. Why do I say that? Certainly because I am banal and have always believed that form must confirm its essence. The poet's soul should have had space like Trelawny's body (which almost carried his stallion up the gangway; whose sense of himself is a melancholy weight at every step). I am not alone in this banality. Lord Byron himself had fomented it when he wrote his oriental tales and let his voice come from heroes resembling Trelawny. Anyone who feels strongly should do so proudly with his skin, with his height, as a cat rules over the grass. He ought to cry hunger and satisfaction with his muscle. Lord Byron was wretchedly thin at this time (in England, on the other hand, rumour had it that he was grotesquely fat and had to support his swollen legs with elastic stockings!). He was small and looked smaller because his clothes hung on him like slack banners, his hair already greying and too thin to be as long as he wore it, his hands in gloves chewed to rags toying wearily with a child's little dog-whip. When I thought about his writing, about everything he had overcome, the words, the thunder and the rumours, it added up to Trelawny. Did it have to? Only his smile was still magnificent.

'. . . sorrowful,' he said. 'The white sand. The small bluish-green thistles. The rivers that once sprang out of the rocks of the Alps and here flow like sluggish tame canals. There was melancholy here long before you and I saw Elba, before these waters drowned Shelley.'

Lerici. A cliff above the caves. A waterlogged house. A story half-whispered: 'Shelley bathed here every morning, naked among the inhabitants of the village patching their nets or hauling up boats or collecting whatever village people collect along the edge of the water. What a sight! A large, ugly, knobbly Englishman, who didn't even swim but paddled peacefully at the water's edge, now and again bending down to admire a pink shell or – tenderly – the jelly-fish that had stung his toe. The villagers interpreted this naked innocence as an expression of religious mania. They were presumably right. Not even young girls were forbidden to watch him. He revealed nothing of manhood.

(I remembered Shelley's widow in that indescribable kitchen, her small square hands washing dishes, the downy lines round her eyes expressing dismissive irony without words. Yes, there were words there when it came to 'Albé, unfortunately he is in a position to entertain real admiration only for poetry inferior to his own, Scott, Rogers, Moore, the kind that can be *set to music* . . .' I turned round to test out that judgement against his face. 'Keats bored him,' the echo of Mary Shelley's voice continued, 'which says everything about his judgement, for Keats was the greatest poet of our time. Shelley never hesitated about that for one moment. Albé, however, always prefers a joke to a truth. His final judgement on poor Keats was that he was the only poet who had died of a bad review, when everyone knows that the whole Keats family – one after the other – have died and are dying of the same consumption. Concerning Shelley's best works, he has surely not been able to bring himself to study them, although he has always said he had read them. Albé wants to be amused, not elevated by others.')

Lord Byron did not change position, but went on looking in towards the caves where the wind turned as if in deep bottlenecks. He went on whispering, half-whispering: 'Shelley was convinced of the *innocence* of the uncorrupted being. There's nothing I distrust more. The first experiences you have in life make all further innocence *conscious.*'

I can't see where guilt comes from in the universe of such people. Where does it come from?

I can't understand his poses or poetry at all.

His anemone Mary was indignant about the nude bathing, ashamed. She suffered when he bent down for a pink shell and in exchange offered the world a view of his. I remember criticising her narrow-mindedness then. If she had chosen to live with – or for – a man who had made it a principle of his life to break all rules he happened to catch sight of, then she couldn't expect it all to happen in rhyme or pamphlets. He had to show the shell as well. Now I have understood that a woman with liberated views in the end needs a tidy life. Sooner or later, everyone needs the feeling that nothing unforeseen can happen. Shelley did not understand her. He said she was cold, and yet she had sacrificed three children to his vegetarian principles, thin little wretches with an unhealthy colour, who died when it grew a little too warm outside. Shelley didn't understand her. He thought she had grown cold. 'I would like to kiss your mouth,' he said instead to Jane Williams, who was easy-going. But what's that got to do with Man and Nature? He couldn't believe human culture is a part of human nature, nor did it occur to him that a displacement in the household would do any harm. After all, it was only 'love'. Which is always healthy? I would like to kiss Your mouth. Perhaps he was innocent after all. The only innocent in the world?

It took us four days and five nights to get from Genoa to Livorno. One morning the long glittering procession of the *Hercules* drew into the great harbour. Everywhere, the ocean-going ships were at rest, at buoys, at poles, at crowded quays. I think of meteors, or animals in the jungle, when I see them, small modest bodies – when they are somewhere else from where they are supposed to be, they lose their colour and shape. Meteors flare only in the heavens, an exotic animal when it wades in the glade where the green river evaporates dusty sunlight. Ships on the sea.

People of all colours were on trapezes mending all those small tame monsters that overwhelm storms. Negroes shouted and gestured at Trelawny's groom, himself a Negro from the Antilles, though he would never go back. All the ships were grey from their privations on the high seas, their eyes closed as if in sleep. Black men perched on trapezes painting blue eyes on the outsides.

In the harbour waters, everything was rippling in reverse, the hulls, the small white clouds, the puffs of smoke as a Greek frigate began saluting the *Hercules* and her passengers.

We stopped for two whole days. Livorno was the best loading harbour on the west coast, so most of our military supplies were waiting there. We also took the opportunity to repair the horses' stalls properly, and while we stayed there, a large sack of mail arrived, forwarded from Genoa. When it was emptied, there was something for everyone and they all retreated to read and quickly write an answer before the sack went back. All except L.B. He had received a goodly heap of letters and small packets, but did hardly more than glance quickly at the various senders' names before pushing them all aside and coming over to stare jealously at the rest of us. This was the first time I was to experience his unreasonable side, and it made me wonder why he ever left England, for his mood was totally dependent on his friends back at home. Nothing could make him as miserable as the suspicion that he had been forgotten. He refused to listen to reason, but was hurt when people he had lived apart from for years wrote letters which showed them to be ignorant of his everyday existence in Genoa, in Cephalonia, in Missolonghi. To be a friend of Byron's seemed occasionally to presume that you lived in his pocket. Now I'm being unjust. He was exactly the opposite – though also just as he was now: he had hoped for a letter from someone on the Committee, naturally preferably from one of his friends, but he had hoped too much. Again! Did we know he hadn't had a word from any of the people responsible since April? They clearly considered he had arranged things for a pleasure cruise for himself! You could see just how much they valued him – men who had themselves urged him to go to Greece! As a political tourist presumably.

All day he poisoned himself with his displeasure, growing more swollen and darker ('a lame poet is of less use in war than a leprous baker!'), subjecting himself to his mood and trying to make the rest of us sing in chorus: did we all now see what our efforts were worth? Was it worth it? Oughtn't we to disperse and each one of us return to our own instead of getting in the way of the Greek freedom fighters who had a serious job to do? Naturally he would personally repay any expenses we had incurred. In two or three months, he had written to the Committee and accounted for requirements knowledgeable people had repeated to him over and over again: light artillery (transportable in rugged mountain terrain) and all kinds of medical supplies. Letters and requisitions in great numbers and no answers, far less confirmations. If they were indifferent to him personally, then they could at least confirm requisitions to his banker. If they couldn't be bothered to write to him, they could in that case let someone they respected know. If they didn't want to send what he requested, they could anyhow refrain from insulting the Cause by forcing on it shiploads of bibles and trumpets. Bibles and trumpets! They treated him like a naive idealist or an adventurer. They knew him, and should

466

know that he was neither. Hobhouse – his oldest friend and travelling companion. Treating him like an idealist! Why had he ever listened to them? Why had he ever opened his mouth? Why do you open your mouth to speak? Why do you open your mouth at all to breathe when you're born? (And so on.)

I was the only one to take his outburst seriously. Trelawny shrugged his shoulders and climbed over on to another boat on which he had seen an acquaintance. Pietro Gamba had just written a long letter to his sister and asked Byron if he wanted to add a few lines at the end (implied – to the woman who had shared four years of his life and was sure to be looking forward to some sign of life. Presuming that he himself wished to . . .) and L.B. said, Yes, yes and absently scribbled something down: my treasure, as Pierino is sure to have told you, we are in Livorno after a tolerable journey and all well and in good heart. No time to write any more as we are soon to cast off, but kiss Papa and Laurina from me. Yours for ever, Noel Byron.

We took on board all kinds of provisions and equipment according to a list composed by several people, and with a degree of detail and complication I could never have guessed or invented. We took on board special ammunition. We took on board two Greeks from the frigate that had saluted us. They wanted to join the campaign but were hardly out of earshot of each other before they started backbiting, one telling us the other had been a spy for the Russians, the other revealing what the first had been paid as a spy for the Turks. Both said that the *Hercules* and her crew were to be annihilated a hand's-breadth inside the Ionian island world. It didn't matter that those islands were British for the time being, for the Turks would not tolerate our presence. We took on board boxes of books. Trelawny's friend appeared with the first part of Las Cases's *Mémorial de Sainte-Hélène* and that improved Byron's temper. He also received several letters and a small packet he forgot to open.

The next morning we were rowed ashore. From the tower, in quarantine, we looked out over the harbour. Hundreds of masts heaving as if by a flock of lancers, by their slow breathing from end to end.

The morning crumbled away before my eyes: the masts had to become something sharp, a lance: a thousand lances rocking, venturing towards a blue enamel sky like a picture of . . . a picture of –

467

Then we climbed down from our survey and came to the alleys at the harbour level of cargoes and stores. Heaps of cargo, houses of cargo, people shrieking in your face to inform someone far behind you. That's what they did. Thoughtlessness and timelessness formed a roof high above people tramping around down there, high above seamen left behind, above deserters, above beggars bumping into us. They saw nothing at all, staring ahead for some uncertain agreement with the future. L.B. stared back. The sun shone through the cracks in the landing stage and lit up the water full of fry in pale yellow stripes. We stood above the reflection in the water at the edge of the landing stage and looked up into our nostrils, dignified small darknesses.

Back on the schooner, an invitation to the American man-of-war *Philadelphia* awaited us, a sloop lying ready to row us over. As eight sailors rowed, the young officer told us that the captain of the *Philadelphia* was a particular admirer of the poet and considered it not only an honour but a highpoint in his life to be allowed to meet the creator of 'etcetera', as Byron surreptitiously summarised the rest of the harangue for those sitting nearest to him. 'My grandfather was an admiral in the British Royal Navy,' he said loudly. The officer looked confused, like a man who has come to the end of his instructions for use but had not been able to get the manikin to function. On the way up the side of the *Philadelphia*, I worried whether the captain would mistake Trelawny, who had climbed up first, for Lord Byron, who was following more cautiously. But the captain took the right hand. It doesn't have to correspond – soul and body. The soul also has a given *milieu* in which it provides itself and its shell with a brilliant tail, a colour, a rigging. And a captain who sails the high seas always sees the little grey boats in harbour, their masts bare.

Parade. Military honours. Commands slicing this way and that, boots stamping down in unison, soles sliding round a half-turn. The soldiers had the long backs of their necks shaven, but were otherwise very unkempt, worse than our English soldiers. To Lord Byron, they might have been angels. He swallowed and turned pale, briskly moved along their lines. He flushed when the captain addressed him as one of the greatest writers of our day and now also 'a man of action'. He *burned* when a group of officers sat down round him and went on congratulating him for this decision, for then he was making an effort to give the praise a striking balance in which all that matters is patience

468

and courage. They said the whole port had been talking of nothing else but his arrival for days on end, and had *waited*. Then we drank arrack out of thin glasses: when the sun managed to penetrate a chink through the dim light of the mess, it played on eight golden spheres swimming to meet each other for the first toast. Lord Byron flushed with pleasure. How I liked him! He accepted all this goodwill as long as he thirsted for it and handed back the rest. 'I don't know,' he said. And that was no false modesty.

He didn't know all that much about those great words Writing and Action. He thought that all their lives, people (those who neither 'write' nor 'act') try to avoid the deadly seriousness in the one by allowing themselves to be drawn towards the other. For him 'writing' and 'action' were two shadow-words, below which he stood – sometimes. He could not embrace them into his person. He couldn't even represent the concept of them, no more than anyone else present there. He, too, could only milk their shadows.

And as he said it, his cheeks still red and eyes brightly searching for words in the darkness, they all understood that he meant it and that it was true. He had both done and invented things the value of which he himself had estimated. But then he had become famous, and the fame had also blown up 'all the worthless things I have done'. Sometimes he could make neither head nor tail of that balloon. Only in his own estimation could a human being be true and sympathetic. Any man devoting himself to fame rattled in its emptiness. 'I know, because I have lived like that.'

How I liked him that afternoon, the hyperboles in his dejection transformed into reasonableness when he was surrounded. And then when they rowed us back, the harbour echoed with more hyperboles as he praised the United States of America and promised to emigrate there (or to Venezuela) when he had done what he now first had to do. Then more reasonableness: two American officers said that several quick successes on our side would clear western Greece of the Ottoman within a year or two. They mentioned semi-abandoned forts and sleepy Turks combing their moustaches along the Bay of Patras. They had recently been to Hellas.

'Ah, but you know,' said Lord Byron, 'they are patient and enduring, even if they aren't energetic. I think they'll return year after year, even if they're defeated a few times. Nothing is ever considered *settled* in the Levant. "The end" is our invention, you know.'

469

After a few more gallant exaggerations while parting from his young admirers, with heavy eyes he smiled silently at the eldest of them. Back on the *Hercules*, he at last opened the little packet and found a letter from an American who had visited Goethe in Weimar, and a few verses, a dedication by Goethe himself:

Ein freundlich Wort kommt eines nach dem andern
Von Süden her und bringt uns frohe Stunden;
Es ruft uns auf zum Edelsten zu wandern,
Nie ist der Geist, doch ist der Fuss gebunden.

Wie soll ich dem, den ich so lang begleitet,
Nun etwas Traulich's in die Ferne sagen?
Ihm der sich selbst im Innersten bestreitet,
Stark angewohnt das tiefste Weh zu tragen.

Wohl sey ihm doch, wenn er sich selbst empfindet:
Er wage selbst sich hoch beglückt zu nennen,
Wenn Musenkraft die Schmerzen überwindet,
Und wie ich ihn erkannt, mög' er sich kennen.

One man in the crew developed a fever just outside Livorno. Perhaps he had concealed it in port so as not to be left behind, and in that deception had been helped by a well-meaning but foolish comrade. At first, Dr Bruno said sunstroke, then some kind of inflammation and prescribed castor oil, bark and blood-letting. That made the man worse. The well-meaning friend refused to have him below deck, but carried him up and laid him in a kind of open shed for which there is sure to be some nautical term. There he became more and more vociferous, a torment to all. Finally, his misery became everything and the only thing. They wanted him to stop his excruciating breathing, which was worse than his lamentations, for it was regular and never took a rest. Hour after hour. Day and night, they listened to him groaning for air, the sound folding the journey into a pocket, a back pocket in which only he existed.

The wind also dropped, pallid beneath the yellow mist. An almost biblical bank of storm clouds climbed up on the horizon, flecked with sun, outlined with golden edges. More and more sea birds came in to rest in the layers of air above the *Hercules*. If you looked across the water, you could follow the circles in the water, slowly playing out from the boat, as if just dropped from the sky.

If we had been on the open sea, he would certainly have died and been buried there. But we had land in sight almost constantly and that seemed to keep him alive, that and Dr Bruno's efforts, which were helped by a great interest in *sickness* in which Trelawny and L.B. were surprisingly united. Both passed the time nursing. Softly, like very sharp knives, they looked into the sick man's eyes. They opened his clothes and looked at a body where everything seemed hopeless, apart from lice nourishing themselves on it. They gave him laudanum from their own supply and felt him, respectfully, as if he were about to give birth, not die.

It was a bad omen for the campaign and the Greek 'spies' took every opportunity to remind them of it. 'But were you thinking of conducting a war with no sickness or death?' L.B.'s eyes widened after reducing them to silence. Finally he cried: 'What do you really want me to do? Murder the man in his bed?'

I, who hadn't said a word, was caught out. For that was precisely what I wanted him to do, to put an end to the torment, the suffering and the wheezing rattling. I turned away. My most beloved pets, all my life, rose before my eyes: those I had put out of their misery as soon as they had fallen sick. They had looked at me as if seeking help and had at once received help, with no mention of any other way out. My love died in face of their suffering, and revived full of regrets when they were dead.

I leant over the side of the *Hercules* and allowed my pangs of conscience to follow my gaze as far down into the depths as they would go. They hung there, fishing. How otherwise can I describe self-knowledge?

Absorbed in this way, I failed to notice how the quarrel arose, but woke up in the middle of it. Voices soared in strength and falsetto, as they do in the south, as when a door blows open. The cause seemed to be that as we passed between Capri and the mainland, Dr Bruno suggested we should make another attempt to put the patient ashore, this time because of the risk of infection. Earlier diagnoses had not mentioned infection; on the contrary. Furious men now crowded round the young doctor, who flushed and shouted incoherent replies, leaning backwards as if he had a swarm of wasps nailed under his nose. The shouting included 'idiot', 'murderer', 'bungler' and 'wife and children' in several languages. The poor doctor was very young and new to his profession. He had an extremely unpleasant moment before Lord Byron came to his rescue and ordered the men to disperse and get on with their tasks. I don't know how he managed it, for his exterior did not impress other fully grown men, and they were indifferent to his rank and birth. Perhaps it was the expression on his face, the profoundest weariness.

(I loathe not being able to sleep. I keep falling asleep. I doze off at any moment. If I lie down, I am lost, dreaming a few scales and then chasing back up into life, of which I've lost a minute or two. What is amazing is waking. Death has an immeasurable craving you give way to, more and more, dozing off into it at any moment. Waking up is a miracle.)

'I never said it *is* infectious, only that as things have developed, an infectious illness *might* arise,' Dr Bruno said, changing his mind, groaning behind his employer's back, tormented by these men digging out the crudest truth from sophisticated medical alternatives.

It was late afternoon, an island like a black saddle on the horizon to the south-west, a precipitous peninsula to the east. In between, the *Hercules* on a course due south, her deck full of Englishmen, Italians, Greeks and a Negro. Some hopping with rage. Their heads hit the sky, which shudders and starts shimmering. A key is taken from its keyhole. The first star is high in the sky, pale blue like a drowsy eye. The next star wakes, then the next, then ten, then a thousand, and a ribbon inexhaustibly pulsates light to the earth. When the night is quite black, the stars are wide awake. The boat's course is now due east, the anger on deck subsided, having said what it had to say, and the voices subsiding, too, suddenly, as they do in the south. At first we try to go into Positano and hours go by while we negotiate with pilots and quarantine, though we are rejected nonetheless. So we go on to Amalfi.

I still have a stone from that remarkable city. It is flat and square with nothing but grainy grey lava on the back. Otherwise it is covered with glaze, white with green squares and nerves, emerald green. It is almost midnight as we climb down the side of the *Hercules* and are given a helping hand by the oarsmen who are to take us ashore. The sick man is hoisted down, suddenly better now he has emerged into darkness and fresh air. Quietly, he named a number of saints and the Virgin Mary, looking from one face to another. He also mentions his wife and children. 'Calm yourself, my friend, you'll soon be back with them,' says Lord Byron, assuring him the same when the man asks him if he really believes it. A confirming nod from Dr Bruno convinces him that they have all knowledge of his life and death at their disposal, and he relaxes.

After a moment's rowing, a large wave comes and takes us on its back. I am sitting in the front of the boat and hold on, watching the steps and towers of the city stumbling towards us. It goes very quickly, the wave retrieving its waters and almost grounding us. I expect us to be washed over as it comes back, but that doesn't happen, the force of the water landing in a cave where it resounds all night like seven hungry wolves. I find the stone. We are helped to get the stretcher up on a cart. The mule is harnessed and Dr Bruno gets up on the back as if on to a load of hay.

It must be a feast day in Amalfi, for the girls have their best lace on their heads and corals as big as pigeon eggs dangling round their necks. We sit half the night on steps that raise the cathedral steeply up above the market square. Well, naturally at first we go up to the top and offer a gift and light a candle, though we do not belong to the religion. We behold the holy finger in the case of relics. We see a withered, almost mummified saint in bridal finery. A moment of stillness tells us that this sight, alien and frightening (and comical) to us, is sacred ordinariness to others. Lord Byron whispers to me that these people are *wise*, for they don't believe in God, but in religion. I myself have my piety elsewhere and look up at the narrow arches, where whisperings turn and come back to my other ear almost simultaneously. All the mosaic reflects the green of the stone I have found. I squeeze it in my pocket with a feeling of being the person who has found what other people have long sought.

We are tourists in Amalfi, just as Goethe was forty years ago. We sit half the night on the high steep steps and talk about him. Lord Byron takes the little poem dedicated from Weimar out of his pocket and asks me to translate it as best I can.

Lord Byron leans his head against his shoulder while I translate the verses in which Goethe says he has long followed him and seen him denying himself in the depths; Goethe also says he perceives great pain, the energy of which the poem overcomes by making use of it. And he wishes Lord Byron could know himself as he knows him. Goethe is warm and gentle and manly. But Byron smiles at the thought of pain being converted into poetry. 'It'd be a wretched poem. I have always written thoughts and images. Certainly not "pain", good heavens.' The stars twinkle grandly. The constant sound of relief as the sea moves ashore. We go up a single cramped street and think we recognise a booth where they sell fine glass to tourists, also a tankard of Bohemian ruby glass, Bohemia and Saxony. Jena and Weimar. Lord Byron calls Goethe the greatest man of his day, the greatest since Shakespeare. It is no original thought among thinkers. Both names roll clumsily like triangles through all that is circular in the night. Corals tremble, Italian girls tremble one long heavy coral. In the square, an orchestra blows circular notes by Rossini. They rise up against the walls behind and grow up the steps where we are sitting, then on up over the sky and break, so that some reach the *Hercules* at anchor and she hears 'music?' And Dr Bruno on the back of the cart rocking up a Parsifal cliff so black it merges into the night – hears shreds of 'music?'

The steps are full of people. So is the square full of them. They go down for a stroll, to eat a pretzel, greet a neighbour in another way, offer the players wine and ask them to play another song about Catalin, about Margherita or Lucia or Gulnare. All the time we see figures moving around each other, a soft alternating flow, but not restless. Restful. Those sitting on the steps fan themselves and fan us, too. They talk to each other. We talk to each other and everything blends with everything else without intruding. Their voices and laughter touch us but we talk undisturbed, as do they. It is peace. Many are widows, other miseries they carry within them and outside them, but today is a feast day, because of the mummified saint – or whatever it is – and faint, oblivious moisture glistens on the downy upper lips of the young widows.

Lord Byron repeats that Goethe . . . after Shakespeare . . . He says that when sitting like this on steps among people eating pretzels, you don't have to be careful about using the word genius. It is true. What that word does to his mouth when he pronounces it is so amusing, I pretend not to have heard. He repeats it, with broad and pouting mouth. He says that sometimes a creature is born who is outstanding for ever, because he is outstanding in his day. Not as a result of natural gifts, more like Nature giving herself away – a few words beforehand – and letting people see into the future of heart and mind. He changes his mind: 'I seem to believe that the future will be wiser than our fathers . . .' He folds up the little poem from Weimar and puts it into his pocket. 'He wrote that to coffee and cognac. But it was kind of him, and a good omen for our journey, is it not?'

Then he listens with attention while I try, with hazy and far too many words, to explain what is inexplicably marvellous in the novel I love most, *Wilhelm Meisters Lehrjahre*, which is not created for coffee and cognac. The novel is as if all Goethe's body and soul and essence had cast impressions in word after word without flagging. Every quiver and every pain, yearning and calm, everything a human being can be, is transformed into narrative, characters, events. I talk of Goethe's breadth of empathy, which makes him give life to characters as if he hadn't *written* them but *given birth* to them, with characters which develop to his own surprise and joy.

I look into L.B.'s eyes, which are glowing (he is also listening to the music and his pupils adopt the beat of an overture) and seek in them confirmation of everything I am saying about the enchanted child Mignon – the little golden spark with black curls? About the complete sense of morning when Philine sticks her blonde head out of the window for the first time? Marianne's red belt? Love, so un-ambiguously sensual and yet so heartfelt, it worms its way into the reader's room? Or does he remember the long sequence about the need for compromises? When the theatre director slowly per-suades Wilhelm into recognising that the five-hour-long, hopeless reading-drama, *Hamlet*, can never be performed in an orthodox manner, but would have to be trimmed for theatre and audiences?

His eyes follow the music to its end, then follow a girl who has what he inevitably has become attached to, large black eyes. Finally he says conspiratorially: 'You know, I don't know any German. I haven't actually read what old Goethe has written. Except a few extracts from *Faust* Monk Lewis translated for me. In as much as Monk is a translator . . .' Why be astonished? In the warm darkness, a few steps above us, are two widows in violent disagreement. Some names, an occupation, fish-drying, a cultivation plot, the rights of three genera-tions, all penetrate into our conversation, and as ours is theoretical, we allow it to be interrupted by theirs, which we have to laugh at, because it is *brutally* materialistic. The warm darkness – it separates us and unites everything, it warms the widows, who consider Tancredi would be worth the eastern slope after twenty years, and la Amilia sticks to it out of pure obstinacy, even though it would be the death of her. He says: 'You take the most important decisions in life on ideas. Why can't you allow me to imagine the greatness of old Goethe, although I can't read him. You do nothing but *imagine* in your well-read monologue. The best and surest opinions are not underpinned but snapped up.'

'I never thought you were such an *Englishman*, Lord Byron!' I exclaim.

No one goes home. When the musicians take a rest, the children run down and do tricks and dance around with coiling black curls, like Mignon's, with uneven ingratiating blandishments, making themselves lovable to their audience. 'Like my poor Allegrina,' sighs Lord Byron but I am thinking about Mignon and see her in front of me, walking on her hands, cartwheeling easily, easily: a wheel with four spokes and eyes bottomless with memory. Glass music. And Mignon with her head on one side for coins. Like the monkey. 'My poor little . . .'

In the body, there is a sense of falling that does away with a sense of rising, and they make each other imperceptible. Life steadies itself ahead in the erosion between them. Sometimes the sense of climbing to cold exhilaration runs wild and rushes on upwards long after the steps have stopped.

And the fall can be free in slanting sleep, which instead of levelling out towards rest, increases speed to a dizzying careening just before the threshold of what in the anguish of waking you suspect to be death itself. You are so close to annihilation, you are constantly separated from it by a wall as thin as skin. It is only in the erosion between rising and falling that you repeat your life, repeating it and continuing it. When you have woken from a fall, you have to collect yourself for a long time before you regain calm. And it is as fragile as a badly thrown pot before our everyday grime grows over it and hides the secret crack.

East was behind us, a beautiful pale strip of light predicting the day. I turned round. What is most obvious appears in the shape of what is most mysterious – you can't stop a new day from coming. It grows. It grew slowly, beautifully, with new shades of blue and gold. The music had long since ceased. The inhabitants of Amalfi had made their way home. Trelawny said that in Africa, after they had all crept up on to their branches and into their caves, the nocturnal animals ruled with base calls and ugly bodies and unmentionable feeding habits. A flock of half-dressed youths raced down the Parsifal cliff, down the steps. Perhaps they had been among us all the time, swallowed by the crowd. Suddenly they stood out like resin torches in the desolate darkness, and hissed. They strode round in a strange dance of thorns, and all that had been so round that night became spiky. They hooted and laughed and *sliced* with their voices. One of them led the ritual – he ran around to hasten on the narrow segment of grey, which widened from the blows of his dirty foot as he danced and kicked.

'Money, coins, louis and paul,' he demanded. He stood astride the widening ravine, a caterpillar creeping into his eye. He came closer, but L.B. was not interested. 'Money! Coins! Louis and paul! Dollars!' He lunged out with his brown calf, but with no result. He shrieked like a bird at his friends, but they had stopped to watch.

Finally L.B. decided to look – slowly – at the arrogant and challenging figure standing there in all the youthfulness that no longer interested my friend. Youth no longer interested him, not the rebelliously arrogant. He said he could no longer stand tedious shrieking.

'Money! Coins! Louis and paul! Dollars! Pounds sterling!!' The caterpillar crawled out of the boy's eye, striped and hairy. He made a grimace that sliced his handsome Latin face in half with a knife. His tongue went out – swish swish – striped and hairy. We walked away. It wasn't interesting. It was no longer interesting. L.B. flung a few paul on to the steps. The boy turned them over with his toes, laughed scornfully and left them there. But two of his friends picked them up, Lord Byron noted. It wasn't interesting. It was no longer interesting.

A week after this, we saw we were nearing the Messina Straits. We were full of expectations – plus and minus: to circle Italy this time was the same as circling the moon. On the other side, the light would be different, would wind its way in an easterly undertaking reaching all the way *there*. We would no longer be protected by the barrier of Italy and all light-heartedness would be behind us.

477

Hot days had followed warm nights, and most on board were tormented by dirt and lice. They considered salt water too 'strong' for the human body – externally as well – preferring to leave their sweat and itching to ripen. The captain was the worst. Broad as two captains and with the seaman's dislike of all water, salt or fresh, inside or out, on principle, he constantly perspired new floods of beer and gin and rum into his gold-embroidered waistcoat, which was the pride of his heart but was now beginning to moulder on his body. One afternoon Trelawny asked to look closer at the handiwork; as he examined it, cries were heard in the rigging, and when the captain responded, L.B. and Trelawny put an arm each in the armholes and jumped into the sea.

Great God! Madmen! Currents and drifts.

'My God! Christ! Like two little rascals.' The captain and passengers and a courageous crewman left their posts and hung over the edge, staring open-mouthed at this baptism. At which two figures swam with one arm each and laughed and yelled and gulped water. A wave carried them far away – a defenceless twin; the heart trembled at the sight, two small heads imprisoned by the sucking movement away. Two waves and twenty strokes, a sudden collision within the water itself and they were back there in the shadow of the hull. Above them the surface of the water was green, satisfying the thirst of their bodies. That annoyed the captain so much, he flung a tankard of beer at them, although it wasn't finished. It hit Trelawny's hair, almost his head, and at 'God Almighty, if they hadn't got something down there that was his own property, then with good conscience he could have left them to the currents and the sharks, without a moment's regret, not *one*!' – the happy rascals were given help and climbed up. Lord Byron had the waistcoat and handed it back with the excuse: 'A little joke that may have done it good . . . my last boyish prank, Captain, what do you say?'

'I say,' growled the captain – having examined his garment and found it undamaged, his relief bringing back some of the polite tone of voice used to address an English peer of the realm – 'the fact that Captain Trelawny is a thoughtless oaf is his business. But one would think, My Lord! And then I was given that waistcoat by a certain lady in Southampton and I know her eyes would fill with tears if she knew the way You had just treated Her gift. And I do not know what will happen when the salt water has dried. But if it is ruined, do you undertake to

478

explain to her, My Lord, for she will feel insulted and hurt, considering that she had carried out that elegant work with her own little hands, sir.'

'Good gracious, Captain. If you restrict your beer ration, within a few months you'll fit into a waistcoat half the size,' snapped Trelawny. But Byron shook the captain's hand and bowed his head, like a schoolboy with orders to take the first step towards reconciliation. It was his last boyish prank. I know that. The captain stayed there with his hand full of excuses, looking at it. Within an hour the precious garment was dry again, except for patches of sweat from armhole to armhole.

Later I heard Trelawny say: 'My Lord, you are excellent company at sea.' Our wash lay like a shiny red train. A louse was born on the end of a hair, grew up the line and came to the root. And bit. It was late at night as I scratched the back of my neck and the first carapace crackled between my nails.

A group of islands lay diagonally ahead of us, an archipelago of shapes standing upright or resting, the upright isles the shape of craters. We sat nearly all night looking at Stromboli. The air blended warmth, heat and cool separately as coffee mixes unstirred cream, but our eyes were full of the pepper-flares of the crater. We sat nearly all night silently following the unique spectacle of the volcano. It was not the ferocity of it keeping us awake, but its regularity, the number of seconds passing between one exhalation and the next. You breathed in time with the volcano, or tried not to. You held your breath as the crescent moon slowly glided across, a chariot going backwards. The mountain was high and the darkness great, at the top a flame of gas hissing out of the mouth of the darkness. Someone had to say bah, of course; they had given him peperoni for dinner, and then suddenly Trelawny had to think the sparks down the mountainside must be molten lava hurtling wildly down. And Lord Byron, now no longer interested in youth, had to reply that it was only the lights in the houses – where fishermen were being woken to go to work. Trelawny said that it was quite definitely fierce and violent lava from the live volcano. And Byron said it was probably father and sons getting up and splashing their eyes with water, being given bread and dried fish and oil and wine to take with them, and, look there! now the boat lanterns are being lit, one by one. Convinced. Ill-humoured and for the moment convinced

479

of the tame and habitual, Trelawny anyhow went off and relieved himself over the edge. And spent a long moment trying to fill the sea.

II

We were losing all sense of time. We whiled away the time. As Loukas Chalandritsanos was running through the last gap in the reeds, he waved his shirt at us. We stood up to catch a last glimpse, and when he'd vanished, we turned slowly back to our waiting. A surrounded life is sleep. For two or three days, we didn't move from the spot.

A fish thrashed around on the end of a line, not once but several times, and you tensed to see if it would be landed. When I played dice with two crewmen with whom I couldn't exchange a word (the language), time and again the six came up on five dice. Below deck, Fletcher was resting comfortably after his fever, scratching himself with grunting pleasure along the lines of 'a bug in a rug'. Tall columns of mist came striding over the water, with no substance but with visible precipices against the mountainside. In a gap in all this greyness, Lord Byron was undressing to go swimming.

When he took off his stock pin, it slipped and he dropped it in the water, where it lay floating on top of the seaweed, his only birthday present from his wife the year they had lived together. The thought of her was a muscle without blood, but with strong sinew attachments. His mouth moved imploringly to make the floating fragment of porcelain stiffen into an image as he stretched out for it. The movements of the water were making the plants rustle, the seaweed caressing and preparing space for the article to sink. The memory of his wife had gathered into something pale and strong, and suddenly intimate: 'Get married later. And obey . . .' A cry from closed lips, he stretched out to reach it. The object was of thin porcelain, the gold

481

frame even thinner; perhaps it would sink slowly, but what happened was that he plucked seaweed. 'Ah,' he said.

In the gap between precipices, he stripped off all he had on above the waist. He looked round. He wished he could be naked. The water was friendly to him, always accepting him, in its superiority shaping itself around his limbs, but it soaked his clothes. It reflected his shadow. His face had aged. He had shrunk in his portrait like a sharp ghost, but his body was the same. He looked down the length of it, white there, here and there warnings usually creeping up on him when some self-inflicted ailment was about to begin. The rider's haemorrhoids. The traveller's swamp fever. All the resolute hyperboles had drawn his route on his face. He looked further down and thought about whether to will the whole lot to the water. There is always someone who learns to act insane, and some who let you do so.

He raised his eyes towards the grey sky for a moment and thought about rusty nails and red-hot iron, the cure for shameful infections. Five times, or so. The pain was of the kind that could hardly be felt when inflicted; it was too white, its rings chasing each other through the body, some lying in wait in a corner, as a reminder. Well, it would never happen again. For four years he had lived as unicorn to Teresa, and for six months now he had abstained, and had missed nothing – except the warm friendship which with luck can be special for lovers. He had thought the urge was inexhaustible, but the source was finite – you don't know it until dry grass starts growing in the bed of the old stream. He would return to his wife and she would prefer him like this.

Nor did this body of his want to remember sickness. He glimpsed his right foot behind the left, but pretended not to at this moment; that had also created lines in his face. When you travel and live abroad, all the ordinary fevers threaten your life. You reckon on something as you lie there. You climb up arms reached down to you. They try to jerk themselves free, worried about being dragged down when you think they can pull you up. One morning, you wake and have slept. The fever has gone as if it had never existed. Its bearing strength has gone, so you lie directly on the cold earth and can feel the stones beneath you.

Byron crept out through the tent opening late one morning in his twenty-second year. They had erected the tent near the town of Tripolitza, but who can remember when. At first he had nursed someone else with fever for a week, then time had swum together into one spot. Fletcher clapped his hands with delight to see him struggling back up to Health. Byron put his hand to his eyes, for the light was strong, drank deeply of the tepid water, then sat down to look. To the north, a wreath of mountains, in front of them a swamp, no doubt the origins of it all. The birds ate the frogs, the frogs ate the mosquitoes, but there were always plenty left. In front of the swamp, four horses and a couple of donkeys were grazing, long sweeping bunches of horsehair ceaselessly brushing away the mosquitoes, helping each other by standing close together, head to hindquarters. From Tripolitza, someone came on the back of a donkey, Niccólo, whom he had nursed to health and whose arms he had climbed on when Niccólo had nursed him, coming from town with necessities. Or was it Euthanasiou? Euthanasiou! But how! Fletcher dived impotently into the tent, talking aloud to himself about not having a say in the company his master was pleased to keep!

The boy waved from a distance, calling out how contento, contento he was to see Mio Viron on his feet again. Hurrah, hurrah. On his knees. When Byron tried to get up, his legs slid against each other with eight, ten joints. He was on his knees to Euthanasiou, who circled round barebacked on his donkey, two large water canisters in front of him, the water clucking metallically. The boy was wearing a little loin-cloth that did not hide the curly hair in his groin. He had taken off the cap that had previously packed in his torrent of hair, long yellow curls sweating a warm glow down his bare back; he shook them out, delighted at the joke of being a pretty and breastless mademoiselle. This equipage was topped by Fletcher's umbrella, open to protect Euthanasiou's skin from the rays of the sun. Byron closed his eyes and opened them. Death is a semi-naked boy of seventeen. On a donkey. With hair hanging loose and a black umbrella. 'How good to see you are better, *mio Viron*. We work, though the whole world, like brothers, goes on turning? You save my life and I yours in ten nights! We'll never be parted?'

But all these minor matters have left traces in his face. His body was saving itself for something more conclusive. He looked down at himself and a thought occurred to him that cannot be truly concluded. Not even the most profound stillness in the living can be compared with death. It is on the other side of a threshold of energy, which is the

483

last thing a man gives of himself, even when he no longer believes he possesses it. All living stillness possesses it.

He swam in grey chilly water at the foot of the cliff and mist and heard the sounds of water echoing in the ravine. Deep down below him, there was a glimmer, not of fish or the bladder out of the fish's mouth, but of gold. As he dived, he stirred up the water so the clasp fell deeper, in the end down into the crack between great stones. A last reflection in his eye reminded him of the picture – he had never thought of it before. He had seen the original on a Greek vase, of a woman sitting on a bench and in vain trying to reach the hand stretching out for her. It was of Eurydice. The water down there settled as the fishing hand was withdrawn. So many sidetracks assembled towards the highway. Omen after omen.

After a few days, we sighted two brigs from Spetzai, and as they came closer, we saw Loukas running back and forth on one of them. Our escort had arrived. The boats looked small, their bowsprits protruding behind small rocks, which then turned out to be huge blocks of stone, offspring of the wall of the laguna protecting us. We were immeasurably small in this confusion of cliffs and stele, in which every manoeuvre was almost soundless. Small reed-covered lagoons opened out, in the middle an island aground, some drawn-up rowing boats, a couple of olive trees and a monastery. The water was green, almost yellow where the muddy sandbanks close below the surface followed the line of an old current. Monks were digging a hole, shading their eyes as they gazed after us, our bowsprits making holes in the mist, drawing with them the mist like skin on boiled milk, and above the sky was blue, flown over by clouds on their way north.

Loukas immediately climbed down into the mistico and unburdened himself of all his news at once, like a dog being sick. He was made to say it all over again.

He had got to Missolonghi without any difficulty. Once he had met some shepherds who had told him of a lone lame wolf roaming around at lambing – all have to live. Once Loukas had lain down in tall grass because at a distance he had seen a mounted troop, but couldn't see which army. He was eventually *woken* in the grass by two girls sitting over him, poking him and laughing and laughing. He would rather have met the whole of the Ottoman army! In Missolonghi, Colonel Stanhope had at once received him and had run with him to the harbour in his eagerness to arrange for the escort without delay. There they also heard that the bombarda had been forced into Patras harbour, but – listen now – she was already on her way to Missolonghi because it turned out that her captain had once saved the life of the Turkish commander in Patras! As a debt of honour of that kind had to be repaid, the boat and her cargo and crew, unscathed, were heading for the same harbour as they were themselves!

Lord Byron's face twitched during the course of the story. At every happy chance, he breathed 'ah' with relief, but at the same time his anxiety seemed to increase for every bit of 'luck'. He used to say he detested 'luck'. He said he preferred it when success bears its own costs. Many lucky chances scoop a large hole in the future, where 'bad luck' balances out. He wanted to know the price. He didn't think 'luck' was free.

Such superstition – as if human lives were each weighed on scales! He explained it to those of us who understood English, in interrupted sentences, while we all helped to keep track of the various elements. He could have raised his eyes. Wherever you saw a house on the mountainside, you also saw ruins caused by earthquakes – or fire, or perhaps some poor devil had abandoned his home, or a whole family had died out. The olive trees wound their roots deep down into the poor soil, embracing the stones below. They say it takes twenty-five years before a tree of that kind bears fruit. Shepherds with crosiers as sinewy as the trees themselves. Black eyes, shallow and turned to stone, they had never seen anything but this bay, its precipices and shards a mere passing impression for Englishmen. He changed the subject to a sudden outburst of delight over 'not having changed clothes for a week!' Herds of sheep and goats billowed over the plain where they found every stem of grass wedged under a stone. 'I've never felt better!' I had never seen a large pit of bad luck later filled with good luck to make up for it.

And yet Lord Byron's theory was almost immediately given substance. We came back to open water, were dazzled, received a huge gust against us and before anyone had time to do anything, we swung round almost a half-turn, the clouds racing northwards, the waves racing in that crafty way they do in a rocky bay. There was a sudden waft of the smell of salt and we saw the brigs slicing out of the depths. After a moment of tramping and stamping, the sister-ship also filled her breast and started roly-polying over the swell, and it was not long before we were in distress. The mistico lay, half-lay, helplessly close to a jagged shore, each wave driving her closer and closer. We crept round, some falling silent in panic, others screaming and trying to help manoeuvre, but the passengers knew almost nothing about boats. The waves seemed like brutal blows to the body– no, like falls from a great height. The faces. We sought help from others seeking help, grimacing mutely.

Memories are images and smells rising up through each other, a flood out of a cave, the most recent thrust dispersing the last and allowing it to sink away in the marshy ground round about. There is no chronology here. Everything now seems random, so I remember nothing of the course of events except spurts of those unreal faces and vainly flapping sails. Wave for wave, in the end the air itself was sliced and sobbing. Then it happened. Four or five voices assembled into a sound that meant 'Now!' and as slowly as she heeled over, suddenly the boat tipped back on to an even keel. The first sensation was that there had been an accident, for the blow had been so terrible, someone hurtling overboard and a cascade of dirt, foam and water flung down out of the sails. But then we saw her steer her way out, with crestfallen stillness, behaving like a boat again. The feeling of great unhappiness was lost as quickly as if we had been animals with no awareness of death. A subdued smile was all.

The brig that had swerved to assist us, tacked along and kept an eye on her sister quivering there on the wave. She struggled up, moved uneasily up there, then thumped down, then it happened again – a valley of wave caught her, became aware of her helplessness and shot her a long stretch sideways before forcing her down to one side.

This time there was no question of silent cries or mute prayers. Experience gave voice to itself. We cut through the roaring of the storm, accepting the blows on our bodies as if in passing. Lyon barked hoarsely and patiently every time he scrambled back after a wave had flung him from his dry patch. 'Loukas!' called Lord Byron. 'Loukas, be quiet and listen to me. I can save you. If we have to abandon ship, then stay close to me, because I've often swum in waves like these and can easily take you to safety. But you must be still and not struggle against it.' Foam flapped by his glowing eyes as he kept repeating this. 'No, no,' shrieked Dr Bruno. 'Save me instead. My God, let me live, my God! I must be helped first, if I can!' We couldn't help laughing at him, clutching at the mast and slipping on boards the salt had turned to slime. We laughed wildly at the most obvious and innocent egoism we had ever heard. Anyone who had lived even slightly less long has such absolute precedence to life, whether only about a year, or two. It was not idealism, even in this reality, that was so. Or was it just that Dr Bruno possessed awareness of death?

For the second time, the crew managed to right the boat and at the last moment fend off the rocky shore. Lyon barked like one possessed. 'We all ought to change craft,' shrieked Dr Bruno, making a funnel with his hands. 'Ahoy' in a headwind came into his eyes. He rubbed them. 'Tell me, My Lord . . .' Both brigs were cruising impatiently, to starboard and to port, like dancing teachers to their ugly sisters. We plunged on. Then it grew calm. Storms test patience and endurance, then they have gone.

Then they have gone. With one single sweep, the waters opened, what had flown and flapped lay down. Everything became a Holland, the water straining up from dark landlock. To the south the snow-covered mountains, to the north again the stony mountains and the long flat shore. Missolonghi lay deep in the lagoon, at the level of the surface of the water.

III

On the sixteenth of February, we were at a meeting no one had called. It just happened.

The lower floor had at last been cleared and no more sounds came from the upper floor. Dr Bruno said his patient had managed to sleep for a while, so we all lowered our voices as soon as anyone raised his, and the 'anyone' was usually Major Parry. We had very little to say to each other. When our eyes met, they turned away, for within them there was no longer the friend on the same level, but a kind of emptiness – the kind that arises in social life when the host leaves the room and silence spreads among the guests, whose illusion of friendship he alone had inspired.

Colonel Stanhope said: 'Of course we feel disorientated today, but there's no reason why we shouldn't be quite collected tomorrow. His importance to the Cause is primarily of a symbolic nature. His name. His health (we will do all we can to ensure he will regain it) is not of total significance, not necessarily. He has no military experience and his political schooling is non-existent. I would be the first to acknowledge his reputation, his nimbus, his personal charm, but neither personality nor luck will decide the destiny of the Greek People. What is required is a great many years' patient work. Studies, time wasted, blood shed. In this respect, it doesn't matter whether he is here or whether he returns to a civilisation better suited to his vulnerable nature.'

He repeated the same thing in different words several times, deliberate defamation, but we couldn't bring ourselves to dispute it. We just listened and remained seated out of some tacit duty to remain

488

together and subdue the sense of collapse that exists in a fruit with no core. The emotion was what was reality, what made sense. What Stanhope had to say we knew perfectly well ourselves. Some people can't help instructing others on eternal truths even when they are least valid.

'Listen to him!' growled Parry. 'God in heaven, or hell, man, must you produce poisoned kindnesses when our friend is lying there defenceless! Sir! If you hadn't gone on tormenting him with your damned newspapers and leaders and freedom of the press and Sunday schools, then he would never have – ' 'Ssh, my dear Major,' said Pietro Gamba, and Parry chose to be silent instead of speaking more quietly. His unspoken opinion won most of us over. Stanhope's uniform was grey. We were of blood royal.

We had our overcoats on, for houses in Missolonghi had no chimneys. Anyone reared in a country where the simplest dwelling is built like a cross round a chimney stack scarcely notices the lack of one until someone says: 'You know, there's no fireplace here. They're content to endure when it's cold.' It was colder indoors than out. From the wall bench I was sharing with Parry and Gamba, we could see the window-pane streaky with rain, and through the streaks we could see semi-dusk or semi-daylight, daylight if you were good-humoured. A cloud that had besieged Missolonghi for weeks allowed neither night nor day to be manifested on earth. More rain from the west satiated the cloud every time it rained and made it so fat and wet, it could capture darkness and light and spread them within itself, rather like a misty moonstone.

How can you describe the kind of rain that fell in Missolonghi? It woke you and put you to sleep, not differentiating between night and day, nor day and night, stopping everything, filling ears, nose and mouth and mould blossoming on boots and harness. It could be a little better at night.

Then the cloud lifted slightly, the barometer trembling off its bottom layer. You could see open water and one night the cloud glowed moonstones in *colour* as a thunderstorm strayed into it. Green marble and red tears. I stood on a roof and watched it.

Three boats sailed in during this suffocating time, swelling broadside on, far away like model boats on a pool; exquisitely shaped, every detail clear in the silent steaming light: 'Look at that, damn it, the

489

lightning struck her,' said Parry, taking a gulp straight out of his flask. It was peculiar. The boat was in the middle of the channel together with two others on course for Patras, moonstone flaring above them, the lightning racing and losing itself, as when you are robbed of a mouthful of air. It struck round the boats, then suddenly stepped down and slowly touched a mast, paying its respects. 'Look at that, damn it, the lightning struck her,' said Parry. We were the only spectators. We saw the fire licking a deep blue membrane down the whole mast and then retreating back up to the top in order to burn. A mast-top fell from its post and the first sail caught fire. Parry handed me his brandy flask and I took a sip to overcome the chaste unreality of looking on in this way.

Suddenly lightning and mast met, paying its respects as we had expected. 'Look at that, damn it, the lightning struck her,' said Parry, handing me his telescope. Another sail was burning, the wind helping, tearing apart burning rags which swirled down towards the tumult on deck, small figures fleeing over the side, a black shower of people falling towards the surface of the water. We were unmoved by this violent course of events, or we seemed to be seeing it slowly, in the jelly of our eyes trying to feed our reason with the experience. The boat was unmanoeuvrable and drifted away from the others, sliding away from the wind which then pursued it with pressure from the fire astern. 'She's burning like a fart,' said Parry, with awe. It all happened very quickly. She sank in that terrible way large boats do, tipping from stern to prow. The last we saw of her was burning rags snapping round in the whirlpools she sucked down with her. The thunderstorm that had been crashing against the mountains to the south came back and the lightning flapped around. A bull in a field seeks the scent from some faint memory. 'One Turk fewer,' said Parry, 'is always in our interest. But that makes us think, doesn't it?' Yes. Finger to finger. The beginning of all destruction.

Every day, the cloud sank down to the level of the lagoon and demonstrated the innumerable shifts existing in monotonous weather. Yesterday we woke to the mist you drink when you breathe.

An hour went by, the mist became rain, scattered drops, overwhelming itself as tears, welling over the edge of tears, becoming a downpour and drowning the lagoon. The lagoon gave birth to the cloud, which always tasted brackish – sometimes you could believe nothing else but that this endless dripping semi-darkness was a conspiracy. The sea birds had long ago moved up on land, reptiles flourishing in the marshes, the fields turning white with gulls growing fat. For one single moment, the cloud reddened from the evening sun and lit up a bird in flight from below. Something yellow came over Lord Byron last night – when the first bird laughed and drew with it the others, in wave after wave – until the whole horseshoe of shore glowed in a bronze of sound.

But now. Through the rain-streaked window-pane I saw the rain had stopped, a ripple running across the lagoon, shuddering and racing back and forth between banks of reeds, the black mooring poles where they hung the nets and the fishing huts far out with no links with the shore, to which you would nevertheless be able to walk had the bottom not been so treacherously muddy.

The marshes surrounding Missolonghi to the east and west were unable to rise above the flood, although the townspeople maintained it was usually dry, 'and fine', from April to October. That must have been the time when the gypsies settled. During our first week, we tried to ride between the ditches, but the horses often stumbled and we came up out of the marsh with the most unmentionable creatures hanging off us; they had begun to take a meal on our necks and wrists.

But the gypsies were still there, their tents round, like garlic, outside them a fire, broken tubs, bellows and other arrangements that added up to a workshop. The gypsy tents were familiar and specific homes, like swallows' nests on town walls, outside the walls, but tolerated in that way. Twice I had seen white clouds of washing. The men sometimes sat in the drizzle outside and worked with metal, the sound of hammers against rivets reaching my ears first when a hand was raised for the next blow: the air resounding, but the copper mute – an effect of echo? But usually people came out of the tents just to discharge their needs into a ditch. Oh well, our comforts were not all that superior. Everything we left behind us in the house – refuse from kitchen and washing – went out of the window and down into a canal used by several houses for the same purpose and so contained every conceivable vermin, the life and death of which contributed to the stink of putrefaction.

I have said 'the lagoon' so many times. The lagoon again, and the lagoon returns like a paunchy mirror in front of its as-good-as-sunken town, and the lagoon turns the world upside-down and puts the cloud in its bed to rest upon. On the morning of the sixteenth of February, we could hardly be bothered to wake up.

We sat together and said nothing – staring at 'the rain' and 'the lagoon'. If the meeting had a purpose, it was to gather all the fallacies of this campaign into a single picture that might indicate the meaning of failure.

On the morning of the fifteenth, Missolonghi's volunteers were to have seen military action for the first time. Everything had been well prepared, but perhaps experience should have overruled optimism.

Our attack on the Turkish fortress at Lepanto was to provide guaranteed progress, not because of our qualities, but because of the failings in their defences. The fortress looked unassailable, but the human eye has a mediaeval view of mediaeval fortresses, and weapons today are tools that have overcome the interpretation of the eye. They cut through stone. They have taken this modern insight back to the brain while ignoring our old senses which have doubts.

Everyone knew it was not possible to defend Lepanto – not least the commander, who had made his view known through envoys who met ours in that shady area in which parties agree on how the battle shall be concluded even before the bloodshed starts. He had made it clear that he had no intention of capitulating without a fight, for that would be foolhardy, but as far as he was concerned, the battle negotiations could well be carried out with gloves on, for he was not such a barbarian that he would evaluate the day according to the numbers of casualties.

Missolonghi was a town thronging with Germans and Danes refusing to submit to each other's orders, and factions of factions of Greek tribes totally opposed to each other's supremacy, or to the German or Polish, for that matter. Macedonians, Russians, Bulgarians and Americans all had their own opinions and presence. 'Not to mention us English,' Lord Byron reminded us sternly, 'who are the most arrogant of all. The advantage of all these factions fighting under the same banner is that no one becomes sufficiently strong to force on to the Greek struggle for independence what has nothing to do with Greek freedom.' All these pious legionnaires thought Lepanto a paltry début. 'Don't worry,' he muttered to a passionate German lieutenant. 'Your hobby-horses will soon become horses dead or alive, your wooden swords bayonets, your bruises shot-wounds and your chickenpox smallpox!'

His words seethed in a crowd of dark heads. The atmosphere among the volunteers must actually be more fanatical and fragile than it is among conscripted soldiers. Byron's ironies roused bad blood and he was forced – how many times – laboriously to take back what he had said so light-heartedly. The English sense of humour was still a foreign language in the exasperated volunteer corps. Are we the only people with a sense of humour?

We talked about it. He said that he could never help seeing the comical side of situations. He said it comes from a feeling that human life is short and of a compromising kind.

The worst feeling of sluggishness in Missolonghi came from neither the weather nor alienation, but from all that waiting.

Added to it all was an earthquake. In northern Europe – where we live – the skullbones of the earth have grown together. In the south, they still move away from and back towards each other, and something gets squeezed and bleeds in between. Are they volcanoes rising to the surface again? Nations never seem to be complete. Then wars come. In Cephalonia, we had witnessed a natural phenomenon that was a kind of reflection of life in war.

The island belonged to the history of Greece but was British territory. We Philhellenes thought this was wretched. Morning and night, the English troops drilled on the exercise grounds. That was wretched. Beyond that, you saw the harbour glistening and beyond that the sea and then the solid bluish land masses at the base of which a crack flashed out.

One night I heard two Italians talking about eroticism, very sensibly, very culinarily, quite alien to an English ear on a grown-together skull. A pale green dust rose and sank in the room, a draught from nowhere dispersing and collecting it. The house smelt of mould, filling the swelling cushions with its green pollen. Everywhere, at slumbering eye level, the cushions tautened into a shimmer of silk, giving the room a roundness that bulged and grew. And the fringes! What kind of instrument was it they were playing, those Greeks and Albanians, as they took on a Jewish note, at eye level, lulling and allowing it to stray and tremble round itself and plait a plait divided into three links. Were they oboes that went so deep, or were they playing on a ram's horn? I eavesdropped.

'. . . ah, things are different with love. You're offered a banquet and

493

choose your diet. You suffer from it, you know. You don't know what to do. It stands like an invisible column in the middle of the room and you can't bring yourself to get round it. An erotic tendency is easy to adopt. Love is off balance, always reminding you of something else . . .'

I eavesdropped and my senses reached out for what remained unsaid, but I found nothing. I knew nothing about these people. When you join together for a Cause, you are not a village but a cell. And yet you are only a villager, who wants to know everything the boundary of the cell keeps from the other members. You are very much alone when you are together with only what is of use to other people.

'. . . is out of balance, always reminding you of something else . . .'

Like a commentary, the rhythm of the music turned over into a new movement, loosening the plait and roughly starting to cut the hair, short swirling tufts working their way upwards, with blades like forks of lightning, right up to the ear. To the scalp. Hair spattered off the head. Someone hissed between his teeth – charged, discharged – and afterwards the rhythm sank into another river of hair and slowly started plaiting it.

The next day we sat on the little terrace watching the English troops drilling. We played with the subject of what period of human history had been the worst. Someone thought 'the first, because man had no knowledge of how to improve things for himself'. Another reckoned wholly originally 'the plague', another 'every great kingdom's rise – for the weak – and downfall – for the strong.'

I myself said the present was the worst period, because you experience it. Every new person experiences both the horror stories of the past and the apprehensions for the future. Like the transitoriness of the short breathing space you have at the moment. More people than ever are suffering now, because more people exist. Now new sufferings have been added to the old ones, while only a few of the old ones have disappeared. The poor suffer from poverty and the rich from what poverty obscures. However many curtains you draw back, people never get as far as the light.

We looked across lines of English soldiers. It was wretched. Below them was the harbour, a flock of sea birds apparently lying stock still, not moving, but their feet must have been paddling against the drift, for they were gently resisting the waves. Suddenly the

494

soldiers did the same. A wave lifted them from right to left and man after man washed over its crest and then stood as before, with fixed bayonets. Another wave washed over them from right to left. They remained standing with the correct distance between them – one by one – over the crest of the wave and then flat.

The birds were now in the sky, where their circling shrieking flight reflected a small maelstrom in the harbour basin. We heard a distant rumble and the house nearest the soldiers slowly started to peel like a fig. Astonished pause, then stones and mortar crashed down, other houses collapsed, but remained where they were round the crack. The soldiers followed the dune of the earth once again. The islanders left their homes. We stayed where we were – like the soldiers – without really grasping what was happening – they made a manoeuvre, their cheeks red. The islanders raced to safety, with no panic, for they were experienced. Then! We all tried to get down the stairs at once. In the crush on the gallery, an impatient junker felt the ground heaving again, and jumped over the top and broke his ankle.

Approximately the same thing happened in Missolonghi. Otherwise it was all waiting. We were waiting for money – for the loan from the Greek Committee in London, the prerequisite for actions on a larger scale. We were waiting for the schooner *Ann*, long since announced with her cargo of arms and mechanical weapons. Months ago, London had forewarned us of her arrival with ammunition, arms and a whole lot of techniques for the manufacture and repair of military materials. In addition, the excellent 'Major Parry, General Congreve's right hand man, with his understanding of all kinds of weapons and projectiles, among them the Congreve rockets, Greek flares and a whole lot more things to strike terror into the Turk'.

We had to wait for the *Ann* before we undertook anything, for in our present situation, we scarcely had sufficient means to defend ourselves. We had a small assorted arsenal of weapons, a crate of trumpets, the printing press, the Bibles and a large quantity of gunpowder that had lain out in Nauplion harbour and been soaked by the rain. They said the amazing Parry could even cure wet gunpowder. When Lord Byron finally saw the *Ann* rounding the reed banks on the horizon, he was overjoyed. At last something would happen. And if anything dramatic happened, opinions would be revived, new idealists would be roused – and his time spent there cut short.

495

But a little schooner from home does not shorten a time of hopelessness so easily. While she was still lying at anchor, two Suliots set about a Dane and killed him, causing immediate fighting between the two camps. Old sins, semi-buried dissensions were brought to light and displayed, and Lord Byron – who somehow had come to serve as the supreme command no one wanted – was half dragged, half invited to administer peace to the extent that the miscreants were imprisoned and the lust for revenge subdued.

He came home and sat down to his diet-meal.

The next day, the *Ann* lay in the harbour. We swarmed, we swarmed all round the famous Parry. He turned out to be a good-humoured matter-of-fact drunk. We all took him to our hearts, in the way you have to with a crudely practical man after having experienced the chronic discontent of idealists for virtually six whole months. But it soon turned out that Parry had no knowledge of assembling weapons worth mentioning – nor of repairing them. He preferred damping his ash to drying gunpowder, and he had brought no materials for Congreve rockets with him, nor anything else that would strike terror into the Turk.

In our first enthusiasm, however, we all helped unload the cargo, as the *Ann* had to return immediately to Zante for repairs. Even the Suliots, who otherwise did not concern themselves with practical labour, carried crates out on to the harbour front.

The next day Lord Byron went to Anatolico. When he came back, it had been raining for hours and the crates were still on the harbour front. Well, what can one say? A few attempts to arrange for their transport to the seraglio had failed. The Suliots refused to do any more work and the rest of us were too few for all those crates.

He came back and shrieked about how lazy we were. He was sick with rage and almost weeping. He came rushing in, striking his thighs in abandoned despair over us all. He came in and flung open the door and emitted hitherto secret opinions on our characters. Then he fell completely silent. He went out and asked the Suliots to help. They replied that it was raining. He went over to the stacks, tried to move a crate, lifted it with an angry jerk and started staggering across to the seraglio. A huddled shadow freed itself from a wall and took hold of the other end of the crate, to help, half-running backwards in front of Lord Byron. It was Parry. He had been drinking all day. What else could we do but help? Even the Suliots stepped forward, muttering. An alcoholic and a world traveller, the latter dissatisfied with everything life had given him for nothing. You just couldn't let them carry things on their own. The next day I lay in bed with a high fever. So did Loukas. But it was to him Byron relinquished his bed.

The town was filthy with rumours – about conspiracies, about spies, Turkish advances, traitors in our lines, the collapse of the Cause in other parts of the country. There were rumours of alliances among the factions which were against Mavrocordatos, rumours about the loss of the Committee's ship (despite the fact that she had been in harbour and unloaded!). We squelched around on bottomless streets and smoked bad tobacco. Suliots drilled as if doing a heathen ritual dance. Byron stood on one side, watching. He was melancholy and played with Lyon.

There was something wrong with his health. When I told Dr Bruno I thought something was wrong, he suggested I should mind my own business and most of all watch out that I wasn't afflicted with 'the same ailment as Major Parry'.

There was something wrong with Lord Byron. A month earlier he had been sparkling, swimming in the cold sea and being pleased he hadn't changed his clothes for a week. Since then, his hair had turned even greyer. His thin face also had become unrecognisably grey – out of its thinness a strange empty fleshiness had been born. He adhered to a strict diet. 'My Lord,' protested Parry, the first time he saw what landed on Lord Byron's plate every day. 'That's all right for a man starved of love, but sloppy muck of that kind will kill you here. What you need is a brandy!' 'So you say, Dr Bruno . . .' muttered Byron listlessly. 'Brandy. Brandy's what you need,' explained Parry, who largely lived off that drink. 'Allow me to mix you a drink – and not too weak. That'll give you your strength back.'

Then the evening of the fourteenth arrived. Then the fifteenth. All memories of those days have merged together. Everything fell apart, separated and fluttered about. It was almost impossible to accumulate a chronology. We were preparing our deployment for the battle of Lepanto. This is what happened.

The Suliots, our main strength and local connection, came in scattered bunches on to the ground in front of the house. A clock struck six, two others replied. Buttoned firmly up to the chin, my hair scraped back so that my scalp crawled, I ate dinner by the window, with my fingers. The Suliots in Byron's private bodyguard lived at ground level, where they went in and out, blowing smoke out through their nostrils, seldom opening their mouths. Suliots from other parts of town were leaping around among the puddles so that their fustanellas flapped like pleated wings. They loved their guns and carried them with individuality, each in his own loving way.

They moved slowly through the jelly of the eye, birdmen in skirts, the folds streaming off their hips, guns and sword-belts and these leaps between puddles, the darkness of their eyes, unreliable – for we don't know what they are directed at. The patch of ground hovering on the edge of a lagoon that has just inclined its small army boats towards the morning, everything open and vaulted. Lord Byron came out with his Suliot officer and they walked to and fro along the quay, kicking a little at the wreck of the boat. They were talking. Lord Byron took out his pistol, aimed and shot the neck off a bottle, after which Lyon ran off and fetched the bottle for his master to judge his aim.

I went to relieve myself thoroughly. I wished to be well prepared. Even if Lepanto were to be a mock fight, you never knew what people might fire off in their eagerness. As I was seated there, alarm arose in the house and it grew noisy. I thought it was time and hurried up. Heard someone storming up the stairs and slamming a door, three voices impinging on each other, rising to a falsetto. Three pairs of steps patrolled across the floor in impatient syncopation, like fingers drumming on a table top. There was a silence, then a bird voice rose out of the cushion and flapped a short way before falling. The door opened again, someone ran down the stairs, where he met another voice and spread the news in wider and wider circles round the house. The throne on which I was seated was like the actual eye of the storm. I stayed there with my forehead against my hand, free to speculate over what had gone wrong – again.

As I came out, I met Tita Falcieri. The huge bearded gondolier muttered something about scoundrels or saints. I did not take it in. He was white round the nose, a feature I had learnt to recognise during our journey as an expression of his loyal rage, but I could understand hardly a word of his Venetian.

They were all in my bedroom, or rather, the office in which I slept. Nearly all of them were there, the last man coming just after me. He himself was leaning against my desk with one knee on the stool, staring at my orderly papers, copies and seals. He was very grey, very gentle. 'So . . .' he said, and wrote his N.B. under a declaration: *Note concerning the Suliots – after vain efforts to assemble the Suliots for the cause of Greece – without on my part shrinking from the expense, trouble and some danger – I have come to the following conclusion: I do not wish to have anything more to do with the Suliots – they can go to the Turkish dogs or to hell. They can cut me up into more pieces than there are factions among them before I change my mind.*

Then the sun dissolved a thin patch in the cloud, a moment of spring gilding the window-panes. The barometer trembled, spirits automatically rising like desire without love. All open eyes underwent the same automatic gilding . . . and the winking membrane of reeds over the sea . . . It lasted a few seconds. You took it with you right through everything that followed – the question of courage to face life and despondency. Is it a tongue of the sun that guides it? Anyone can answer that question. No one. On my way home from Greece, I spoke in Italian to a woman planting rice and she said the sun is projected shadow and when the clouds gather, the soul also rests in the shadow.

'Won't it happen?' The patch of sun was blown away and all eyes were as grey as before. Lord Byron made an effort to work up his rage, but you could see the wave turning down within him before it had taken hold. 'Yes, it's over,' he said. 'As far as I'm concerned, humanly speaking, it's over. I was prepared to fight the Turks, but not the Greeks. I cannot see a united and free Greece. When not even a situation like this can make them think otherwise than of the day, then I give up. Anyhow for the day.' (Good heavens, he can't resist framing his words even now!) A similar wave of protest rose in the room and turned before it had had time to take hold of anyone. 'Over?' I whispered to the nearest man. Whispering he told me what had happened. While he was speaking, several newcomers began to listen, so he raised his voice in embarrassment and stammered out a version of what Lord Byron had said, finally also for Lord Byron himself, who was peering as if he were trying to see troops on a very distant puddle.

The Suliots had once again changed their minds. Their particular demand for marching against Lepanto was double pay to start with. Three of them were to be appointed generals and a corresponding number promoted to officers according to the army hierarchy, this new responsibility weighed against gold, of course. With all these conditions fulfilled, however, it was still uncertain whether they might consider risking their forces at Lepanto, as Suliots preferred to fight against men and felt it went against their honour to fight against walls.

Some are silent, others commenting on everything. The most realistic of us was Parry, who predicted what would happen the next day – the Suliots accepting rejection of their conditions and saying they were willing to fight under the original conditions. 'Those fellows try out how far they can go with tourists. How can they take us seriously, when we devote ourselves not to our own concerns, but to theirs?'

But many of us thought that from the start L.B. had been an incurable optimist – blinded – when it came to Suliots. In Cephalonia, he had already handed out money to them indiscriminately, and immediately on arrival he had decided to give them the élite rôle in the struggle for freedom, as well as taking fifty of them as his personal bodyguard, generously paid and installed on the ground floor of his house. At that moment I also remembered – in a gap in a conversation – how delighted he had been over how cheap it was to maintain a small army in Greece. 'About the same amount as a month's bill from your tailor in England. A soldier costs twenty-five piastres a month, about two dollars, and in Greece the dollar fetches four and tuppence, as opposed to London, where the rate is two and sixpence.' But nevertheless I did not want to mention gaps in a conversation. They are perhaps characteristic of what drives a man, but not of his endeavours. And Lord Byron expressed his endeavours like this:

'My friends . . . I know I have an unfortunate tendency to see things with the eyes of a man in love. But that tendency has inconstancy as – a tendency.' He was speaking slowly. If anyone reacted to a word, he started back as if he were speaking a foreign language whose few words in common with ours had another meaning. '. . . a tendency. So I wish to defend myself by reminding you that I did not select the Suliots because of their costumes. The Suliots are the local warriors in this war of local wars. You know that I have always tried to bind our presence to something that is living and will go on living here. If we come here in the capacity of ourselves, then we would be yet another faction among the others: a faction of *Adventurers and Idealists*, which we also are the moment we act – on our own.'

Pale and gentle, he said: 'But all that is . . . now. It is because we are strangers that we expect . . . Those who live here have time. Perhaps we'd better . . . But if I'm wrong . . .' He began leaving out words. You hardly noticed it because everyone was talking at once. Perhaps he was leaving out words that were obvious – and chewing them over in disgust.

He chewed them over during the endlessly long day of the fifteenth. It ought to have been short, the day when he evaded the argument over what rôle those sent out by the Committee should play in Greece: A military rôle, or shouldn't we consider Colonel Stanhope's viewpoint, that the *Idea* was our most important contribution?

Stanhope had used the printing press we had with us to start up the liberal newspaper the *Greek Chronicle*. The fact that the majority of his intended readers were illiterate did not worry him, for he had prepared a plan to start schools according to the excellent Lancasterian system, which, briefly, starts out from pupils at a higher level contributing to the teaching of those at lower levels. (L.B. said diffidently: 'Don't you find it strange that of us two, the soldier wants to spend money on educational reforms while the poet intends to spend it on military purposes?' 'I find that typical,' said Stanhope. With permission to joke at L.B.'s expense, he said that scribblers are the most bloodthirsty of the lot.)

But obviously the question was discussed and gone over again and again, particularly on this day. He chewed it over and kept grimacing. The fact was that Stanhope had one or two pupils for his school and one or two readers for his *Greek Chronicle*, and Lord Byron had nothing but failure to show. Stanhope had travelled around meeting other leaders of factions in order to form impressions of their personalities to add to his own impression of the situation. L.B. had met only Mavrocordatos, had listened and lapped it up. He chewed over his boiled vegetables as if life should be like this, but Parry took out his flask and said: 'Brandy is what you need. Allow me to mix you a drink – and not too weak.'

He was still chewing when evening came. I was with him taking dictations to England, to Genoa, to bankers and friends. I tried to feel with him, feel the weight of his disappointment. But there was no weight there. It was pupa-light all round him, weariness the only thing that replied. When you put your weight behind a goal and neither reach it nor reach resistance, then you ought to feel rage or disappointment. They are healing emotions. Devotion purges. But he was already ill. He smiled. I smiled back. He smiled more broadly (I wondered why) and went on chewing, something white now, as if they had given him blubber and it was coming out of the corner of his mouth. The other corner started to grow tragic. He stared at me with his only eye before turning up the white of it. The first spasm went through his body. Everything started from the back of his neck and raced on in short waves, and I saw his fingers curling up as if the sinews were shrinking.

'What's he playing now?' I asked. He replied by letting the whole of one half of his face succeed the tragic grin, while his teeth went on chewing blubber into foam. At first I laughed at this demonstration of disgust, then I breathed in most of the laugh and leant forward. He fell rhythmically and endlessly; leaning back against the cushions and with his heel against the floor, he fell deeper and deeper. The room was as purple as a plum and he was drowning in the colour. He did not reply to my enquiry as to whether he was all right.

Even later, when I knew he was ill, when he had regained consciousness and told me his mother had died of an apoplectic fit, part of me went on wondering whether he hadn't acted it all the same. It was a performance; the creature had now begun to make growling noises, snoring and sobbing. I stood watching it. Cautiously, on the outside of my foot, I walked over to the door and closed it behind me. I was going to go out. I wiped the sight off my body, off my forearms and the backs of my thighs. 'Hullo, Dr Bruno, can you come?' I shouted and walked slowly round the gallery.

It took three men to hold him and I had to see that he couldn't have been acting, for he was not strong enough to fling people about in the way he did. Four voices emitted hoarse sounds. Only Fletcher spoke, if you could call it speech. 'My Lord, oh, can you hear me, My Lord, wake up, can you hear my voice. It's Fletcher, My Lord, oh, who's been in your service for fifteen years. Oh, my God, come back, My Lord! What shall I tell My Lady. And little Ada.'

That's the kind of thing you have to say to your friend when you're afraid of losing him. Very old, much beloved, sick or ecstatic friends must be allowed to be addressed with such fervent stupid strings of words. They exist in a flabby or a taut time alongside ours. They aren't afraid there, but you yourself are afraid and frighten them awake if you can.

Fletcher walked alongside and called forth memories in the unconscious figure, whose convulsions were now slowly calming, whom they now carried up to his bedroom. 'Think of your little Ada, My Lord, and Mrs Leigh who is so fond of you. She said at least ten times that she was entrusting you to me for better or worse. What will she say . . . only a word, one that you can hear me.'

The room was in darkness. Some candles came in, with them people. It became a wake. We stood nodding, like water weeds. 'Out, everyone,' hissed Parry, but we stayed in a shapeless faceless oval. An oval face, pale blue, it hovered in the middle of the room. We stared at it like moon-madmen, for suddenly it was very small in the darkness. Suddenly you noticed it and stared intently to prevent it disappearing altogether. Someone had already dissolved into tears. The beginning of a quarrel was already going on ('You've tormented him every single day and made him ill with your damned Lancastrian method!' 'Don't speak to me like that! I really do question your title of major. You're utterly untrustworthy and you've given him alcohol against doctor's orders!') but every expression of emotion came to a stop.

At the head of the bed, Tita stood on guard. Fletcher held the right hand. 'Speak to him, go on talking!' said Dr Bruno, trying to find the pulse in the left, and Fletcher obediently went on reminding him of everything that can be so dear to a man that he wishes to stay alive. It was as if the facial oval, cog by cog, was clicking down into smaller sizes, smaller and smaller, more and more brilliantly pale blue. Feathers and smelling-salts. A movement ran through the room for the flame and the smell. Everyone leant over to see his anguish. His face shrinking to a pinhead – ready to go through the eye of a needle into the next world – regained one size, then another. Fletcher spoke gently about Mrs Leigh and Countess Guiccioli and himself and little Ada and Lady Byron. The face started drinking the words and growing from them. A single sigh. A whispered question. The great eyes roamed, frightened, over the oval that was us all, inquisitive. Lord Byron felt the fall in his body and tried to rise, but couldn't even press his elbow against the mattress. 'I wasn't present,' whispered Dr Bruno as he put cold compresses over Lord Byron's temples. 'A kind of attack. Do you remember anything yourself? Do you remember what you felt before the convulsions?'

The face was now only slightly smaller than usual – as far as I remember, it never again completely filled out. 'Have I . . . did I have?' began Lord Byron, and ended, 'I am tired,' as if he had never been tired before.

The least of our problems was finding leeches in Missolonghi. If you go on foot in the marshlands, a tussock soon gives way and you're up to your knees, or on your knees, or lying flat out in one of the innumerable ditches that branch off there. When you get up, you are colonised. During my few months of medical studies, I had learnt to handle molluscs, and also the use of leeches. I had become really intimate with some of them as they sat there in the glass jars in the laboratory contracting and extending their greyish-black bodies from knob to trail and back in their efforts to suckle the sterile glass. They no longer revolted me, but many of the others were frantic when they found a soulless life clamped to their necks or wrists, eating. Dr Bruno had a whole set of leeches in his store and was longing to make use of them.

'I must take a few ounces of blood,' he said sternly, well prepared for the deep 'No!' that was to follow. 'Yes!' During the journey, he had several times had to listen to his patient's scepticism over blood-letting. Byron had actually forbidden him to use the method should he himself fall ill. 'All that talk of black, thick and fatty blood is nonsense,' he had said. 'Every time they cut me, it looks the same, red, possibly sometimes a little thin, and I consider it the same blood all the time and fundamentally the best medicine for all ailments.'

But now he was helpless, wriggling and humping like a leech himself as Dr Bruno prepared him for them. 'No, no,' he whimpered piteously, frightening the doctor with his eyes starting out of his head. 'They are creatures of God's creation, too,' muttered Dr Bruno, insulted, as if he himself had been the creating god. 'Do you prefer the scalpel, My Lord? It must happen one way or another. If you refuse, I shall leave the room and remove my hand from you, as you clearly consider you can get better on your own.'

'Is there really no other way . . . ?'

Everyone then had to leave the room, the leeches allowed to grow

504

and shrink discontentedly in their glass jar. Everyone else left the room. Only we who were to adminster the blood-letting were allowed to stay behind. His arm was bared. The top was covered with pale freckles and hair, the underside white, just as reluctant as everything in the animal kingdom to be turned on its back, but that was done, and Dr Bruno made two lips. 'Aha,' he said, as a sluggish shiny darkness rose from that mouth in a curve as if the blood really had become so thick and hot that it had to force its way out.

A moment went by in that dreamy pause in which you care for the very sick and everything is for them, and they are calm. It is a small sacred moment of co-operation; the light must not be too strong, strong feelings must not penetrate. We spoke, incoherently but not quickly. The memories made their way past his almost closed eyelids and out of one of them; he suddenly said: 'Evidence of true friendship is betrayal, did you know that?' I collected his blood in a tin bowl, sometimes a steady stream, sometimes a spurt. The flow pushed out its own pool in sluggish circles from the middle, and layers of various colours were formed in this way like the rings of age in a tree. It was unutterably peaceful and time could have stood still. Something fell on my foot, something fell on the same place, and a third time – I looked down. The rusty spot at the bottom of the bowl was a hole, and at once all shadows rushed from the green lampshade up into the ceiling and his life ran out of his arm, out of the bowl, on to the floor.

We had to send for another doctor, one from the German camp, for Bruno needed help to close the artery. Sometimes we thought we had stemmed it – we breathed out, held our breath, then the lips smiled again and pressed out their lip colouring, the pulse labouring and squeezing up yet another red ribbon, which fell. The German doctor laboured so that his spectacles slowly slid down his nose and fell off the tip. Dr Bruno was sweating with the effort and anguish. Their goal was as small as a little finger nail, small and elusive. All under one single green lamp in the darkness: we were crowded; nonetheless at an immense distance from each other. Lord Byron agonised and twisted and turned. I wiped his face, wiped sweat and tried to wipe away that expression showing that he understood. He knew that his conscious-ness was lying here on a pillow, further down the lips of his bloodstream parting however wildly the doctors tried to force them together again. And everything between those distances belonged. So

505

absurd! His arm emptying heart and mind. His own lips opened for
'ice!' I bent over him. 'Of course,' but there was no ice in Missolonghi.
With pressure, with pressing, with all physical strength concentrated
on that little mouth, at last the doctors managed to silence it. Then the
room was white and widely spattered with blood and water. They
collapsed and breathed out. Then they checked in some confusion
whether their patient were alive.

Someone had knocked over the tin bowl, the bed was wet, the
German doctor sitting exhausted on the edge of it, bleary-eyed, long-
nosed – the glasses he was looking for hidden in his cravat. Dr Bruno
tried to wake the patient. Is the sense of smell the sense that lies closest
to consciousness? Sleeping people mumble to sounds, arch at a touch
and try in their sleep to find the hand touching them. But a smell wakes
them with promptly wide-open eyes, and to the doctor this un-
researched secret seems to be as obvious as customary law and
servitude is within the kingdom of justice. As I knelt massaging those
icy hands, I tried to think myself into the dialogue of waking:

'. . . why burning feathers?'
'. . . no one knows, but it has always had an effect . . .'
'. . . then it must be good . . .'

Not even on that night did calm and dignity reign in Missolonghi.
Soon after midnight, Fletcher and I had been relieved of our watch
over the sickbed, and while I was still dipping in and out of the surface
of sleep, I was brought wide awake by shots firing. It was quite close,
and I eased my way indifferently over the side of the bed to find out
what in hell was happening now, again.

It was trouble outside the seraglio, where one group wanted to get in
and another was resisting. A whole barrel of bad cantankerous wine
was part of the scenario, which also began to spread colonies all over
the town and one of them was to be found by our gateway, where two
men were poking at each other in an attempt at fighting; the exchange
of blows struck the air and their own balance; they were so drunk, they
were pedantic. As no Suliots were left, neither was there anyone to
chase them away. Fletcher poured something out of the window, but
missed. Gamba stood at another window, yelling in Italian.

A cry of anguish penetrated up out of the skirmish further away and was followed by a chorus of oaths. This was the pitch black night of Missolonghi. It had been raining again and the earth kissed your foot as in the most terrible dreams in your childhood. The bird laughter breathed its hairy wreath round all other sounds. Here we had the whole sky above us, the stony Kleissova mountain behind us, and Lord Byron's reduced face in a bubble of memory, in which the light would not go out and grow dark. And then this paltry and unnecessary row, in which unnecessary people brag about what seems important in their anger. Sometimes you wonder what people are for!

By the time I had reached the seraglio, the troublemakers had already fled. A Scottish nobleman had been stabbed in the thigh and was being carried groaning away. The guards were standing like crossbeams in front of the seraglio entrance, and talking to them were the very two men who were supposed to be watching over Lord Byron. They explained that he had been sleeping very peacefully and they considered it more important to watch over these interesting events.

He was awake when we came back. The first thing we saw was his great frightened eyes turned on the combatants, who had somehow made their way through the entrance, shot two lamps off the walls and frightened all the heroes in the house behind lock and key. They had sealed a drunken friendship and decided to go up and cure the sick man with a drop of wine. He looked at their shadows, staggering across the walls like giants to the accompaniment of 'eternal fidelity', belch. What he saw in those shadows, I do not know, but his expression was confused, misty, veiled, as if he had been attacked by butterflies, dragonflies.

And so it was that we came to be sitting together on the morning of the sixteenth. At first we were fairly controlled, then less and less so. Guilt started being apportioned – first outside, then all the more generously inside the house.

What was distinct in our mortification was the sight of the goddess of noble struggle that had lured us to her and then climbed up on to a piece of scenery, from where she gave us neutral looks. Byron's illness, the lethargy, sluggishness and reluctance of the war of liberation – all were manifestations of her challenging neutrality. Life was neutral. Where we had taken sides, life was neutral and forced our side-taking into by-roads. Stanhope talked about brandy and Parry went on about the *Greek Chronicle* and the Lancastrian method, as if everything that had gone wrong stemmed from the individual use of drink and liberalism.

Less than a month earlier, we had still had our illusions. We thought we could see the goddess. She shaded her eyes with her hand in our direction and sat heavily astride an anthill. That was the fifth of January, the day before our arrival in Missolonghi. The last lengths of a long slender monoxylon were racing across the lagoon. A few days of confidence remained.

Lord Byron had stood in the boat in the red uniform coat invented by his tailor in Genoa, Lyon at his feet. The little aft sail shuddered cheerfully as the boat was poled into harbour. Around us spread the intensely brilliant flat land which then still seemed worth mentioning, a metallic world, a dull metal that cannot be polished. On the water line, the town shimmered, and just as we hove to, a cloud of black and white birds rose out of the marshes: crows, jackdaws and gulls. They rose suddenly, frightened by their numbers and the disharmony of their voices and movements. Sea birds and land birds in a single flock, the sky full of squabbles and the irritable movements they made with their bodies.

We went ashore and walked to the grave where they had buried the murdered Suliot chieftain, Marco Botzari. With this ceremony, the town of Missolonghi adopted Lord Byron. (Towards the end, he used to say that everything would have been different and better if Botzari had lived.) I am not much one for ceremonies – am moved by them, something which never seems to afflict those who say they take such things seriously. Lord Byron made a short speech. I saw the criss-cross pattern of wrinkles below his eyes as he leant over. The listeners were standing in the pale sunlight with the semi-open expressions of those trying to catch something from a foreign language. And yet he was speaking modern Greek, the patriarchs of the town in a semi-circle behind him. Ordinary people repeated – constantly, like a stream repeating its leaps and bounds – whoever was able to understand, who understood . . . what the man said?

Colonel Stanhope was standing beside me, laughing quietly as he translated what was being said by this man who knew to those who didn't know: 'This is Colonel Viron. Who has come to Missolonghi with many dollars.'

L.B. devoted the first day to familiarising himself with the place. He received everyone wanting to speak to him and visited those he wanted to talk to. He rode far into the countryside. The first week was wonderfully spring-like. The swallows arrived, thin after their trek from Africa. The goddess sat on her anthill with her hand over her eyes. One morning, she was gone. By then, the collaboration between Lord Byron and Colonel Stanhope had also come up against a problem of differing insights.

Stanhope was the Committee's second-in-command in Missolonghi, a position he was forced to resume after having ruled absolutely for a month or two. It was not just a matter of wounded vanity. He truly considered himself – perhaps with some justice – to be more capable than the noble and renowned number one. They were divided on point after point. Stanhope's idea was to school the Greeks. Byron's idea was his Practical Task: to see to it that the Committee's money – should we ever see any sign of it – went entirely towards arms and medical equipment. We others were divided on this difficult matter, our commanders, on the other hand, so definite in their respective extremes, they often preferred to correspond rather than take a step up or down the stairs to talk. I was one of those who ran with questions and answers from Colonel to Lord and from Lord to Colonel. I found Stanhope sulking by means of familiar formalism and Byron briefly unpleasantly affected.

Stanhope: *'Pro primo* – does Your Grace recommend handing over a limited quantity of Cyrillic and Latin style typeface to the editor of *Greek Chronicle?'*

Reply: 'Yes.'

Stanhope: *'Pro secundo* – does Your Grace aim to advance a sum of fifty pounds as support for this Greek publication?'

Reply: 'Yes, yes, yes.'

Stanhope: *'Pro tertio* – will Your Grace permit me to take the printing press to the seat of Greek legislative assembly in Tripolitza?'

Reply: (What does the man mean? They might suddenly decide to support another faction and start a civil war against Mavrocordatos, whom the Committee is expected to support now we happen to be here.) 'We'll have to discuss the matter.'

Stanhope: *'Pro* – fourthly – will Your Grace advance one hundred pounds as support for the German artillery?'

Reply: 'Yes.'

Stanhope: 'Fifthly – would Your Grace consider allowing a hundred pounds of your loan to the Greek government to be transferred to the German Committee, with regard to the fact that they advanced that sum to the government on the basis of my guarantees of its repayment?'

Reply: 'Yes.'

Stanhope: 'Sixthly – would Your Grace recommend that Mr Kesketh be appointed Superintendent of Stores?'

Reply: 'Yes.'

Stanhope: 'Seventhly – would Your Grace recommend that I exchanged the Greek Committee's printing press for the one belonging to the editor?'

Reply: 'I don't quite understand that point. Must discuss it with you.'

When the unresolved points had reached such huge numbers that a meeting became unavoidable, the contracting parties first placed, then seated themselves as uncomfortably as possible, looking preoccupied. The conversation touched on questions of the printing press, press censorship, school systems, systems matters and matters of persons. Witnessing this, you understood quite clearly the way the same war had different courses and bases of conflict for different people. To Stanhope, Greece – Hellas – was an established nation which was to free itself from slavery because the slave system cannot continue when the people have been taught history and had a Christian-philosophical education. He considered no military power subdues the power of knowledge. The wars between factions, as far as he could make out, were a stage of development and nothing to despair about as they would soon be united, for the factions were nonetheless different fingers on the same hand.

To Lord Byron, the factions were the main problem, evidence that no 'Greece' existed. He feared that any man who got used to fratricide and found that action reasonable, would not necessarily give up the habit with better education, but instead would motivate it better. So you had to unite the factions or persuade each of them to be responsible for its own part of the country, federally, instead of trying to knock each other out.

These separate conceptions, on the other hand, did try to knock each other out: they were expressed in strangely clumsy conversations, in which the Colonel argued with logic and conviction, coolly and internationalistically, while the Lord asserted his intuition and finely tuned concentration on time and place – though never so that the one understood the other or even made any effort to do so.

One evening Stanhope was looking particularly displeased and when, with artificial joviality, Lord Byron tried to extract the reason out of him, it came with no circumlocutions.

S: 'I've thought about our conversation of yesterday. You told me you'd said to Count Mavrocordatos that if you were in his place, you would have brought in censorship of the press in the liberated areas. And he is said to have replied that freedom of the press in Free Greece is guaranteed by the constitution. May I ask, My Lord, if you made that statement in all seriousness, or simply to provoke me? For if you are serious, I consider it my duty to communicate this matter to the Committee in order to clarify to its members the difficulties I have in pleading the cause of freedom in Greece, when Your Grace puts the weight of Your Considerable Talents on the opposite side of the scales, and that is a matter of central importance.'

B: 'My dear Stanhope, communicate with whoever you damn well please. I *burn* for all kinds of writing and the press; but I am personally not so certain now that those freedoms in particular are applicable in this particular society. Or of any great importance, for that matter. Considering the minute number able to read, perhaps it would be possible to transform it instead into some kind of freedom of thought?'

Stanhope pretended not to have heard this concluding attempt at wit.

'Those freedoms are applicable in all countries and utterly essential in conditions such as these in particular, for an ordered written form of information would be the only way to put an end to the existing state of anarchy. No one in Missolonghi complies with anyone else. They all act only in their own short-sighted interests. Does Your Grace really not think a little orderly thinking would cure that?'

B: 'What I think is that precisely that little bit of ideology for the ignorant would lead to defamatory writing, scandals and unseemliness.'

S: 'It is the actual aim of freedom of the press to spread essentials and restrain the kind of emancipations you suggest.'

B: 'I repeated that conversation I had with Mavrocordatos so that you would realise that he – after all, he exercises power over this plain of Greece – is *not* an opponent of your Free Press.'

S: 'He certainly is, though he refuses to admit it. And now you are encouraging him. He knows Your Grace has the right to make decisions on the Greek Committee's hundreds of thousands of dollars and that he now does not have to comply with any of the Committee's demands when Your Grace authorises his most primitive statesmanship.'

B: 'We still haven't seen a single dollar of those hundreds of thousands, and I sometimes wonder whether my task out here is to contest privately the costs of a war while the members of the Committee sit drinking toasts in front of a nice warm fire. No, forget it. My dear Stanhope, I can make no decision whatsoever on press freedoms in Greece. On the other hand, my opinion is what it is. I am always game for experiment when something has stagnated, but here nothing ever stands still sufficiently long for you to be able to fix your eyes on it.'

Three weeks later, the tone had become even more strained. They discussed the constitutional consequences of Mavrocordatos' pursuit of a Turkish boat and crew up – and across – neutral Ithaca. Lord Byron considered that you could close one eye and handle the matter with sensitivity and a will to compromise. Stanhope thought neutrality had been violated, and what is more, British neutrality, and that the affair had to be dealt with according to international principles of equality and consideration for international law. The candles smoked, pungent in the indoor damp, and we were all watery-eyed and tired. Byron asked impatiently whether Stanhope hadn't observed that law and order played no part whatsoever in Greek local politics. Stanhope replied virtuously: 'Maybe, but personally I will not expend my energies on what I regard as wrong . . .'

Lord Byron stared at him for a long time, his eyes red-rimmed, a meditative musing look in them. He said later that at that moment he had seen Stanhope's 'ideology' in his clean handsome face. Liberalism. And Stanhope's model: Jeremy Bentham – anti-religion when it came to the mysterious and religious, but *religion* when it came to the *materialistic*. The bear-like look shrank to a red glint as he summarised what he had seen, and thought: 'That Bentham is nothing but a lot of nonsense!'

S: (controlled) 'I find it highly inappropriate of you to attack Bentham in the presence of a friend who esteemed him highly.'

B: 'I am not attacking your friend, but his official principles, which are simply theories, and as such can cause immense damage in the hands of uncritical admirers. What becomes of theories when they are put into practice? Look at the misery Bentham caused in Spain! And in Greece, his ideas would cause chaos and catastrophe to the same extent.'

S: 'I am not protesting against your criticism of principles but against your personal attack. You don't argue about Mr B's writings, but joke about them. Which of them, more precisely, do you have objections to, if I may ask?'

B: (long pause) 'His Panopticon is just a vision.'

S: 'Experiences in Pennsylvania and Millbank, however, have shown it to be a vital force . . .'

(As far as I could make out after having studied Stanhope's library regarding Bentham, this Panopticon is a form of institution or way of living in which Mr Bentham has sketched a kind of arena with residential cells round large common spaces – I couldn't grasp the idea.)

Mr Bentham has a true English heart. You, Lord Byron, after having championed liberal ideas in your earlier years, in the moment of action have turned out to be a *Turk*!

B: 'What! What basis have you for making such a statement?'

S: 'Your behaviour in everything to do with freedom of the press, your attempts to crush the press by pronouncing negatively about it to Mavrocordatos and your general scorn for liberal principles.'

B: 'If I had waved a finger I really could have crushed the press.'

S: 'With all that power – which actually you have never possessed – you have gone to the Count and poisoned his ear.'

Lord Byron then devoted a moment to speaking ill of all liberals and Utopians – people who wrote pamphlets and at the same time cultivated their own interests which were contrary to the contents of the pamphlets ('All radicals advocate principles which they themselves do not observe because they consider themselves to have already made their contribution to a better world by means of the Idea Itself'). People who had a chequered cloth of ideas unrolled and imposed, but then sold themselves to the tailor and allowed him to cut it out, provided he paid well.

S: 'Which liberals are you thinking of, My Lord? Have you acquired your ideas from the Italian bourgeoisie?'

B: 'No, I'm thinking of people like Leigh Hunt and Cartwright, people with "English hearts".'

S: 'And yet you took part in driving through Cartwright's electoral reforms in the House of Lords and helped Hunt by praising his poetry, looking after his family and giving him the publishing rights of several of your works.'

B: 'I simply don't know what you're doing here in Greece. This is already the home of Freedom, where everyone does what he wants and no one does what he ought to. You're worse than Wilson and should leave the army.'

S: 'I'm only a simple soldier, but I will never abandon my principles. Our principles are diametrically opposed, so in future let us avoid the subject. Let me simply declare my motto in this context. The world is our realm and to do good is our religion. If you live up to the ideals and pronouncements of your youth, you will be the foremost of men, otherwise the most wretched.'

B: 'Then I really do hope my obituary will not be dependent on your judgement.'

S: 'Your poetic genius has made you immortal. Nothing could deprive you of that.'

B: 'Poetry!!! You'll see. Judge me by my actions.'

The conversation petered out. Again, I had to start running up and down the stairs with questions and answers. Stanhope seemed to have won the argument, but when later on that day I saw him squelching along the bottomless street, taking foolish little leaps from stone to stone, it did not appear that convincing argument had been of any great help in life. When Lord Byron established that there was nothing more to add, he got up to leave Stanhope's room. The latter picked up a candle to show him out into the corridor. 'What!' L.B. raised his eyebrows. 'Are you lighting the way for a Turk?'

We also had the usual household squabbles. Lord Byron had asked Pietro Gamba to order a length of red material and ditto oilcloth from Zante, and shortly afterwards arrived a voluminous consignment and a bill for six hundred and forty-five dollars. Long black silence. Hands tore off the customs seal and out came article after article: Hessian boots, some bales of royal blue cloth for parade uniforms, horse whips from London, cut-glass salt cellars, silver tankards and so on. Eyes met for terrible moments. Our rosy Gamba turned bright red, from defiance and resentment as well. The quarrel went on for hours, the combatants following each other from room to room. Each time one of them delivered the last word and slammed the door behind him, the other found another opening, fragments of accusations partially reaching us through open and closed doors. Gamba was finally told that all his patriotism and idealism could be concentrated in his dream of a sky-blue uniform. 'Bairon' heard that he lacked both patriotism and idealism and that he was a rootless adventurer who exploited people and situations until he no longer had any use for them.

Then they could not be stopped, the tears. The depressing weather facilitated – a first marital quarrel. Provoked by nothing but money, it appals the parties as it progresses: had he had this image of me in his real eye (the smiling one), so detailed that he had to work it up in secret while holding out the prospect of friendship and intimacy? Is this the real truth about him, the one that breaks through, so obvious and detailed?

All those squabbles in the house. They passed, were actually forgotten, for loathing and hatred are nothing to maintain when living so restrictedly. But they trampled on enthusiasm more effectively than the rain did, than the silence from the Committee and the non-existent arms supplies did. Once Lord Byron said to me that his misanthropy was the only thing that flourished here. Everyone in the household, the Suliots and other groups of volunteers – they all wanted his money and services and promises. He said none of them enquired of anyone else what that person had received – for the purpose of adapting his own demands afterwards. They all demanded the maximum of him and supported each other, preserving a hard-won internal friendship at his expense. With a thousand demands, they forced him to become a person who said no, and demanded his sympathy in exchange for the displeased sight they themselves displayed. Well, what did he ever receive in exchange?

You have to have something for something. You have the same longings even in a very restricted existence. Every emotion exercising its tyranny over your senses when you lived in London now tested its modest best on Missolonghi. But only *one* thought about love; no one else demanded that it should manifest itself there.

515

The first evenings in January, when you could still go on foot with some pleasure, we walked around to get a feel of the town. It consisted of a street and a few parallel ditches, two side alleys and the bazaar – the smell of dried fish soaking first into clothes, then hair and mucous membrane, then muscles, and finally skeleton. All meat tasted of fish. We saw it, red, flayed, hanging on hooks in the roof in the meat bazaar, sheep, bullocks, heathen in their nakedness. Long half-bodies swinging in the darkness of the caves, the butchers' arms equally naked, everything smelling of warm blood, meat, but tasting of fish. Dusk came early in the bazaars. We used our sticks to disperse the colours. Were the women scaly? Grey glistening faces with no courage to look at us; all the peoples round the Mediterranean must have blended with each other, once the seaway was the only practicable route. They were very dark, and in the place where the men had their deeply cloven moustaches, the women had youthful down.

Dogs chased cocks which had annoyed them and which laughingly escaped from them as easily as they had escaped all previous dogs and small boys. Old Greeks sat directly on the street stroking fat beads. Yellow lamps up in the sky caused shudders in the puddles, smiling warmly, the reflection wrinkling and the men letting the fat yellow beads slip through their fingers, raising all hairs and a movement in the slits of their mouths. Those who had put their beads in their pockets were holding a hen in their arms, for the necessary stroking, large, stupid, downy birds feeling the wind ruffling their breast feathers and a gentle greedy hand fastening in the rich scum below. We walked to the town wall, to the gateway and back, the dogs leaping their dog-leaps around us and Loukas his boy-leaps ahead of us.

'I am *lonely*,' said Lord Byron to Loukas. We had had enough of the town. Instead, if the rain held up, a rowing boat came across the lagoon every afternoon and took some of us over to the strip of land opposite where you could ride. The oars fluttered slowly over the glass surface – mountain ranges all round – but the glass surface bore us and brought us home as quietly as if it had given itself a slight slope.

We landed. We stepped ashore, into an ankle-deep powder of lagoon mist. It was quiet, completely. In Lord Byron's immeasurably large mirror-globes of eyes, I saw Loukas trying to escape. Slowly. Slowly, he strode in this powder, an island creature. With his head on one side and his gaze turned away, he let every step fall like a pure,

pure note in the silence, forming a scale of thin steps. A scattered melody of rain along the wide mist shifting in opal away.

In April, I collected up some papers left by Lord Byron, intending to add them chronologically to the letters, bills and official papers to be sent to his executor, Mr Hobhouse. Then I found what must be the last piece of poetry he ever wrote. And in the middle of all salutes, all tears and big words, I realised that a human being never ends grandiosely, but tries to the very end to start again. Finiteness expressed in a spoonful of diluted soup:

> I watched thee when the foe was at our side,
>   Ready to strike at him – or thee and me.
> Were safety hopeless – rather than divide
>   Aught with one loved save love and liberty.
>
> I watched thee on the breakers, when the rock
>   Received our prow and all was storm and fear,
> And bade thee cling to me through every shock;
>   This arm would be thy bark, or breast thy bier.
>
> I watched thee when the fever glazed thine eyes,
>   Yielding my couch and stretched me on the ground,
> When overworn with watching, ne'er to rise
>   From thence if thou an early grave hadst found.
>
> The earthquake came, and rocked the quivering wall,
>   And men and nature reeled as if with wine.
> Whom did I seek around the tottering hall?
>   For thee. Whose safety first provide for? Thine.
>
> And when convulsive throes denied my breath
>   The faintest utterance to my fading thought,
> To thee – to thee – e'en in the gasp of death
>   My spirit turned, oh! oftener than it ought.
>
> Thus much and more; and yet thou lov'st me not,
>   And never wilt! Love dwells not in our will.

Nor can I blame thee, though it be my lot
  To strongly, wrongly, vainly love thee still.

Oh, yes. Here and now. The only thing on offer. Love is itself and in all
circumstances finds an object. Incomprehensible to the spectator. And
the love poem is the invocation of the hopeless. It is also hopeless if you
'are given', 'have', for nothing is met as it desires. You melt together by
going through the extraordinary amount of emptiness contained in the
body you desire. Every love poem is about something fleeting that has
fled, a moment that did not allow itself to be enjoyed in the depths of
the promise, one day, a carp that is not caught.